Born in Melbourne, Patricia Shaw has worked as a teacher, a political journalist and an oral historian, but gave all this up to pursue a literary career. Having won awards for her poetry and short stories, Patricia went on to write her first book, and *Brother Digger* was published in Australia in 1984. This was followed by *Pioneers of a Trackless Land, Valley of Lagoons, River of the Sun, The Feather and the Stone, Where the Willows Weep, Cry of the Rain Bird, Fires of Fortune* and *The Opal Seekers*.

Apart from her writing, Patricia spends her time researching political history, reading and swimming. She lives on the beautiful Queensland Gold Coast of Australia and has a grown-up son and daughter. She is also a devoted fan of native birds and is concerned with animal welfare.

THE GLITTERING FIELDS

Patricia Shaw

HEADLINE

First published in 1997
by HEADLINE BOOK PUBLISHING

First published in paperback in 1997
by HEADLINE BOOK PUBLISHING

10 9 8 7 6 5 4 3

ISBN 0 7472 5421 4

Typeset by Palimpsest Book Production Limited,
Polmont, Stirlingshire
Printed in England by
Clays Ltd, St Ives plc

HEADLINE BOOK PUBLISHING
A division of Hodder Headline PLC
338 Euston Road
London NW1 3BH

To the Daniher family,
bless us all.

My thanks to Sally Milner, who published my first two books; to Sue Fletcher, who took over from there; and to my stalwart minders, Clare Foss and Sarah Thomson.

Cromwell I charge thee,
fling away ambition:
By that sin fell the angels.

Shakespeare, *King Henry VIII*

Chapter One

Everyone on board yearned for the long voyage to end;
everyone, that is, except the boy, Clem Price, who gloried
in this great adventure. He loved the ship, from their snug
little cabin to the swaying decks above, where a boy could
scuttle about as nimbly as the sailor men. Every day was a
new excitement. In good weather there was so much activity
up top. Passengers played quoits or deck tennis, some did
their physical jerks, others strolled about or set up deckchairs
to read or chat with passers-by, while the crew worked under
the Captain's watchful eye. But when the weather turned foul,
passengers stayed below, squashing in for meals at the long
mess tables, or wasting time just lying on their bunks. Clem
could never stay still that long. He roamed about with the
stewards, or slid into the galley to talk to the cook, who could
always be relied on to produce a slice of apple or a piece of
bread and dripping for the boy.

And then there was the ocean itself, a never-ending delight
to Clem, who clung to the rails watching the endless surge,
revelling in its moods. He was there when they first sighted
dolphins, and he would never, ever forget the massive whale
that surfaced near the ship like a great steam train bursting
up from the depths. Clem's father had grabbed him, thinking
he'd be frightened, but the boy thrust him away, not wanting
to miss a second of this awesome spectacle.

At night, as he lay in his bunk, the sounds of shipboard life
captivated him. Back home on the farm, nights were still and
silent, but here, darkness came alive. He could hear the swish
and swirl of the ocean, the creaking timbers, the clink of steel
rings on the masts, the call of the watch, the unlovely whine of

winds that were much gayer in daylight. Clem liked to listen and identify all these sounds, adding them to his repertoire as if to distinguish instruments in an orchestra.

And over all this were the less disciplined sounds of the voices of his fellow passengers, raised in fun and laughter or community singing or even, at times, angry shouts, followed by the buzz of earnest talk. All of which told the boy that he was safe, that the fine clipper with its three tall masts was bearing him across the oceans as surely as a bird on the wing.

Then, one night, the voices ceased. Disturbed by the sudden quiet, Clem waited, straining. For a minute he thought the world had stopped, but the ship was still ploughing on, rising and dipping, and the ocean sounded louder than ever.

He sat up in his bunk and peered about him. The others were still up, his mother and father and even Alice, his sister. She was nine, allowed to stay up later than he was because he was only six, but even so, she should have been abed by this. Slowly, he slid to the floor and opened the cabin door to peek along the narrow passage.

He saw two ladies down the companionway, talking quietly, and watched as they disappeared into their cabin. At least now he knew he wasn't the only one left on board.

Only slightly reassured, he returned to his bunk, allowing himself to be lulled to sleep by the comforting whispers of the ocean rather than dwelling on the vague concern that was stirring within him.

In the morning, his father, Noah, woke him with a mug of pale tea and then sat heavily on the low bunk to talk to him.

This was a rare occurrence and Clem was uneasy. 'Where's Mother?'

'You know your mother has been bad sick, son,' Noah said with a sigh, and Clem nodded, sipping his tea.

'So poorly, she's been in the ship's infirmary for the last week,' he continued.

Clem heard Alice sniff, as if she was crying, and he peered up at her bunk. 'What's the matter with Alice?'

'She's upset, leave her be. I want to talk to you. Here, finish your tea.' Noah held the thick mug as Clem swallowed the tea. 'There, that's better. Now, Clem, it's as hard a thing as I've ever done to have to tell you that your dear mother has gone to heaven. God saw she was suffering and in his kindness took her to where she can rest in peace.'

Clem stared. He didn't believe a word of it, and he was angry with his father for making up such a lie.

Above him Alice was sobbing loudly now, and Clem wished she'd stop. She might be a big girl but she could be a real cry-baby at times. His father was still talking, explaining, apologising, and Clem didn't dare contradict him. Noah was a huge man with a loud voice, not one to cross. So Clem said nothing, nodding dully like the loose head on Alice's doll, until Noah resorted to prayer, with both children kneeling beside him, cramped over the bunk.

Ladies came to the door, whispering, conferring with Noah, crowding in, patting Clem on the head, calling him a brave boy. They said Alice was a brave girl – which she was not, she was howling – and Clem didn't trust any of them.

When he finally escaped from all the suffocating clutching and patting and sweet talk, he ran headlong up top, barging into the Captain himself. That was the best thing to happen all morning. Captain took him into the wheelhouse, normally out of bounds to passengers, and let him steer the ship. *He* didn't go on about heaven and death, he had more important things to do, and Clem appreciated that. Standing on a stool, he steered the ship into the steep waves with care, to show he was a serious person, mindful of duty, and beside him, Captain smoked his pipe with patient respect.

The next day Alice stepped out in a shiny black dress, and Clem stared at her. It was an ugly dress, with a lopsided collar big and flappy across the front, and an uneven hem that scraped the floor at the sides.

'Where'd you get that funny dress?' he asked her.

'Some ladies made it for me.'

'Take it off, you look like a dwarfie old lady.'

To his astonishment Alice burst into tears.

3

'You don't look like a dwarfie old lady, Alice, truly you don't,' he offered, but she was not to be consoled.

'I do so. It's an awful dress but I have to keep on wearing it because we're in mourning. I'll always be ugly now.'

He tugged at the dress. 'You're not ugly, Alice. I heard the ladies saying what a pretty girl you are.'

'They did?' She looked at him in pleased astonishment.

'Yes, cross my heart.' It was true, but they'd added 'except for . . .' and Clem reasoned that was best left unsaid, if he was to make up for saying the wrong thing in the first place.

He wished his mother hadn't gone to heaven; she wouldn't have made Alice wear a dress like that. But she'd gone all right. After he'd looked for her in the infirmary, Clem had searched the ship. He'd looked everywhere, using his diminutive size as a cloak for spying into cabins and deep in the hold. He hoped she'd be all right in heaven but he missed her, he'd been her favourite.

Just the same, if she had to go it was a pity she hadn't taken Alice with her. He and Pa would be fine, but it was hard on Alice. She cried a lot, probably because the family had become uneven: two men, counting himself as one eventually, and only one girl now. Alice had no one to plait her hair or make her dresses or sit sewing with her, all those ladies' things she'd have to do on her own now. Poor Alice.

'Don't you worry,' he said stoutly. 'I'll look after you, Alice. When I grow up I'll always look after you.'

'Which lady said I was pretty?'

'Mrs Cathcart, and the others all agreed. I told you true, I did.'

Despite his brave words it was Alice he clung to when the ship docked at Fremantle, the first port of call in Australia, and he found himself in the bewildering confusion of the wharves, a very small boy intimidated by the noise and the crowds.

They waited an age, staring at nothing but sheds as their father made sure all their luggage was ashore, and then, to their astonishment, they had to join a queue to board a barge.

'Where are we going, Pa?' Alice asked nervously. 'I thought we had arrived.'

'We have, girl. From here we go upriver to the city of Perth. This is only the port.'

Alice was tired, and she dozed leaning against Noah as the barge plied upstream, but Clem ran from side to side, looking out at the green forests that lined the wide, calm river. Hours later they rounded a bend and came upon Perth.

Noah roused Alice. 'Look up, girl. Here we are now. End of the journey.'

Shipboard companions raised three cheers to celebrate their arrival and everyone looked eagerly at the scattering of white buildings among dusty green trees.

'Doesn't look much like a city to me,' a woman complained, but Noah laughed. 'And there's the beauty of it. A fresh country and plenty of land for all. A city doesn't have to be all smoke and clutter.'

Ashore again, Noah and Alice were busy. A wagon appeared from somewhere and Clem was told to sit on it and wait, but he sat there so long in his sailor suit, he thought they'd forgotten him, and in a panic went looking for them among a welter of luggage and hooped skirts.

Alice came running after him with that funny wobbly run of hers. She had a turned foot. Noah always said it was a perfectly good foot, it just liked looking at the other neat foot instead of the way ahead, but Alice was shy of it. Her dresses were always longer than need be, to keep it hidden, but the good ladies on the ship hadn't allowed for it, so her black boots were in full view, in all their oddity.

Her brother sighed. Adding a black shawl and black bonnet to that clumsy dress, she did look like a miniature old lady, but this time he did not tell her so.

'Give us a go, Clem,' she puffed, yanking his arm. 'You were told to stay on the wagon.'

'You took so long! Where have you been?'

'We had to fill in a lot of papers, and then there was an argument over the horse and wagon. A man claimed it was his but Pa wouldn't have that. It was the one he'd ordered to meet us, well in advance. We'd have been in a nice fix if we'd got here with all our stuff and no transport.'

'Where is our stuff anyway?'

'It's coming on the next barge. Now come back to the wagon and sit, and I'll get you a raspberry drink from the kiosk by the jetty.'

He didn't sit, but stood on the high German wagon, watching people collect their goods, and after hugs and kisses and tearful farewells march up to the town. For some reason the departures reminded him of Mother, and he hoped she knew where they were.

Noah seemed to know exactly where they were. He soon had the wagon piled high with as much as they could cart in this load – the rest of their furniture was in store, he said – and they too were on their way. They drove slowly along sandy streets until, on the outskirts of Perth, he stopped at a roadside café and bought them steaming bowls of thick soup.

'We must say grace,' he told his children.

Obediently Alice and Clem clasped their hands and lowered their eyes as he prayed.

'We thank you, Lord, for our first meal in this land, which I am pleased to say was splendid fare, and we thank you for delivering us in safety to these shores. We ask you to keep Lottie Price, our dear departed wife and mother, as close to your heart as she will always be in ours, and further to bless my little family in this our new life. Amen.'

He picked up his hat and grinned broadly at his children. 'Come along now. We're off to our new home. The farm is ten times bigger than any in our county, with a ready-made farmhouse. 'Twas a pity to have to leave Old England but we'll prosper here in the new world.'

Clem heard the excitement in Noah's voice as he lifted them into the wagon and took the reins, giddy-upping the new horse, and he grinned too, pleased to see his father in such high spirits.

But then they hadn't seen the farm.

★ ★ ★

Using the map that had been sent to him, and asking directions all along the way, Noah finally found his land at the end of a bush track that could hardly be rated as a road. But there it was, a sign nailed to a post that read: Winslow Farm.

By this, Noah's mood had changed, and he didn't seem too pleased at all, but Clem thought it was because they'd come so far and it was nigh on dusk.

'Where's the house?' he asked.

'Not far now,' Noah said, and they followed another track across this unfenced land, assisted by arrows nailed to tree trunks, until they came to a collection of broken-down sheds.

'Which one is the house?' Alice asked, but Noah handed her the reins. 'Hold on here. I'll look around.'

When he came back he had a face like thunder, and the children quaked. 'This is it,' he said. 'Get yourselves down.'

'It doesn't look much to me,' Clem said, but Alice shushed him.

'Be quiet. Don't you think Pa knows that?'

Dismayed, they followed Noah into the foremost shed, and when he lit the lantern they saw that it was indeed their new home, just one large room with four windows, no glass, each covered by hessian bags. It had a bare corrugated-iron roof and an earthen floor. The furniture consisted of grubby bunks lined against the far wall, a bare table and chairs at the other end near a large open fireplace and, surprisingly, a new pine kitchen dresser.

Clem sniffed. This place stank, and underfoot he could feel the scrunch of animal droppings, mice or rats maybe. He looked to Noah who stood, arms folded, surveying their miserable home, seething with rage.

Suddenly he went into action. 'No point in us standing staring,' he said. 'We have to bunk down here for the night, but first we light a fire and clean up this place.'

As they worked, sweeping and dusting, hauling buckets of water from the well to wash away the grime, throwing out the musty mattresses and carrying in necessities from the wagon, Clem worried. He was hungry.

'There's no food in this house. What will we eat?'

7

Alice managed a smile. 'Don't fret. Pa bought a box of starting-up provisions from a vendor at the jetty. He'll buy the rest tomorrow. There must be a shop round here somewhere.'

That night there was no grace, before or after their meal of bread and bacon, their father being in no mood to give thanks to anyone.

Clem slept fitfully, beset with cares, knowing that his father was not sleeping at all – he could hear him tossing and turning on his creaking wooden bunk. Screeching birds woke him in the morning but the others were already up. He smelled toast and that cheered him.

'What's for breakfast?' he asked Alice, who was busy at the fireplace.

'Fried eggs,' she said shortly, and Clem jerked up, listening.

'Who's Pa talking to? Outside there?'

'Shush! Hisself.'

'Why?'

'He's angry.'

Clem thought that queer and deemed it wise to stay right where he was until summoned. Noah's anger could be alarming.

When he did come in, the burly bearded man was still glowering. He ate his breakfast quickly, gulped his tea and stood.

'I have to go to town. You'll be all right here, but don't wander. I'll be back as soon as I can.'

He grabbed his town hat and coat and stormed out of the door, only to turn back and stare at them, a new softness on his rugged face. 'You be good.'

He was in a real hurry. Within minutes he was on the horse, galloping away across the uneven fields.

The children hoed into the eggs, adding some fried bacon and the last of the bread to the wide pan.

'I'm the cook now,' Alice said officiously. 'I should have given Pa a list, he won't know what kitchen provisions to buy.'

'Sure he will,' Clem said. 'But why did he have to go right back to town to get supplies? Aren't there any shops out here?'

'I don't know. You'd think there would be. If he finds one nearer, then he'll be back sooner.'

They explored the empty barn and the smaller sheds, unimpressed by this dilapidated farm, as yet bare of stock, and finding the day very hot, repaired dismally to the shelter of their hut.

Noah was back and he had a man with him. At gunpoint!

The children watched, bewildered, as he ordered the man down from his horse and set off across the fields with him. They ran to keep up as Noah hustled him more than a mile, first in one direction and then another, shocked that Noah didn't care about the stranger's city clothes when he stumbled and fell to the ground. Appalled when their own pa shouted his rage, and with his boot pushed the man's face into the dirt.

'Taste it, you bastard! Taste the land you sold me! Salty, isn't it? And why? Because it's mostly sand. And why? Because it's too close to the ocean. I'll bet this land was once covered by the sea, and I'll bet you soon woke up to that too.'

The man was red-faced, spluttering. 'You let me up, Price! I'll have the law on you.'

'No you won't. I haven't got time for that foolery. I'm not waiting years to get my money back from a land shark like you. I know all about those sort of tricks. I'll shoot you right now if I have to.'

'Pa! No!' Alice screamed.

Noah squatted on his haunches and grinned, but the grin was loaded with menace.

'This here gentleman,' he said to his children, 'is Mr Clive Garten. He got this land free, all fifteen hundred acres, because he's a clerk in the gov'mint. Then he wakes up it's crook country, useless for farming, so what does he do?'

The stranger, still on the ground, was edging away like a crab, but he stopped when Noah tilted the rifle at him with a click.

'He can't sell it locally because folks know, so he advertises it in a London paper as prime farmland, the best, handy to Perth and all that, with a cottage to boot.'

Noah looked back over his shoulder. 'Now that there hut's neither a cottage nor a farmhouse, but that I could overcome. I could build us a decent house, but I can't do anything about the soil.' He poked his victim with the rifle. 'I can't turn sand into good soil any more than I can turn water into wine. So there you have it, Alice. We've been done, good and proper, us new chums. We'll starve out here. All because of him.'

'Shoot him, Pa!' Clem was all for shooting, and even Alice was wavering.

'There's another way out of this.' Noah's voice was soothing. 'If I get my money back, every penny, then you, Mr Clive Garten, could survive this day.'

'You'll never get away with this.'

'Yes I will. I've had time to think this out. You give me your IOU or you die out here. If you renege on that, I'll come to town and shoot you dead in the main street. You can take that as my solemn oath, for I'm a man of my word.'

Back at the hut, Garten signed the IOU and, encouraged by Noah, left his gold watch for good measure.

As soon as Noah received his refund and returned the watch, they packed up the wagon and moved on, but this time Noah chose his own land.

They travelled a long, long way, over the ranges from the coast and on east in an interminable straight line for days and days, because Noah wanted land, plenty of land, at his price. There was no shortage out on these massive plains.

They came to a tiny village called York and went still further east from there until Noah was satisfied.

He bought his land, built a stone farmhouse, stocked his property with sheep and called it Lancoorie. He always referred to it as his farm, but as the children grew up they insisted it was a sheep station, not a farm. Their father was not much interested in what it was called; he went on acquiring land and more land, because there was no end to these wild acres.

Chapter Two

It was shearing time. Noah had managed to scrape enough cash together to hire three shearers to help him and Clem to get through the job while the weather was clear and warm. They only had about five hundred sheep this season, thanks to a sudden cold spell that had killed off more than seventy newly shorn sheep in one night last year, so they were going at it hard, with Alice working too, mustering them into the runs and dashing inside to collect and pile the fleece.

Nineteen now, Clem loved shearing time. He was a good shearer himself. He loved the smell of sweat and dust, the noise, and the clip, clip of the shears, the heavy hunched backs of the men, and their talk, their cursing and swearing and the irreverent laughter that seemed to dance in the air with the shower of sun particles in the shaft of light from the high window. It was a good working day, running smoothly, when one of the men coming back from the outhouse noticed a new horse at the rail.

'You got a visitor, Noah?'

'Yeah. Vicar Petchley. Bloody hangers-on, those blokes.'

'Trying to convert you, is he?'

'Fat chance!'

Clem saw the men exchange winks, and grinned, feeling part of it, though he wasn't sure of what. Shearers liked to gossip, and even more, they were great teasers, taking good-natured rises out of people.

'You ought to listen to him sermonize, Noah. It'll do you good.'

'I got no time for sermonizing.'

11

'You could get him to recite his latest while he's here. A free sermon from him and no chance to pass the plate.'

'Nothin's free. I reckon he only turns up here for a feed.'

'That's not kind, Noah. The poor feller's spreadin' the word of God.'

Noah released his ram, nudged it out the door, stood up and stretched his back. 'Well, he ain't spreading it on me.' He laughed his deep, throaty laugh. 'He can spread it on Dora. She can do with it. What is he anyway? What bloody church?'

'He's of the Wesleyan denomination, they say.'

'Never heard of it.' Noah took a rolled smoke from behind his ear and stepped outside for a break.

The grins were passed about again, and Clem watched, feeling a nervousness in the pit of his stomach.

'That vicar spreads himself round all right,' one winked.

'Has a hard time keeping it in his trousers, they say.'

'Kind to the ladies, is he?' A leer.

'Ah, terrible kind. Skinny as a link but he must have somethin' working for him, there's a few don't mind his style.'

'He's probably spreading it on Dora right now.'

Noah was in the doorway. Filling the doorway. Blocking the light. He didn't say a word. He didn't have to. They could feel his rage engulfing the shed. Then he turned and ran.

Clem dropped his animal. 'You stupid buggers! Now look what you've done!' He sprinted after his father.

'Don't take no notice, Pa. You know how they go on. Half of what they say ain't true, the other half you can't believe.'

It was a farce. Like the silly stage play they'd seen in York, in the days when they could afford to take time off to go into the village.

All the way across the paddock Noah was roaring: 'What's going on up there? By Jesus, you little apology for a dingo! If you touch Dora I'll make tripe of you!'

'Pa! Shut up!' Clem was running along beside him. He truly didn't believe that talk. 'He's a vicar, for God's sake.

He wouldn't be doing any wrong. He's a man of the church! He wouldn't!'

But as they ploughed up the back steps, the vicar was off out the front, his shirt tails hanging out of his pants. And there was Dora, her blouse askew, one large drooping bosom visible as she shot for their bedroom.

'No you don't,' Noah shouted. 'What have you got there?'

She was clutching a piece of clothing, but he tore it from her and Clem gaped as Noah held them up. Her bloomers! They really had been up to no good, the pair of them! Noah was enraged that the vicar had touched his woman, but that didn't stop him. He clouted Dora across the face, sending her flying, then he upended her, displaying her big bare bum, pushing the bloomers into her face. 'You bloody hussy! Where do these belong? Not on the bloody floor when we've got a vicar in the house, do they? You whore! By Christ, I'll deal with you when I get back.'

Clem hung back, enjoying the show. Years he'd waited for the old man to wake up to Dora, and it had to be with a vicar of all people. He wished Alice could have witnessed Dora getting her come-uppance at last. And he was still laughing as he watched Noah take off after the vicar. He wouldn't ever want to come back into this district again after Noah had finished with him!

'Bad luck, eh?' he said to the weeping Dora before he went off to find Alice, to tell her the good news.

The shearers found his body. 'His neck's broke,' one of them told Clem. Then, with a shuffle and a shift of sad eyes, 'He wouldna suffered, Clem. He'd a hit the ground. Bang! Gone! Movin' that fast, you see. Cuttin' across country. The horse took a tumble. Broke a fetlock. We had to shoot him. We're real sorry, mate. Real sorry. You come on back with me, the boys'll bring your pa in.'

'No. I'll get him. I'll bring him in.'

'I reckon we'd better get on back to the homestead. Break the news to the missus and Alice. Young Alice, she'd be best off hearing it from you than any of us.'

13

'The missus can go to hell, and there's no kind way to tell Alice. Whichever way, it'll be a shock. He's my pa, I have to be with him.'

He wished he hadn't insisted. He fought against a faint when he saw the men loading the slumped bulk of his father, Noah Wolverton Price, on to a horse, heaving him across the beast's bare back like a large, ungainly sack. But the horse, spooked, would have none of it. As they tried to strap him on she shied, bucked, snapped angrily at them, and when the body slid to the ground for the second time they kept their curses to a mutter in deference to the bereaved son standing by, the indignity of the scene a terrible embarrassment. In the end, with Clem's help his father's body was firmly aboard, covered in a saddle blanket, and they set off on the long ride back to the homestead, a good nineteen miles by Clem's reckoning.

Noah would have known that his old horse was no match for the vicar's fine mount, so he'd left the track to try to cut him off on the west road into York. Obviously he hadn't caught the bastard, Clem thought grimly. But I will one day. Not for the likes of Dora, but for the life of my father. Reduced to this.

As he rode behind the small procession, two of the men doubling on one horse, he looked out over the wide, flat sweep of country. 'Flat as a tack,' Noah used to say, with wonder in his voice. 'Flat all the way to the horizons, no matter which way you look. Bloody uninteresting I call it, but great pasture land.'

Clem had never thought about it one way or another, because he knew no different. He was a plainsman, and he took the vast country for granted. As much as a farmer could here, with one eye on the water supply. But now he looked at the huge overhang of pale-blue sky and wondered what was to be done about all this land, most of it still virgin bush. He supposed it was dull country. Sometimes you could be riding along for ten miles or so, dreaming, thinking of things, and when you looked up you'd swear you hadn't moved, it was that much of a sameness.

Other farmers had put in wheat, they had huge wheat fields,

14

and Noah had considered it, talked about it to Clem, but then he'd claim he was a sheep farmer, his family had been sheep farmers for generations, and he might as well stay one.

'You clear this land,' he told Clem, 'and the bloody trees keep coming back at you. Try burning them out and they grow even better.'

'Not if it's properly cleared. Get all the roots out.'

'And that takes money. We'd need an army of men to clear Lancoorie.'

'Not if they did it acres at a time.'

'We'll see when we get some spare cash.' He never did have enough spare cash, and then Dora and the house took what little he did have.

Alice came running down the track, hair flying, skirts bobbing, calling, 'Did you find Pa?' Then stopping so suddenly she tripped over herself.

Clem was down in an instant to help her up. 'Come away, love, Pa's had an accident.' But she wrestled free and ran on, to stand staring, speechless, at Noah's lolling head brushing the horse's flank, white hair, scraggy with sweat and grime, set loose at that angle, to resemble another beard on the wrong end of his head, eyes open in a grotesque gaze.

'He's dead!' she screamed as Clem took hold of her. 'What did that terrible man do to him?'

'Nothing. I don't reckon he caught him. Now let's you and me go and have a cuppa tea. They'll take Pa over to the shed.'

'They'll do no such thing. Bring him to the house.'

'Is that the right thing to do?' Clem asked uncertainly.

She nodded, needing his support as they stumbled past the three big oak trees that Noah had planted with acorns he'd had sent from England. He'd planned a row of them as a windbreak against the hot, dry winds that swept across the plains in the summer, but only three had survived. And only then by Alice's constant watering and nurturing.

'We'll come back tomorrer,' the shearers said, clutching their hats, their sad duty done, addressing the missus, who was prostrate on the couch, loudly bewailing her loss.

15

'No you won't.' Clem interrupted her performance. 'We'll get back to the sheds. We have to get the shearing finished.'

'Oh, you cruel boy!' Dora screamed at him. 'Have you no respect for the dead? Let them go!'

'The sheds,' Clem said, and the shearers, practical men, nodded, knowing he was right.

Women came swiftly to lay out the body, to sit with Alice in long, mysterious conversations, women's talk, while they prepared for the funeral; while Dora, in her best black taffeta with the wide gold stripes, sat obstinately on the front veranda, snuffling into a large handkerchief; while their menfolk, at a loose end, busied themselves giving a hand. They milked the cows, they mended fences, they fixed the wheel on the dray and the roof of the storehouse, and they sheared the strays that kept being found. They packed the bales of wool and set them under cover, waiting for the wagoners to come for them and take them into York. With their women and children they camped nearby like a miniature settlement, not wanting to intrude on the small family in their long stone farmhouse, but Clem felt their strength as if they were right in here with him and Alice. And it astonished him. Although he'd been called up, with Noah, for similar service over the years, he never thought these people would bother with the Prices, who were so poor-looking, compared with the other farmers and the townies. Not much of a cut above the selectors who struggled to survive on pocket-handkerchief acreages that had no place out here, ill-chosen blocks parched of water.

A new pride grew in him when he was asked to choose a site for the family graveyard and when, at the burial, several men stepped forward and spoke of Noah Price in glowing terms. 'An honest man, upright and true,' they said. 'A hard-working man who will long be remembered as one of the pioneers of the district. Taken too soon,' they said, heads nodding. 'A great loss.'

The women were distantly polite to Dora, referring to her, Clem thought gratefully, as the housekeeper, and on packing up their baskets reminded Clem and Alice that they were always welcome to visit.

16

'Don't shut yourself in now, you young people,' Mrs Gordon Swift said to them. 'Nothing to stop you coming in to the dances in the church hall.'

Alice blushed, on account of her foot, and Clem answered quickly, to cover the gaffe, 'I can't dance.'

She laughed. 'Why, Clem Price, no one can until they try, and there are pretty girls in York who'd be lining up to teach a fine strapping lad like you. How old are you now? Nineteen?'

'Yes, ma'am.'

'Then we'll be expecting you. All you young people should support the socials.'

Clem agreed he would go, knowing he'd have to find the money for a decent pair of boots if he were to do any socialising at all.

'What are we going to do about *her*?' Alice asked him when the last of the mourners rode away.

'Get rid of her.'

'She says she's not leaving.'

'Does she?' He strode into the kitchen where Dora was polishing off the last of a donated fruit cake. 'Tomorrow you leave. Pack your things up. I want you out of here!'

'This is my house, I'm staying! My brother is coming to stay here too, we got the farm to look after.'

'If you are ready by dawn I'll take you as far as York in the dray. If not, I'll dump your stuff at the end of our track and you can walk.'

Dora threw one of her tantrums, screaming abuse at Clem and at Alice, but he ignored her. When she flew at him, scratching and biting, he slapped her hard. 'That's for Noah, and a taste of what you'll get tomorrow if you're not out there in the dray first up. Now get packing.'

'Watch what she takes,' he warned Alice, 'or you won't have a pan to cook with.'

'I'm watching. She gets nothing from the kitchen, but she can take all her fripperies out of the sitting room. I'll be glad to be rid of them.'

That night, when the two women had gone to bed, Clem

17

dragged out Noah's old sea box, not surprised to find the books and papers in a jumble. Dora had been ferreting about looking for something worth taking, but since she couldn't read, there'd have been nothing in here to interest her. He found the land deeds, neatly tied with ribbons, and then lost himself in memories as he sorted through their old school books. Not that he'd ever been to school. Alice had been given the task of teaching her young brother, and at night, Noah gave them lessons in reading and writing and sums as they sat round the kitchen table. He'd been very strict about their 'learning' and they were only let off the irksome tasks on Saturday and Sunday nights. Clem smiled. Alice was the good speller, but eventually he could beat them both at sums. He was still a good counter.

As he looked over at the big old chair by the fireplace where Noah used to sit, he was overcome by the enormity of what had happened. Noah was dead. Their father. He couldn't imagine their lives without him. Until now he hadn't seemed to have time to let this sink in. It had been so sudden. He recalled laughing as Noah raced out after the vicar, not realizing it would be the last time he'd see him alive. Noah. His Pa. God, he'd miss him. Clem slammed the box shut as if to stem the tears that were welling up from inside him.

'Damn you, Noah!' he muttered. 'You spoiled our last years together as a family by bringing Dora into the house. I'll not let you foist her on us permanently.'

Dora didn't go easily. As soon as she'd unloaded her things at a friend's shack by the bridge, she made straight for the police station, demanding Clem Price be put in charge for throwing her out of her own home. Discomforted, Constable Fearley, with Dora in tow, waylaid Clem at the bank.

This was Clem's first stop in town. He felt Mr Tanner would be the best person to talk to about the station.

'I'm sorry to hear about your dad,' Tanner said. 'I always liked Noah. I couldn't go out to the funeral, it would have

18

meant closing the bank for the day and we can't have that, can we?'

'That's all right, Mr Tanner. I've come in to ask you how things stand . . . like.' He wasn't sure exactly what he wanted to know.

'Yes, I've been expecting you. Or Alice. Carty lodged the death certificate. He'll bring a copy here for you. And here's the bank statement. We've got a few papers for Alice to sign . . .'

'I'll sign them.'

'You're under age, son. How old's Alice?'

'Twenty-two.'

'That's all right, then. Did she come in with you?'

'No. There's the milking. We got no one else.' As he spoke, Clem glanced down at the neat figures on the sheet, scanning swiftly to the bottom line. 'What's this? It says five hundred pounds, three and seven pence.'

'That's right. In credit.'

'I thought we was broke.'

'*Were* broke,' Tanner corrected. 'Ah, no. Your dad called that five hundred his "sleeve". He always liked to keep it up his sleeve, he'd say, against bad seasons. Many's the time he had to dig into it, and you'd think the end of the world had come. I used to tell him we'd stand him for a loan, but he was a proud man, your dad. Asked nothing of anyone.'

'Only his kids,' Clem said angrily.

Tanner brushed at his dark beard, and leant his chin on his hand. 'Did you want for anything, Clem?' he said quietly.

'We got fed, but we lived poor,' Clem said defiantly. He looked about to make sure no one was listening. 'Look at me! I'm bloody embarrassed to come into town. I got nothin' but work clothes, and these old boots don't come any worse.'

Tanner shrugged. 'Clothes aren't the worth of a man, Clem. You'll learn that in time.'

'We needed farm hands. We got a thousand acres going to waste out there.'

'I'm aware of that, but Noah was a careful man. He saw

too many go under by overextending. The plains can be dangerous in drought seasons.'

'What about the ones who didn't go under? What about the Pedlows, and O'Mearas, and Cadmans? What about their big wheat fields? They got rich. They didn't go under.'

'They had a bumpy time though, bush fires nearly wiped out the Pedlows years back . . . One day, when I have time, I'll tell you the history of those properties over the last twenty years.'

'All right,' Clem insisted. 'But tell me now. How did they get out of it?'

'Loans. Mortgages. I can't discuss any of our clients, but a lot of farmers have debts to cover. That's what Noah couldn't, would not even consider. Do you understand?'

'Not properly. I haven't got a grip on it yet. I'd like to see the loan business on paper. Do you reckon you could show me?'

Just then Dora bounced into the bank, taking up more space in her hooped skirt and high bonnet than was spare. 'There he is, Constable! Arrest him!'

Clem sat stolidly facing a picture of the main street of Perth on the back wall, but Tanner stood, smoothing out his coat tails. 'What is the meaning of this?'

'He threw me out!' she snapped. 'Done me out of house and home, the bloody blighter he is. My husband dies and I get treated like I'm nobody.'

Constable Fearley intervened. 'She wants to prefer charges, Mr Tanner.'

'I was not under the impression that you were married to Noah Price,' Tanner said.

'Well, I was.'

'She was not,' Clem said, still looking at the picture of Perth. He hadn't been back there since they left the first miserable farm, a hundred years ago, it seemed now. He'd only been a nipper.

'Do you have a marriage certificate?' Tanner asked.

'Yeah, I got one somewhere.'

'She hasn't,' Clem said.

20

'Noah loved me!' she cried. 'For all intents and purposes I was his wife. Where's his will? That's what I want to know. Wait till you see his will. He wouldna left me out. Not Noah. He never cared about those kids of his.' She banged on the desk, plump hands bulging from their black lace mittens.

'Did you bring in your father's will?' Tanner asked Clem.

'He didn't write a will. There's no will. How could there be? He didn't expect to die while we were shearing. Or when he was chasing that dirty bastard out of his house after he'd been fucking *her*.'

Tanner stiffened. 'That's enough, Clem! We won't have that sort of language here. Since there was no will – nor was there a marriage, or I most certainly would have known of it – I suggest you escort the lady from these premises, Constable.'

'You're all the same, you men!' Dora shook a faded parasol at the bank manager, tears forming grimy rivulets through the dust that had accumulated on her cheeks during the long, awkward hours on the road. 'You think you can use women and throw them away. Well, let me tell you, Noah was different! He wasn't like that! Noah would never have seen me scorned, thrown into the street. I want my entitlements.'

Fearley took her by the arm. 'You're disturbing the peace, Dora,' he warned. 'So you just settle down now. I don't want to have to take you in charge.'

'Take me in then,' she wept. 'At least I'll have somewhere to lay my head.'

Clem had no sympathy for her. 'You can stay with your mate Mrs Penny, you were never short of excuses to come into town and visit her when Pa was alive. She's a good drinking partner, and you won't be short of company there.'

'Now, now,' Tanner said nervously, obviously afraid that Clem would commit another indiscretion in the presence of the law, since Mrs Penny was known to entertain more than her share of gentlemen callers. 'This is my place of business, Constable . . .'

The policeman took the hint and backed out, waiting for Dora, who had to have the last word: 'This is a terrible thing you're doing, Clem Price!' she hissed at him. 'I've been like a mother to you and your sister. And you take that sneer off your face! You'll never be half the man your pa was.'

She shoved through a trio of curious bank customers who were gathered at the front step, in no hurry to see the end of this juicy little drama, and swept across the sandy road, her parasol pounding the ground in dudgeon.

'Perhaps you could come back?' Tanner said to Clem, indicating the growing queue.

'Yes. In the morning.' He was glad to escape, to savour the events of the day.

As he headed for the Duke of York hotel, he felt like throwing his hat in the air and doing a little jig right then and there. Not only was he rid of Dora, he owned Lancoorie and had money in the bank! He was rich! What an old miser Noah had been. Cashed up all this time, while having them all think he was broke. Including Dora. Just as well she didn't know the truth, or she'd have put on even more of a turn. She hadn't demanded money from Clem, believing he hardly had a penny to bless himself with.

He stopped to tighten the laces on his boots, Noah's boots. He had balked at admitting to Tanner that his own boots had been resoled so often, by his pa, the uppers were grey with age.

Come to think of it, he mused, I should have asked Mr Tanner for a few quid from Noah's stash, since I've got to stay over and see him tomorrow. If Noah had left any money in the house, Dora must have grabbed it. Alice never found any. So here I am now without a bean in my pocket.

He had intended to drop Dora and go straight back to Lancoorie, eating his cut lunch out there on the road. Now he might stay a day or so. Alice would be all right.

He braced himself, strode into the dim bar and bought a beer.

'Put it on the slate, Chas,' he said to the publican. 'I'll be in town for a bit. Have you got a room for me?'

'Of course we have, Clem,' the man said kindly, pushing a beer across the counter. 'This one's on the house. Real sorry to hear about your dad, mate. He was a good bloke, old Noah.'

Clem found himself the centre of attention, friends and strangers alike treating the bereaved young man with due deference. He had never been permitted to 'knock about the district', as Noah put it, with lads his own age, so he had no real mates.

When Les and Andy Postle swaggered in, they claimed him as if they'd been friends for years, not just neighbours separated not only by a distance of thirty-two miles, from homestead to homestead, but by parental disapproval. 'Wild pair of brutes,' Noah called them, referring to their well-known leering and leching after girls, ignoring the fact that he was hardly a beacon of virtue in the drab landscape.

'Orphans!' Les intoned after several rounds of commiserating drinks. 'By Jesus, it just hit me, Clem! Youse two, you and Alice, you're orphans now. You poor buggers.' Fascinated, he worried the subject until his brother put a stop to the maudlin conversation.

'Cut it out, Les. We gotta cheer old Clem up, not make him feel worse. Come on, Clem. Have another drink.'

When the pub closed they repaired to Clem's room with two bottles of beer and a bottle of whisky that Clem had added to the slate in reckless abandon, profoundly grateful in his drunken state for the company of his two new mates.

Miraculously, Clem thought, the barmaid appeared a little while later carrying her own tribute of a bottle of beer. Her name was Jocelyn, a beautiful name, Clem told her, several times, as they made room for her curvy presence on the side of his bed. She was older than any of them, he guessed, pretty, with rosy cheeks and a mass of glistening black hair, and playful as a kitten. They drank from the bottles and laughed and teased her, and Jocelyn, with a quick tongue, gave as good as she got.

Clem hoped she favoured him over the others but it was Andy who was really making the running. He was getting more free with her by the minute, whispering in her ear, plucking at the buttons on her white blouse, even managing to undo several of them without complaints from Jocelyn, Clem observed jealously. But at the same time Clem and Les were engaged in an earnest quarrel over the merits and demerits of wheat farming, and as Jocelyn and Andy fell back, giggling and wrestling, on the bed, they merely moved aside to make room for them.

Les was ignoring the cavortings of the pair, and Clem, trying to do likewise, pretended that a man kissing and cuddling a woman right here beside him was an everyday event. It was nothing to this all-important conversation he was having with Les Postle, because the fate of Lancoorie was at stake. But out of the corner of his eye he could see the open blouse, and Andy Postle's heavy hand roaming inside. The room was hot. Sweat stood out on his face and he shifted uncomfortably.

'You'll get your turn.' Les winked at him, and Clem shuddered, shocked. He'd never been with a woman and he was petrified of trying it in front of this pair, who'd never let him live it down if he made a fool of himself.

'I've got to take a piss,' he said, and bolted for the door.

He took his time down the steps and back again, and stole along the passage, trying to think of an excuse not to return but it was his room. He wished he had gone home. But then he couldn't do that, he had a business appointment with Mr Tanner. And he had to see the clerk of the courts. Les had given him some interesting advice: 'If you can't afford to pay farm hands, get convicts. There are still some around and they're no worse than the rest of the layabouts that wander out this way. We had one for a while. Until he knocked up my sister.'

'Who? Elsie?'

'Yeah. Pa took the horsewhip to him and packed her off to Perth.'

Clem was astonished, Elsie had always seemed so dull and staid. He found he was still thinking about Elsie, standing outside that door, when he realized that a row had started inside and they were making enough noise to have him thrown out with them.

Jocelyn was sitting up on the pillows at the head of the

24

wide bed, her legs tucked under her, snarling at both of them like a cat at bay. 'I told you no, Andy Postle, so get away from me!'

'You been asking for it,' Andy snapped, and in one lunge lifted her with both arms and threw her back down on the bed, flipping her skirts up over her head and falling clumsily on top of her.

Clem stared at Les, who was tilted back on a chair with his long legs up on the dresser. 'Wanna take a bet, Clem? I'm five to one on Andy.'

At least the noise had stopped. Now there was just this muffled struggle coming from the bed.

'She'll settle down,' Les said, as casually as if he were commenting on a mare being put to stud, and Clem was appalled. He didn't know what to do. He advanced on the bed.

'Are you all right?' he asked the woman smothering under her own skirts and Andy's hefty flannel-checked back.

'Of course I'm not all right,' the voice came back. 'Get this bastard off me!'

So Clem did just that, more in a reflex action than a considered decision. He didn't know the rules of this game. He moved as fast as Andy had done, grabbing Andy by the legs and yanking him down the bed. Then, with a twist and a shove, he sent him crashing to the floor from the high bed.

His new friend leapt up from the floor, clutching his pants. 'I'll have you, you bloody maniac, Price! You coulda broken me back.'

'Go on, try it,' Clem said, shaping up, fed up with this débâcle, with Dora, with Noah and his hypocrisies, with the weight of a huge property being run like a suburban farm. With everyone!

'You try me,' he warned Andy, who, he knew, couldn't match him in size and strength, 'and you'll get the hiding of your life.'

'Listen to him!' Les, the elder of the brothers, laughed. Everything seemed to amuse Les. 'I reckon he could take you, Andy old pal. But not here, if you don't mind. Jocelyn's not in the mood, so we'd better get down to Mrs Penny's before she shuts up shop.'

Having buttoned herself up again, Jocelyn slid off the bed, bristling with resentment. 'You can go to hell, Andy Postle!'

Boldly she pushed Les's legs aside with a thump so that she could make some attempt to tidy her hair in the dresser mirror, and then she was gone.

'Well, what about it?' Les said, picking up his hat. 'Are you two coming with me, or are you gonna go down and thump it out in the yard?'

'I'll get you another time,' Andy growled at Clem, in tacit agreement with his brother's suggestion.

In a panic, Clem felt them willing him on his way to Mrs Penny's. The whorehouse was bad enough at the best of times, but what if he ran into Dora? Les would have a field day with that one. Not to mention what another confrontation with Dora would result in. He descended the back steps of the hotel for the second time that night, and suddenly let himself sprawl to the ground.

Les went to help him up, but let him fall again. 'God dammit, he's passed out.'

'Couldn't drink to save his bloody life,' Andy responded, cheered.

'We better get him back upstairs.'

'No, bugger 'im. Leave him there. Puttin' on airs, he is, with the old man still warm. And that floozie in the house. I bet he's on with her already.'

'No fear. I heard he chucked her out.'

'Ah, go on!' Andy pushed Clem with his boot. 'He wasn't that drunk a minute ago. He's probably shamming. They're as poor as church mice, the bloody Prices. He couldn't afford the couple of bob we'd need for the whores.' He kicked Clem harder, but as the pain shot through his ribs, Clem clenched his teeth and refused to react. He hadn't thought of that. Andy was right. He didn't have the money to pay a whore.

When the Postle brothers left, he gathered himself up and went back to his room, thoroughly depressed. But in the night he felt Jocelyn slip into the bed beside him, and despite the pain in his side he drifted pleasantly from a voluptuous awakening to a full realization that she was there. In the flesh. Bare flesh at that! No argument now about modesty. Nor about her intentions. Jocelyn was all over him, kissing him passionately, so frantic for him that he was astonished. He'd always understood that women needed coaxing, cajoling, but not her. Excited, wildly excited at this wondrous turn of events, Clem rolled over on top of her and took charge, afraid that she'd change her mind at the last minute.

In the morning he lay on the crumpled sheets in the dim room with the blinds still down, reliving every minute of their love-making. She'd stayed a long time, and they'd made love over and over. That in itself was another revelation. Clem felt strong and proud, especially since she'd whispered to him before she left: 'You've got a beautiful body, Clem Price. I knew you'd be good.'

He grinned, contented. Had she known he was a virgin? He hoped not. Anyway, it didn't matter now. He wondered, maliciously, how the Postle boys had got on at Mrs Penny's. They couldn't have done better than he had. It would be fun to crow over them, but unwise. He could do without the inevitable gossip.

When he emerged from the shower block beside the laundry, towelling his dark hair, he was startled to see Jocelyn pegging clothes on the line. He didn't know what to say to her. What would be the right thing? But she merely waved to him as if nothing had happened and went on with her work. Clem nodded, relieved, tucked his shirt into his trousers and marched, barefoot, over to the back staircase, past the spot where Andy had booted him. He didn't care now. He'd won the fight after all.

While he was waiting for the bank to open, he called in at the courthouse to make enquiries about hiring convicts as farm hands, believing that Les had probably been talking through his hat.

A death in the family certainly made all the difference. The clerk, knowing his circumstances, was kind and considerate. He was a busy little fellow, pale and middle-aged, working in a cupboard of a room surrounded by open shelves, tipsily piled with papers.

'We'll see what we can do for you, Clem. I've got the application forms here somewhere.' As he searched he talked: 'A shame about your dad. A terrible shame. What happened to Vicar Petchley? I heard he was out at Lancoorie that day.'

'No idea,' Clem said shortly.

'Haven't seen him around,' the clerk murmured as Clem stood stiffly, making no comment.

'Here we are. These forms have to be filled in. In triplicate. Alice will have to sign them. She has no objection to using convicts?'

'No.'

'Oh well, I daresay it will be all right. We'll find you some reasonable types. How many do you want?'

'I dunno. Er . . . two. We'll try two.'

'Yes. I think that's sensible. You being on your own. You don't want them ganging up on you.'

Clem wasn't sure that he wanted convicts at all, but he had to get someone. On the way home he'd see how Ted Cornish was placed these days too. Now that he could afford to pay workers, it would be handy to know he could call on Ted.

'These days the convicts get bed and board and they are entitled to sustenance of two and six a week,' the clerk said, passing over another form. 'These are the regulations attendant to the employment of prisoners of the state. Me, I can't see why they had to stop transportation. Convicts made a huge difference to our work force, I don't know how we'd have got along without them. And it's not as if we don't need them any more, what with the size of this state and the expansion that's going on all the time.'

Eventually, Clem was on his way again, a confusing array of forms neatly tied in a cardboard folder with thin red cord.

Dr Carty was in the bank, enjoying a cup of tea with Mr Tanner. 'Ah, Clem. Just the one I wanted to see. You all right now?'

'Yes.'

'And Alice?'

28

'Yes, thank you, Doctor.'

'Well, I've got the death certificate for you.'

'What?'

Clem was hard put to drag his mind away from Jocelyn and the intriguing notion of maybe being in a position to borrow some cash from this bank. He scarcely heard what Dr Carty had to say.

Carty reminded him, 'Your late father's death certificate, Clem. If it's all right with you, I'll leave it with Mr Tanner.'

'I'll need it to transfer the deeds of Lancoorie from your father's name to you and Alice,' Tanner explained.

'Oh yes. Of course.'

'Are you staying in town this evening?' Carty asked him, and Clem blinked, surprise tinged with a whiff of guilt. Did they know about last night? They couldn't! He already had it in mind to stay over if he could be sure that Jocelyn would be available. Beyond his bland expression, an imp of a smile was hovering. He'd stay a week if he could be guaranteed her company.

'I don't know,' he replied. 'Hadn't given it much thought. I've got some things to sort out with Mr Tanner. And I have to get some provisions for Alice.' He searched his mind for more excuses. 'And I've got some calls to make. To thank people. You know, the ladies, especially, who came out to the funeral. They were very kind, bringing food and all.'

Carty nodded, pleased. 'And so you should. Good manners seem to have gone by the board these days.'

Tanner provided another reason. 'Don't forget the headstone, Clem. Old Henty was asking, the stonemason. He does a good job and will give you the best price.'

'Yes. I'll have to do that too, won't I?'

'Then it's settled. You'll have to stay over. I was asking because it's Mrs Carty's birthday and we're having a party at the house tonight. I realize you're in mourning, Clem, but I don't think the Lord would frown, or your dear departed father. You're so rarely in town, you're entitled to a little time off. You've been through a lot lately. We'd like you to join us.'

Clem stared at him. He'd never liked Carty much. He was a short, plump man with a shock of white hair and red, womanish lips accentuated by wispy white sideburns, but his eyes were cold. Pale blue and as cold as charity. As if, people said, you were a damn nuisance inconveniencing him by getting sick. And he was very wealthy, one of the richest men in the district, dealing in land as well as owning the lucrative Carty Coach and Carrying Company.

'He'll be there.' Mr Tanner answered for Clem.

'Good. We'll expect you at five,' Carty said. 'Don't bother to bring a present, Clem. It's not expected.'

'What was that all about?' Clem asked the bank manager when the doctor had gone. 'I don't even know him very well. And I've never met his missus.'

Tanner laughed, removing the tea cups from his desk. 'Think about it. You've got a fine property out there.'

'Who says so? Three-quarters of it is still scrub. The wool clip just keeps us afloat. Better than I thought, I have to admit, but that don't make me no shapes for the likes of him.'

'Doesn't make me any,' Tanner corrected. 'You have to watch your speech. Noah knew better and so should you. It's just laziness.'

Clem slumped into a chair. 'Are we talking about Carty or my manner of talking?'

'Both. You'll be twenty in a few months and you're "landed", Clem. Lancoorie might be under-developed but it's still a fine sheep station. You shouldn't underestimate yourself. Especially where men like Carty are concerned. He has three daughters, all of marriageable age. I'd say Carty's got an eye on you as a possible son-in-law. There aren't too many really eligible young men about. We have a shortage of single men and among them few that Carty would even consider for his daughters.'

'And he's looking at me?'

'I'd say so.'

'Jesus! That's a turn-up.'

'Possibly. And you could begin to watch the company you keep. I heard you were drinking at the Duke of York last night

30

with the Postle boys. I'd avoid them in future. No harm in it, I'm sure, but could you imagine Dr Carty lining up one of his girls with either of them?'

'I suppose not.'

'Noah might have been strict, but you've got a good reputation. All I'm saying is, keep it that way. I don't want to sound like a Dutch uncle . . .'

'You're not doing a bad job.' Clem grinned and Tanner sat back in his chair.

'I'm glad you're not taking offence. If my customers do well, then so do I. You get the picture? A bank is a business and so is a sheep station. It's in both of our interests that you get it right.'

For the first time Clem took a good look at this man: a bank manager, high and mighty on the York social scale, an important man. Almost unapproachable, he'd thought, giving due deference to the neatly trimmed beard and the serious dark suit. He now began to get the measure of Tanner. Man to man, for God's sake! Wait till he told Alice about this revelation. Tanner was human after all, and only about forty.

'You reckon I should go?'

'Definitely. I'll be there, with my wife. We don't have any children to worry about, so that's not my ulterior motive.' He opened a tin of peppermints and passed one to Clem. 'You won't let me down?'

'I can't go. I haven't got any decent clothes. And what's more, I walked out of here yesterday with no money. I'm on the slate over there at the Duke of York for bed and board and a few drinks. Can I draw some of Noah's money?'

'Not until Alice signs the papers, but I'll give you an advance on it.'

'Jeez, that's a relief. Can you give me enough to get some gear? I can't arrive at Dr Carty's place like this.'

'Lunchtime. Meet me over at the draper's and we'll fit you out. In the meantime you'd better go and see Henty. You can order a really nice gravestone for Noah. He'd like that.'

He stood, his usual move to dismiss customers, and Clem

31

stood too, reacting, but there was that other matter. 'One more thing, Mr Tanner. Once I get things sorted out, I'll need to borrow some money to expand. I've decided against grain.'

'That's fair enough. Go with what you know.'

'And you'll give me a loan? So's I can keep some cash up my sleeve?'

'We'll see.'

'I've applied for convict labour, to clear some country.'

Tanner was delighted. 'You have? Good for you. I was thinking of suggesting that. I'll put in a word for you.'

'And another thing.' Clem was losing confidence. 'I don't want to go to the doctor's house on my own. Can I come over here at five o'clock? Go with you and Mrs Tanner?'

'Of course. The bank will be closed. Come to the house at the back and walk up with us.'

'I'm still not too sure about this. I've never been to a party.'

'Don't worry. No one will bite you. Now run along.'

Forewarned, Clem went along to the party prepared to withstand the advances of three marriage-bent girls, but he had no need for concern, they hardly noticed him.

He was quite proud, sporting new trousers, a striped shirt with a stiff collar and bow tie, and a short-back-and-sides haircut that made him feel like a shorn sheep, but which he had been assured was fashionable. And arriving with the Tanners was a boost to his confidence. As soon as they walked in through the gate, people converged on them from all directions, anxious to ingratiate themselves with the bank manager. Clem wondered which of them were bound to the bank by mortgages.

The Carty house was an imposing two-storey brick building with a small porch at the front where Dr and Mrs Carty and their three daughters waited to welcome the guests once they had disentangled themselves from meetings and greetings of their own in the garden.

He vaguely knew the girls, having seen them at gatherings

over the years, but Dr Carty reminded him: 'Clem, you know Thora, and Lettice and Felicia?'

One by one, the girls bobbed and dropped their eyes and chanted: 'Sorry to hear about your father, Clem,' in such a way that he knew they were following instructions.

They all wore pretty white dresses, with coloured sashes and deep flounces that brushed the polished floor, and they looked very gracious indeed. Thora was the tallest of the sisters, very aloof, with long blonde hair and cool blue eyes like her mother's. She had real style about her, Clem thought. Lettice and Felicia, younger, had curly hair, rosy cheeks and pink pouty lips. They were all about his own age, give or take a few years, and as he filed down the passageway with other guests to the rear of the house, the venue for the party, he contemplated the girls, at the same time casting furtive glances into spacious sitting rooms (two of them), a gleaming dining room, past a white-railed staircase and a large kitchen, over-crowded with busy ladies. Given a choice, if the occasion ever arose, he decided he'd choose Lettice. As he'd moved on he'd noticed her expression change for the next guest into merriment, her brown eyes twinkling. Thora had remained aloof, nodding curtly. But Lettice? Imagine being married to someone called after a plant. Her name had been a constant joke among the kids in the district.

Mrs Tanner disappeared into the kitchen and Clem walked on with his escort across the wide back veranda, where tables were already set for supper, into a yard where the trees were decorated with colourful ribbons and Japanese lanterns, not yet lit. Even the dunny right down the back looked festive, its pointed red roof peeping over a brush screen garlanded with flowers.

Clem was impressed, and not a little awed. He'd never seen such a display, and there were so many people out there, all dressed to kill. Especially the ladies, hooped skirts mushrooming in gay groups. He followed Mr Tanner to where the men were gathered about a keg of beer and a white-jacketed waiter dispensed the hard liquor and jugs of wine. He stayed there most of the night, leaving only to converge on the supper table, obeying the call, and returning later to stand about with other young men, eyeing off the girls, listening to jokes and rude comments. Becoming bored. Thinking of Jocelyn.

At one stage Mrs Carty invaded their clique and dragged them over to mix with the young ladies who were gathered by the back steps, and who giggled furiously, sharing a common awkwardness.

Clem managed to station himself by the middle Carty daughter, determined, now that he was in the presence of the girls, to make some sort of a showing.

'How are you, Lettice?' he asked firmly, as if he were a veteran at parties.

'I'm very well, thank you, Clem. How is Alice?'

'She's very well.'

'You should have brought her.'

'There wasn't time.'

'Oh well. Another time.'

Her sister interrupted. 'Lettice, Mother wants you in the kitchen.'

Clem was surprised when Lettice touched him on the arm with a disappointed shrug. 'I'd better see what she wants.'

One of the lads nudged him. 'You're doing all right, Clem. She likes you.'

And so it seemed to him for that fleeting moment, and he was sorry she'd been called away. He could get to like Lettice.

Loud voices from the house caused a sudden rent in the air, and people turned, curious, glancing about for an explanation.

'What's going on?' Clem asked a girl who had replaced Lettice by his side.

'Thora's missing,' she whispered, 'and Dr Carty's furious.'

'Missing?'

'Yes, she's got a boyfriend and he wasn't invited. Lettice thinks she probably ducked off to meet him.'

'Thora!' Clem was amazed.

34

'Yes. She's got a crush on Matt Spencer. Do you know him?'

'No.'

'He's not a bad-looking bloke, but he's a stable hand at Dr Carty's coach company. He might as well be the nightman to Dr Carty, absolutely beyond the pale. They say the doctor has threatened to horsewhip him if he comes near Thora again.'

'And Thora's gone to meet him!'

'I reckon so. I bet he'll be grilling Lettice and Felicia, but he won't get anything out of them.'

Thora never did reappear, and Clem drifted away, hoping that Lettice would seek him out later, but that didn't happen. Eventually he concluded it would be prudent to disengage from the now-rowdy lads, some of whom were at the staggering stage, so he thanked his hosts and left with the Tanners, a model of propriety.

'Did you enjoy yourself, Clem?' Mrs Tanner asked him as they walked down the road.

'Yes, thank you. Did Thora come back?'

She pursed her lips. 'That's not for us to discuss.'

'Oh! No, I guess not,' he mumbled.

'I thought it was an excellent affair all round,' Tanner said breezily, slowing to restoke his pipe, and Clem grinned to himself, realizing that the bank manager was a bit tipsy.

'Rather too much alcohol,' Mrs Tanner sniffed. 'I don't know why people need liquor to enjoy themselves. Dr Carty should know better.'

'Ah, now.' Tanner exhaled heavily. 'That's not for us to discuss.'

She turned on him. 'Are you mocking me, Mr Tanner?'

'Not at all, my love.'

Angrily she quickened her pace, and the men strode out to keep with her, their footsteps crunching into the stillness of the night. A dog barked as they turned into a side street, and Tanner woofed back at it. Clem laughed.

They crossed over to the manager's residence at the rear of the bank, where Mrs Tanner exacted her revenge.

'Finish your pipe out here,' she instructed her husband. 'You know I can't stand that smell in my house. I'll say good night to you, Clem, and remind you that you have a duty to bring your sister in to church whenever possible.'

'Yes, ma'am. I'll do that,' he replied to placate her. It was a full day's travel in the dray from Lancoorie to York and back, and it hardly seemed sensible for a church service, when all the stores were closed. It would be faster to ride, but in Sunday clothes? Alice would be mortified. Come to think of it, she didn't have any Sunday clothes. He'd have to see to that.

'Did you see Henty?' Tanner asked him, leaning against the fence, ready for a chat while the pipe still glowed, and Clem's heart sank. He'd been hoping to hurry back to the hotel now, in case Jocelyn was still up.

'Yes. It's all fixed. He's going to send the headstone out when it's ready.'

'Good. You know, you don't want to think too badly of Noah over that Dora woman. Men get lonely, and he wouldn't have given himself the time to go courting. He was a fine man.'

Clem looked at him curiously. 'I never imagined you knew him that well.'

'He did me a favour once. A long time ago. When I first came here.'

'What sort of a favour?'

'He got me out of a bit of trouble.'

'What trouble?'

Tanner hesitated, taken aback by the direct question, then he shrugged. 'Money trouble. Gambling. I got carried away, lost too much at cards and couldn't pay.' He warmed to his story. 'I was in a real fix. Could have cost me my job. And just at that time Noah Price walked into the bank. He only came in once in a blue moon, so that was my lucky day. And he never mixed much in town, so I knew he wasn't one to gossip. Anyway, I took a chance on him. I told him the spot I was in and mentioned I'd appreciate a loan.'

'Couldn't you have borrowed it from the bank?'

'I did. Madness. The road to ruin for a bank man, with

inspectors breathing down your neck. I had to replace the money quickly.'

'I'll bet Noah got a surprise.'

'He did indeed. He loaned me the money, refusing to charge me interest, claiming it was ungodly. But I had to put up with a lecture on the error of my ways. I remember him saying: "There's a time to sow . . ."'

'". . . and a time to reap",' Clem responded. 'I got that one plenty of times.'

'Yes. Back then I wasn't sure what he was getting at, not being a farmer. He said a farmer smells the air, smells the soil, and he knows exactly when to start sowing a crop, and so it had to be in my business. I gave up gambling on the spot – that wasn't hard after the fright I got – and eventually I woke up to what Noah meant. I began to study banking very carefully instead of regarding it as just a job, and I got very good at smelling the air. Picking which of my customers were fertile soil.'

Clem moved in on the opportunity. 'Do you think I'd be fertile soil for a decent loan?'

'I couldn't say, as yet. You're bold enough. But I owe it to your father to give you careful consideration.'

Clem slept well. It didn't seem to matter any more that Jocelyn chose not to visit him again. He was eager to set out for Lancoorie.

In the morning he paid his hotel bill, returned to the drapers and bought presents for Alice, then turned the dray to the general store, splurging on groceries to please her. He'd had a great time in the little town and he wanted his sister to share some of his excitement, as a reward for staying behind at the lonely homestead. He had so much to tell her about everything that had happened – all except his night with the Postle brothers, and with Jocelyn. He blushed. His Dora! Because he knew now in the clear light of day that Jocelyn was of the same ilk as Dora. He could almost hear his father laughing.

*　　*　　*

37

Alice couldn't believe her eyes as he unpacked the dray and piled his presents into her arms. As well as a blue dress and bonnet, he'd bought her linen for the house, to replace the old patched sheets on the beds and towels so thin and worn they were reduced to threads. A dozen of everything, pillowcases and shams as well. Laughing, teasing her, he piled them so high they spilled to the dusty ground and she floundered to retrieve such precious booty.

'For God's sake, Clem. What have you done? Robbed a bank?'

'No need, sister mine! We ain't, I mean we're not broke at all. Noah was holding out on us.'

He carried in a box and she stared as he unloaded hams and jams and tinned peaches, boiled lollies, cakes and sweet buns; big red apples for them, and green apples for the horses.

'My Lord, Clem, what's all this?'

'I went to the store too.'

'I can see that. But next time, if you don't mind, I'll do the providering. We could do with fresh tea and flour and sugar, and you bring home this peculiar fare.'

'Don't you like these things? This ham is sugar-cured, the very best.'

'Yes, of course, but Clem . . .'

'Don't worry. Help me unpack and I'll explain it all to you. Over a party.'

'A what?'

'A party. You and I, Alice Price, are going to have a party. I know all about parties now, I went to one in York.' He handed her a flagon of wine. 'This is what they served, so I bought some for you as well.'

Alice frowned. 'Are you sure you're not still under the influence?'

'Never let it be said. I'm stone-cold sober. And look here . . .' He hauled out two unwieldy parcels. 'Blankets. Not grey old things, real wool. One for you and one for me. I was thinking, if it's all right with you, I could move out of my room into Pa's room. Mine's just a sleepout. We can keep it for visitors.'

'What visitors?'

'You never know. People might come to visit.'

'Let's get all this stuff inside, Clem. Or should we leave it on the dray so that you can get the money back? I knew I should never have let you go to town on your own. I've been worried sick.'

Alice sat like stone at the kitchen table as he set out all their party fare, slicing the ham, opening a tin of peaches with a knife, spilling sticky boiled lollies on to a tin plate, producing the squashed buns. 'I should have bought a tablecloth,' he commented casually. 'I remember we used to have pretty tablecloths. Our mother embroidered them herself.'

'They wore out.'

'I suppose they did. We used to have nice things.'

'So?'

He uncorked the wine. 'This is called claret. It's what Dr Carty serves to guests in his house. The very same thing.' He reached for two thick tumblers. 'We'll have to drink our claret from these . . . Dr Carty served the wine in nice glasses, and at the store, in a cabinet, I saw fine glasses. They had two, real crystal like our rose bowl, Mrs Hannigan showed them to me. They sing when you plink them with a finger. They're a bit rich for us but one day I'll buy you crystal glasses, Alice. For now, though . . .' Clem poured her wine.

She took it with a sigh. 'If you're talking about the rose bowl in the sitting room, the one that Mother and Pa got as a wedding present, it's not crystal, it's cut glass. Now, Clem, you tell me the truth about all this.'

Piece by piece, Clem related the tale of his visit to York. Good news and bad news. Alice was upset to hear that Noah did have money in the bank. More upset than he'd expected. His reaction had been surprise, irritation and then delight, but she was hurt.

'That was cruel of him.'

'I suppose he knew he couldn't refuse Dora, so best to shut up.'

'You've given me a lot to think about, Clem.'

39

'That's right,' he said eagerly. 'We've got such a lot to think about. I've got all these papers to sign. For you to sign, I mean, me being under age. And I've put in an application to employ two convicts.'

That took some explaining.

'I don't understand,' Alice said. 'We give them jobs out here. Miles from anywhere. They're not imprisoned. Why don't they just bolt?'

'Where to? In all these years only one prisoner has escaped from West Australia, and he was an Irish political. He had help. Stowed away on a ship bound for America. Everyone heard about him.'

'But these fellows? Why don't they just run away?'

'That's what I keep saying. Where to? Take me, for instance, Alice,' he said magnanimously, quaffing more of the splendid claret, wishing he'd gone for this at Carty's party instead of sticking to the best-known beer. He'd know better next time. 'Where was I? Right. Now, I'm a bushie. Been out here since I was six. Know the country. Now, I ask you, if I was on the run, where would I go?'

She was intrigued, leaning forward, sipping on the wine as she contemplated the problem, her eyes, always intelligent, roving over the possibilities. 'Not east,' she replied. 'Heading for endless desert. No way out.'

'North?' he asked.

'Dangerous,' she said. 'Even from York. You'd need a gun and ammo and a lot of know-how to live off the land, but where would you be going?'

'That's right,' he encouraged her. 'A few thousand miles on foot to hit a coast if the Abos didn't get you. Try south.'

'A man could hide out in those big forests there . . .'

'Forever?'

'Make for the port of Albany.'

'After journeying hundreds of miles on foot, a stranger would stand out in a small town like that.'

She smiled. 'All right then. I'd make for Perth.'

'Good. That's only a hundred miles, with the same worry of seaching for water and a feed, and by then every man and

40

his dog would be searching for you. The police would grab you in no time. But that's not our problem, so cheer up.'

'It doesn't seem right to be celebrating, with Pa just buried up there.'

'He wouldn't want us to be miserable.'

'Nor would he want us to go spending his savings like this. He'd expect us to be just as cautious with our money.'

'That's it, Alice. Our money. It's ours now, and there's more where that came from.'

'God in heaven! How can that be?'

As he sliced the ham, Clem outlined the conversation he'd had with the bank manager. 'So you see, I'm sure Mr Tanner will give us a loan if we ask.'

'A mortgage, you mean. Pa was always afeared of mortgages.'

'It's the only way to get ahead. Everyone gets loans, that's what banks are for.'

'I'll have to think about that.'

'Of course you will. We'll have to decide the best way to use a loan, to make it work for us.'

Ham sandwiches, more wine, followed by the cakes and buns moved Alice into a less nervous frame of mind, and Clem jollied her along with the gossip from York until he had her laughing.

'One thing we can be thankful for,' she said fuzzily. 'That Pa didn't write a will. I was petrified you'd find it at the bank. He'd have made provision for Dora, he couldn't see past her. Not until the last day, anyway.'

'He did.'

'Did what?'

'Make provision for Dora in his will. He left her half of everything.'

Alice stared, stunned.

'I thought you said he didn't leave a will.'

'I lied. He did. I found it in his box, it was in the Bible. I burned it.'

'Oh my God! You looked them in the eye and lied like that!'

'Not exactly. I threw in some really foul language about the vicar and Dora. That got Mr Tanner in such a spin, he shut down the talk quick fast before I got arrested, what with the Constable standing there.'

Alice blushed. 'You didn't mention what went on here between those two?'

'Sure I did. It caused such a fluster, they forgot to pin me down, to ask me again if I was sure there wasn't a will.'

'Why didn't you tell me you found it?'

'Because you might have owned up. Now you can't. Not without getting me into a lot of trouble.' He looked earnestly at her. She really was quite pretty, much like the photograph of their dear departed mother, with her heart-shaped face and big brown eyes. Admittedly, unlike their English mother, Alice's skin was browned and freckled from the sun, but that didn't matter; most of the girls out here on the plains looked like that. If the sun didn't get them, the hot winds did. He and Noah shared different features, with high cheekbones and hawk noses and wide mouths that held good, even teeth. Noah used to boast he still had all his own teeth. Clem hoped he would too at that age. False teeth were a great mystery to him.

'Now you listen to me, Clem Price,' Alice said eventually. 'You promise me you'll never do that again.'

'Do what?'

'Swear in front of a policeman. You really could have been arrested.'

In the morning he walked outside to take a look around. He had a lot of thinking to do.

The house, for instance. It was a long, low stone building with an iron roof and an awning along the front, for shade.

Some of the properties had brick or timber houses, two storeyed, like the swell houses in York, but they were in the minority. On the other end of the scale a lot of families still hung on in slab huts, no better than small cow sheds. They were the very poor settlers, like Ted Cornish, who'd been sold a useless pocket of land for a sheep run on the east boundary of Lancoorie, into the more arid country. Ted was a shepherd, and his dad before him. And probably back further. He was no farmer, he never should have tried it, but he asked no advice of anyone as far as Clem knew. He just bought land, the dream of so many. Noah's dream, too. All these people coming from Britain, seeing land as space, not just land. Because that was all it was out here, just bloody space with a million acres more behind it if anyone was mad enough to keep going. And they did.

'A bloomin' shame,' Noah had said about the misfortunes of Ted Cornish. 'He's stuck. Land's too poor to carry enough sheep and too small to sell. He'll end up walking off too.'

And yet he, Noah, had bought more than three thousand acres out here because it was going cheap, more land than he knew what to do with. Clem wondered if he should sell a thousand acres. Get in some cash.

The inside of the Lancoorie house had begun with an earthen floor, a rock-hard mix of termite mud and water that was easy to care for, but not good enough for Dora. She had to have floorboards, even outside under the awning to make a real veranda, though Noah had balked at that extra expense. But she got her floorboards inside, and Alice got the job of keeping them polished. Then she had to have a sitting room, so Noah added another room on to the end of the house after the kitchen, made a bench and a few chairs to put in it and let her order all sorts of cheap fripperies from the catalogues to put in there. But he still preferred his heavy old chair by the fireplace in the kitchen, and the family still sat round the kitchen table at night as they'd always done.

The sitting room became known as Dora's room. In the meantime there was no money for their clothes. Clem wore Noah's hand-me-downs, and to her acute embarrassment Alice was given Dora's gaudy cast-offs. Her complaints fell on deaf ears. To Noah, if the material wasn't 'wore out' then it was wearable. They ate mutton three meals a day, hot, cold and in soup with the vegetables that Alice managed to grow in her small garden. Dora never seemed to care about their diet – 'Knows no better,' Alice would comment angrily – as long as she had her grog and the tins of biscuits and sweets hidden under her bed.

Now the sitting room, swept clear of the wall pictures and old calendars, hanging scarves and shawls, frothy dolls and music boxes, tin spittoons, china ornaments, piles of empty chocolate boxes and all the rest of Dora's hoard, looked bare, but fresh and clean. Clem wished it had looked like that when all those neighbours had come for the funeral.

He turned to gaze across the cleared land to the surrounding bush, a wall of trees that, to survive, never grew too tall in this parched land. Beyond, there were water holes, a few fresh but mostly salt. For a while there he and Noah would collect and bag the salt for sale, but too many other farmers had the same idea, so their hard work was not worth the effort.

He leant on the fence and whistled to his horse for company. The animal trotted over and blinked at him curiously.

'I'll get money,' Clem said. 'I'll raise a mortgage so I'll have money to pay the labourers, but what to do with them? Clear more land? Raise more sheep? But what if we have a couple of dry years again?' That was always the bugbear.

He'd often argued with Noah about building a real dam, but Noah had said there wouldn't be enough rainfall to fill it. Now his son wasn't so sure. He'd been riffling through Noah's *Countryman* magazines and come across a rainfall listing of recent years. Allowing for evaporation, Clem was fairly certain a dam could be maintained.

He shrugged and headed for the woolshed to get the bales ready for the carriers, wrestling with that other question. Wheat? The seasons here were known as summer, winter and hell. Hell was high summer, temperatures up over the hundred mark, dust storms and lightning and fire. The bush could shoot flames skywards without warning and farmers could only watch helplessly as fires roared into life, burning out in their own good time. Clem had seen wheat fields go up like that, caught in the path of destruction, and he'd pitied the farmers. All that work for nought. And the fear writhing in your gut year in and year out that it would happen again.

Alice came out to help him, tying her long hair up and tucking it into a checked scarf as she limped along.

'You know, Alice,' he said, weary as an old man. 'I wouldn't mind selling up the lot here and moving to Perth.'

'What would we do in Perth?'

'That's the trouble. I don't know. But I can't see myself breaking my back clearing land for the rest of my life just so's I can break my back shearing more sheep.'

She laughed. 'More sheep means more money, and money's comfort, they say. I wouldn't be too keen on selling Lancoorie, I think we'd live to regret that, but oh . . . Clem, I'd dearly love to see Perth. They say it's grown into a fine city, the jewel of the west.'

Clem looked at her, surprised. Somehow it seemed out of character for his sister to have such dreams, any dreams. Alice was too stolid, too matter-of-fact, too set in her ways. He felt a rush of fondness for her, pleased that she'd confided in him. After all, there wasn't much chance of Alice marrying, what with the gammy foot, so he guessed she'd always be with him. It would be his duty to look after her.

'One of these days I'll take you, Al,' he said, her proud champion now. 'We'll go there, you and me. We'll have a holiday.'

'Where will we stay?'

'In a hotel, a grand hotel. And we'll go and look at the sea again. We haven't seen the sea since we left the ship. Wouldn't that be something?'

Alice loved Lancoorie, she loved living out here in this breathtaking endless expanse. She was old enough to remember the bitter cold and the dampness of their cramped farmhouse back in England and the constant fights and arguments staged by her parents. It hadn't been Noah's idea to migrate, it had been Lottie Price who'd wanted to come to Western Australia. She'd read about it in a magazine and had her heart set on living in a sunny clime. Noah had tried to tell her that these places were not all they were cracked up to be, but she wouldn't listen. Not her. Lottie had it in her head that migrating was a superior thing to do, it made her a cut above everyone else in their village. Or so she thought. That was what was at the back of it, Alice knew, nothing to do with whether or not a drastic move like this was viable. Lottie just wanted to be able to crow, to be able to write home to friends and families of how much better off she was than everyone else.

Grandma had accused her of it straight out. 'You're a devious miss, Lottie. Good or bad you'll be writing back your glowing tales about life over the seas. You don't give a damn about your family, about your husband, a good man and a good provider. You'll have these little bairns growing up with no notion of us, none at all, and it's wrong, I say.'

'It's for Noah to make the decision!' Lottie retorted.

'And that's what you call it, do you? Nagging the man day and night, sulking, throwing those tantrums. I'm awake up to you, my girl. Ever since Alice was born with that poor sad foot of hers, you've been wailin' inside, ashamed of her, believin' people think less of you because of it.'

Alice could hear the banging of pans, indicating that her mother was trying to drown out Grandma's voice. 'You're all for the limelight, my girl, and you shun that child because . . .'

'Shut up! Shut up!' Lottie screamed. 'Leave me alone. You're just jealous, you all are!'

Outside the window Alice had cringed. She'd always known her mother was ashamed of her; she always walked ahead of her as if trying to disassociate herself, and it was her idea to dress her daughter in skirts that were too long, but Alice understood. She didn't mind. What hurt now was for Grandma to be saying so. Out loud. She huddled against the wall, humiliated.

Lottie got her way, and they started to pack up for the sea voyage. Noah was no match for his wife any more than, years later, he could control Dora. He was a strong man with strong opinions, but when it came to the women who shared his bed, pleasured him, he was weak.

Alice, even more than Clem, had hated the woman her father had brought into the house, but she'd held her tongue, recognizing the danger. Noah had cut himself off from his family back home to please his wife, and she knew he'd do the same for Dora if his now-adult offspring forced him to choose. And hadn't Alice been proved right by that outrageous will, leaving half to that whore? She moved quickly about the shed, opening out the bark shutters and securing them with sticks, letting the light in, nodding gently to herself. She'd ever be grateful to Clem for that swift move. He'd solved the problem that was not with Dora, as he thought, but with their father. She wondered if he would turn out the same as Noah, letting a woman lead him about by the nose like a bull in a ring. She hoped not. Although she day-dreamed of having a handsome suitor sweep her off her feet one day, Alice knew that her chances of marriage were very poor, so eventually she could be faced with this same situation again, when Clem brought home a wife. But Lancoorie was half hers now, she was a woman of means and she intended to stay that way.

Right from the start she'd taken to this property, even though they'd lived in a bell tent until Noah and the two farm hands had built the house. Not that she and Clem had minded living in the tent. It was fun, better than the first place, that was gloomy and stunk and had rats. But nothing could ever erase from her mind that first morning at Lancoorie. When she awoke, all was quiet, Noah was off somewhere nearby, Clem was asleep. Alice had stepped outside in the tingling early light to find they were completely surrounded by the old bush she was already well acquainted with after that tiring wagon journey over the range and straight east, but a wondrous change had taken place! All about, in every direction, the bush was carpeted with sheets of colour, on and on, everywhere! It was spring in this topsy-turvy land, September, and wild flowers were blooming gaily. Yellows and pinks and purples and blues, in myriad shades, had turned the dull undergrowth into a fairyland.

Delighted, the girl, in her white nightdress, her hair stream-ing, had run out into the midst of all this beauty, to be part of the romance, the loveliest experience of her life.

Still is, Alice thought fondly. Still is. Of course, now she knew the names of all those delicate flowers, the fringed lilies, coral vine, Queen of Sheba orchids, wild gladioli and all the rest . . . the cornucopia of the west. Every year she looked forward to their return. They were always there in the bush by their thousands. To gather them by the basketful for the house wouldn't so much as make a dent in the profusion. They were there, delicious, smiling, heartwarming in their sweet constancy. Even with clearing, all along the sandy roads the mischievous blink of colour would reappear in scattered, untidy array, and seeing them Alice felt she could hear the little rascals cheering.

Local women often boasted of their wild flower collections, poor brown, dead things pasted into the pages of books, but Alice was appalled by this insensitivity. To her it was as disgusting as collecting the superb butterflies that fluttered about the wild flowers and pinning them to parchment, stealing their short and fragile lives. For years now, Alice had refused to pick any of the wild flowers, to deprive them of their massed glory. That was what they were all about. They were not garden flowers, they were wild and free and not meant to be captured and taken from the light.

Ah yes, this was Lancoorie. Her Lancoorie. And she had other tales to tell herself, her own tales, never shared. Clem was too young, Noah too busy. And anyway, Alice had always tried to be motherly, helpful, not a silly girl, though she knew there was a lot of silliness in her. Secret silliness. Romantic, if you like.

Take the time she came face to face with a kangaroo out by the horse trough. That was early days, with the house half built. She'd seen them before, bounding across country, but never so close, only a few feet away.

It had been drinking from the trough and it looked up at her, not startled, but its doe eyes were mildly curious.

Under the stare, by habit, Alice had shifted her twisted foot out of sight and the kangaroo had moved its head sharply to note the action. It stared at her and Alice had a sudden lilt of glee, a cheekiness foreign to her.

'What are you looking at?' she said boldly. 'You're a

funny-looking thing yourself. Your legs are all bent. Your knees are backwards.'

The kangaroo stayed and Alice sat down. She stayed too. The sweetness in the face of this docile animal that dared not breach the gap engendered loveliness in the moment. Love. Something she yearned for so desperately in this matter-of-fact, lonely world. She longed to pat the animal, to cuddle it, but she dared not. In the end she moved first, and the kangaroo, released, bounded away.

Alice's love of wildlife was just part of her growing up at Lancoorie. She'd had pet dogs, lambs, joeys, kookaburras, magpies, but when Noah found she had a dingo pup, he'd killed it, and that was the day, unknown to anyone else, when he lost his daughter. And now he was gone, and that stupid woman too. No one had noticed that Alice hadn't shed a tear on the death of her father. She was the elder of the two children. It had been her role to keep her chin up, as they had expected, which was convenient.

In the kindness of the women of the district who'd come together in their hour of need, she'd seen their pity for her and their conclusion that here was a young woman destined for spinsterhood because of her deformity. She too knew about animal husbandry: important to the survival of livestock, defects were eliminated, not passed on. The Postles, neighbours, had an elderly aunt with webbed fingers. A spinster, naturally. And the Aborigines who wandered in small clans about this land which once had been theirs, were even more adamant in correcting nature. They killed deformed babies at birth. Old Sadie, an Aborigine woman who occasionally came by the homestead with her motley collection of relations, had even remarked on Alice's foot with wonder that she had survived.

'You missus got plenty good spirits, eh?'

'Yes, Sadie. I've got plenty of them. So you better watch out. Don't get me cranky, eh?'

'No, missus. No fear.'

Even though transportation of felons to Australia had ceased, there were still men serving out the last of their sentences, some in the dreaded Fremantle jail, others less dangerous and more trustworthy given tickets-of-leave to work for chosen employers.

Alice Price's application, witnessed by Mr Tanner and Dr Carty, was approved and two convicts were delivered to Lancoorie by an officious Constable Fearley, who bade them stay on the trap until he had attended to the paperwork.

Alice thought that was a bit much, to be telling grown men to stay in place like kids, but they grinned, tipped their caps and pulled out tobacco tins, so she hurried into the kitchen after Clem and the Constable.

Being of age, it was for Alice to sign all the papers again on behalf of the owners of Lancoorie, but she insisted on studying them first.

'Which is which?' she asked, looking at the names and then out of the open door at the two silent men.

'The big feller is George Gunne, and the lighter chap on the other side there, with the red hair, he's Mike Deagan.'

Alice gazed at them nervously. 'What did they do?'

'It's all there, you have a copy of their records, Alice, and they have to be kept up to date. Like how they're behaving. Clem can do that for you.' He turned to the man of the house. 'I don't have to tell you, Clem, they got their rights, villains though they might be. Give 'em plenty of work but make it reasonable. Same goes for their tucker. Keep 'em reasonable fed. You got guns in the house?'

'Yes.' Clem blinked.

'Good, see you keep them hid. With blokes like this it's as well to have protection.'

Alice looked up, startled. 'Surely they're not dangerous?'

'You have to be wary of all strangers,' he replied cautiously.

'But all strangers are not felons. It says on Mr Gunne's papers that he was transported for assault and robbery, and he's twice had his ticket-of-leave revoked for theft.'

Fearley shrugged. 'What can you expect? It's only the hardliners that's left now. The majority have done their time and gone free, the real crims will never get out of Freo jail, that leaves blokes like this. The tail-enders, we call them, just plain rogues, but harmless enough. They've both had extended sentences, but the judge has given them one last chance to work out their time. If they act up again they're back in jail for at least another seven years. So you see, it's up to them.'

'You never told me this,' Alice accused her brother.

'I didn't want to worry you. They'll be all right. It's in their own interest to behave.'

'That's right, you got the picture,' Fearley chimed in.

'But they're so much older than Clem. Those men are both about forty,' Alice complained.

'It doesn't make any difference,' Clem snapped. 'They're here, and we need them.'

Unconvinced Alice searched the papers anxiously. 'It says here the other one, Mr Deagan, transported as a Fenian. What's a Fenian?'

'Irish troublemakers,' Fearley said. 'There were fifty-six of them banished out here for life. They can't never go back. He's got a big mouth, that one, knows his rights, but don't give him no mind. He's done extra time for absconding.'

'And a few other things,' Alice said primly, noting several convictions for forgery while working in Perth, but not sure what the man had to gain from forgery.

She followed Clem outside and watched as Fearley formally handed over the two labourers, with dire warnings to them about pulling their weight and doing as they were told. The men listened, deliberately affecting boredom. They took their swags from the wagon, waiting disconsolately for further orders, looking to Alice less like rogues than men who had learned to handle humiliation, not let it get to them. That cheered her immensely, and since the Constable had only introduced Clem, the man of the house, she stepped forward firmly, a hand outstretched.

'I am Miss Price.'

Surprised, Gunne rubbed a dusty hand on his trousers and responded, 'Pleased to meetcha, miss.'

Deagan followed suit. 'And meself, Miss Price.'

'I've got lunch ready,' she said, looking about, uncertain of the protocol in this situation. Her eyes came to rest on the weather-worn cane chairs on the veranda. 'If you gentlemen would like to sit yourselves down there, it won't be long. Clem, you take Mr Fearley inside.'

This was the first time that Alice had ever had a chance to assert herself as mistress of a house, and she enjoyed the sensation. 'I hope you'll be happy here,' she told the prisoners as soon as the other two had stepped inside. 'We really do appreciate your coming out to help us.'

'To tell you the truth, miss,' Deagan said with a grin, 'we didn't have a lot of choice. But it's a nice thought for you to welcome us.'

Alice looked at him curiously. 'I know you're not exactly volunteers, but have you any objection to farm work?'

'It wouldn't make any difference if we did.'

'That's not what I asked you.'

The Irishman nodded. 'That's true. Put it this way, Miss Price. Farm work is a sight better than the roads, and the roads are a sight better than the quarries, and the quarries are a sight better than the cold cells in Fremantle, so there's your answer, as best I can offer. But all things being unequal as they are, don't be worrying. We'll work for the lad.'

She was glad Clem hadn't heard that; he was earnest in his new role of boss. 'Thank you, Mr Deagan,' she replied. 'But just remember one thing. Don't underestimate my brother.' That remark was sheer bravado, to put him in his place. She hoped she was right; Clem was untried as a boss.

Alice served them cabbage soup, bacon and egg pie and steamed treacle pudding with custard, deliberately eschewing mutton in a subtle message to the Constable, which she knew would go back to York, that the Prices could afford a decent table. He ate with Clem at the kitchen table while she took the other two their meals on a tray. She was thankful that the labourers had the sense to drag up a rickety old bench that had sat at the end of the veranda for years, not minding the dust.

Jim Fearley was pleased with his day's work. 'You're a fine cook, Alice, I'll say that for you. I never expected a feed as good as that. Most times at farms, this time of day, I'm lucky to get a plate of cold meat. But can I give you a bit of advice. Them prisoners. Feed them out the back door . . .'

'There's no shade out there,' she objected, but he turned to Clem.

'And there's no need for them to have full meals like this. A plate of stew, slice of bread, that'll do them. They don't know any better. You'll break yourself, young Clem, feeding them up like Alice has done just now.' He sat back and lit his pipe. 'Just remember, give them an inch and they'll take a mile. I know blokes like this, they can be cunning too. So you watch out. The magistrate, I can tell you now, wasn't too keen on letting you young people take on a couple of lags like this, but Mr Tanner, he said you were a special case, having just lost your dad. He said you were entitled, under the law. That bloke might be a bank manager, but he's a real bush lawyer thrown in. I suppose he sees enough . . .' He glanced over at Alice, who was making a pot of tea. 'Do you reckon I could have the recipe for that pie you made, Alice? For my wife. We never think to have a pie of eggs and bacon, that was a real beauty.'

'Certainly.' She smiled, aware that her brother was fuming. She would feed her workmen where and what she pleased and there'd be no argument from the boss, who'd just been called 'young Clem'. Alice reasoned that it was imperative to get the men on their side. The opinions of a policeman had no bearing on their situation, which was desperate to have to employ convicts in the first place. You get more with honey than vinegar, she'd told herself when she'd turned a toolshed into a bunkhouse for them, with new mattresses and blankets, a table and chairs, a good lamp and some reading matter, a pile of Noah's old *Countryman* magazines. She even put a cloth on the table and two ashtrays cut by hot wire from the bases of bottles.

As Fearley left, he reminded them that their neighbours, the Postles, had been warned that there were convicts at

Lancoorie. 'You get any problems with them, young Clem,' he said, 'you ride like hell over to Charlie Postle. He'll be over and sort them out pretty damn quick.'

This was an exciting time for Clem. His property. His labourers. He had made his decision: he'd stick with sheep. It was easier and cheaper to clear land for pasture rather than crops. He was still determined to build a dam, and he'd need more fences and bigger sheds, but so did the wheat farmers as they extended their fields. All in all, he hoped he was on the right track.

He took Deagan and Gunne on a tour of some parts of the property, riding out to the salt lakes, their thirsty horses standing disconsolately on the white-caked shores, staring at the shallow green water.

'Not much of a place, this,' Gunne said, as unimpressed as the horses, warding off sticky bush flies.

'No,' Clem responded, but then he realized that Gunne meant the whole place, Lancoorie, and was irritated. 'I just wanted you to know your way about. So you don't get lost. There's nothing wrong with this country; cleared, it makes excellent farmland.'

'With salt water?'

'We've got fresh water closer to the house. But I'm going to build a dam out here. *We're* going to build a dam out here once we clear some more land.'

Deagan laughed. 'That'll teach you to belittle the man's estate, George me boy. Where to now, boss?'

The day's ride, with billy tea and sandwiches at a small water hole by a granite outcrop, taught Clem a lot about these men, the main thing being that they automatically referred to him as boss, regardless of the disparity in their ages. Their last job had been as gangers on a railway line, but they had been seconded to Lancoorie for no other reason that any of them could fathom but the whim of a clerk.

'You put in your application,' Deagan said. 'Some little bloke in an office picks our names with a pin, so lo and behold here we are. It's nothin' to him that the gang was already short-handed. They like the glory of bein' able to push people around.'

'Would you rather be working on the railway?' Clem asked.

'Gawd, no!' Gunne said. He didn't enlarge. He didn't say much at all. Deagan was the talker, the spokesman. And he was curious about everything. How the Price family came to be here in the first place. What had happened to their dad.

Clem censored that reply. 'Killed in a fall from a horse.'

'Ah, that's bad luck. Hard on you an' the miss. How much land do we have to clear?'

That was the way with Deagan. Mike, as Clem came to call him. And the other one George.

Mike would toss pertinent questions in among innocuous talk and then never comment on the reply. As if he was weighing things up all the time. That made Clem wary. He was never sure what Mike was thinking, but he knew that brain was ticking over all the time, taking stock. George was a glum fellow, in contrast; he just seemed to accept whatever came his way with a shrug.

But they could work, and work hard. It seemed second nature to them. When the clearing started on from the west paddock they took the axes and crowbars and went at it so steadily that Clem was hard put to keep up with them. It was weeks before Gunne happened to mention that he'd spent years clearing scrub outside Bunbury, and that was where he'd met Mike.

From the house, Alice could see the curls of smoke in the distance where the men were burning off, and she smiled. Life had taken on an entirely new dimension. As the lady of the house her time was her own now; no more nagging and carping from Dora, no longer did she have to suffer Noah's irritation when Dora complained to him about his daughter's lack of attention to the chores. And strangely, her attitude to those chores had undergone a miraculous change. These days she went at her work with a will and had all the housework done in half the time it had previously taken her. And it made her proud to see the house so spic-and-span, a tribute to her new status.

Clem had mentioned, casually, as if by right, that he would move from his room into the larger bedroom previously occupied by Noah and Dora, but gently, without fuss, Alice had made light of the idea, suggesting they toss for it. She had won. The main bedroom was now hers, and Clem had taken her small success in good part.

'Fair enough,' he'd said, and forgotten about it, but to Alice, as she scoured and aired her new abode, this was part of a growing resolve to stand firm in her own right, not just as Clem's spinster sister.

The two farm hands – she refused to think of them as convicts – had settled in well. They were cheerful fellows, quite funny at times, and didn't seem to mind what they did in the way of farm chores. Every so often they surprised her by doing the milking before she arrived at the shed; and George was interested in her vegetable garden.

On Sunday mornings he liked to potter there. 'Something to do,' he'd muttered when Alice first found him digging and weeding, but then it became his hobby, offering her advice, extending it to double the size.

Mike teased him unmercifully, claiming he was turning into a Chinee gardener, but George took no notice.

'Water off a duck's back!' Clem observed, grinning. 'They're like that all the time,' he told Alice. 'Mike likes to stir. If it's not George, it's me.'

'He doesn't give you any trouble?' Alice asked him anxiously, but he shook his head. 'Not at all. It's just his way of getting through the day. I think farm work bores him. He's a clever fellow. Educated.'

'Not educated enough to keep himself out of jail.' Alice sniffed. But that was a cover-up. A matter of self-protection. For Alice really liked the Irishman. He was tall and slim and the red hair that Constable Fearley had referred to was dark auburn, thick and wavy, with a soft lock that often dropped on to his forehead, as unruly as the man himself. And he had the merriest smile. In fact, she found him such a charmer that she had to force herself to stop thinking about him.

With the house chores under way, Alice relieved Clem by

riding out to check on the sheep, taking the dogs with her, since the pastures weren't fenced. Many a time she found it difficult to keep her mind on the job, resisting the temptation to visit the men, who were hard at it clearing scrub.

It seemed churlish of them, of her and Clem, to have their Sunday dinner alone in the kitchen, with George working out there in the garden, so she'd invited the two men to join them, pleased that it didn't bother Clem.

'You're the cook,' he'd said. 'Please yourself. I've always thought it a bit mad to be feeding them out on the veranda while we're in here.'

'I'm sorry, I thought that was the correct thing to do.'

'Fearley's rules, not mine.'

Then she realized that Clem appreciated their company at meals, since brother and sister didn't have all that much to talk about. Sunday lunch was just the beginning. After that they took all their meals in the kitchen, Alice telling herself it was a much simpler arrangement.

Lancoorie was a livelier place these days, she mused as she spread the mashed potato across the mince in a large baking dish; Mike's favourite meal.

Only last night, in the big double bed, she'd dreamed of him. Of him taking her in his arms, kissing her, and she'd awoken with such joy. Knowing, at last, for sure, that she was madly in love with him.

When they finally came in, her three noisy men, she counted herself the happiest of women, so content. But carefully, she hid her feelings, afraid Clem might disapprove, and, more importantly, not wishing Mike to think her foolish. So far, he'd treated her the same way as George did, politely and kindly. Maybe one day he'd come round to seeing her in a different light. There was plenty of time.

And then, one Sunday, Dr Carty came to visit.

Chapter Three

They both walked out, hesitantly, to greet him as he alighted from the smart black gig with its shiny hood; a nervousness akin to guilt dogging their steps, for what would the doctor want of them? Had he guessed their secret about Noah's will? Alice let her brother take the lead.

She could almost feel Clem's relief as the doctor straightened his soft black hat, a sort of velour, and ambled over to them with a cheerful smile and a quick studied sweep of their farmhouse.

'Place is looking good, Clem. I heard you're doing a good job out here.'

Alice made morning tea and served it in the sitting room with scones that, fortunately, she'd made only yesterday. She apologised for the battered kitchen cups. 'I'm hoping to buy a proper tea service the next time I'm in York,' she told the doctor, 'but we've been so busy.'

She blinked when, instead of telling her such things didn't matter, as any polite guest should, he agreed with her. 'Yes. You should do that. Tea sets are not expensive and there are some passable items at the store. Little things make all the difference, young lady.'

Maybe he caught Clem glaring at her for having introduced the subject and caused embarrassment to all, because he then went out of his way to congratulate Alice on being such a neat housekeeper. 'A credit, my dear, for one so young, with no parents about to guide you.'

But Alice was hardly mollified. What did he want? Why was he here? She wished he'd get on with it instead of quizzing Clem about the property and how he was coping with the convicts.

Neither of whom had put in an appearance, preferring to retreat to their bunkhouse. Alice hoped they'd stay there. What business was it of Dr Carty's to be sticky-beaking about their home?

'Is someone ill out this way?' she enquired.

'Only Grandma Postle,' he said, 'as far as I know. She took another turn and the boys came riding in hell-for-leather to get me, but by the time I arrived she was on her feet again.'

'They say she hits the brandy,' Clem laughed, but Alice was shocked.

'A ninety-year-old woman. Never!'

'That's probably why she's a ninety-year-old woman,' Carty remarked. 'She's had more accidents than a circus tumbler, but she keeps on rallying.' He touched the corners of his mouth with a neatly folded handkerchief. 'What about a walk, Clem? Stretch these legs of mine before I start back again.'

Clem was up in a rush, grabbing his hat, eager to please, leaving Alice to stare after them, wondering what was going on. She washed up and doused the small garden by the back door with the dishwater, so absorbed in her thoughts she let the basin fall in among the hydrangeas. Mike seemed to appear from nowhere to retrieve it for her.

'Would that be the local doctor come to visit?' he asked.

'Yes. Dr Carty.'

'No one's ailing, I hope?'

She shook her head. 'No. It's just a social call, I think.'

He grinned. 'I see, as the blind man said, and the dummy said he didn't see at all.'

'Yes.' Alice forced a smile. 'I don't see what they've got to talk about that I can't hear.'

'Might be just passing the time of day.'

'Not Dr Carty, he charges for his time.'

'Does he now? Well, don't be bothering your pretty head. You've nothing to worry about, so shift the frown there. Something interesting could come of it and Clem will tell you all about it.'

Alice hurried into her room, her heart singing, for hadn't Mike called her pretty? She forgot about Carty and Clem as

she practised frowning to see what that did to her face, vowing
never again to introduce those lines to her smooth features.
Her pretty features. What a lovely man Mike was.

Men always seemed to end up surveying horses, Clem had
noted, as they walked about the farm. Nothing much else to
see in flat country like this, he supposed. Dr Carty was no
different. He stood at the fence by the home paddock and lit
his pipe.

'They're in good nick,' he commented. 'You bought a
couple from the Postles?'

'Yes, I needed them, what with the two full-time farm
hands. We had to shoot Pa's horse.'

'Ah yes. I remember. There's something I wanted to talk
to you about, Clem.'

'Yes, sir. I thought that likely.'

'I was wondering. A young man like you, well set up now,
have you given a thought to getting wedded?'

'M-me?' Clem stammered, his thoughts flashing to Lettice
Carty. 'No. Can't say I have as yet.'

'You're twenty?' Carty asked.

'Next month. Christmas Eve, that's when I was born.'

'Go on! The best of gifts, I always say, to have a Christmas
babe, rather than tell that being dragged out on Christmas
Eve is no fun for the doctor. But that's by the by. I'll put
it to you straight, Clem. If the right girl came along, would
you be thinking of marriage at this stage?'

'I don't know.'

'Let's say a girl with a decent dowry?'

'Ah! You're trying to tell me that when I get married I ought
to stand out for a dowry. I'd never given that much thought.
It seems to me that when a man marries it'd be the girl that
counts.' He shuffled his feet. This conversation was making
him uncomfortable. 'And whether the girl would have me,'
he added morosely.

The doctor sighed. 'You young fellows, you're all the same.
You all need a bit of a push along when it comes to this
business. Too shy, that's your trouble.'

'Well, I suppose there's time yet,' Clem said, hoping to shut down the subject. He truly wasn't considering marriage yet, even if it was Lettice. He hardly knew her.

But the doctor had other ideas. 'We've always been friends, haven't we, Clem?'

That was news to Clem, but he nodded obediently.

'Then I'll put my cards on the table and it'll be up to you. You're a decent young man, of good stock, and I wouldn't say no to having you as a son-in-law. I could be a great help to you, socially and financially. Keep that in mind for a start. I was never blessed with a son,' he added plaintively, 'but I have three daughters . . .'

As he rambled on about a father's duty, Clem recalled the bank manager's comments. He couldn't wait to tell Mr Tanner he was right, Carty was winding him up to marry Lettice. It was becoming difficult to keep a straight face with the laughter bubbling up inside him.

'Now you take my Thora,' his prospective father-in-law said, and that stopped Clem in his tracks.

He composed himself to offer a polite response when Carty finished outlining Thora's good points. A charming girl, good-looking, well mannered, with all the social graces, an excellent housekeeper . . .

'Dr Carty, you forget. Thora's older than me.'

'Good Lord, man. Only by a year. That's neither here nor there.'

'But she hardly knows me.'

'She knows you well enough. Many a marriage is arranged with the couple never meeting at all before the ceremony, and they turn out just as well.'

Clem was intimidated. He didn't dare mention he'd prefer Lettice. What if Lettice didn't want him? That would be too embarrassing to contemplate. But the thought had lodged, and it provided him with an answer.

'I'm sure you mean well, Dr Carty, and I'm real flattered, believe me, that you'd think of me, but what would Thora say about this?'

'She agrees.'

'What?' Clem was astounded. Something was wrong here. Something was very wrong. Why would Thora, the stuck-up one in the Carty family, want to marry him? She already had a boyfriend. Suddenly he felt older, no longer the lad Carty thought he was talking to, knowing he'd have to step very cautiously here.

'Why?' he asked.

'Why what?' The doctor's response sounded ingenuous but Clem knew it was bluff.

'Why would Thora want to marry me? Was it her idea? Did she suddenly come to you and say she'd like to marry that Clem Price who lives out at Lancoorie?'

'Who owns Lancoorie,' Carty reminded him.

'Not the point. Of all people I can't see Thora wanting me.'

'You underestimate yourself, Clem.'

'I don't think so. What's really going on here, Doctor? Is Thora in the family way?'

Clem had his answer as Carty's pink skin exploded into a blush of red that subsided just as fast. He felt sorry for the man then, all the puff and bluster gone out of him.

'I've got some claret in the house,' he said. 'Would you like a drink, sir?'

'Not claret,' Carty growled. 'There's a good Scotch whisky in my gig. Would you get it for me, lad?'

They were back in the cool of the sitting room with the beer glasses and a jug of tank water and the bottle of whisky. The door was firmly closed. Clem noticed his sister's irritation at being left out again, but that couldn't be helped. He'd explain later.

'So you see the position I'm in,' Carty said, having taken a large gulp of whisky.

'Is Matt Spencer the father? I heard he was Thora's boy-friend.'

'Yes. He's the father all right, and he's bolted. But Clem, no one knows about this yet. Only Mrs Carty and I, and that bastard Spencer, of course. Now you. I'd appreciate your discretion.'

Clem drank his whisky too. It was good. The best he'd ever tasted. 'Look. I hope you don't mind me saying this, but you're a doctor. Couldn't you . . . like . . . do something for Thora?'

'I could not! It's against all I stand for. Out of the question.'

'I'm sorry. I didn't want to offend you.'

'That's all right. But see here, Clem, she'd make you a good wife . . .'

'But what did she say? Thora. About me.'

'She's rather distraught, naturally. I mentioned several local young men to her that I might approach . . .'

'Ah, poor Thora. Wasn't that a cruel thing to do?'

'She has no choice!' her father snapped. 'But I can tell you true, Clem, she did say she thought kindly of you. Apparently other girls at our party spoke well of you. You know, the way young girls talk.'

Clem didn't know, but it was nice to hear.

'If you agree to marry Thora, you'll be saving her reputation, Clem, as well as gaining a good wife.'

'What about my reputation?'

'Eh?' It was Carty's turn to be surprised.

'It won't take long for people to figure out that Thora was pregnant before we were wed, and bang goes my reputation too.'

'I'll make it up to you, Clem.'

They used a silence, broken only by the distant shriek of a cockatoo, to shore up their arguments. Clem was tempted to go for it, tempted only by this talk of a dowry, though he knew in his heart it was a miserable excuse to marry. He disliked the idea of being bought and decided to say just that.

'Dr Carty, I feel it's not a dowry that's on offer here but a bribe, and that doesn't say much for me. What sort of a man do you think I am?'

Carty's response was the reassurance he'd hoped for. A smoothing-over of ruffled feathers that hid the excitement brimming within him. What a coup it would be to win Thora Carty! Who was by no means an ugly girl, even

63

if she was pregnant, and who would bring him rewards he couldn't hope to gain marrying any other girl of his acquaintance.

'My dear fellow, forgive me,' Carty was saying. 'I have the greatest respect for you. At best, this is a delicate matter, and perhaps I've presented it clumsily. With any one of my daughters the subject of a dowry would be raised, so please see it in that light. Were Noah alive, I should work this out with him . . . It's a normal arrangement, Clem. You mustn't think for one minute that I'm belittling you. I had hoped that you would see it as a compliment that Mrs Carty and I would welcome you into the family.'

'Ah, I see,' Clem admitted grudgingly. And for extra leverage added: '*I* wish Noah was here. He'd be able to tell me if this is the right thing to do. I'm a bit bemused, you could say,' he continued, picking up a phrase often used by Mike Deagan because it sounded appropriate.

'Then you will give this your consideration?' Carty asked earnestly, reaching for the whisky.

'I'd rather talk to Thora first.'

'You shall. I'll bring her out tomorrow. No.' He looked about him. 'On second thoughts I'd be obliged if you could visit us tomorrow, Clem. Now don't get me wrong, but this house could do with some . . . er . . . alterations.'

'Like what?' Clem was genuinely interested.

'Just a bit here and there. You know what women are like. It's a solid house. It won't take much to spruce it up. And it's on me. Will you come to York tomorrow?'

'I'd have to bring Alice. It wouldn't be right to leave her here with the men.'

'By all means. You bring Alice and stay over. Do you realize what you'd be doing for Alice too? She's a fine young lady, but she's isolated here. My girls would welcome her into the family.'

That was true, Clem mused. The Carty girls would be excellent company for Alice. This was opening up a grand new world for her too.

Dr Carty took his leave of Alice with a hug and a warmth

that astonished her and left her standing in the kitchen as Clem accompanied him to the gig.

'If it's not a rude question,' Clem asked him, 'how far gone is Thora?'

Dr Carty looked stricken. 'Two months, Clem, and Mrs Carty is beside herself with worry. For her sake I hope we can sort this out as soon as possible.'

'After I talk to Thora,' Clem said with a firmness he did not feel. After having come this far he was petrified of confronting Thora. He had visions of that tall blonde girl looking at him as if he'd emerged from under a rock like some blind beetle.

'I am fully aware of what you said regarding your reputation, Clem,' the doctor said as he led his horse over to the trough, watching it drink greedily. 'And I admire your stance. In fact, this talk has shown me your mettle. You're Noah's son all right. A good man. But it is beholden on me to spell out the dowry, not, as you so wrongly think, a bribe. Thora will bring with her two hundred pounds, and land I own at Birimbi. Do you know that district?'

Did he ever? Birimbi was the most fertile and sought-after land over the ranges from Perth. Clem nodded as if this had to be expected. Didn't Carty know the cash would have been good enough? Was the man made of money?

Deliberately he stood at the gate until Carty was well out of sight and then he ran, back to Alice, back to the kitchen to tell her all this astonishing news.

Sunday-night tea was more like a council of war. Everyone had something to say except George Gunne, who listened in his usual taciturn manner.

Alice was appalled. 'They're using you, Clem. Making a fool of you. People will think you're the one got her pregnant!'

'I told him that. He apologized. Said he'd make it up to me.'

'How? With a shotgun wedding?'

'No. With a big dowry.'

'You're selling yourself for money? You're too young to

marry. You're only nineteen, Clem. And you're not in love with her, or she with you. I know Thora better than you do. She's the most awful snob.'

'Not any more.' Clem grinned. 'How the mighty doth fall!'

'Listen to you. Fall's right. She'd be thinking she's taking a mighty step down marrying you.'

Clem flared. 'Are you saying I'm not good enough for her?'

'I'm saying you're too good for the likes of Thora Carty, but she won't see it that way.'

'But she wants to marry me.'

'Any port in a storm.'

'Just a minute,' Mike said as he finished off the last of his cold corned mutton, placing his knife and fork neatly together in his mannered way. 'Don't you two be making a fight of this. Let's talk it over. What's she like, this Thora?'

Alice was only too pleased to report. 'She's tall and skinny and got fair hair and a nose stuck up in the air like there's a bad smell under it.'

'Try again,' Mike urged her with a smile. 'Now, is she a fair-looking lady? Or an ugly one they're trying to push on you, Clem? You answer me, Alice.'

Much as it hurt, Alice had to admit that Thora was the best-looking of all the Carty girls, and, pressed, that she was probably the prettiest girl in York.

'Not so much pretty as elegant,' Clem added. 'I never thought I'd be able to get anywhere near her. Tell him true, Alice, she's got skin like cream, not a freckle in sight, and I'm darned if I know how she does that. And her hair is long and sleek and white.'

'It's called blonde,' Alice snapped.

'In other words she's some prize,' Mike said. 'Out of range at other times, Clem. You said so yourself.'

'A flawed prize,' Alice sniffed.

'Ah now, have a little pity for the girl, Alice. Do you not have it in your heart to offer her refuge? Do you have no idea of the ferment troubling her now? Put yourself in her position.

Wouldn't you be heartfelt grateful for a kind word from a decent young man like Clem? Can you imagine the rant and ravin' the poor lass has been bearing from her social-climbing parents? And can you not see what a refuge Lancoorie will be for her with a decent man as her husband, and a fine young woman like yourself to stand by her? She'll need you as much as him, Alice, she'll need and appreciate your friendship. This is the sister you never had who'll be relying on the strength of a woman like you to tell her: "To hell with the gossip."'

With astonishment, Clem watched Alice back down. He knew that Mike was a Fenian, something to do with politics, and he'd had plenty of excursions into Mike's opinions while they worked, allowing them to go in one ear and out the other as conversational fodder, but never before had he heard Mike in real action, and the power of the emotion convinced him too. Until later.

Carty had left the whisky, so Clem and Mike sat on the veranda in the moonlight, making it last.

'Now what's with the dowry?' Mike asked him.

Clem was glad of the company. 'He says she brings two hundred pounds and land. A king's ransom, Mike. How could a man refuse?'

'A man doesn't refuse, he sets it in stone first.'

'What do you mean? He couldn't renege.'

'It's been done. Your old man would have wanted to see the paper.'

'Is that right?'

'And watch it, lad. Get it set in that aforesaid stone. Not in the Carty family name. I'd say, without wanting to put you down, that they're using you. What say she has the babe and then she goes home to Mum? Says you were a bad husband. There's none of you Catholics. She can legally split from you and take what's hers. And everyone back to the starting post.'

'But what a wife owns belongs to her husband.'

'That's your old man talkin'. Not in this country, Clem. The women are too tough, too free-thinkin' for that old game. It works back in the auld countries but not here in Australia.

You put your foot down before you sign any weddin' papers. Alice is right. You don't know the woman and she sounds to me like a little filly who'll have her own way.'

'She's not getting her own way now. She's in trouble.'

'Temporarily, lad. Pregnancies have a way of not lasting. You're doing that snotty family one hell of a favour. Make it worth your while.'

'You think I should marry her?'

Mike raised his drink to Clem. 'Don't blarney me, son, you've been for it from the time the dowry was mentioned. I think we'll go a long way, you and me.'

Manners prevented Clem from asking this fellow, a convict, a sort of friend, how *they* could go a long way, but he did remember Mike's warning when it came to the discussion of the dowry.

'When it comes down to tin tacks,' Mike had said, 'pretend you're your father. Place his mantle upon you and work from there.'

Alice hated the visit. She was uncomfortable sharing a room with Lettice Carty and wished she was anywhere else but in this regimented household, with maids dashing about, parents behaving like bereaved royalty and daughters giggling furtively in corners. Thora, who had her own room, had nothing to say at all. She emerged that first noon, when Alice and Clem arrived, wearing a remote expression and a splendid summer dress.

It was yellow. Swiss organza, the sisters said, figured with embroidered bouquets of tiny flowers. A blossoming full skirt, wide sash at the waist, fitted bodice with a scooped neckline and a romantic swathe of georgette replacing a collar.

Alice felt dowdy beside this vision, who also wore her hair swept up, as older ladies did, into the rich classic style. And a necklace of pearls! The sight of this person, who might shortly invade her home, almost reduced Alice to tears.

But would Clem listen? Not him. For propriety he had been billeted with Mr and Mrs Tanner, and so he left, promising to return later.

Mrs Carty asked Alice if she'd like to take a nap after lunch, and although the idea was foreign to her, she agreed that she was tired from the long drive in the trap from Lancoorie and was glad to lie in her petticoat on Lettice's bed until, at last, she heard Clem's voice outside.

Even then he didn't rescue her. She whispered to him that she'd like to take a walk through the town, just the two of them, but he'd hissed back at her, 'Not now, Alice. Please.'

So she went back to the bedroom, where she sat miserably on her own, listening to the younger girls playing ball outside, wondering what was going on in the front room, and feeling forgotten by everyone.

Mrs Carty sat in on Clem's initial conversation with Thora, so he was never clear in his mind what ensued. Thora seemed even more nervous than he was.

He did manage to extract from her that she would be pleased to marry him, even though Mrs Carty, in her black beaded dress, seemed to dominate the room.

She did most of the talking, telling them how well suited they were, and how happy the families would be if a union could be arranged. A lot of ballyhoo, Clem thought, but he only had eyes for Thora. She was like an ice maiden out of those fairy stories. He couldn't imagine how Matt Spencer had the cheek to have gotten so close to her. Let alone do the deed. It was impossible to contemplate. She still looked so virginal.

There was only one chance of reality. When Mrs Carty went off to find her husband, who was probably lurking just behind those double doors, Thora turned to him anxiously.

'You don't have to do this, Clem, if you don't want to.'

His heart went out to her. 'Thora, what do *you* want?'

'I don't know what to do. It's a mess, isn't it?'

Clem looked at her. 'It shouldn't be. You're very beautiful, and I mean that. Seeing you today I was completely bowled over. I never thought I'd have a chance with you.'

'Until my parents offered me. I hate them.'

Clem walked over and threw the bolt on the door. 'Let's have a talk, you and I.'

'You locked them out! Good!' She ran to the door and leant against it. 'Oh God, this is so awful.'

'Sit down, Thora. What can we do here? Do you want me to find Matt Spencer and bring him back?'

'Don't you dare! Please, Clem, you wouldn't do that to me? When I told him, he was so cruel . . .' Her eyes brimmed with tears. 'The things he said . . .'

'Never mind about that now. Obviously he's gone. But now I don't know what I'm supposed to do. This has all been sprung on me so suddenly.'

'Of course. I bet they offered you plenty to take me off their hands. I'm the most awful embarrassment to them.'

'Don't you think I'm embarrassed too? I like you, Thora. But you've always been up there on a pinnacle to me. Out of reach.'

'Now I'm not?'

Clem remembered Alice's similar comment and fought against it. All he could see now was this lovely girl. He wanted Thora as he'd never wanted anyone before in all his life. To hell with her father and her mother. And Matt Spencer, for that matter. This was his wife, right before him, if only he could convince her that he was worth her attention. Not just some bloke roped in for an emergency.

'Thora,' he said, 'we've grown up together, you and I. All the kids in the district. I don't know you all that well, nor do you know me, distance being what it is, but I know who you are, and if you've heard ill of me, then say so.'

'I can't say I have.'

'Then I would ask you if you would do me the honour of becoming my wife.'

'Even though you know I'm bearing another man's child? Have you no shame?'

Clem walked over to the window and looked out into the street. 'That's a worthy question, Thora, that I keep asking myself, with not a lot of time to think it over. Your dowry is not to be sneezed at, but your sisters could expect the same.

70

Probably more with a better-placed suitor, if you see what I mean. In other words, I think they're selling us both short. They think I'd grab at the best cash offer and you'd have to do the same. Circumstances being the way they are.'

He came back and sat in the chair, confronting her, their knees almost touching. 'But we can make our own rules, you and I. The truth is I want to marry you and I promise you I'll see you no ill. What do you want?'

'I want this child,' she said fiercely. 'Did my father tell you he could do nothing to put a stop to this pregnancy?'

'Yes, of course.'

'Then you've already been fooled by him.' She wept. 'He lied. He tried to bully me into aborting.'

'Never mind about that now.' He wished he could reach out and stroke that troubled face, soften those frightened eyes with a kiss, but she was still intimidating. Battling like a cornered calf for she knew not what.

'Why don't we give it a go, Thora? You know what the Abos say round here: "You walk to the sunset and you walk to the sunset. Just another day." We might as well walk together. What have we got to lose?'

When Clem admitted her parents, Thora had stopped weeping and had composed herself. To all appearances the matter had been settled, but Clem was more determined to strike a better deal with the father who had no pity for his daughter. Who had lied to him.

They hadn't wasted any time, the Cartys. A preacher was waiting in the dining room to make arrangements for the marriage, and the couple were led in to confer with him. Or rather to listen as Dr and Mrs Carty discussed the venue, his tiny rural church out on the long east road that bypassed Lancoorie.

'It's the sweetest little church,' Mrs Carty enthused, 'I couldn't think of anything nicer.'

Clem looked to Thora for her reaction but she kept her eyes cast down, hands clasped neatly in her lap.

'What's wrong with the Anglican church here in town?' he asked. 'It's a fine church, the people of York have every reason to be proud of it. They say it's the best church outside of Perth.'

'I think St Luke's would be better,' Mrs Carty said quietly. 'After all, it is out your way.'

'Out of sight, out of mind, do you mean?' he asked. 'If you're thinking to stop the gossip, it won't work. Thora and I will be married and there's nothing shameful in that.' He turned to the preacher. 'With all due respect to you, sir, my wife and I should walk out of a church with our heads high. We don't need to be hiding out there in the bush. I would rather we marry right here in York.'

'You don't understand, Clem. A wedding in town would mean a big reception, invitations would have to go out, there'd be so much to do. It would take time.'

'Then don't bother with the reception. To my mind family is enough. It just sounds like an excuse to me.' He looked to Thora. 'What do you think?'

'St Luke's will do,' she whispered.

Her reply angered him, but rather than argue with her in front of them, he shrugged. 'All right. If that's what you want.'

'It's the bride's day,' the preacher said brightly, and grabbed for his book to take down the particulars as Clem glared at him.

'Is it? You could have fooled me!'

In his heart he knew this was a mistake. A serious mistake. Admittedly Thora was in a panic over her pregnancy and nervous of facing people, but was she ashamed of him too? If she had any sense, she should just be herself, and let him stand by her. But now this wasn't about to happen and the dissonance of it would echo throughout the marriage. Clem was hurt; he'd offered her his friendship and support and she wasn't woman enough to take his lead.

Later, Dr Carty invited him to seal the bargain with a drink, another of those fine Scotch whiskies. The dining room looked bigger now with just the two of them in residence; the long glossy table, that he noted could seat twelve people without crush, like a barrier between them.

'Well now,' Carty said, 'I don't think there's any more to discuss. I've given Thora a cheque for a hundred pounds, so she can't be feeling hard done by. It's been a wearing time for all of us, I can tell you, Clem, but I hope you two young people will be happy together.'

'You said two hundred,' Clem stated firmly.

'Did I? Got a bit carried away in the fret of it, I guess.'

'Yes, I suppose so. You can make the other hundred out to me.'

'Eh?'

'By the sound of things I've saved you a lot of cash by cutting out the reception. I'm still not happy about marrying out there in the bush. It's a dodge and you know it.'

'But you won't renege?'

'Not if you don't. Then there's the house. It was your idea that the house should be done up for Thora, and I agree with you. Coming from a beautiful place like this, Thora would need a little more comfort than the Lancoorie homestead can offer. We've got time. The banns have to be read.'

'I'll bring some tradesmen out and we'll have a look at it,' Carty said grudgingly.

'Then there's the land in Birimbi.'

'Ah yes. I hadn't forgotten that. The child will be my first grandchild. You take care of Thora, see that she gets plenty of rest – she's very stressed and run down – and when the baby is born I'll sign the property over. At the christening.' Then he added: 'To Thora, of course, as the child's mother.'

'I will be the child's guardian, Dr Carty. The land is to be signed over to me. And I'll want that in writing and lodged with Mr Tanner before I leave York tomorrow.'

Carty stood up. 'You're getting a little above yourself, Clem.'

'No I'm not. This is all your idea, don't forget. Unless we have the dowry arrangement met right now, then the wedding's off. You can start searching all over again. If you hadn't insisted on hiding this marriage away as if I'm just some ring-in, I might have been able to make it easier for you, but now . . .' He shrugged. 'A deal's a deal.'

Clem knew all that was simply bluff, but the irritation had given him enough courage to hold his ground as Mike Deagan had advised.

'It'll be done,' Carty said stiffly. 'Now, if you don't mind, I have some calls to make.'

Because it was inevitable, Alice made no fuss about moving back to her own room.

'That didn't last long,' she sighed, and Clem kissed her on the cheek. 'You're a brick, Al.'

The brick also watched without comment when Carty arrived with some carpenters to discuss the house with Clem. No one asked her advice, which was just as well, since she had been in a state of utter confusion from the day the date was set. She disapproved of all the arrangements, from the out-of-town wedding to the wheeling and dealing that was going on between the doctor and her brother, but out of loyalty to Clem she kept her thoughts to herself. A bigger problem was looming. Another woman in the house. Of all people, Thora Carty, who'd hardly spoken two words to her while she'd stayed in their house.

As she was leaving, Alice had made an effort. 'I'll be pleased to welcome you to Lancoorie, Thora. We'll get along fine.'

Thora had bitten her lip, nodded, and thanked her. That was all.

A great start, Alice thought bitterly. What is to become of us?

The men decided to enclose the long veranda completely, turning it into a habitable room with louvred windows along the front wall to allow a view. Alice smiled. One step further than what Dora had wanted. She heard they were also to have a bathroom in place of the old washhouse, and she had no objections to that. She was more intrigued listening to Carty and Clem arguing, laying down the law about what was required and what was not. It dawned on her eventually that they were enjoying themselves like a couple of horse-traders, battling for the best price, and she would have felt sorry for Thora were she not reserving her opinions for a later date.

The wedding was a disastrous affair, made worse by the massive dust storm that rolled across the plains from early morning, covering everything in web-like silt and adding to the dry, choking heat. It was the worst of times for fresh flowers, but the pastor's wife had tried, massing dusty gum leaves on the miniature porch rather like the preparations for a bonfire, Alice thought.

She was feeling quite hysterical as she waited with Clem and the Postle family outside the windswept chapel, miles and miles from anywhere, with nothing to view but that endless sandy road that shot out from the coast like a bullet. This was no laughing matter, Alice kept telling herself as they huddled round the side of the church for shelter, but her innards were beset with an awful threat to send her off into fits of laughter.

Gulping, she addressed Les Postle, who was to be Clem's best man. It was a poor choice – Mike Deagan was the better man – but to have a convict stand up with Clem would have insulted the Cartys.

'Where does this road go to, Les?' she asked.

'I dunno. It just heads east, on and on. Settlers keep addin' to it. It must just come to a dead stop somewhere out there.'

Alice went into a fit of laughter, disguising it as a cough, choking and spluttering, while Les, helpfully, banged her on the back. 'You all right? It's this bloody dust!'

'Yes.' She nodded. But she'd been thinking a convict as best man would have been a nice touch to really annoy these people who had inveigled her young brother into this undignified charade.

Eventually, the Carty entourage came out of the whirling silt like a misty desert caravan, first the gig and then one of Carty's passenger coaches.

The biting wind defeated protocol as everyone barged into the church together, and then Thora emerged and Alice gasped. She had never seen such a beautiful woman in all her life.

'Oh my God,' she whispered to herself, in fear for Clem.

That time, back at the Carty house, when marriage was being discussed and approved, Lettice, the talkative one, had told Alice that Thora had decided she would be married in white even though her mother had been shocked at the very idea.

'Only virgins get married in white,' Lettice had whispered.

But Thora had won. Despite the heat and the sand and the wind and the dried-out dejected gum leaves lining the short aisle, Thora Carty, in a magnificent white satin gown, looked cool and composed, like an angel. A misty veil, held in place by a band of tiny roses, gave her an ethereal air as she glided forward on her father's arm. Sunday-suited men and ladies in guarded bonnets leaned back in awe, but Alice's eyes flung to Clem.

There was no music – St Luke's didn't run to an organ – and Clem had turned to watch Thora's progress, at first gazing with a wonderment that was swiftly replaced by sheer joy. Involuntarily he stepped towards her, hands outstretched, but Les, determined to observe protocol, jerked him back.

Lettice, in a sweet gown of pink silk, tripped prettily after the bride, almost as an afterthought, with no train to carry.

In no time the ceremony was over and they all milled outside again, braving the searing wind.

Eventually Mrs Carty called her chattering girls to order. 'Come along now. We must get back.'

Alice was dismayed. 'But I've prepared a wedding breakfast at home.'

'We wouldn't put you to that trouble, dear,' the woman responded, edging away.

'It's no trouble!' She'd been baking for days, and Clem had bought the most beautiful china and silver for the occasion.

'Don't worry about us,' Dr Carty put in. 'You people go along and enjoy yourselves.'

Hastily he summoned his family and friends to wave the bride and groom off to Lancoorie in his gig and then made for his vehicle to transport them back to York.

'Well! I say! What a cheek!' Mrs Postle struggled to anchor her hat with a strip of muslin. 'You mustn't mind them, Alice.

I always said them townspeople don't have no manners. Let them go. Les will drive you back in your buggy and we'll follow behind.'

Her husband was uncertain. 'Do you still want us to come, Alice?'

'Yes, of course.'

He whistled to his sons to bring up the buggies while Alice thanked the preacher. 'Pastor Dodds, it was a lovely wedding. You and Mrs Dodds are welcome to join us for the breakfast.'

'It's very kind of you, Miss Price, but we wouldn't want to intrude. I hope you'll remember us now. St Luke's is your nearest church, and we'd be honoured to have you as parishioners. Perhaps you wouldn't mind if we called on you?'

'You'd both be very welcome.' She was about to add that he could have a christening to perform in the near future, but checked herself in time.

Nobody seemed to mind that she'd invited George and Mike to attend the fine breakfast she'd set up on the gleaming new veranda room with its polished floor. After a few drinks were downed and Clem produced champagne, it turned into a jolly party. They were all more relaxed without the 'townies'. Even Thora managed a smile now and then.

'No honeymoon?' Mike whispered to Alice.

'It hasn't been mentioned.' She shrugged.

Another couple, passing St Luke's in their dray, slowed to stare at the collection of vehicles waiting outside the church.

'What's going on there?' Lil Cornish asked her husband.

'A weddin'. Clem Price is gettin' hooked.'

'Who to?'

'One of Dr Carty's daughters.'

'Well, I'll be blowed! Can we go in and have a look?'

'No we can't,' declared Ted. 'Bugger them. Clem don't mind callin' on me when he needs a hand but he's too hoity-toity to invite me to his bloody weddin'.'

'Which one of the Carty girls?' she asked, peering back wistfully.

'The eldest, Thora. And he wouldn't have got her only she's got the same complaint as you.' He laughed, reaching over to pat Lil's stomach.

She was amazed. 'Clem Price got her pregnant?'

'They reckon not. They say it's Matt Spencer's kid, and Clem got hauled in to make an honest woman of her.'

'Well, what do you know! Wonders will never cease.'

'You can say that again. They say he's in the money now, so next time he wants me, he can pay me decent wages. I don't come cheap no more.'

Chapter Four

Dutifully, Thora allowed him to make love to her on their wedding night, but Clem was nervous. And clumsy. The next few nights weren't much better because she was so tense. He wanted to talk to her about the matter but couldn't find suitable words, and to be truthful he was afraid that she would put a stop to the lovemaking altogether, because of the baby inside her. Finally he took her in his arms and lay quietly with her, telling her how much he loved her, how happy they would be together, outlining his plans to expand Lancoorie, promising her that when the baby was born he'd take her to Perth, where they'd have a holiday with the best of everything,

He'd thought she was listening, hoping the gentler approach would make her more responsive, even have her turn to him, kiss him voluntarily for a change, but his heart sank when he found she was asleep. Rather than disturb her, Clem remained still, thinking of their wedding day, and how foolish he'd been to have ever thought her plain, compared to her sisters.

As the weeks passed she became more and more listless, still in bed when he left the farmhouse, and lying down when he came home.

'It's as if she doesn't live here,' he complained to Alice. 'Even on Sundays she doesn't join in, lazing about on the veranda like a dying swan.'

'Oh, for heaven's sake.' His sister smiled. 'Leave her be. She has terrible morning sickness and the heat isn't helping.'

'Why didn't she say so?'

'She doesn't want you to know. She's bilious all the time and it embarrasses her. These thing usually clear up in time.'

But the sickness did not abate, and though Clem wanted to send for Dr Carty, she wouldn't allow it.

'I'm not that bad really, Clem. There's nothing my father can do, it's a normal state.'

When Carty did come to visit, he said the same thing, but Clem was troubled. 'Perhaps Thora should go back to town with you for a while. It might make her feel better.'

'Nonsense. She's quite well. She's earning the wages of sin, teach her a lesson.'

Clem was incensed. 'What a miserable bloody thing to say, and about your own daughter! Call yourself a doctor!'

'Being a doctor has nothing to do with it. And I'll thank you to watch your tongue. You've done all right out of me.'

'No more than you offered. And isn't it time you were heading home?'

'Are you dismissing me, you young brat?'

'This is Thora's home. She's a lady and I can't allow her to be insulted in her own home. Next time you come to Lancoorie I hope you remember that.'

When he'd left, Thora took Clem aside. 'I heard that conversation you had with my father. And I want to thank you, Clem.' She laughed. 'I've never heard anyone stand up to my father like that before. It was just wonderful.'

With that she kissed him on the cheek.

'By God, you must be feeling better,' he said joyfully. 'It's a real tonic to hear you laugh.'

'I'm sorry, I must be such a drag about the place. You're all so kind to me, I wish I could be more helpful.'

'Just keep well, look after that baby, that's your job.'

Thora looked at him, surprised. 'Are you happy about the baby?'

'Of course I am. Aren't you?'

'Oh yes, Clem. I love babies, and to have one of our very own will be wonderful.'

This was a tender side of Thora he'd never known before, but it was overshadowed by her remark about 'our' baby. Clem was so delighted he did not dare draw attention to it for fear it had been a slip of the tongue. Their baby, a son or a daughter, had now become a reality to him, not just a vague entity that would eventually put in an appearance.

Thora's health did not improve, and Alice cared for her the best she could, sitting with her while they made baby clothes, taking her for walks, making her bland meals so as not to upset her digestion. She was prone to colds when the summer waned, and Mrs Postle came over with potions and eucalypt rubs to ease the racking coughs. Dr Carty returned for his monthly examination of the patient, declaring she might be a bit thin on it but otherwise quite well. 'Everyone gets colds this time of year,' he said. 'Nothing unusual. And the baby's sitting well in there. Nothing to worry about.'

But Alice did worry. She even consulted old Sadie, the matronly Aborigine woman, next time she and her family came padding up to the house.

'That one skinny,' Sadie said. 'Not much milk comen on. I send over one of my girls when time comen.' She jerked her thumb in the direction of her entourage. The tribal people were squatting in the shade of a tree, and among them were two pregnant women. 'My girls got plenty milk,' she added proudly.

'Sadie's got some stuff for you,' Alice whispered to Thora. 'She wants to give it to you herself. Just take it. You don't have to use it, whatever it is.'

'I'll try anything,' Thora said. 'I'm so worried, Alice. I'm six months. I should be feeling better.'

Politely she accepted Sadie's offering, and later even rubbed the mixture of muddy leaves on her stomach as she'd been bid.

'My God, it stinks!' Alice cried, but Thora had the country-woman's faith in Aborigine cures, so she had to try it. She was disappointed to find no improvement.

When Thora was seven months along and still ailing, Alice sent Clem into York to fetch Dr Carty, but Thora's family had left on their annual holiday to Narrogin and were not expected back for at least a month. The scheduled locum had not arrived as expected.

Clem found Mr Tanner in a great state of excitement.

'Gold,' he whispered to him. 'Keep it under your hat. But I've heard from our head office in Perth that there's gold at Fly Flat. I'm waiting for confirmation, then we'll have to see how big a strike.'

'Ah, they're always talking gold somewhere,' Clem said, 'and nothing comes of it. The gold's in the eastern states. Where's Fly Flat anyway?'

Tanner pointed to a map. 'It's only a hundred and twenty miles east of the town of Southern Cross. Just out there!'

'Just out there?' Clem echoed. 'It's about four hundred miles east of here, by the looks of it, into desert. A man'd be mad to go there in the off chance of picking up a clinker or two.'

'We'll see,' Tanner said, attempting to appear calm, but the gleam in his eye reminded Clem that this man was a reformed gambler. Though what gold strikes had to do with a bank in a little country town like York was beyond him. There had been gold strikes in West Australia before this but they'd all fizzled out.

At the apothecary he obtained a large bottle of recommended medicine for Thora, and some mineral salts for her bath. A relaxant, he was assured. Searching for a gift, he eventually found some sweetly perfumed soap for her, and then disconsolately set out on the long lonely road home.

Gold! He wondered what would happen if a big strike did eventuate at Fly Flat. There would be a rush! Thousands of people came from all over the world to trek the gold trails. He'd read amazing stories of the multitudes that poured through the port of Melbourne, making for the Victorian goldfields. Would the same thing happen here?

Clem shuddered. He wouldn't like to be on that road to Fly Flat, hundreds of miles of parched travel into terrible country, with few suppliers along the route and none at journey's end. He'd heard of Southern Cross, just a village at the end of nowhere. Water would be as scarce as hens' teeth.

As the horse cantered along he couldn't keep his mind from the possibility of a gold strike. It must be more than a rumour to have Tanner so het up.

A man could make a mint selling water, he thought, mulling this over. Then he grinned. What water?

It crossed his mind that he did have a head start. Travellers from Perth would have to cross the ranges to get this far.

'I wonder if it would be worth a go?' he murmured.

With his knowledge of the land, he began to work out what supplies he would need. Two new horses, for a start. Packhorses. And enough basics like tea and sugar and flour to last at least three months. Prospecting gear . . .

'And for what?' he murmured. 'What if you failed? Time lost, conditions close to hell, all for nothing.'

Clem Price was no gambler. He knew that gold-prospecting required more than muscle and sweat; he'd need Lady Luck on his side, and there was no guarantee of that.

Nevertheless, there had to be opportunities to make a quid somewhere in this.

A few more miles down the road he stopped the horse with a jolt. To gather his thoughts, make sure he was clear in his mind of what he could do, he dismounted, took a gulp of water from his canvas bag and poured some into his hat. While the horse drank gratefully, he made his decision, turning back to York.

Tanner was surprised to see him again. 'I was just closing. It's been a long, quiet day today.'

'Any news yet?'

'No. But I feel it in my bones, Clem. It's on, I bet.'

'That's what set me thinking. If there's a gold rush, wouldn't you have a rush on your hands here too? Like people borrowing money to buy supplies and equipment to get themselves out there?'

'Without a doubt.'

Clem nodded. 'It seems to me a bank would only have so much to lend. I mean, you can't go on forever.'

'True.'

'Then I'd like my loan now. I'm not a prospector, I'm a grazier. I need the cash to build up Lancoorie. While the cash is still here.'

Tanner lit a cigar and blew out the match. 'You wouldn't even have a go at the gold?' he asked incredulously.

'No fear. While the going's good I need a thousand pounds for Lancoorie. I'd rather keep my money safe, not spend it on a pipe dream.'

'I admire your tenacity, Clem. Gold's a big temptation. You could do well to invest in a goldmine, but if you're set on sticking with Lancoorie, then that was what we originally discussed. You're right. You'd better have the loan now. Is a thousand enough?'

Clem stared. 'Enough? You mean I could borrow more?'

'Make it two if you like,' Tanner said cheerfully, and Clem agreed, although something about this arrangement made him uneasy.

'It's all right, is it, then? The two thousand?' he asked nervously.

'Yes.' Tanner took a folder from a neatly packed drawer. 'I'll need your signature on a few papers here, and the money will be put into your account. You can draw on it whenever you need it.'

'Jesus! Thanks, Mr Tanner. This is terrific. I won't let you down, I promise.' He signed on several dotted lines, watching as Tanner put his signature to the pages too.

'How's Thora?' Tanner asked.

'Not too good. I've got some medicine for her but I doubt it will make much difference. Alice is looking after her. I came to town for her father but he's away, the bastard. Couldn't even wait a month or so until the baby is born. And the locum hasn't turned up.'

'Yes, I made enquiries by telegram. No one seems to know about a locum. Didn't Carty know Thora isn't well?'

'Of course he did.'

'I see.'

See what? Clem wondered as he watched Tanner locking up the bank.

'I'll let you out the back way,' Tanner said.

'You had a funny look on your face just then,' Clem said. 'Do you think Carty doesn't care about Thora?'

'Peculiar time to go to the coast on holidays,' Tanner commented. 'The Cartys usually go in the summer. I wouldn't put anything past that old wretch.' He ushered Clem out of the back door, padlocking it behind him, then he turned and shook Clem's hand. 'Good luck then. Give my regards to Thora, tell her to hang on. It's not much longer.'

It was well into the night when Clem arrived home. He said nothing about the money and made excuses for the missing doctor so as not to upset Thora, but he was seething with anger. Had Carty deliberately left Thora with no professional care? Tanner seemed to think so. But surely not? Women died in childbirth. The babies died if they lacked proper care. Even with. Surely Carty couldn't be so vicious as to wish more punishment on his daughter? Did he want her and the baby out of the way altogether? An end to the scandal? Could be. Apart from the doctor, not one member of the Carty family had visited Thora at Lancoorie. Too far, Carty had said, and Thora hadn't complained. She seemed to accept their absence, as she accepted her father's attitude these days, listlessly.

'Well, not me,' he muttered as he heated cocoa on the stove for her. 'Thora will come through this. And she will have her baby. And then I'll deal with you, Carty. I'll have you grovelling one of these days.'

He sat by Thora all night, soothing her restlessness, keeping the eiderdown about her for warmth, taking her hand and talking quietly to her as she cried out in her sleep.

Suddenly there was more activity at Lancoorie. Clem hired the two Postle brothers to pitch in and help with the dam. He wanted it completed as soon as possible. Then he rode to another property and bought a hundred sheep, calling in on Ted Cornish to bring them over to Lancoorie.

'I get six bob a day now.' Ted scowled at him. 'I got a family to support too, you know.'

Clem glanced over at Mrs Cornish, who was chasing chickens down the yard. He'd never been introduced to the woman, but although heavily pregnant, she looked hale and hearty, and he felt a tug of envy.

'Your wife doing all right, is she?' he asked.

'Yeah. Nothin' wrong with her that a good hidin' wouldn't fix. Bloody women, always whingeing with their aches and pains. I keep tellin' her she don't know she's alive. She's got tucker and a roof over her head, she ought to take a lesson from them Abos. They turn out kids like layin' eggs. They don't need all the home comforts.'

Clem didn't think of their shack as any form of home comfort. He pitied the kid this dirty, miserable bugger brought into the world.

'Six bob a day it is,' he said. 'Bring them on to Lancoorie and I'll have another job for you.'

'You bought a hundred of Cochrane's sheep,' Ted said. 'He saw you comin', mate. Poor-grade bloody wool in his mobs, he don't know nothin' about wool.'

'Never mind, bring them over just the same, but take them quietly. There's no hurry.'

For the next fortnight Clem roamed the district, buying up all the sheep he could find.

'You're overstocking,' Alice warned him. 'I've heard the men talking. They think you've gone mad. When it comes to shearing you'll need a full-time wool-classer in the sheds. And a lot of them will hardly be worth shearing. I don't know what you're doing. If you bring in any more they'll starve here. We haven't enough pasture.'

'Don't worry, Alice. When I've got in enough I'm going droving with Ted. We'll take them over to the property at Birimbi. It's lying empty.'

'But it's not yours. It still belongs to Dr Carty.'

'It will be mine, and besides, Carty's away. How will he know? I need that land now.'

'Do you know how to find it?'

'My oath I do. Tanner gave me the description, it sounds a treasure. There's no crook land up there. Besides, it's near Northam.'

'What's that got to do with it?'

'Northam's on the road to Fly Flat.'

'So what?'

'So let's just wait and see.'

86

If the worst comes to the worst, Clem told himself, I can fatten them up and sell them, keeping the best wool-producers at Lancoorie. I could lose a bit, that's for sure, but it's best to be prepared.

Eventually, he and Ted went on the road with a thousand sheep and three slick dogs, and he leapt about in delight when he located the property, known as Carty Downs, and found it to be fenced.

'Do you own this place?' Ted asked him.

'No, I'm leasing,' Clem lied. 'Let's get them in and settled.'

It was indeed a beautiful property, with the ranges to the west and only a few miles from Northam. He would have liked to look over that little town but he was worried about Thora and eager to get home.

Not so his drover. As far as Clem could ascertain, Ted's wife was due any day but he didn't seem concerned.

'The Abos'll turn up if she needs a hand. They get wind of everything that's going on. She can't expect me to be hanging about. I didn't want no kid in the first place.'

Clem looked at the lanky man with his straggling, unkempt beard and thick hair tied back with string and wondered how any woman could marry the wretch in the first place. He'd like to get hold of him and shear off that wool to see what sort of face it hid.

'The way you talk,' he countered, 'you'd think you had nothing to do with it.'

'Ar . . . women are supposed to know.'

Clem turned away in disgust. 'You stay here. I'll ride up to that house on the hill and introduce myself. They'll be wondering what's going on over here.'

'We could go into Northam for a drink.'

'No, we'll camp here tonight and head back first thing in the morning.'

'How long are you leavin' this mob here?'

'I haven't decided.'

He was glad to be rid of Ted for a while at least. Next time, he decided – if there's a next time – I'll bring one of my own men, they're better company than this brute.

★   ★   ★

Lil Cornish, too, was glad to be free of her husband for a while. She took a rickety chair out of the shed that was her home and placed it in the warm sun by the back door, and then sat with a blanket over her knees, just resting and dreaming.

Her parents were drovers. For as long as she could remember they'd been travelling the stock routes in the south-west of the state, moving sheep great distances to properties, to stockyards, and on to other properties, wherever the work took them. Bud and Bonnie Roper were never short of work. They were good, reliable drovers, living under the stars with their wagon as their home.

Everywhere they went they took their daughter with them. By the time she was seven she had her own horse, a quiet mare that seemed to know she had a child in her care. Lil could still remember dear old Floss, trudging behind the wagon, more in command than her rider, resisting any of Lil's attempts to break loose and gallop off after the men. And sadly she recalled the terrible morning she'd found Floss lying dead in a field of purple wild flowers.

'She'd had a good run, Lil,' her father said, trying to console her. 'And look all about here. She died pretty like she lived, no fuss.'

By that time Lil was ten, and they gave her a real stock horse called Pip.

He could go, that Pip, she reminisced. No holding him, he was as keen to go a-droving as I was.

From then on Lil joined the team. She rode well and knew her job, whistling the dogs to keep the mobs tight on the long trails through the forests, scouting out on the plains, checking with her parents from all points. Mostly there was just the three of them, but with bigger mobs her father hired extra drovers to go on the road with them.

'It was a good life,' she murmured, watching the skinny chooks scratch about her. 'Mum and Dad were happy moving about all the time, and at nights round the camp fire they'd yarn about this and that, and all the people they'd met. When other men joined them it was fun; they'd have singsongs at night and jokes and more yarns.

'Not a worry in the world,' she said.

But as she grew older, Lil began to yearn for a proper home, for a home of her own. Especially when she saw all those neat homesteads, safe from the rain and the cold, and girls her own age, so secure and confident, knowing who they were and where they were every day of their lives. All members of communities Lil longed to join.

Then they met some drovers on the Great Eastern Road. Lil hated roads like this. Endless, boring roads with nothing to see but plains and more plains, not like the lovely scenery further south, and no protection from the cruel winds. Burning in summer and biting cold in winter.

Ted Cornish was one of the drovers. Since Bud was short-handed he hired Ted, who had no objection to turning south with Bud's new mob of sheep, although he kept saying he owned a farm on from York.

When he began courting Lil she wasn't all that keen, but he was persistent, and at least he had a farm with a house on it.

'She's got the nesting instinct,' her father laughed, but her mother was cautious.

'It's not all it's cracked up to be, Lil. Why don't you wait a while, you're only eighteen.'

'You just don't like Ted,' Lil complained.

'I'm not saying I don't like him. He seems polite enough, but I don't know him.'

'How am I to get to know anyone, moving on all the time like we do?'

Her mother sighed. 'Have you made up your mind?'

'Yes.'

'Then you can get engaged and we'll see about the wedding later on.'

'No! Ted's going home when we finish this drive. He wants me to go with him.'

They were married in a little village called Brookton, and their honeymoon was a long, leisurely ride up to Ted's farm, which she'd thought was in the Avon Valley.

'Barely on the outskirts!' she said bitterly, looking about her.

'And oh yes, he was polite,' she added, 'until we got here. And then he turned into the boss and I'm just his lackey.'

She hadn't expected a grand house but Ted's home was a shock. 'We can't live here,' she exploded. 'This place is filthy.'

'Because no one's been living in it for a while,' he said angrily. 'What did you expect?'

'From your talk I expected better than this.'

'The bloody cheek of you! What did you have? Nothin'! Nothin' but an old wagon. You never had a roof over your head in your life and you go whining to me about my place. Well, if it's that crook, you clean it up. I'm going to York for supplies.'

Lil supposed he was right. In a way. To outsiders, the Ropers' nomadic lifestyle might seem queer. And hadn't she wanted to stay in one place, put down roots? It was too difficult to explain to him that none of their camps had ever been in such a decrepit state as this, and she didn't want to start trouble, so as soon as he left, she began to clean up.

How she'd worked! Her new home was a wattle-and-daub shack with an iron roof and a floor of rough boards. It was only one room, with a log-and-canvas bed at one end, a kitchen table with four chairs and a huge brick fireplace over which hung blackened pots for cooking. There were deep cupboards either side of the fireplace but they held little more than rubbish, food remnants in one and old clothes and linen in the other. Lil found some books and a dartboard belonging to the previous owners and fortunately, in the outdoor washhouse, a bucket, bars of soap and a worn broom.

'You'll do,' she said resolutely, and began by sweeping the cobwebs from the shack. She boiled the copper to scour the grease from the pots and cleaned out the fireplace. Then she scrubbed the house from top to bottom. The activity seemed to give her courage – for years after that, whenever she was angry, Lil took to scrubbing and cleaning until every muscle ached, as a means of working through her emotions.

When Ted arrived home late that night she informed him, in no uncertain manner, that she would be going to York herself the next day, to order a proper mattress, some linen and a few other necessities for the house, and he could start cleaning up the yard.

'You were quick,' he said when she returned mid-afternoon.

'That's because I don't hang about pubs,' she said, unstrapping the saddle and releasing the horse. 'You haven't done much here. The yard's still overgrown with weeds. I want it properly cleaned out and we'll build a chicken run.'

'Who says so?'

'I do.'

Lil shifted uncomfortably in the chair, feeling the weight of her stomach. She'd told the local midwife that she was due at the end of this month, but she was afraid it might come sooner. When Ted came home she'd send him back to St Luke's to alert the pastor's wife, who'd become popular as an excellent midwife.

'The lazy bugger,' she groaned, thinking of her husband. He would work in the fields when she made him, ploughing and planting the wheat, but she had to work with him to keep him moving. It was a small farm but some crop was better than nothing. In return he expected her to attend to all of what he called the 'house' jobs – the chooks, the milking, the cooking and the rest of the chores attendant upon a farmer's wife. Life with Ted was a constant battle, especially since she told him she was pregnant and caused another row, but Lil refused to give in. Her mother had told her that if things didn't work out she could come back to them, but pride kept her on the lonely farm. She hated to admit she'd made a mistake, and besides, this was her home now. It was quite pleasant when he was off droving, and that brought in extra and badly needed cash.

Lil liked to daydream about her wedding day. She'd stood in front of a mirror at a friend's house, staring at how two women had transformed her from a bushie in her baggy pants and shirt into a pretty lady. It had been miraculous! The brown hair that she usually kept in neat plaits had been washed and brushed until it shone and allowed to fall down to her shoulders in natural waves. Mrs Barell, their friend, had made Lil a fine white muslin dress with a lacy bodice and a skirt of three layers, each edged with a border of white satin. To finish off the picture they produced a lovely hat of delicate straw covered in wild flowers. And she'd carried a bouquet of wild flowers.

'She's beautiful!' Mrs Barell had said. 'Good skin, smooth, even features and eyes the colour of cornflowers. Plenty of girls would give their eye teeth to look like Lil.'

'Too good for him,' Bonnie Roper had muttered, but Lil pretended not to hear. She was too excited to care.

Besides, Ted had shone up well too. Everyone said so. His beard was neatly trimmed and his wiry hair plastered down. He looked very smart in a borrowed black suit with a striped shirt and bow tie.

Lil's greatest disappointment was the photographer. He never arrived, and so there was no one to capture for ever the picture of this fine young couple on their wedding day. Of her looking prettier than she'd ever been in her life.

'Oh well,' she sighed. 'It can't be helped. When the baby comes along things will be different.' She had decided to prevail on Ted to sell this farm for whatever he could get for it. They were just surviving here. She wanted to move to a town where she could get a job and he could go droving as much as he liked. I'm working for nothing here, she thought. If I had a job I could start saving some money so that we can buy our own house. He'll sell if I have to nag him until he does.

As the sun moved across the house, Lil journeyed into the future, where she embraced visions of her dream home. She saw herself with her baby at the door of a neat cottage deep in the magnificent karri forests, or, with the licence of mind travel, chatting with neighbours over the fence of one of those semi-detached houses in central Perth, or even in a white stone cottage high on a hill, looking out over the wild beauty of the Indian Ocean, watching whales at play. The baby was always with her in these wanderings, but never Ted. He hadn't yet earned a place in her secret life.

★   ★   ★

The dam was progressing, growing wider and deeper every day under the watchful eye of the self-appointed foreman, Charlie Postle, who rode over every few days to check on the work.

'You young blokes,' he said, addressing his sons as well as Clem, 'wouldn't know the first thing about digging dams. Neither would them two ring-ins you got working for you, Clem. I been diggin' bloody dams all me life. I'll show you how.'

He also insisted that the four men camp at the site during the week. 'You gotta keep men working, Clem! They can't spend half the day ridin' over here and the other half ridin' home. Time's money, and while the rain holds off you got a sportin' chance of gettin' the job finished. Then while the going's good you have to reinforce the walls. Mind you, the work would move faster if the boss stuck around more often.'

'I can't, Charlie, I've got business to attend to.'

'Yeah, I heard, buying sheep fit for the slaughterhouse and moving them about the countryside. What's got into you, lad?'

Clem made vague excuses, grateful for Postle's help but not ready to confide in him. After he placed the sheep on the Carty property he put in a few days working close to home because he was worried about Thora, who seemed to be suffering a lot of aches and pains and spent most of her days in bed.

'I think she's getting close,' Alice told him. 'Her stomach's dropped.'

'But it's too soon.'

'Babies can come early. You'd better have a talk to her. She won't listen to me.'

He sat with Thora. 'Do you want me to go into town and see if your father is back?'

'No!' she cried, her voice hoarse and tired. 'I don't want him near me. Alice should have told you. I won't have him here!'

'All right then. Don't get upset. I'll go and get the midwife, Mrs Dodds. You remember her, the vicar's wife from St Luke's? They say she's very good.'

'I don't want her. Not yet. It isn't time.'

'But it could be, Thora.'

She was crying. 'No. It's too soon, people will talk. Keep her away.'

Alice was waiting outside. 'I told you. She seems to have some silly idea that she has to hang on as close as possible to the nine months. Although in her case what difference it makes is beyond me.'

'Do you think I ought to get the midwife?'

'Yes, I'll feel happier with her here, even if it is a false alarm.'

'I don't want to bring her here for no reason. Is Thora close to giving birth or not?'

'I think she is.'

'Good, then I'll get her.'

That morning Lil Cornish woke with no doubts at all.

She roused Ted. 'Quick, get the wagon. I want you to take me to St Luke's.'

'Why?'

'Why do you think? Because the baby's near and it will be quicker for me to go there than wait for you to bring Mrs Dodds here.'

'What's wrong with bringing her here? You ashamed of this place?'

'No,' Lil said, although there was that in it too. But recently she'd heard that a woman had gone into labour on the way home from York and Mrs Dodds had delivered the baby right there in her own house behind the church. And cared for the mother for some days afterwards. That sounded like heaven to Lil. She didn't fancy being left to Ted's ministering.

'Just get me there,' she said. 'And hurry.'

But when they arrived, Mrs Dodds wasn't home.

'She went off this morning to see to young Mrs Trafford out on their south property. I'm not expecting her back today. Mrs Trafford hasn't been well, she had a fall.'

'What are we going to do then?' Ted asked angrily.

'Just do your best, Ted. I'm afraid Mrs Dodds will be busy

when she comes back, Clem Price has been here looking for her as well. She'll have to go to Lancoorie first.'

'Yeah, of course she would. Moneyed folk come first, don't they?'

'That's not a worthy remark, Ted. My wife can't be in two places at once. And Clem was here earlier.'

They walked out to the wagon to break the news to Lil, who burst into tears. 'But I must have her. I'm near to my time. What can we do now?'

Dodds relented. 'This is an emergency, and I'm sure Alice won't mind, she's got room there. Take Mrs Cornish to Lancoorie, Ted, and I'll send my wife out there as soon as she arrives.'

'We've just come past there,' Ted complained.

'What does that matter?' Lil gulped. 'I have to go somewhere, and at least I'll have Miss Price to help me.'

'Is this your first, my dear?' Dodds asked her, but Lil could only nod. The pains were draining the last of her energy.

To Alice these were the most exciting two days of her life. During all the events, she had shone through. In the absence of the midwife she had surprised herself that she'd been able to keep calm and go about her duties steadily and responsibly. After all, she'd kept telling herself at the time, you've helped cows to calve and many, many ewes. The main thing is to keep the mothers working, pushing, but not wasting their strength.

Poor Lil Cornish had the worst time of it. She was thin and malnourished, soon weakened by her exertions, but Alice had petted and encouraged her, bathing her red, blotchy face with cool cloths, helping her to hang on to the iron rails of the bedhead for support. When the baby was born it was Alice who almost faltered.

'Oh God,' she prayed, 'help me now. And help this poor woman.' She cut the cord, swaddled the child, a little girl, and rushed to the door.

There was no sign of Ted, but her brother was pacing about.

'Come in here, quickly, Clem.'

'Me?' he cried, backing away.

'Yes, you. Get in here! Hold this baby. There's another one. She's having twins. Oh my God! Oh my God!'

She went back to the exhausted, weeping mother. 'You can do it, Lil. You've done it once, you can do it again. Now breathe in, big breath, breathe out. Hard. And push! That's it, keep pushing.'

'I can't,' Lil wept. 'Leave me alone, I'm done. It's over.'

'No, no, no! It's not, you've got another baby there. Come on, Lil. Keep pushing. Bear down.'

Alice, in a wash of perspiration, kept glancing at the door in the hope that Mrs Dodds would walk in and take this responsibility from her, and when it opened she gave a sigh of relief, only to find it wasn't Mrs Dodds but old Sadie.

The plump Aborigine woman bustled forward, ignoring Clem to take in the situation.

'She keeps passing out on me,' Alice whispered, glad of the company of this woman, any woman.

Without a word, Sadie climbed across the head of the bed, her legs straddling Lil. She took her in her strong arms, lifted Lil up so that her head was resting on the ample chest, and hung on tight, whispering to Lil in her own language. Then she slid her arms forward and took hold of Lil's hands, providing her with support and a new fund of strength.

The labour began again and Lil bore down with renewed energy, time and again, until Alice gave a cry of joy. 'It's coming, Lil. It's nearly over.' And so she delivered the second child.

Clem went to find Ted.

'Congratulations! You've done well. You've got two fine baby girls.'

'What do you mean, two?'

'Mrs Cornish had twins.'

'Twins! Strike me bloody pink! What are we gonna do with two? We can't afford one.'

'Ah, you'll be right. Do you want to see them?'

'Later.'

Clem shrugged and returned to the house, meeting Sadie and another Aborigine woman on the way.

'Where are you off to?' he asked.

'Your ladies not much good feeders, Mr Clem. This one she feed that other bubby.' She looked darkly at Clem, as if he were somehow responsible for this state of affairs. 'I brung her to feed your bubby when it comes. Now what we're gonna do?'

'One day at a time, Sadie. We'll worry about it when it happens.' He laughed. Sadie was wrong. Thora's breasts had swelled; she could feed her own child.

But Sadie stopped and glared at him. 'Lot you know. Your missus put out that bubby tonight.'

He rushed inside to Thora. 'How are you feeling?'

'I don't know,' she said listlessly. 'Has that other woman had her child? She looked so wretched. I know how she must feel.'

'Yes.' He didn't want to frighten her with the thought of twins. 'She's fine.'

'I am so uncomfortable. Could you get me some tea?'

'Yes, of course.'

When Mrs Dodds arrived there was a general sigh of relief. Thora went into labour at nine o'clock that night, with the midwife and Alice in attendance.

Clem sat in the kitchen worrying the hours, as Ted dozed in Noah's old chair. He felt sorry for Ted's wife, who was weak and weepy, not helped by Ted's sour attitude. He hadn't minded them coming here; in fact, he considered it a sensible move. Mrs Cornish could have been in serious trouble left to the far-from-tender ministrations of her husband. But now he wished they'd go on their way. The sooner the better. He had his own wife and child to worry about.

It was Alice who came out to break the news, tears tumbling down her cheeks. 'Thora had a little girl, Clem, but it was born dead.'

Clem was shocked. 'It can't be! What went wrong?'

Alice shook her head. 'I'm glad Mrs Dodds was here too. I'd have felt it was my fault. But it was the cord, she said. It got tangled up somehow. It seemed such an easy birth, too, everything was going so well at first, not such a worry as it was with Ted's wife. And then . . .' She burst into sobs.

'How is Thora? Can I see her?'

'Not yet. Mrs Dodds said to let her sleep. She's given her laudanum. Mrs Dodds wants to fix things up in there herself . . . Poor Thora, she'll be devastated.'

'Give her one of mine,' Ted grated, and Alice turned on him.

'How could you be so cruel!'

Hours later Thora awoke, screaming at Alice to give her the baby, but then she fell asleep again.

'She's going to take it hard,' Mrs Dodds said, and Alice agreed, but having had time to think about the situation, she had a long talk with Ted.

When Clem joined them and the suggestion was put to him, he couldn't take them seriously. 'Your wife would never agree to this, Ted.'

Alice took her brother into the sitting room to discuss the matter in private. 'If Mrs Cornish agrees to let you adopt one of her little girls, it will be a godsend to Thora. She's very high-strung, Clem. Losing the child will be a terrible blow to her after all she's been through.'

'But would she accept another woman's child?' Clem was confused.

'Don't tell her.'

'We have to!'

'Not necessarily.

His sister's cold reasoning astonished Clem.

'What difference will it make to you if you bring up one of those little babies in there? Thora's child was never yours in the first place.'

'But what about Mrs Dodds? What will she say to all this?'

Alice smiled. 'We'll see. She thinks you're a saint, Clem. I've been listening to her. Mrs Dodds is the wife of the vicar, remember? And she's got hard-core religion, very severe on morals. Not much sympathy for Thora there. Muttering about the wages of sin. She was so mean and nasty I'm glad Thora couldn't hear her. I almost told her off at one stage, and I'm glad I didn't now. We need her. Let me have a talk to her.'

Mrs Dodds drank her tea and nodded thoughtfully. 'I believe it is God's hand working here, Alice. Your brother would be doing one of those little baby girls a great favour if he was to take her on. I've seen where the Cornishes live. God knows what sort of a life those children would have. At least one of them would have a good future with this family. An excellent future.'

Alice sighed. 'I worry about Dr Carty. He would probably object to his daughter adopting a strange child.'

'What's it got to do with him? Why wasn't he here instead of running off on holidays? The locum still hasn't arrived and I've had to ride all over the countryside looking after the women he should be caring for. I'll give him a piece of my mind when he gets back. But you listen to me, Alice, I still say the good Lord has been at work here putting everything right.'

'It seems so.'

'It is so. The little baby that died wasn't Clem's child.' She sniffed. 'I'm well aware of that. God asked him to step forward and be the father, and he did. Now God is asking him again to be his servant and provide for another. He cannot refuse. As a matter of fact, I've already been speaking to that Ted Cornish. He's not fit to parent either of them. You must rescue at least one of those children in the name of the Lord.'

'We'll see,' Alice said again. 'It will be up to Mrs Cornish.'

'No, it will be up to God. Let us pray on it, Alice.'

Their voices were all part of her dreadful fatigue, churning over her like the relentless crunch of wagon wheels, crushing her. Mrs Dodds persuaded and prayed, Ted whined and insisted, Miss Price thought it was for the best.

'They're dear little girls,' Mrs Dodds said, 'but the smaller one is in need of extra care. You want to do the right thing by your babies, don't you?'

'I'll sell the farm if that's what you want,' Lil thought she heard Ted say.

Lil was confused: she'd heard of girls having their babies adopted, their only babies, that must be hard. Heart-breaking. Eventually she heard herself saying, 'At least I'll have one.' And she clutched her baby to her breast for fear they'd want to take this one too.

'You're a righteous young woman.' Mrs Dodds' voice was smug. 'God will watch over you for the pity you've shown Mrs Price in her darkest hour, and he will reward you, my dear, never doubt that.'

When all the talking was done, Lil was caught up in their elation, proud that she was strong enough to make the right decision, thanking the Lord that her two babies would be loved and cherished by their real mother and by the adoptive mother. She would have a better chance of coping with just one. And Ted had said he'd sell the farm. She hadn't forgotten that.

It was Lil who made the decision not to see the other baby, afraid she would upset them all by changing her mind. Mrs Price, they said, wasn't coping so well. She was high-strung. Hadn't been the best for a while, and Lil nodded. That sounded like Thora, the hothouse flower.

Miss Price was so happy with Lil that she brought her two beautiful layettes and a shawl for the baby, whom Lil had decided to call Caroline, a name she'd chosen months ago. Everyone agreed it was a most beautiful name, and Lil glowed with pleasure. On her third and last night at Lancoorie, she sank back into her daydreams. Ted had kept his promise, the miserable farm was already sold, to Mr Price, since the land adjoined his property, and they would be moving on.

Mrs Dodds was right, Lil mused, God is good. She'd never had much religion, but now she was afire with it, and she had her own Bible, a gift from the midwife. Quietly, together, just the two of them, they christened the baby Caroline Cornish, and they went on their knees to thank the Lord. It was a beautiful ceremony without Ted to spoil things, and Mrs Dodds read psalms to Lil, wonderful words full of joy. Lil was happy, uplifted, the path of a true Christian ahead of her.

'What do you want for your farm?' Clem asked.

Ted cocked a sly eye at him. 'Well, that's something we have to discuss, isn't it? I take it you want us to move on?'

'Yes. I think that would be a good idea under the circumstances.'

'It's gonna cost you. We've made a big sacrifice for your missus.'

'How much?'

'Fifty quid for the farm.'

'It's not worth fifty!'

'To you it is. Under the circumstances, as you say. Then there's our fares.'

'What fares?'

'I've got a cousin. He's got a big sheep station outside Adelaide. I always wanted to go to Adelaide.' He grinned. 'Is that far enough away for you? We wouldn't want my wife to have a change of heart and come traipsing back here, now would we?'

Clem had intended to give the couple a gift of money to see them on their way, and he wasn't surprised that Ted was trying to wring as much as he could out of him. It was typical of the man, who would have sold them both children given a chance. But he was still wary. If they went to Adelaide then that was a bonus, the further away the better.

'Very well. I'll pay your fares to Adelaide.'

'First class.'

'Fair enough, it isn't a long voyage. I'll write to the head office of my bank in Perth and they'll buy the tickets for you.'

'You're a good man, Clem Price. I always said so. You'll fix up the midwife, I suppose?'

'Yes. That's not a problem.'

'Good. Then there's only my missus. She ain't got nothin'. She'll need clothes and things to go on a big ship.'

'How much?'

101

'Well, fifty quid for the farm, and fifty quid for her. She did the work. She gave you a bloody healthy kid.'

'Very well. I've got some papers for you to sign, though, and they'll be witnessed by Mrs Dodds.'

'That's all right. Lead me to the pen, mate.'

As they were leaving, their wagon laden with supplies and the lovely gifts for Caroline, Lil looked back at the house in silent salute to her other baby. Mrs Price was still unwell, confined to bed, but they'd said she'd be up in a day or so. Lil knew her baby would be safe with Thora and Clem Price; she'd be well cared for. And Alice had promised to watch over her too.

She was pleased that her daughter would grow up with the nobs on this big property, wanting for nothing.

Clem Price surprised her, handing her an envelope once she was settled. 'What's this?'

'It's for you,' he said. 'You take good care of yourself and your baby, Mrs Cornish. And you hang on to that money.'

Lil knew she looked a wreck in the loose cotton dress, her skin was still puffed and blotchy and she cringed, ashamed. Over these days she'd hardly glanced at Clem Price, but seeing him now, out here in the clear, she was taken with his good looks and gentle smile. This was the man who'd married the pregnant Thora Carty that day, to rescue her from scandal. A truly God-fearing man, Mrs Dodds had said, a gentleman. And he was that. Lil wished Clem Price could have seen *her* on her wedding day, could have seen the real Lil Cornish.

Her husband was angry, jumping up in front to whip up the horse. 'What'd he give you?'

As the wagon rolled down the long drive to the gate, she hitched Caroline aside and opened the envelope. 'Great heavens, Ted. There's fifty pounds here. Fifty pounds!'

'It's mine!' he cried, trying to snatch it from her. 'It's payment for the farm.'

'No it's not, you liar. Miss Price told me they'd already paid you for the farm. And they're paying for our fares to Adelaide, by ship. Why are we going to Adelaide?'

'Because I've got a cousin there. We can get jobs on his station.'

'I don't mind going to Adelaide. I've always wanted to go on a sea voyage. But I hope you're telling the truth, Ted Cornish, because God help you if you're not. We're going to lead a much better life now, a Christian life.'

'Jesus! What's got into you?'

'Nothing. Just slow down, I don't want to upset the baby.'

Alice was so excited at having a baby in the house that she fussed over mother and child every waking hour.

Mrs Dodds had taken the other tiny soul to be buried by the vicar in hallowed ground by St Luke's church. 'Baby Cornish' was only the second burial in their new cemetery.

When the men eventually came in from the work camp, Alice brought out the baby, as delighted with their compliments as if the child had been her own, but then Thora had to spoil everything by appearing and taking it away.

But Mike didn't seem to mind. 'My word,' he said, 'Mrs Price is surely looking well again now. The babe's put a real shine on her.'

Even George muttered agreement as they trudged back to their quarters to wash up before dinner.

They were right, of course. Thora had ceased to be the invalid and become a mother, a beautiful mother, who spent a great deal of time attending to her appearance. She washed her hair in rainwater and brushed it until it shone, leaving it loose. She took a bath every day in water perfumed in lavender. She had milky lotions for her body and rosewater and glycerine for her flawless skin. Special creams were produced from her small travelling bag to rub into her hands, and daily she filed and buffed her pretty nails.

Nothing had changed really, Alice mused. Prior to this Thora had been too unwell to help much about the house, and now she was too busy with herself and the baby. Clem was still, or even more, madly in love with his wife, and Thora accepted his fussing over her as her due. Alice didn't object, it suited her to run the household without interference, and as long as Clem was happy, that was fine with her. But now it was beginning to dawn on her that there was no more to Thora. Her aloofness, her tall, statuesque beauty was probably all men needed, Alice thought dismally, to go gaga after her, for there was nothing else endearing about the woman. She had no conversation, no interests, not even in Lancoorie or Clem's latest activities. She never spoke of her family nor was she interested in Clem's background. She never read a book or a newspaper, although women's magazines took her fancy, and she found cooking beyond her.

'We always had cooks,' she said vaguely to Alice. There was no malice in the remark, just further indication that Thora was content to waft about the house in pretty dresses with her baby.

At mealtimes she sat sweetly by Clem, when he was home, happy to congratulate Alice on her cooking, which pleased Clem, and saying little else.

'Thora's a good listener,' he said to Alice, 'I'll say that for her.'

Yes, in one ear and out the other, Alice thought darkly.

It was impossible to dislike Thora, she mused. Nothing there to like or dislike. She's just being the good little wife. But she's so damn vain. I wonder how long this will last.

Thora named the baby Lydia May, and Alice laughed.

'Lydia may what?'

'I'll thank you not to make fun of me.' Thora sniffed, resentful, and Alice had to remind herself that her sister-in-law had no sense of humour.

'I'm sorry, Thora. I think Lydia is a lovely name.'

At Sunday dinners, though, she did notice that Thora could raise a smile at Mike Deagan's jokes, whether she got them or not. And that concerned her; it made her feel drab and uninteresting beside this lady.

The Cartys came out, *en masse*, in one of the doctor's horse coaches; all the same people, it seemed, who had attended the wedding. They adored the baby, showering it with gifts, fussing over mother and daughter, congratulating Clem, who embarrassed Alice with his constant enthusiasm for his lovely wife, kissing and hugging her so much that Thora was seen to pull away from him at times. But he was mad for her, and there it was.

Everyone was happy. Carty was delighted with his grand-child, claiming Lydia looked like his sister, while Mrs Carty said no, she looked like Lettice.

Thora smiled possessively. She still thought she had borne this lovely infant, and neither Clem nor Alice would ever disillusion her. They enjoyed her pride, her almost defiant attitude to her family. It was as if she was saying to them: 'There! I was right all along. I had my baby and it's mine, not yours.'

Dr Carty presented Clem with the deeds of the Birimbi property without demur. 'We're all grateful to you, Clem. It's a joy to see Thora so happy and I know you'll be a good father to my granddaughter. You'll have to bring her to town for the christening.'

'As soon as we get time,' Clem said. 'The dam is nearly finished.'

But before they could arrange the christening, big news came through.

Intermittent rain had fallen while they were building the dam, but now, with storms threatening, they all worked feverishly to complete the retaining walls.

'It's as fine a dam as ever I saw,' Mike puffed as they hauled the last of the rocks into place.

'I reckon so.' Clem grinned. 'I had a mind to build one all along, but my old man would never hear of it. Now I can run more sheep.'

'Will you be bringing back that other mob now?'

'I hope not. I want to buy more.'

'They're saying you got more money than sense, boss . . .'

'I know.' He called to the other men. 'It's a good job well done. What say we all make for my place and christen the dam?'

'A party, is it?' Charlie Postle said. 'Count us in, Clem. You can pay the lads, too, then we'll get back to our own farm.'

By the time the six men rode back to the Lancoorie homestead, the storm had burst and heavy rain was sweeping across the plains. They were all in a riotous mood, cheering the soaking rain, wallowing in the rare pleasure of having beaten the elements for a change.

Clem recognized a jinker belonging to Pastor Dodds and growled: 'What's he doing here?' He was nervous that Dodds might have come to reveal the truth about Thora's baby, but none of the others seemed to have heard him, they were too busy stabling their horses.

Alice came running. 'What's going on? Is there anything wrong?'

Andy Postle took hold of her and swung her around. 'We're here to celebrate. Clem's got his dam and we've all got a mighty thirst. You gonna join us, Alice?'

She escaped from him, laughing. 'Of course, that's wonderful. Come on up to the house, all of you. Pastor Dodds is there, Clem, he has some news for us.'

'What news?' Clem asked suspiciously.

'I don't know. I was just about to get it out of him when he saw you coming in the gate. He wants to tell you himself now.'

Clem walked with her. 'Is everything all right? He hasn't been talking to Thora, has he?'

'Yes, he's been fussing over the baby, but I don't think it's that. He's in an excellent mood. I think he's a bit of an actor.'

Whatever it was Dodds had to say, he dragged it out, congratulating them all on their hard work and agreeing to take a glass with them.

'Did you want to talk to me?' Clem asked anxiously. 'We could go into the sitting room where it's quiet.'

'No, my news is for everyone, Clem.' He raised his voice to address them. 'Obviously none of you has been into York in the last few days.'

'No, why?' they chorused.

'Because the whole town's in turmoil. There have been big gold strikes at Fly Flat, out west from here! And not just

106

fly-by-night goldfields. They say that whole area is rich with gold. This will really put West Australia on the map.'

'Not to mention York,' Charlie Postle said. 'By Jove that's gonna cause a few changes round here.'

'Why here?' Les Postle asked his father.

'Because a gold rush will bring thousands of diggers and the price of everything will skyrocket. We'd better get into town tomorrow and grab supplies while we can.'

'Me, I'd rather go to Fly Flat,' Andy said. 'I want some of that gold.'

'What's happening in York?' Clem asked the Pastor.

'Gone mad. Men downing tools everywhere and leaving. Joining the rush. Even a bank manager.'

'What bank manager?' Clem asked.

'Mr Tanner. I'm quite shocked. He just shut the bank and left. His wife is distraught.'

Tanner, Clem thought. The gambler! He recalled the bank manager's excitement at the talk of gold, and realized, now, why he'd been given that loan. Tanner had known he wouldn't be there to face the responsibility if Clem defaulted.

'Mr Tanner went?' Alice was amazed.

'My dear, gold fever doesn't differentiate,' Dodds said. 'All sorts of men get the fever, from workmen to professionals.'

Thora had joined them. 'Then why is Mrs Tanner distraught? I should think she'd be pleased if he came home with gold. Clem, you ought to go too! Can you imagine it? Coming home with all that gold? I think it would be simply wonderful.'

'Not for Mrs Tanner, I don't think,' Dodds told them. 'He must have had some advance notice. They say he had a couple of horses packed and ready to leave, in Crombie's stables. He left her a note of some sort. He hasn't just gone . . . he has left her. Taking their savings.'

'What about the bank?' Clem asked. 'Will they reopen it?'

'Oh yes. Apparently a replacement is on his way. But the Tanners occupy the bank residence. Mrs Tanner will have to leave. A dreadful shame. I feel for the poor woman.'

'She bossed him around a lot,' Clem remarked.

'Obviously he needed it,' Dodds said primly.

When Dodds left, the party deteriorated into shouted arguments. The two Postle brothers were all for leaving for the goldfields right away, but their father was dead against it.

Mike was also keen to go.

'You can't!' Clem said. 'You're contracted to me. You have to stay here.'

'Not if we go with you, George and me. You're still the boss. It's the chance of a lifetime, this is. We'd be a team.'

'What about the farm?' Alice cried.

'Oh, pooh! There's nothing much to do here until shearing time,' Thora said. 'Mike's right. This is a golden opportunity.' She giggled at her own joke. 'We could be rich, Clem.'

'A lot you know about Lancoorie,' Alice snapped.

'Heavens, you'd think they were going for ever,' Thora rejoined. 'They just have to ride east a while . . .'

'Hundreds of miles,' Alice reminded her.

'So? We're already on the right side of the range, it shouldn't be all that difficult. With three of them they could dig for gold and be back in no time.'

'We're not going,' Clem said, 'and that's the end of it.'

It was the end of the party too. Appetites were not affected as Alice served rissoles in gravy with hunks of bread, but a brooding silence had taken over the company, broken only by the long rolls of thunder that accompanied the steady rain.

Later, as they were preparing for bed, Thora had more to say. 'You should give this more thought, Clem. You'll never make much here. You've got a chance to make us rich and two men to help you. What more do you want?'

Clem doused the lamp. 'Don't ever contradict me in front of people again!'

The next day Clem was moved to apologize to Thora for snapping at her; he couldn't bear to see her so withdrawn and upset, refusing to address him.

'You're looking beautiful, darling,' he said. 'Let's go for a walk.'

'I don't feel like a walk. I have to watch Lydia.'

'She's asleep. Alice will keep an eye on her. Here's your shawl. Come along now, don't be cross with me. I know I can get a bit cranky at times, but I wouldn't hurt your feelings for the world.'

They walked down the bush track at the back of the house, through a grove of lemon eucalypts that lent a sweet fragrance to the air.

'I have to go away for a while,' he began.

'Where to? The goldfields?' Thora forgot her sulks at this prospect.

'No. To Northam. I'm hiring a woolshed there. As soon as this weather clears there'll be some real warmth in the sun, so the shearers can start here at Lancoorie. When they're finished I'll take them to shear the mob I've got on the new property.'

'Oh yes. Carty Downs. My father knows you're grazing sheep there. One of the neighbours let him know.'

'So?'

'So nothing. I don't care. It's ours now and I want the name changed.'

'By all means. To what?'

'To my name. We can call it Thora Downs.'

Clem shook his head. 'That doesn't seem to fit. What about Thoravale?'

'Wonderful! I love it!' She pecked him on the cheek. 'Will you put the name on a sign over the main gate? A big sign.'

'Consider it done. I wanted you to know that I wasn't just buying sheep for the fun of it. With this gold rush, I'll sell those sheep in Northam as soon as they're shorn. Prices are climbing all the time. I don't think . . .'

Thora interrupted him. 'I'll design an archway to be built over the gate with "Thoravale" printed across the arch in large letters.'

'All right. You do that. If I get this right, Thora, I could make a huge profit on the sheep I bought. There could even be time for me to . . .'

'When you make the sign, don't have the name painted on. Paint washes off. I want it burned into the timber. Signs like that are very smart. Won't my sisters be green when they hear?'

Clem looked at her fondly. Thora was so sweet and feminine. Why should she have to listen to his boring talk of sheep and prices? He took her arm to assist her round a rocky patch, overgrown with hardy cut-leaf banksias, watching warily for snakes. 'I know I promised to take you to Perth, so I thought that when I come back from Northam we could go.'

'Oh no! Not while I'm still feeding baby. It would be too much of a tie. I wouldn't be able to enjoy myself. And I couldn't buy any new clothes with my bosoms so horribly puffed out.'

He smiled and turned to gently squeeze her breasts. 'I don't think they're horrible; they're lovely and soft and sexy.'

Thora pushed him away. 'Don't be vulgar. Is Thoravale a nice property?'

'My word it is. Lovely country, the pick of the district.'

'Good. I was thinking we could build a really nice house and go there to live. Lancoorie is too big and isolated. We'd be so much closer to Perth.'

'We couldn't do that. It's only farm land. Your father bought it on spec. It's handy grazing land for my purposes, now but it's fit only for a small farm. Being on the river it would probably suit a dairy farmer with a small herd.'

'Or a lovely residence.' She pouted. 'With grounds that could be landscaped, I'm sure. You wouldn't need to stock it at all.'

Clem laughed. 'That would be a terrible waste.'

'Don't laugh at me.' She scowled. 'Other people, like the Forrests, have residences on big estates. They build beautiful houses and they don't ruin the surrounds with smelly stock.'

'The Forrests! Good God, Thora! Sir John Forrest is the Premier of the state. He'd have a government residence.'

'There are others. My father says six families run this state, and they've all got wonderful residences. I don't see why we can't. I was led to believe you were well off.'

'Don't be silly, Thora, we're not in that league and we never will be. And I'm not well off, as you put it.'

110

'My father says you would be if you sold Lancoorie.'

'I don't need your father's advice and neither do you. Since when have you cared what he says?'

'Since I realized that you have more land here than you'll ever need. And you just want to stay in these backblocks, never caring what I want.'

She began to cry, and Clem attempted to comfort her. 'That's not true, dear. I was just trying to tell you before, that I can build Lancoorie up into . . .'

'Oh, leave me alone!' Thora twisted away and flounced back along the track, stumbling on slippery exposed roots, and Clem ran after her.

'Please, Thora. Would you like to go into York for a while and stay with your family?'

'York! Never! I never want to go there again as long as I live. They do nothing but laugh and gossip about me. I don't know how you could suggest such a thing.'

Completely at a loss, he walked disconsolately behind her. He wished he could make her understand that he did have ambitions, that he would do well without selling Lancoorie, but it would take time. He was already planning carefully and working hard. The harvest of his endeavours was still a long way off but he was on his way. Clem figured he'd make a handsome profit on that extra mob of sheep, and he'd reinvest in something else. He grinned. Too late to buy any more on the cheap. He'd got into that market just in time, thanks to Tanner.

As they neared the house he ran after Thora with renewed exuberance, tickling her, teasing her. 'Come on, my darling. By happy! Let me see you smile.'

She fended him off. 'Don't muss me up! You don't really care about me or you'd listen to me, and you wouldn't call me silly.'

'I didn't mean that, Thora. Tell you what. We'll hang on to Thoravale and one day I'll build a house there for you. A big house. A mansion, if you like.'

'Can I design it?'

'Yes. Why not?'

'Good. We'll have a house something like my family's house in York, only better and twice the size, with real reception rooms and a guest wing. Won't that be something? We can have people to stay over for house parties, and maybe a tennis court too, that's the latest thing . . .'

Clem wasn't listening. He'd remembered the bank overdraft that he'd been digging into rather freely. He decided that he'd repay a token amount to keep the bank manager happy, when he sold the sheep, but he'd keep the bulk of the money to invest. But invest where? That was the problem. He'd heard that Carty was selling his passenger coach company for a song because the railway line from Northam was being extended to York, and he wondered if it would be any use buying that company. Having it cover outlying districts, bringing people into York to connect with the trains. Then he shook his head. Carty would have thought of that idea. It probably wasn't viable.

'Oh well,' he murmured to himself as he closed the gate behind them. 'I'll think of something.'

Chapter Five

The auctioneer came striding over as Clem and Mike drove the big mob of sheep into the Northam sale yards.

'By God! You're a sight for sore eyes, mates. Where did you spring from?'

'York. I'm Clem Price from Lancoorie Station, and this is Mike Deagan.'

He'd brought Mike with him to assist with the shearing of the sheep from Thoravale, and all had gone well. The shearers were paid, the wool bales were at the railhead store to be auctioned off and now all he had to do was dispose of the sheep. He looked about him. This was Friday, sale day, but there wasn't much on offer, just a few sheep and cattle, some pigs and no horses.

'Are we too early?' he asked innocently. 'Or are you having a quiet day today?'

'Quiet?' the auctioneer thundered. 'It's bloody hopeless. I've got more buyers than stock. They've come from Southern Cross and even as far as Coolgardie itself.'

'Where's Coolgardie?' Mike asked.

'Cripes! Where have you two been? Fly Flat has been declared a town and renamed Coolgardie. The Abo name for the place. They named it after some kid way back in time who found a water hole there.'

'Then you can sell my sheep, can you?' Clem asked.

'And your horses too if you like.'

'I'd expect a good price,' Clem said. 'I've gone to a lot of trouble to bring this mob here.'

'You'll get it, mate. There's no end to the mobs of fossickers streaming through here, some even with their poor bloody families. They're like a plague of grasshoppers munching up everything in sight. You won't have any trouble getting three quid a head for your sheep.'

'Make it four,' Clem said. 'I want a reserve of four quid a head. They're all newly shorn and ready.' He could hardly hide his excitement. He'd bought the sheep in lots, often well under five shillings a head, but he'd taken care of them and they'd fattened up on the better pastures of Thoravale.

'I'll do my best,' the auctioneer said.

'I can wait. The rush is only beginning, the papers are full of the gold strikes at Fly Flat, or Coolgardie, or whatever they call it now. If they don't buy now, they'll pay more next week and more the week after, and the buyers would have to know that.'

He and Mike repaired to the nearest pub and sat in the crowded bar, listening to the endless talk of gold.

'I've been thinking all along you had a tip-off on this gold, Clem, and that's why you've been herding in all them sheep.'

'I heard a rumour.'

'You'll make a lot of cash today, by the sounds of things.'

Overhearing them, the publican intervened. 'You blokes brought in that mob of sheep this morning?'

'Yes.'

'Then watch out, mates. Insist on cash up, no cheques or IOUs. There are more spivs and crooks on this road now than in the Fremantle jail. I've been caught more than once and now I won't even look at a piece of paper. Half of the blokes that are bidding at the sale yards these days aren't real buyers or butchers, they're just fly-by-nights. They take the sheep out on the road, miles from anywhere, and sell them off one by one to the bloody stupid gold-chasers what have run out of grub.'

'How many towns between here and Coolgardie?' Mike asked.

'Only two, to speak of, in the whole four-hundred-mile trek, Merredin and Southern Cross, and they say they're in uproar.'

'But they're finding plenty of gold out there?'

'Sure they are. And paying a heap for water and getting bowled over by typhoid.' He laughed, swabbing down the counter. 'They say half the diggers are busy burying the other half.'

'Nice place!' Clem commented, but Mike was still keen to go.

'You'd be able to make it with a wagon and your own provisions from Lancoorie,' he urged Clem. 'I'll come with you. George can stay on at Lancoorie to look after the ladies, and your property. We're so close it's mad to miss out.'

'Four hundred miles isn't close, even to me. And you'd get a shock trying to dig in that country. It'd be bloody hard work.'

'And convicts aren't used to hard work?' Mike said bitterly.

Clem laughed. 'Don't give me your sad story. We're not going and that's that. It's not my fault you're still on parole. When your time's up you can go where you like.'

'There'll be no gold left.'

A bell rang and they joined the crush in the small dining room that had been cleared of tables and chairs. Instead there was a bench by the kitchen door where sandwiches, boiled eggs and potatoes were snapped up by hungry customers as soon as they appeared. In the end they managed to buy a few potatoes before the supply ran out, and left the pub still hungry.

'I was sure we could get a feed there,' Mike complained. 'I'm so starved I could eat me boots.'

Clem made no comment, rather than point out to his companion that they'd just been given a mild indication of the hazards of the long, arid gold trails. Compared to the rest of the journey, Northam was paradise.

The two men forgot their differences when the bidding for Clem's sheep began, with as many buyers as spectators. Clem could pick the experienced men who'd taken the time to view his stock prior to the sale and were hanging back, aware that the best were being kept until last. Not so the other bidders, who were so desperate for the mutton they pushed the price up and up, past the reserve to five pounds per head for the first lot of a hundred bony sheep.

Clem had a word with the auctioneer, warning him to take only cash, but even that regulation didn't slow the frantic bidding, with men shoving and jostling to be heard.

Mike was thoroughly enjoying himself, shouting encouragement to the buyers, throwing in an extra bid himself, to keep up the pace. As the price of his sheep went up to six, then seven pounds a head, sometimes only by the haggling over a few more pence, Clem listened in amazement, wishing he'd worked harder at assembling more stock. The last lots of his sheep skyrocketed to eight pounds then ten pounds per head, with arguments raging in the crowd about racketeers ruining the chances of decent buyers, who were trying to do the right thing by the residents of their country towns.

But the cash poured in, and Clem was glad of Mike's company when they lined up at the auctioneer's shed to collect, both men now armed with rifles.

The auctioneer, too, had guards as he took his commission, and paid the owners of the stock sold that day.

'You did all right,' he grinned as he counted out more than three thousand pounds in battered notes to the man from Lancoorie. 'You got any more, mate?'

'Yes,' Mike said eagerly. 'Sure he has.'

'No I don't,' Clem retorted. 'I'm a wool-grower, my sheep are too good for the slaughterhouse.'

'At these prices?'

'At any price,' he said. 'I'm not stripping my station of stock.'

The money was wadded with rubber bands and placed into calico bank bags, which Clem stuffed into his strong leather saddlebag. 'Let's go,' he told Mike. 'I have to get this into a bank right away.'

They ran to their horses, not from any need to hurry, but out of sheer jubilation, laughing and whooping like a couple of tearaway lads.

'By Jesus! You pulled it off!' Mike gloated. 'What a bloody windfall! Me and George, we talked over why you were buying up so many sheep with no eye to their condition, and guessed you were building up to go for a high price out this way, but we never guessed you'd make so much.'

'Neither did I. It wouldn't have surprised me if half of those bidders couldn't come up with the cash, but it's here. Every damn penny. We'll bank it and stay in Northam tonight. I feel like celebrating.'

As they turned into the main street of Northam they were confronted by a huge crowd surging noisily in front of the shops.

'Looks like they're celebrating too,' Clem said, slowing his horse to a walk.

'Like hell they are! Protesting, more like it.'

'What about?'

They urged their horses to the edge of the crowd to listen to a man who was standing on a box addressing the mob. He was a strange-looking fellow with a gaunt face and a mane of long, lank hair.

'Hold back, mates,' he was yelling. 'You can't be taking the law into your own hands. It'll go against you in the long run!'

Voices tried to shout him down but he persisted. 'There's a lot we're needing, from here to Coolgardie, in the way of services. Don't show the bosses in Perth we're nothing but rabble, or we'll get nothing.'

Mike leaned over to Clem. 'The town's ready for trouble. Do you see, the shops are all closed and barred. The banks too.'

'God, no!' Clem groaned. 'Who's this chap?' he asked a bystander.

'Name of Vosper, mate. Fred Vosper. He's a reporter. Don't know why he's interfering. Folks have had enough.'

'Of what?'

He didn't hear the reply. There was a shower of rocks, and Vosper ducked, but they weren't aimed at him. Shop windows were smashed, and the crowd roared their delight.

But Vosper wouldn't give in. 'No more!' he shouted. 'Don't do this, don't make it any worse for yourselves! You're only the first wave, every ship that comes in now will be bringing diggers from the eastern states and the lack of supplies will be far worse than now.'

He had a powerful voice and was making himself heard again. 'If you wreck this town, you'll put the bosses offside. It's the rich politicans in Perth I'm talking about. They won't send help, they'll send troopers.'

'What help can they give us?' a man shouted.

'They've got the cash, mate. You haven't. They can sink wells for water at Coolgardie where you'll be paying more for water than for whisky. And if you think the price of tucker in this town is outrageous, you ain't seen nothin' yet. They've already got the means to take the railway on from here to York. I say it should be redirected on to the town of Southern Cross and then to Coolgardie, to stop the tragedies already happening out there on that awful eastern road.'

'You're a lunatic,' shouted a man standing by Mike.

'No he's not,' Mike retorted. 'He's trying to tell you diggers that if you demand your rights in a body, united, they'll have to listen. He's trying to help the situation.'

'What would you know, redbeard?' the man spat and pushed forward. 'I say we teach this town a lesson,' he shouted, waving a heavy stick. 'We're not even halfway to Coolgardie and these bastards are bleeding us dry, charging us to the hilt for every morsel of food. We'll starve out there on the road if we listen to mad Vosper and his pipe dreams.'

'They're not pipe dreams,' Vosper shouted, 'I've been to the goldfields in the east, we can learn from what happened there. Rioting did no good . . .'

'Let's get out of here,' Mike urged as the mob surged forward, intent now on attacking the butcher's shop, but Clem worried about that speaker.

'Will he be all right? Those buggers are pulling him down.'

'Not our worry.' Mike grabbed the reins of Clem's horse and jerked him away.

Within minutes a full-scale riot was underway, and as they

looked back, missiles were flying in all directions. Torches were flung into the butcher's shop and it was soon ablaze, firing the adjoining buildings, one of them the Bank of Western Australia, Clem's original destination.

'They've gone mad!' Clem said. 'What will that achieve?'

'Nothing. Provisions will be in even shorter supply. But they'll feel better having punished someone for their sufferings.'

'And you wanted to go prospecting with that lot? They *are* rabble.'

'They're confused, that's all.'

'Tell that to the poor people who own these shops. The butcher would have had to bid like everyone else at the sales, no wonder meat's expensive in the shops.'

'Don't shout that about or they'll be after you too.'

'What am I supposed to do? Tell the buyers I'll only sell at the pre-gold prices?'

'Just don't be trying to fathom economics. We'd better head home.'

'Home? We've been camping out for more than a week. I promised myself we'd stay in a hotel tonight and celebrate. I've earned that.'

'What about all that cash?'

'We'll keep it with us and put it in that other bank in the morning. Too many people saw us with the money from the sales; we'll be safer in a hotel. We could get bushwhacked on the way home.'

'We could ride fast for York and stay over the night there.'

'Jesus, Mike. You'd think it was your cash. I'll keep the saddlebag with me. That's nothing unusual. We'll stay in a pub, have a couple of drinks, get a feed and a good sleep and we'll be gone before any of these madmen wake up.'

They found a hotel that was just reopening, the publican nervous but relieved that his end of the town wasn't involved in the rioting.

'You blokes diggers?' he asked.

'That we are,' Mike said, rather than admit to profiteering in this town.

'Where are you from?'

'Perth. On our way to the fields. That's a nasty bit of business we saw down there. Does it happen often?'

'No.'

'What was it about?' Mike persisted, making conversation, but the publican was wary.

'Buggered if I know. What are you drinking?'

'Beer.'

'We're out. Rum or whisky?'

'Whisky. Can we get a bed here tonight?'

'Sorry, mate. Booked to the rafters already.'

'Looks like we're going home,' Clem said, and the publican glanced at him, a question looming.

Mike covered the mistake with a laugh. 'What can I do with him? First setback and he wants to go home to Perth! Took me enough time to talk him into heading for Coolgardie. There is gold out there, isn't there?'

'More than most folks know,' the publican whispered to them. 'Word is they're picking up scores of ounces in their bare hands, even further on from Coolgardie. There's a bloke staying here, a scribbler, name of Vosper, he reckons that this'll be the biggest gold strike the world has ever known.'

'Where does he get that from?' Clem asked, realizing it would be wiser in this touchy town to know nothing about the riot. Or Vosper. Who he hoped, was still alive. He felt guilty about leaving that poor fellow in the hands of the rabble.

'I dunno. Geologists maybe.'

'But further on from Coolgardie has to be right on the edge of that desert, doesn't it?' Clem asked.

'Nothing comes easy,' Mike intervened. 'We'll have those two whiskies.'

'Can you pay for a bed?' the publican asked as he served their drinks.

'So far so good,' Mike replied easily.

'Then hang on and I'll ask about. You staying for a feed?'

'I could eat a horse,' Clem said.

'Righto. Money up. That'll be ten shillings. My missus will be bringing out mutton stew and potatoes shortly. That's all we've got. You diggers coming through have to understand that we're all in the same boat. I have to pay a bloody fortune to even feed my family.'

'But the pub's doing all right,' Mike said mildly as customers began streaming in from the excitement in the street, but the publican had moved away.

'See!' Clem said, following Mike down to the end of the bar, their backs to the wall. 'We can relax. If he can't find us a room we'll bunk down in his bar. At least we can have something to eat. And this whisky isn't bad, although I've tasted better.'

'Go on!' Mike said, annoying him, patronizing him, his sharp eyes moving over the faces of the men crowding about them.

Suddenly Clem looked down. 'God Almighty! What the hell are you doing? You've got your rifle with you. And it's bloody loaded! I don't know where you come from, but that's illegal in this country! Keep it hidden!'

'I am. Calm down. You've got the cash. I've got the minder, that's all. You left yours in the stables with the horses.'

'That's where you're supposed to leave your firearms.'

'Ah, well, nobody told me, did they?'

The hours they spent in the Northam Hotel were a welcome relief to Clem. Neither he nor Mike drank heavily; they sat with their whiskies and enjoyed the company of the strangers about them, who were all hopeful gold prospectors. The locals, as someone remarked, were using their wisdom to remain out of sight for fear of a lynching.

They had bought and devoured a second serving of the watery mutton stew before the publican remembered them.

'You can get a bed at the Avon Hotel,' he informed them. 'It's right in town, but he doesn't want any trouble, so he's shut down today, and he's not reopening. It's a good room, with two beds, and it'll cost you two quid. I told him you look a decent pair of blokes, so don't go causing no trouble. He's not serving any booze, even to boarders, so you can buy a bottle here and take it with you if you want. Go to the back door and

121

tell him I sent you. The name's Barclay. And no women.' He glared at the tarts who had infiltrated his bar, especially the two gaudy young women who had targeted Mike and Clem.

'That's a great pity.' Mike nudged Clem. 'The ladies are hot to come with us.'

'Well they're not!' Clem said primly.

'Have a heart! Do you not know how long it is since I bedded a woman?'

Clem pretended not to hear that as he hunched the saddle-bag on his shoulder, making for the door. Mike followed him, his rifle slung casually under his arm.

'I think your rules are a bit out of date,' he commented to Clem. 'Several fellers in there were armed. I suppose it's the times.'

'Or the publican is too busy to notice.'

With dusk settling, the deserted street was gloomy, two dark gaps in the row of shops an ominous reminder of the day's events. Debris still littered the street and the smell of burned timbers lingered over the town. They found the Avon Hotel locked and barred as expected, so they made their way around a side street to the rear of the hotel, only to find that the gate leading to the stables and the back yard was chained shut.

'Dammit!' Clem rode up and down the high fence, trying to attract the attention of someone inside.

'I don't think shouting at them will help,' Mike said. 'Wait here, I'll rouse them.' He jumped down and handed Clem his horse's reins, then he ran forward and scaled the fence.

The hotel was two-storeyed, brick. A fine-looking building, Clem thought. No wonder the publican shut down today, with more respect for his premises than the marauders in the town. At least we'll have a decent room.

'What are you doing hanging about here?' A man hurrying round the corner caught him by surprise.

Clem twisted about in the saddle to reply. 'It's all right, mate. I'm just waiting to be let in. We're staying here.'

Where the blow came from, he hardly knew. He hadn't seen the other man come up behind him. In shock he clung to the reins as a heavy club smashed across the back of his neck. His horse reared, the bit tearing at its mouth, and Clem crashed to the ground under another agonizing blow. They were pulling the horses away and he tried to hang on to the leather straps, but he was being dragged along the rough ground.

His hands were slippery, from sweat or blood he couldn't tell, and then he could hear them running, with his horses! Getting away! He tried to shout but could only raise a croak.

The chain rattled and the heavy gate swung open. It seemed a long way back from where he was lying.

'Now where the hell is he?' he heard Mike say. 'He was here a minute ago . . .'

'Did he go round the front again?' a voice replied.

'No. Jesus! Why would he do that? Hey! Clem! Where have you got to?'

'Who's that?' the voice asked. 'Up there by the fence?'

Clem groaned a response.

'Holy Mother of God, what's happened to you? Where are the horses?'

Dazed, he staggered into the hotel, supported by the two men.

'Did they get my saddlebag?' he asked Mike urgently.

'Yes. A bonus, I'd say. The boss here reckons they'd have been after the horses.'

Clem groaned. His wrists were wrenched and bleeding and his head felt as if it had been cracked open. 'We have to go after them!'

'On foot?' Mike said. 'We'll clean you up and you'd better get some rest. No point in even looking for police tonight. The horses have your brand; that could be a start in finding the bastards.'

'I can buy more horses,' Clem said bitterly.

'Not round here,' the publican said. 'You've got a nasty gash on your head. Will I send for the doctor?'

'No,' Clem said angrily.

Two days later they learned that their horses had been found wandering in the scrub near the road to Perth, and troopers were bringing them in. Just the horses; none of the owners' possessions were located.

'That's it then,' Mike told Clem. 'They thought they'd just scored two fine mounts, but one look at your cash and they'd have known they had to ditch branded horses fast and head for the hills. They're gone! You'll just have to put it down to bad luck.'

'Is that all it is to you? Bad luck? Jesus, I'm bloody ruined, and you talk as if I've only lost a few pounds!'

'We'll have the horses. We won't have to walk home,' Mike said. 'That's something!'

'It might be to you. Get out of here and leave me alone. And by the way, stop referring to yourself as my partner. Everyone who comes up to this room calls you my partner. It's bloody annoying.'

Mike shrugged. 'Since I'm doing the talking and the explaining, and the chasing about with the troopers, they're taking it for granted I'm your partner. I've said naught. You're doing yourself no good lying doggo up here, snorting and sulking. You're not that bad hurt, it's the pride as well as the cash has got you fair paralysed, so don't take it out on me.'

Left alone again, Clem knew Mike was right. He'd made money and from sheer carelessness he'd lost it. He should have been on the alert. Jesus, he thought angrily. I was armed. It should never have happened. Bloody stupid, that's what!

'Had it been Mike who was robbed,' he muttered angrily, 'I'd have given him a few more bruises from sheer rage. But I've got no one to blame but myself.'

It irritated him even more to realize that the older man, the convict who had survived tough years in this country, would not have fallen prey to a couple of muggers. He wouldn't be surprised if Deagan was laughing at him behind his back. What a tale he would have to tell his mate George when they got back to Lancoorie!

Clem had considered saying nothing to the women, but eventually decided they might as well know, rather than hear it from someone else. At least he could expect some sympathy from his wife and his sister.

'But by God,' he muttered savagely, 'this won't happen to me again. I'm not sure what I can do from here, but I'm going up in the world somehow. I've promised Thora and I'll not let her down. And I'll not give anyone an inch, ever again.'

He was still berating himself for letting the mugger surprise him with that challenge while his mate attacked from the rear, when another caller came to sympathize with him.

This time it was the reporter Fred Vosper, who introduced himself and brought Clem a bottle of brandy.

'Thought I'd commiserate with you, my dear fellow. Have a brandy now, cheer yourself up.'

Clem stared as Vosper dug into the pockets of his shiny black coat and produced two glasses, pouring hefty drinks.

'Weren't you up there addressing the mob before the riot?'

'The very one.'

'I thought they'd lynch you. I was worried about you.'

'Not me. I know when to bolt. But it's gentlemanly kind of you to be concerned, Mr Price.' He took off his hat, releasing the longest hair Clem had ever seen on a man. 'Don't take this hair amiss, sir. The bosses jailed me on the Queensland goldfields for writing the truth about their iniquitous treatment of the diggers, so I vowed never to cut my hair again in protest.'

'I see.' Clem nodded, bewildered.

'You're famous now, Mr Price. I've written your story. Of how the bosses are allowing mayhem on this gold route by refusing to pay extra police, and therefore leaving honest citizens like yourself to the wiles of thugs. You were robbed of a great deal of money and I place the blame at their feet.'

'You're putting me in the paper?' Clem felt sick.

'My word. It's done. Losing ten thousand pounds to bush-whackers out on the unprotected roads . . .'

'It wasn't ten thousand, it was three, and I was at the back gate here.'

'The same thing. This is only the beginning. The roads are not safe. The banks had to shut down to avoid being raided in broad daylight, with the local sergeant and constable out on the track trying to keep law and order, and no law left in the town.'

Clem listened, fascinated, to Vosper's diatribe about politicians who were sitting on their tails in Perth, enjoying the good life, while any fool could foresee the tragedies that were befalling diggers and their families struggling to reach Coolgardie.

'You've been out there? To Coolgardie?'

'Of course I have. I always get the facts first-hand; that's why I couldn't leave without meeting you.'

'But you said you'd written the story?'

'Oh yes, your partner gave me all the details. He said you're a wealthy grazier and the loss of thousands of pounds was a drop in the bucket to you.'

'He did?'

'Yes. But that's not the point. You are a citizen of note. You have every right to lodge a complaint at the highest level, pointing the finger of blame at the Premier himself. He's to blame, you know. I'm writing an open letter from you to the Premier and it will appear in the *Perth Western Mail*. You have to demand protection, an efficient supply of provisions, water, all sorts of things, not just for yourself but for everyone out here . . .'

Clem drank the brandy to ease his throbbing head. Vosper wasn't helping. But the man did have some interesting information.

'Will the gold hold out?' he asked when he could get a word in.

'Bet your life it will. And there's been another strike twenty-four miles on. Place called Kalgoorlie. All of that country is a mile deep in gold. You only have to look at it, wasted away by the elements until the hard gold is left lying about.'

'Why don't you dig for gold?'

'Because I'm a writer and a patriot. That is my calling. Why don't you? You're a lot younger than I imagined. I had the impression you were a middle-aged chap. Or older. But you won't go because you're settled, you have your property and your family, why would you bother?'

'It might be fun.'

'Let me tell you for free, Mr Price, gold-digging might be a lot of things but it is never fun. Even if you made a big strike, that's only a ticket out of hell.'

'What was it you were saying yesterday about the railway line?'

'That's as plain as the nose on your face. They won't build the railway to York now, they'll be forced by me and by the multitude of diggers' voices to take this rail line straight on through Southern Cross and on to Coolgardie. You mark my words.'

'I thought you said they won't listen to the diggers.'

'Aha. But when they see how much gold is out there, they'll be investing their own money, then we'll get results. I'm just trying to hurry it up for the sake of all the poor folk struggling out there now.'

They talked until they finished the bottle. 'We'll get our letter written tomorrow,' Vosper said, 'your open letter to Forrest, our rich and greedy Premier.'

'Good-oh,' Clem said. But when he was advised that his horses had been brought in to Northam, he told Mike that they'd be leaving for Lancoorie at sun-up.

'Glad to hear it,' Mike said. 'You're not achieving anything sitting around here.'

His boss scowled. 'Don't be so sure.'

Lancoorie was so peaceful, with the sheep grazing quietly on the rolling plains, that Clem was filled with nostalgia for the untroubled days of his childhood, when it was just Noah and Alice and himself and their ordered, isolated existence. But those days were well gone. Now, he knew, it was time for him to sow again. His harvest had failed, Noah's 'sleeve' money was gone and Lancoorie was hobbled with a mortgage.

Alice was dumbfounded by his tale of success and failure, but she was hopeful. 'We still have the wool cheques, Clem. From here, and from the sheep you had at the Carty property. We'll manage.'

His wife was a different matter. Thora raged, 'You sold all those sheep and let yourself get robbed! Were you drunk? Have you no sense at all? Three thousand pounds down the drain! That's a fortune. I can't believe you were so stupid. Now I hear you have a mortgage on this property. I didn't know you had a mortgage. You don't seem to have any idea how to run a property, Clem. You'll have to speak to my father.'

'Yes. I'll do that, Thora. Don't be worrying. It will be all right.'

When at last, with Lydia asleep, he had her to himself in the privacy of their bedroom, he took her in his arms.

'You're so beautiful, Thora. Every time I come back from only a few days away you look better than ever. Motherhood becomes you.'

'Did you do what I asked? Did you put up the sign over the entrance to our property? The sign that says "Thoravale"?'

'Yes,' he lied, afraid to antagonize her further.

'And it's burned into the timber?'

'Yes. It looks very smart.'

'Good. At least you managed to get something right. When will you take me to see it?'

'As soon as I can. It's a long, tiring ride.'

'I suppose so. Do you have to maul me like this?'

'I've missed you so. You're so soft and lovely to the touch. Why do you have to wear such big nighties? I can't find you in all the linen.'

Thora bristled. 'You're not even wearing pyjamas! What if someone comes in?'

'No one will come in,' he laughed, tickling her, kissing her, sliding up the voluminous skirts. 'Come on now, let's get this off. Darling, we don't need all these clothes, it's a lovely warm night.'

By dint of teasing and gentle persuasion he had at last removed the nightdress, not minding that she kept the sheets clutched about her. 'Now isn't this better?' he whispered to her. 'You and I together just as nature made us, just as nature wants us to be.'

'No,' she said angrily. 'It's vulgar. You're deliberately humiliating me.'

As fast as she rewrapped herself in the sheet, he eased it away. The feel of her long, slim body with those jutting breasts was sheer heaven to him, the homecoming he desperately needed from the disaster at Northam. 'No one's humiliating you,' he smiled, retaining his good humour. 'You're just bashful, that's all. I can understand that. But you have to take pride in yourself, be proud of your body and the joy it can give you.'

He tried to make a game of his teasing and fondling, wanting her to enjoy it, hoping by encouragement to arouse her. Then what followed would be enjoyment for both of them. 'If you give yourself over to love,' he whispered, his hands exploring gently, tentatively, 'you'll be wanting more, I know you will.'

'Don't,' she said, pushing him away. 'You're so common. If you must have your rights, for God's sake do it and get it over with. I shouldn't have to endure all this vulgarity first.'

'What did you say?' he demanded.

'I don't know. Just do it, Clem. I want to get to sleep.'

'Did you say I was common?'

Released from him, Thora turned away with an audible sigh.

All of Clem's frustrations of the previous day culminated in real anger. 'Common, am I?' he grated, dragging the sheets from her. He threw himself at her, forcing himself on her, abandoning any pretence of gentleness.

'This is sex, Thora, this is what it's all about, and the sooner you get the hang of it the better,' he snapped.

In the morning, though, he fled from their bedroom filled with remorse, knowing it would be useless asking her to forgive him.

Alice noticed that Thora was cool, even rude to Clem, and she thought it grossly unfair of her sister-in-law to be punishing him for losing all that money. It wasn't his fault, it was just the times, with all of those terrible people out on the roads.

And to make matters worse, for days now she'd been playing up to their workmen, the men she'd previously despised as convicts. It was all a ploy, Alice knew, a payback, with her husband as victim, making him look small in front of the men.

'We'll all be in the poorhouse soon,' she'd smirked at the dinner table last night, 'the way Clem's going.' And Alice had felt like smacking her face.

But Clem hadn't reacted. Not even a blink, so Alice made no comment either. She supposed it was for the best. One should ignore such spiteful remarks.

Something else bothered her as well. She didn't like the way Mike was looking at Thora these days. She hoped she was imagining it, but he seemed to be responding to Thora's wiles with no little appreciation. More than was necessary, Alice felt. Distressed, she had to admit that Thora was a beautiful woman, and it would flatter the workmen to have her batting her eyelids at them, but Mike shouldn't encourage her.

Clem was talking about going into York for a few days, and Alice had suggested that he take Thora and the baby with him.

'She doesn't want to go,' Clem retorted abruptly. 'She wants to take up riding again now, and that will be good for her. She'll be able to see a lot more of Lancoorie, being free to ride where she pleases.'

'Oh yes,' Alice said numbly as she went on with her scrubbing. But she wondered what had brought this on. Thora had given no prior inkling that she liked to ride. But still, it was something for her to do, Alice supposed. Better than hanging about the house all day, primping and posing.

Once out on the road, Clem slowed his horse to a trot. He was glad to get away but in no hurry to reach York, there being so much to think about. Thora was still not speaking to him; she even put the bolster down the middle of the bed to separate them as much as possible.

He wished she'd told him off, yelled at him, said something. Her silence was unbearable. He'd tried to apologize: 'Thora, about the other night, I'm sorry, I didn't mean . . .' But she'd brushed past him as if he didn't exist.

Finally when he'd offered to take her to York she'd stopped to stare at him with contempt. He only knew that she intended to take up riding because he heard her discussing the horses with George, deciding that the young chestnut mare would be suitable. Afterwards, as if he'd known all along that the mare was her choice, and it was to be left available for her, Clem groomed the horse, prettying it up for its mistress, and he cleaned and polished a light saddle until it shone, hanging it with a new blanket by the stable doors.

He was so depressed it was hard to concentrate on his next move. In fact, even now, he wasn't sure if he wanted to do a damn thing but stay home at Lancoorie and take life as it came without trying to be too clever. But he knew he couldn't hide from the looming demands of the bank and from the promises he'd made to Thora. There was still loan money available and he'd use it, but this time he had to get it right.

His first call was on Dr Carty, seemingly a social call from a dutiful son-in-law.

Carty was pleased to see him. Too pleased, a mean grin puckering his plump face, but Clem was prepared.

'Heard you had a spot of trouble,' Carty said, handing him a whisky, not the good brand.

'Yes.'

'It was in all the papers, son. You lost a fortune, they say.'

'I took a hiding as well.'

'You young' uns! You get yourselves into strife. Nobody would have robbed me of that sort of money. You had those sheep hidden out there on my property!'

'My property.'

'Whatever. You should have told me what you were doing. I'd have given you a hand. I'd have made better arrangements than you did, planned it better. I don't know what you thought you were doing with all that cash and only that bloody convict for an offsider . . .'

Clem endured the lectures, the conceited crowing, until Carty was done.

'How are you going with your passenger coaches? Thora says you're selling.'

'Yes. With the railway coming to York it won't be any good any more.'

'Why not? I don't understand why you're selling. Horse-drawn buses will still be needed to bring people to the railway station from the outlying districts.'

Clem was watching. He knew that what he'd said was not a viable proposition: most people had vehicles or horses, at least, to bring themselves that far, and for that matter the population was sparse. It was one thing to transport passengers from the town of York on to the railway at Northam that would take them through to Perth, entirely different to try to collect enough starters just to get to York. But he saw Carty's expression shift.

'You're right of course,' the doctor said. 'But to tell you the truth, I'm sick of the business, Clem. I'm getting too old to be bothered with it.'

'You don't have to do much bothering. Your manager does a good job, doesn't he?'

'Oh, sure. But Mrs Carty is all for selling it. So I might as well.'

They sat silently in the dim dining room for a while, and Carty replenished their glasses.

'It's a pity to see a good business go out of the family,' Clem commented. 'Got any buyers?'

'Not yet. Everyone's heading for the goldfields. They don't know a good thing when they see it.'

'Well, if you really want to get rid of it, why don't you sell it to me?'

'You? Have you got any money left?'

'A bit, I didn't lose it all.'

'You didn't, eh? Is that right? What did you do? Split the cash? Keep some on you?'

'Something like that.'

All of a sudden, according to his father-in-law, Carty's Coach and Carrying Company was the best business on the plains.

Clem listened innocently, nodding patiently as Carty explained how little expenditure was needed to keep a coach company going, compared with the profits, and he allowed himself to be drawn in as a possible buyer.

'I'll think about it,' he said. 'It sure sounds like a good business, but I'd have to look at the books and the condition of the buses and so on, wouldn't I?'

'Don't call them buses. They're coaches. Cheaper to ride on top, that's all. Why don't you stay for dinner, Clem?'

'No, I can't. I've got business to attend to. I'm staying at the pub.'

The barmaid, Jocelyn, was thrilled to see him. She waved to him, indicating that she'd come and talk to him when she had time.

Clem bought a drink and stood at the end of the bar, striking up conversation with a group of men who were on their way to the goldfields. They had travelled more than a hundred miles on foot to York and were headed across country to the great eastern road.

'We nearly missed York,' one prospector told him. 'We hit that bang-long stretch of road out there and headed east into the sun before we woke up this town was behind us. Wasted a day. You on the march too, mister?'

'Thinking about it.'

He had been thinking about that gold ever since he left Northam, but the spectre of failure loomed large. From his hotel window in Northam he'd watched the never-ending procession of fortune-hunters making for the goldfields. Men humping their swags like these fellows; others, on horseback, mingling with the carts and wagons, even wheelbarrows, that crowded the road. Some had their families with them, dusty women and children with blank, weary expressions, already strained from the long journey over the ranges with no idea of the hardships ahead.

And he'd seen the spring carts pulled by two horses with their escort of six armed horsemen, galloping strongly on to Perth to deliver the cargo of gold. They gave heart to the marchers who cheered their progress.

But on the other hand he'd also seen the forlorn stragglers who were moving west against the flow, going home, defeated.

Already these hopeful men in the bar were showing signs of wear and tear. Their clothes were shabby, their boots giving way, and it was obvious they'd set off without too much thought and less cash. They were three fishermen, a bank clerk, a tailor, and a baker's apprentice, all from some little coastal town; none of them, he realized, with any knowledge of the bush.

But he'd always enjoyed the company of strangers, hearing about faraway places, so he stayed with them, lingering, as they did, over only two drinks.

Times had changed too, in York. Previously this hotel had served meals in a neat dining room beside the bar, but now, with an excess of customers, the tables were shoved aside and drinks were served in there too. Meals of sausages or stew were being sold in a rush over the counter as the clock struck six.

'Smells good,' one of the prospectors said, but the others frowned at him. 'Can't afford to eat here. Let's get back to camp.'

'York's famous for its pork sausages.' Clem smiled, feeling sorry for them. 'You have to try them. I'll shout.'

'We couldn't ask you to do that,' the tailor said, picking up his hat, but on Clem's insistence they accepted.

'We're beholden to you, sir,' the tailor said. 'Most appreciated.'

'You're very welcome,' Clem replied, spying Jocelyn, who was beckoning to him. 'Think kindly of York.'

She had a half-hour dinner break, so he sat at a table outside with her while she made short work of a big plate of stew.

'It's lovely to see you again, Clem,' she said. 'So many people have gone off to the goldfields. Even Les and Andy.'

'Yes, I heard. I hardly know anyone in the bar these days.'

'We're worked off our bloody feet with all them grasshoppers coming through. They eat everything in sight. I heard you had a spot of bad luck at Northam?'

'Yes. The bastards. Put me in a hell of a hole.'

'Why don't you go after the gold too? If I could figure out how, I'd go there meself.'

He laughed. 'What would you do there?'

'I'm strong. If I had a partner, a bloke, I could dig.'

'No you couldn't, it'd kill you. You stay here safe, my girl.'

Jocelyn looked at him, her eyes twinkling slyly. 'Are you going home tonight?'

'No, I thought I'd stay here if there's a room.'

'That we have got. None of the grasshoppers pay for rooms, they sleep under the stars. Maybe I'll see you later.'

And of course she did. This time she knocked, and Clem let her in, relieved to have a woman who had no inhibitions. They made love and they talked. He could talk to Jocelyn. He spoke about the goldfields, and the horrendous trek prospectors would have to face.

'A man would have to be well prepared,' he said, 'with supplies, equipment, water. A wagon would be essential, and two horses.'

Jocelyn listened as he listed the necessities for a well-planned expedition, and she laughed. 'You're going! You are going! You just haven't made up your mind when!'

'I suppose I am.'

'Of course you are. What will your wife say?'

'She wouldn't care.'

'Oh! Like that, is it? Then you'd better get yourself out there before the gold runs out. I'll come with you.'

'No you won't,' he laughed, pulling her down into the bed with him. 'Forget about the gold, you're much more interesting.'

Morning brought resolve, and resolve engendered enthusiasm, because Clem loved to plot and plan. The lethargy of the previous weeks disappeared in a flurry of activity. He bought three large empty beer kegs from the publican, to contain water, the first priority, on the dry route to Coolgardie.

Then he visited Carty's Coach Company and had a long

talk with the manager, appreciating his warning that the business would collapse once the railway reached York.

'You're talking yourself out of a job,' Clem said. 'If Carty can't sell he'll have to shut down.'

'I wouldn't have it on my conscience no matter who he sold to,' the manager replied. 'I'm honour-bound to speak the truth, regardless of what the boss has to say, but that done, Clem, I'll show you round. Then it's up to you.'

Clem began buying supplies where he could, and storing them in the hotel shed. He avoided the bank rather than face an uncomfortable conversation with the new manager, whom he had not yet met. Fortunately.

He grinned as he strode down the street. Not having made his acquaintance, Tanner's successor wouldn't be able to spot him in town.

But he was spotted by Mrs Carty, who rushed over to him. 'I'm so glad to find you, Clem. I hope you're not going home today, I absolutely insist you come and stay with us. What will people think, our son-in-law being forced to stay at a hotel!'

Clem was aware of the reason behind her eager invitation and allowed himself to accept. 'Thank you. I'll be along later.'

He dined with the family, listening without comment to their talk of the town, and the gold rush, and all the queer types passing through. The meal was served quickly and the girls were dismissed immediately after the dessert of stewed apples and cream.

Carty could hardly wait. 'I hear you've been looking over the coaches,' he said when there were only the three of them left at the table.

'And the books,' Clem said.

'You'll find them in order.'

'Yes. It's certainly a good business.'

'Of course it is. You won't find a better money-spinner.'

'You can't just rely on farming,' Mrs Carty said. 'What with the worry of the seasons, a young man like you should diversify your interests as Dr Carty has always done.'

'That's true,' Clem admitted and settled down to be persuaded and then to haggle over the price, changing his mind, backing away from the purchase, claiming to be unsure of the viability of the firm once the railway came to York. Gradually the price came down, with Carty insisting he was not desperate to sell, but he should make allowances for family.

Later, with pencil and paper, Clem argued about the value of the six coaches, the horses, the price of maintenance and feed, the value of the depot premises, which were in need of paint, and finally agreed to pay four hundred and fifty pounds, less than half of Carty's orginal price.

'I think Alice will agree to that,' he said eventually. 'If you can have the contract ready tomorrow I'll take it out to her.'

'Alice?' Mrs Carty asked, surprised.

'Yes. Alice will buy it.'

'But I thought the business was to be kept in the family.'

'Alice is family,' he said firmly.

'What are you thinking of, Clem?' she asked, staring at the contract he put in front of her. 'Everyone knows that business will be ruined.'

'No it won't,' he said quietly. 'Keep it under your hat. The railway won't come here, it will go on from Northam straight through to Coolgardie. The goldfields are more important than York.'

'Lord heavens! Shouldn't you have told Dr Carty that, if it's true?'

'No, he's enjoying himself, taking me for a duffer. I can't say for sure this will happen, so why should I mention it? Sign it and you'll own a good business. The manager is a fair and honest fellow; you can go into town and meet him whenever you like. After that it will be up to you to keep an eye on it.'

'You should have put the contract in both of our names. Why didn't you do that?'

'Because I won't be here. You have to have full control.'

Alice was bewildered. 'Where will you be? You can't buy any more sheep at the old prices.'

'I'm going to the goldfields.'

'Oh no! You wouldn't be so foolish.'

'I have to go, Alice, so there's no use trying to talk me out of it. I've planned all this carefully and I'll take George with me.'

'George? Why not Mike?'

'Because Mike's too volatile a character. I never know where I am with him. George is a plodder. He'll go along with whatever I say. Anyway, you seem to like our Mr Deagan. You won't have any trouble with him.'

'Let me read what this contract says.' Alice was stalling.

In Clem's absence, his wife had been behaving badly. On the last two nights she'd gone for evening walks with Mike, and while Alice had to admit there was nothing really wrong with that, it made her nervous. And not a little jealous. Mike had never taken her for a walk, day or evening. What would happen if Clem went away and threw that pair together for months on end?

She signed the contract and looked thoughtfully at Clem. 'I'd still rather you left George here. He's really more useful about the property. When they knock off work, Mike likes to rest and to read. Nothing wrong with that, he's entitled. But George likes the kitchen garden, he's got green fingers, we've never had such a supply of vegetables before. And he doesn't mind doing odd jobs about the house . . .'

'So you don't mind if I go?' Clem obviously didn't really care which of the men went with him as long as Alice was happy.

'If you must, but be careful, Clem, please. They say those goldfields can be dangerous places. You've already had a taste of the sort of company you'll be mixing with.'

He threw his arms about her. 'I'll be careful, don't worry. Just pray that I'll have good luck.'

His wife found that she could talk to him after all.

'How long are you going for?'

'Three months. No longer.'

'And do you think you'll find gold?'

'Why not? Other people do.'

'Oh, marvellous! Bring me back some. When are you leaving?'

'As soon as we can put up a supply of salt meat and preserves. Alice is starting a big cook-up tomorrow. I'll need every bit of food I can carry in the wagon. In the meantime, we have to arrange Lydia's christening. Your family will be coming.'

'Why? I don't need them.'

'Never mind, the christening is important. It will be a happy day for us, Thora. And by the way, we bought your father's bus company.'

'The coach company! Oh God, you're such a fool. How did you let them talk you into that?'

'Don't worry, it'll be all right. Another asset for our family.'

Thora shook her head and wandered away to attend to the baby, and Clem nodded, feeling better. At least they were talking. Before he left he would patch up the row between them with an apology, and the pretty gold pendant he'd bought for her in York. She'd cooled down now and he'd never force himself on her ever again. Thora was sexually immature, he decided, remembering that exciting night with Jocelyn. I'll just have to be more patient with her, he told himself, and certainly not upset her before I leave. I'd be too miserable to go if she was still cross with me.

He needn't have worried. Thora was thrilled by the thought of the gold, she even helped Alice bake cakes that would keep, and packed them in tins for the men.

'I swear you've got the gold fever too, Mrs Price,' Mike teased, and she giggled.

'If I were a man I'd be riding out there myself. It would be sheer joy to be able to pick up gold nuggets for free. An absolute dream.'

'It's not like picking flowers.' Clem smiled.

'Nonsense. I heard the streets are paved with gold.'

'What streets?' Alice muttered as she wrapped boned slabs of salted mutton into strips of muslin.

Lydia's christening, held at home, turned out to be a very happy occasion, the women fussing over the beautiful baby, and Dr Carty chomping on a cigar, mightily pleased that he'd off-loaded his coach company, beaming on Alice, the new owner. Everyone was intrigued by Clem's preparations to take on the goldfields with Mike Deagan.

'Are you sure you know what you're doing?' Carty asked Clem.

'No,' Clem laughed. 'But I have to give it a go.'

'I mean, taking that convict as a partner. He could bolt on you.'

'No he won't, he's as keen to go as I am. And he's in for a half-share of whatever we find.'

'Are you mad? Legally he's only entitled to his pay while he's still indentured to you.'

'Then I would lose him.'

Clem had traded his wagon for a heavier German one, and when the day came to depart, the two horses were well rested and, sensing adventure, slid into harness in eager anticipation, matching their masters. The wagon was loaded carefully with provisions and equipment, leaving room for the rest of the stuff Clem had to collect from his store in York, and Alice double-checked her list that nothing had been overlooked.

George presented them with a bag of pumpkins that would keep for months, and Thora gave them both woolly caps that she had knitted. Even old Sadie was there with her mob. She took Clem aside and insisted he take a message stick, a flat piece of timber about a foot long, decorated with strange daubings.

'Thank you, Sadie,' he said politely. 'It's very pretty.'

'What you mean, pretty?' she snapped, insulted. 'That keep you safe allasame strange blackfellers out there. Them angry, white fellers shoving them off.'

'How do you know this?'

'People know. This says you a good feller, Mr Clem.' She began to weep. 'You doan go and get your'nself kilt by them cranky blackfellers. You keep the message stick.'

Clem took the big black woman in his arms and kissed her, ignoring Thora's frown. 'What would I do without you? I'll be all right. You look after my three girls, you keep them safe.'

He embraced Alice, grinning at her blushes as Mike gave

her a hug too, then he turned to Thora, kissing her. 'Goodbye, my darling, wish me luck,' delighted that she responded, throwing her arms about him in a rare display of gaiety. She too blushed when Mike kissed her on the cheek, and Clem felt a lump in his throat at this sentimental leavetaking. He would miss them all.

Mike climbed up into the driver's seat, signalling to George to let the horses go, and Clem swung up beside them.

With a 'Giddyup!' from Mike, the horses plunged forward. Clem turned back to wave, but Mike looked straight ahead.

'Righto, boss, let's go and find that gold.'

Chapter Six

Lil Cornish still yearned for the little baby she'd left behind. No matter how many times she told herself it was for the best, it didn't help. And it was no use talking to Ted about it. He was heartless, he didn't understand how much she was suffering. The loss was physical. Every time she thought of her lost little girl, pains wrenched at her stomach, pains that were identical to the spasms that dragged through her stomach when she fed this little one.

In the end, by the time they reached Perth, Ted forbade her to even mention the other baby again.

'I'm sick of your whingeing,' he said. 'You've got Caroline to look after, that's bloody enough. You keep complaining your milk's low; how would you go with two? This one's always bawling as it is. Shut her up.'

That was true. Caroline did cry a lot. They'd taken a cheap room in Perth while they waited for a ship to carry them on to Adelaide, and Lil was really looking forward to the sea voyage – travelling in style too, thanks to Mr Price – but the baby was a worry. Other boarders complained at Caroline's constant crying, and in desperation Lil sat up nursing her through the night to try to console her. Often she wondered if the child knew her sister had been taken from her. After all, they'd spent all that time in the womb together. But she did not dare mention this to anyone for fear they'd tell her she was stupid. Ted told her she was stupid often enough.

He went out every day to hang about in pubs, while she sat in the room with the baby or walked round the block carrying Caroline in her basket. She was afraid to go too far afield in case news came from the shipping company when she was out.

Once they boarded the ship for Adelaide everything would be all right, she was sure. To put an ocean distance between her two babies was like crossing over to another world, being reborn as she had been into the life of the Lord. Her previous life would be put behind her as, humbly, she accepted the will of God.

On Sundays, when the hustle and bustle had died down and the streets were quiet, Lil ventured a little further with Caroline, down to the Church of All Saints, where she sat in happy harmony with the Lord. She prayed that Ted would be blessed with the call too. Her husband was wasting his life now, hanging about pubs and gambling saloons, spending his new-found wealth as if there was no end to it. So far, despite his angry demands, Lil had hung on to her share, although paying for their bed and board was making a hole in it. Still, she consoled herself, it wouldn't be long now and they'd be on their way.

After church she took the baby in her carry-basket down to the river bank, where she loved to sit and dream in the shade of the red gums. The river was beautiful, wide and soft-flowing, and black swans drifted elegantly near the shores. Lil had learned that to board the ship they would have to go by cutter downriver to the port of Fremantle, and she was looking forward to that. Then they'd reach the familiar Indian Ocean; that would be exciting. In their travels her family had often followed that wondrous coastline, looking out to sea, and now she'd have a chance to view the coastline from the deck of a ship. As a child, running wild on those great surf beaches, Lil had never dreamed she'd have such an opportunity.

The Sundays always calmed her, putting to rest her fears and trepidations, helping her to cope with the long, lonely days she spent in their room.

I'm just not a city person, she told herself. I miss the bush, but it will be all right when we get to Ted's cousin's sheep station. Then I'll be myself again. I can cook and I can ride and there's little I don't know about sheep. I can make myself useful enough to earn a wage as well.

When the letter came advising Ted to collect the tickets, Lil left the baby with their landlady and went into town with him, walking with new confidence along the wide streets, past imposing buildings. They found the shipping office in Barrack Street and emerged with second-class tickets.

'We were supposed to get first-class tickets,' Ted growled.

'You heard what the man said,' Lil explained. 'Most of the ships come from England with passengers for the east. The cabins are full up. We were lucky to get these.'

'Then we should have waited.'

'But we could wait for ages. Anyway, as he said, second class is still a lot nicer than steerage. I think we're very lucky. When do we leave?'

'Next Friday, I think he said.'

Lil shouted them meat pies and pudding in a café while they examined the tickets to find they would be sailing on the SS *Silverton*. Afterwards they strolled about enjoying the sights, the grand town hall with its clock tower, the National Bank building, two-storeyed, neat and cool. They even peeked in among the trees at magnificent Government House, awestruck that one man lived in such a palace. It was the best day they'd ever had together, a turning point in their lives, Lil felt, looking to the future of the little Cornish family. Ted didn't even object on the way home when Lil bought herself a coat and a straw hat with ribbons to wear on the ship.

With only a week to go, Ted seemed to think he had to make the most of his last days in Perth. He was hardly ever home, not even for meals, which were paid for, and to Lil it was the last straw when he staggered in well after midnight, waking the whole household. Rather than upset the other boarders any further, she waited until morning to have her say.

'We'll have no money left, the way you're going,' she cried angrily. 'Don't you ever come home at that hour again! And there'll be a stop to this drinking.'

'Ah, shut up!' He pulled a blanket over his head. 'Get away, you stupid bitch. I'm tired.'

'I'm not surprised. You can sleep for another hour and then we're going for a walk to Kings Park. I'm entitled to see round this town too! I don't have to wait in any longer.'

She was in the washhouse when the landlady accosted her. 'You tell that old man of yours this isn't a dosshouse. I expect my boarders to come in at a respectable hour. And sober.'

'Yes, I'm sorry. I've spoken to him. It won't happen again.'

The tall, scraggy woman shook her head. 'Where have I heard that before? You'd better keep an eye on your husband, my girl, and the company he keeps.'

Lil sighed. 'Pubs! I don't know why some men have to spend all their time in pubs!'

'You'd be better off asking him where he gets to when the pubs close.'

Lil was genuinely surprised. 'What do you mean?'

'I'm not one to mince my words. Never was. I'm telling you this for your own good. Mr Cornish has been seen round town with a couple of floozies. One of them used to live here. She was here when you first came, name of Polly, you remember her?'

'A dark-haired girl. Dressed up a lot?'

'That's her. I threw her out. On the game, she was.'

'A prostitute?'

'Yes. Real bad news.'

Lil dumped her washing and ran up the passage to confront Ted, who denied knowing Polly.

'Then where do you go when the pubs close?'

'Anywhere and everywhere,' he sulked. 'There's always parties. A man's got nothin' else to do here. Now get away and leave me alone.'

'I want to go out.'

'Then go. I'm not stopping you.'

'You could get up and come with me.'

He turned his back on her and Lil was left fuming. But later, determined to see the famous Kings Park, she persuaded the landlady to mind Caroline while she set off on her own. It was a fair trek up the hill but well worth the effort to be able to stroll about the lovely gardens and enjoy the splendid view over the riverside city. Things didn't seem so bad up there, surrounded by all the native trees she knew so well. It was like being back in the bush, with everything so quiet except for the chattering of birds. And Perth looked so pleasant from the heights.

Only a couple more days to go, she told herself, and we'll be leaving here. Once Ted starts work he won't have a chance to be taking up with bad company.

She hurried home, more concerned for Caroline than for her husband, relieved to find the baby sleeping soundly.

'The child was restless. Hungry,' the landlady said. 'So we gave her a bottle.'

'But she doesn't have a bottle. She's breast-fed.'

'She does now. Me and the other ladies have been saying that kid's hungry, and now we've proved it. Give her an extra feed from a bottle. That'll fatten her up.'

Even before she reached her room Lil sensed trouble, as if her morning had been too blue and sunny. The scent of a storm, nature's warning, was in the air. She opened the door with a rush to find that Ted had gone. Not gone out. Gone! His canvas pack that hung on the end of the bed was missing. He'd cleared the washstand of his shaving mug and brush. Lil placed her hat on the hook behind the door, where Ted's winter jacket should have been, and lifted the baby into the centre of the creaking bed, then slowly she checked the dressing table drawers, leaving one until last. The top one that contained her underclothes.

He'd taken all of his clothes. Forgotten nothing. Closing her eyes, she drew out that last drawer and almost had to force herself to open it, to face what she hoped was not inevitable. Her neatly ironed cotton petticoats and bloomers were all of a jumble, and Lil shook her head painfully as she slipped a hand under them, but they were not there. The tickets. The precious tickets for the SS *Silverton* that would take them to a new life on a South Australian sheep station were missing. He'd taken them too.

'Call me Merle,' her landlady said. 'I tried to warn you.'

'A bit bloody late,' Lil snapped.

'Ho, listen to you swearing! The God-botherer! Head in the clouds, you people. Don't go blaming me.'

'I'm sorry. I'm not. I'll go to the police, that's what I'll do.'

'A lot they'll care. Go down to the shipping company and tell them you've lost your ticket. Yours. Get them to issue you another one. Then he can't leave you behind. That's if you still want to go with the bugger.'

'I have to.'

Lil ran. Even in her town skirt she was fast, nothing ladylike about this dash. She hurtled past pedestrians, dodged across busy streets, not for Ted, but for Caroline, and for the other little one. She had her heart set on putting half a world between them so that the mystical bond would be severed, so that they could bloom and blossom in their own fields. Lil, in her confusion, truly believed she was running for their lives.

The shipping office was crowded. People jostled her and she jostled back, pushing her way to the counter, where she found she was on the wrong queue; there was another ship in port. The next clerk was not helpful until she shouted at him. Even then he considered her request preposterous.

'I suggest you go home and look for your ticket, madam.'

'Listen to me, you bloody scarecrow,' she snarled at the black-suited gentleman. 'I'm a passenger on the *Silverton*. I wouldn't be here if the ticket wasn't lost. I can't go aboard without a ticket and if you don't replace it I want to see your boss.'

'I presume it's paid for?' he said with a shrug for the benefit of interested onlookers.

'Would I have a ticket if it wasn't?'

'Oh well. Wait a moment and I'll see. What was the name again?'

'Cornish. Mrs Ted Cornish.'

'This is highly irregular.' He turned to wooden filing cabinets behind him and drew out a folder. 'Cornish. Second class. Here is the passenger list. I'll have to look up the number of the ticket now. Even then I can only give you a duplicate slip.'

'Will that get me on board?'

'It will have to, won't it?'

Apparently he found what he was looking for, but he took his time conferring with another clerk before he returned to announce, in a supercilious voice, 'Mrs Cornish, I don't know what you think you're up to, but whatever, it won't work here. Your husband sold those tickets this morning.' He pushed a page across the counter. 'Here is his signature. Next, please?'

Humiliated, Lil retreated through the crowd, head down, fighting back tears.

She couldn't go back to her folks. Ted had dumped her, not the other way around, and that would be an awful admission. For weeks she answered advertisements, to no avail, and finally found a live-in job through a mean little employment agency in a back lane.

'Here's two bob for your fare upriver,' she was told, 'and a slip explaining who you are. You can take the kid. Mr Warburton don't care. He's got a few black gins there, they'll give you a handout. All they're good for is minding kids.'

'The job? A dairy maid?'

'Yes, you can milk cows, can't you?' the bored agent said.

'Yes.'

'Well. Take it or leave it.'

'What's he like, this Mr Warburton?'

'Who cares? He's got a big farm up there and a whacking great big house, but you won't see much of it.'

'You haven't got anything better? I was hoping for a job in town.'

'With a kid? Forget it. Do you want this job or not?'

'Yes. Thank you.'

On the way home she called in to the church to make amends for her bad language. Not that she was in any mood to apologize; there were things that just had to be said with the only words available.

She'd seen a sign outside that read: *God loves the cheerful giver.* 'Well now,' she replied to the Lord. 'I'm trying to be a good Christian but you're making it hard. I've nothing left to give except Caroline . . . no home, no husband. I even missed out on that lovely sea voyage. But no one is taking Caroline from me. It's about time you gave a little yourself.'

Lil found printed texts on the pew and read the prayers with solemn appreciation. They were excellent prayers, worth keeping, so she tucked the slim pages into her handbàg. 'Look kindly on us now, Lord. Help me in this new place to do well. I'm feeling really down.'

The journey upriver in the open boat was, to Lil, sheer delight. It was a cutter, with a single mast and sails, and it swept easily round each wide bend, collecting the cool breezes, a welcome relief for the seven passengers who had waited for it on the wharf in temperatures of over a hundred degrees.

Lil learned that her destination, Minchfield House, was the second last stop, so she had several hours to enjoy the scenery and watch the crew putting passengers and goods ashore and reloading at various jetties. There were some fine houses, set miles apart on the banks of the Swan River, but none of them matched the mansion that finally came into view. It was huge, two-storeyed, constructed of rose-coloured brick, surrounded by wide verandas that were supported by slim white pillars, and it was set in the most beautiful grounds. She stared in awe at the lawns and gardens, as fine as in any parkland.

Lil gaped. 'Is this where I go?'

'Yes, missus, this is your stop,' a crewman told her.

'I thought it was a farm.'

'It is. Mr Warburton owns half the countryside round here. Come along, I'll carry the bub for you.'

At this jetty, as at the others, people were standing about, some work-bent, others simply curious, and Lil felt all eyes on her as she stepped ashore.

A heavy-set man greeted her. 'You Mrs Cornish? I'm Jordan, the farm manager. You're here to work as a dairy maid? You done this work before?'

'Yes,' Lil lied, crossing her fingers.

'Righto.' He beckoned to a black girl. 'Here, give this lass a hand with her case.' And to Lil, 'What are you called?'

'Lil.'

'Good-oh, Lil. Mercy will show you your digs. You start tonight with the milking.'

They avoided the house, taking a bush track that veered well away from it into open paddocks with cattle grazing quietly, then they followed a fence that took them past imposing outbuildings at the rear of the house, and tramped on again . . .

'Not far now,' Mercy said, striding ahead, swinging Lil's case. She was a skinny girl with a gaunt face and stringy black hair, and she was wearing the usual cotton shift allotted to 'house' blacks, but Lil noticed she walked with confidence. As if she had a place in life and knew it. Lil felt a little envious of her.

Having circled round the house, they came in sight of a long stone building with a shingle roof and an awning that shaded a row of doors. Lil guessed this would be the staff quarters, Minchfield Farm being set out in much the same manner as the big outback sheep stations she'd visited often enough.

Mercy opened the first door and dropped Lil's case. 'This is your room. Can I nurse the baby now?'

'Of course.' Lil smiled proudly, handing over Caroline who was awake, having slept all the way in the boat.

'She's so pretty,' Mercy gushed, taking the baby's tiny fingers.

Lil agreed. 'It's not just because I'm her mother,' she said fondly. 'For she is pretty. Her name's Caroline. Her hair is so fair and silky, and she has lovely dark eyes. And look at the dimple.'

'Two dimples,' Mercy said, sitting on one of the two bunks to rock the baby in her arms.

'Who do I share this room with?' Lil asked.

'No one. The dairymen ran off.'

Lil didn't like the sound of that. 'Why?'

'Gold. They gone chasing gold.' She grinned. 'You the first dairy girl here. They couldn't find more men.'

'I see.' Lil realized why, even with a baby, she had been given the job. Scraping the bottom of the barrel. Not a job too many young girls in Perth would volunteer for, especially with this property so far from town.

'I hope I don't have to do the work of two men,' she said.

'No, me and Beth have to help you. She don't like it neither.'

'Who's Beth?'

'One of the housemaids. And there's Tom, he's a dairyman, but he's old. That's why he didn't run off.'

The room was surprisingly clean. Lil had seen some awful staff quarters in her day but this one, though sparsely furnished, was really a credit to the owners. Even the china basin and jug on the washstand were immaculate. Not a chip in sight.

As she unpacked her meagre belongings, she noted that the dresser was lined with white paper and the mosquito nets knotted over the bunks were fresh white muslin. In fact, though smaller, the room was better kept than the one she'd had with Ted in Merle's boarding house, and she felt she ought to say so.

'At least the room's nice and clean,' she said chattily.

'Yeah. And you better keep it that way or Miss Lavinia, she'll get after you.'

'Who's Miss Lavinia?'

'The boss's sister. Old maid. Cranky, she is.'

Lil smiled. 'Well, I guess she's entitled. There can't be too much wrong with her if she likes to keep things nice.'

A grizzled workman peered in the open door. 'You Miz Cornish?'

'Yes. Call me Lil.'

'I'm Tom. What are you doing here, Mercy?'

She pouted. 'Minding the baby.'

'It's a long trip on that boat. Did you get Miz Cornish something to eat?'

'I'll be all right,' Lil said, rather than cause trouble, but she was hungry.

Tom ignored her. 'You go get Miz Cornish afternoon tea,' he told Mercy, 'and bring it down here. She has to go to work soon.'

'I can go,' Lil said, but Mercy put the baby down by a pillow and shrugged. 'What if Cook hasn't got nothing?'

'Go!' Tom said, and she sped away.

'Where do we eat?' Lil asked. 'At mealtimes, I mean.'

'There's a staff refectory at the back of the kitchen. I'll take you up when we finish the milking.' He was staring at her hands. 'They don't look like work hands to me, missus. You sure you can do this job?'

She laughed. 'They've been resting lately. Don't worry about me. I'm a drover's daughter.'

'Is that right?' he said with a glimmer of appreciation as he rolled a smoke. 'I was a drover meself for years. Got too old for the saddle.' He glanced down at Caroline, who was becoming restless. Hungry too.

'Where's your old man?'

'Gone.' She shrugged.

'Gold?'

'I think so. Yes. He just took off.'

'Well, he won't want to be coming round here.'

'He won't. He doesn't know where I am.' She pushed her case under the bunk. 'He left. He can stay away.'

Tom nodded. 'That's the shot, girlie. Don't give them buggers a second chance. I reckon we'll get along all right. I'll come and get you in an hour or so.'

When Mercy returned with tea and sardine sandwiches, Lil was feeding the baby but she still managed to enjoy her afternoon tea. 'I think I'll have a rest now,' she said, and Mercy took the hint. She looked about the room. 'I could take the baby for a walk but you got no pram.'

'Friends in Perth are sending one on,' Lil told her. Merle had insisted that she could find a good cheap one at the Saturday markets, and Lil knew she was reliable.

'By boat?' Mercy asked enthusiastically. 'I'll watch. I'll bring it up for you.'

As Lil was later to discover, Mercy's favourite pastime was

to meet the boats, and waiting for the pram gave her a new excuse to be down on the jetty.

All in all, Lil mused, a week later, she was content with this job for the time being. She worked hard, what with the milking and the ensuing dairy chores, but she had a friend in Tom, who made sure she always had time to see to Caroline, whether in her room or nearby in the basket. And the other women who worked in the house – the cook and the four domestics – were always willing to care for Caroline in their time off. In fact Beth, the young housemaid, vied with Mercy for the honour of minding the baby, and it became a joke among the women, who were a pleasant lot. Considering that they all lived in this row of rooms, Lil thought, like nuns, they all got along very well. There was a nice cheerful rapport between them that Lil appreciated.

She hadn't met Mr Warburton and she hadn't seen inside the house. There were large gaps in her knowledge of Minch-field Farm and its inhabitants, but that would take time. Miss Lavinia had come down for a spot inspection and Lil stood quietly by as one of her employers strode grandly into her room for the first time, checking every corner.

Miss Lavinia was a tall, thin woman with greying hair tied in a bun, and sharp, darting eyes. She wore an old-fashioned hooped skirt under a heavy black dress, apparently unperturbed by the heat, and a jumble of keys hung from her belt.

'Who are you?' she asked, acknowledging Lil for the first time.

'Mrs Cornish, madam.'

'From?'

'York.'

'Not with a voice like that, you aren't.'

Lil blinked. 'It's in the Avon Valley, madam.'

'Stuff and nonsense.' She opened drawers, studying their contents, and took out the prayer texts that Lil had brought with her, reading them carefully as if searching for some sedi-tious element. Then she nodded. 'Good Christian, are you?'

'I try, madam.'

'One doesn't try. One is or one is not. I, for instance, am a good Christian. I do not equivocate.'

With that she turned on her heel and stalked grandly out, making for the next room.

Lil was astounded. The woman could not possibly have missed the baby, who was sleeping peacefully in a neat bundle on the spare bunk, but she ignored Caroline. It was as if the child was invisible to have been passed over like that! Lil didn't mind the intrusion, but she deeply resented Miss Lavinia's attitude to her baby, compounded by a mother's expectation that any woman would find a smile for such a sweet little being.

'Damn her,' she muttered. 'If she's a good Christian I'm a bishop!'

But at least it seemed she had passed muster, and that was important. She had soon learned that the formidable Miss Lavinia ruled the roost here, while Mr Warburton busied himself in his library with his stamp collection and other gentlemanly pursuits. Lil had only sighted him a couple of times in the rose arbour at the side of the house, and only from a distance, but he seemed an elegant fellow with white hair and a white goatee beard. No one talked about him much; they were all too busy keeping on the right side of his sister.

I can do that easily enough, Lil smiled to herself. I've got her measure. Eyes down, keep clean and keep the Bible on show. For already Lil's ambition was to have herself moved up from the cow sheds to a job in the house, and the only person who could help her was Miss Lavinia.

The pram duly arrived with a little baby blanket, a gift from Merle, which made it easier for Lil to move the baby about, and after that she settled down to the daily routine of Minchfield Farm. Life without the depressing presence of Ted Cornish had taken a turn for the better, and she was earning her own money now. The discipline of the work didn't bother her, in fact, she'd grown stronger and fitter and her blotchy skin had disappeared. After a couple of months Lil realized that she was very happy to be working at Minchfield, her bed and board taken care of, and wages accumulating.

Until the day she found Beth, the housemaid, cringing in a corner of the dairy, badly beaten.

Chapter Seven

Driving the wagon, their progress across the hundreds of miles of increasingly arid plains was excruciatingly slow at the best of times, and maddening when they were hampered by broken-down vehicles and mobs of foot-sloggers.

''Tis like the retreat from Moscow,' Mike commented. 'I never saw such a miserable lot outside of a chain gang. We should have come on horseback, we'd be there by now.'

At times Clem almost agreed with him, but he hung on grimly, refusing to leave the wagon and their precious supplies, even though they could have sold them at ten times their value. All along the track, scavengers searched through refuse dumped by the columns ahead. Not only were there empty boxes and bottles, but an astonishing array of effects, thrown off like ballast as the journey became harder. Chairs, bedheads, all sorts of household furniture marked the miles, lying starkly awry in confused desolation as if they were only lost, waiting to be found. Tin trunks lay upended, gaping, coloured gowns flapping and fading in the onslaught of scorching winds. Clem hated looking at the miserable debris, but to Mike it was entertainment. A joke that people would be crazy enough to push into the desert with all their worldly goods. If they stopped near any of these derelict items, he'd hold mock auctions, starting at a hundred pounds, to the vast amusement of fellow travellers.

But when men begged for a lift on the wagon, he sternly overrode Clem's kinder nature, refusing all comers. 'Don't be a bloody fool. They're on foot, they're carrying hardly naught. What happens when we make camp? Would you tell them to stand apart while we eat? And it wouldn't be for a mile or so, it'd be all the way. Extra weight for the horses.'

It took them nearly three weeks to reach the last outpost, the village of Southern Cross, which was now under siege. Clem stood in line to buy what few supplies the town could offer, and Mike waited in another queue to replenish their water supply. Then they were on their way again, but outside the town there was another hold-up. Troopers barred the way, forcing vehicles to halt in a long line on the track, and the foot-sloggers to mill out on all sides in angry groups.

Clem ran up front to find out what was going on, rather than accepting the second-hand information being offered by men about him. He climbed over a rope to address one of the mounted troopers.

'What are we waiting for?'

'We're checking everyone who leaves here.'

'Why?'

'Because there's more than a hundred miles to go from here to Coolgardie, and they're dying out there on that track. You'll see the graves for yourself, mate. No one leaves here unless they've got enough water and grub to get them through.'

'My partner and I, we can go, we've got a wagon and plenty of water. If I can get the wagon up here will you let us pass?'

The trooper dismounted and hitched his horse to a heavy stake driven into the ground by the track. 'I'll come with you and have a look.' He signalled to other troopers who were patrolling right across the front of the crowd to make sure no one dodged out into open country to escape them, and tramped back with Clem.

On the way, he stopped at a dusty jinker carrying a couple and a small boy. 'How much water have you got?' he asked the driver.

'Our water bags are full, three of them!'

'Then you're not going any further, mate. Your bloody horse will die before you do. You might as well turn back now.

'See what I mean?' he said to Clem.

When he sighted the three kegs he laughed. 'Jesus! Have you got beer there?'

'No. Water. And we've got grub and shelter.'

'Well, you're all right. Swing your wagon out and bring it up the front, but you'll still have to wait a while.'

'What for this time?'

'We're not letting them loose to straggle into the desert like Brown's cows. They're going in groups of sixty, some with transport and some walking, so that if anyone gets into strife there's help. It's not much of a track . . .'

'I didn't think it would be.'

'Where are you from?'

'York.'

'Ah. Right. Then you've got some idea of what you're in for. A lot of this mob are city folk, they seem to think that a hundred miles is just a matter of tramping east. They're straying all over the bloody countryside, getting lost, so we have to put a stop to it somehow. Your horses fit?'

'Yes. We've taken good care of them.' By this time Clem wasn't too confident either; he knew there'd be no such thing as dead-flat country in this already stony terrain, and it would be easy to stray off the tracks.

'Are there any guides?' he asked.

'No. You're on your own. But watch for the worn track and never move at night, even if it is cooler. That's been their downfall.'

As they waited for their turn, they listened to the angry and sometimes violent confrontations between the troopers and would-be prospectors, who complained bitterly that they'd take their chances, that the military had no right to bar their way, but the troopers were adamant, riding down men who tried to dash past them.

When they were, eventually, on their way, travelling slowly so as not to tire the horses and keeping within view of their fellow travellers, Mike looked out over the hard barren land and shook his head. 'Jesus,' he said, wiping the sweat from his face. 'It's the end of the bloody world! Hardly a tree worth its

158

keep in sight, just rusting rocks. If it's this bad here, what'll it be like a hundred miles on?'

'I don't know what you're talking about, Dr Carty, and I would appreciate it if you'd keep your voice down. You'll wake the baby.' Primly, Alice continued to set the table so that she could give her unexpected guest morning tea.

'How long will Thora be?' he asked, reluctantly quieter.

'Quite a while, I should think. She rode over to the Postles' to see if there's any news of the lads; she only left a half-hour ago.'

'The Postles!' he snorted. 'There was a time when Thora wouldn't have been seen in their company.'

'Maybe so. But if Thora sees something to her advantage, she can adjust.'

'Are you criticizing my daughter?'

'Not at all. We are both eager for news of the goldfields. Clem should be there by this.'

The doctor moved the cup and saucer aside and clasped his hands firmly on the table. 'Alice, that contract you signed was illegal, but I'm prepared to return to you the money that you paid for my coach company, and forget all about the incident.'

'In what way was it illegal?'

He sighed. 'I have just told you. It is obvious that your brother had prior knowledge to which I had no access. In other words, he knew that the plans to build a railway to York had been cancelled. He bought that business under false pretences.'

'That's not a very nice thing to say, Dr Carty. We all expected the railway to come to York. We bought your business on your assurance that it would still be viable even then, using new routes.'

'And it would be. It would be! But your brother has tricked me and I won't have it. I want that business back.'

'Milk?' she asked, proffering a jug.

'No! Yes! Just a little. Now, Alice, all you have to do is get that contract and we'll tear it up. Call it a misunderstanding.'

'I'm sorry, I couldn't do that.'

'Why not? Your brother tricked me into selling to him. He's a damned cheat, and if you don't give me that contract I'll have him up.'

'You mean you'll have me up. You sold to me. I hope you're not calling me a cheat.'

'I'm giving you the benefit of the doubt, but you have to realize that your brother has put you in a nasty position. You could be in serious trouble here. Surely a young lady like you wouldn't want to be hauled into a courtroom?'

'Heavens, no.'

'Then you have no choice. We'll just call the whole deal off.'

Alice nibbled on a biscuit. 'I'd rather not, Dr Carty. I can't understand where anything illegal has taken place.'

'You don't understand business. That's why. He should never have placed you in this position.'

'Oh well. Let's just wait and see.'

'Wait for what?' he snapped. 'Don't be wasting my time, girl. I've done you a favour coming all the way out here. I could have put my solicitors on to it right away.'

'That's good of you, but I'll have to wait and see what Clem says.'

No matter how much he argued, Alice refused to budge, and she was relieved when he finally stormed out.

'You'll hear more of this!' he shouted.

She went back to the table and poured herself another cup of tea. He's only bluffing, she told herself, hoping she was right. Almost sure she was right, because he had been very convincing.

Weeks passed. Thora received a letter from Clem to say that they were in Kalgoorlie and had begun work on their claim but with no result so far.

'Why didn't they stay in Coolgardie?' Thora moaned. 'The Postle boys are there and they've found gold. They didn't actually say how much but quite obviously it's considerable. If they come home rich men and Clem doesn't, I'll scream.'

'Give them time,' Alice said. 'It's early days.'

'It could be last days too. The gold could run out. Mrs Postle said men are already coming back through York, filthy rich, and that's a worry.'

'Why?'

'Because if there's more gold they'd have stayed, wouldn't they?'

'I think they work on their mines until there's no more left in that patch, then they have to start somewhere else. And Clem did say it was an awful place to be: no shade to speak of and the temperatures well into the hundreds.'

Thora shrugged. 'They've got their tents. It can't be any hotter than here. This has been a horribly hot summer and the flies are the worst I've ever known.'

In her letter to Clem, his sister wrote about their daily routine and told him the good news that the new dam was still holding water, a boon for stock out that way. She added an extra page about Lydia, his beautiful daughter, whom she loved dearly. The child was Alice's joy, a good baby and an absolute delight. She did not mention Dr Carty's visit.

When an official-looking letter did arrive for her, Alice was startled, worrying that Carty had engaged a solicitor after all, and when she saw that it was from their bank manager she was further concerned. She had made all the repayments she could on the mortgage – not enough, she knew, but he'd have to wait.

She gasped when she read the letter. The bank manager had a client, a successful gold prospector, who was in York, looking to invest. The manager suggested that Alice sell Lancoorie to this gentleman, who was well able to pay a high price. He asked if the gentleman could come out and inspect the property, seeming to take it for granted that Alice would be willing to sell.

Alice didn't waste any time replying that Lancoorie was, most definitely, not for sale. Then, as an afterthought, she added that the passenger coach company *was* for sale, setting an outrageous price on 'this excellent business'.

Within a month Alice had sold the former Carty's Coach Company for fifteen hundred pounds to the gentleman who had also paid a fortune for the Victoria Hotel. He saw those two businesses as complementary in the solid little town.

'How much did we get for the coach company?' Thora asked her.

'Enough to recoup our expenditure,' Alice murmured cautiously. 'It was too much of a worry with your father upset.'

'Him! You shouldn't take any notice of him. When the railway line comes here it will be worthless anyway.'

'Thora! The building of the railway has been postponed. You know that.'

'I don't know any such thing. What's for lunch?'

Alice stared at her. 'Lunch? We've had lunch!'

Thora had a tablecloth in her hand, ready to set the table. Hurriedly she stuffed it back in the drawer and rushed outside.

'Really!' Alice muttered. 'That girl is so vague!' She retrieved the tablecloth and folded it neatly before returning it to the drawer.

The party that was travelling with them soon disintegrated. One by one, men with wheelbarrows holding their possessions, turned back; some trudged on after casting aside the unwieldy barrows. Then the foot-sloggers began to succumb to the exhausting march. Several had the sense to go back in a body, others sank down by the track time and again, demanding to rest, holding up the two wagons and causing heated arguments. Eventually Clem and the other wagoner agreed to carry their swags but when first one man and then another collapsed, they were forced to take them on board. To make matters worse, horsemen galloped past them, having obviously deserted their comrades. Then, during another enforced rest, a long string of camels carrying massive loads of provisions clomped haughtily past them, their Afghan drivers waving cheerfully.

Mike watched them with a jealous eye. 'Camels! Why didn't we think of that?'

Clem couldn't be bothered replying. He shouted to the

stragglers to get a move on, losing patience with this laboured trek. Already the other driver, worried by the very real fear of catastrophe, was preparing to desert. They were only halfway to Coolgardie and the sight of two wooden crosses set in a pile of rocks had unnerved him. He had his wife and two children with him as well as a sick man, and the scorching heat was taking its toll on them too.

'If he goes, we go too,' Mike said, but Clem looked back anxiously at the weary foot-sloggers. 'We can't do that. Those blokes are almost done in.'

'Then what? One by one we have to pick them up off the track? Those troopers knew what would happen, that's why they sent the walkers with the wagons.'

It was a harsh decision, but they couldn't afford so many delays waiting for the stragglers, miles back on the lonely track, to catch up. The stronger, more determined marchers were able to keep with them, with an occasional lift, but the others were left to take a day's rest and wait for the next contingent. By the time they reached the chaotic goldfields at Coolgardie, only twelve marchers were still with them. None of their travelling companions had any heart to go further but Clem and his partner pushed on to the newer goldfields, where there'd be less competition.

Disappointment followed. Thousands of people had flocked to Kalgoorlie ahead of them. They drove into what appeared to be the main street of a bustling tent city, except that it was more of a dusty wide divide than a normal street. Later they learned that this great gap was to allow camel trains with their lumbering wagons to turn in the street.

'We've made it,' Clem said, trying to boost his sagging spirits. 'That's the main thing.' He studied the haphazard signs that hung from canvas and corrugated iron walk. 'Pull in over there, Mike. They're selling grog. That's our first stop. I've never had such a thirst in my life.'

'And meself,' Mike laughed. 'The Welcome Inn, they call their little watering-hole, and never was an inn more welcome.'

They found a camp site outside the town and spent a day

exploring Kalgoorlie. Apart from the jumble of business premises and rough living quarters, the goldfields were massive ant heaps on the pancake-flat land, with men crawling over them, disappearing into narrow pits, or filing in zigzag lines to crouch with their booty over sieves and sluices. At dusk they returned to the make-shift tavern.

Dusk was for company in Kalgoorlie, for talk and for listening, not to the confusion of sound emanating from this overpopulated, raucous settlement, but to the hints and winks of where 'colour' might be found. Over and over again they heard of men who'd left Kalgoorlie with their saddlebags packed with gold, and they were caught up in the wild optimism, rushing out the very next day to stake a claim beside other diggers.

The pace was frenetic. Every morning they stumbled from their tent as the stars faded to hurry over a breakfast of tea and warmed porridge before making for the diggings and beginning work. Their neighbours were generous with advice and with their help, so the two men soon fell into a routine of digging and searching. Water was scarce and expensive, so they had to forgo sluicing and learn the difficult art of dry-blowing for gold, but drinking water had to be bought from the owners of condensing plants who drew it from brackish bores. All about them was good and bad news, accompanied by shouts and curses, but they kept digging, past the dusty brown surface into the greying pit, with not a sign of gold. Inevitably, they argued, as the mine went deeper, as to whether they should proceed with this claim or move on, but as neither of them could make a decision, for fear of making the worst mistake of their lives, they stayed hammering away with pick and shovel as the temperature soared.

When they did find gold, when Clem found traces in his sieve, it was an anticlimax, because the question now was how much. They had grown weary of new chums dashing mad at the sight of smidgeons of gold dust.

'Well now, boyo,' Mike said, picking out a tiny gold pebble, 'it's a start. I guess we'd better hang on here for a while longer.'

As the weeks passed their finds became a cruel joke. More and more strangers poured into the town, and every night some lucky digger burst into the Welcome Inn to shout the bar, which had now been extended to a long corrugated-iron shanty, while Mike and Clem glanced at each other ruefully. Like many others they were barely earning enough alluvial gold to meet expenses. And oddly, they seemed to have exchanged attitudes.

When they first arrived, Mike was the cheerful one, still the larrikin Irishman, ready with a joke, popular with the other diggers and a charmer to the 'ladies' who enjoyed his company when business was slow. He insisted on educating Clem, taking him on a riotous tour of the brothels one night, until they arrived back at their camp at daybreak, too drunk to work. Then he began to change. He lost interest in the nightly revels, even in the women, and preferred to drink a bottle of beer in the relative quiet of their camp rather than join their friends after work.

'I've a low level of boredom,' he told Clem. 'Those fellers are getting on me nerves.'

'But you can't just sit here on your own,' Clem argued. 'We work hard; we're entitled to enjoy ourselves.'

'When you speak of that, let me say we're not working hard enough. First up we worked right through to dusk, now we're downing tools early in the afternoon . . .'

'Jesus, Mike!' Clem was amused. 'We can't keep going at that pace. We'd die of thirst.'

''Tis the beer thirst that gets you, mate. And the good times to be had up the road with them fools. We're not short of water. But it's your money, you spend it. I'm here for the gold, not for that bastard of a town.'

'Is it because that bloke recognized you and blurted out you were a convict?'

Mike shook his head. 'You're not hearing what I'm saying.'

Clem didn't want to hear. He was having the time of his life. Never before had he met so many amazing people. Never before, coming from his isolated property, had he met so many *people*, for that matter. Regardless of Mike's opinion, he found them great company, especially the Easterners, old hands who'd come from the eastern states in their hundreds to join the rush. He hung on their every word, fascinated by their talk of those far-off states of which he had little knowledge. And the women made such a fuss of him, telling him how handsome he was, calling him their 'Yorkey'. Clem had no qualms about the life he was leading; it was all for Thora's sake. He was still working hard, a slave to the sweat and toil of that mine, and missing the comfort of Lancoorie, so what he did of an evening had no bearing on his love for her.

Right before their eyes, Kalgoorlie began to change. Every scrap of timber in the vicinity was cut down for firewood and for building materials as the diggings extended to an area called Boulder. The main street was transformed so swiftly it was hardly recognizable day by day, as stores, banks and even a stock exchange emerged. The Welcome Inn widened to a real single-storey tavern with prepared timbers brought in by camel train, and a newspaper *The Miner*, appeared, owned and operated by none other than Fred Vosper. Clem couldn't get back to the camp fast enough to tell Mike. His friends were impressed that he knew the famous hell-raiser!

Then the rain came. The newcomers to this parched land ran out into the streets, leapt up from their mines, stood outside their tents, blessing the Lord above, thanking him for their long-overdue bounty as the precious rain filled their tanks. And their cellars. And their mines. And as the rain teemed down on them, celebrations were the order of the day. Mud-wrestlers replaced tent-fighters. Drench parties were an instant and innovative success, with tables and chairs set outside in the wondrous teeming rain, and women – and men – discarding their clothing to the excited handclaps of enthusiastic audiences. It was an orgy of thanksgiving to the rain god, whoever he was. No thought was given to the lack of river courses in the area; it was just a grand time, a momentous occasion, and Clem, in soggy trousers and bare chest, won the slippery foot race down the main street only an hour before the flood crept upon them.

Now water was more precious than gold. They rolled out their unused beer kegs and dipped water from their flooded mine, because as fast at it had come the flood evaporated and the red soil cracked and dried. Before they had finished dipping water from their mine, the precious liquid had slipped away into the hard depths, lost to them. Mike examined the slimy walls.

'I think it's time to move on.'

'Yes, but I want to have a look further out. What say we peg out a new claim and you get started on it? That way we keep something going.'

'All right with me.'

Three days later, Clem rode out into the bush north-east of Kalgoorlie, carrying enough supplies to last for ten days' prospecting. Always with him were the stories of men like Bayley of Coolgardie and Paddy Hannah of Kalgoorlie, who'd examined these scrub lands and come upon enough surface gold to instigate this rush and change their lives for ever. Clem, an acknowledged bushman, saw himself as another Bayley, riding back into town, his saddlebags laden with nuggets.

He began his search at a twenty-mile mark, working in an arc around his central point through lonely, desolate country that gave ample warning of the fearful desert beyond.

On the third day he sighted a cave worn into the side of a jutting rock formation, and decided to shelter there from the cold night winds. But when he came closer he changed his mind. An Aborigine rock painting loomed over the entrance and Clem stared at it in amazement. The massive ochre-red and white figure on the roof of the cave was at least fourteen feet high, and the head, with its huge white eyes, glared threateningly at the stranger. He would have liked to examine the other paintings that adorned the inside walls, but thought better of it, knowing that places like this were sacred to the Aborigines. Clem had no wish to upset the local tribes, so he put a good five miles between those rocks and his next camp site.

In the morning he began poking about the scrub, looking for 'colour', overturning rocks, pulling up young bushes, chopping into cracked ground with his tomahawk, and so intent was he on his work that he didn't hear the Aborigines approach. It was only when he sat back on his haunches to ease his back that he saw them. He wasn't afraid of blacks – tribal people had often crossed his land – nevertheless he stood up quietly with a smile and a nod of respect towards the five heavily painted men who were standing in a line a good fifteen feet away from him.

'G'day,' he said cheerfully, but they offered no response.

They all wore headbands to keep back their matted hair and long knotted beards, and were naked except for thin fur belts, the wildest-looking tribal men he'd ever seen.

Clem waited as they stood studying him, holding their long hunting spears beside them, their faces giving no intimation of their attitude. To break the impasse he looked down at his tomahawk and then took a step forward to place it on the ground.

'For you,' he said to a tall man with greying hair, an elder, traditionally superior, but still no one moved or spoke. They would have had any amount of time to discuss him before they showed themselves, so they had no need to comment to one another now.

He shook his shirt free and held out his palms to show that he was not armed. 'Friend,' he called, holding his smile. 'Friend.'

The grey-haired leader motioned to one of his men to go forward and grab the tomahawk.

This done, Clem beckoned to them to come with him, pointing to his camp, making hand signals indicating eating.

'I have food at my camp. You are welcome to share. Food!'

The elder nodded, understanding, and waved at Clem to go ahead, but he still took care, making sure that was what they wanted.

When he was waved on, he turned, inviting them to follow him, with a sigh of relief. This would mean the end of his expedition – he had not counted on sharing his supplies with five big blackfellows – but it couldn't be helped. He was on their land and had to pay his dues.

When the blow felled him, he thought he'd been struck across the back by one of them, but a scorching pain followed and Clem lay flat on his face with a spear in his back, unable to move without making it worse. Out of the corner of his eye he could see the tall spear wavering above him, twitching when he tried to draw a breath, so he lay very still, trying to summon the courage to make an attempt to get rid of the thing.

That problem was soon solved. Black feet padded past him and suddenly the attacker wrenched his spear free. Clem screamed, feeling the hot blood gushing with the pain, but they didn't stop; they left him in the scrub with ants already swarming over him. He tried to push himself up but instead had a sensation of falling, falling. He closed his eyes, steeling himself against the crash, and passed out.

The Aborigines rummaged through his camp, examining everything. They smashed tins with the tomahawk and tipped the contents into their hands, eating with relish. They made bundles with his blankets, collecting tools and cookpot and his canvas waterbags. They emptied his pack, throwing aside notebooks and pencils and clothing, and at the bottom of the pack, they came across a message stick.

They handed it from one to another, staring at it in astonishment, and then they began to laugh. They doubled up laughing, tossing it in the air, catching it, staring at it again and shaking their heads until the elder intervened.

He shook his head sadly. Message sticks carried from tribe to tribe, even across nations of ancient peoples, bypassed diverse languages. From eons past, the same signs spoke of meetings, conferences, celebrations; of traders and warnings, even of war. They requested permission to enter lands, as protocol required, and a response was delivered in the same form, each cut and mark clearly understood.

But this one! Obviously the sender was from some far-off tribe who had never learned or who had lost the art. And that to Mulwalla the elder, was a tragedy. Just another indication of the destruction of their culture by the flood of white men that now threatened even the inland people.

He saw nothing funny about this message stick which was a jumble of unrelated signs, but he understood that someone had tried to communicate on behalf of the white man. There seemed to be some indication, perhaps, of safe passage. Well, it was a bit late for that, but as an honourable man it behove him to observe the law while there was still time. Grumbling that the foolish white fellow should have produced the message, such as it was, in the first place, he ordered his men to get the horse, which they did, not without some effort because, sensing trouble, it shied away from them.

Eventually they managed to undo the hobbles, and with a lot of argument, interspersed with directions from Mulwalla, fitted the bridle on the frightened animal.

Nervously they approached the horse with the saddle, but the familiar scent of leather had a quietening effect and the animal submitted to the rough, clumsy hands that settled it in place and secured the girth. Mulwalla was pleased that they had mastered the strange tasks, something new learned.

Clem was only semi-conscious when they picked him up and carried him through the scrub. They were by no means gentle bearers, so when they dumped him over the saddle he thought he had crashed to the bottom of that fall with every bone broken, so terrible was the pain.

Using his tent ropes and strips of canvas, they lashed him to the horse, and one of the men took hold of the bridle and began loping towards the white settlement at a steady, rhythmic pace. He covered mile after mile with ease, but with no care for the moaning white man thrown over the horse like a dead kangaroo. He had his instructions and would carry them out.

Several miles from the outlying diggings, he thrust the message stick under the white man, tied the bridle to the saddle knob and sent the horse on its way with a slap. As it cantered away he shrugged and turned to the east, without even checking to see if his charge was still aboard. He had done exactly as he was told and now he had to catch up with the others.

*   *   *

The bridle had worked loose and was trailing as the horse trotted towards the mines, smelling water. Men rushed at him, yelling, and he swerved away, nostrils flaring, eyes flat and confused, as the saddle and its dead weight began to slip over his flanks. The message stick dropped into the dust, unnoticed.

One man caught up, grabbing the bridle, halting him, soft words pacifying: 'Good fellow, there's a good fellow. Settle down now. Who's this you've got?'

Willing hands slashed the ropes and lifted the heavy man down.

'Who is he?'

'Get out of the way, he's still alive.'

'What happened to him?'

'Bring him to my tent. Over here.'

'Someone get a doctor.'

'Where did he come from, for Christ's sake, trussed up like that?'

'Where are his mates? Who'd send him in like that?'

'Some bastard has shot him in the back.'

'Get a bloody doctor!'

The news spread like wildfire, and even before a doctor was located Fred Vosper was on the spot, pushing through the curious crowds for first-hand information on the incident, but a burly digger refused him entry to the tent: 'Keep out. No room in there for stickybeaks. My mates are looking after him. He's in a bad way.'

'Was he shot?'

'No, but he's got a bad wound in his back. Been stabbed, I reckon.'

A shudder went through the press of onlookers. They were accustomed to fist-fights, murderous brawls with clubs of any sort, even gunfire, but knifings were unheard of, considered unfair, never tolerated.

Fred took the digger aside. 'I'd be surprised if he's been knifed. They say he came in from the bush lashed to a horse. It sounds more like a spear to me.'

'How would you know?'

'I'm from Queensland, I've seen spear wounds aplenty. You'd better let me have a look. I'm betting the doctor wouldn't know either.'

'What difference does it make? He's still badly wounded.'

But the long-haired journalist finally managed to gain entrance to the tent, where he stood over the patient and stared.

'By God, I know him! It's Clem Price. From York.'

The caring diggers had stripped and bathed their patient, and he now lay unconscious on a low bunk, his chest swathed in bandages that were still seeping blood. Fred thought better of disturbing him then, and decided to wait for the doctor. But at least he'd been able to identify Clem, and so he was permitted to stay.

'No doubt about it,' he said when the young doctor examined the ugly, festering wound. 'It was a spear. The skin's all torn where the head was pulled out. Must have hurt like hell.'

'You're probably right, but he's lost a lot of blood and he's got a bad fever. I'll have to get him to the hospital so that I can sew up the wound.'

Fred had scant respect for the shanty hospital that was known as the death house, last refuge of men dying of exposure, malnutrition and exhaustion, but there was no alternative. He went in search of the Irishman, Clem's mate.

Mike held off writing to Thora. If her husband recovered, then he might have to get him out of this place and take him home to recuperate with decent food and care, because his body had been wasting this last week as the fever took its toll. Clem was barely conscious, delirious. Shock too, the doctor said. If he didn't recover, then Mike figured she'd hear that news soon enough. No use worrying her, or Alice.

A girl came to see the patient. One of the prostitutes from the Black Cat brothel, Mike was told, and he thought that was very kind of her. On his next visit he found her sitting anxiously by Clem's bed.

'You used to work for him. At Lancoorie,' she said.

172

Mike was surprised. 'How did you know that?'

'I'm from York. I heard Clem brought one of his . . . his farmhands with him.'

'One of his jailbirds, you mean,' he laughed.

'I'm sorry. I didn't like to say.'

'It's all right. As a matter of fact my glorious career as a guest of the Crown ended a while back, but I never bothered to tell the lad. It didn't seem to matter any more.'

'How long was your sentence?'

'It was life, but by the time that was rescinded I'd blotted the copybook a bit so I'd almost become a permanent parolee.'

'You must have been young when they sent you out.'

'I was a master forger at fifteen,' he grinned. 'See what education does for you. I didn't mind being shipped out, I was such a smart aleck I thought I could beat the system.'

'Well, you have,' she said stoutly. 'You look all right to me.'

'Time wasted,' he admitted. 'I've a chance now to pull up and not a moment to spare. Your name's Jocelyn, is it?'

'Yes. I'm a friend of Clem's.' She looked wistfully at the still figure in the bed. 'He's a lovely fellow. Do you think he'll get better?'

'Sure.' He took a damp cloth and mopped Clem's face. 'Come on, boss. Wake up there. We've got work to do.'

The patient stirred in the bed, muttering incomprehensibly, and his two friends stayed anxiously by him until the doctor came with the same news. 'The wound is healing. We just have to wait until the fever breaks.'

The smell worried him, fetid, mouldy, yet laden with a sharp tang that was vaguely familiar, phenol maybe, but too strong. He flung his arm across his face to ward off the foul odours, and pain seared, punishing him. Why? He tried to focus on the source, but it was tiring and he drifted back to sleep again.

Mike hated the wretched hospital. He'd seen better accommodation in prison dormitories, where at least the furniture was regular. The beds here were all shapes and sizes, as if gathered from a rubbish dump, which, he mused, was quite possible. There were high iron beds, squat bunks, canvas foldaways, rickety wooden contraptions, all pushed together along the timber wall. Every bed was occupied though, with miserable patients sweltering under the iron roof. He wished he could take Clem out of here, but it wasn't possible yet, not until the fever ran its course and allowed his brain to take control. He prayed it would be soon: fevers were dangerous, freaky things, perverse in their antics . . .

He saw the nose twitch, the restless arm and the grimace of pain. 'By God, you're there,' he cried. 'I know you are. You have to wake up now so I can get you out of here. The mine's showing colour, better than the first one, I'm still only filling matchboxes, no nuggets yet, but I made twelve quid this week and that's not to be sneezed at. And you've got people waiting to see you, friends from York. There's the girl Jocelyn, and the Postle lads. They can't wait much longer, they've made a pile, picked up nuggets worth a fortune and are heading home when they come down from the roof of celebration. And another fellow has been in, name of Tanner, read about you in the paper. He's a bit of a swell, a sharebroker, opened an office and all, juggling the new mining syndicates that are buying up big leases. He says there's money to be made in that business.'

He watched the doctor bending over patients down the end of the ward. 'Then there's our mate Fred Vosper. He's been in here too and now he's raising hell, calling up public meetings to make the government build a proper hospital. He's never short of causes. Demanding that the goldfields get due representation in the parliament, and the way the population is doubling and trebling here every day I wouldn't be surprised if he does make that happen. Now don't go away, I'll be back in a minute.'

He approached the doctor. 'Would you come see Clem, sir? I think he's waking. I'm sure he is.'

The weary man shrugged. 'We'll see. Don't get your hopes up.'

'Hope's never wasted, I can afford it. He hasn't been

174

washed yet, that'd cool him down. Could you ask one of the women?'

'They're busy, he has to take his turn. We haven't got enough nurses for all these patients.'

'Then get more.'

'Will you pay them?' The doctor leaned over Clem, taking his temperature, and consulting his notes. 'His temperature is down, that's a good sign.'

A nurse called him urgently and he rushed away. Mike nodded, watching them pull a screen round a patient. 'Yes,' he said, 'I can do just that.'

He went outside and found another nurse, a neat woman with an efficient air. 'Do you know the patient Clem Price?'

'Yes, I do.'

'He's bad in need of a good wash. Here's ten bob. I want him washed and cleaned down twice a day, with fresh sheets, and each time you get ten bob in your pocket. All right with you?'

'Certainly is,' she grinned, slipping the money into her apron pocket.

'Then bless you.'

There was a woman by the bed, a shadow against the yellow glare of light from a window, but she was there and Clem gave a sigh of relief. She was holding his hand, comforting him, helping him from this dark confusion, telling him that everything was all right, and he was so grateful to her for just being there when he needed her.

'Thora,' he whispered, wondering why his tongue felt too big for his mouth, but he tried again, clasping her hand tightly, his voice stronger. 'Thora, darling.'

'What brought you out to this awful place?' Mike asked her as they ambled down the middle of the road to dodge the confusion of lorries delivering building materials to the noisy workmen who were transforming the centre of Kalgoorlie into a street called Hannan.

Jocelyn took his arm. 'I wanted to go gold-digging. I had

my heart set on it. I even asked Clem to bring me, but he wouldn't.'

'I can't imagine why.' Mike grinned.

They gravitated to a small tavern next door to the Black Cat whorehouse, one of the first buildings to have replaced tents in the town, and he followed her through the dingy bar to seats set outside under canvas.

Jocelyn seemed to know everyone. He bought two ales and settled himself on a log bench while she did her socializing among the rough-and-ready clientele. This tavern, like every other liquor outlet on the goldfields, did a roaring trade, and Mike looked about him enviously. It had always been his ambition to own a pub of his own, and to own one packed to the rafters – or in this case the canvas – would be a dream come true. But not in Kalgoorlie, not yet anyway. The cost of bringing liquor into a place like this would equal freighting it into the Sahara, so the price of grog over the counter was outrageous. He looked ruefully at his pint, which had cost two and six, and considered downing Jocelyn's pint mug, but manners got the better of him.

Having completed her rounds, Jocelyn came bouncing over to him. 'We're on for free drinks, Mike. My pal, the Englishman over there – his name's Teddy – he struck it rich today, we're drinking champagne.' With that she tipped the precious ale into the dirt, grabbed his tall enamel mug and dashed away to fill it with golden French champagne, while Teddy, tall, slim and very young, stood on a tree stump and sang his triumph to the world.

'I wasn't always a whore,' Jocelyn said to Mike.

'And that'd be a fact,' he agreed.

'Well, it's not my fault,' she insisted. 'I came here to be a gold-digger. I did. I came with Joe Parsons, a bloke I met in York, and I worked his claim with him. My word, I did, so don't look so disbelieving.'

'It's interested I am, not disbelieving.'

'We'll drink to poor Clem,' she announced. 'Now, as I was saying . . . I worked hard with Joe. We were finding colour, not a lot but enough to keep us going, and then one day, he just took off. Left me. He'd sold the claim. I had to move off. Nowhere to go. That's how I ended up at the Black Cat. I didn't even have the cash to buy a meal, let alone get myself back home. That was cruel of him, don't you think?'

'Indeed it was.'

He gave himself over to contemplation while Jocelyn talked about her new home, the Black Cat. He decided that he'd have to remove Clem from that wretched hospital as soon as possible. He'd heard rumours of various infectious diseases infiltrating the town, and knew that in his weakened state Clem would have no resistance. All he could do was take him back to their tent and leave him there while he worked. But cash was short. Alone, the work was too slow, and he was barely finding enough alluvial gold to cover their expenses. He was even considering selling their horses. With little grazing land available out here in this bloody desert, he'd been reduced to buying hay for them. But he dreaded the infamous walk back to civilization, knowing that even if he could make it, Clem could not.

To keep the women at Lancoorie from knowing their predicament, he wrote to them claiming that Clem had hurt his hand, so he was doing the honours. But all was well.

'The Black Cat is a rotten place,' Jocelyn was saying. 'It's filthy, and you wouldn't give a cat the grog she serves. When I think of the lovely hotel in York, with everything spotless and the kitchen scrubbed to gleam, I could just cry. And our rooms there! I mean, there'd be hell to pay if the sheets weren't fresh and ironed. And a stained mattress! By George, it would have been burnt right away. I could tell you a lot more about that place,' she added ominously, 'if I had a mind to, but Madam Glory – what a name for a hag like her – she doesn't care. No one knows her real name. Do you know where the money goes? Gambling! While we work she plays cards with that cigar hanging out of her mouth like a man. Some say she is a man. Wouldn't surprise me. She knows nothing about keeping the place clean. Some of the other girls – real whores, you know – they say proper whorehouses they've worked in have baths and housemaids and laundresses, and everything is clean. Not like that rat's nest!'

She glared at the clumsy timber house where lamps were already beginning to glow in the windows.

'They say any day the police will pull her in, and then where will we be? The other brothels have got their own girls.'

'What would they pull her in for? Brothels aren't illegal here.'

'You're not listening. I told you, she never pays anyone except us, and that's hard to drag out of her. She gambles away the cash, never pays for the grog or even for the horrible cheap grub her cook gives our clients. And her taking at least a thousand pounds a week at the Cat, and throwing it about worse than Teddy there . . .'

Mike was suddenly alert. 'How much does she take?'

'Used to take a thousand, but the other brothels are beating her now. The customers are getting choosy. I tell her if we cleaned the place up we wouldn't be losing the better types. But do you know what she says to that? "Keep the lamps dim and they won't notice." Did you ever hear such a thing? And her so slummocky the girls are getting just as bad. No one cares. I wish they coulda seen the hotel at York, then they'd know how the place should be kept.'

While Jocelyn expounded upon the graces of a hotel where you could eat your dinner off the floor, Mike was more interested in her present employer.

'Sounds as if Madam Glory has lost interest in the business. Why doesn't she sell?'

'That's another thing we're feared of. The bank wants to buy, but naturally they don't want the business, nor even the building. They only want the block, being so central. They'd pull the house down and rebuild. But they're offering her next to nothing. I mean, an empty block is only worth about fifteen pounds.'

'So it would be. For the time being,' he murmured. 'I presume that's your boss over there, Jocelyn. Why don't you introduce me?'

178

She laughed. 'Sure. She's old but she's still got an eye for handsome men.'

Mike grimaced at the tactlessness of youth. Madam Glory would be around forty, he guessed, about his own age.

Jocelyn was right, he noticed as he sat in Glory's front room the next morning, the harsh daylight exposing a tale of grime and neglect.

'Let's get this straight,' she said. 'You want to buy the brothel?'

'No. There are too many brothels here already. I want to buy the premises to open a rooming house.'

'That won't make you much.'

'I know. But in ten years' time the town block will be worth money.'

'Ten years! What's the point of that? You could be dead. Here, have a cigar, Mike. If you really want to make money, come back with me to Perth. We'll open a brothel there.' She sat back, puffing on her cigar. 'Mark my words, in ten years they'll have given this place back to the Abos and it'll be nothing but a windswept sand heap again, but Perth, that's the place. It'll be bigger and better.'

He scratched his head. 'Maybe so, but I have to start small. I can't afford a place in Perth.'

'And you can afford to buy the Black Cat?'

'The premises,' he corrected.

They haggled all morning over a bottle of whisky, which was treating Mike to a return of his morning hangover, but it did help to give the impression that he was a little drunk and therefore vulnerable to Glory's pressure.

He laughed when she mentioned a figure of two thousand pounds, and Glory laughed when he mentioned that the bank had offered her fifteen pounds. They were both enjoying the morning, despite the contest.

'Would you take a cheque?' he asked.

'Do I look mad?' she hooted.

'Cash then. Five hundred pounds. Not a penny more.'

'Five hundred pounds? Is that all you've got?'

'That's it.' He shrugged.

'Well, it's no deal. I owe more than that. Bills to pay. It'd leave me with nothing, Mike.'

'Ah, now there's a great pity. Five hundred is a lot of money; I'd have thought it would be well enough for you to start again in Perth.'

'So it would be, but if that's your last offer I'm stuck here. God, how I hate this fly-ridden hole. It's the bloody end of the earth.'

He commiserated with her. 'It's surely no place for ladies. But keep in mind that to raise the five hundred I'd have to write a cheque and wait until it is approved by the bank. Then I'd have the money in cash.'

'I told you, it wouldn't help me.'

'But what if we kept quiet about the sale? Said not a word to anyone? You'll never get the two thousand you're asking.'

'So?'

'So, I'll quietly make arrangements for a lady to travel through to Northam. Returning supply wagons are taking passengers just a few at a time, and they carry enough water and eats to get them through without hardship. You could go on one of them.'

A grin spread across her powdered face, and her green eyes gleamed. 'You mean I should just go?'

'The drivers are experienced journeymen. They leave well before dawn to beat the heat.'

'You're a rascal, Mike,' she chortled. 'No one would know I've gone.'

'Something like that. You'd leave smiling, with the five hundred in your purse.'

Glory sat back on the worn sofa, wrapped in a warm glow of smugness. 'Sold.'

'Then you'd better put it about that you've changed your mind and you're not selling, so snoopy creditors won't be watching. And I'll have the contract ready tomorrow.'

Mike had a spring in his step as he strode the mile out to their tent. It's like old times, he told himself cheerfully.

He searched through Clem's belongings for the claim form

180

that carried his signature, and sat down with pen and ink and a notebook to practise copying *C. Price*.

'Not hard at all,' he murmured. 'Child's play, this one.'

He hoped that Clem had enough in his bank in York to cover it, otherwise poor Glory wouldn't be going anywhere.

With a wink and a flourish Glory lent her correct name to the contract that disposed of the Black Cat, handing it over to Messrs Deagan and Price.

'Who's Price?' she asked.

'My partner. He's the one speared by the blacks but he's coming along nicely now. I'll have him out of that hospital tonight. Now, don't be sleeping in tomorrow morning. The lorry driver will be expecting you at Padgett's stables no later than half past four.'

She folded the notes into a brocade purse and kissed him on the cheek. 'I'll be there. You're a real pal, Mike. Look me up in Perth next time you're in town.'

Two days later he cooked breakfast for his patient and began to collect his tools to make for their mine.

'I can't thank you enough for the way you've looked after me,' Clem said, standing groggily with the aid of a tent pole. 'I should be coming with you.'

'You will,' Mike said cheerily. 'Now you're on your feet I'll be handing you the pick any day.'

'That'll be a relief. It's terrible sitting about here with nothing to do.'

'Write some letters.'

'That's all I seem to do. I told Thora I've had an accident, hurt my arm, so we'll have to stay longer. When you wrote to Alice you didn't mention the spear, did you?'

'I didn't think you'd be wanting them to worry.'

'No, I don't. I'll have a real tale to tell when I get home. They won't miss the great scar on my back. I still wonder why the blacks half killed me and then put me on a horse.'

'A warning to others, I guess.' Mike waited awkwardly, the pick and shovel slung over his back, and Clem waved him on.

'I'm sorry. I'm holding you up. No point in us both hanging about doing nothing.'

'You're not doing nothing, you're making progress. Keep out of the sun or you'll get giddy. I scrounged some books if you feel like reading. They're under my bunk. I'm off now to make our fortune, you just wait and see.'

Clem watched him tramp away and then looked about him at the lonely scattered tents, feeling like the last man on earth. All the other diggers had left for the fields and here he was, the lone inhabitant of this shabby camp. The smell of dust, ancient dust, was always present, but now it mingled with the stink of primitive quarters. He hadn't noticed it before, when he too was up and off, hurrying over to the fields, coming back at dusk, caring only for a feed and a rest, or a trot into town, but now he saw his temporary home as it truly was: a collection of ragged, fading tents slung among a growing pestilent heap of human waste. There was not a tree in sight, or even a bush to soften with a glint of green. There was no birdsong, no flash of parrot wings, no piping little birds about their business, no black-and-white magpies marking out their territories and cleaving the air with their glorious notes. Clem missed them all; he yearned to hear them again. He walked a few paces up the track, trying to force his legs back into working order, but the sight of rats scurrying among discarded tins and bottles and snivelling into empty tents disgusted him, so he turned back.

You're just weak, that's all, he told himself. And depressed from the sickness. And by the two facts staring you in the face: that Mike is doing all the work and that neither of you is doing any good out here.

He decided it was time to pull himself together. He pushed back into the shade of the tent and with a determined effort began to stretch his muscles, remembering the body-building exercises that Noah had taught him when he was a little kid.

'You will get fit again,' he said aloud, 'and you'll get back to that mine and work the hell out of it. Others have struck it rich here, and by God, so will you. And you're not going home until you do.'

182

Recalling that his neighbours, the Postle boys, had struck gold had a lot to do with Clem's decision to remain at Kalgoorlie. He'd already made a fool of himself in Thora's eyes by getting robbed. He dreaded returning to Lancoorie having failed again, with those Postle louts crowing over him. Thora would never let him live it down.

He'd already checked. Nearly all the cash he'd brought with him had gone, except for a couple of pounds. They'd been living on the small amounts of alluvial gold that Mike had been able to glean from the mine, after he'd paid the hospital and doctor's bills, so there was nothing for it now. Clem knew he'd have to draw more money from the bank. Alice would see the statement and know they weren't doing as well as they pretended.

I'll just have to make some excuse. Tell her we're expanding the mine or something, he worried. I hate to lie to Alice but Thora will be bound to want to read her letter . . .

After the exertion he did need to rest. He took a swig of water and lay on his bunk, fighting off despondency with plans of staking a new claim somewhere, maybe further out towards the newer fields.

One worn track led down a stony incline to the first of the mines and meandered raggedly through the rutted landscape for more than a mile before it became a furrow itself among man-made hillocks. Another track, widened by cartwheels, turned away towards the town, and it was this route Mike chose, leaving his implements with a mate at the water-condensing plant on his way.

At the Black Cat he soon located Jocelyn, who came rushing at him with the news.

'Mike, you'll never guess what's happened! Glory's done a bunk!'

Other girls gathered about them, worried and confused.

'We haven't seen her for days,' cried a slight girl with tumbling black hair. 'What are we to do? We'll get thrown out now.'

He held up the keys. 'Don't be fussing. The house is under

new management, that's all. You've no cause to be worried. Jocelyn, can you spare me a minute?'

She stared as he crossed the hall and opened the door to the front room.

Still not comprehending, she backed away. 'That's Glory's room.'

'Not any more. Come on in.'

To settle her rush of questions, he shut the door and insisted she sit down. 'If you listen to me now, I'll tell you what's to be. Glory has sold the business. To me. So we are under new management and things are about to change round here.'

'Where is Glory?'

'Somewhere round town. I don't know where she's staying, but that's not our business.'

'You bought the place? You?'

'That's what I said. Now, will you give me a chance to tell you what's to be, or will I call one of the others?'

'No, no. I want to know.'

'Good. Firstly, the Black Cat will keep going, and secondly, I want you to run the place. To take over. You'll be the boss. Can you do that?'

'Me?'

Jocelyn sat overawed as he told her that the premises would be closed for a week but the girls would still be paid. During that week, he wanted them all to get to work and clean the place thoroughly.

'I want it gleaming like your hotel in York,' he grinned. 'You've got ten housemaids waiting outside there, you'd know how to put them to the scrubbing brush, wouldn't you?'

'Yes.'

'Anyone who isn't interested in our cleaning work is to be fired. Kicked out.'

She was recovering from the shock and beginning to see light. 'They'll work,' she said grimly. 'I'll see to that. But there's stuff here – curtains, linen, mats and things – that's past cleaning.'

'Then replace them. Book them up to the Black Cat, they'll be easily paid for once we're making money again.'

184

They continued to discuss the transformation of the run-down house, until Jocelyn broke off from her enthusiasm to remember his original offer.

'You want me to be the madam?'

'Why not? You'll be well paid.'

'And I don't have to take customers myself?'

'Certainly not.'

She hesitated, trying to take this in, and then she jumped up and threw her arms about him. 'Oh, Mike, thank you. I promise you I won't let you down, I'll make this the best house in town. With elbow grease and a slap of paint, I'll have it all lovely. And I'll run it proper so we bring in the best customers.'

Mike extricated himself. 'That's what I had in mind. Once we start earning real money we'll make this a showplace, with furnishings that'll knock their eyes out.'

With almost all of her questions finally answered, he had to go, he wanted to get back to the mine.

'If you can spruce the house into good condition by next Saturday, you should put up a sign: "Grand reopening". How does that sound?'

'Marvellous! But what am I to call myself? Madam Jocelyn doesn't seem much of a name.'

With everything falling neatly into place, he allowed himself a good laugh. 'You'll think of something.'

'Maybe just Madam,' she mused. 'Yes. Just Madam. That'll give me respect and let them all know who's boss. Wait till the girls hear all this, they'll be blown over . . .'

'For the time being, I don't want them to hear that I'm the new owner. It'll get around soon enough, but there's no hurry.'

'I won't say a word. Cross my heart. Maybe I should call myself something better than just Madam . . .'

He left her to it and headed back to his own work. There was still plenty of gold in Kalgoorlie.

By the time the Black Cat was re-established and doing a roaring trade in the firm hands of Madam Jolie, a name suggested by one of the girls, Clem was back at work and the two men were beginning to eke out enough alluvial gold to encourage them to persevere with this claim.

Clem knew his limits, though, and by the close of the day he was glad to turn in, no longer interested in the pals and parties of previous days. He felt he'd wasted enough time.

It was when he was sitting by their camp fire, finishing his evening meal of mutton and potato stew, that the subject came up.

'Do you know what I'd like?' he said to Mike. 'I'd like a house by the sea. I haven't seen the sea since I was a little kid. I can remember it, though, the ocean. Staring down at it from the ship, so deep and clear and clean, with the wind whipping up flecks of white. Wouldn't it be something to be able to run down and plunge into the sea whenever you felt like it?'

'Sure would.'

'It's this place. I never feel clean, not with water so short. I reckon I'd need an hour in the ocean to ever feel clean again.'

'Well, why don't you come into town with me and we'll find a bath?'

'In three inches of water! But better than nothing, I suppose. Yes, let's go.'

'I know a place where we can buy a full bath.'

'Where?'

'The Black Cat.'

'That rathouse. No thanks.'

'Don't be like that. Glory's gone, your friend Jocelyn's running it now.'

'Jocelyn! I couldn't believe my ears when she told me she was working in a brothel.'

'She was good to you when you were sick. She'd be pleased to see you again. And the Black Cat's changed with her in charge. She's got it looking nice now.'

But Clem hesitated. 'I have been thinking about Thora a lot. I don't want to go to brothels any more, it's wrong.'

'You only want a bath, she wouldn't object to that,' Mike

186

laughed. 'In fact, I'd say she'd not be wanting either of us visiting her in our scruffy state. A bath is in order. Come on, let's go.'

They were well past the condensing plant, striding out with other miners town-bent, when Mike decided to break the news.

Clem stopped dead in his tracks, causing a rift in the stream of thirsty men coming along behind him.

'We've what?'

'You were too weak and ill to be making any decisions, so I made them for you. That's all.'

'This is a joke? Right?'

'Not at all. We're going to be rich.'

'Where did you get the cash? Have you been lying to me about the mine?'

'I have not. The mine is still a matchbox pay, but the Black Cat will bring us cash by the trunkload. There's a pub over there, I'll buy you a drink and explain.'

'You can explain right here. Where did you get the cash?'

'I wrote a cheque.'

'On what? You haven't got a bank account.'

'No, but you have.'

Clem grabbed him by the lapels of his thin jacket. 'What have you done, you bastard? How could you write a cheque on my account? My Lancoorie account, that's the only one I have . . .' Then it dawned on him. 'You rotten, stinking bastard! Did you forge my name?'

The diggers were intrigued to see a punch-up on the road at this early hour, before the drinks were even poured, but not that keen to stop and watch with the sundown temperatures still in the cruel nineties. They marched on past, grinning.

Mike held him off as best he could, dodging and feinting.

'This is bad for your health, lad. Calm yourself.'

'I'll kill you, you thieving bastard!'

'Give over, you fool. You're outmatched, and it's too bloody hot to be fighting.'

Clem kept on punching, rarely connecting, but his outrage, mixed with confusion, wouldn't allow him to stop. He would have punched anyone or anything that came within range. In the end he dropped down on to the road, on his knees, exhausted, but by no means finished with this thief.

A digger came forward and helped Mike take him, staggering, down to the pub, where he was shoved into a chair and handed a whisky. He tried to take in his surroundings. They were on a narrow veranda by the pub window, and there was a lot of noise inside. Drinks were lined up on the windowsill. A lorry lumbered past. In the distance he could hear the thump of crushing machines that worked day and night, so continuous that the sound became unheard, but now they were striking at his head, and all the time Mike, lodged on a wooden stool beside him, was talking, explaining. Clem refused to listen.

'I'll kill you,' he said at length, when his head began to clear, thanks to the jolt from a fiery cheap whisky. 'How much did you rob from me?'

'It cost us five hundred quid.'

'I'll have you jailed. I'll have your parole revoked.'

'Forget the parole. I've been a free man for a while now. My term's up. Try to see the sense of what I'm telling you. And you don't want to be jailing your partner. You'll be telling the world we own a brothel. I've been trying to keep your name quiet.'

'My name? My name is written down somewhere as the owner of a bloody whorehouse! Are you trying to ruin me?'

'Think of the money we'll make.'

'We? You buy a bloody brothel in my name and you talk of we. You're mad. I'll have you in the deepest cell in Fremantle jail, and you'll never get out.'

The worst thing about this outrage was that Mike ignored his threats. It was like punching air again.

'Your money, but my idea,' Mike said, shoving his stringy red hair back from his face. 'Fair's fair. There'll be enough money for both of us, and if you're feeling hard done by, I'll give you back your bloody five hundred in due time. But I won't let you buy me out.'

Clem was shouting. 'Buy you out! I don't want a bloody

188

brothel! I'll shut the place down, that's what I'll do. Then I'll have you up for forgery.'

'No you won't. Wait till you see the arithmetic. Jocelyn, the dear girl, keeps a fine ledger. Come with me now and I'll show you.'

'I won't go near the place. You're a rotten, conniving bastard!'

'What happened to all those thank yous, for me looking after you?'

Clem stood up. 'You're a criminal. A convicted bloody criminal. I want nothing to do with you.'

He stormed into the bar, shoving through to the rickety counter, where he bought himself another whisky. The second one didn't taste so bad. The blind rage was still with him, hand in hand with his determination to see that forger, that crook, behind bars. But there was also a wailing in him, a wailing of horror that he was the owner, like it or not, of a filthy brothel. He'd heard enough to know that his name was on the contract, that the solicitor Mike had used would know, and his clerks; that bank tellers here in Kalgoorlie, the source of all financial gossip, would know. That Jocelyn, for Christ's sake, was his employee as manager of the Black Cat. So how long would it be before all of York knew? Even if he did sell the unwanted brothel swiftly. Which he couldn't do if Deagan, his so-called partner, wouldn't sell.

'Oh, Jesus!' he said, and jumped nervously as a barman approached, as if he'd been caught out in a sinful act.

'Same again?' the barman asked.

'No.'

Clem struggled back down the road to the camp, past shadow-lit tents, past groups of men yarning round soft fading camp fires, ignoring their calls to join them, and found his way to their tent. He lit the lamp and threw himself on his bunk, wanting to die of shame. He was a respected sheep farmer. The owner of Lancoorie. And the owner of one of the most notorious brothels in the west. What would Thora say if she knew? She'd be mortified. Humiliated. He doubted if she'd ever heard of a brothel. When she found out, she'd be furious. She would probably leave him. And she'd have every right to.

The imagining of reactions from Thora, her family, the people of York, turned away any hope of sleep.

Chapter Eight

Sweet animals, cows; understanding, Lil mused, as she rested her head against a warm flank. She felt the animal sigh as she began milking, relieving the heavy udder of its burden.

'Good girl,' she said. 'You're a nice girl.' And then she added darkly, 'Not like the two-legged cows I have to live with.'

For, after the initial welcome and curiosity, her status among the staff of Minchfield Farm had deteriorated. It wasn't the job. She liked her work; old Tom even said she had a real way with the dairy herd, they'd come to her whistle whether it was milking time or not. The dairy and the creamery had become her province, always kept clean and no waste. She came down hard on spillages and any of the girls who slackened off with the churn or let any of the cream go sour. Miss Lavinia knew she was doing a good job too. Not from what she said, but what she didn't say on her excursions. And that was what had caused the trouble in the first place.

Mercy had said she was as bossy as Miss Lavinia. 'She used to shout at us, now she doesn't have to. You do the shouting about every little thing.'

'I do not! I just have to see everything is done right.'

'Why? You're not the boss!' That was Beth, the ungrateful little turncoat.

Lil thrust on with the milking, her hands working rhythmically. The cheek of Beth! Who looked after her when she was beaten? I did. And who tried to find out what happened? I did. But no one would say a word, not even Beth. She'd even lied, days later, saying that she'd fallen down the steep river bank.

No crumbling banks would leave weals like that over her back and legs. It was a mystery, but the others had made it clear that this was not Lil's business. Like she was an outsider.

'What do I care then?' she said to the cow, who lowered her head by the bale and looked back at Lil with big, soulful eyes, commiserating. 'They can all get bashed, for all I care.' On another Sunday morning she'd seen the scullery maid, usually a bold little piece, looking tearful and the worse for wear, but no one had said a word. They'd all sat in their places in the staff room, eating their porridge, gossiping, taking no notice. So Lil hadn't commented either.

And that was another thing. The staff room. Miss Lavinia was insistent that the table was set properly for all meals and that they observed their manners like toffs.

It took a while for Lil to realize that they were laughing at her because she'd never learned table manners and had no cause to bother about using the right spoon or fork. It wasn't as if they were seated in the big flash dining room in the house with Mr Warburton or Miss Lavinia! When she did wake up to what was amusing them, Lil resorted to watching, trying to learn, rather than asking any of them. And when Miss Lavinia came in one morning to check on them, Lil had sat, eyes down, leaving her meal for fear of being spotted as clumsy.

'You still feeding that child?' Miss Lavinia had asked her.

'Yes, miss.'

'Then you should eat more.'

'Yes, miss.'

Lil had breathed a sigh of relief when that ordeal was over, but the next morning Miss Lavinia was waiting for her at the gate to the staff quarters.

'It's time you weaned that baby. I've nursed a lot of babies in my time, so I've written out the instructions for you.'

'Yes, miss.'

'Read them carefully. Start with a mix of milk and water in the ratios I've stated. You can heat the milk in the kitchen as you need it. Is that understood?'

'Yes. Thank you, miss.'

She had feigned gratitude, but inside she was fuming. What right did that old maid have to be telling her how to care for her baby? And then she answered her own question. The right of power. You either obeyed Miss Lavinia or you were sent off on the next boat without a reference.

That new ruling brought her into conflict with the cook, Mrs Morgan, who did not take kindly to anyone intruding on her kitchen, let alone wanting room on her stove to heat milk several times a day. Unable to complain to the mistress, since Lil was acting under orders, Cook had made her resentment plain by causing Lil as much inconvenience as possible, making her wait, elbowing her out of the way.

'It won't get you nowhere sucking up to Miss Lavinia,' she sneered. 'She's as mad as a hatter.'

'And you'll be sailing down the river if I tell her you said that,' Lil snapped.

The cook dumped a heavy saucepan on the table with a thump. 'You wouldna!' she cried fearfully.

'Wouldn't I? Don't bet on it.'

From that day, the second most powerful woman in the house became Lil's ally. She defended Lil when the others laughed at her constant sermonizing about the Lord, and the long road to goodness, and she put in a good word for her with Miss Lavinia.

On this day, when the milking was finished and the cows were making their way up to their paddock, Lil was a little sad. She'd miss them. Thanks to her friend Mrs Morgan, she had been promoted to housemaid, retaining her charge of the creamery at her own request.

Sucking up to Miss Lavinia? She smiled as she took off her apron and heavy boots and walked out into the quiet of the evening. This was the hour she liked best, when the beautiful house and its leafy surrounds took on a reflective air, softened by the misty glow of sunset. Of course I am, I'd be a fool not to. Lil knew that her hard work and her cheerful manner had not gone unnoticed by the mistress. She never had to be told to get on with her work or to stop standing about gossiping, because she deliberately kept clear of the others.

Lil Cornish soon became the senior housemaid, making certain that everything was in order for the boss and Miss Lavinia, allowing no cause for complaint.

Her darling Caroline was no trouble at all now. No need to dash back to her room to care for her. The pram, with its mosquito net, was taken for granted, left in the back courtyard under the wisteria, or in the staff room on chilly days, and Miss Lavinia, though never stooping to pick up the baby, watched her progress with satisfaction, due, of course, to the strict diet she prescribed.

Mr Warburton was an absent-minded sort of chap. He never noticed the staff. He wouldn't be able to name any of them, but then, Lil decided, that was the way with gentry. Why should he?

For her part, no matter how hard she tried, Lil could not break down Miss Lavinia's reserve. The woman was as hard and distant as ever. Except when it came to religious instruction. Lil was beginning to regret her first show of religious fervour that had so pleased the mistress, because now Miss Lavinia had become a nuisance. Each Sunday a church service was held in the rose garden or on the nearby sheltered veranda for the Warburtons, and the house and field staff were expected to attend. Lil endured the Sunday meetings but afterwards she was summoned by Miss Lavinia, who chose a chapter from the Old Testament and instructed Lil to learn it.

Miss Lavinia meant well, Lil was sure, but she found the study onerous. The stories confused her – there were some peculiar people in this book of God's word – but the more she applied herself, for fear she might be examined on the text, the less she understood. In fact, the short burst of religion that Pastor Dodd's wife had bestowed on her was beginning to fade. Lil was reverting to type, trusting in God as the Almighty who controlled the seasons, and therefore the livelihood of all country souls. He didn't seem to have much relevance in this opulent world. Mr Warburton, she had discovered, was a gentleman farmer, too wealthy to have a minute of his leisurely days disturbed by a bad season.

Nevertheless, as Lil confided to baby Caroline, her only confidante, she could not let slip her Christian zeal. In Miss Lavinia's eyes, constant reference to all the boring pages of the holy book was proof of piety, so she couldn't afford to upset her mistress by neglecting her duty. Besides, the staff were watchful. She could never allow any of them to discover that she was finding the trappings of religion tedious. She hadn't bargained on all this irksome reading, nor on the long, dreary Sunday services, listening to incomprehensible singsong sermons, delivered by the local Anglican minister.

To retain her fortunate position in this household, Lil increased her missionary fervour, claiming it was her duty to bring the other women closer to God, unconcerned by their impatience and sly efforts to escape her prim homilies. After a while it simply became habit, and it bothered Lil not at all that she was known as the Bible-thumper. Minchfield was her home, and she would do whatever was necessary to remain here.

As head housemaid she now had the run of the house, and after her first awestruck ventures into the splendid rooms, tiptoeing along the polished passageways and up the wide cedar staircase, she fell in love with it. Minchfield House, with its wondrous furnishings, chandeliers, paintings, silver, precious china and all the other wildly expensive things that a house could possibly need, was, to Lil, more blessed than any cathedral. It deserved the loving care that she alone could bestow on it, and she became obsessed with its upkeep. Nothing escaped her eagle eye, not a spot on a mirror nor a handmark on polished timbers, nor a figurine an inch out of place. As she had driven the dairy maids, the housemaids and waitresses now came in for her wrath if they let her down. It was as if Minchfield House had replaced God as her latest compulsion, but this was reality, things she could see and touch and treasure.

Sometimes, if the baby was restless, Lil would slip over to the kitchen before she went to bed to heat some milk for her. This night, strong winds blustered through the trees as she cut across to the kitchen door and let herself in without bothering to light a lamp. She knew the kitchen so well, pale light from the moon was enough for her to put her hand on a small pan and move quietly to the stove, relieved to find the last of the embers still smouldering. She hooked a central iron plate aside and put the pan directly over the heat, and had gone into the pantry for some milk when she heard a crash from the dining room above her.

For a second it gave her a fright, but then she decided a shutter must be loose, so she went up the stone steps, intending to secure it before it woke Miss Lavinia, whose bedroom was directly above the dining room.

Leading from the landing above the steps there was a swing door with a glass panel, a convenience for the waitresses designed to avoid collisions, and as Lil put her hand on the door to push it aside, she saw movement in the dim room. She jumped back guiltily when she realized that Miss Lavinia was already in there.

Curiosity held her hand, for this wasn't the Miss Lavinia she knew. In the light of a tiny red lamp that sat on the table she saw an elderly woman in a long white nightdress, her grey hair no longer in the neat bun but wild and straggly round her face.

Lil stifled a giggle, noticing that Miss Lavinia had knocked over a chair on her way to the window. Then the woman veered, staggering, towards the sideboard.

Interested, Lil watched as Miss Lavinia bent over to open the sideboard door and lost her balance, tumbling backwards, muttering to herself.

Even before the woman reached for the bottle, Lil knew. The old villain was drunk!

Lil stared in amazement. Nobody had to tell her about drunks. She was married to one, and she'd seen plenty of women worse for the drink. But not gentry! Genteel women like Miss Warburton took their tipples of fine wine at dinner, maybe a little more when they gave dinner parties, but they didn't slosh into it. And not in the quiet of night on their own.

Or did they?

Bewildered, she drew back a little, keeping the nocturnal tippler in sight. Still sitting on the floor, Miss Lavinia took a swig from the bottle. Lil couldn't see what she was drinking, but it would have to be spirits of some sort, she noted, because wine was always decanted if the bottle was opened. She couldn't have removed a cork so easily.

Eventually the mistress managed to climb to her feet, but not before she'd sent a figurine crashing to the floor. Involuntarily, Lil jerked back in fright, as if she herself had smashed the pretty china shepherd. When she looked again, Lavinia was busy shoving the broken pieces well under the low-set sideboard. Still clutching the bottle, she began her stumbling retreat from the dining room, straightening the chair with exaggerated care, blowing out the tiny lamp after several attempts, and moving on to the drawing room, still muttering to herself like a demented ghost. Then all was quiet again.

The pan hissed as Lil quickly heated the milk, wondering if Mr Warburton had heard the noise. Probably not. He had a suite of rooms at the far end of the house, over the library and the big sitting room. She was soon back in her own quarters, the baby sleeping contentedly with the help of the warm milk.

Well I never! Lil said to herself, for the umpteenth time, and as she climbed into bed, she smiled. That's something to know. She recalled that Cook had said Miss Lavinia was as mad as a hatter, and wondered what that really meant.

The next morning the trouble started.

All the household staff were hauled into the dining room, where a furious Miss Lavinia was pointing with her cane at the broken china hidden under the sideboard.

'Who did this?' she shouted. 'I demand to know who did this.'

While the others quaked, shaking their heads, Lil gazed at the floor, listening to the sham with shrewd indifference.

One by one they were made to step forward, as the mistress raged and swung her cane about, and it was then that Lil knew who had whipped the girls. She'd had an inkling it might have been Miss Warburton at first, but had dismissed that as hardly being likely for a lady who might have a sharp tongue but who was very circumspect and very much a Christian woman. Instead she'd decided on Jordan, the farm manager, who was known to be hot-tempered and often called on the house girls to help out sorting and packing fruit and vegetables in the big storehouse. Lil didn't have much to do with him these days. He'd kept a close eye on her work in the dairy when she'd first started, but finding no cause for complaint, had let her be. He was none too pleased when she was moved to housework, but Jordan couldn't overrule Miss Lavinia.

'Very well,' the mistress said, permitting Cook to leave, since she'd pointed out that she never went into the dining room. 'The rest of you will be punished until the liar among you comes to me with the truth.'

Eventually they were released to file, scowling and arguing, down to the staff room, scattering blame indiscriminately.

'We're all on bread and water until someone owns up,' Lil told Mrs Morgan, who nodded.

'That's the usual.'

'And she's taking four bob off our pay at the end of the month to cover the breakage.'

'That's bad luck.'

To Lil it was more than bad luck, it was outrageous. The bread-and-water diet didn't bother her, for Cook would see that she didn't go short, but losing four shillings from her precious savings so bloody unfairly really hurt. For that vicious old woman, who had more money than she knew what to do with, to prise more than a pound out of the staff like this was nothing short of theft. 'She's a drunk and a thief and a bully,' Lil muttered to herself, resentment festering.

She could see no point in telling the others what she knew of the incident. To accuse the mistress would be a short cut back to Perth.

'I didn't do it,' she told a hungry, angry gathering that night as they met under the tree by the women's quarters. 'It's unfair that I should have to suffer too. If I didn't have the baby, I'd leave.'

198

Lil caught glances among them and guessed that option had already been discussed.

Mrs Morgan spoke. 'Whoever broke the little figurine should say so now, to save a lot of trouble. The worst that could happen is that you'll get sacked, but Jordan will write you a reference.'

'You've never had a hiding!' Beth cried. 'If someone doesn't own up soon, she'll give me another beating, I know she will.'

There was a hush, as if they'd been caught in the act of some foul deed, and Mrs Morgan hastened to close the gap.

'No use going back over past history,' she said. 'We just have to sort out who broke the thing and get this over with.'

'What do you know?' Mercy sneered. 'Miss Lavinia takes her cane to anyone she feels like, and no one says a bloody word because they're all scared stiff of her. You and your bloody references! No one gives references to Abos. Me and my mum are getting out of here.'

Her mother darted forward from where she'd been sitting under a tree. 'No, Mercy, no! She didn't mean what she said. She's just het up. Mercy didn't break nothin'.' She turned to her daughter. 'Come away, don't get mixed up in white women's business.'

'I won't shut up,' Mercy said. 'I've had enough of this place. You all whine and go on about your bloody jobs, but we don't get paid. We don't get paid nothin'. We're just let live here! And don't none of you pretend you don't know. You all know. You too, Mrs Bible-thumper! We're goin' and we don't need to wait for no bloody boat. We'll find our own way. And you can go to hell, the lot of you!'

'Don't say that,' her mother cried, but Mercy, the adolescent Aborigine girl, had suddenly come into her own. 'My mum and me have taken enough beatings from her. Beth's right, and I tell you what, if she don't get a hiding because of one of you liars, then I will. And I'm not waitin' around!'

Mercy, tall and haughty, grabbed her mother's arm and marched her away from them, down across the cleared block where horses grazed, and the pair disappeared into the night.

'That's very sad,' Lil said, but one of the waitresses stood up and confronted her.

'Why don't you shut up! I'm sick of listening to you. And to old Miss Folderol. She's got us living out here like prisoners. Going for walks on Sundays, our big outings!'

'You're paid better here than anywhere else,' Mrs Morgan reminded her.

'Yeah! Sure we are. Because no one else will put up with the place. I'm getting out too.'

Lil was on her feet. 'Oh, please, Vera, don't. If you go, everyone else will go too. You're the mainstay here.'

'Since when?' Vera snapped. 'Since you got to be teacher's pet? I'll be on that bloody boat on Friday, and when I get to town I'll tell that employment agent what goes on here. You, Beth, better come with me. I know the law. If you'd had the guts to speak up earlier, you could have charged the old bag with assault.'

'Oh dear, fanciful thinking,' Mrs Morgan clucked.

The next few days were chaotic. Bread and water at each meal fuelled the fires of mutiny. Mrs Morgan tried to calm them by unlocking the pantry and handing out cold pie and cakes, but their minds were made up. The scullery maid clanged pots about and left vegetables half peeled. Priceless carpets, hung outside to be beaten for dust, were left in the rain. Windows were left open, dust swept into heaps uncollected. Curtains were dragged down to be washed and not returned. Food was dumped on stained tablecloths in front of Mr Warburton and his sister, and at every meal something was forgotten, be it salt or sugar or even Cook's superior Yorkshire pudding.

Mr Warburton actually complained – rare for him – and Miss Lavinia stormed about the house, given a real excuse now to lay down the law, her law, slamming her cane on doors and walls, and threatening dire punishments.

Lil watched, knowing drunks, knowing that the woman would break out soon. Understanding Miss Lavinia now, knowing that any time, given the opportunity, the mistress could react violently against one of the staff, Lil knew she had to be vigilant. But that time never came.

On the Friday morning all of the household staff lined up before Jordan for their pay, less four shillings, which he considered none of his business, and all, except Cook and Lil, quit without giving notice.

They took their belongings and ran gaily down to the boat, shouting gleefully to Jordan that he could serve the missus himself.

Lil refused to serve Mr and Miss Warburton at dinner that night.

'I'm not a waitress. I wouldn't know how.'

So, apologetically, poor plump Mrs Morgan climbed the stone steps to serve the four courses to the master and the mistress, who sat in dead silence in her presence.

'What did they say?' Lil kept asking.

'Nothing. Not a word. Not for me to hear. It wouldn't be right. But I'll bet the master gives her an earful. Jordan will have told him why they left, and it'll be the talk of the district. Them boatmen carry gossip up and down the river.'

'Why did everyone keep so mum about the beatings? Someone should have told the master before this.'

'They did, but he wouldn't interfere. Loyal he is to her, since she runs the house. Perhaps she promised him it wouldn't happen again. Who knows? But the last girl that complained had to go. Miss Lavinia got rid of her double-quick. And you wouldn't want to try working for her, after you'd dobbed her in to the boss, now would you?'

'I suppose not.' That put a damper on Lil's vague plans. She'd hoped to catch Lavinia out on the booze again, by accident of course, and report her to the boss, but if he stuck by his sister despite her behaviour, she'd only come a thud. And end up next on the boat.

Nevertheless, she was curious to know how Lavinia really would react to the day's events. She was willing to bet that the woman would be smarting from the affront to her dignity. It was not every day a mistress had to face the embarrassment of having nearly all her staff resign. What better time for her to reach for the bottle?

Later that evening Lil knocked on Cook's door. 'It's spooky here with just us two now. Would you listen for Caroline while I go up to the kitchen and heat some milk?'

'Yes, of course. Bring the little darling down to me.'

'Did you set the table for breakfast?'

Mrs Morgan was stricken. 'Oh, dear Lord, I forgot. How am I supposed to think of these things?'

'Never mind, I'll do it while I'm waiting for the milk to heat.'

When she handed over Caroline, who was still wide awake, Mrs Morgan reminded her: 'Don't forget. You use the Irish china for breakfast, and the plain silver.'

'I won't forget.'

Now she had an excuse to barge in on dear Miss Lavinia, if she came down.

All the way up to the house, Lil prayed she would, but if not tonight, there would be other nights, and she'd be watching. She wasn't sure what she could achieve, but no one could be allowed to steal four shillings from her and get away with it.

This time she lit the lamp at the far end of the kitchen and dawdled about, setting up the tray of Irish china as the milk warmed, but all was quiet. She was just about to give up when she heard a noise in the dining room and darted up to her spy window. Lil smiled with satisfaction. Here was the night drinker again.

Lavinia had come down with a candle, placing it on the table. She bypassed the crystal decanters and made for the sideboard, from habit, Lil supposed. But she couldn't get the door open. It was locked. Where was the key?

In the top drawer of the sideboard, Lil prompted silently. In the green felt top drawer where it's always kept, you silly old chook.

But Lavinia battled and scratched at the door, even trying to use a knife to prise it open, and watching, Lil wondered what liquor she took upstairs to start her off and where she disposed of the bottles.

Eventually her mistress stood up, puffing from the exertion. She leaned on her cane, staring about the room, and then she sighted the decanters.

The nearest glass from a water set was soon put into action as, standing, Lavinia poured herself a stiff drink from a decanter and gulped it down. She was pouring a second drink when Lil walked in and calmly placed her lamp on a side table by the window.

'What are you doing here?' Lavinia cried angrily, her words slurring.

'I won't be long, madam,' Lil said. 'I'm just setting for breakfast. There's no one else to do it.'

Soon she was back with the tray, making a deliberately slow job of setting the two places.

'Get out of here! You're spying on me!'

'Why would I do that?' Lil asked, continuing with her work.

When the heavy cane struck, Lil was forewarned. She leapt aside, but knocked over a pedestal, and a large crystal vase full of roses smashed to the floor.

Now Lil regretted her foolhardy interference. But there was no going back, it wasn't in her nature to slink away.

'Look what you've done!' Lavinia hissed at her. 'You'll pay for that.'

'No I won't,' Lil said, putting the heavy table between them. 'You get a hold of yourself, you're drunk! And put that cane down or I'll take it from you.'

'How dare you speak to me like that!'

The cane swished again, slamming into the table, but as Lavinia recovered from that effort, she lurched back against the small table. The lamp thudded down and within seconds it had ignited the curtains that were drawn across the french doors leading to the veranda.

'Look out!' Lil called. 'The curtains are on fire!'

Lavinia, with her back to the exit, was too set on her course to grasp what was happening.

'Get out of here,' she demanded. 'I'll deal with you in the morning.'

'Don't be ridiculous!' Lil shouted. 'The curtains are on fire!'

They were dry with age and they were going up like matchwood. Frantically Lil looked about her, and hoisting a mat from the floor, ran with it, hoping to smother the flames, but in her befuddled state Lavinia saw only the mat.

'It's a Persian! Put it down!' she screamed.

She was still hampering Lil's efforts when Mr Warburton appeared at the door.

'What's going on here?' he wailed.

'Fire!' Lil yelled. 'Fire. Can't you see that!'

By this time the flames were hurtling towards the ceiling, the heavy side drapes also well alight. Lil tossed the mat aside and began pulling furniture away from that end of the room, amazed at the swift progress of this fire.

Although still confused, Lavinia began shouting orders at Lil: 'Not that chair! The other one! Get that picture off the wall. Open the french doors.'

'I can't,' Lil puffed. Smoke was choking her and the heat was forcing her back. She couldn't shift the heavy sideboard, which was already being seared, bubbling varnish adding acrid fumes to the smoke, so she pulled out a deep drawer laden with the beautiful silver table settings, and ran with it, dumping it in the passage. Returning to rescue the second drawer, she saw Lavinia run towards the french doors, which were already crumbling, glass cracking like pistol shots.

'No!' Lil screamed, cursing the jumble of dining room furniture as she climbed over it to get to Lavinia. In the distance she heard the clang of the fire bell that merged with Lavinia's shriek of pain as she put her hand on a brass door latch that must have been white-hot by this time. Through the smoke she could see the stricken woman, standing clutching her hand, not seeming to notice that her skirt was on fire.

'Come back!' Lil yelled at her as she quickly unbuttoned her own heavy skirt and petticoat, dropping them to the floor, memories of fierce bush fires flooding back. She wrapped the soft calico petticoat round her head, and taking a deep breath, plunged into the fire that had taken over half of the room. She moved fast, barrelling forward to grab her mistress round the waist and crash with her through the shattered doors, to fall on to the tiled veranda, surprised to find that ceiling, too, was alight.

She rolled Lavinia about, trying to smother the burning cloth, and then men came running, shouting.

Jordan, the farm manager, was there. He picked up Lavinia and carried her out to the lawn, well away from the house, and Lil hurried after him, her shoulder aching from the heavy fall and her throat and lungs burning from smoke inhalation.

'Get a stretcher!' Jordan shouted as he tried to revive Lavinia. He bent over her to blow air into her lungs until she began coughing and spluttering, and then he pulled back with a grimace.

'Has she been on the booze again?' he whispered to Lil, who nodded.

'Just as well,' Jordan said softly as he gently examined Lavinia. 'She's been burned but she mightn't be feeling too much yet, what with the shock as well. You all right?'

'Yes,' Lil gulped. 'Just a bit of smoke and I banged my arm.'

Jordan looked keenly at her. 'I saw you come through those doors with her like a battering ram. Why didn't you go the other way? The other side of the house isn't alight.'

'No choice,' Lil puffed. 'She headed for the french doors. Look at her hand; she marched into the fire and tried to open the door and got stuck there.' Lil stopped for breath. 'I'm sorry. I hope I didn't hurt her but it seemed the fastest way out then.'

'Good girl. You stay with her until they bring a stretcher. Take her down to my house, but don't let anyone try to remove any of her clothes, they'll be stuck to her. See that they wait for the doctor.'

While she waited, Lil watched the horse-drawn water carts rattle up to the house and groups of men fight the fire with hoses and buckets. She shook her head, horrified to see that the flames had spread. An awful thing to happen to such a lovely house. A terrible shame.

She heard Miss Lavinia moan and spoke to her, trying to offer words of comfort, but she didn't dare touch her for fear of hurting her, their previous battle insignificant now.

It was only when she was trudging down the path towards Jordan's house with the stretcher-bearers that Lil realized she was dressed only in a blouse and bloomers and torn black stockings. Mortified, she hung back to trail behind them, but neither of the men made any comment, even when they entered the lamp-lit cottage. Before they placed Miss Lavinia on Jordan's bed, Lil grabbed a cover and wrapped it about herself.

'We ought to get back,' one of the men said, 'unless there's something we can do here for you, miss.'

'No, you go. I'll sit with her. I have to wait for the doctor. He only lives on the next property, he shouldn't be long.'

When they left, Lil sat in the neat bedroom, thoroughly depressed. Now what? After that fight with the mistress, her days here were numbered. But where to go? She wished she could leave the cottage and run down to Mrs Morgan and the baby, because she too desperately needed comforting, and she was exhausted from the night's work. She wished now she'd stayed in her own quarters and minded her own business, then none of this would have happened.

Fortunately, Mr Warburton was not of that opinion. He was very grateful to Lil for her bravery and resourcefulness in rescuing his sister from the fire.

'Had you not been there,' he told Lil warmly, 'the whole house might have gone up.'

Lil's version – that she had been in the kitchen and heard something break, then smelled smoke – had been accepted by all, but she had yet to face Miss Lavinia.

That morning, with the east wing of the house in ruins, Mr Warburton and the doctor took Miss Lavinia to hospital in Perth, so Lil and the cook were left to their own devices. The pantry and kitchen, being of stone and at a lower level than the main house, were not affected by the fire.

'This is part of the original cottage, I'd say,' Cook told Lil as they settled down to a quiet cup of tea. 'When the Warburtons made their money they built the main house.'

Lil was curious. 'How did they make their money so fast? Miss Lavinia's only about fifty, and he's just a couple of years older.'

'Not them. Their uncle, Thomas G. Warburton. He was an importer, had big warehouses in Fremantle and owned half of Hay Street. They still do. He bought this farmland and he and his wife lived here in the cottage until he built her the big house. It was a labour of love, they say; he wanted to make up to her for the years they'd lived poor while he was making the fortune. He wanted her to have the best house money could provide.' She sighed. 'Poor man, he'd turn in his grave if he could see the mess out there. But isn't it always the way, Lil? Poor Mrs Thomas Warburton didn't live long enough to enjoy her house.' She lowered her voice. 'They say she died of the cancer.'

'Ah, no!'

'It's true, I tell you. She lingered on a year or so – that's when Miss Lavinia came here. She nursed her to the end. But the old gentleman pined so bad for her, it weren't but a year or so before he went to join her.'

Jordan stuck his head in through the door. 'Can you spare me a cup of tea, Cook?'

'Of course I can. Have you had any breakfast?'

'Yes, but we'll have to make some arrangements for the workmen to keep them on the job.'

He pulled up a chair and sat down. 'How are you faring, Lil? That was quite a night for you.'

'I'm well, thank you, Jordan. I hope Miss Lavinia will be all right.'

'She'll have the best of care, that's all we can ask. Mr Warburton will be staying in Perth for a while, to be near her, so I have to get the house in order.'

'How can you do that?' Mrs Morgan asked. 'Lil can look after the undamaged sections, keep them nice, but that lot up by the steps there, nothing but ruination.'

'We'll clear it out, see what we can salvage and pull the whole wing down. It will have to be rebuilt.'

'Oh, God help us,' Mrs Morgan cried. 'Is it that bad?'

'Yes, but we're harvesting and I don't want to use my field workers, so I'll be bringing labourers upriver from Perth. That's what I wanted to talk to you about. It's an ill wind, but it's just as well the other women quit. I'll need those staff quarters for tradesmen.'

Mrs Morgan bristled. 'We can't live down there with strange men! They could murder us in our beds. Or worse.'

Jordan grinned. 'There won't be room for you down there. You and Lil will have to move into the house.'

'Upstairs?' Mrs Morgan breathed, awestruck.

'Not in the family suites, but there are plenty of guest rooms.'

'Well! For heaven's sake!'

As Jordan discussed with Cook the problems facing him – finding tradesmen who had chosen not to join the rush for the goldfields, finding the materials necessary to restore Minchfield House to its former glory, the provisions required to feed an influx of men for several months – Lil weighed up her own situation. She decided she might as well stay awhile to enjoy the luxury of living in this house, until Miss Lavinia came home and ordered her out. In which case it would be a good idea to keep sweet with Jordan. He could write the all-important reference.

'I can help Cook in the kitchen as well as look after the rest of the house,' she volunteered, 'but what about the milking?'

'That's about the only good news I can tell you,' he said. 'Everyone in the district has been so upset about Miss Lavinia and the fire, I've got volunteers coming from all directions. This is where good neighbours become invaluable. We'll get by until it's time to start looking for new staff.'

He poured his tea into the saucer and drank it quickly, wolfing down the slices of custard pie Cook had put before him, and left, hardly bothering to take his leave of them, with too many other things to think about.

'He likes you,' Mrs Morgan whispered. 'You should go for him. He's a widower. Got a nice cottage over there.'

'Yes, I've seen it,' Lil said. 'But you forget. I'm still a married woman!'

'These mistakes can be undone. You told me your husband's a no-hoper. You can't say that about Jordan.'

Lil shook her head and went outside to watch the volunteers dragging burned and soaked furniture out on to the lawns. The dear house looked crippled, as if it were struggling to stay upright, and she felt a surge of pity, for she so much loved this beautiful place.

As for Jordan, she knew that Mrs Morgan was right. He'd been so gentle last night, escorting her back to her quarters after all the fuss had died down, enquiring after Caroline, who was still with Cook, dashing back to the house to bring the baby the milk she'd been denied. And early this morning he'd been very nice, singing her praises to Mr Warburton. But Lil wasn't attracted to him. She never had been, even though she'd noticed his kindness to her before this. And where would he stand when Miss Lavinia came storming back to her house? Would he take her part against the inevitable accusations of their mistress? Not likely. He hadn't stood up for the girls who had been beaten by Lavinia, what chance for someone who had defied her?

Ah, no, she said to herself. I don't need a fair-weather friend, Jordan. You're no use to me. Her thoughts went back to Clem Price, the owner of Lancoorie and the father, now, of her other baby. He was tall and handsome, with fine features, not a bulky, rough gent like Jordan, who was no more than an overgrown farm boy. Clem Price had class. He would even stand up well against Mr Warburton in later years, for men like Clem Price aged well. To this day Lil could never understand how such a virile man could have been persuaded to marry a prunes-and-prisms girl like Thora Carty. But then she remembered that Thora had been in the family way, and she giggled.

'See, you just never know who's up to what!' she murmured. 'Who'd have thought it of Thora?'

Lil walked in through the front door of Minchfield House and up the grand cedar staircase that, mercifully, had been spared, turning away from the gaping hole at the end of the long passage to investigate the other rooms at various levels, coming finally to Mr Warburton's suite of rooms. She explored them lovingly, touching the wide mahogany bed and the matching suite of furniture, the exquisite inlaid table, the fine china in his bathroom, the big rocking chair in his sitting room that faced out over the river, a sublime view.

What must it be like, she wondered, to be so rich? To have a part of your lovely house burn down and just give orders to rebuild? To live in rooms like this with servants to wait on your every whim?

Mr Warburton was staying with friends in Perth but he came upriver once a week, to oversee the work in progress and confer with Jordan. He took his meals in the library, seemingly unconcerned by the hammering and banging under way at the other end of the house.

Every time Lil delivered his lunch he was absorbed in papers that were scattered about the long table, but he would have no fuss, merely pushing pages aside to make room for the trays. He seemed to be enjoying all this activity. It was quite a change from his previous meditative lifestyle; in fact, as Lil reported to Mrs Morgan, he was rather cheery.

She always made a point of enquiring after Miss Lavinia, with the ever-present spectre of being banished from Minchfield, but his responses were confusing. He'd shake his head and murmur: 'Oh, poor Miss Lavinia.' He was able to tell Lil that yes, the dreadful burns were healing, but she was still seriously unwell.

Lil and Cook mulled over the news.

'Must be her chest,' Mrs Morgan decided. 'Fogged up with smoke, burnt her insides.'

'But she should be over that by now. Maybe she got pneumonia, but you think he'd have said so, if that's what it is.'

'You never know with them hospitals. She could have

caught a contagion, poor lady. Bad enough the burns without a sickness on top of them.'

Lil supposed Cook was right, but she still dreaded Mr Warburton's visits. There was nothing to stop Miss Lavinia ordering Lil's sacking from her sickbed, unless she was too ill to talk, and a woman like that, used to throwing her weight about, would have to be dying to shut her up. And somehow Lil didn't think she was.

Then came the day. Lil's heart sank. Mr Warburton sent for her not long after he arrived with another gentleman.

They were both in the library, looking very serious, indeed, and Lil quaked as they instructed her to be seated.

As it turned out, the other gentleman was a solicitor who had some questions for her.

'I want you to answer truthfully, Mrs Cornish,' the master said gently. 'Don't be afraid. We just want to sort a few things out.'

Both men took their places across from her, and the solicitor looked down at his notes. 'Now, Mrs Cornish. On the night of the fire you came up from the kitchen when you smelled smoke?'

Petrified, Lil nodded.

'And at that point could you tell what had started the fire?'

'The lamp,' she whispered. 'It was knocked over, broken. The curtains caught and were going up fast.'

'Who broke the lamp? Who knocked it over?'

Lil looked to Mr Warburton, who gave her a wan smile. 'You must reply truthfully, my dear.'

'Miss Lavinia,' she said nervously.

'Think about this carefully,' the solicitor said, when he had finished recording her previous answers on a long form. 'Would you say Miss Warburton was intoxicated at the time?'

Lil drew a deep breath. She felt she was finished at Minchfield now, so she could say what she liked, damn them.

'Yes.'

He nodded, writing. 'And have you seen Miss Warburton intoxicated before?'

'Yes. When I came up for milk for my baby. She was in the dining room, drunk.' Lil sat straight in the chair and gazed loftily at Mr Warburton. 'As a matter of fact, I heard someone in the dining room and looked through the glass of the door to see what was happening, and I saw her break a china figurine. The one she claimed someone on the staff broke.'

'Why didn't you speak up then?'

Lil sniffed at him. 'Would you call Miss Warburton a liar?'

The solicitor coughed and bent to his page. 'Is that why all the staff except you and the cook departed?'

'Partly. They were fed up with her. She beat them.'

That interested the solicitor, who had Lil give details, which he added to his page in a careful hand.

Eventually the interrogation was over and Lil was asked to sign her statement. By this time she was intensely curious about the official-looking page, so she fumbled with the pen to give herself time to glance over it, since neither of them seemed inclined to explain. Her answers were written under a printed statement, and above that again she saw the heading: Perth Mental Institute. Instantly she guessed what they were up to, but she pretended to be unaware, writing her full name carefully.

'Is all this necessary?' she asked, innocence in her eyes. 'The fire was really only an accident.'

'Just a formality,' Mr Warburton said, sliding the form away to add his signature, which was countersigned by the solicitor. 'It's just between ourselves. While we're here, would you mind witnessing these other papers, Mrs Cornish?'

'No.'

The other papers were pink-bound legal documents, and Lil's eyes raced over them while appearing to be lowered in humble submission. What she discovered amazed her: 'The Property known as Minchfield Farm, of Miss Lavinia Grace Warburton . . .' was being transferred to her brother, Robert Jamieson Warburton! They were putting old Lavinia away! Obviously he didn't own a chair in the place. What had Cook said? Miss Lavinia had come to Minchfield and nursed her aunt. And probably the uncle too. No mention of Mr Warburton. So the uncle had left everything to her.

No wonder this Mr Warburton never intervened, never took sides against her. She could have thrown him off too.

Time to go. Lil was dismissed with thanks and Mr Warburton escorted her to the door, where she stopped suddenly.

'I was wondering, sir, about the future. Once everything is in order again, you'll be employing more house staff, I suppose?'

'Oh yes, indeed.'

'Then could I apply for the position of housekeeper? I love this house and can run it well for you.'

There, it was out. She was letting him know she was aware that Miss Lavinia would not be returning.

No doubt Mr Warburton was pleased with the morning's work. He smiled benignly. 'Yes, you may. I was intending to offer you the position.'

'As housekeeper I can hardly live in the staff quarters. I would need a room in the house.'

'By all means,' he said jovially. 'When the east wing is completed I think a bedroom and a sitting room upstairs would be appropriate.'

'Thank you, sir, you're very kind.'

'What did they want?' Cook was quick to ask.

'Nothing much. They were making up lists of all the furniture and things lost in the fire. I was hard put to remember all the stuff they had in those rooms.'

'Insurance, it'd be. Rich people can get their money back for goods wrecked and damaged in fires; poor people just have to put up with it. All wrong, I say.'

Months later the building was completed, the rooms plastered and carpeted, and the furniture began arriving, so Mrs Morgan took two days off to go to Perth.

When she returned she had news for Lil.

'Miss Lavinia's been put away! I heard it in town and it's a fact!'

'What do you mean, put away?'

'Just what I said. They've put her in the loony bin, they say she's mental.'

'Good Lord! It must have been the fire sent her off her head.'

'Not likely. Not her. There's talk of her being done by the booze, and I think it's bloody disgraceful. Just because a woman takes a few drinks at times, she shouldn't be locked up. There's more to this than meets the eye. You mark my words.'

Lil did. But for the time being it was best to say nothing about the new arrangements. She'd wait for Mr Warburton to move back in.

'How much longer am I expected to wait for him?' Thora complained to Alice. 'He said he'd only be away a few months and it's nearly half a year. I've become a grass widow, that's what I am, and at my age! It's positively tragic!'

Alice smiled to herself. 'Tragic' was her sister-in-law's latest favourite word. Everything was tragic: the baby's sniffles, mud on her skirt, burned toast. 'It is sad for you, I know,' Alice comforted her, 'but I'm sure Clem will be home soon. Then everything will be back to normal.'

'That's what I'm afraid of,' Thora sulked. 'He says in his letters he can't wait to get back to Lancoorie . . .'

'And to you, my dear.'

'Yes, yes, whatever . . . He'll be so glad to be back from those frightful goldfields, I'll never shift him. I'll just be stuck here again.'

They'd had this conversation many a time and it was beginning to worry Alice, because Thora's threats of leaving Lancoorie were becoming more constant. She tried to change the subject.

'Poor Clem, he is obviously trying hard. Don't forget he's had setbacks. The injury he sustained put him in hospital. I'm glad we didn't know about that at the time, I'd have been worried sick.'

'Then he should have come home!'

'I doubt he would have been well enough to travel, but it

was obviously for the best. He seems to be doing well. He has already sent two money orders for five hundred pounds each. And he says there's more to come. Isn't that exciting!'

Thora stood by the front door, staring down the track to the road as if hoping someone would appear. Anyone.

'It's just not the same,' she said miserably. 'The Postle boys brought home gold. I expected him to come home with gold too.'

It bothered Alice that Clem's wife always referred to her husband as 'he' or 'him', never by name, but to keep the peace she refrained from commenting. Thora wasn't the easiest person to live with.

'The Postle boys sold most of their gold in Coolgardie,' she said. 'I'm sure Clem will bring home samples too. Really, Thora, the worst is over. Clem says his mine is yielding well and I'm to keep banking the money orders. I think it's wonderful. That means there's more to come. It's my guess that when this gold runs out he'll be home, because he's missing you terribly.'

'Missing Lancoorie, more like it.' She turned suddenly and confronted Alice. 'It's no use. I have decided to take Lydia and go. I'm a town person, I really can't stand it out here, with or without him. It's not fair. I had no idea how lonely these places could be. We haven't had a visitor in weeks, and that was only the Postles.'

Alice was devastated, but she tried to keep calm. 'Are you going into York to visit your family?'

'No, I am not! They never bother to come near me. Lettice writes, that's all. And you know perfectly well my father is still furious about the coach company. Not that I care; we made the money on the deal, not him. Lettice thinks it's a scream.'

'If you're feeling so lonely out here, Thora, we could go into York and stay at a hotel for a week. You could visit all your friends, show them Lydia. She's such a darling, they'll be thrilled to see her.'

Thora frowned. 'Really, Alice. I keep saying this and you keep saying that. We go round in circles.' She leaned on the back of a chair as if placing a barrier between them and took a deep breath. 'I want you to know, Alice, that I've never really had any friends. I'm not a demonstrative person.' A pink blush visited her fair cheeks for a second as she continued. 'I never really got along very well with my family, except for Lettice, but she gets on with everyone.'

She sighed. 'What I'm trying to say is that you are a nice person. A really nice person. Oh dear, this is so embarrassing, but you have been so patient with me and so good to Lydia and to me that I felt I had to speak before I go. I don't want you to think badly of me.'

Astonished, Alice jumped up and put her arms about Thora. 'Goodness me, Thora, you're family. I'm very fond of you. Why would I not be?'

But Thora was in tears. 'This is your house, Alice. Not mine. I was terrified when I first met you that you'd give me a bad time, but you haven't. You love it here, I hate it. I have to go.' She sniffled into a handkerchief. 'Do you think I could have a glass of wine? It's after five o'clock.'

'I think we both could have one. What about the claret? It's your favourite and it will cheer us up.'

'Something has to.'

As she prepared the tray with the decanter and glasses on a white damask cloth with savoury biscuits, the way Thora had taught her to serve visitors, Alice prayed that Clem would come home. She knew she was losing control of the situation. But she also knew her brother. When he made up his mind to do something, he did it. Nothing would turn him aside. He had gone to the goldfields to make money with his wife's blessing, and there he would stay until he had succeeded. Obviously, having drawn money from their account some months back, he hadn't any luck, but now the tide had turned. Clem knew as well as she did that Thora wanted more out of life than years on an isolated property and he was working towards that end. If it hadn't been for Thora he probably wouldn't have cared about the gold. But there it was, and Alice also knew that if she confronted her sister-in-law with that argument she'd simply drive a wedge between them.

She'd have to be very careful, because Clem was in a no-win situation. If he came home now, life at Lancoorie would go on as planned. They would have to irrigate a lot more of their land to take on more stock and work the property at its full capacity, and that would take years.

If he stayed chasing the gold, he'd lose his wife.

Alice poured the wine. 'Let's drink to us, you and me,' she said cheerily, but the toast ended in a dismal silence as the sun drooped beyond the vast scrub.

'George should be home soon,' Thora said absently.

'No. He's fencing the Postle boundary. They can afford it now, so we have to go halves. He's staying over there tonight.'

'Oh.'

Alice swallowed the rich claret. She didn't care for it herself, she much preferred white wine these days, but anything to please.

'Now let's get this straight,' she said. 'You want to go somewhere. And York is out. So what do you have in mind?'

'Perth. I want to live in Perth. I'll rent a house there until he buys me one.'

'Lord, Thora. Apart from the fact that this would be rather expensive, have you thought of me? I couldn't live here with just George. Good God, I'm not particular about proprieties, but that's a bit much. To use your own expression, what would people say?'

'Don't worry, I've thought of that. You'll have to come with me. We'll go, all three of us. We'll have a wonderful time, just you and me and Lydia.'

'But I don't like cities.'

'Oh, go on. You haven't tried cities, and everyone says Perth is the most beautiful place in the world. All the important families in the west live there.'

Alice shook her head. 'You know I wouldn't do that.'

Thora shrugged. 'I'm sorry, Alice, I've made you the offer. I want you to come with me, but if you can't, I do understand. Which doesn't alter the fact that I am leaving as soon as I can get packed. I am taking the baby and moving to Perth. I will, of course, let you know where I am. I will stay at a hotel until I can find a house.'

'And what will you do for money?'

Thora's face hardened. 'As long as I have been here I have been content for you to run the finances, since my husband seems also content with that arrangement, but as the actual mistress of Lancoorie, I doubt you would or could in all honesty deprive me of upkeep.'

'No, I would never do that.'

'The two amounts that my husband has forwarded from Kalgoorlie are not inconsiderable. Half of those amounts should go to me, for a start. But that's beside the point. Don't let me down, Alice. I cannot stay and that's that. You are not the sort of person who would force me to remain here from lack of money, and I expect to live in Perth in such modest style as I am accustomed to.'

'Oh my God! What will Clem say?'

'That is not your problem. You can tell him where to find me and our baby in Perth.'

'Can I not dissuade you, at least until Clem comes home?'

'No.'

Alice was in tears when they left, and Thora did feel sorry for her. Apart from the family disruption, Thora knew how much her sister-in-law loved Lydia and how much she would miss the baby, but she had made the offer. There was nothing more that she could do. Or maybe there was.

George had been seconded to drive her into York, with the baby snug behind them in the gig, and he too was depressed that Thora was making such a move. He took the opportunity on the long drive to try to talk her out of it.

'It's not right, Mrs Price. If you're unhappy, you should wait until Clem comes home and talk it out with him.'

Thora, furnished with a purse of crisp notes and a holiday mood, chose not to take offence. 'Oh, George! Don't be so tragic! Who said I'm unhappy? I'm just going to Perth. It's not the end of the world.'

He stared gloomily ahead. 'It's not next door either, missus.

And what with Clem hundreds of miles in the other direction, he's not going to like it.'

'Nonsense!' Thora retied the bow on her best blue bonnet and smiled brightly. 'He'll be glad to see city lights after those awful goldfields. Although I don't know how they can be much worse than here, the dust this year is appalling. Worse than I've ever known. We badly need rain too.' She laughed. 'But not now, please God. I don't want this suit ruined.'

As the gig spun along the sandy road, she was lulled to silence by the monotony of the plains until they turned on to the road into York.

'I asked Alice to come with me,' she said, 'but our Miss Price wouldn't leave Lancoorie.'

'She knows her place,' George grunted, and just then an idea struck Thora. She was cross with herself that she hadn't thought of it before, and now time was running out.

'Alice is a very nice woman,' she announced.

'That she is.'

'It will be awkward for her now with just the two of you out there. Especially if my husband comes on to Perth.'

George set his jaw hard in an expression of irritation, and slapped the reins harder, but Thora was not to be deterred.

'You like Alice?'

'Who would not?' he snapped.

'That's true, but the poor thing is doomed to live a very lonely life back there.'

'She don't seem to think so.'

'Of course not. But she'll be hard put to find a husband, since she rarely socialises, and then there's her limp.'

'What's that got to do with it?'

Thora turned to him with her most angelic smile. 'Nothing, when it comes to a kind man like you. Why don't you marry Alice?'

He shot up in his seat as if he'd been jabbed with a hatpin. 'What? Me marry Miss Price? What are you up to now, missus? It wouldn't do at all.'

'And why not? We're not in the Old Country now. You get

along well. I think it would be a good match, and I'm entitled to my opinion.'

'You are that, but it's Alice's opinion that counts.'

'Ha! I knew it! You are keen on Alice! Well, I've said my piece. Even if Alice did marry someone else it would be a wrench for her to leave Lancoorie. If you married her, everyone would be happy.'

She could see he was relieved to be driving her down the main street of York, to be rid of her and this conversation, so she left it at that, sitting grandly in her stylish blue travelling suit as they passed familiar faces.

Thora had timed the drive carefully to connect with the Northam coach, so that she couldn't call at home. She wouldn't dream of admitting to any of the family that she was bored silly with Lancoorie. They'd be full of questions, wondering why she was off to Perth without her husband, even for a holiday. It would be more fun to send them postcards. The girls would be absolutely green.

Once settled in a good seat by the window, facing the front, Thora smiled with delight. She prayed that George and Alice would marry; that would give her the perfect excuse not to live at Lancoorie. She knew Clem. When he came home he would hotfoot it to Perth to find her and then, if that marriage was in the air, they could both leave Lancoorie behind them for good.

She looked down at Lydia, who was gurgling in her basket and being fussed over by two women passengers, and was pleased with herself for making this move at last. As the coach raced towards Northam, one of the women leaned forward. 'Have you been visiting York too, dear?'

'No, I'm on my way to catch the train to Perth.'

'On your own?'

'Yes.'

The woman adjusted her spectacles and peered at Thora. 'I don't know what the world's coming to. In my day young ladies never travelled unaccompanied.'

Thora returned her gaze. 'I'll be quite all right. I believe the train is very comfortable.'

'Really? Then you have been mightily misinformed. It might have been so before the rush, but now the journey is a nightmare, shockingly overcrowded.'

'I won't have to worry, I'll be travelling first class.'

'Then you'll enjoy the company of the worst type of riff-raff and vulgarians returning from the goldfields. The other carriages will be packed solid with unfortunates who've lost everything out west but who can scrape up enough pennies to get aboard the train. Take my advice, get the next coach home.'

'I can't,' Thora said tersely.

'Where's your husband?'

'In Perth,' she lied.

'Then you'd be wise to telegraph him and tell him to come and fetch you. My sister, Mrs Cowper here, would not object, I am sure, if I offered you the hospitality of our home in Northam until he arrives. A country girl like you can't be left wandering the streets . . .'

'Indeed not,' Mrs Cowper said. 'Not with that little baby. The hotels would not be fitting, even if you could find a room.'

Thora was slightly taken aback at being referred to as a country girl, when she was sure she was dressed in the height of fashion. Their warnings were making her nervous, but she was still determined to continue on to Perth.

As it turned out, she was grateful to be able to spend several hours at their house near the station, to freshen up and feed Lydia, when the women discovered that the train was late. Even then it was only because Mrs Cowper knew the station-master that Thora managed to obtain a ticket on the crowded train, and as they helped her on board she shared their dismay, and almost backed out.

Her fellow passengers were a raucous mob, many of them smelling suspiciously of liquor. The men were a motley lot, some in ragged, dusty clothes, others well dressed, even wearing top hats. The women were a gaudy, noisy collection in fancy dresses and huge hats that seemed to Thora more appropriate for the stage.

'Don't talk to anyone,' Mrs Cowper whispered.

'And don't accept any refreshments from them,' her sister warned. 'If you have any trouble, pull that red cord and stop the train,' was her fleeting advice as the whistle blew and they retreated to the rear of the platform to wave Thora off.

She looked up at the red cord and knew that even if there was a murder on this train, she'd never dare touch it, and she cringed into her corner as the train gathered speed, trying not to notice that the revellers were already producing bottles of liquor.

As usual Lydia attracted attention, unwanted by her mother in this company, and an awful painted woman decided to befriend the young lady with 'the kid', embarrassing Thora even more.

Those women were right, she thought miserably, these are the most vulgar, dreadful people I've ever encountered. For once she was not impressed that several of the men were very much taken with her, inviting her to join the party, calling her 'my beauty' and causing others to look over at her with undisguised interest.

Rather than risk offence, Thora smiled as sweetly as she could manage and, shaking her head, clutched Lydia to her. When the singing started, the poor child, unaccustomed to such a racket, wailed incessantly until she finally slept, exhausted. With nothing better to do, Thora stared out of the window as the train chugged into the ranges, wondering about all of these people, who were obviously celebrating success on the goldfields.

Clem's letters had given her the impression that the fields were a male outpost on the edge of the desert. It hadn't occurred to Thora that women might be out there too, especially women like this. She wasn't inclined to put a name to them, but she knew they were the sort hell-bent on leading men astray. And yet Clem hadn't mentioned any women at all in his descriptions of the place. This boisterous lot, singing with the men, were wearing satins and silks and bows and well-made hats, even if they were horribly vulgar. What would they do with clothes like that in the desert? Where did they stay? On closer examination she saw that quite a few of them, about her own age, were rather pretty, and she felt a thrust of jealousy. Was Clem – and Mike, too – mixing with women like this? Was this why he was in no hurry to come home?

Everything had seemed so simple when she'd explained her plans to Alice, who worried far too much.

'All I have to do,' she'd said, 'is to walk outside Perth station, and hire a horse cab. I've seen photos: they line up outside the railway station by the dozen, waiting for passengers. Then it will take me to the Palace Hotel, which is famous, just the best in Perth. I'll have a lovely room and servants to help me with Lydia. Nothing could be easier. I wish you'd stop wringing your hands. You'd think I was some sort of nincompoop, not capable of managing in a city.'

When the train pulled in to Perth station, all of those drunken passengers had dashed away as if there was a fire in the carriage, leaving her to struggle out and find a porter for her luggage.

It was teeming with rain and growing dark as she stood outside the station where the cabs ought to have been, but they'd all been taken by the time Thora emerged. She waited by the kerb in damp misery, buffeted by cold winds, until a porter took pity on her and went to find transport.

A town clock was bonging six and Lydia was crying again when the kindly cab driver delivered them into the mayhem of the foyer of Thora's palace of dreams. Ladies swished by her in stunning gowns, and gentlemen in evening dress detoured around the woman with a mound of luggage and a baby on her hip. Thora was tall enough to see a fine staircase over the sea of faces, and a magnificent chandelier above that, but at this level she was just stuck in the crowd and it was another struggle to push her way through to the reception desk, where, when she was finally noticed, she was told the hotel was full and she would have to go elsewhere.

'Where?' she asked desperately, but everyone was too busy to reply or to care. Then she realized that all the other people beside her were also clamouring for rooms, some even offering the clerk money.

Finally she retreated to a sofa against the far wall, trying to hush the baby, trying to think what to do next.

A porter approached her. 'Excuse me, madam. Is that your luggage?'

'Yes. And I'd like a room, please.'

'I think you've already been told there are no rooms. And that luggage is inconveniencing people.'

She looked over to see that her basket, hatbox and two heavy suitcases certainly were in the way. People were stumbling over them, and that gave her some small pleasure. Serve them right.

'So they are,' she said haughtily. 'You'd better shift them.'

'I'll call you a hansom cab,' he replied, 'so that you may take your luggage and leave.'

Thora was shocked. 'How dare you tell me to leave, you rude fellow! Where am I supposed to go? Are there any other decent hotels in this town?'

'Not that would have spare rooms on a Saturday night,' he said calmly. 'Or any other night, these times. Could I suggest a boarding house?'

'A boarding house!' Thora was appalled. The only boarding house in York took in itinerant workmen, like shearers! She burst into tears.

Nonplussed, the liveried porter glanced about him, no doubt hoping that none of the other guests had noticed this sad little drama that was spoiling the tone of the Palace. But a gentleman did approach, and stood staring at the weeping woman.

'For heaven's sake. Thora Price! What's the matter?'

Thora looked up at the elegant gentleman with hair slightly greying at the temples and a small, trim moustache. 'I'm afraid I don't know you, sir.'

'Of course you do! Edgar Tanner, at your service! What's the problem?'

Then she recognized him. Mr Tanner! The bank manager from York. The one who'd run off on his wife! But he looked so much smarter and well-to-do! However, she thought swiftly, any port in a storm . . .

'Oh, Mr Tanner. I'm so pleased to see you. I'm in a dreadful fix.' He listened quietly as she poured out her troubles, and eventually offered a solution.

'We can't have you galloping out into the night with young Miss Price here in need of care, Thora. You can have my suite.'

'Thank you, but I couldn't do that. Where would you sleep?'

'Don't worry about me, I'll have someone else move up. We're all friends here.'

In no time she was spirited up to his two-room suite, a bedroom and sitting room, as she had expected to have. He even ordered a cot for the baby while he collected a few of his own things.

'I believe Clem is doing very well,' he said.

'Yes. His goldmine is succesful. And about time. I was almost giving up on him ever finding gold.'

Tanner coughed. 'His goldmine, eh? I must look into it when I go back to the fields.'

'Did you see Clem out there?' she asked.

'Oh yes, several times. I visited him in hospital when he was speared and called on him quite often after that, when time permitted.'

'When he was what?'

'Um! I think I might have put my foot in it. You didn't know?'

'He hurt his arm, that's all.'

'Rather more than that, my dear, but he's over it now. Tell you what, why don't you and the baby get yourselves settled down for the night? Just tell the maids what you need and have them bring you up a nice dinner as well.'

'Gracious! That would be heaven. I don't know how to thank you.'

'No need.' He took her hands. 'Old friends should stick together. Why don't you have lunch with me tomorrow and we'll catch up on all the news?'

Thora was thrilled. 'I'd love to, but there's the baby . . .'

'Speak to the maids. They'll find someone to assist you. I'll call for you at one, if that's convenient?'

'Oh! Goodness. Yes, that would be wonderful.'

When he left, she swanned about the big sitting room in ecstasy, then, collecting herself, pushed the brass button on the wall to call for service. This was how it should be. This was city living at last! Thora applied herself to the next vexing question, of what to wear for luncheon tomorrow, when she'd be sure to meet other elegant people. Mr Tanner had improved since his York days. Maybe he had found gold too. It was all as exciting as she'd known it would be. Perth was a wonderful place.

Chapter Nine

Mike Deagan stood at the head of their mine, known as S Block 75, and watched the prospector examining the deep trench.

'Give it to the poor bugger,' he said to Clem.

'No. You don't give away your luck.'

'What luck? It wouldn't keep a man in socks. Jesus, man, we don't need the money, the Black Cat's a goldmine in itself.'

The brothel was still a sore point with Clem. It was making money, a great deal of money, with Jocelyn proving to be an excellent manager – he refused to refer to her as the madame. For weeks he'd anguished over being associated with such a business, but he couldn't bring himself to relinquish his share while Mike kept crowing about the burgeoning profits. Instead, he just went along with the arrangements, accepting Mike as a full partner when he solemnly handed him two hundred and fifty pounds, half of the purchase price, that he'd borrowed from someone. Easily repaid from his share of the first month's takings.

Clem knew he should have demanded complete ownership, since his money had bought the business, but it salved his conscience a little to be only a partner. Besides, Mike was such a gregarious character that the Black Cat soon came to be known as Mike's place, the other partner forgotten. That suited Clem, who was no longer seen there.

At the end of the month he was astonished to learn that the brothel was grossing a thousand pounds a week, as Mike had declared it would, so Clem began sending money orders to Alice, with notes saying the mine was doing better.

But then Mike had another idea. 'We have to rebuild the

brothel, Clem, or we'll get left behind. Kalgoorlie's getting too rich for a rough old place like that.'

'It's making money, why bother?'

'Come on now. You can see what's happening in the town. The old corrugated-iron walls painted white inside might have been genteel in a canvas-and-hessian town, but not any more. The lads will move on as soon as someone builds a decent brothel . . .'

'Is there any such thing?'

Mike ignored his remark. 'There are builders here, and plenty of labourers down on their luck. We've got enough cash to go for a fine house, two storeys, with a veranda looking over the main street. Stop sending money home for a while, and then you can double up.'

The argument raged for days, with Mike demanding that Clem buy him out so that he could rebuild, but now Clem didn't want that either. 'Do what you like!' he said, rather than admit that financially it was a very sensible move.

'I'll give you a fiver!' the prospector called from the trench.

'Not on your life,' Clem retorted. 'That mine's still showing.'

'Then why are you selling?'

'Because he doesn't need it,' Mike said.

But Clem was persistent. 'Twenty.'

'I'll give you ten. No more.'

'Done,' Mike said. 'He'll take ten.'

Clem shrugged. 'All right. Ten.'

When the papers were signed over, Clem took Mike aside. 'Get the horses, I want to show you something.'

'What?'

'You'll see. While you've been harrying those builders, I've been prospecting. I've staked a new claim ten miles south of the town.'

'Not in the blacks' country again?'

'No. I've told you dozens of times. It was my own fault I got speared. I wandered on to one of their sacred sites.'

'Maybe so, but there's still a lot of blackfellers out there none too pleased they've lost their hunting grounds.'

'Do you want to see it or not?'

'I suppose I'd better or you'll nag me to death.'

'You talk about nagging! I've got nothing but nag from you, from the day you took on the Black Cat. We're still miners, remember?'

They rode out into undulating scrub country scattered with salmon gums, past the desolate remnants of isolated camps, where other miners had tried their luck and failed.

'What's the point of this?' Mike said. 'This scrub has been turned over.'

'I just went that bit further.'

Near a low-lying mound of granite, Clem pointed to a shallow soak. 'See, we've even got water. That's why I stopped here and started nosing about.'

They dismounted and Clem strode over to where he'd left an old faded shirt hanging from a branch. 'Come on, it's a hundred yards direct east from here.'

As he paced out, with Mike following reluctantly, he was still talking. 'I wandered about, seeing nothing of interest, and finally I sat down and tapped a few rocks. I was just about ready to give up when I chipped some quartz.' He bent over and dug two pieces of rock out of the earth. 'So I split this fellow, and then I buried it again quick. Take a look.'

'God help us!' Mike almost fell on the glowing white quartz streaked with gold. 'Jesus! You've done it! Is there any more?'

'I don't know, I haven't looked.' Clem was jigging about with excitement now that his secret was out. 'But it was worth staking a claim, wouldn't you say?'

'Right here? You found it right here?'

'Yes. I reckon we ought to bore a hole in the quartz here and fire it, to see what we've really got.'

'God Almighty! When did you find this?'

'A while back. But I wanted to sell that mine first, otherwise the others would think it suspicious that we just upped and left it, even though it's poor. We don't want anyone following us out here yet. I went to see the warden and claimed an acre.'

'An acre? What's to be done with all that land?'

'A precaution, that's all. I've drawn up a rough map with the trees marked. So. Are you in?'

'Try and keep me out.'

Clem strode about, pleased with himself. 'I've named the claim Yorkey.'

'It'll be tough work here,' Mike commented, kicking at the rocky ground, 'but worth a go, lad. I'd say there's a couple of hundred pounds you've got there already. We'd better keep it under wraps for a while.'

The following day they packed their wagon and left the tent settlement, driving casually through the town and then heading south, well off the beaten tracks, to take up the Yorkey claim.

One side of the hole had a bank of similar gold-bearing quartz that sent them scrambling for their picks, and soon Yorkey mine was a reality. The rocks they collected from around the mine were stowed under brush, away from the soak where they'd pitched their tent, in case anyone came by, and day by day they added more to their supply.

It was hard work, battling rock, and at times just as heartbreaking as the other mine. The first good bank soon ran out, but they had to keep going, searching relentlessly for even the smallest lump of the elusive quartz, cursing the vagaries of nature.

'Why couldn't He have put it all in the same place?' Mike groaned.

'He probably did, then the earth convulsed and crunched, just to make it hard for us.'

Once a week, they took it in turns to ride into town for supplies, the other guarding their store of quartz. When it was Clem's turn, he posted his letters and looked in vain for a letter from Thora, but as usual the one envelope only contained Alice's weekly report. After leaving his order at a general store – including new picks, since Yorkey was as hard on the metal as it was on their muscles – he marched down to check on the progress of the new building. To himself, he admitted curiosity, but this inspection was being made on a promise to Mike, who had threatened him he'd throw the Yorkey area wide open if Clem did not do his duty as part-owner.

When he saw the skeleton of the building going up, Clem was impressed that the builders were making such good time. He'd imagined that it would take months to erect from the plan, with good timber in short supply. But then he remembered that Mike had said something about placing themselves first in line with the Afghan camel drivers whose teams brought in heavy loads.

'The villain! He bribed them,' Clem muttered to himself as he climbed about, examining the timbers and testing stays, wondering how much extra that had cost.

The carpenters, obviously accustomed to curious visitors, took no notice of him, for which Clem was grateful. He could see no reason to confer with the boss, since all appeared to be going according to plan, and was just about to leave the premises when Jocelyn arrived, throwing her arms about him.

'Clem! How marvellous to see you. Where's Mike? God, you look so well! And there we were a while back, scared stiff you'd go and die on us. I reckon you look better now than you ever did back home.' She squeezed his arms. 'Look at you. You've got muscles I bet you never knew you had.'

He noticed the grins of the workmen as the now well-known Kalgoorlie madame, dressed for the part in a large feathered hat that matched her incredible lime and black dress, made such a fuss of him.

'We're prospecting,' he said, anxious to move on, but Jocelyn would have none of that.

'Come and have a drink with me,' she said gaily, taking his arm. 'You've been too much the stranger.'

She sensed his reticence. 'No, come on. I insist. I'd never have got the job running the Black Cat if it hadn't been for you. I know you put Mike up to asking me. I can see your hand behind it all. Mike's the front man, but you're the brains. I never tell people that; Mike said you'd prefer to stay quiet on the sidelines and you don't have to spell it out for me. Wouldn't they have a fit in York if they knew what we were up to!'

On that he had to agree. 'They certainly would. What on earth did you tell your family?'

'That I'm cooking in a hotel. What have you told Thora?'

'Oh, Christ, nothing. Mike got me involved in all this.'

'Never mind. We're mates. Our secrets are safe. But it's good of you to pay the girls while we wait for the Black Cat to open up again. They're the best, and I'd have lost them otherwise.'

'I did?' he said weakly as she dragged him into a new hotel across the road. It was easier to go with her than stand out there, publicly, and argue.

Trying to retain some dignity when they were esconced in the saloon bar, separate from the noisy public bar, he insisted on buying the drinks, and as he ordered her gin and his whisky, Clem realized that the layout of this hotel was almost identical to his own place across the road, except that the street front of the hotel featured bars, while 'his' building had a small foyer and spaces that Mike called reception rooms either side of the front door. It occurred to him that they could easily turn the Black Cat into a hotel, but even he knew that a brothel was a much better investment than a pub in a town where males out-numbered females more than twenty to one.

'Where are you prospecting?' she asked.

'Just out of town.'

She laughed. 'That was a silly question, wasn't it? Are you staying over tonight?'

'No, I have to get back.' He drank the fiery whisky, realizing he'd forgotten to ask for 'the good', because this was definitely the bad stuff, and stood. 'I'm sorry, Jocelyn, but I have to pick up our supplies. I really must go.' He saw her disappointment and relented enough to pat her on the shoulder reassuringly. 'Mike says you're doing an excellent job managing the business.'

She cheered up considerably. 'Why, thank you, Clem, I appreciate that. You can trust me, you know, I won't be skimming cash like a lot do out here. I take my pay and the rest goes in the bank.'

232

'Of course, I wouldn't think otherwise of you. And you can look forward to a bonus at Christmas.'

He grinned as he headed back up the street. If Mike could throw money about, so could he. And Jocelyn was *his* friend. It was important to keep her on his side.

They considered building a primitive kiln to extract the gold themselves, but that meant hiring labourers to keep the work going and thus complicating the ownership of the gold, so there was nothing for it but to take their precious heaps of rocks and stones to a government plant in Kalgoorlie. They hired a horse and dray and hauled in the first load on the day they had chosen for the gala opening of the new Black Cat.

It was a fine building, painted white, with gutterings, veranda posts and railings picked out in brown, a prim façade that belied the gaudy interior. Clem had taken fright at the preponderance of red plush, but Jocelyn was quick to tell him that it was all cheap stuff.

'The girls dyed it,' she said. 'This town is so drab, the lads appreciate a bit of colour.'

From the street the 'house' looked bigger than it really was, due to the blinding white paint, but it conformed with the common trend of new buildings in Hannan Street; a blessing, Clem thought, relieved.

To please Jocelyn, he did attend the celebrations for a while, mingling with the crowd. Mike took on the role of master of ceremonies, thoroughly enjoying himself, as a pianist pounded on a tinny piano and a fiddler raced ahead at his own pace. He introduced all the girls, who were dressed in their finery, serving free food that they had prepared, and parried calls for free drinks.

'You'd be joking, me friends,' he laughed. 'I don't want the place wrecked on the first night.'

Having done his duty, Clem retreated to the pub over the road, where he'd taken a room, more interested in the results from the plant that would be revealed the following day.

★　　★　　★

Yorkey mine was a far better proposition than their previous workings, but even so Clem was disappointed at the return on the ore.

'Why such a long face?' the plant manager said. 'You've hit paydirt, Clem. Three hundred ounces of fine gold! How long have you been working Yorkey?'

'A while,' Clem said, calculating what he could probably get for the gold once it went on the scales at the bank. Somewhere around a thousand pounds. They'd hoped their quartz would produce a lot more gold, carried away by the glint of it.

He took cash for the gold, twelve hundred pounds and nine shillings. Then he went back and paid the plant manager, after which he needed time to think, so he drifted over to a pie shop and settled on a bench by the side door to eat his breakfast.

Greed, that's what it is, he told himself, as he munched on a large meat pie doused in Worcester sauce. Just sheer greed.

He was depressed, and very much aware that if their first mine had returned such a sum so soon, with more to be gained, he'd have been over the moon. A thousand pounds was a great deal of money. To receive such a gift from the earth was normally every man's dream, but this town, with its constant talk of gold and money, money and gold, had thrown normality out of the window. Added to which, the profits of the Black Cat far outshone the glow of success from Yorkey. Clem knew that he had lost perspective. He had become a front-runner in the game of greed, sitting nonchalantly with a small fortune in his pocket.

He stood up and made a decision as he left the shop. I'm going home. It's time to go. It's not fair to Thora to have her husband away so long.

There were men at Kalgoorlie now from all over the world, men who had left their wives and families behind. They could be away for years, and that too was insidious. Time meant nothing in the search for gold, the end result was all that mattered. Until now, Clem hadn't given a thought to staying on, postponing his return month by month. Kalgoorlie was like that. Only the losers surrendered before the race was run.

That's it, he vowed as he went in search of Mike. Time's up. I'm getting out of here.

Still smarting from her ignominious arrival at the Palace Hotel, Thora Price was determined to make up for it on this glorious Sunday morning. She was up early, quizzing the housemaids on all manner of things.

She discovered that the hotel served midday dinner on Sundays and high tea at six, and to her delight, the noon gathering was a well-known social occasion.

'Everyone that's anyone comes to the Palace on Sundays,' they told her proudly. 'And the ladies dress to the teeth, trying to outdo each other.'

'We used to be better known for our afternoon teas,' an older maid said. 'They were lovely, so refined, but that's gone by the board these days, the big spenders stay too long over lunch. It's the gold, you see: the gentlemen are either fresh from the goldfields, or connected with them somehow through the big companies.'

They were interrupted by the housekeeper, who introduced herself as Miss Devane. She was a stylish, grey-haired woman, an authoritative person who did not fit Thora's experience of housekeepers, not like a servant at all.

Miss Devane was not pleased with the haphazard arrangements regarding this room that had been thrust on her.

'Who is occupying twenty-six, might I ask? You, madam, or Mr Tanner?'

'I am.'

'Then why are his effects still here?'

Thora knew she could not allow this woman to intimidate her, and that a tantrum would not work. Miss Devane would have been challenged by stronger women than her. Even though she resented the attitude of a woman who was, after all, a servant, she resorted to the time-honoured honey to deal with vinegar.

'Oh, Miss Devane. I'm so pleased you've come. I'm in such a tangle! It's so difficult to be in this awkward situation with my baby to care for as well.'

'Yes, I heard you have a child with you.' The reply was terse, and then Thora realized there was more to the housekeeper's cold attitude.

'Oh!' she said, startled. 'Good Lord, I hope you don't think Mr Tanner and I are sharing?'

'One doesn't know what to think.'

'No! Heavens, no. I came here last night, after a long journey by train, looking forward to taking a lovely room at the Palace, only to find there were none available. I was devastated. It was then that Mr Tanner came forward, with the kindliest intentions, and allowed me to have his rooms. He has taken accommodation elsewhere.'

'You came here by train? From where?'

'Northam.'

'I see. From the goldfields.'

Thora was shocked. And angry. Evidently this person was lumping her with the sort of women she'd suffered on the train. How dare she? Nevertheless, in her determination to remain in the hotel, either in this room or another, Thora remained calm.

'Why the goldfields? I couldn't think of anything worse. My husband and I own Lancoorie sheep station outside of York. It's a sad state of affairs, I think, when country people can't come to Perth and expect to be treated with civility. Instead, I stumbled into a foyer that was more like a cattle sale. Of course, I suppose, it's my own fault. I said I was capable of coming on ahead, before my husband, who is frightfully busy, to settle into a nice room at the Palace and start looking about. We intend to purchase another house in Perth. But that's beside the point. I'm afraid I've made a mess of things. I can just hear him now . . . "I told you so." But I did try. Women should exert themselves, don't you think?'

Miss Devane's face softened. 'York? You're from York? My father was the Mayor of York.'

'Was he? I thought the name was familiar,' Thora lied.

'Long before your time, Mrs Price.'

'Perhaps my father mentioned him. Dr Carty.'

'Dr Carty. Dear me, I remember him. How could I not?

236

He attended my dear father, and your mother was very kind to me. She had a young baby at the time . . .'

'I'm the eldest of the girls, that must have been me,' Thora enthused. 'What a small world it is.'

'Was,' Miss Devane said, sadly. 'My father was a widower. When he passed away I came to Perth to earn my living. Men who give their all to public life in a voluntary manner, as did Mayor Devane, leave little for their families.' With a wave of her hand she dusted that aside. 'But as I was saying, here in the west it used to be a small world. Everyone knew everyone, but since the gold, my dear, we're inundated by strangers. They're pouring in at a rate of a thousand a week, heading for the goldfields, and one hardly dares mention what returns, their pockets stuffed with new money.'

From that morning Thora led a charmed life at the Palace. Miss Devane arranged for her to keep the suite, since Mr Price would be arriving shortly. Thora hadn't counted on having to pay for a double room, but since her new friend instructed someone in the depths of the hotel to forward all her accounts to Lancoorie Station via York, there was no need to think about money. One just signed. Which was as well, since Miss Devane advised her that it was usual for ladies travelling with babies to have their own nursemaids, who were put up in the staff rooms next door to the hotel.

By Monday morning Miss Devane had searched through her list of stand-by staff and assigned a young girl called Netta as Lydia's permanent nursemaid.

But in the interim other matters had to be sorted out. The housekeeper was curious about Tanner.

'Do you know this gentleman?'

'Of course. He was our bank manager. In York.'

'Oh. Well, you should have said. You mustn't take up with strangers. Not that I have anything against Mr Tanner, it was very courteous of him, and I'll see that he has a decent room. He's quite well known in Perth, a stockbroker.'

'Is he really? I was so flustered I didn't ask.' Thora resisted a giggle. Her very proper mentor obviously had lost touch with York or she'd have known that Mr Tanner was a wife-deserter.

Not that Thora cared. The Carty girls had always regarded Mrs Tanner as a battleaxe.

She stood aside as the flurry of removing all of Tanner's effects took place under Miss Devane's supervision, and her clothes were unpacked, pressed and closeted. Such luxury, Thora thrilled, forgetting that Alice did all of her laundering at home.

Another maid was given nursemaid duties for the day, on a temporary basis, for which Thora was grateful.

'It'll go on your bill.' Miss Devane shrugged. 'Now, is there anything else?'

'Yes. I hope you don't mind me asking you this. But Mr Tanner is a good friend of my husband's. Seeing that I was on my own, and looking such a fool, Mr Tanner invited me to lunch today, to cheer me up. And now I'm alarmed. The chambermaids tell me that ladies dress up here for Sunday dinner. We never dress up on Sundays. You know that. What on earth should I wear?'

Miss Devane was up to the challenge. She strode into the bedroom and opened the wardrobe.

'Well now, let me see.'

As she examined her outfits, Thora added: 'I'd hate to look countrified.'

'Not with these clothes you won't, my dear. You have excellent taste, which can't be said for the majority of our new patrons.'

'I buy them by catalogue and my sister-in-law alters them to fit me.'

'What about this?' Miss Devane took out a cream silk dress buttoned through to a high collar overlaid with fine lace. It had a nipped-in waist, and a gently flowing long skirt.

'Don't you think it's rather plain?'

'Not plain, my dear. Elegant. Do you have a hat to match?'

'Yes. Several.'

When Edgar Tanner marched up the stairs to collect Thora Price he was regretting not the offer of his suite – a man could hardly do less, and besides, he had been allocated instead a front room with a veranda over the street, far more interesting than the highly priced suites along the side of the hotel – no, he was regretting having invited her to dine with him, forgetting that the morrow was Sunday, since he'd been slightly inebriated when he'd made the grand gesture.

This Sunday dinner was important and today, of all days, Lord Kengally was due to attend. He was yet another of the English aristocracy, representatives of big syndicates, recently arrived in Perth in the wake of Lord Fingall, who had invested in the fabulous Londonderry mine south of Coolgardie, a quartz blow.

Tanner had discovered he hadn't the muscle nor the perseverance of a gold miner, so he had turned to stockbroking and promoting. He had offices in Kalgoorlie and in Perth, under the bold title of E.G. Tanner & Co., and he was doing fairly well, but he kept missing out on the big one, which had to come along sooner or later. With the optimism of a gambler he was sure it would happen, and the best way was to guide men like Kengally to his own projects. To do that, he needed to keep the newcomers happy.

He soon saw that Kengally was a sociable fellow, fond of good food and wine and bright company, so Tanner was hosting this Sunday dinner. The three other men were high-level public servants from the Mines Department, not averse to grand company, jolly good times and free meals, especially when the host indicated they were welcome to bring along their girlfriends and another lady to entertain Lord Kengally. Tanner had met these four ladies before: definitely not the type you'd take home to Mother, but good sports who could be relied upon to make this function a very gay occasion.

But Thora Price! Good God! What had he been thinking of? She'd be like a fish out of water in this company, not being known for her wit and humour, even in a dreary little country town like York, where there was no competition.

But there was no retreating now, so he knocked lightly on her door.

When she emerged, he was taken aback. The tearful woman

clutching her baby in the foyer had been transformed into a composed, willowy beauty. She'd always been a good-looking young girl, he had to admit, but now she looked gorgeous. It crossed his mind that marriage and motherhood agreed with Mrs Price. She'd improved out of sight.

'My dear, you look charming,' he said spontaneously.

'Thank you, Mr Tanner, that's very kind of you.'

He could see she was excited. The flawless skin had a slight becoming blush and her lovely blue eyes danced, but her voice gave no indication that the country girl had stars in her eyes at this, her first outing in Perth.

As he descended the stairs with her, Tanner was aware that this stately blonde, elegant in cream silk and a large hat that bore a garland of apricot-coloured roses, was gaining quite a bit of attention. Women glanced and glanced again, men smiled her way, eyes followed her as they made for the dining room.

'I have several other guests,' he said, 'including a British lord. I hope you don't mind.'

That was a mistake. Thora pulled back in fright. 'A what? You should have told me. I wouldn't know what to say.'

Edgar could believe that. 'Well, just smile.' He almost had to drag her across the room, where he inspected his table with care. 'What do you think? Does it look all right?'

She gazed at the round table set for ten, with its fine napery and silver. 'It looks wonderful. Is this your party?'

'Yes, we'll sit here, and I'll put Lord Kengally beside you.'

'No. Put him down the other end,' she cried frantically.

'I can't do that. He's the guest of honour. Here he comes now.' He nodded towards the head waiter, who was escorting a group of people in their direction.

'Which one?' she whispered.

'The old fellow in the white duck suit. To the English it's what one wears in the tropics, I believe, so don't comment on it.'

She bristled. 'I wouldn't dream of commenting.'

He could see she was still very nervous when the others

gathered at the table to be seated, because she was fidgeting with her gloves as she took in the other women, who had really dressed to be noticed in a gala of colours.

'I feel a frump,' she whispered to him behind her handkerchief, as soon as he took his place beside her, and all he could offer in a surreptitious aside was: 'It's the other way around. You look fine.'

Fortunately, Lord Kengally thought so too, and as the courses progressed he seemed to be more charmed by the lady he took to be his hostess than by the other females. To Edgar's relief, Thora had little to say beyond being agreeable. Whether she was still in awe of the Englishman or could find nothing to offer in this jovial group, he didn't know, or care, as long as she continued to please.

By the time the main course of roast duck arrived, Edgar began to relax. In contrast to the woman on his other side, the girl from York drank sparingly. In fact, she was showing up the other women to some extent, with her quiet manners. She even seemed to be self-assured at last, although Edgar remembered, with a grin, that Miss Carty had always struck a haughty pose. Now, toned down by awe, it was rather fetching.

When the merry party broke up, Edgar was in high spirits. He had secured another meeting with Kengally and his associates to discuss the good prospects of the new Lady Luck mine at Kalgoorlie. Edgar had promised the four owners that if they kept their mine quiet, he would produce a buyer, a personage who could form a company and open up the mine in a big way. There was still so much gold on that great Kalgoorlie ridge, the days of the individual miners would soon be over. Already companies were buying up big leases, poppets were dotting the horizon like skeletal trees, and the shores of salt lakes were home to huge condensers. As he kept telling Kengally, there was still a wealth of gold underground – there had to be – and only companies with the machinery and manpower to go deep could recover it.

Lady Luck was his best bet. It was still bearing, and Edgar hoped that Kengally would be interested enough to buy not only that mine but all the surrounding leases that were still current, then go public with shares to draw in enough investment to allow a big operation to get under way. But it was a battle: there were promoters everywhere, and Kengally had been approached by several of Edgar's competitors.

The assayer would be arriving in town tonight, with a report on Lady Luck which Edgar was sure would clinch his deal.

'A delightful day, Edgar,' Kengally was saying. 'Thoroughly enjoyable, the duck à l'orange about the best I've tasted. You must dine with me here again, as my guest, and do bring the charming Mrs Price.'

'I'd be glad to,' Edgar said, a little too quickly, and Kengally frowned.

'If Mr Price has arrived by then,' the Englishman said firmly, 'I should be pleased to meet him also.'

Edgar realized then that he had made a serious mistake, providing that female partner at table for his important guest, and that Kengally was letting him know. However, it didn't seem that any harm was done, since Kengally chose to overlook the gaffe.

They arranged to meet at the National Bank in the morning.

'Ten o'clock. Will that be suitable?' Kengally asked. 'The manager has kindly agreed to allow us the use of a board room.'

'Yes,' Edgar said. 'Eminently suitable. I'll have some good news for you by then.'

Kengally turned to Thora. 'Now, Mrs Price, since we're both strangers to Perth what say we do some exploring tomorrow afternoon? That is, if Edgar can spare the time to accompany us.'

'I'd love to,' she said. 'It's very kind of you to invite me. Where would we go?'

Edgar was delighted. The more time he could spend with this man, the less time there was for other promoters to get their hands on him. 'Kings Park is very beautiful at this time of the year,' he said. 'The wild flowers are out.'

'Capital,' Kengally enthused. 'I'm an amateur botanist, you know.'

'Then you'll find Kings Park extremely interesting,' Edgar said. 'We could take a leisurely drive through – it's a large area – and then perhaps you might enjoy an afternoon picnic.'

'I adore picnics,' Thora said, 'but what should I bring? I don't know how I can prepare a picnic from a hotel room.'

Edgar laughed. 'The hotel will prepare picnic baskets for us. Would two o'clock be convenient, Mrs Price?'

That night Thora wrote to Alice to let her know that she had arrived safely, and that, despite warnings, she hadn't had a speck of trouble. Two kind ladies at Northam had delivered her and Lydia to the train and the journey to Perth had been extremely pleasant. She chewed the pen as she continued with her tale.

It was neither a lie nor a fact, she mused, any more than her intention of moving to Perth had been a lie or a fact when she'd told Alice. A holiday, permanent residence, these notions were all part of her daydream, and just because she'd stepped out into her daydream, she saw no reason why she should try to unravel her thoughts. It was too delicious the way things were. She didn't want to think past the day. If she wrote fact – that on her first day she'd dined with an English lord – that would be construed as a lie; and if she lied and said she'd had no trouble booking into pleasant rooms at the Palace Hotel, that would be accepted as fact.

'See,' she said to the page, 'I'm blessed if I know what's real any more. I'm supposed to have a husband, but he left me. Then again, I didn't much like being married anyway. And I'm a mother now, but Alice was a much better mother to Lydia than I am. Lydia will miss Alice: maybe I should have left her there instead of bringing her with me, the poor child. For some reason I associate her more with Alice than with me.'

Thora knew she was in a confused state. She had known that for quite some time, finding that hours had passed that she couldn't recall; becoming lost in the bush and having to rely on the horse to bring her home; believing that there was a man in bed with her, only never Clem. It was either Mike, kind, funny Mike, or Matt Spencer, the man who'd raped and abandoned her. She still had nightmares about him.

They'd been kissing and canoodling in the park one evening; he was so handsome, all the girls had eyes for Matt, even though he was only a stable hand. And there was something extra about him. He was strong and intense, sexy, some of the girls said, but Thora disliked the word.

He'd become angry with her, called her a tease. The park had gone quiet, people had left and she'd wanted to go home too, but he wouldn't let her, and she was too ashamed to find herself in such a predicament to call out. He'd held her down, torn at her clothes, forced himself on her. And he'd laughed when she'd gathered herself up and run from him.

But she hadn't cried, she couldn't afford to. Someone at home would have noticed her distress, and there would have been awful embarrassing questions.

Thora brushed her hand across her face as if to brush away the terrible memories of that time. She never wanted to think about it again. It was gone. Over. Buried. Except that Lydia, sleeping peacefully there in the cot the hotel had provided, was always there to remind her of the outrage she'd suffered at the hands of Matt Spencer. Sometimes she'd thought she should have let her father do what he wanted to do, to abort the pregnancy, but she'd taken so much abuse from him and from her mother that she'd refused. And besides, in her resort to daydreaming, she'd never really believed that it would happen.

Lies and fact. It was a monstrous lie against her that she had sinned grievously, and a fact that even her dreams lied, whispering that Lydia was not her baby, confusing her. It was such a relief to escape from them.

As she turned back to her page again, Thora smiled, immersed happily now in the reality of her daydream. What would they say if they knew that she'd been rescued in the hotel foyer by none other than the infamous Edgar Tanner, and that he'd invited her to hostess a divine Sunday dinner in the grand dining room of the Palace Hotel in Perth? And that she'd made a very good impression on a new friend, an English lord?

'They' was everyone back there at Lancoorie and York, and even Clem. Why should she tell them anything, allow them to intrude on her present gloriously dreamy existence in these luxurious surrounds? Even Edgar Tanner had been reviled by the people of that hated town, York. So what if he'd run off on the dreadful Mrs Tanner? And from York? Thora felt an empathy with Edgar now. He was suave and sweetly spoken, kind, as shown, and he had the sort of friends whom her mother, one of his chief detractors, would have killed for.

Oh yes, Thora decided, she and Edgar had a great deal in common.

She took up the pen again and wrote a glowing account of her first day in Perth, in this lovely hotel, where maids were about to see to her every whim, and invitations were already pouring in.

Tomorrow, she enthused to Alice, she was going sightseeing to the botanic gardens, known as Kings Park.

They're just beautiful, I'm told, she wrote. *What a shame you're not here to share my enjoyment.*

For the first time in ages Thora slept soundly. By the time she signed her name to the letter, she had convinced herself that the page was fact, and she felt very relaxed after such a pleasant day. All her former confusions, she decided, in self-analysis, could be put down to nerves. And with good reason, after what she'd endured in York. Her reputation ruined. The shock of pregnancy. The hasty, out-of-town marriage. And all the rest.

Now she was repairing those shattered nerves. Thora wished she'd come to Perth earlier. The isolation at Lancoorie had simply given her more time to dwell on the humiliations.

The esteemed visitor was ecstatic about Kings Park, referring to the large expanse overlooking Perth as a botanist's dream. This was not the type of park he was accustomed to, well designed and laid out in symmetrical terms. Instead he found the opposite, where the accent was on natural flora. The bushland had been disturbed as little as possible, and native plants and bushes had been artfully planted near paths so that the visitor could view them, while still giving the impression that they'd sprung there from seed.

Within minutes of arriving at the park, Kengally had jumped down from the gig to examine this plethora of strange plants, and his two companions were happy to join him.

Edgar was all smiles. He didn't care if Kengally walked all afternoon. The meeting had been successful, his report accepted as promising. Now he had to persuade Kengally to make a decision and come with him to the goldfields to see for himself, but the man was cautious.

'I believe it's a long and arduous journey, Tanner,' he'd said. 'With respect, one can't afford to go off on a wild-goose chase. Are you sure we can lease enough land thereabouts to make a large operation viable?'

'Certain. As shown on the section map, there are several acres still available surrounding the Lady Luck mine, with only a few individual mines within the boundaries. My main fear is that other large companies might encroach before we lodge our claim.'

'That's a chance we'll have to take. But the owners of Lady Luck have agreed to sell, haven't they? On paper?'

'Oh, yes. A copy of the option is with the other papers I left with your clerk, plus a note from the warden that he would not oppose our application.'

'But the smaller mines that remain on our proposed lease-hold . . . what if their owners won't sell?'

'Men working on their own can't go down more than a hundred feet on company land, and I believe the law is being changed to ten feet. That will force them out.'

'And create a great deal of ill-will, I don't doubt,' Kengally murmured. 'Don't you think it would be a better idea to buy them out? See what you can do, dear boy.'

Edgar knew he should go out there himself, but Kengally was the centre of his universe at the moment. Out of sight was out of mind, and he intended to stay well in sight. He solved the problem by wiring the owners of Lady Luck to sound out a couple of their neighbours.

For a portly man, Kengally was light on his feet, and as he bounded from one exotic plant to another, Thora trotted obediently beside him, looking as lovely as this fine blue day. She was wearing a graceful white dress and a straw boater with blue ribbons trailing over her sleek blonde hair. Edgar couldn't take his eyes off her.

'Are you staying at a hotel?' she asked Kengally.

'No, my dear. A friend of mine has been kind enough to allow me the use of his house while I'm in Perth. A charming residence.'

'Where is he?'

'He's taking a holiday in London with his family.'

'How wonderful. I might do that too.'

Listening, Edgar raised his eyebrows. Clem Price must be doing very well. Come to think of it, she never mentioned Clem at all. And what *was* she doing here on her own? She didn't seem to know anyone, or if she did, she wasn't in any hurry to see them.

Kengally was collecting specimens of wildflowers, but when he told her that he would press and keep them, Thora looked pained.

'Alice says that's a dreadful thing to do to plants. Cruel.'

Edgar froze, but Kengally took it in good part. 'Ah, your Alice must be a sensitive lady,' he smiled. 'But you wouldn't begrudge me taking some to show people at home how extraordinary they are, now would you?'

'Oh, no.'

They did have an enjoyable afternoon. Thora was scatty – she kept losing the collection of specimens she'd offered to carry, and Edgar was sent to retrieve them – but that only endeared her to Kengally, who found her a delight. So did Edgar, but from a different point of view. The Englishman had taken a fatherly attitude to her, while Edgar longed to touch her, to stroke that long hair, to have his hands about the slim waist, to feel the warmth of her.

When they delivered Thora to the hotel, Kengally extended another invitation. 'A friend of mine has a splendid yacht. We're sailing upriver on Thursday, a day trip to visit another old friend. A Mr Warburton. I haven't seen him for years. We're to be his guests for lunch. Would you care to join us, Mrs Price?'

She nodded vaguely. 'I think I'll be free. That will be very nice. Will it be another picnic?'

'I shouldn't think so. I believe his house is rather grand.' He turned to Edgar, as if in an afterthought. 'And you too, of course, Tanner.'

Even though he knew the invitation to him was issued merely from good manners, Edgar hung on. 'I should be delighted.'

On the morning after the gala reopening of the Black Cat, Jocelyn invited Clem to breakfast, unconcerned that several of her girls were wandering about in skimpy kimonos, and less.

'No thanks,' he grinned, eyeing them. 'They don't shine up too well in the mornings, do they?'

'Hard night,' she said wickedly. 'You must be the only bloke in town who had an early night. The takings will be a goldfield record.'

'That's good,' he managed to say, with little enthusiasm, but he spared a kind word for Jocelyn. 'You're looking well then, considering you must have been up very late.'

'Haven't been to bed yet. I've just thrown out the last customer. I like to see everything shipshape before I turn in. Are you looking for Mike?'

'Who's taking my name in vain?' Mike stuck his head in through the kitchen doorway. He tramped in, bent down and gave Jocelyn a kiss on the cheek. 'Well done, lady. That was a party to end all. And what do you think about this fella slopin' off on us?'

She was wise enough not to offer an opinion, turning back to the kettle.

'I've got the papers you wanted,' Clem said to him, with a

jerk of his head, and Mike followed him through to the front street. 'What papers?'

'For the sale of the gold.'

'You've been out and about already? What's the verdict?'

'Three hundred ounces.'

'What? That's brilliant!' He slapped Clem on the back. 'Bless you and your Yorkey, I never thought we'd bagged half that. Wait till I get my gear. We'll have to stand guard over Yorkey now that the word will be out.'

'If there's any more gold there.'

'What are you saying? Of course there'll be more. A swag of it.'

'We didn't see much the last week.'

'That doesn't mean a thing, and you know it. What's the matter with you, lad? What with this nice little business here, and Yorkey, we'll be rolling in cash.'

'I'm going home,' Clem said flatly.

'Fair enough. It's about time you went to see Thora. You've been away from the marriage bed too long. I've no quarrel with that. Once we get Yorkey . . .'

Clem interrupted him. 'No, now. Today. I'm leaving today.'

'What about the mine?' Mike was shocked.

'I couldn't care less.'

'Jesus, have you got a fit of the glooms. Hang on and we'll go to the pub and talk this over. What did you do last night, you silly bugger? Sit on your own and drink mother's ruin?'

They argued for an hour or more, once again attracting amused attention as they shouted at each other, but this time it was Mike upbraiding his partner for being a welsher.

'It's your luck found Yorkey, you have to stick with it,' Mike insisted.

'Don't be so bloody superstitious. I'm just fed up with this place. I want to go home.'

'You and a thousand more, but this is not the time.'

'I'll sell you my share.'

'Ah, no, you won't. You started it, you have to finish it.

Write to Thora and tell her you'll be home shortly. That's a start, isn't it?'

'I could sell my share to someone else.'

'And shove some loafer on to me, some Johnny-come-lately with powder-puff hands? Like hell you will. We're not a company, you don't have a share to sell without my agreement, and I won't sign.'

Clem appealed to him. 'You haven't got any ties. I have.'

In the end he agreed to stay on for a few more weeks to see if Yorkey was still bearing, on condition that they bring out an assayer for his advice, but only because Mike hit a nerve.

'It's not just Thora,' Mike said, 'think about your daughter. You two might be missing each other, but you're young and you've got the time. Don't you want the best for Lydia? The money we're making at the Black Cat won't last for ever. When the gold peters out, this place will go back to dust. You didn't come out here just to make a quid, and if you did, you're dumber than I thought. We're here for the big money. You have the chance to set the Price family on its feet for generations. Don't chuck it in now.'

Before they left town, Clem checked the post office, disappointed that there was no mail for him. Even Alice seemed to have let him down this week. But he took the time to write a letter to Thora, sitting at a table in the new post office, telling her that he was making arrangements to return home as soon as possible, and how he was yearning to see her. He sent his love also to Lydia, not that a baby would know.

Lydia had a nanny, not a nursemaid, her mother chided people, since she had picked up the word from her dear friend Lord Kengally, and Nanny had taken charge altogether, thank God, since Mrs Price *was* inundated with invitations.

First and foremost in Thora's mind were her two beaux, the secret name she had for her gentlemen. Lord Kengally was elderly but just divine, and Edgar, younger but still old, being in his forties, was the perfect escort, so distinguished looking! He was fun, she could relax more with him, but then Lord Kengally was extremely light-hearted for a man of his age. Her own father, she thought darkly, could take lessons in social graces from both of them, for all his pretensions. Wouldn't he just die if he knew who his daughter had snared to introduce her to Perth society?

Word had flared round the Palace like a bushfire that Mrs Price was a friend of the titled Englishman, and by Tuesday morning neatly printed cards and invitations were being delivered to her door. She didn't know who these people were, but because of that, unwittingly, they had entered her dream world; they too were her friends. She went shopping, with an eye for the best, for new clothes and shoes and lovely hats, flattered by the ladies in those expensive establishments who gushed over her excellent taste, and at Edgar's suggestion had the bills sent to the Palace, thence to Lancoorie. Edgar liked to accompany her on her buying sprees so that he could take her to luncheon afterwards, and that was as it should be. A woman alone in a big city needed a companion.

Having purchased hand-made stationery with wild flowers painted in the corner, Thora accepted all of the invitations, to luncheons, teas, soirées, without another thought. One morning she found herself surrounded by ladies at a tea in the Palace dining room. As it turned out, the only one she actually attended.

She couldn't quite recall how she'd got there, not that it mattered, for they were all so sweet, placing her at the top table behind a bank of roses. They were raising money to build a hospital somewhere for a charity called St John of God, and when the call came for donations, Thora happily volunteered a hundred pounds, which was utterly delicious because everyone clapped her.

Afterwards, the ladies gathered, anxious to be introduced and it was all going so well until a woman, some person, approached her and said: 'Aren't you Thora Carty? From York?'

Thora turned on her, screaming: 'How dare you! I don't know you! I am not from York! How dare you say such a thing! Who is this person?'

Later, when she was dressing for dinner with Edgar, a

tête-à-tête this time, she recalled a shot of silence in a room heavy with perfume, when time had stood still with a hundred gaping faces turned towards her, for some unaccountable reason, but she shrugged it off. There had been so many women, all wanting to talk to her at once, a little stage fright was understandable. After all, she was a celebrity.

Thursday morning was tragic. She awoke to the solid thud of heavy rain and ran to the window. 'Oh, no!'

So it wasn't surprising when a note was delivered from Lord Kengally, with a bouquet of roses and an apology that their river trip to a place called Minchfield House would have to be postponed on account of the weather. But to make up for it, perhaps he could persuade her to lunch with them at the Palace, rather than have her face the elements.

Thora accepted, wondering why another foray into that dining room should make her nervous.

When she arrived, looking stunning in a shapely blue silk gown with a softly flowing skirt, Edgar remembered Clem Price with jealous resentment. Her blonde hair was swept up under another of those large hats that were all the rage. Edgar always thought they buried small ladies but Thora was tall enough to carry them with style.

'By Jove!' Kengally said, impressed, and Edgar nodded before he hurried off to greet her. 'She is something, isn't she?'

It was just the three of them, and Edgar had the pleasure of escorting the lady across the room as heads turned, while Kengally stood, dazzled.

'My dear,' he said, 'if I were only twenty years younger!'

'What would happen then?' she asked innocently. Edgar knew she was in a scatty mood and he groaned. Thora was his mascot and he needed her to play her role and not wander into the dippy remarks that sent Kengally off into hurtles of laughter. He adored her naivety, while Edgar wanted to keep his mind on the main game, with Thora as only an inducement to procure the Englishman's company. The reply from Kalgoorlie had been bad news. Only a cryptic:

'No chance on the other leases stop When do we get our money stop'

Didn't the fools realize that their sale depended on the viability of the surrounding leases? He'd been hoping Kengally would overlook that element, since his company would be into deep mining. And what did they mean, where was their money? They'd signed the option, they'd get paid when it was taken up. By Kengally.

Nevertheless, to allay Kengally's fears, he was able to produce a replacement telegram, which he'd written himself on the appropriate form, stating that the owners of the neighbouring mines were willing to sell, and he'd handed it to Kengally just before Thora made her entrance.

She decided that today she would drink only champagne.

'And so you shall,' Kengally said. 'It's the least I can do, considering I ruined your day.'

'You didn't,' she cried. 'The rain did. I should have cancelled all my other engagements, but I forgot.'

Kengally found that an hilarious witticism, but Edgar wasn't so sure. Maybe he'd missed the joke. Her reply had to be a joke; it didn't make any sense at all. The only engagement cancelled was the river trip.

They'd settled down to their champagne and ordering, when Kengally delivered the body-blow. 'I had another assayer check Lady Luck mine, Tanner. I'm sure you are acting in good faith, but this one wired me that Lady Luck is a rather shaky proposition. I'll explain later.'

'That's nonsense. Lady Luck is bearing, and there has to be more deeper down.'

'We'll talk about it tomorrow, old chap. Needs a bit of unravelling, I think.'

Edgar was devastated. He knew that Lady Luck was a viable mine. He knew it. Someone had got to them, offered them more money, and they were pulling this trick to get out of his deal. But they'd signed. By Christ, he'd hold them to it. But could he hold Kengally? Who had by this time turned his full attention to Thora. He liked to hear about sheep stations, as exotic to him in their sheer size as the flora from Kings Park.

The champagne flowed. With Kengally, as host, insisting that they sample the very best French, Thora was a willing starter. To Edgar, they were like a pair of juveniles, an old man and a young woman, prattling away through the meal while he sat there, fraught with worry, and not a little jealous that Thora seemed to be ignoring him.

He tried to turn the conversation back to more serious matters. 'Have you heard, Lord Kengally, that there has been a huge rush in England for shares in Londonderry?'

'What's Londonderry?' Thora asked.

'A gold mine.'

She laughed. 'Oh, you two with your fishing about for gold all the time. If you want gold, you should ask my husband.'

'Is he interested in investing?' Kengally asked.

'Why should he? He owns a gold mine. A fabulous gold mine. He's always sending Alice money, lots of it.'

'Alice is your sister-in-law?'

'Yes, she looks after our banking.'

Kengally was still curious. 'I thought Mr Price was a station owner?'

'He is, but he had to go out and investigate those gold places. It would be silly not to.'

'Of course, and he's done well?'

Irritated, Tanner shook his head. 'Last time I saw Clem he was pottering about with an alluvial mine. He's doing better with sheep.'

'And that goes to show,' she said tartly, 'how far behind the times you are, Edgar. I received a letter this morning. Clem has a new mine now, called Yorkey, and he's finding lots of gold. But it's a secret, so you mustn't tell anyone.'

'We won't,' Edgar grinned. 'Where is it?'

'Oh, heavens, I don't know. Out there somewhere.' She turned to Kengally. 'He says the goldfields are perfectly ghastly. I can't believe you'd even think of going there, Lord Kengally.'

'Business, my dear, one has to do these things.'

Later he spoke privately to Edgar. 'Secrets interest me. Perhaps we should seek more information.'

'Yes, I could send a telegram to a friend at Kalgoorlie. Price was there last I heard. I'll have enquiries made.'

'And tell the world? Telegrams are notoriously fair game. You know Price, why don't you go and see him personally?'

'But what about the Lady Luck deal?'

'We've got three weeks left on the option. Time enough to find what this Yorkey mine is all about. You can telegraph me your findings, but make it cryptic. No names.'

But Edgar wasn't to be dismissed that easily. Nor did he believe Thora – she was given to exaggerations, he'd noticed, but as long as her tales amused Kengally, he hadn't minded. Somehow it was all part of her airy-fairy nature.

'Why don't we both go? We can visit both mines and talk to assayers on the spot.'

'Not possible for me, dear boy. I have made arrangements for the weekend. Going up to stay with Warburton. I tell you what – you go on ahead, I'll follow on Monday. *En route*, perhaps you could set up an itinerary for me. I'm told each leg of that journey gets more hazardous.'

'Yes, it does take some arrangements if you don't know the ropes. They've started the railway out to Southern Cross, but it won't be open for a long while.' He was so jubilant he made a mental note to take Thora a gift. 'I'll book your hotel accommodation at Northam and Southern Cross, and at Kalgoorlie, of course, so that you can do the trip in three stages. You do ride?'

'I'm not in my dotage yet.' Kengally grinned. 'Sat a horse before I could walk. You arrange the safari and I'll be on the train on Monday morning. It'll be quite an adventure, what?'

Edgar went back to his office, more than pleased with the day's work, and sent his clerk out to buy a box of chocolates for Thora. It was seven o'clock before he completed all the work that had been pushed aside while he paid court to Kengally. He hurried back to the hotel. Living at the Palace was an expense far beyond his means, but that was where the action was. A few shillings to the porters produced a run-down on the who's who of visiting personages. And that had paid off:

he'd met several important gentlemen in the billiard room, including Kengally. The Palace was good to him, a fount of information, as was his other home, the Albert, in Kalgoorlie. It could be said, had anyone thought to enquire, that Edgar had no fixed address.

He met Thora's nanny in the passageway. 'Is Mrs Price in?'

The girl glanced at him uneasily. 'She's always in.'

Edgar thought that reply peculiar. He blinked at her and moved on to knock at the door.

The nanny's name was Henrietta Barnes, but everyone called her Netta. She'd applied for a job as a housemaid and landed this one as a fill-in while she waited for a vacancy. Netta was chosen by Miss Devane because she had excellent references and, more importantly, because she was the eldest of eight kids, so minding babies was second nature to her. And Miss Devane was pleased with her because she adored Lydia, who was such a good little child, no trouble at all. It was the mother who bothered Netta. Worried her. She was peculiar.

Netta had been in service long enough to know never to criticize her employers because it always got back. Someone would tell. And then you got the backlash. What she'd said to that gentleman, Mr Tanner, had just slipped out, and it sounded stupid, she knew. No wonder he'd stared at her funny.

What she'd meant was that Mrs Price rarely left the room. In the mornings she wrote responses to invitations, which Netta posted for her. Mrs Price gaily accepted them all, but then didn't bother to go. She'd only attended one morning tea. When she went out with her two 'beaux', as she called those gentlemen, that was fine, but they didn't take up all her days, or evenings, for that matter.

No, the rest of the time was the weird bit. She sat in a chair by the window. Just sat there. 'Away with the pixies', Netta described it to herself, because the woman took no interest in her baby, she didn't read, she never talked, and of all things, she never had a meal, refusing Netta's offers to have something sent up. On Wednesday, for instance, Netta could swear that Mrs Price had nothing to eat at all. Not a thing. Perhaps, she'd thought, the poor lady was too shy to eat alone in the dining room, and that was understandable, but when she'd offered to bring the lady a nice lunch to have in the room, Mrs Price had gone all haughty.

'I wouldn't dream of it,' she'd said. 'One has so many engagements it is difficult to keep up with them.'

Which was hardly the point, but Netta wasn't one to argue. In the meantime Mrs Price just sat in that chair, in another world.

Earlier Netta had suggested that they might take Lydia, in her new pram, for a stroll, but the missus had a lunch engagement, which was something, at least she'd eat. And it gave Netta a chance to get out of those rooms.

Now, with luck, Mr Tanner would cart the lady off to dinner.

Thora wasn't surprised to see him, and she accepted the chocolates with such delight, she didn't seem to notice that the gift was accompanied by a warm kiss on the cheek.

'Where are we dining tonight?' she asked him.

Taking Thora out hadn't been in his itinerary this evening, since he had to leave town in the morning and there were several of his clients downstairs in the bar. He'd be better served keeping in touch with them, but Thora did look lovely. And anyway, she was already searching among a scatter of hats on the sofa for something suitable.

Eventually she chose a soft brown velour to match her trim outfit, and they were on their way.

He took her to a small café on the river bank, where they had a quiet meal.

'You seem tired,' he said. 'And so am I. Too much wine at lunch.'

'I suppose so. It has been a busy week.'

Afterwards they strolled out into the garden, lit with Japanese lanterns, and he took her hands. 'Have I told you how beautiful you are, Thora?'

'No, but you may,' she said demurely, and Edgar couldn't resist her. He took her in his arms, very gently, and kissed her, and Thora looked up at him, smiling. 'Isn't this just so romantic?'

'Just being with you is romantic,' he murmured, kissing her again, but then another couple came out from the café, so they moved apart, the moment lost.

On the way home he told her he would be going out to Kalgoorlie in the morning, disappointed that she didn't seem concerned. Not about his absence, anyway.

'Oh, you poor thing, having to go on that horrible train,' she said at her door. 'You must remember not to talk to people. Thank you for the chocolates, that was very sweet of you.'

And she was gone, closing the door softly.

Try as she might, Alice couldn't bring herself to write to Clem and tell him that Thora had gone to Perth with the baby. She felt it was up to Thora to break the news to him herself. Instead, at the end of the week, she wrote again to her sister-in-law, begging her to come home. She was glad to hear, in a letter that had just arrived today, that Thora was enjoying herself staying at that fine hotel, and she had good rooms. That was all very well, but by the time this request reached her she would have been away two weeks, and that was long enough. Clem would be furious with Thora for taking off like that, but when he heard she was on her way home, that would take the edge off a bad situation.

She finished the letter, refusing to add her own news, which would only distract Thora. It was important to keep her mind on coming home.

The second letter, to Clem, was no easier to write. With no mention of Thora and Lydia, it seemed dishonest.

'Oh, damn!' she said. 'I'm not your wife's keeper,' and set her pen to work. It was time to tell him that she and George had had a long talk, and that they had decided to marry. She could not mention that their first evening alone here, with Thora away, was extremely awkward. As she served his dinner in the silent household, Alice wished she could throttle her silly sister-in-law for leaving her in a spot like this. It had even occurred to her that she should telegraph Clem to come home, but that would have meant giving a reason, and she'd soon dismissed that idea.

'Have you looked at our papers lately, Alice?' George had asked her.

'What papers?'

'Our paroles.'

'Goodness me, no.' Why did he have to bring up that subject, tonight of all nights? She was embarrassed enough as it was.

'Then you should do,' he said, his face quite red, but maybe she imagined that. Men didn't blush, did they?

'If you'd looked you'd have seen that both Mike and I are free men. He was clear soon after he left here, and I finished my time a month ago.'

'Oh, George. I'm so pleased for you. I'm sorry, we should have had a celebration. But why are you telling me now? Are you thinking of leaving?' Damn Thora! Now they were going to lose George, the best hand they'd ever had at Lancoorie. He wasn't stupid, he must know being alone at the station with her would cause talk.

'That's up to you, Alice.' He changed the subject quickly, maybe hoping she wouldn't dismiss him, and began to talk about his young days in Liverpool, about the hard life he'd led back there. 'I won't give it to you wrong,' he said, 'I was a bad lad, I wouldn't have been fit to talk to a lady like you in those days.'

She supposed he had to think of something to say, since all the others had left them at this table alone, but she'd never heard George talk so much. He had been married, he told her, to a convict woman he'd met on the transport ship, a girl from London. They'd been sent to work for a farmer down Bunbury way, but he'd treated them worse than his animals.

'We tried to make a go of it,' he said, 'but Jane – that was my wife – she was poorly. She never got over that transport ship, I won't tell you how cruel that was, bad enough for

259

men.' He sighed. 'Jane got thin and sick, but she battled on. We'd heard how convicts could get free and make good lives out here, us being the last lot to ever be transported, and we wanted that. In the end she was too weak to get up, but that bastard – sorry about the language, Alice, but he was . . .' He shook his head miserably. 'He sacked us, even though I was doing Jane's work in the orchard as well. I told him, all right, we'd go, as soon as she was well, and asked him to get a doctor to her. But not him. He wanted her up and out of there. He was taking us back into Bunbury . . .'

George pushed his meal aside as if it pained him to eat. 'Jane died that night.'

'I'm so sorry.'

'So was he,' George said grimly. 'I didn't care any more. I gave him the hiding of his life, raided his kitchen for some grub, found a pound in a drawer, took that and ran. I headed for a southern port to try to stowaway on a ship, but I got caught and ended up in Fremantle jail on the same charges that got me here. Assault and robbery.' He smiled. 'A dismal tale, eh?'

'Sad.'

'Well, puttin' that aside, and one thing and another, I ended up here. I can't say I learned my lesson, I've no regrets for bashing that farmer . . .'

'Neither would I,' she said.

'The thing is,' he continued, 'working about this country I came across bosses that had more respect, and I came to like this country. Even if you weren't free, you felt free, if you know what I mean.'

She didn't, but she nodded wisely.

'Then I came to Lancoorie. What I'm trying to tell you, Alice, is it's the best place I've ever been in my life. Jails didn't reform me, you're too busy keeping ahead of the game, I just sort of learned self-respect. You see what I mean?'

'Yes.'

He cut a slice of bread and handed it to her, spiked on the end of the knife. 'It's like this,' he said heavily, slicing again at the bread, 'I might be just a farm hand but I'm not a felon any more. Would you agree with that?'

'My word, I would.' She smiled. 'And you've got papers to say you're not.'

'Papers don't always tell the truth. I've known men who should never have been in jail and men who should never get let out. I'm asking about me. Would you say I could be a respectable person now?'

'Without a doubt, George. And you're not just a farm hand, you're our friend.'

He looked at her earnestly. 'Then, Miss Price, I hope you don't take this as a cheek, but we get along well, you and me. I was wondering if you would consider marrying me. Becoming Mrs Gunne.'

That weekend was bliss. Alice was pleased there was no one to intrude on them, to bother them with mundane chit-chat, because they just got on with their work and sat together by the fire after dinner as if nothing stupendous had happened. On the Sunday night George took his cocoa to his room as usual, but before he left the kitchen, he stood awkwardly in the doorway.

'You can change your mind if you want.'

'I won't be doing that, George.'

'You know I love you, don't you?'

Alice kissed him, a soft brush on his lips. 'You're very nice, George. I'll be honoured to be Mrs Gunne.'

A wide grin lit his face. He returned her kiss with enthusiasm, and Alice laughed. 'Look out, you'll spill your cocoa.'

They gave themselves the day off and went to town on the Monday. He called at the police station, where Fearley wished him good luck as he signed and stamped two sets of papers, making both George and Mike free men.

'Where's your mate?' he asked.

'Out at the goldfields with the boss. Doing well too, the pair of them.'

Fearley sighed. 'Sometimes I think I ought to chuck this in and have a go too.'

'Yeah,' George said, interested only that he was now free, and even Fearley was treating him with respect. It felt good. He went to the store and ordered supplies for Lancoorie, then called on the Stock and Station Agent to lodge a call for shearers. They wouldn't be needed for months yet but it was as well to get in early because of the shortage of working men in the district.

Alice was shopping. They both needed new clothes for their wedding, she'd said, so he joined her at the draper's shop where she was quietly gathering up her purchases. She had bought herself a new dress, brown, and a fine brown felt hat swathed in copper-coloured ribbons, and there on the counter were two white shirts, trousers, men's clothes which, he knew, were for him, but he made no comment.

She took him aside. 'I have to buy some stockings and things. You go next door to the bootmaker and get a pair of shoes. Not boots. You can't wear boots to the church.'

He nodded, noticing the draper watching them curiously, thrilled that she was calmly going about her business not inclined to enlighten the shopkeeper. She was a one, that Alice.

It wasn't until they were on their way home, looking forward to the all-important call at St Luke's to make arrangements for their wedding, that Alice remembered she'd forgotten to call at the post office to see if there was any mail waiting for delivery to Lancoorie.

'Oh well, never mind,' she said. 'We'll hear the eruptions soon enough. Clem will know by this that Thora is in Perth. She'll have written and told him herself.'

But Clem did not know. He was hard at work at the Yorkey mine, where they'd struck more gold-bearing quartz. The assayer had been out and given them an excellent report, but hard on his heels were other prospectors, angrily surveying the clear markings of the acre that Price had claimed. To make certain the boundaries were observed, Mike had tied rags to trees, and they flapped untidily in the wind, a constant source of annoyance. Some claimed it wasn't legal to grab such a parcel of land but, being new to the fields, they were unsure of their rights, so they began to dig at the perimeters.

Tanner arrived, reopened the office that he rented in a ground-floor room of the Albert Hotel, and began making enquiries about Clem Price.

He found that their mine out at the block had been sold, but, more interesting, that Mike Deagan had bought the Black Cat. He'd seen the building being demolished just before he left but had been too involved with his own affairs to take much notice. It took a lot of time and tenacity to search for a mine with real expectations, checking the maps at the warden's office and then riding miles in all directions to see for himself, camping out with miners, listening for tips. That was how he'd found Lady Luck.

But Deagan was a convict. Where would he get the cash? The mine he and Clem had owned only produced gold by the pennyweight, and the new owner wasn't doing any better. And look at that building now! The old iron and canvas brothel had made way for a fine two-storey premises that looked positively decorous. Glory was a sly old bawd. She wouldn't have sold for pennies. So where had Deagan found the money? How long had they been working the Yorkey mine?

He went to the new courthouse to examine ownerships of property in Hannan Street, found that block, and sat back with a grin.

Clem! He'd bought it and put Deagan in as front man. The big overdraft he'd given Clem at the York bank had come in handy. The lad knew his onions all right. What better investment than a good brothel? It was hard to imagine Clem as a brothel-owner, but you never knew with people. At least he was smart enough to keep quiet about it. Tanner bet that Thora had no idea. He began to laugh. Jesus! She'd have a fit. Maybe all that money she was talking about was coming from the brothel and Yorkey was just a blind. Well, he'd have to do a little more checking . . .

Three hundred ounces! From Yorkey? The plant manager was amused. 'You'd think I told Clem his mine was a dud.

263

He didn't look too pleased at all. He's a strange bloke, that Clem Price.'

At the warden's office, Edgar learned the exact position of Yorkey, and early the next morning he was riding out to visit his friend Clem.

Chapter Ten

Mrs Morgan, still indignant at the fate of Miss Lavinia, resigned. The new cook, installed by Lil, had references from good hotels and experience with 'functions', which Lil knew would please Mr Warburton. He had made it clear to her that there was a new era at Minchfield, and he expected to be entertaining guests more often, so the wine cellar, which Lil hadn't known existed, was cleaned out and restocked.

She thought his first garden party was a stodgy affair, with ladies and gentlemen parading about the lawns in their finery, looking rather bored until refreshments were served and then descending on the tables like a plague of locusts. After that, many of them took the opportunity to wander about the house, even upstairs, just plain inquisitive, and the house-keeper was far from impressed. Judging by the conversations she heard, they were all aware of the Warburton story.

'Had the sister put away,' a woman said. 'Took over the property himself.'

Another whispered, 'He's peculiar himself,' as she peered into the library, and it dawned on Lil that these people were not really friends of the formerly reclusive Mr Warburton, they were just folk from around the district who had accepted his invitation out of curiosity. They left rather early, in a rush, leaving only the dedicated imbibers in a small group, concentrating on the excellent wines and ignoring the host.

Eventually Mr Warburton stormed inside, instructing his housekeeper to clear them out.

'How?' she asked.

'Remove the wines.'

Quietly Lil told the two waitresses who were clearing the

tables to take some wine with them on each trip back to the house, so that the tactic wouldn't be too obvious. She was as disappointed as the host. They'd gone to so much trouble to make this a truly grand party, and Mr Warburton had spared no expense for the enjoyment of his guests, and yet at times she'd seen him standing alone, as if bewildered, not knowing what to do next.

You're not a good mixer, sir, she said to herself as she passed the closed library door. Perhaps he'd forgotten how.

At first, copying Miss Lavinia, Lil had worn black all the time, with keys jangling at her belt, but black didn't suit her at all, and with her thick black curls pulled back in a bun, every mirror she passed told the same story. So, gradually, she began to make a change. She wore a white blouse for a while, then a coloured blouse, and then she took a chance and came downstairs in a neat blue-and-white-checked dress with crisp white cuffs and collar. Observing some of the ladies at the garden party, she had cut the front of her hair so that the dark curls fell on to her forehead, and piled it up at the back, securing it with combs.

He noticed. He looked up from the breakfast table, squinting at her over his glasses. 'You do look nice today, Mrs Cornish,' and went back to his newspaper.

She was thrilled. 'Thank you, sir.' But he didn't seem to hear.

Lil decided she couldn't take her meals with the staff any more – she didn't want to be involved in their gossip – nor could she eat in the dining room. The kitchen was out of the question. In the end she solved the problem by having her meals brought up to her small sitting room where she kept her accounts. She had been disconcerted, at first, to find there was more to housekeeping than constant forays to detect dust or default, but a quick search of Miss Lavinia's room turned up the books she needed. To her astonishment Lil found meticulous records going back years. Not only the contents of the house, from the fine linen to the lowliest teapot, but a history of every stick of furniture purchased, repaired or replaced, as well as copies of menus and recipes and a wealth of other information. She decided she had better follow suit. Assiduously she attended to that task every evening, adding to the pages in the large ledgers with equal precision, finding she quite enjoyed the time spent keeping everything in order. Mr Warburton couldn't be allowed to find fault with his new housekeeper.

Eventually he overcame his disappointment over that garden party and seemed happier to be pottering about on his own, as he had always done. One day when he came across Lil at the linen press, he walked on past and then stopped.

'I've been wondering, Mrs Cornish, where do you take your meals?'

'In my room, sir. I hope you don't mind.'

'No, not at all. In fact it would be more convenient for all concerned, I'm sure, if you ate in the dining room.'

Lil thought that was a silly idea. The table was always set for him before meals; she could hardly mess up the settings, so she'd have to wait until he'd finished. And that could be hours.

'If you wish, sir,' she said dutifully. 'I'll wait my meals until you've finished.'

'No, no. Tell them to set another place. It is rather foolish for us both to be sitting in lone state. You take your meals with me in future, unless I have guests, of course. I'm sure you understand.'

Lil was delighted. This was a promotion and a half! And from that minute on, she knew. She just knew.

Came the day when he was almost beside himself with excitement. 'A dear friend of mine has arrived in Perth, on his first visit to Australia, and he's coming to visit Minchfield with several friends. I'll put on a grand luncheon for them. I want Lord Kengally to see Minchfield at its best.'

Lil almost fainted. 'Did you say "Lord", sir? The gentleman is a lord?'

'Indeed I did. We were great pals during the time I spent in London, and he was immensely kind to me. Now, you and

Cook work out the best possible menu, six courses, and I'll attend to the wines.'

This, to Mr Warburton, was far more important than the garden party, and he dashed about the house checking everything in a frantic burst of activity.

By the Wednesday night, everything was in readiness. The extra pieces were fitted into the dining room table so that it sat fourteen, and apart from the flowers, the table was set with the very best Minchfield could offer until it fairly glittered. Gardeners toiled, clipping and pruning for days, until there was not a leaf out of place, and the jetty was festooned with red, white and blue ribbons. Looking over all of this magnificence, Lil was impressed. The house was beautiful, and on this eve it looked better than ever.

'You must be very proud, sir,' she said to him, and she meant it.

'I am, Mrs Cornish, and I have you to thank for all your efforts. It can be no mean task keeping a house this size in tip-top order.'

But that night, from her window, Lil sniffed the air. There was a strong wind blowing, a sea wind, laden with salt. By midnight she was up again, closing the shutters, as the first signs of one of those massive storms that originated out there in the Indian Ocean became evident. Preliminary winds blundered about all night, and in the morning the full force of the storm struck, rain lashing as they battened down. Trees were uprooted, the roof of the staff quarters blew off, but worst of all, the river was in torment, whipped up by the winds. Lil had never seen the Swan River turn into such a swollen, dangerous rush before, and she feared the worst.

'They won't come,' Mr Warburton said dismally as the storm raged, battering at the house with mean, whining winds and spattering the lawns with layers of hail. 'A yacht can't come upriver in this weather.'

To confirm the dread news, a soaked messenger made his way to Minchfield with a telegram of apology from Lord Kengally himself, expressing his great regrets.

Mr Warburton was devasted. The jetty looked pitiful,

lashed by the angry river, and the ribbons flailed about in pathetic disarray. The grounds were a sodden mess, but inside, the table, the beautifully set table, still glittered in the storm-darkened room, patiently waiting.

He was in such a state, he was almost in tears. 'Throw everything out,' he shouted at Lil. 'Clear the table, throw out all that food. I don't want to look at it.'

'Yes, sir,' she said, thinking the staff would eat well for the next few days; he'd never know.

'Why is it,' he appealed to her, 'that everything I arrange goes wrong?'

'No accounting for the weather. It's just bad luck.'

'I'm sick of this place. I ought to sell it. Move into Perth. There's no one of note living round here. I'm surrounded by country bumpkins full of booze and bad manners.'

That frightened Lil. Sell Minchfield? What would become of her and Caroline? She'd never find a job like this again. Her grasp on authority here had given her the right to delegate the minding of Caroline to various maids, who were always eager for that gentle task because it got them out of their everyday duties. They loved to feed the housekeeper's baby and take her on long walks about the estate in her pram. In fact, they were thoroughly spoiling the child. Not that her mother cared. God help them if they didn't.

'They won't come again,' he was saying. 'Lord Kengally is a busy man, he's in Australia on business. An investor, in gold, steel, those sort of things.'

As the thunder rolled over the land and rain swept at the windows, he sat slumped at his desk, a picture of abject misery, Lil took a chance. She put an arm about him, surprised at the feel of him in his unpadded lounging jacket, firmer than she'd expected for a man twice her age. 'Don't take it so hard, sir. These things happen.'

'Yes, they do. They happen to me.' His voice was hard. 'Do you know, I wanted to be an artist? I went to London to study. My family disapproved. All of them. My father was in business with my uncle, the man who built this place, and neither of them would give me a penny. But I hung on there, studying, selling enough to bring in a pound here and there, relying on what my mother could send me. That's when I met Gerald Kengally; he was very encouraging.' He stopped. 'I don't know why I'm boring you with this, Mrs Cornish.'

'Oh, no!' she said. 'I've never met anyone before who has ever been overseas, let alone to London. One day, sir, when you've got some free time, would you tell me about London?'

'You'd really like to know about it?'

'Why not?' She was genuinely surprised that he'd ask. 'But about today. Your friend the lord might be a busy man, but all the offices close down at the weekend. Why don't you send him a telegram inviting him for the weekend?'

'He'd have a host of invitations. No, he'd be booked up.'

'Just ask. The storm will pass. If he can't come, he can't come. But one would appreciate the invitation, surely?'

It struck Lil that she sounded like Miss Lavinia then. Never in her life before had she used the expression 'one'; it had just slipped out. But she liked it. The word sounded very smart. Polished, like Miss Lavinia. These days she was taking a lot of leaves from Miss Lavinia's book, not the least a recalling of the way she spoke, to improve herself in Mr Warburton's eyes.

He was distracted, staring moodily at the persistent bad weather. 'When my father died,' he said, 'my mother came to England, so thrilled to be able to see me and to find her heart's desire in touring the mother country. Too late I discovered that she'd sold my father's share of the business to our wretched uncle for a few hundred pounds.'

'He diddled her?' Lil asked, awed.

'Well put, my dear. Diddled,' he said bleakly.

There was a small tweak in Lil's mind that diddling could be a family trait, since Mr Warburton had wrenched ownership of Minchfield from Miss Lavinia rather harshly but it was not her business.

'I still think you should invite your friend for the weekend.'

With the passing of the storm, joy burst on the household.

Lord Kengally had accepted his invitation. He was coming for the weekend. The whole weekend. On his own.

Telegrams being what they were, purveyors of none-too-private information, Mr Warburton's neighbours knew by the Thursday afternoon that Minchfield would be hosting a distinguished guest. He received a sudden onslaught of cards and invitations pertaining to that particular weekend, and that night, dining with Mrs Cornish, he took delight in burning them over the candles, one by one, while they sampled the wines he would serve his friend.

So it was hardly unexpected, Lil thought, that, given the fun they'd had over dinner, he ended up in her bed after escorting her to her room. She had known all along it would have to happen, since the day he'd invited her to take her meals with him.

Mrs Cornish knew her place. She did not meet Lord Kengally, but she saw to it that the two men were served the most delicious meals, that their beds were warmed, that the crystal decanters in the library were topped up, that the hot scones in the afternoon were served with blackberry jam and clotted cream, that the guest's clothes were laundered and returned to him immaculate in seemingly miraculous time. Everything Lil could think of to make this weekend pleasurable was done, and she smiled serenely, standing at her window, watching them marching together across the fields, deep in conversation as two friends should be. When they returned from their walks, maids took their tweed coats and walking sticks, and wherever they chose to sit, roaring fires welcomed them.

On the Sunday afternoon she saw the two friends embrace on the jetty, before the lord boarded the river boat for the return journey to Perth, and she saw the marvellous smile of satisfaction on Mr Warburton's face as he walked back up to the house, triumphant.

Mrs Cornish was there waiting for him. Asking anxiously if everything had gone off all right. As if she didn't know.

They had tea that Sunday night in the library, by the fire, while he reminisced about Gerald Kengally.

'He is such a good friend,' he told Lil. 'A decent man. I can't speak highly enough of him. It was much better having him here on his own than Thursday would have been with all those other people about. And he was very pleased that I'd invited him on his own so that he could have a pleasant break from all his business concerns in Perth.'

Robert lit a cigar, recalling his London sojourn at length. 'I wasn't regarded as a colonial,' he told her. 'Not at all. I was accepted as being a cut above the ordinary Anglo-Australians who bob up over there. So I had a glorious time in London town.'

Lil was a good listener. 'Did you see the Tower of London?'

'Of course. Visited there often. And I was invited by the Queen to a garden party at the Palace.'

'Heavens!'

'Oh, yes. Even though I was a struggling artist, Gerald Kengally befriended me. Introduced me to all the right people. He is still a patron of the arts, he tells me. So you see, it was quite amusing that in my turn, I was here to rescue him from the deadly dullness of Perth. He found Minchfield a splendid retreat. Next time he comes I shall introduce you.'

Still savouring the success of the weekend, Robert sat by the fire sipping his brandy, while Lil closed up the house, then he escorted her upstairs, not to her room, but to his own. From then on they shared his wide, comfortable bed. Lil was aware of the talk below stairs, aware that the more they talked the more the district would learn who was who in this household, and take note.

Having told Alice that she'd attended the church service at the great cathedral the previous Sunday, Thora convinced herself it was true, so to the nanny's great relief she took herself off again this morning, a little bewildered that she'd forgotten the way. But it was a beautiful morning and the new hat looked splendid with her navy travelling suit, so it was a pleasure to be out walking.

I don't know why I've been stuck in that room, she told herself as she strolled quiet streets, looking in the windows of closed shops, smiling at a few passers-by. I don't have to if I don't want to. I can do anything I like here in Perth.

Nevertheless, she was hurt that Edgar and Lord Kengally had deserted her. 'Not a word from either of them since Friday,' she muttered, forgetting that Tanner, at least, had told her he was returning to the goldfields. 'They don't care about me any more, they've probably been partying with other ladies all the weekend, leaving me to rot. I'll never speak to them again.'

She turned down the hill towards the river and joined others walking along the promenade. There was so much to see – ferries and small yachts on the river, children playing by the banks, fishermen sitting dreaming in the sun while black swans manoeuvred nearby, hoping to share the catch – and yet Thora could feel a knot of nerves deep in her stomach. She forced herself to keep walking, turning her attention to other ladies strolling amiably along, until she realized that she was the only unaccompanied lady present, they were all with gentlemen or other ladies.

Frantically she peered about her, hoping to see at least one person on her own, noticing only the gaiety and laughter of the other promenaders, certain they were laughing at her. Sneering. She moved faster to escape their ridicule, hurrying along this seemingly endless path until it became too much for her and she broke away to scramble uphill through scrub country that bordered the river.

Her skirt caught on bushes and she tore her stockings, but she couldn't turn back. She was headed for the comfort of those indifferent city streets and thence home, back to the hotel, but she'd long passed the commercial centre of the neat city. She crossed a busy road, hanging on to her hat as gusts of wind snatched at it, teasing her, bothering her, making her look even more foolish, and began hurrying through wide residential streets, turning somewhere, anywhere, at every corner, lost. Completely lost.

The woman who opened the front door of a large house stared at this odd person who had come knocking, asking if Lord someone lived there.

'No! Who are you? What do you want?'

'Are you sure this isn't his house?' Thora pleaded.

The door slammed in her face, and it was her mother who was on the other side, locking her out, refusing to listen to her, casting her into a world of strangers.

Later that afternoon a mounted policeman riding by saw the woman sitting huddled on the stone steps of the town hall.

'Are you all right, miss?'

The face that looked up at him was as pretty a picture as he'd ever seen, but she was clearly distressed. 'I've broken the heel of my shoe.'

He dismounted. 'Let's see.'

Timidly she took off her shoe and handed it to him with the errant heel.

He managed to fasten the heel on again by jamming the nails back into place. 'It's still loose, miss, but it should hold for a little while. Where do you live?'

Her hands fluttered vaguely and she looked wildly about her, as if seeking escape from him, but he persisted, sensing something was wrong. She was too well dressed to be hanging about the town on her own. 'I'll walk you home,' he offered. 'Is it far from here?'

'I don't know,' she whispered. 'Where's my hat?'

There was no hat to be seen. 'Must have blown away,' he said. 'It's turned into a real windy old day, hasn't it?'

'Yes.'

He helped her up. 'I'm not in any hurry, miss. Sundays are always quiet. We'll walk you back, Dandy and me. You like horses?'

'Yes, I like to ride.'

'Good for you. Now, where did you say you lived?'

The warmth and familiarity of the big horse that nuzzled her hand as she reached out to it was comforting, and she felt her head clearing as if she'd just wakened from a heavy sleep.

'The Palace Hotel.' She blinked and glanced back to the policeman, appreciating his sturdy presence. 'I was lost,' she added quietly, a weight lifting that she had actually said so. It was the first time she'd ever admitted the frailty. Nevertheless,

274

taking in the lateness of the day, she couldn't further admit that she'd also lost many hours. The last thing she could recall was rushing away from the esplanade that bordered the river.

At the entrance to the hotel she thanked him for his kindness and limped up to her room, where Lydia's nanny was waiting for her.

'Oh, Mrs Price! There you are! I was so worried about you. Goodness me, you look all blowed about. What happened to you? Let me get you a cup of tea.'

In her shattered state, kindness from two strangers was too much for Thora. She burst into tears and gave herself over to Nanny's ministering.

From that day life changed again for Thora, and became more difficult for the nanny, because Mrs Price clung to her. There were no more grand luncheons – Mrs Price would not go out without Netta – so they took the baby for long walks in her pram, often stopping for tea or even lunch at nearby cafés, but all other meals were served in the rooms. Mrs Price would not go down to the dining room, even for breakfast, without an escort, and since the flow of invitations had ceased, she seemed to have no choice.

So why does she need me? Netta worried. It's crazy for two women to be sitting within these walls most of the day, minding a baby. Perhaps she thinks I'm not capable and doesn't like to say so. Not that she says anything much at all. If she's not sitting staring out the window, she spends her time reading ladies' journals and magazines from cover to cover and back again. Is the husband coming? She never mentions him. Nor does she say how long she's staying. It's not my idea of a holiday. So what is she doing here?

Tanner's progress out to the Yorkey mine was slow. He talked to everyone he met, and visited various mines along the way, searching for information. Dizzying gold finds in all directions only increased his frustration. He'd been one of the early birds on the goldfields, but not among the lucky few who struck wealth beyond their dreams. Sharebroking had kept him afloat after all five of the mines he'd leased had hardly been worth the trouble.

Financial crises in the banking world overseas had seen investors fleeing shaky banks for gold shares. Commodities were falling but gold was holding. And out here, so were breweries. He had a good turnover in brewery shares. All very fine but he had to find the big one, like that Golden Hole mine that had been taken over by the Londonderry Company, with investors queueing for shares as the prices skyrocketed.

One of these days I'll be on Easy Street, he told himself. It's just a matter of time. Edgar was convinced, as were many others, that this massive ridge was laden with gold, a treasure chest that would outdo the Rand. Already a stretch outside Kalgoorlie was being referred to as the Golden Mile.

By the time he located Clem and his mate at their lonely camp surrounded by dry scrub, he knew all he needed to know about Yorkey, but he kept that to himself.

'I was out this way, Clem, and I heard you were here. How's it going?'

Clem was pleased to see him but unhappy with the mine. 'Bloody awful! You wait for rain for months on end and then when it comes it's a deluge. The bloody mine's flooded.'

His mate, Mike Deagan, laughed. 'We've bucketed most of it out and the rest's draining off. We'll be back at work tomorrow.'

'But are you doing any good?'

'More or less,' Clem admitted. 'I just hate wasting time.'

'What's the rush?'

Clem led him over to view the muddy mine surrounded by slippery hills of mullock. 'You'll find out sooner or later,' he admitted. 'This mine's a goer. We're doing all right. The first pay was three hundred ounces to the ton, bloody hard work, though . . .'

'Three hundred! You're on a winner, Clem!'

'I know. But I want to go home. I've been away too long as it is. Mike's all for staying, but then he hasn't got a wife sitting at home waiting for him.'

Tanner was confused. 'Where's Thora?'

'Home. At Lancoorie, of course. Alice is there, and George Gunne. I believe he's running the place now. Turned out to be good fellows, both of them.' He looked back at Mike and grinned. 'For a couple of ex-cons.'

'Ex?'

'Yes, they've served their time. Mike says they're both free men now. I hope to God George stays on, at least until I get home.'

Edgar scratched his head and stepped carefully round the mine. Didn't Clem know Thora was in Perth? Better give that subject a wide berth.

He accepted their invitation to camp out with them, waiting for his chance, which came as they shared a meal of tinned meat and potatoes. He told them he was fixing up a deal with British investors to buy the Lady Luck mine, emphasizing that the owners would make a fortune now without ever having to lift a pick again. 'They not only get the money for the mine, payment includes a parcel of shares in it, so they go on earning. They're happy gents, they are.'

'Find us some British investors then,' Clem said glumly.

'How much would they give us for Yorkey?' Mike asked.

'I'd have to know more about it.'

Mike was cautious. 'If a man can go on digging up his own gold, why sell?'

'I quite agree,' Tanner said. 'But the deeper you go, the tougher and more dangerous it gets. Companies can afford engineers to set up the works and employ miners, they can dig for ever. Just the same, if you're happy to go on the way you are, then stick with it. Companies need plenty of ground anyway, to set up their works.'

'Would an acre do?' Clem asked.

'I suppose so. Why?'

'Because he went and leased a whole bloody acre,' Mike said triumphantly. 'I thought he had more money than sense at the time. You won't find me working like a mole over a bloody acre! But we've got an acre here. All marked out legal.'

Tanner pretended surprise. 'An acre? You haven't!'

'Sure we have.' Clem grinned. 'I just wanted to bag it for prospecting if the Yorkey didn't work. But maybe now it will come in handy. Why don't you mention us to your company people?'

'They're too interested in the Lady Luck, but I'll see if there's anyone else who might take a look at Yorkey. I'll need the latest assayer's report. But in the meantime, you keep going and we'll see what happens.'

Kengally stood watching a flock of budgerigars lifting and swirling above him, one minute flashing green and yellow and the next, against the sun, a black swarm.

'Magnificent!' he cried. 'There must be thousands and thousands of them, and yet they're flying in perfect unison. Why don't they bump into each other?'

'They flock,' Edgar said patiently. 'It's the flock that counts, their central system. Less danger for them that way, the blacks say, frightens off birds of prey.'

'Well I never!' Kengally watched until they swirled away into the distance. 'What a sight. I must remember to put that in my diary.'

His abounding enthusiasm for everything about him was a trial for Edgar, who was finding it hard to keep Kengally's mind on the purchase of gold leases. He hadn't minded the train journey: 'Never seen such a cross-section of the world, all bundled in together,' he told Edgar. 'Had a most interesting time. My word, the lure of gold is a great leveller!'

Even the hard ride between Southern Cross and Coolgardie hadn't dampened his vigour, and far from upsetting this fastidious man, the wild, chaotic town of Kalgoorlie fascinated him. Order, in the form of new buildings, was beginning to emerge from the great spread of iron and canvas under the hard sun, but nothing could disguise the rough-and-ready characters who thronged the few wide streets.

'I heard there's nigh on a hundred thousand souls here now,' Kengally said. 'Isn't that remarkable? An instant city far out in a desert.'

'That can't be right,' Tanner said, disbelieving.

'My word, it is. I had it on good authority from a civil servant I met on the train. And the majority of them are poor people. Think what privations they must have endured to get here. A great many of these people walked here from the coast . . .'

'No one forced them to come,' Tanner said, tired of Kengally's insistence on learning everything about the area, as if he were here as a tourist.

'Easily said but hard done,' Kengally said gravely. 'I think they're all incredibly brave.'

But he wasn't so soft-hearted when it came to his role as investigator in search of a promising mine site before he made a decision on behalf of his two English partners. Having made all the enquiries he could in town, he visited the Lady Luck mine, climbed down into the depths, quizzed the owners endlessly, visited the adjacent mines, gave nothing away. That was Edgar's role. When Kengally decided to buy, it was up to Edgar to negotiate a deal, but so far he hadn't been given the nod.

'What do you think? Is Lady Luck the one?'

'Probably,' Kengally said. 'But what about the Yorkey mine? Why are you suddenly so silent about that?'

Edgar had hoped that Kengally would take Lady Luck and give him a chance to line up other investors for Yorkey, and now he had a perfect excuse to keep him away. No use lying about the output of Yorkey, he'd soon be found out. The truth was convenient.

'We've a bit of a problem there. It is owned by Clem Price and his partner. I've been talking to them and I got a shock. It's about Thora. Her husband doesn't know she's in Perth. It would be awkward for you to meet him without mentioning you have met his wife.'

'Really? And did you mention that you'd seen Thora in Perth?'

'God, no. I didn't want to rock the boat. He wants to leave anyway. If I told him that, he'd be gone in seconds.'

'Why did it occur to you that I might be so tactless? Thora is a very lovely woman. If she chooses to take a harmless little holiday in Perth then it's her business. Unless, of course, you have something to hide?'

'No, not me! I've known Thora and Clem since they were kids. I was just trying to look after her. She's really rather shy.'

'Yes, I think she is,' Kengally said. 'Surely I'm capable of discussing business without involving myself in other people's personal affairs, wouldn't you say?'

Edgar smarted a little at the reprimand, but he was accustomed to that from his wife, from years in the banks, and from others more powerful than he, so he put it aside for the time being, vowing that one day he'd not take cheek from anyone.

The meeting at Yorkey mine with Clem Price and his partner was cordial. Too cordial for Edgar's liking, since Clem made it obvious that he was anxious to sell. On the other hand, Mike Deagan, knowing eagerness would lower their asking price, feigned indifference.

Kengally thanked them for their time, and left. As he and Edgar rode back to town he had a battery of questions about the Yorkey mine, but not once did he mention Clem Price, to say either that he found the man pleasant or that he disliked him. No comment.

'One thing you forgot to tell me,' Kengally said, reining his horse in at a general store.

'What would that be?'

'That the nights here are bloody freezing. The last thing I would have expected in hot desert country. Wait here.'

He emerged from the shop wearing a huge sheepskin jacket and a large smile. 'I want an assayer's opinion on Yorkey's gold-bearing capacity, an up-to-date one, and if it's as good as the first, we'll take Yorkey.'

But later that night he received one of the owners of the Lady Luck mine in his room.

'How much did Tanner offer you?'

'Fifteen thousand pounds, sir,' the miner said, clutching his battered hat.

'And how much is his cut?'

'Five, sir.'

Kengally smiled. 'Commission's a bit high, what?'

'Is it? I don't know, sir, we're new at this game.'

'Too many people are new at the game,' Kengally murmured, 'but that's no reason to take advantage.' He sat at a desk and wrote a cheque for thirteen thousand five hundred pounds, and handed it over.

'Would you sell for that?'

The miner stared. 'Yes! By crikey, we would. But what about Mr Tanner?'

'I'll pay his commission. Don't worry about him. He's working on another deal. Your mine has been bought, as you see, by the Brompton Court Company, London. This means you're not entitled to dig any more, you have to shut it down right away. You will not discuss the price, just go. Two of my men will be out at Lady Luck tomorrow to see that this is done and to talk to your neighbours.'

The miner stumbled to his feet, a treasure on paper in his hand.

'Take my advice,' Kengally said. 'Lady Luck will go public, you will have a parcel of shares. Leave it at that. You've done well. Take your money home.'

'We'll do that, sir. And thank you. Thank you.'

When the miner had left, Kengally turned his attention to the notes he had on Yorkey. It seemed to him to be as good a bet as Lady Luck, and would do very well for his other mission, a syndicate of Scottish players, the Edinburgh United, of which he was also the chairman. Depending on the assayer's latest report, of course. But it had started off as well as the famed Londonderry, which now was not only shut down, but cemented to keep out fossickers, until the real work started.

Clem Price, he'd noticed, trusted his friend Tanner, but he was so anxious to sell he was being quite reckless. His partner, though, the Irishman, was a different proposition. He'd sell all right, but he was an educated man, a hard-head. Interesting fellow. Kengally thought he recalled Tanner saying something about the fellow being among the last of the felons transported to Australia from Britain, and he was absolutely fascinated. What an experience to meet a real live transported convict! And find him flourishing!

And that same Mr Deagan, he knew, would no more fall for Tanner's outrageous commission than fly in the air. He was the type that would blow up his mine before he allowed himself to get skinned by the likes of Tanner.

We'll keep you honest this time, Edgar, mused Kengally. I don't like to be associated with underhand dealings.

'Ten per cent, no more,' Mike said. 'I don't care what agreement you had with Clem. His mind's in his britches these days.'

'You don't know the work I've put in to get Kengally interested,' Tanner argued. 'Or what it has cost me.'

'And I'm not carin'. 'Twas you brought the man here, so you can have a reasonable cut, and the going rate is ten per cent. Take it or leave it. If there's one buyer about there'll be two.'

'With the cash up front? Not too many, mate.'

Mike took his time lighting his pipe. 'You don't seem to get the picture here. I'm in no hurry. I like Kalgoorlie, I've bought me a block of land in town and I'll be building a fine house on it real soon. Time I settled down, and this place suits me.'

'You mightn't be in a hurry, but Clem is.'

'That's our business. If he has to go, that's all right. We'll work something out.'

'Twenty per cent!'

'Don't waste my time. Ten or nothing.'

When Clem heard that the deal had been struck at last, with Tanner to receive only ten per cent of the eight thousand sale price, he was immensely relieved, but disappointed that Mike had been so hard on Tanner.

'He's been very good to me, we could have been a bit more generous.'

But Mike shrugged. 'If you feel that way, toss him some of

your share. He got the going rate, nothing to cry over. The man's a con, he was trying to rob us.'

For the first time in a very long time, Clem laughed. He threw his head back and roared, partly because he was so relieved that he was finally going home and also because of Mike's comment.

'That's ripe, coming from you!'

'Ah, but I'm a reformed character.' Mike grinned. 'Amazing what money can do for a man.'

'And you've really decided to live here? Are you mad as well as reformed?'

'Not at all. I like this country. After being locked up so long I love the feeling of space out here, it's all so vast. And this town, she's never dull. It's fair roarin' along. Besides, I have to keep an eye on our Black Cat.'

'Don't remind me,' Clem groaned. 'I don't know what to do about that.'

'You don't have to do anything. I'll be straight with you, Clem. I owe you more than I can say. You're a good mate. Every penny of your share will be fed into your bank as long as the house runs.'

More reticent than the Irishman, Clem wished he could find the words to tell Mike, now that he was leaving, that he was the best friend he'd ever had. They'd had their ups and downs, some furious rows spawned by the monotony of the work and their isolated camp, among other disagreements, but somehow they'd managed to battle on, relying on each other for support.

'Kengally gave me a bottle of whisky. Since this is our last night at Yorkey, why don't we drink it?'

'The lord gave it to you? Why you and not me?'

'He probably thought I was a good bloke,' Clem laughed.

'Ah, get out with you! Where have you got it hid?'

The fine whisky warmed them as they sat by their camp fire in the cold night air.

'Will you look at them stars!' Mike said. 'It's as if you can see the whole universe out here.'

'I've seen enough of them. The Southern Cross is just as

clear at Lancoorie as it is here. What will you do with yourself once the mine is closed? You can't be just playing happy Jack at that brothel.'

'You haven't been listening. I told you it's the town I'm staying for. No more digging, I'm getting too old for that, but there are opportunities everywhere as she grows. I'll be in on the ground floor. Once the railway comes through there'll be no end to it. More pubs, more shops, more land to be bought. I'll give you the tip if you want to invest with me.'

'No. I'm just going home. The mortgage is cleared. Lancoorie's safe and I can even fence more of the property now. But I have one great idea. The sea!' He reached for the bottle and poured himself another drink. 'Every time I spat dust out here, dying to take that water bottle and drink it dry, I thought of the sea. As soon as I get home and have everything sorted out, I'm taking Thora for a slap-up holiday in Perth, and I'm going to surprise her. I'll buy or build a beach house overlooking the ocean. It will be wonderful for us to be able to take a break from the heat in summer, and Lydia will grow up with the best of two worlds. When I was a kid I always wanted to go to the beach, it was my greatest ambition. Do you know, Perth has the most marvellous beaches, and I've never seen them.'

'Am I invited?' Mike asked.

'Any time, mate. And if we're not there, you can have the run of the place.'

This was the day he'd been waiting for. It seemed to him he'd been in Kalgoorlie for an eternity. Mike could take care of the assayer, who was to give his final opinion on Yorkey within a few days, the delay caused by the shortage of qualified men to examine the mines that were still springing up everywhere. But Clem didn't care. Daily, the Black Cat, the best brothel in town, was bringing in more money than he could spend. To his mind, Yorkey was no longer bearing as well as they'd hoped, but Mike, the optimist, argued it was just a temporary setback, and the last loads they'd sent off to the plant would prove, on average, to be just as valuable as before.

Not that it mattered. Clem was leaving, and Mike had accepted that. If the assayer's report was poor then Mike would become sole owner and make his own decisions.

He'd meant to leave at dawn on his new horse, a good fast mount, but he hadn't been prepared for the surprise send-off party that Jocelyn and Mike had organized for him at the Black Cat. It had been quite a night. Everyone he'd ever met on the fields seemed to be there, singing and dancing and wishing him well until he'd passed out, smiling, on a couch, with the party raging on about him. A couple of times he'd opened his eyes to find they were all still celebrating, and closed them, content to leave them to it. He had a faint recollection of a fight of some sort, but since that was nothing unusual in the gold town, he'd forgotten what it was about, if he'd known at all.

Jocelyn and Mike managed to stagger out to see him off, with Jocelyn making certain he had enough food and water for the hard ride to Southern Cross. He kissed her goodbye, shook hands with Mike, and he was on his way, with one last call to see if there were any letters for him at the post office.

There was just one. From Alice. Dear Alice, he could always rely on her. Crowds jostled him as he walked across the porch, acquaintances causing him more delay, asking about Yorkey, bidding him farewell, and a fair run home, given the aggravations of the route.

One man warned him: 'Stock up at Southern Cross, mate. That town of Northam's got to feed mobs of railway workers now, on top of diggers still pouring in from the coast.'

'That doesn't bother me,' Clem said. 'I'm heading south from Southern Cross. Going home to York.'

'Travelling alone? Watch out for bushwhackers then.'

'I've learned that lesson the hard way,' Clem said as he strode away. He was only carrying enough money to buy supplies on the return journey, and this time a handgun had replaced the unwieldy rifle.

He waited until he was out on the road to open Alice's letter, scanning it quickly for the note Thora often added, rather than have to write a letter herself, but there was no postscript, so he turned back, with a sigh, to see what Alice had to say.

Married! He jerked the reins so hard the horse almost stumbled, so he drew it back to a trot as he reread the letter.

Alice had married George! What was she thinking of, marrying a convict? He'd never given a thought to the fact that his sister might marry, always too busy with his own affairs, and now that it had happened, and while he was absent, Clem was furious.

She'd said something in here . . . 'under the circumstances, we decided not to wait'. What circumstances? Had that bastard got her pregnant? No, not Alice, that would never happen. Unless he forced her. Even then she wouldn't have been forced into marriage, she was too strong-minded. She was a sweet, gentle woman but not lacking in backbone. If he'd attacked her, Alice Price would have ordered him off the property with a shotgun. Angrily Clem urged his horse to the gallop, covering mile after mile as he tried to make sense of this sudden marriage.

By the third day of his long, lonely trek he'd calmed down to a certain extent, accepting that Alice was entitled to marry, and to marry anyone she wished. And maybe George wasn't such a bad idea after all. The devil you know, he mused. Except for that peculiar line about circumstances. Hadn't they received his letter telling them he was coming home?

Then again, he allowed, several times before he'd written that he'd be home soon, and even though this time he'd said it was definite, maybe they'd not believed him. And Thora? What did she think about this wedding? Not a word from her about it, and yet her other letters complained there was never anything much to write about.

Why hadn't they waited for him? That still annoyed him. Had they forgotten him altogether? It was a bloody mean thing to do, to cut him out of such an important occasion. And they'd stolen his thunder! Here he was, coming in like the conquering hero, with his great news that he'd made enough at Yorkey to set them up for life. Yorkey, he reminded himself. The story is that all the cash has come from Yorkey and other investments. There'll be no word of the Black Cat. Mike will keep his mouth shut and no one else out there knows or cares. Kalgoorlie is worlds away from quiet little York, and there it stays.

That night he was restless, sleeping hard in the open, rather than seek shelter in one of the distant homesteads he had passed now that he was re-entering arable country. Prospectors surging in from the eastern states were disembarking from ships at the southern port of Albany and marching north, rather than continue on to Perth. He'd seen quite a few on the bush roads, but had avoided them by travelling cross-country with the unerring eye of a homing pigeon. Clem didn't feel he should add to the burdens of these homesteaders by knocking on their doors. They'd have had enough of strangers by this. He was glad that Lancoorie was far enough out of York not to be bothered by tramps.

All night wild notions harassed him. Had George taken over as head of the house? Replacing him? After all, Alice was older, and she shared ownership of Lancoorie with her brother. And what would be their 'circumstances' now? It dawned on Clem that as his brother-in-law, George now had equal authority to him. He was no longer the boss! He had been usurped. After all he'd gone through out there on those bloody goldfields, he had been demoted to just a partner on his own property!

What was Thora doing to allow this to happen? Why hadn't she wired him? Had she been displaced too? Thrown out of the only double bed in the house to make room for the newly-weds? By God, he'd see about that! If they'd upset Thora, he'd have their hides.

With his mind in turmoil, the days dragged, and the great plains seemed endless. He couldn't urge the horse any faster and he begrudged the times he was forced to give it a spell, pacing about impatiently, trying to make plans, trying to think what he could do about them. Worrying about Thora. Disappointed that the fortune he was bringing home was no recompense for this disaster. If he went ahead with his plans to spend up big on Lancoorie, he would only be putting money in George's pocket, and he was damned if he'd do that. Had that bastard married Alice for her money? Before this, he thought meanly, with her gammy foot, she'd have been handicapped in the marriage stakes. But that would be no obstacle to a man like George, bent on leaping from destitution to landowner through a wedding ring.

Sullenly he rode through York, his heavy collar high over his chin, and his hat pulled down hard. He noticed that the Mayor's house was for sale, and wondered idly what had happened to him. A sign said that this fine property could be bought for sixty pounds, and he shook his head, disgusted. In Noah's day, sixty pounds was a fortune. When Tanner gave him that huge overdraft with a mortgage on Lancoorie, that had been a fortune, and he'd lain awake at night sweating, remembering what happened to farmers who got too deep into banks, afraid he'd fail. Now, he could buy a dozen houses like the one he'd just passed without making a dent in the bankroll, but he felt no joy, no exhilaration, no excitement that he was coming home a winner. They'd even robbed him of that.

While Mike waited for the assayer's report he mulled angrily over that conversation with Tanner, the night of Clem's send-off. They were all in their cups by then and he was looking for Clem to join them in a barbershop quartet, but Tanner told him that the guest of honour had passed out in the front room.

'Get him up,' Mike had said. 'I'm needing the foursome.'

Tanner shook his head. 'Leave him be. He's got a long road ahead of him tomorrow.' Then he wagged a finger drunkenly at Mike. 'And he'll need his strength. He's in for a shock when he gets home.'

'What sort of a shock?'

'Didn't you know either? His wife's left him.'

'You're talkin' rot.'

'No fear. She's run off on him, I tell you. Thora's staying at the Palace Hotel in Perth and having a high old time.'

'How do you know?'

'Because I was staying there too. Kengally knows her, he thinks she's an angel. No getting away from it, she's a beautiful woman, knocked spots off the society ladies strutting about there.'

Mike was sobering fast. 'If Kengally knows her, why didn't he say so?'

'Tact, my dear fellow. Tact. It was obvious to us that Clem had no idea his wife was on the loose. He said she was home at Lancoorie, and we weren't about to argue with him.'

'I don't believe you.'

'You don't? Then how do you think we heard about Yorkey? Thora boasted her husband was making a fortune out here with his mine.' He laughed. 'She's left him all right. We had a good time with her, parties and picnics.' He nudged Mike. 'She was all very ladylike with Kengally, but not with me. Thora never was the ice maiden she pretends to be. I mean, Matt Spencer got into her bloomers, she was pregnant when she married Clem.' He sighed, reminiscing. 'I was sorry I had to leave her to come back here. Thora's not averse to a little slap and tickle, believe me.'

Mike punched him in the face, sending him sprawling over a table laden with bottles and glasses that crashed to the floor with him. There were shrieks and shouts as people in the crowded room shoved each other aside, trying not to trample on him, but Mike pulled him to his feet and dragged him outside.

'You've a dirty mouth,' he gritted. 'Get out of here!' And threw Tanner, reeling, into the street.

Clem was still asleep, so Mike left him there. He had to believe half of the story, at least, that Thora was in Perth, but as for the rest, it was surely no more than drunken boasting. Thora could be a little flirty – he'd seen that for himself, that was probably what had got her into trouble in the first place – but also nervy and skittish. He didn't believe for one minute that Tanner had got his hands on her.

So what to do? In the end he said nothing. Had Clem not been leaving that morning, had he been staying, Mike would have been obliged to mention that someone had seen Thora in Perth, and encouraged her husband to go home. Clem was right, he mourned for his friend as he rode away. He had been away too long. Thora had probably got fed up and gone for a holiday, but she should have had the sense to tell him. He hoped that was all.

He was among the early crowd jostling to be served by the overworked clerk in the front office of the assayer's domain, where miners were already demanding attention. They wanted advice, directions, application forms, maps, reports and all manner of information, and the clerk flapped about, adding to the disorder by trying to serve several men at once, hoping to break down the crush.

Mike stood for a while, watching the clerk rifling through overflowing cupboards, boxes on the floor and trays on his desk, searching for requirements as the men milled about him. A request for an assayer's report sent him to a tray on the desk where he licked a finger and snapped through pages until he sifted out the right one and handed it over. Not given to patience, Mike moved closer to that tray, peering at the pages carefully as they were sorted through to retrieve reports, and spotted the name Yorkey. As soon as the clerk turned his back, Mike quietly helped himself to the Yorkey report and backed away. Pleased with himself, he pushed out of the office, eager to read the assayer's final report, but he soon came to a halt, staring at the page in shock.

The returns were poor. Yorkey quartz still showed some gold but the level had dropped considerably from the first excellent finds. In the assayer's opinion, that mine had deeped out.

'Damn blast it!' Mike spat. This would mean thumbs down on the purchase.

He was about to go on his way, resigned to the inevitable, when he was reminded of Kengally and Tanner. He was still angry with them, feeling that they'd made a fool of Clem, that they were laughing at him, pretending they didn't know his wife. And Tanner! That slimy bastard with his remarks about Thora! Boasting that he knew her better than a man should! Clem's wife.

'Tact be damned,' he growled, remembering very clearly that when Tanner had come out to Yorkey he'd given the impression that he knew nothing about it, though he'd already heard from Thora that it was yielding well. Obviously, Mike now knew, the buyers had checked Yorkey's original gold-bearing returns with the gold register before they'd come near the place.

'Think you're bloody smart, don't you?' he muttered.

He went back into the assayer's office and asked the clerk if he could look at a map of the Boulder area, a district just outside Kalgoorlie that was turning up awesome gold finds.

Obligingly, the clerk searched a cupboard for the map, complaining that new areas were opening up so fast it was hard to keep track of them, but that he did have one somewhere. While he was busy, Mike pocketed several sheets of official notepaper with the state crest at the top, the same paper that the assayer used.

When the map was produced, he looked it over and plunged a finger in the centre. 'That's it, thanks, mate, that's all I wanted to know.'

He stopped by the store and picked up a fine pen and black ink, identical to the squat bottle on the clerk's desk, and hurried back to the Black Cat, where he settled at Jocelyn's neat desk to get down to business.

As soon as the new report was finished, he burned the other one and sped back to the assayer's office.

The crowd had swelled, overflowing down the steps into the street, but Mike edged his way further and further into the office until he was standing by that tray again. Then it was easy. He slipped his own version of the assayer's report in among the others waiting to be collected, and left the office unnoticed.

By the time Tanner arrived to request the Yorkey report, the rush had eased. As the clerk shuffled papers again he looked up: 'Gee! You're Mr Tanner, aren't you?'

'Yes,' Tanner growled, in a mean mood after that alter-cation with Deagan the previous night, and too much booze. His jaw had hurt far more when he awoke this morning than it did when the blow was struck, and two teeth were loose.

'By Jesus,' he muttered to himself, 'I'll get you for that, Deagan.'

'Don't you remember me?' the clerk persisted. 'John Beardley. I used to work in the Lands Department in York.'

'No,' Tanner snorted. 'Can you find that report or do I have to look for it myself?'

'It's here! I've seen it here this morning. Just a tick.' He fished the page out. 'Here it is, Mr Tanner.'

Without a word Tanner took the report and turned away, reading, nodding his head in satisfaction. Yorkey was all that he'd expected it to be. A winner! Feeling slightly better, he set off to hand it over to Kengally.

The sale of Yorkey went through without a hitch, and Mike deposited the other half of the sale payment into Clem's personal account.

If the worst comes to the worst, mate, he mused, we'll have to hand back that cash, but it's not going to break either of us. It's more important for you to find your wife right now. He laughed. And you, Tanner, with your big mouth. Talk your way out of that!

'You forced her out,' Clem shouted. 'My wife! You forced her out of her own home.'

Alice was in tears. Clem had been home two days now and still his anger hadn't subsided. She had tried to explain what had happened, quietly and truthfully, but he wouldn't listen.

'I'm surprised you haven't taken over our room as well,' he added. 'But I suppose that's just a matter of time.'

George came into the kitchen. 'Don't speak to Alice like that,' he said grimly. 'I've had enough of your bad temper.'

'No, George, it's all right,' Alice begged. 'This is between Clem and me.'

'You can't expect me to stand by and listen to him yelling any longer,' he said. 'That's no way to keep the peace.' He turned to Clem. 'If you've got any more to say, say it to me.'

'I've said all I'm going to say to you.'

'Good, then it's my turn. I haven't got any sympathy for you. Your wife has left you . . .'

'Not really.' Alice tried to soften the situation.

'She's left him, Alice,' he retorted grimly. 'And it's his own fault, leaving a young bride for so long. But that's nothing to do with us. She left before we even thought about getting married. As a matter of fact, it was Thora's idea that we should.'

'What?' Even Alice hadn't known that.

'Yes, she knew she was placing us in an awkward spot, leaving us alone here. I wouldn't have had the courage to propose to you if she hadn't encouraged me.'

'I don't believe you,' Clem sneered.

'And I don't give a damn what you believe,' his brother-in-law said. 'The thing is, Alice and I are married, I love Alice, and if you can't accept that as truth, then we're at a dead stop.'

'What does that mean?' Clem charged.

'It means, if we all can't live here peaceable, then we'll leave, Alice and me.'

Alice was on her feet. 'No! You can't mean that, George.'

'Of course he doesn't. What will you live on? He's got nothing.'

But George was determined. 'I do mean it. We'll leave, Alice. I can get a job. I'll look after you.'

'Go ahead then,' Clem muttered. 'I'm not stopping you.'

Alice intervened. 'I'm sorry to have to say this, Clem, but have you forgotten that I own half of this property?'

'No, and I bet he hasn't either.'

He stepped back in shock as Alice slapped his face. 'You behave yourself, Clem Price. And before we go a step further, you apologize to George.'

'Why should I? He marries you when my back is turned . . .'

'Your back? Who do you think you are? We are adults, able to make our own decisions. I'm thinking that no matter who I married you'd have found some objection, because you think you own Lancoorie. Well, I own it too and the sooner you get that through your head the better.'

Clem slammed out of the room without apologizing.

'Well,' George shrugged, 'I think we'd better start packing, love.'

Alice looked sadly out of the window. 'I'll really hate leaving here, but if I'd married a man with his own property I'd have had to go with him, wouldn't I?'

'But I don't own anything,' George said miserably.

'We will, though. Clem will have to buy my share of Lancoorie. He can afford it with the money he's been sending home from the goldfields. I don't want that money. That's his. With our share of Lancoorie we'll have quite enough to buy a nice property of our own.'

'Are you sure? I never thought to break up the family.'

'You haven't broken it up. He has, he's so damned pig-headed.'

'Ah, he'll cool down, lass.'

'Yes, and so will Thora, no doubt. This is her home. I don't want to be involved in their upsets any more. I want my own home.'

'You're really going?' Clem said.

'Yes.'

'But I apologized to George.'

'That's beside the point now. We've made up our minds.'

'What if I asked you to stay?'

'Clem, we need our own home. We can all stay friends. We'll be living in the district and we can visit. It'll be very nice. You won't begrudge me my money from Lancoorie?'

He put his arms about her. 'No. That's as good as in the bank for you. I'll be sorry to see you go, both of you. But you've got to let me help you find a good property. I can't have you buying a dud. It might take time. You will stay on until then?'

Alice smiled. 'Of course we will.' She turned to face him. 'Now, what about Thora?' she asked anxiously. 'You haven't even written to her.'

'I've been too busy putting on extra farm hands.'

'But it's been two weeks. When are you going to Perth?'

'I'm not.'

Alice was stunned. 'You can't just leave her there!'

'Why not? I'm paying the bills. She can stay there as long

as she likes. Until the Palace throws her out, and then she'll have to come home.'

'That's cruel. I'm sure her leaving was just to get your attention. She'll want you to come for her.'

'She wanted me to make more money for her and I did. You say she was lonely; well, I was bloody lonely too. Kalgoorlie isn't the Palace. I don't think any of you realize what it was like living in that stinking tent city.'

'You don't look any the worse for wear,' she said, unimpressed. 'After your illness, I was surprised to see you looking so fit.'

'Just the same, the monotony of a mine gives a man plenty of time to think.'

'What about?'

'Water, mainly,' he said. 'Water and home. And what a haven Lancoorie was after that dust bowl. And how good it would be to get home to you and Thora. And what do I find? Everything's wrong. You should have written to me.'

'That was Thora's responsibility. I hoped she would be home before you.'

His face hardened. 'Well, she's not! And she's got my daughter with her. Lydia might be adopted, but she's mine as well as Thora's. How dare she take my child from her home?'

'That's unfair. She could hardly leave her here. And you're forgetting, Clem, in your anger, that Thora thinks that baby is her own. You be very careful what you say there.'

No matter how hard she tried, Alice could not persuade him to go to Perth. She wrote to Thora, telling her that Clem was home and waiting for her, hoping she'd enjoyed her holiday. She could do little else. Clem kept saying he had his own plans about Perth, but that he would go in his own good time. And that was that.

The fencing gang was working well. They were older men than the usual run of hefty labourers, but they were experienced, and Clem was relieved that he could let them get on with the job unsupervised. He headed home, feeling strangely at a loss. And it wasn't only Thora, although his thoughts were constantly with her.

Lancoorie seemed to have lost its gloss. It was hard for him to maintain interest in the place, although nothing had changed, everything went along with the seasons as usual. But like it or not, the property was no longer the centre of his universe. He'd griped about the hard days at Kalgoorlie often enough, but there was also the excitement, the extraordinary mix of characters, and the camaraderie. He couldn't bring himself to admit his restlessness to Alice and George. They'd laugh at him. Tell him to bring his wife home, to own up that he was missing her.

If they only knew how much he was missing her! Facing the truth, Clem knew he was afraid to confront Thora. He wanted her to come home of her own volition. Deep in his heart he was sure that Thora had left him, that this was not just the holiday that Alice, peacemaking, claimed that it was. Obviously she had no idea that Thora wasn't interested in sex. That their sex life was practically nonexistent.

He had listened to their subtle references to the marriage bed, to the expectations of a young bride, as if the poor girl had been sadly misused by his desertion, and he could have laughed in their faces. If Thora had missed him at all, it wasn't in the bedroom, not in the room that Mr and Mrs Gunne had tactfully not disturbed. They had bought themselves a double bed and installed it happily in Alice's smaller room, making a joke of the cramped conditions. And they were happy! Surreptitiously curious, he'd not failed to notice that his quiet, shy sister was blooming. She had a sparkle in her eyes now, and a loving smile every time George gave her a cuddle, which was often, and Clem was pleased for them but not a little jealous.

Why couldn't Thora be like that? It wasn't that she was a stranger to sex before they were married.

'For God's sake,' he muttered as he led his horse down to drink at the dam, 'Alice was a virgin and she's enjoying married life. Why can't Thora?'

'Because she's not in love with you,' an inner voice replied.

296

'You were just a port in a storm. Now that she has overcome the social stigma, and is a married woman, you've served your purpose, she has left you. And you handed her the excuse on a plate.'

He shuddered. That was why he was afraid to confront her. What if he went to Perth and demanded that she return? If she agreed, under duress, that would drive another wedge between them. And worse, if she refused, what then?

'Them fellers stuck a spear in you, boss!'

Clem jerked around to see old Sadie sitting cross-legged under a tree.

'How did you know that?'

The strong white teeth gleamed a smile on her weathered black face. 'Blackfeller talk. What you do with my message stick?'

'I'm sorry, Sadie,' he said. 'I think I must have lost it. What did it say?'

'Not say, I bin told you. Just speak. People business and you, damn fool, lose it! Your missus, she sick lady, eh?'

'No. She's just having a holiday in Perth. A good time.'

Sadie glared at him. 'She bin sick long time. You give her another bubby. That make her better.'

'Good, I'll do that,' he said, to appease her. More bubbies was Sadie's answer to all female ills.

'How have you been?' he asked. 'How are all your family?'

'Them good. I got two boys, you ask George give them white man's jobs? They gotta learn, I tell them, people country gone.'

'Your grandsons?' he asked, to cover the statement he had just heard, that he was no longer the boss here. Was it true? How could that be? Maybe she had just become accustomed to having George about.

'Yes, good boys. Smart.' She tapped her head. 'Up here. They no lose no sheeps.'

'Tell them to come to see me,' he said, reclaiming his authority.

Sadie looked at him, surprised. 'When this happen? The boss feller come for you soon.'

'What boss feller?'

The dark eyes widened as she gazed at him, deep, velvet eyes glistening with the mysteries of the ages, and Clem looked away. Sadie seemed as old as the distant hills. She and her mob, the remnants of their tribe, had been here long before Noah laid claim to the land, so he'd known her all his life. He'd learned to take a lot of what she said with a grain of salt, because she was a wily old sod, but sometimes . . .

That night at dinner he quizzed Alice: 'Tell me truthfully. Has Thora been well? I mean, she hasn't been sick or anything?'

'Oh, no. She's been in excellent health. She was riding quite a bit, Clem, and she rides extremely well. In fact, she hasn't had a day's sickness since you left. I went down with a bad cold but Thora didn't even get that. And neither did Lydia.'

Clem nodded, sorry he'd mentioned the subject, because Alice took the opportunity to plead with him again. 'Don't just leave her there, Clem. Go and get her. I know she'll be glad to see you.'

He reached for another helping of mashed potatoes and made no comment.

George listened to them. In his opinion that wife of Clem's was one card short of a pack. She wasn't just the scatterbrain that Alice thought she was. Years of incarceration had introduced George Gunne to every level of madness the human mind could devise, and he'd recognized as a 'condition' the vagueness, the lapses, the odd bewilderment in Thora. That was how the degrees of madness were passed off in prisons, as 'conditions', beyond the expertise of the physicians and amateur apothecaries, and therefore shunted aside, teased or ignored. Who cared?

He had cared enough to try to talk to Thora alone, but the opportunities were rare and Thora's conception of her status as mistress of the house could not allow her to address any problems with her convict farm hand. Nor had he missed the cunning in her eyes when she'd suggested he marry Alice. The trouble with loonies, he'd told himself, genuinely bowled over by the idea, but not against it, was that they could be boldly sane at times. If it suited their purposes.

No, not a full-time loony, he told himself. Just a card short, but as the newest member of this family, far be it for him to make such mention. He watched as Clem poured the last of that rich brown gravy on his potatoes, and sighed. George was not an ambitious man. He was always grateful for whatever came his way. But he would have liked more gravy.

The dining room at the Palace was in uproar.

Mrs Price had swept in looking a dream. She was wearing a low-cut ivory satin dress with a bustle and a tightly corseted waist, a dress that, Miss Devane learned later, she'd bought on a sudden foray with Netta into the most expensive dress shop in town.

Her blonde hair was padded out to frame her lovely face, and one long curl was allowed to slide voluptuously down on to her bare shoulder. She wore no jewellery, but the bodice of her dress flashed richly with a shower of blue and gold beading, and all eyes were on her this Saturday night. Diners turned to stare as she was greeted by the head waiter. There seemed to be some difficulty.

The string quartet played their lovely romantic airs, and she smiled, appreciating, waiting, until, in whispers, it appeared she had been turned away.

She raised her voice and the guests strained to hear, creating a hush. The manager was called. The tall, elegant woman with eyes like the western skies stood her ground until a well-meaning gentleman in an immaculate dinner suit thrust aside his chair and came to her rescue.

'Madam,' he said, 'there appears to be some misunderstanding. Would you care to dine with me and my family?'

'Thank you,' she said graciously, with a cold glance at the hotel manager and his minions, and followed him across the room, cutting a swathe through a forest of eyes.

A kind lady in a neatly buttoned black dress smiled her welcome, and her two adolescent sons sprang to their feet to provide another chair at their table, but Mrs Price stared at them.

'Who are you? What are you doing at my table? This is my table. I don't know you.'

To their dismay, she signalled to the head waiter to attend her.

He came rushing over, skirting the large, busy tables. 'What is it, madam?'

'This is my table,' she said imperiously. 'Send these people away. When Lord Kengally hears about this he'll be furious.'

'I think you've made a mistake,' he whispered. 'Perhaps it was another night.'

'Sit down, my dear,' the kind lady said. 'You're creating a fuss.'

'I am not creating a fuss. I simply wish to sit at my own table. Is that too much to ask?'

The head waiter retreated to firmness. 'I'm afraid I shall have to ask you to leave, Mrs Price.'

After a considerable flurry, it was the kind lady who escorted Mrs Price from the dining room.

'She's not drunk,' she said staunchly as she went with Thora into the adjacent lounge and handed her over to Miss Devane, who had been called for assistance. 'I've seen plenty of drunks in my day. This girl is confused, that's all. Call her husband.'

In conference with the hotel manager, Miss Devane agreed that Mrs Price would have to leave the Palace, but it was a difficult situation. The pastoral community was the backbone of the leading Perth hotels. They came in with their families for months at a time in the summer, to escape the inland heat, and they were respectable, reliable guests. They came from the big cattle stations in the north, and from sheep stations in the south, and their loyalty to hotels that gave them service spanned generations. They were beloved of the hotel fraternity, not only because, with their spontaneous good humour, they were the most undemanding guests, but also because their cheques and countrified IOUs were always met, unlike those of the gold-involved creatures who now roamed the city. Of these, it was hard to tell who could pay and who could not. The Palace manager had been burned too many times by gentlemen who wore a façade of affluence. The last thing he wanted to do was offend any of the pastoralists or their women.

'What do you suggest, Miss Devane?'

'One of the cottages might be suitable.' The block at the rear of the premises was also owned by the hotel. Designated for future expansion, it was presently occupied by two cottages which were leased in the summer to country visitors and their families.

'But they're closed up.'

'I can soon remedy that. I'll have one of them cleaned and aired within a few hours.'

'She mightn't be happy about moving back there.'

'Then I'll have to convince her. She can't stay in the hotel, we must not have any more of her tantrums. Besides, her demands are becoming an irritation. She seems to think the staff have nothing better to do than run up and down to her with meals and teas at her convenience. Sometimes I think we should charge for all that extra service.'

'Charge to send up meals! Impossible. That would cause a dreadful outcry.'

'It might encourage them to use the dining room instead of dragging the waitresses away from their downstairs duties.'

'Heaven forbid that Mrs Price be encouraged to grace my dining room more often. I hope you will inform her that there is no room service to the cottages. The summer visitors who occupy those premises bring their own cooks.'

She nodded. 'I quite understand that. Her nanny is reliable. She can cook for her if Mrs Price doesn't want to run to a cook. I can't see that flibbertigibbet dirtying her hands in a kitchen.'

He was unimpressed. 'Why bother with the cottages? Why not just tell her we're booked out and resettle her in another hotel?'

'Won't do. I mentioned something like that and she wouldn't have it. She insists on staying at the Palace. Status, you know.'

'Where is the damned husband?'

'Still out at their sheep station, obviously. The bills are being paid. If we wait until he arrives, we're still stuck with her. She might even be more demanding with him to back her up. Let me talk to her again. I have to convince her that the cottages are still part of the hotel.'

The manager stood, straightening his waistcoat. 'Tell her she has to sign a lease on the cottage. Three months is the usual, they're never let by the day or the week. That will put her off. Explain we are going to great lengths to accommodate her, what with the child and the nanny, but if she can't accept this compromise then she goes to another hotel forthwith. We'll be seen to have done our best, so there should be no repercussions.'

Mrs Price was suffering from anxiety pangs that knotted her stomach, but for the life of her she couldn't remember why. They had something to do with the beautiful satin dress that was now back in its tissues in her trunk.

She had a glass of cognac with her lunch, at Nanny's suggestion, but that didn't seem to help much. It was only when Miss Devane came to chat to her that Thora remembered her original plan to find a house in Perth. Her own house.

Thora liked Miss Devane – she was so sensible, so much a woman of the world – and she tried to concentrate on what she was saying, but it was rather complicated, all this talk about a busy hotel. Everyone knew the hotel was busy. All the best hotels were busy, Thora was sure. To please Miss Devane, though, she went with her on a pleasant stroll round the block to visit a dear little cottage that had a view of the park.

'It's nice,' she said. 'Is it yours?'

'No. It is still part of the Palace Hotel. We keep it for our élite clientele. For people who don't wish to be bothered by strangers dashing about all the time. Come and see, it has three bedrooms and a kitchen, and the sitting room opens out on to the veranda. And it has its own bathroom. I often think it is so difficult for ladies having to take their turn in the hotel bathrooms. Quite embarrassing at times, don't you think?'

'Positively tragic,' Thora replied. 'I find it horrible to have

302

to wait in line in my dressing gown while some other woman takes her time. I've told them off, you know.'

'So I've heard,' Miss Devane murmured. 'Of course, we only have the right people staying here, people who prefer to have their own bathroom. More hygienic, they say.'

'Of course it is. I've always found it rather disgusting having to use a bath after boarders. Who's staying here now?'

'No one as yet. We'll be taking the first bookings shortly.'

Thora wandered about, impressed by the fresh linen on the beds, the pictures of scenes on the walls, even the old-fashioned lounge suite in the sitting room. The starkness appealed to her, as if no one really lived here, and the thought grew in her mind that this was an empty house, the one that she'd known she'd find. She knew Miss Devane was impatient to leave, but Thora stalled, caught up in her fantasies. This was her home. She'd never have to go back to York, to all that humiliation. In the progress of time she'd forgotten Lancoorie completely, and her hotel room was receding too.

When she signed the lease it was as if she'd come directly from the misery of the Carty household in York to this dear little haven set among high wild grass and familiar gum trees. In her eyes, this wasn't an old workman's cottage on the street front of a block that hadn't been cleared since last summer. Standing at the top of the three back steps that overlooked a dilapidated laundry, she laughed at the red and green parrots that scuffled in the trees, and then she saw the other cottage down by the back fence.

'Who lives there?'

'No one, Mrs Price.'

'That's good. I don't want neighbours calling. They're such a bore.'

The next morning Mrs Price, her daughter and her nanny took up residence in the cottage, and the manager was delighted. The bills still went to Lancoorie – more money in the Palace Hotel's till – and the changeover had been effected with no fuss at all. He invited Miss Devane to dine with him that evening.

★　　★　　★

Cook said that Mr Warburton was the artistic type, since he'd recently taken to setting up an easel on the river bank, and Lil didn't disagree. To her he was more than that, and less.

Times had certainly changed. Robert was unlike his departed sister in every way. He was not the slightest bit interested in her household journals, he had no interest in the running of the house, as long as his needs were attended. He no longer made a pretence of overseeing Jordan's management, and it was to Jordan's credit, and Lil's, that no one took advantage.

Lil was surprised to find that Robert was a very weak man. His dismissive attitude towards the local people was all bluff. He really did want to be the social centre of the district, since Minchfield was the grandest house along the river, but he couldn't make up his mind what to do about it. When Lil suggested he invite selected people to a dinner party he agreed enthusiastically, and then backed off, inventing excuses, whining about the sort of folk that he'd have to entertain.

'Just not my sort at all,' he said to her.

He complained about the size of the bill for the renovations necessary after the fire, and Lil agreed that the builder's charges were outrageous. But when it came to the showdown, he buckled and paid up.

A weak man, she told herself. No backbone. But that could be useful. Now she knew why Lavinia had ruled the roost. Her brother had lived here under her rule, beholden to her for his roof, ignoring her excesses for fear of expulsion. The strongest thing he ever did was to make that move on his sister, but that was only because she was in hospital, out of his way. In a strange turnabout, Lil had come to respect Miss Lavinia, and, gradually, to despise her own lover, this cringeing, whining man who wasted his days being neither fish nor fowl. He was not, as he pretended to Lord Kengally, a gentleman farmer, because he took no interest in Minchfield Farm, nor was he the intellectual he professed. Trying to improve her own education, to impress him, Lil had taken books from his library to her room, only to discover that most were soiled with mould, the pages stuck together from disuse.

He had one frequent visitor, Henery Whipple, who came from Perth once a week to lunch with Robert and discuss business, Henery's business, which was to advise Robert on the purchase and sale of shares. He was a large, paunchy man, with a booming voice; a necessity, Robert explained to her, for his profession, because Henery had been an auctioneer and then progressed to Parliament, where he was now the Speaker of the House.

At first Lil had found Henery comical, with his bald head and huge waxed moustache, and his habit of finding his way to the piano to accompany himself as he sang the silliest of ditties, but she soon learned that Henery was no fool.

They were so different, in every way – Robert quiet and querulous and Henery so boisterous and outspoken – that she wondered how the friendship could have developed, until she learned that they were somewhere related. And, it was interesting to discover, Henery disliked Lavinia intensely.

Then it all began to fall into place. While Lavinia was in hospital, Robert had stayed at Henery's home in Perth, and it was in that stronger, more decisive company that he'd found the courage to have Lavinia committed and establish himself as master of Minchfield. Now, of course, Henery was being repaid by the commissions he was earning while he wore his other hat, that of sharebroker. Lil was intrigued by the machinations of these men, and, a schemer herself, vowed to stay on the right side of Henery, no matter what, beginning by serving his favourite dishes at lunch.

For his part, Henery soon became aware of her relationship with Robert, and to Lil's relief, simply took it for granted. He even went so far as to compose little ditties about the beautiful Lillian being 'one in a mill-i-on', and from that day on, the name stuck. Both Robert and Henery referred to her as Lillian.

'I am retiring from the House shortly,' he announced one day. 'Give me more time to attend to business. All power and no pounds in politics. Time I paid more attention to the sharebroking while it's at its peak with the gold rush. Those shares you've got in the steel company will skyrocket, Robert, with that railway line under way.'

'The line to Southern Cross?'

'Not just to Southern Cross, old chap. I have it on good authority that that line is going to Coolgardie and on again to Kalgoorlie.'

'What on earth for?' Robert said. 'Those goldfields will be ghost towns in a year or so.'

'Just trust me, Robert. I've got a swag of steel shares myself. But, getting back to my retirement, they're giving me a send-off at the town hall, and you must come.'

'I don't know about that,' Robert said. 'I'm fairly busy here. I wouldn't know anyone.'

'You know me.'

'But you'd be caught up all the time, being guest of honour.'

'That's true. I might be a poor host. Bring Lillian, she'll keep you company until I'm free of official duties.' He turned to Lillian. 'What do you say, dear girl? I think you'd cut quite a dash.'

She tried to keep the excitement from her voice. 'That's up to Robert.'

'What about it, Robert? She's a beautiful woman. You can't keep her hidden up here for ever.'

'If she wants to go,' he wavered.

'I'd adore to,' she said. 'Thank you, Henery. I'll have to get a new dress for the occasion, though.'

'Then that's settled. You both come up to my place and stay a few days, and we'll all go to the party. It should be great fun.'

His hand squeezed hers warmly, and Lillian wondered why she hadn't noticed Henery's real interest before.

Later that night she examined her face and figure in the long mirror. There was no doubt she'd come a long way since Ted Cornish. She was no longer a skinny, downtrodden girl; she'd filled out in all the right places. Her dark hair was thicker, well cut now, and elegantly dressed in the wide, high fashion of the day, swept up round a roll of fake hair and pinned into place. And now, her eyes looked darker, brighter, against clear fair skin that was no longer tanned by the sun. Those days were over. Lil took great care to stay out of the sun, and with her general appearance for that matter, even adding a touch of powder, and a little rouge to her lips. As mistress of Minchfield she had to look her best, and it was paying off. She swirled about, admiring her tightly corseted figure, the real hourglass look that was all the rage, according to ladies' journals.

You're looking good, she told herself. You must be, or the likes of Henery Whipple wouldn't be making passes at you, nor would he want you at his party with all his fine friends.

Perth! Lillian hugged herself with joy. She was going to Perth, to mix with all the most important people! It would be wonderful. She'd have to be extra specially nice to Robert now, to make sure he didn't change his mind.

Caroline would be safe here. Gladys, one of the house-maids, an older woman, very reliable, would take care of her while her mother was away. This opportunity, to be acknowledged in Perth as Mr Warburton's lady, was important. Too important to miss. Lillian knew that her future, and Caroline's too, could depend on the outcome. Though she hated the thought of parting with Caroline, even for a few days, it had to be. It just had to be.

He came out of the dust storm like the ghost of a long-dead explorer returning at last from the bitter trails of defeat, and he frightened the life out of Alice. She stood petrified, peering through the slats of the shutters, hoping this spectre with its white face stark against funereal black would pass on by, but it moved steadily ahead, its horse barely making a sound over the whine of the wind. It seemed to take ages coming into focus from the gloom, heading straight for the house, and she was only slightly reassured as the vision took the shape of a stranger, a weird-looking fellow with long black hair hanging lank under a dusty black hat.

'Oh, mercy,' she whispered, wondering if she had time to run out the back door to the sheds, where the men were working, but he was already dismounting and striding towards her, his heavy coat so long it was brushing his boots.

Rather than wait for him to bang on the door, she rushed out on to the veranda and spoke to him through the murky, dust-laden flyscreen, with all the cordiality she could muster.

'Good afternoon, sir. Are you looking for someone?'

He swished off his hat. 'I am indeed, madam. Is this the home of one Clem Price?'

'Yes.'

'Then would you kindly inform him that F.C.B. Vosper has come to call?'

'Yes. Yes, of course. Would you come in, Mr Vosper?'

She ushered him into the sitting room and then ran for the sheds.

'Well, for crying out loud!' Clem said. 'It *is* you, Vosper. What are you doing in this neck of the woods?'

'Making my way to Perth.'

'You're off the track a bit, aren't you?'

'Not at all. I had to go to York, and then I remembered you were in the vicinity, so here I am.'

'What's doing in York?'

'That's a long story if you have the time to hear me out.'

Alice raced to make afternoon tea so that she wouldn't miss anything, and she sat mesmerized by this odd character as he explained.

'Sold the paper,' he said. 'Too much competition. Six daily papers and ten weeklies are being printed on the goldfields now, all of them except mine servants to the God greed, filling their pages with nothing but mines and shares. I tried to tell the fools the truth, that miners should stand up for their rights and not allow themselves to be stamped on by jewelled promoters and their fat bosses in cities from London to Sydney. But they wouldn't listen.'

He turned to Alice. 'Excellent rock cakes, Mrs Gunne. My favourites. I'm not a bad cook myself, you know.'

She studied him as he talked. For all his strange appearance, especially that hair, he was a very interesting man. And for his age, only about thirty, he had certainly covered a lot of ground, from the eastern goldfields to the wilds of the west.

Mr Vosper was the first person she'd ever met who had more than a passing interest in politics, and he was adamant in his opinions, especially when it came to the rights of miners, who, he claimed, had no representation in the state parliament.

'Hard-working diggers count for naught as long as they keep burrowing out gold for the bosses. There's precious little water out there, and what is the government doing about it? Nothing!' He banged the table vehemently. 'There's cholera and typhoid and men are dying by the score, but will they give us decent hospitals? Not on your life. I heard you sold Yorkey, Clem. You got out just in time. Companies are buying up land now, land already leased by diggers.'

'Does that matter?' Clem asked. 'As long as they can keep digging. No individual miner can go down deeper than a hundred feet, it's too dangerous, so the companies might as well take over from there, with their heavy equipment and engineering know-how.'

'That's what you think. The law is changing. They'll only be able to go down to a depth of ten feet on company land. Every speck of gold from that point down belongs to the companies.'

'But that doesn't give the miner a go at all. What if he's struck a reef?'

'Too bad. Mark my words, there'll be big trouble on the fields when the diggers wake up to that. I've been trying to tell them what's in the wind. Why they ought to have representation in Parliament, to air those grievances and a lot more, before the situation gets any worse. My paper, the *Coolgardie Miner*, spelled it out for them until I got sick of trying to make them pay attention. So . . . this is why I've been visiting country towns.'

'Why?' Alice asked, intrigued.

'Because if you can't beat them, Mrs Gunne, you join them. I intend to stand for Parliament, and I'll get in too. I've been calling on editors of country newspapers to introduce myself and make sure that they publish what I have to say.'

'And will they publish?' Clem asked.

'Oh, yes. I write the articles myself – that's a saving for them – fill up a column here and there, and a different voice is always news. Get my name about, you see, spread the word like a preacher.'

They invited him to stay over, and Vosper was pleased to accept the offer. After dinner he sat up late with Clem, reminiscing about the bad times and the good times on the goldfields, for he was not without humour.

'And how are you settling back into farm life?' he asked Clem. 'Bit of a change from those rowdy days, eh?'

'It surely is.' Clem nodded. 'I'm finding it rather quiet, in fact.'

'Thought so. Adventure gets in your blood. Why don't you come to Perth with me?'

Clem laughed. 'I wouldn't hardly call Perth adventure.'

'Something different. Have a look about. You could give me a hand for a while. You don't have to hang about if you get sick of it.'

'Doing what?'

'Talking to people. Rustling up backing. You're a miner, you know what I'm on about. You could be a big help.'

'I'll see,' Clem replied. 'Let me think about it.'

But he was already almost convinced. Here was his excuse to go to Perth without appearing to be chasing after Thora, and to look for that house on the beach he'd already mentioned to George and Alice. They thought it was a wonderful idea, though their enthusiasm was heavily influenced by a desire to see him reunited with his wife, and that irked him. Held him back. He ought to go with Fred. He should. Why not? He was his own boss. Why not? It could be fun.

It wasn't until they arrived in Perth and booked into the United Services Hotel that Clem broke the news to Fred that his wife was in town with his daughter.

'I thought you had a wife somewhere,' Fred said. 'Are you separated?'

'No. She just got fed up with me being away so long and took off. She's staying at the Palace.'

'I say! High living. But don't let me detain you, Clem. If you'd rather be there with them . . .'

'No. It's a long story. My wife wants the world on her terms. I didn't appreciate arriving home to find she hadn't waited for me. She can come here.'

Fred laughed. 'Well, you sort that out. I've got some real organizing to do now.'

Instead of going straight to the Palace Hotel, Clem walked the streets of Perth, trying to remember how it had been when he'd trundled through these same streets on the back of a wagon as a child. But there was nothing familiar to him except the river. He couldn't even recall where they'd come ashore.

Exploring the busy gaslit streets, he gave himself the excuse that he wanted to get his bearings before he confronted Thora. If indeed he did at all. He was still in two minds about that.

Nevertheless, he was glad he'd come to Perth at last. He was truly impressed by the stylish city and its inhabitants.

'This might be the most isolated city on God's earth,' he told himself, remembering the taunts of easterners at the goldfields, 'but that's not so bad. There's substance here, and pride in the place.'

Damn Thora! Clem thought how much more enjoyable this visit would have been if only she'd waited and allowed him to bring her, so that they could see all the sights together. And what had she been doing here all this time? Digging up acquaintances, he supposed, people he'd never met.

He looked up, admiring a fine building half hidden by trees at the corner of St George's Terrace and another street, and then stepped back, caught unawares. It was the Palace Hotel!

What to do?

Before he could allow himself to think about this, he'd charged in through the double doors and made straight for the desk to enquire after Mrs Price.

The clerk looked at him oddly, glanced at another person

behind the desk and, without bothering to consult the lodger's book, referred Clem to 'the cottages'.

'The what?'

'Mrs Price is staying in one of the hotel annexes. A cottage. You go outside and round to the back street. You'll find madam there.'

'Thank you.'

Clem was irritated that now he had to make the same decision all over again. He considered leaving her a note, telling her he was at the United Services Hotel if she wanted to see him. But if she ignored the letter . . . Better to keep moving, he supposed. Go to see her and be done with it.

'Was there something else, sir?' the clerk asked, and Clem shook his head, barging out of the lobby as heavily as he'd entered.

Nervousness kept him pacing the dim street outside the cottage, which was as dissimilar from the splendour of that hotel as he could imagine.

'Annexe,' he sneered. 'That's a fancy name for a run-down cottage waiting to be demolished.'

But there was Thora, looking so sweet his heart gave a bump. He could see her through the window, sitting in an armchair by a lamp, the soft light glinting on her fair hair in such a tranquil atmosphere, the picture gave the impression that this woman lived here. How dare she settle in like that!

He stepped over the narrow veranda, boards creaking, and a young girl answered the door.

'I'd like to see Mrs Price, please.'

'Who shall I say is calling?'

'Mr Price!' he said tersely.

'Oh, it's you!' Thora didn't even get out of the chair. 'How are you?'

Clem stared at her. You'd think he'd just been out for the afternoon. Dumbfounded, he looked to the girl, whom Thora wasn't bothering to introduce.

'I'm Lydia's nanny,' she said quickly. 'She's asleep, Mr Price, but I'll get her for you if you like.'

'No, it's all right,' he muttered. 'I'll see her later.'

She bobbed and made herself scarce, for which he was grateful.

'What the hell are you doing in a place like this?' he said to his wife. 'I thought you were staying in the hotel.'

'I like it here. Do sit down, Clem, and stop making such a fuss. We've had our tea. Can Nanny get you something?'

'No.'

'Very well. Now tell me all about your adventures.'

'Bloody adventures!' he exploded. 'I want an explanation from you. How dare you leave Lancoorie without a word to me! What have you got to say for yourself? You're bloody lucky that I'm still paying your bills or that precious hotel would have sent you packing. And what are you paying for the privilege of living in this dump?'

Thora burst into tears. 'Don't shout at me. I can't stand it. I wish you'd go away.'

'You wish I'd what?' He was in such a rage, her tears meant nothing. 'Crying won't get you off the hook. Look at me, Thora. I want the truth. I haven't heard a word from you in months, and I'm forced to come looking for you. I demand an explanation, and it had better be good.'

'What explanation? she cried. 'I simply wanted to live in Perth. What's wrong with that?'

'Everything, you stupid woman. And since when do you need a nanny for Lydia while you sit on your bum all day? Or are you too good for her too, now?'

'I have my social engagements, and you couldn't expect me to live in this cottage on my own. I need Nanny.'

'I don't expect you to live anywhere on your own,' he fumed. 'And what about us? I'm your husband, what sort of a welcome is this?'

'It's not my fault,' she wept. 'I didn't know you were coming.'

'Would it have made any difference?' he asked bitterly. 'I've had enough of this. I'm going. You get packed, I'm moving you and Lydia to my hotel in the morning.'

That had some effect. 'I am not leaving here. Nanny can move into Lydia's room and you can sleep in her room, but we're staying. I'm very happy in my cottage. You'd like it too if you could see it in the daylight. I can't see any point in moving from one hotel to another.'

Clem gave up. He pulled a chair over and sat by her, taking her hand. 'Thora. Don't you care about me any more?'

'Of course I do. What a silly question.'

'Then why are you putting me through this? Am I being punished for staying away so long? If so, I'm sorry, it just couldn't be helped. But you know I love you, I'll always love you. I missed you terribly.'

For a second there, he thought he had her. She looked at him with sorrowful eyes. 'I love you too, Clem. Don't be unkind.' Then, just as quickly, the moment was gone. 'How long are you staying?'

He stood up so abruptly he knocked over the chair. 'I'm back,' he shouted. 'I'm finished with the goldfields. And the sooner you get that through your head, the better. I'll see you in the morning.'

But in the morning, calling at the hotel to settle her account, he discovered that Thora had taken a three-month lease on that cottage, and there were two months still available to her.

Clem was so stunned by the implications that he blundered his way outside, into the fresh air, away from the suffocating condescension of that elegant foyer, where he'd made a fool of himself for the second time. Where she had made a fool of him.

Hadn't Alice insisted that Thora was just taking a holiday, that she'd be home any day? Like hell she was! He stood uncertainly at the street corner. Thora had left him.

No, wait. Why then had she invited him to stay in the cottage, albeit in a separate room?

Stalling for time? His arrival must have come as a complete surprise to her. That was only a gesture when she found herself cornered.

He knew that if he'd been thinking straight, he should have paid out that ridiculous lease and to hell with whatever it cost. Then packed Thora up and taken her straight back

314

to Lancoorie, where they could sort this out in a normal atmosphere, away from the eyes of strangers.

She stayed in bed that morning, fretting. It was just too bad of Clem to come by, making all that noise, spoiling everything. Nanny had brought her morning tea and taken Lydia to the park so that she wouldn't disturb her mother, and the cottage was serene again, but Thora was nervous that Clem might come back.

The weeks she'd spent here had been very pleasant, although she hadn't been out much. She did have relations in Perth, an aunt and uncle, and having found their address in her little journal, she had actually taken a cab to visit them, but when she arrived at the house in Wellington Street, her nerves let her down and she just wasn't up to it. On impulse, not knowing where else to go, she instructed the driver to take her instead to the cathedral, where she sat for hours. Just sat, losing all sense of time, grateful that no one bothered her.

This became routine. These outings were her social engage-ments. She'd take a cab, allow herself to be driven about for a while, and then, as if on impulse again, ask to be taken to the cathedral, after which, with a little difficulty, she would find her way back home. Sometimes, confused, she wandered into the hotel, unable to find her room, and was escorted from the premises.

Thora did have a vague recollection of a porter talking about some woman who was drunk again, but that, of course, was no business of Mrs Price, who abhorred drunkenness.

Sometimes hotel girls, waitresses and chambermaids, would call to see Nanny, and Thora loved to hear them gossiping about the goings-on at the Palace; it made her feel part of the hotel family.

She heard him knock, and then he came into her bedroom, opening up the curtains, showering her with light.

'Please don't do that, Clem. I have such a headache. I'm not feeling at all well.'

He was sorry then. And so he should be. 'What's the matter with you? Should I call a doctor?'

'You bring my father in here and I shall scream.'

'Not your father. A local doctor.'

'It's not necessary.'

He sat on the side of the bed. 'Then you ought to get up. You'll feel better to have some air.' He bent over and kissed her, and Thora felt consoled. It was nice to see him again. He could be very sweet.

'Later. I'll get up later.'

'We're going home, Thora,' he told her. 'We can catch the afternoon train. We'll go home and start all over again. Forget about Perth.'

She sat bolt upright. 'Forget Perth? Are you mad? You can go, but I'm not. I can't possibly.'

'Why not? Is it me? Last night you said you loved me. If you love me, then for God's sake stop all this nonsense. I need you, Thora.'

'It's not you,' she fretted. 'I just don't want to go back there.'

'Why not?' he insisted. 'Is it Alice? Or George? Did they upset you?'

'No. I told Alice she should come with me. She would have had a lovely time.'

'Did you know that Alice and George are married?'

'Yes. She wrote and told me.'

'And are you unhappy about that?'

Thora felt her nerves giving way again and she was frightened. She didn't want Clem to see her in one of her states. 'Of course not. Why don't you go and find Lydia? She'd love to see you.'

'In a minute. I just want a straight answer. Are you coming back to Lancoorie with me?'

'No,' she whispered fearfully.

'And if I insist?'

'Leave me alone. We don't have to go back. You can stay here.'

He argued, cajoled, took her in his arms, tried to make love to her, but she wept and thrust him away, terror building.

When he finally left, she cringed under the covers, bunching

316

the sheets into her mouth to try to stop the echoes of someone screaming.

He found his daughter with her nanny in a small park across the road, but the child didn't know him, adding to his depression. Lydia had grown into the sweetest little girl, with dark curls and soft blue eyes. The nanny soon sized up the situation: 'Come on, darling, this is your daddy.'

Before long she was gurgling happily, showing him her doll and her new bangle.

He tried to make conversation with the nanny, without resorting to embarrassing questions about his wife, but she had nothing to offer except to chat about Lydia, what a darling she was, so in the end he kissed the child and left.

To go where? Not back to Lancoorie without his wife, and certainly not to move into that cottage on her terms.

Thora was his wife, and he wasn't about to lose her. He would stay right here in town until she came with him willingly.

That afternoon he confided the problem to Vosper, who proffered advice. 'Seems to me the lady is just teaching you a lesson. She feels you abandoned her. At least she's talking to you. Why don't you take her out and about? Court her all over again? That'll put you back in the good books.'

Sadly, Clem remembered that it would not be all over again. That no courtship had ever taken place, nor had there been a honeymoon. At the time he'd been too shy, and too busy, to suggest a honeymoon, nor had Thora seemed interested in so obvious a beginning to what was in fact a shotgun wedding. He was overwhelmed now by his own selfishness. Thora had been deprived of all the sweetness a new bride could expect, regardless of the circumstances. He would try to make it up to her.

The very next day he arrived at the cottage with a flourish. He had hired one of the larger horse-cabs – a curious affair, he thought, with steps at the back, like a miniature covered wagon, all the rage in the busy streets – and called for his family, including the nanny. He asked her to prepare a picnic lunch while he jollied Thora into dressing so he could take them on a mystery day out. Since she had been in town so long, she had probably seen most of the sights of Perth, so he was taking them to the seaside. As a child – young and old, he smiled to himself – he'd always wanted to go to the beach; now he could take his daughter.

'How will you find it?' Thora worried.

'The driver knows. You get ready while nanny packs, and we'll be off.'

For most of the journey to Cottersloe beach they had to travel slowly over a bush track, but the horse was capable and the driver in great good humour to be hired for the day. Thora made Clem laugh, worrying that they might get lost, but Lydia was the centre of attention, climbing from one to another, wanting to sit on Clem's lap, then changing her mind, moving back to Nanny, then reaching out for her mother, picking up on the excitement.

'Hold her, Nanny,' Thora said. 'She'll crush my dress.'

'I'll take her.' Clem was only too pleased to hold Lydia so that she could look out of the window, telling her about the sea even though she couldn't comprehend.

When they trudged to the top of the huge sand dunes and looked out over the ocean, Clem forgot his troubles for a minute. He stood, awed, staring at the great sweep of beach before him, hearing the thunder of the surf and smelling the salt air at last.

'Will you look at that!' Nanny said, wide-eyed.

Clem turned to Thora. 'Isn't this something! Look at that great ocean, it's so blue.'

'It's very hot up here,' she said.

'Yes, but it'll be cooler down on the beach.'

'I can't go down there. I've already got sand in my shoes.'

'Then take them off. And your stockings too.'

Soon they were all paddling, dashing away from the waves as they surged up the beach, and Clem knew his first family excursion was a success. Despite Thora's protests that he might drown, he decided to go for a swim, but in deference to the presence of Nanny, he walked well away from them until he was almost out of sight, discarded his clothes and forged in, battling the huge waves that seemed bent on keeping him out. He'd only ever swum in tangy river water or mud-laden dams, and now this crystal-clear water, full of energy, was sheer joy.

As he lifted with the rise and fall of the waves, he studied the shoreline, where two bungalows nestled at the edge of the scrub, and he envied the owners. This was where he would build his beach house, with a view of the ocean and his own beach, right at the doorstep. Obviously the good citizens of Perth preferred their river, even though the surf beaches weren't far out of town, but as far as he, a lad from the west, was concerned, they could keep their river. He had found his dream with a bonus – the land would be cheap, thanks to an obvious lack of interest in the area. It wouldn't cost much, he decided, to upgrade that bush track; he wouldn't mind working on it himself. But only after he'd bought a few blocks, he told himself cannily. No point in making life easy for other buyers until he was ready. Clem could see another excellent investment in the making.

Thora interrupted his calculations, shouting to him to come out. Embarrassed by his nudity as he waded ashore, she threw a towel on the dry sand and fled, and Clem grinned. That would change, but he'd have to take things very quietly, one day at a time.

Two weeks later, her frustrated husband remembered his overconfident expectations. There were days when Thora was too lethargic or too disinterested to want to go anywhere. Other times, when he invited her to lunch or to dine with him, she became quite excited, taking ages to dress and fussing about, but after that she had little to say, and even after several glasses of wine, which she enjoyed, she seemed to be on her guard. There was only one bone of contention. Thora kept insisting that they dine in the Palace dining room, but he flatly refused. He'd come to hate the hotel. But fortunately, once they were on their way to other cafés or dining rooms, she forgot the argument.

'This courting business is heavy going,' he told Fred. 'I'm almost inclined to grab her by the hair and insist on the conjugal rights.'

'Not a good idea, old chap. You'll turn her into the enemy. Or rather, you'll be the enemy. Do you think there's someone else?'

Clem was startled. 'No!' But he'd been thinking the same thing. Thora had changed. One minute she was friendly and warm, more so than ever before, and the next she retreated into that cold, aloof person he'd barely known in York. She seemed happy to have him about as a friend, but more often than not as a friend who had outstayed his welcome. Sometimes, too, the young girl, Netta, who obviously liked him and was always pleased to see him, gave the impression that she had something to say to him, but when he gave her the opportunity to speak privately, she clammed up. That was the beginning of his suspicions.

In the meantime he'd been busy. Fred had managed to place him on the Board of Agriculture and Mines, by introducing Clem to a board member who was pleased to lobby on his behalf.

'Why?' he'd asked. 'What do I want with them?'

'For crying out loud! You're a sheep farmer, it won't hurt to keep your eye on your own interests.'

'That doesn't sound like you.'

'Maybe not.' Fred grinned. 'But that board is becoming unwieldy, with mining leases doubling by the day. They'll have to split it soon. You're a miner as well as a pastoralist. If you can pull the numbers, you'll be in the box seat for chairman of the new Board of Mines, reporting to Parliament. From that position you can do a lot to assist the cause of your brother miners.'

Because of the pace of change in the state, the meetings were being held weekly, and Clem found them very interesting. Most of the members were retired graziers with limited knowledge of the mining industry, so Clem soon found his voice, which in turn brought him a load of paperwork that was pushed in the direction of the new enthusiast.

But he hadn't forgotten Cottersloe. He bought ten large blocks, only recently surveyed, at fifteen pounds each, and began discussing plans with a builder.

He tried to tell Thora that he was building her a lovely house overlooking the ocean, but to his astonishment she was not interested.

'How nice,' was all she could say to his news of his business interests and the house, as if none of it had anything to do with her.

Finally he gave in. He knew he would have to sooner or later.

'All right, Thora. You win. I'll buy you a house right here in Perth. Right in the main bloody street if you like. Will that do?'

'Win what? I really don't know what you're talking about, Clem. If you want to buy a house, do so. I'm not stopping you.'

'Good. Then you'll come and live in it?'

She flapped about in the irritating way she had affected. 'I don't know. I'll have to think about that.'

It happened gradually. He was becoming thoroughly fed up with her refusal to allow him to go further than a few kisses, and with her inconsistent attitude. Teasing him, he felt. Arguments were inevitable, ending with his anger and her tears, and so Clem, moving easily into Vosper's world of political campaigning, which meant meeting as many business people as possible, began to call at the cottage less and less as the days slipped by.

When Tanner found that Lord Kengally had gone ahead with the owners of Lady Luck, without advising him, he was furious. He had other irons in the fire now, and he wasn't so beholden to Kengally that he could allow an insult like this to pass. It would make him a laughing stock.

He found the Englishman in the billiard room of his hotel.

'I'm disappointed in you, sir. I didn't expect a man in your position to double-cross me.'

321

Kengally chewed on his cigar. 'You get what you give, Edgar.'

'Meaning what?'

'I shouldn't have to spell it out to you. You were cheating those miners. Your commission on the sale of Lady Luck was far too extravagant.'

'What's that got to do with you? They agreed. I object to being called a cheat.'

'But you don't mind accusing me of the double-cross. You should choose your words more carefully. I simply disassociated myself from your foolery. As you well know, I am engaged in setting up public companies in London. The subscribers have to trust me, to know that my dealings are beyond reproach.'

'All very well, but what about my commission? I set this deal up for you!'

'Simmer down. I'll pay the commission at ten per cent, which is what you charged Price and Deagan. Isn't that correct? No need for us to fall out. I simply ask that you watch your step in future.'

Tanner laughed. 'You're a hard man, Kengally.' But he soon departed that company, by no means amused. He hated Kengally's patronizing attitude, treating him like a naughty boy who only needed a slight slap to bring him into line.

'We'll see who has the last laugh,' he gritted as he strode out into the night. 'One of these days you'll pay for that, Kengally.'

Already he'd heard whispers about the fabulous Londonderry mine, that was now closed down, concreted over and guarded until the company was ready to mine.

The diggers had unearthed a lump of quartz weighing two hundred and fifty pounds, and more than a third of it was gold. That mine was so rich it became known as the Golden Hole. On one June day those same diggers turned up more gold from that dazzling white quartz than a hearty man could lift on to the bank scales. They sold their rich mine for one hundred and eight thousand pounds, plus a sixth of the shares in the Londonderry Gold Mine Company being floated in London.

Tanner hadn't missed that windfall. He'd been out like so many others to view the mine, but it was surrounded by a fence and guarded by two men. He'd bought and sold shares himself. Kengally had a substantial parcel, but a few of these 'rolled gold' shares were seeping back on to the market on the sly in Coolgardie.

So what was up? The first float had been wildly oversubscribed. Closing the mine, as he had done with Yorkey, was a good move. Share buyers knew they were on to a good thing if the mine was a known treasure chest, not just a prospecting foray, and Londonderry was money in the bank.

Or was it? Tanner couldn't figure it out. Nor could he find out who was in the know. Londonderry was as safe as a bank. But Tanner had been on the fields a long time. There was a smell in the air, just a sniff, nothing he could rightly explain, so he followed his nose. He sold all of his shares in Londonderry to eager buyers at a profit, then he bought more, turning them over fast. And he didn't forget two men who owed him: Kengally and Mike Deagan. He hadn't forgotten Deagan's attack, any more than he'd forget Kengally's double-cross.

He scoured Coolgardie for Londonderry shares, still unable to arrive at any conclusions except that the sellers, always miners, needed the cash.

Eventually he was satisfied. He'd unloaded all his remaining shares in that company on to Kengally and Deagan. His Lordship had only spent one thousand, but Deagan was holding two thousand.

'No hard feelings, mate,' he'd said to Mike Deagan, rubbing his chin. 'I was out of line. Thought I'd let you in on a good thing.'

Mike, though, was a great believer in the old adage that leopards didn't change their spots. 'I should know,' he grinned.

'I nearly knocked his block off,' he said to Jocelyn. 'Why would that bastard want to do me a good turn?'

He went to another stockbroker and sold all of his shares in Londonderry at a profit.

'Why would you want to sell Londonderry?' the broker asked him.

'It's the house I'm building,' Mike said. 'Costing me a bloody fortune. Twice as much as I'd bargained for.'

'Isn't it always the way?' the broker said, pleased, very pleased, to be of assistance.

Back in Perth, welcome civilization again, Edgar Tanner loved the excitement of the Stock Exchange. He experienced a thrill every time he walked in those doors; here was gambling at its best – more robust than cards, more powerful than a racecourse – and better still, he was winning at the game. Despite that disagreement with Kengally and his overblown righteousness, he had a good name in Perth as a broker with real knowledge of the goldfields and a nose for worthy investments, and even as he approached the building he was met by gentlemen anxious for news.

This, too, was the place for him to do some prospecting of his own, ever on the lookout for new clients. He saw Clem Price there, with Fred Vosper, and soon learned the gossip about them. Vosper, he heard, was making a run for Parliament, which was of no interest to him, for Vosper never had any money. Price, however, did.

Price, he was told, was a grazier from out west making his mark on the town as a member of several important boards, but no one seemed to know much else about him.

Good, Edgar mused. He wouldn't draw attention to Price by going over to have a chat with him; he'd catch him on the quiet. What with one thing and another, his young friend Clem was a wealthy man these days, just the sort of client he needed. Disappointing, though, that Thora's husband was back in the picture. He'd have liked to be able to spend more time with that lovely lady, but that couldn't be helped. There were other women.

He took his room at the Palace again, and that was where he picked up something really interesting. Mrs Price was still at the hotel! She'd moved with her child and the nanny into a cottage on hotel premises known as the annexe. But her husband hadn't joined her.

So they *were* separated! Excellent! Now he had the perfect excuse to call on her, to find out where Clem was staying in town.

Thora was delighted to see him. She no longer associated Mr Tanner with York. All of those people, with their dark memories, were fading and she was feeling much better. Mr Tanner was part of her new life, and for that matter, Clem was too. It was so nice to have Clem call and take her out, take the family out. They all had a most enjoyable time. It was only when Clem made demands on her that she felt herself slipping back into that terrifying nervous state, because allowing him to make love to her would, in her mind, mean a return to Lancoorie and, by association, York. Every time he mentioned going home, she was struck with a fear that she knew was unreasonable, but she simply couldn't control it. Nor could she explain it to him, because she was afraid he'd think she was going mad.

At first she'd wanted him to take her to dine in the hotel, but one afternoon, while she was sitting quietly with him in the park, she'd had a sudden flashback. She'd seen herself in the hotel dining room causing the most awful commotion, with shocked faces staring at her and people in the far corner of the room standing to watch.

Thora had clutched her mouth in fear, her knuckles white, her whole body shaking as she recalled being escorted from the dining room. It had happened, it must have happened, it seemed so real. But when? There were times now when Thora felt she really was going mad.

The horrible scene passed, and Clem hadn't noticed anything, but Thora was frightened. She reached over and took his hand, holding it tight, for reassurance. Clem was there. Everything was all right, she kept telling herself. Clem will look after you. He's a good man.

He beamed and put an arm about her, and Thora wished they could stay just like that forever.

Lately, though, Clem hadn't been calling so often. He was a busy man, of course, with meetings and what have you.

That was the way with city men, they all had business to attend. Thora didn't begrudge him, but she had come to depend on him for company and found it rather lonely sitting about waiting for him.

Which was why she was so happy to receive the visitor.

'Why, Mr Tanner! Do come in. How nice to see you again. Have you been away?'

He grinned. 'Ah, how soon you forget me, my dear. Yes, I've been out at the goldfields.'

'And Lord Kengally too?'

'Yes, he's been plunging about out there like a tourist, but he's back also, so I'm sure he'll call.'

Over tea he managed to bring up the subject of her husband, when he could get a word in, since she was full of chat about how much she was enjoying Perth, the splendid weather and the exciting social life. He thought she said she enjoyed *living* in Perth, but he must have misunderstood.

'And how's Clem?'

'He's very well. He might call in later. You must wait and see him.'

'He's not staying here?'

'Oh, no! He can't stay here, this house is too small. I mean, I like living here, it's very convenient, but there are only three bedrooms, and Nanny and the baby have the other two, so you see, it's quite impossible.'

Tanner didn't see, but he nodded wisely, convinced she was covering the fact that man and wife were separated.

'Where is Clem staying?'

'At the United Services Hotel. He's very busy. And he's building a house, you know. It will be very grand. I can't wait to see it.'

Maybe she was telling the truth, he mused, bewildered by the conversation. Maybe this peculiar pair really thought the cottage was too small. After all, it was only a holiday house, but the double bed he could see reflected in a dressing table mirror in a bedroom off this sitting room, would have room for a married couple. Definitely peculiar.

'Where is he building the house?'

'Out of town,' she enthused. 'Overlooking the ocean.'

'Up on the hills?'

'No, silly, right on the beach. At Cottersloe. It's divine. I've actually been there, we had a picnic and paddled in the sea.'

'That's a long way out.'

'No, it's not. Clem is having the road fixed. He's buying a lot of land there, I think.'

That was interesting. Tanner decided to check, land was always a good investment for a quick turnover if it had something to offer like ocean views and a beach. He'd never thought of looking as far out as Cottersloe.

'That'd be Clem,' he said. 'Ever since I first met him I've known he'd go places. And I wasn't wrong, he's doing very well.'

He was reminded then of York, and enquired politely after Thora's parents.

'They're very well,' she said.

'We weren't the only ones from York out at Kalgoorlie,' he continued. 'I did say, didn't I, that I saw Clem there? I arranged the sale of his Yorkey mine. An excellent arrangement, he won't be sorry. But I suppose he told you about that.'

'Yes, he did,' she said, fidgeting. 'Yes, he did say you were very helpful, now I come to think of it. He's very fond of you. He says you've always been a good friend to him.'

'I'm glad to hear it. I must look him up now that we're all back in town. Kalgoorlie is quite a place. You know those two Postle boys struck gold out there?'

'Who?'

'The Postles. Didn't they live next door to you?'

'I don't recall,' she said nervously.

Conversation was flagging, so he kept on in the hopes that Clem might come in, come home, or whatever odd arrangement this pair had.

'Tell you who else was there,' he said, relying on reminiscing with her to stall for time. 'Jim Forgan and his son. You remember Jim, the bootmaker. He wasn't so lucky with the gold, so he turned round and opened a bootmaker's shop there, and he's going great guns. Better than he ever did in York . . .'

She was standing, looking very pale. 'Would you excuse me, Mr Tanner. I really have to rest now.'

He stumbled to his feet. 'Yes, of course.' She disappeared into the bedroom, leaving him to let himself out.

As he walked away he wondered what he'd said to upset her, and then it hit him!

Oh, God! How could I be so stupid? In his efforts to please her he'd completely forgotten his wife. He hadn't given a thought to Mrs Tanner since he left York. She was an ignorant fool of a woman with an overdeveloped sense of her own importance. Very easy to forget.

He shouldn't have mentioned York. No doubt his sudden departure had been a great scandal in that one-horse town, and now he'd embarrassed Thora, who would be aware that he'd deserted the woman. Come to think of it, until he'd just put his foot in it, Thora had been very tactful in all of their meetings prior to this, in never mentioning York. Never mentioning a subject that, from her point of view, might have embarrassed him.

Damn!

Never mind, Thora was so scatty, she'd forget. But he would have to be careful not to make a *faux pas* like that again. She was an unsophisticated young married woman. According to her lights, unsavoury subjects like that were best avoided in polite circles.

He went in search of Clem and found him in the lounge of the United Services Hotel.

'There you are!' he cried heartily. 'I've just been to visit Thora and she directed me here.'

'How did you know where Thora was?'

'Didn't she tell you I rescued her from a fate worse than death?'

'No. What's this about?'

Tanner laughed. 'There's women for you. I'll bet she wouldn't admit to you that when she arrived in Perth, with it raining cats and dogs, there was no room at the inn.'

'She didn't.'

Tanner related how he'd come across Thora in the foyer and given her his room.

'I'm beholden to you, Edgar,' Clem said. 'Why didn't you tell me about this before?'

'There wasn't time. You were off, remember? And Kengally was there. He took quite a shine to Thora. Not surprising, your wife is a lovely woman.'

'Kengally?' Clem said. 'When I mentioned he'd bought Yorkey she said she knew him. Oh, Lord! I took that with a grain of salt, Thora's apt to exaggerate. But she really does know him?'

'Yes.'

Clem frowned. 'Then why didn't he say so?'

'Because he didn't put two and two together,' Edgar lied. 'Your name isn't exactly rare. It didn't occur to him. To tell you the truth, he had such a crush on Thora I wasn't about to inform him he was dealing with Thora's husband. She told him you were a grazier, which is true. And it sounds better than saying your husband is a miner. I only got back yesterday, I couldn't wait to tell you.'

'To tell me that my wife has been meeting Kengally on the sly?'

'No. To tell you that he didn't wake up that Thora's your wife.'

'And you say that old coot has a crush on her?'

'Has he ever? But Thora's blameless. There were no meetings on the sly. She's very circumspect. He arranged lunches for her but she always insisted I come along as her chaperon. He never got to see her privately.'

'As far as you know,' Clem grated.

'Don't say that, I reckon I could vouch for Thora.'

'And him?'

'He likes a good time, and he's got a way with the ladies, the title and all . . .'

'The bastard! You should have bloody told me.'

'What's there to tell? I had the fish on the line to buy Yorkey, I wasn't about to let you or Kengally wreck the sale for private imagined differences.'

Shed of Tanner, Clem stormed over to the cottage, only to find Thora was in bed.

'She had one of her turns,' the nanny said.

'What sort of turns?'

'Mrs Price gets all upset and dizzy-like. She has to lie down. And she has bad nightmares. She gets to scream sometimes.'

'What about?'

'The nightmares, I suppose.'

'Has she seen a doctor?'

'No, she won't let me call a doctor.'

He went in to see her, sitting by the bed. 'What's the matter, dear?'

As soon as she heard Clem's voice, Thora felt better. He was there to comfort her, and the demons that assailed her fled swiftly. She smiled. 'Just a headache, that's all.'

'Should I call a doctor?'

'Heavens, no. Ladies get headaches, Clem, he'd laugh at you.'

'Nanny said you have nightmares.'

Thora shuddered. Why was Clem reminding her? And Nanny. How dare she have discussions behind her employer's back? Were they all against her?

'Stuff and nonsense. You know I never dream. Nanny is such a silly girl. She snores, you know. She should have her adenoids seen to. Pass me my dressing gown, I should like to take a bath. And while you're here, the front garden needs weeding, could you do it? I've asked them to send a gardener, but they're so lackadaisical, it's tragic. And be a dear, tell Nanny to put the kettle on.'

He helped her put on the robe. 'Remember you told me you met Lord Kengally?'

'Yes?'

'I didn't realize you knew him well.'

'Because you don't listen to me. You're always too busy with all your own affairs and your new friends. You don't stop to think that I have friends too.'

There were no gardening tools, and the so-called garden at the front was overgrown with scraggy shrubs that clung precariously to the tired soil.

'What weeds?' he muttered as he waited for her. 'No self-respecting weed would be seen in this sad patch. It needs to be totally dug out and given a fresh start.'

Despite Tanner's excuses, he still thought it was underhand of Kengally not to have mentioned Thora, and that left seeds of doubt. How friendly were Thora and Kengally?

Clem shook off the question. For all her irritating ways, Thora was his wife, she was entitled to his trust.

God knows, he said to himself, the marriage is precarious enough without these suspicions creeping in.

It did not surprise him, as he gave the matter more thought, that Kengally found Thora attractive. She was. And whatever Kengally's intentions might have been in squiring her about, impressing her with the title, he'd left his run too late. With her husband on the scene, the silly old goat could look elsewhere for lady friends. Besides, Clem recalled, her husband had more pressing concerns.

The house he was building was modest, bungalow style with an open terrace in front to take full advantage of the sweeping views, but Thora had it in her head that it was very grand. No matter how often he reminded her that it was only a beach house, for use mainly in the summer, she couldn't or wouldn't take that in. She dragged him to various stores in her search for the 'right' furnishings, changing her mind daily, insisting they must have the best. So far she hadn't even settled on the curtain fabric, let alone something to sit on, as Clem wryly observed, but there was time yet, and she was enjoying herself. She also loved poring over a copy of the plans, and that gave Clem the chance to refer to the main bedroom as 'our room', delighted that she had no objections.

Vosper had laughed when he'd told him. 'Looks like the courtship is working. When you take her to your new house, leave the nanny and Lydia behind for a few days, so that you can carry your wife over the threshold and have a real honeymoon.'

Clem grinned. 'I've already thought of that.'

Nevertheless, worry still lodged. Thora was as skittish and as easily spooked as a young horse. And increasingly moody. One minute all up in the air about the new house, the next vague and disinterested. He wished Alice was here: the company of her sister-in-law might settle her down.

Also, Thora had taken to referring to the beach house as their home. He wished she wouldn't do that. Lancoorie was home. George and Alice would be moving on. Clem knew he'd made a bad mistake right from the beginning with Thora, expecting a girl who'd grown up in York, surrounded by family and friends, to bury herself on a lonely station, but now he was remedying all that.

They'd go into York more often, and now that they both had interests in Perth, there was nothing to stop them becoming frequent visitors to the city. He'd put on more farm hands, build better quarters for them and employ a cook to keep the staff separate from the homestead. Thora could keep the nanny, who was working out very well, a nice girl who was extremely fond of Lydia. All of this would take place in the near future, after they'd rounded off their sojourn in Perth with a holiday at the beach. And he wouldn't make the same mistake again, he'd encourage visitors to Cottersloe to share the good times.

For that matter, he recalled, I was restless at Lancoorie after the hectic days at Kalgoorlie. I'll enjoy the breaks too.

At last she was dressed, looking lovely. In a rush of emotion he decided to break his own rule. It had been foolish of him to refuse to take her into the hotel, just because he'd got off on the wrong foot there.

'My, you are looking beautiful, my love. Blue suits you. Why don't you put on a hat and I'll take you to dine at the hotel.'

'Which hotel?'

'The Palace, of course.'

He saw her flush, and apologized. 'I know. I've been difficult, but you were right. Everyone says they serve a great meal.'

'I'd rather not.'

'But you said you enjoyed dining there. There's plenty of time. We'll stroll over first and collect Fred. He'd like to join us, I'm sure.'

'You needn't go to that trouble. We can eat here.'

'No, I insist. I want to show my wife off.'

Thora couldn't talk them out of it, especially since Fred Vosper was keen on the Palace too.

Escorted by the two men, she was filled with an awful sense of foreboding as they walked across the bustling foyer towards the door to the dining room. The well-lit room yawned in front of her like some evil chasm, and the noise from within sounded raucous and cruel. She clutched her hands together in front of her, nails cutting through her gloves, telling herself there was nothing to worry about, she'd been there several times before and always enjoyed herself. That she was safe with Clem and his friend. But the fear gnawed at her, of something that had happened here, or something she had imagined.

The head waiter spoke to them, a shadowy figure, out of focus like the strained, misshapen faces that glared from all about her. She stumbled, but Clem steadied her, taking her relentlessly right across the great expanse to a table by the wall.

In a daze Thora sat with them while they discussed the menu, fighting anxiety, trying desperately not to panic.

Kengally saw them come in, and his first instinct was to go over and pay his respects, but he hesitated, remembering Yorkey. He was annoyed with himself then, that he hadn't come straight out and told Clem Price that he was acquainted with his wife. A stupid thing to do. What if Price hadn't known she was in Perth? What difference did it make to him? He should never have allowed Tanner to confuse him. It was simply not good enough.

With that, he excused himself from his table and went to greet them, believing it would be ill mannered of him not to do so.

Mr Price stood to introduce him to the other gentleman, but his voice was cold, by no means welcoming.

'And I believe you know my wife.'

'Ah. Yes. I have had the honour, And now that I am blessed with the opportunity to meet you both together I am doubly honoured. You have a charming wife, Mr Price.' He turned to Thora. 'And you, my dear, you're keeping well, I hope?'

'Thank you.' She nodded, and then suddenly, out of the blue, added, 'The house is extremely pleasant. It has a terrace in front, for the views, you know, but I think we shall need a wind guard, as I'm sure we'll need protection from the sand, but Clem says we'll think about that when we come to it. I have to admit it would be a shame to shut out the view. Dust storms can be bad enough, but I should imagine sand would be worse, and there we are set amid those great dunes . . .'

She rattled on, seemingly unaware that she had their visitor trapped standing by their table, wondering what house she was talking about, until her husband gently intervened.

'Thora, we can tell Lord Kengally about the house another time. I'm sure his friends are waiting for him.'

She stopped mid-sentence, colour flaring on her cheeks, and lapsed into a silence as sudden as her outburst.

Kengally tried to rescue the situation. 'It sounds delightful, Mrs Price, and I should indeed like to hear more of it. Perhaps we could join forces and arrange another picnic at Kings Park one day.' To Price, he said: 'It was such a pleasure to see you again, and I mean that about the picnic. I have become the most ardent fan of those magnificent gardens, you see.'

'Count me in,' Vosper said gallantly, placing the conversation back on an even keel. 'I love picnics but no one ever invites me.'

Kengally looked at this strange fellow with his long, flowing hair and smiled. 'So do I, sir. You shall be at the top of our list.'

His friends were all agog when he returned.

'Do you know those people?' a woman asked, disapproval in her voice.

'Had I not, I should hardly have spoken to them,' he retorted.

Admittedly, he mused, I had a degree of awkwardness to overcome in approaching them, but Price is a business associate, and Thora is a friend. I could do no less, but what went wrong? Price had been just as shaken by Thora's wildly inappropriate chatter as he had been, but he'd made no apology. Kengally liked that.

'I hope we will see you again,' Price had said to him before he departed, and Kengally recognized the genuine inflection in his voice. At least the breach was healed. But Thora, he felt very uneasy about Thora. She hadn't been talking *to* him about that house, she'd been talking at him. Her eyes, those lovely blue eyes, had a curious glitter, and yet she had laboured on, as if what she had to say was entirely necessary.

'Who was that weird fellow?' someone asked him.

'Vosper. His name is Vosper.'

'Is that Vosper? He's a newspaper man, you know. With socialist leanings, Lord Kengally. And political ambitions. As if anyone would vote for a curiosity like that.'

There was laughter. 'Would they cut his hair before they allowed him in the House?'

'No fear of that. The occasion won't arise.'

'But the woman. You know who she is?' Gladys Hunnicutt, wife of the Deputy Premier, said breathlessly.

'Mrs Clem Price,' Kengally said, wearying of them.

'That's what I'm saying! She's famous. Thoroughly spoilt, they say. A hugely demanding woman. She put on the most awful performance in here one day.'

'What sort of a performance?' her host asked testily.

'Oh, demanding her own table. Demanding people be shifted. So rude! It was just dreadful.'

'Mrs Price?' Disbelieving, Kengally stared.

'Mrs Price indeed. That same woman sitting over there now. It's a wonder they let her back in.'

'I'd let her in.' Hunnicutt grinned, looking over at Thora. 'She's a dream walking.'

His wife frowned. 'Then you'd be making a big mistake. I saw her, I was here that day, and I heard her shouting at the top of her voice. They threw her out.'

'Threw her out?' Kengally said, his voice ominous. 'Mrs Price?'

'Well, not physically, one should say. They sort of encouraged her out, obviously glad to be rid of her. And who wouldn't be? God knows where she came from.'

'She comes from York,' Kengally said. 'They have a sheep station out that way. Mrs Price is a very sweet woman and a good friend of mine.'

Hunnicutt glared at his wife as the other guests fell silent, concentrating on the dishes now being served.

'What was that all about?' Clem asked her as they parted company with Vosper on the hotel corner.

'What was what?'

'All that talk you foisted on Kengally. You behaved like a silly schoolgirl.'

'I did not. I don't know what you're talking about.'

'If you're such a good friend of his, why did you go all gushy when he came over?'

Thora remembered Kengally had been there, early in the evening, but she'd been so horribly nervous about that dining room she couldn't recall what she'd said to him.

'It must have been the wine,' she said gaily.

'You hadn't touched a drop at that stage.'

'Oh well, I made up for it afterwards, didn't I?' She laughed, taking his arm. 'Don't be such a bear!'

She had enjoyed the evening after all. Once she realized the roof wasn't about to fall in on her, and aided by the wine, her confidence had returned. She'd coped very well. In fact, she was pleased with herself, convinced she'd finally cured her nerves.

Clem was still in the cottage as she prepared for bed, and when he came in to say good night, he was apologetic. 'I'm sorry. I didn't mean to be a bear. I just get plain jealous, especially when you're looking as lovely as you do tonight. Fred said I'm a very lucky man to have such a charming wife.'

'Did he really?' Thora was thrilled.

'Of course he did, and why wouldn't he?' Clem took her in his arms, kissing her passionately, and moving her towards the bed.

'Don't, Clem, please. Don't. Nanny might hear.'

'No, she won't. I've sent her home. She'll be back in the morning.'

The thought of him being jealous of Lord Kengally excited her, gave her the sense of power that she'd lost somewhere along the line, and she purred as Clem undressed. 'He's very fond of me, you know. Lord Kengally, I mean. The first time I met him he quite ignored the other ladies at the table, making it clear that they were not in my class.'

'How could they be?' Clem murmured, slipping into bed beside her. 'At least Kengally has good taste. You're so adorable. I love you.'

They made love. Thora was hesitant at first, but he was so gentle and pleasurable that she threw her cares to the winds, needing him to excite her even more, delighted at his joyful reaction to her fervour. He smothered her with kisses and soft words and intense loving, and she clung to him, not wanting this night to ever end, realizing how much she loved dear, sweet Clem Price.

In the morning, Nanny was all smiles as she brought in Thora's tray, and then Clem came in, looking very manly in an open shirt and belted trousers.

'Good morning, sleepyhead.' He kissed her. 'I've had breakfast. I'm riding out to Cottersloe this morning, but if you want to come, we can make a day of it.'

'No.' She smiled. 'I'm a little tired, I think I'll rest.'

'You do that, my darling, and I'll come back this evening. What say we have a quiet dinner here tonight? I'll bring you a nice present.'

Thora stirred voluptuously in the warm bed, in love with this new-found romance. 'A box of chocolates?'

'The biggest box in town if that's what my darling wants.' He kissed her again and left.

Chapter Eleven

His name was Walter Addison. A qualified geologist and minerologist with the Department of Agriculture and Mines. He was a thin, bladey sort of fellow, who gave the impression that a gust of wind would blow him over, but Walter, in his quiet, self-deprecating way, had trodden the backblocks of West Australia, from the Kimberleys in the far north to the great forests of the south, at the behest of his employers, without a word of complaint. He had followed prospectors and miners into the fierce tropics to give his unemotional opinions on the value of mineral discoveries, and trekked hundreds of miles back to civilization to lodge his reports without fear or favour. He had seen gold strikes illuminate the land like lightning and just as soon die out, but he was unimpressed, for Walter was, at heart, a clerk. Folks might regard him as an expert, a whiz, and he supposed he was, having spent years studying his subjects and maintaining that interest, but the field work was, to him, simply an extension of his office duties no matter how hazardous. He had his own office in the Government Buildings in St Georges Terrace, and of that he was proud, therein lay status, real respect, despite shelves piled with dusty rocks and specimens and the constant odour of cheap cigars.

Walter had two homes. One was his office, the other the brick house in Hay Street that he and his wife had managed to buy with savings accumulated over twenty years. They were a frugal pair, content with their lot, and well liked in the neighbourhood, for Walter was a kindly man, devoid of artfulness, and Mrs Addison mirrored his quiet goodness.

When the gold rush began at Coolgardie, Walter's superiors

dispatched him to the warden's office as government assayer, expecting this to be another short-term stint away from Perth for their valued employee. Contrary to expectations, the rush did not fizzle out; more and more gold was escorted back to the coast and more and more prospectors journeyed west.

Other assayers were sent out to assist Walter in competition with private assayers who'd set up shop, because it was essential to keep pace and assure the gold register was accurate. Government taxes on every ounce of gold discovered had begun with a trickle, and now they were pouring into the Treasury coffers, where they were received with absolute glee.

The rush widened to Kalgoorlie, to the Golden Mile of treasure, and money flooded in, boosting the flagging economy and creating more wealth than the battling treasury officials could ever have imagined they would control.

Doggedly, the Secretary of Mines kept adding staff to his offices at the front line, and it was finally decided to appoint Walter Addison as Chief Assayer, based permanently in Kalgoorlie.

This was a disruption Mr and Mrs Addison did not welcome, but dutiful as always, they closed their house in Hay Street and took up residence in a block of small flats that was hastily erected to accommodate government officials.

After an exhausting year, Walter applied for leave. Although he wouldn't dream of mentioning it in an official letter, he felt that his wife had been such a brick, coping with the discomforts of this rough town, that she was entitled to a break. When there was no response, his letters became firmer, and at last leave was granted.

They hurried back to Perth, reopened their house and settled back for a well-deserved rest. Most of all, coming from the arid west, they missed the Swan River and liked nothing better than to stroll down to the Esplanade and sit quietly on a park bench, gazing out over the placid waters.

One somnolent afternoon, they were sitting there, enjoying this precious time, when Lord Kengally came by, and recognizing Walter, greeted him warmly.

Slightly thrown by this interruption, Walter sprang to his feet to return the greeting, and agree it was a fine day. Not being much of a conversationalist at the best of times, Walter reached for the only subject that he had in common with this fine gentleman.

'Sorry about Yorkey mine,' he said. 'I thought that would have been a goer. But then, Lady Luck will prove very worthwhile.'

'I beg your pardon?'

'I said Lady Luck will prove a good investment.'

'No, about Yorkey, Mr Addison.'

'Oh, yes. That started off with high hopes, but these things happen.'

'Are you saying that Yorkey is no good?'

'Well, of course.'

Kengally planted his walking stick firmly in front of him. 'You must be mistaken, Mr Addison. Yorkey is the goer, better than Lady Luck, in fact.'

'Heavens, no, sir. I did that report myself. Checked the yield carefully. I was sorry to have to disappoint you.'

'But I saw that report. I have it on my files. We are going public, the company is registered in London and we have an excellent response already.'

Addison shook his head. 'I would strongly advise against it, sir.'

When he saw that Lord Kengally was confused, he turned to his wife. 'My dear, would you mind? We could go home via my office, where I have a copy of the report in question. It won't take long.'

'Not at all,' she said, with a smile for Lord Kengally. 'I'm sure my husband can clear this up for you, sir.'

Kengally produced his card. 'Would you please send your findings to me at this address?'

It was evident to Walter that the gentleman was sure he was wrong, but Walter knew he did not make mistakes. 'It shall be done forthwith,' he said kindly, not wishing to prolong the argument.

★　　★　　★

Kengally was puffing by the time he reached the house, anxiety gnawing. He rushed into the sitting room that he used as an office, and riffled through his papers several times before he found the report signed by Walter Addison. Then he sank into an armchair with relief. 'By God, the fool had me going there for a while.'

He poured himself a brandy and was sitting savouring it when the messenger came with a brown envelope from the Department of Mines.

Shocked, he read an almost identical report, signed by Walter Addison, except that the results were vastly different. Comparing them again, he found that the dates were the same.

'What in God's name is going on here?'

He ordered a cab and went first to the Mines Department, where he learned Addison's home address. He was soon at the fellow's house, banging on the door.

'I demand to know what this is about, sir,' he said angrily, waving both reports at the Chief Assayer.

Walter fetched his glasses and studied the pages there and then, on his doorstep, since Lord Kengally was too agitated to bother with pleasantries.

'This one,' he said, 'is correct. I distinctly remember that I was quite disappointed to find Yorkey had fizzled out. It gave good promise at first.' He squinted at the other one, bewildered. 'I don't know where this came from. It's quite wrong.'

'But you signed it, man. The one you claim to be correct is only a copy. This is the original, handed to us by your clerk.'

'Lord Kengally, I signed the other one too. I always do my own copies to make sure there are no mistakes. As you can see, in the right-hand corner, I have noted "copy", with the number of the assay.'

'Then what do you make of this one?'

Walter took the report and walked down his path into the broad sunlight, studying it carefully. 'What I can tell you is this. Yorkey deeped out. Of that I am sure. As for this report, I am sorry to have to tell you, it is a forgery.'

'What?'

'If you look more closely, you will note differences in the shape of the figures, not my method of writing twos at all, and the eights are not even.' He sighed heavily. 'But I have to say the signature, the forging of my signature, is extremely well done. Perhaps you should come in and we'll discuss this.'

Mrs Addison brought the Englishman a sickly sweet sherry, but Kengally was grateful for it.

He turned to Walter Addison, desperately in need of this man's advice.

'How could this have happened?'

'Well, let's see,' Walter said quietly. 'I completed the report and left it with my clerk at the front desk to be handed, among others, to the relevant persons.'

'Could your clerk have tampered with it?'

'Not to this extent. I despair of that fellow's handwriting as it is.'

'Then who?'

'Who collected it from my office?'

'Edgar Tanner. He brought it straight to me.'

Walter sighed. 'Then perhaps Mr Tanner could throw some light on it. You are sure this forgery is the only one that reached you?'

'Certain. What on earth can I do now?'

'I'm afraid this is a matter for the police.'

'Not yet, not yet. Could someone else have done an assay after you, disagreeing with your report?'

'Not with my signature.'

'Oh, dear God. I'll have to telegraph London immediately to halt all sales of Yorkey shares. Any money that has been paid will have to be returned. And what about the payment I made to the owners, purchasing the mine? That will have to be returned to me, surely.'

'Did they see the report you hold? The forged report?'

'Yes. I showed it to Mike Deagan. One of the owners.'

'Then he sold to you in good faith. Under those circumstances it would be difficult to overturn the contract.'

'So I've bought a dud mine?'

343

'Yes. Might I say that it could be in your interest, however, to employ miners to turn over every speck of that claim, which was rather large, if I recall. There's always a chance of recovering the reef. In the meantime, for your own protection, for your good name, Lord Kengally, I'd waste no time in telegraphing London, with, unfortunately, very bad news.'

'And the police?'

Walter leaned on the table, making a spire with his long fingers. 'Talk it over with Mr Tanner. Find out what went wrong. If your company shows goodwill by returning any money accumulated by pre-sale of shares, then you are safe from charges. It is your right, however, to request a police investigation of this forgery. I'm very sorry about this. Forgeries are not unknown, people get up to all sorts of ruses on the goldfields. It is a great pity that you have been so inconvenienced.'

His manservant was sent to locate Tanner.

'Where shall I look, sir?'

'His office. The Palace Hotel. Any bars in the vicinity of the Stock Exchange. Ask about. Find him.'

Kengally needed several brandies to calm his nerves. He had just made it to the telegraph office to lodge his message before they closed. He was appalled that he should have to cable this sort of information, but letters took months. Aware of the sharp eyes of staff in the telegraph office, who were often known to tip off mining interests with information gleaned in the course of their duties, he used the code word *clubs*, prearranged to mean negative. *Hearts* meant affirmative. Given the minutes that were ticking away, he did the best he could.

No clubs here worth their salt. Abort that plan immediately. Yorkey main interest.

Three particular words in the cable would be enough to alert his colleagues in London and give him time to make sure this was not just a mistake. Tomorrow he'd have to advise them, and the Stock Exchange, formally, if Yorkey was not the winner that he believed it to be.

'And led others to believe,' he groaned.

Tanner arrived in great good spirits, this being the first time Lord Kengally had invited him to his temporary Perth residence.

'What can I do for you?' he asked heartily, taking the opportunity to glance about this very comfortable, well-appointed house.

'Quite a lot, I believe,' Kengally said. 'Did you know that Yorkey deeped out?'

'How could it? It's shut down.'

'Before we shut it down.'

'Is this a riddle or something?'

'It is no such thing.' Kengally went on to explain the events of the afternoon, and then handed Edgar the assayer's report on Yorkey. 'That is a forgery.'

Tanner was furious. 'Who says so? This is our report, straight from the hands of Addison himself. What's he trying to pull? Do you realize what ramifications this could have? If this got out Yorkey would be dead in the water right now. I can't believe you'd fall for this trickery.'

'Do you think it's a trick?' Kengally needed to be reassured.

'Of course it is. If rumour gets out casting doubts on Yorkey, the shares will hit bottom and someone, whoever's at the back of that phoney report you're talking about, will spring up and start buying. Well, we won't let that happen. This is no forgery, this is the real thing. You haven't done anything about it, have you?'

'I had to. I cabled London to abort Yorkey.'

'Jesus! What the hell did you do that for? They've got you spooked. And I should appreciate a drink.'

'Yes. I'm sorry,' Kengally said, absently pouring him a brandy from a well-stocked drinks tray without bothering to enquire about choice.

'Addison insists that this is a forgery. He insists that Yorkey deeped out and this is his real report. A copy, of course.'

Tanner grabbed both pages, staring at them. 'Christ! Which is which? No . . . this is ours, the excellent report. See the other one has "copy" on it.' He stared at the damning report.

'Stuff and nonsense! We hold the original, this other thing is rubbish.'

They argued, compared pages, worried the figures, searching for an explanation, until it developed into an angry confrontation.

'Addison admits this stupid report is just a copy,' Edgar shouted. 'He's made a mistake. He mucked up the copy, that's all.'

'It's not only the reports. He insists that Yorkey failed, fizzled out. He also declares that this is a forgery and it is a police matter.'

'The man's off his head. He does so many assays he wouldn't remember one from another. How the hell could it be a forgery? I picked it up from his office and took it to you.'

'You tell me,' Kengally said. 'That's the question Addison will be asking. Don't think he will let this pass. He was adamant he's right. He claims someone must have tampered with it between his office and mine.'

Edgar slammed his glass on the sideboard. 'Are you looking at me? Are you implying that I tampered with that report?'

'I'm not looking at anyone. I am just totally mystified as to how I could be faced with two such wildly differing reports.'

'They got to him,' Edgar said meanly. 'Deagan and Price. They could have paid Addison to produce the report they needed. Bribed him.'

'Addison doesn't seem the type.'

'Anyone's the type with cash on the side.'

'Then why would Addison file a copy contradicting his own report?'

'Because he's bloody stupid, that's why.'

In the end Kengally had the last word. 'I shall look into this matter first thing tomorrow.' He walked Edgar to the door. 'Addison strikes me as being a very efficient man of great integrity. I am inclined to believe that we have been holding a forgery.'

'Believe what you bloody like!' Edgar shouted at him and strode into the night.

'The bastards!' he stormed as he headed back to town. It was too early to pin anyone down yet, but if there was some funny business going on, he thought he knew exactly where to look. The only explanation was that Deagan and Clem had bought Addison. They'd paid him for a glowing report so that they could sell Yorkey and let Clem get out of Kalgoorlie. Hadn't he been bloody eager to get home?

After all I've done for Clem Price! fumed Tanner. The rat! Well, all bets are off now, Clem. I'll put you in so fast your head will swim. It'll be a cold day in hell before you ever see Lancoorie again. You and your mate, and that holier-than-thou Addison! Our report better be the right one, or the three of you are in big trouble.

He had a restless night. Too much to drink and too much worry over what was probably just a stupid mistake. In the morning he would check with the Mines Department. Check it properly, not go off in a sweat as Kengally had done.

'Mr Tanner.' The chambermaid was knocking at his door. 'Your morning tea.'

'Go away,' he yelled and turned over. Why hotel managements felt their patrons were in need of tea and biscuits at this ungodly hour he'd never understand. For the next few hours he enjoyed the sleep that had eluded him through the night, but when the heat of the day began to seep into his room he gave up and staggered from the bed.

'Ten o'clock! Damn it!' He hadn't meant to sleep this late. He should have been over there checking on this Yorkey business by now. Although in the light of a new day, he couldn't regard it as serious, just two old codgers getting their lines twisted.

He bought a paper from a newsboy in the street, glancing absently at the headlines, and stopped to stare at the shock announcement. Doubling back, he hurried into the hotel to spread the broadsheet on a reading table.

LONDONDERRY CRASH! the bold letters screamed, and Edgar pored over all the details, congratulating himself. 'I knew it,' he said. 'I knew something was wrong.' Reading

347

on, he found that the principals of the company had arrived at the mine to reopen it and turn the first sod, in a symbolic gesture heralding the commencement of happy days for all the fortunate investors. A grand luncheon was planned at a Coolgardie hotel to celebrate the occasion after the Earl of Fingall had completed his duties on behalf of the syndicate.

Tanner raced through the rest of the article. Capital was seven hundred thousand shares at one pound each, a third of which were owned by Fingall and his friends. Londonderry had been promoted as being unsurpassed in rich quartz, at the present time, in the universe. At a meeting in the Cannon Street Hotel, London, the Earl of Fingall had spoken and said that if experts were right, and they usually were, the mine would be worth three hundred thousand pounds for every twenty feet of sinking. And if the reef went down a thousand feet, it would be worth fifteen million.

The Perth daily even featured a photograph of Fingall, in evening dress, being farewelled at Charing Cross Station as he left for Australia.

'Cripes,' Tanner said with a grin, staring at the photograph. 'I bet he can do without that right now.'

The fence had been removed and the mine reopened, but diggers looking for work were puzzled to be turned away. A cloak of silence descended over the activities in the mine until eventually Fingall strode into the Coolgardie post office and sent the damning cable to London.

Regret in the extreme to have to inform you . . .

Tanner turned the page. Already arguments were raging about what had happened to the famous mine. Some said that Fingall and company had been duped, others claimed that Londonderry must have been looted. Still more called it bad judgement. *Whatever it is that has gone wrong,* Tanner read gleefully, since he had disposed of his shares, *the Queensberry-Wilde libel case has been quite forgotten in London and Paris due to the consequent furore.*

The startling news took up several pages, and Edgar was amazed to read that Lord Fingall and two of his partners were promising to recompense investors from their own funds.

The editor lauded the promise as decent and honourable, but Tanner scoffed.

'What about the original miners, the discoverers?' he sneered. 'They ought to refund the purchase price.' No way, as a promoter in the same business as Fingall, would he repay a penny under these circumstances.

'Sharebuyers take the risk,' he muttered, believing that Fingall was setting a nasty precedent. 'It's the name of the game. And what about all the buyers who turned over their shares for a profit, as I did? We've walked clear of the disaster. It's only the shareholders at the end of the line who've got caught holding the bag, and that's their bad luck.'

He scanned the rest of the editor's comments, irritated by his gushing comments of honour among gentlemen, and looked with little interest to the wind-up paragraph at the bottom of the page. He'd read enough of this juicy story, time he went on his way, first to the Stock Exchange, where Londonderry paper would be flying about like confetti. Investors would be looking for somewhere else to place their cash now that Londonderry had gone down. He should have been there hours ago, on this busy day. Addison's stupidity could wait, there was money to be made.

But just as he was preparing to fold the paper, the last lines in that article sprang out at him.

Unconfirmed rumours give rise to doubts on the viability of the Yorkey mine, which has also received a great deal of publicity here and overseas.

Stunned, he slammed the pages on to the table, twisted them into a heap and threw them into a waste-bin.

'Where the hell has that come from?' he muttered angrily. 'Kengally and his bloody cable, of course. The idiot jumped the gun. Said his message was coded. That means bloody nothing to the blokes tapping away in Morse. It's a game with them to figure out what the sender is really saying.'

He stood uncertainly at the front entrance to the hotel, trying to decide where to go first. The newspaper could wait. He could sue them. The Stock Exchange was the one place where he could begin to scotch the rumours, or his own shares in Yorkey would be worthless, but he'd need back-up.

'Lord Kengally was here earlier,' Rivett, the departmental head, informed Edgar coolly. He was a plump little man with a wad of fair curls that looked as if they'd been acquired rather than grown atop his shiny face, and he had the demeanour of a bantam hen, chest thrown out to demonstrate his importance. Edgar took an instant dislike to him but curbed his annoyance.

'So I believe. But I am an associate of Lord Kengally and I haven't had time to catch up with him. I should appreciate your considered opinion on the Yorkey matter, given that one newspaper has made an outrageous statement regarding this mine.'

'I presume you mean as to the assayer's report and decision on the worth of Yorkey quartz.'

'Exactly.'

'Mr Tanner, this is extremely unsettling. We do not appreciate promoters challenging our official reports.'

'Did Lord Kengally do that?'

'He did indeed. He seemed to think that his title somehow gave him jurisdiction over my department, but I can tell you it does not. Every application is treated on its merit and, may I add, in order of presentation. Big companies have no more push here than the lowly miner, and I reminded him of that.'

While he listened to this bustling bureaucrat, nodding in agreement to please the fellow, Edgar was reminded of Fred Vosper, who was running on the theme that Jack was as good as his master. Fertile ground here. He made a mental note to donate to Vosper's campaign in case the worker's friend got in.

'Why did he challenge the report? I'm only concerned because of what I read in the paper this morning. Are there any grounds for such a malicious statement?'

'I can only present the facts to you as I will do for my Minister, even if he does happen to be a personal friend of Lord Kengally. In the light of viewing two differing reports on the Yorkey mine, as shown to me by that gentleman, I was forced to recall Mr Addison.' He gave an aggrieved sigh. 'As you would know, Mr Addison is highly regarded in the mining world, but he is also on leave. I consider that being forced to call him in here is an intrusion and a great inconvenience for poor Mr Addison.'

'That's a shame. So what happened?'

'Mr Addison, in the privacy of his office, and in the company of Lord Kengally, a Justice of the Peace, and myself as witness, made a statement to the effect that the report held by the Yorkey syndicate is indeed a forgery. I am sorry to be the bearer of bad news, Mr Tanner, it must be hugely disappointing to you, but let me make one thing clear. The rumour that was mentioned in the paper this morning did not emanate from this office. We are very much aware of our responsibilities. A statement on this rather unsavoury matter would have to come from our Minister.'

Tanner wished Rivett would shut up. He was in a daze, wanting to run from here but unwilling to go yet.

'A forgery?' he breathed. 'Are you sure?'

'No doubt about it. I noted the differences myself once they were brought to my attention.'

'What does that mean?' Tanner asked, though he knew full well. He was still searching for an explanation.

'It means that Yorkey's not what the promoters say it is, no offence intended. You look shocked, as well you might be.'

'Addison couldn't have made a mistake?'

Sigh. 'Please don't burden me with that again. To make doubly certain, Mr Addison has curtailed his leave and will this very day be on his way back to reassess the Yorkey mine. He has volunteered to do so, which is extremely generous of him, but that's our Mr Addison.'

'I appreciate your time,' Tanner said miserably. 'What do you think will be the outcome?'

'The Yorkey mine has deeped out. Mr Addison doesn't make mistakes.'

'No. About the forgery. You know about these things. How could it have happened?'

'The only way that forgery could have taken place was after the report was collected from the Chief Assayer's office in Kalgoorlie. I told Lord Kengally that he ought to look to his own personnel if, as he asserts, he had no knowledge of the crime, but I object to the suggestion of any wrong-doing on our part. You would understand that, Mr Tanner.'

'No, I don't,' Tanner snarled, released from any necessity to be polite to this pompous know-all. 'I would prefer to look to your personnel. You're not Caesar's wife, none of you. You bloody mob are always screaming you're underpaid. A bit on the side would come in handy, wouldn't it? Don't try to tell me your Mr Addison is above suspicion, because I'm wondering about you too. You tell me he's such a saint, so I'm wondering if you're in it with him.' He wrenched open the glazed glass door and called over his shoulder: 'You haven't heard the last of this!'

No sooner had the roof of Mike's house been completed than a doctor, new to Kalgoorlie, offered to buy it.

'Name your price, Mr Deagan,' he said, 'and I'll try to match it. My wife and I are at our wits' end trying to find a suitable place for a residence and a surgery, and this house would be perfect. To tell you the truth, my wife has already been poking about inside, and I hear how cool it is and how new, from dawn to dusk. She's not impressed with Kalgoorlie at all, the heat and dust has been getting her down, and she has her heart set on a new house, this house.'

Mike made a few quick calculations and then shook his head, looking proudly at his new home. 'Wouldn't I be the first, sir, to agree with her? After working out here for so long, I dreamed of a clean place meself. The smell of new is a welcome change from all these shanty buildings. There'll be no creepy-crawlies in my house, and I've had the whole place wired against the hordes of flies that could carry off a side of beef on their own.'

'I've noticed that,' the doctor said dismally. 'It's essential for a surgery to be spotless, and the flies out here seem to be in plague proportions. Are you sure you won't change your mind? I'll make it worth your while.'

'I was looking forward to moving in,' Mike said, matching the doctor's dismal tone. 'It would be a cruel disappointment for me to have to start over, even if I could find a block in town as good as this. The real terror out here is that blazing afternoon sun burning down, but this block faces east, away from the worst of it. The front of my house, you'll be noticing, gets the morning sun, and that's a bonus on cold winter mornings.'

'That's where I thought of putting the surgery. Why don't you give this more thought? I'll come back tomorrow.'

'I'd have to think hard about giving up this fine house. But we'll see. Yes, give me a day.'

He went and found Jocelyn. 'Looks like I'll be moving back into my room here.'

'Why?'

'Because I've got a fish on the hook. He wants to buy my new house.'

'Lord above, Mike. You wouldn't sell your house?'

'Everything's for sale at a price, my girl. If I can double my money he's got a house.' He followed her into her office.

'I'm glad you're here. I wanted to have a talk to you,' Jocelyn said.

'What about?'

'The Black Cat.'

'Why? Anything wrong?'

'No. But about Clem wanting to offload his share . . .'

Mike lit a cigar. 'I thought we'd settled that. I've written to him to tell him that you're buying his share. That'll make him happy. And me too. I don't want any other partners.'

She looked about her unhappily. 'Mike, I appreciate what you're doing. But I don't want to put all my savings in here. And I hate owing money.'

'What owing? I said I'd stand you for the difference. You can pay me back in your own good time.'

Jocelyn took a deep breath. 'Why don't you buy Clem out yourself? You can afford it.'

He stretched and put his feet up on a nearby chair. 'What a question! You're the mainstay of this establishment. You're entitled to go for half-share, my love. It's not fair at all that you should be on a wage.' He grinned. 'We're all mates. This is a good investment for you.'

'Is it? Or are you just making sure I don't leave? Protecting your investment?'

'If you put it so harsh, I suppose you're right. But you have to look after yourself same as I do, Jossie love. You stick here as my partner and you'll end up a wealthy woman.'

'Then what's to become of me?'

'Eh?'

'You heard me. What would I be then? Some rich old crone with dyed hair, turning to the drink for company?'

'Ah, never. Not you.'

'Then what? I never started out to be a whore or a madame. I just wanted to do better than being a waitress married off to some farm boy . . .'

He butted the cigar and stood up. 'Come along now. Have you got the miseries this morning? You have done better. You're not short of a quid, nor ever likely to be now.'

'Money isn't everything,' she said sadly.

'Since when?' He walked round the desk and kissed her on the cheek, persuasive as always. 'Don't tell me you want to back out? That'd be the silliest move you ever made.'

'Do you think so?' Jocelyn walked over to the window, pulling back the curtains to stare out into the street. 'Tell me this, Mike. You've slept with the girls here, you've even got your favourites, but you've never slept with me. Why's that?'

He blustered, running his hand through his thatch of red hair. 'Well, you're the boss, aren't you? Out of reach, so to say.'

'No, I wouldn't say. Not where you're concerned.'

'Ah, come on now, Jossie. What's this? We've always been mates. I didn't think you'd be minding that I take my pleasure. Besides, I always thought you were keen on Clem.'

'I was, true enough,' she said apologetically. 'But I grew up. You can understand that. This is hardly the place for romance, and anyway, he never noticed. He's too gone on Thora. But that's beside the point.' She drew her shawl about her as if shutting herself off from him. 'I'm sorry, I really am. I don't want to let you down, Mike, but I'm leaving. I can't stay here any longer.'

Having made up her mind, Jocelyn was immune to his arguments, to his sweet banter, to his blarney.

'Don't you see? I come from decent folk. The money means nothing to me any more. It did at first, it was exciting. I never even had a bank account before I came here. But with my wages and tips, and mining tips as well, I can afford to get the hell out of this life while I still can.'

He followed her across the room. 'Is that all there is to it?'

'Why wouldn't it be?' she asked angrily. 'I don't want to wear the stink of a whorehouse all my life.'

'Where will you go?'

'East. As far away as I can get from my reputation. Melbourne, they say, is a beautiful garden city. I want to get on a ship and sail right round to the other side of the country. I want to see places, Mike. I want to be like other women, decent women.'

'Who ever said you were not a decent woman? Not I, for one. Would you just be wanting a holiday? Then you shall have a holiday. And a bonus to travel first class. I'd not be holding you back.'

'Jesus!' she cried. 'Do I need a hammer to bash it into your head? I'm in love with you, Mike Deagan. There! It's said. But it's too late for you now. I told you. I'm leaving!'

'You never gave me a chance,' he said quietly. 'I've twenty years up on Clem, and you. And with my record I'm not much of a bargain for any woman. Don't be belabouring me, girl, for what I can't change. I'm no catch. No hard feelings. I'll help you. You go east, Jossie, and forget the Cat ever existed.'

She took a long time to reply. 'Then it's agreed,' she said stiffly. 'I'm not buying into the Cat. And I'll leave as soon as you find someone to take over.'

'You'd leave me? Just like that.'

'Yes. You'll end up one of the richest men on this heap,

355

I don't doubt that. But here in the west you'll always be an ex-convict. And I know why you want to stay on the goldfields. Because no one cares here. Because respectability means bugger all. You're not living here, Mike Deagan, you're hiding. With all your talk, you're so bloody beaten down, you're afraid to raise your head. And you know what? If I stay here I can see myself going the same way. And it won't do. It won't do at all. I won't live with shame.'

She burst into tears and he put his arms about her. 'Oh, my darlin'. Don't go on so. Is it all that bad?'

'Yes, it is,' she wept.

In her bed that night they talked long and lovingly.

'What with costs going up like bushfires,' he told the doctor the following day, 'I think I'm making a horrible mistake here that I'll live to regret, but pals of mine tell me doctors are desperately needed in this town.'

'You'll sell?'

'Looks like I'll have to.'

With the profitable proceeds from the sale of his house, Mike bought a brooch of a golden horseshoe for the lady soon to be his wife. Then he called on an estate agent, showed the gentleman the figures on the Black Cat, together with the relevant bank statement, and listed it for sale.

The agent stared at those figures, familiar greed lighting up his eyes under the green eyeshade fashionable in bank and business circles these days. 'Leave it with me, Mr Deagan,' he said. 'I'll see what I can do, discreetly, of course.'

Mike smiled. Knowing the town, he'd picked his mark carefully. 'Of course. Discretion is all-important, you realize that.'

And so he did. Six days later, the estate agent purchased the Black Cat. He was unaware that the madame was leaving, but when he did hear, after he signed the contract, he didn't consider it important. Mr Deagan had given him the name of another lady who had recently arrived in Kalgoorlie, and who would help him out if he ever needed assistance, because she had experience in this business. Her name was Glory. A suitable name for a lady in charge of a goldmine like the Black

Cat, the agent told himself gleefully, having been assured that Glory was the soul of discretion. He had already decided not to mention to his wife, a pillar of the Methodist church, that he had extended his investments. She would reap the benefits, he consoled himself wisely.

Jocelyn saw to it that her wedding reception was a sedate occasion, held in the new Catholic church hall and catered for by the Women's Guild. The gifts showered on them were typical of the goldfields. Sentimental diggers, sad to see them leave, gave them the customary souvenirs of gold trinkets fashioned into various shapes, from rings to delicate pickaxes, or just small lumps in their natural state.

Mr and Mrs Deagan travelled first to York, where they were welcomed by family and friends, and then on to Lancoorie, to stay with George and Alice for a while. After that they would move on to Perth, their last stop before embarking on the most exciting leg of their long journey, the voyage from Fremantle to Melbourne.

Kengally was at the Stock Exchange amid the uproar over the Londonderry crash and suspicions about Yorkey.

'As far as I know,' he said to reporters, scowling as Tanner approached, 'Yorkey is still viable. I have simply suspended dealings for a few days to check. I am a cautious man, as you all know, and on behalf of our investors I have to make certain everything is above board.'

'Are you saying there's foul play here?' a reporter asked eagerly.

'Not at all. Poor choice of words perhaps. Rather a mix-up, that's all. Here's Mr Tanner, ask him.'

They turned on Tanner. 'What's the real story?'

'All I can say right now is that a mistake has been made, that's all. The assayer has made some sort of mistake, to put it mildly, and it is up to him to reassure all of us that Yorkey is as good as we know it to be. I'll keep you informed.'

Disappointed, they drifted away.

'Why are you making things worse?' he demanded of Kengally. 'Addison has mixed up the reports, that's all.'

'I think not. I was at the department this morning and I am now convinced that the report we held was a forgery. The original stated unequivocally that Yorkey was not worth our consideration. And I want to know how this happened.'

'It's clear how it happened! Right there in that department. They're the ones who need investigation.'

'They are already investigating. And they're sending another assayer to check that mine. I don't hold out any hope. We've been duped, and my duty now is to our investors.'

'What investors? They'll have been warned off by this. We ought to charge that assayer with forgery.'

'I wouldn't rush into that. You should look at your own position. I received that report from you, and acted upon it. Somewhere along the line a switch was made.'

'Not in my hands.'

'Then whose?' Kengally asked angrily.

Another man interrupted them. 'I want to talk to you, Tanner,' he shouted. 'You sold me a heap of useless shares in Londonderry!'

'I sold them to you in good faith!'

'Yeah! Did you? How many shares are you holding?'

'That's my business.'

'None! You haven't got any. You're a cagey character. And what's this about Yorkey? You mixed up in that too?'

'You watch your tongue, slander's a costly business,' Tanner retorted and stormed away, making for his office.

At another office, in Kalgoorlie, the clerk, John Beardley, was being questioned by his superiors as a result of telegrams they'd received from Perth. Mr Addison's report was dated 6 June, so it would have been available on the 7th, and they needed to know who had collected it from this office.

John scratched his head. 'I dunno. A lot of reports go out. And it was a while back.'

'Think very carefully. This is extremely important. Mr Addison completes his reports and places them in that wooden tray, that one there. Now, in the mornings, being the first one here, you unlock the offices, and then what?'

'I unlock Mr Addison's office, take the tray, ready for people to come for those reports, and lock his office again until he arrives, or being now, with Mr Addison away, until you arrive, sir.'

'You couldn't say his office had been broken into?'

'No, sir. Well, I'd have seen, wouldn't I? Mr Addison's office is always neat, the windows are locked too, because his safe's in there. Yorkey, was it? The Yorkey mine?'

He sighed. 'Something rings a bell. About Yorkey. Yes, I know. I do remember. *He* picked it up. Mr Tanner, from York. He didn't remember me, though, but I knew him. Why? Does he say it weren't him?'

'No, he does not. We're just making certain everything is in order from our end. There have been some unfortunate mishaps but I'm sure Mr Tanner can explain. That will be all.'

They sat then, the Acting Chief Assayer, the Mines Warden and the Registrar, looking at the empty chair as if it alone could solve the mystery.

'If Mr Addison says there's been a switch, then there has,' the assayer said loyally. 'But not in this office. You heard what Beardley said. He remembers giving Mr Addison's report to Tanner. So it's out of our hands.'

'According to the telegram, Tanner claims that this so-called forgery was collected from here,' the Registrar said.

'Not so-called at all. We know he took a forged document to Lord Kengally, so the responsibility ends with him. I won't have them casting aspersions on this office or on Mr Addison.'

'No need to get upset,' the Warden said. 'My money's on Tanner himself. I could write a book on the scams that have been pulled out here. It's the land of tricksters. Some of them devilish clever.'

The Registrar was still concerned. He undid a stud in his stiff collar and rubbed at the red graze on his neck. 'You realize, gentlemen, that what with the Londonderry débâcle, we're all in for a hard time. We don't need this business as well. I don't understand why Tanner would pull a stunt like this when he had to be the obvious suspect.'

The Warden had no such qualms. 'They get too smart, you see. Nothing new about this one, forgeries are thick on the ground in this motley populace. I reckon Tanner was in for the quick kill. Forge a brilliant report on Yorkey, pull in the investors and then do a bolt. My bet is that Kengally was in on it too, but somehow Mr Addison got wind of it and blew the whistle.'

'How did he find out?' the other two wanted to know.

'I've no idea, but thank God he did, or this office would be in real trouble. As it is, the assayers in Coolgardie have to face a police inquiry over Londonderry.'

The assayer was nervous. 'What's to do then?'

'As the most senior departmental person here, if you all agree,' the Registrar looked to them, 'I shall reply to the Secretary that our investigations fully back Mr Addison. If any switch has been made, then it was so done after that report left this office.'

They nodded agreement, relieved.

'I shall also point out that the clerk, John Beardley, distinctly recalls handing it to Tanner, but I shall leave it at that. One has to beware of libel. From that point it is out of our hands. However,' he turned to the assayer, 'the Secretary wants an official examination of the Yorkey mine, so you'd better get out there as soon as possible. And take one of the junior assayers with you to countersign your report, for your own protection. We can't have any more mistakes. Mr Addison is returning also.'

'I don't believe Mr Addison made a mistake in the first place!'

'Of course not. But let us all make sure. If Yorkey really is a goer, then this has been an unfortunate mistake.'

'All right, I'll go,' the assayer agreed. 'But it's a bloody waste of time. Mr Addison doesn't make mistakes.'

Tanner was in his office assessing his probable losses on Yorkey when Kengally confronted him again.

'Is it true that you had prior knowledge of a problem with Londonderry?'

'For Christ's sake, what now? I buy and sell shares all the time. What's it got to do with you?'

'Everything.' Kengally slammed his walking stick down on Tanner's desk. 'Everything you do reflects on my reputation. I have just been back to the Mines Department to speak to the Secretary himself. He has had a reply from the Kalgoorlie offices. He insists that the report handed to you regarding Yorkey was unfavourable. The clerk even recalled you as a person he knew from York. Is that so?'

'It could be. That doesn't mean a thing. Sit down. I'm sorry I've been so cranky but this is all too much. Don't you see? We've been conned.'

Kengally remained standing. 'All I can see is that *I*, to use your expression, have been conned. On your own admission, you are the only person who had charge of that report from the Mines Office to my hotel room. The Mines Department issued an unfavourable report and yet you were able to present me with a glowing report that caused me to go ahead with the purchase. Did you alter that report in any way?'

'I did not!' Until now Edgar had been so annoyed by this turn of events and Kengally's panicky attitude that he hadn't wanted to believe that the finger of blame could be pointed at him. He was shocked. 'You still think I had a hand in it?'

'What else? You were keen for your commission and for sales. If I hadn't bumped into Addison, by sheer coincidence, we'd have been well down the road before the truth came to light. Maybe, like Londonderry, not even until the mine was reopened.'

'By which, you think, I'd be long gone?'

'Something like that.' Kengally shrugged. 'As it is, you have cost me a fortune. As soon as that mine is reopened and reassessed, which will be very shortly, I shall make a decision.'

'What sort of a decision?' Edgar snapped.

'I found Mr Addison an upright gentleman, and I can't say the same for you. I don't really need a reassessment to know that Yorkey is a dud, but I'm prepared to give you the benefit of the doubt for the time being.'

'Then what?'

'I will, of course, prefer charges against you for forgery, and for fraud.'

Edgar felt a cold shudder run through him but fought against the obvious sign of fear. 'You do that,' he said, his voice hard and menacing, 'and it will cost you a bloody sight more in libel and reparation. I'll have you run out of town. I'll also sue you for going behind my back, as agent and promoter, to make a deal on the side with the discoverers and owners of Lady Luck mine. You thought you were teaching me a lesson, didn't you?'

Kengally was appalled. 'I did no wrong there.'

'The courts won't see it that way. I have your signature on your approval for me to act on your behalf.'

Maliciously, Edgar was pleased to see Kengally visibly shaken, clutching the back of a chair for support.

'If that is what you intend to do, then go ahead,' he said stiffly.

'I will, milord, I will. You can count on that. In the meantime I intend to find out who forged that bloody report, because it wasn't me. Despite your schoolboy trust in civil servants, I know exactly where to look. Addison was bought, you bloody fool. It's as plain as the nose on your face. Price and Deagan were desperate to sell, so they roped in Addison, who saw that I got a favourable report.'

'I find that difficult to believe.'

'Of course you would. It's easier for you to blame me than take on the whole bloody Mines Department, isn't it? You don't want to fall out with your mate, the Minister of State, do you? Better to let Tanner take the fall. Well, it's not going to happen. You're wrong, you're all bloody wrong, and I'll prove it. After which you'll have another bloody slander case on your hands!' He was pleased to see that this verbal battering had Kengally seeking refuge in the chair, but he was so enraged, he hadn't finished.

'You can sit there all day as far as I care,' he shouted. 'If you want anything, a cup of tea, a brandy, just ask my clerk. You'll rue the day, Kengally, you ever pointed the finger at me. Your reputation! Hell! What about mine? You won't look so good either when word gets out that you've been romancing Clem Price's wife. The owner of Yorkey mine. That adds a twist that reporters will love to hear, doesn't it?'

He took his hat from the stand. 'By the way, Clem already knows about you and Thora, and he's not amused. If you sit there long enough I'll come back and tell you what really happened with Yorkey.'

Lord Kengally did accept the brandy, and the kind ministrations of Tanner's young clerk, who had heard the shouting.

'Will you be all right, sir?' he asked as the gentleman mopped his brow with a silk handkerchief.

'Yes, thank you.'

'Call me if you need anything else.'

'Thank you. I'll be on my way shortly. I just wish to catch my breath.'

He sat in that seat for a long time, looking out at a peerless blue sky, marvelling that it was a perfect day. A pigeon rested on the windowsill, murmuring contentedly in that familiar way, unimpressed by the surge of the city below, and Gerald Kengally wished he could disassociate as easily.

He hadn't wanted this assignment in the first place, but his friends had insisted and prevailed. They had elected him chairman of their investment companies and had every confidence in his ability to take control of their affairs out here in the Antipodes.

But why had he accepted?

Ambition, he told himself. Just ambition. He didn't need the money, he'd only agreed because he'd wanted to make a name for himself in the city. London was the centre of his universe, and he'd felt himself slipping to the sidelines, being overtaken by younger men in bowler hats. The famous, massive wealth of these goldfields had the capacity to catapult him back into the mainstream, and thence on to important corporation boards, and at the same time give him a voice to be reckoned with in the House of Lords. Prior to this he'd only been a whisper, unable to find an issue to grasp that was within his field of competence, but the colonies, especially Western Australia, loomed large these days, and he'd expected to return home not only as a successful promoter of desperately needed gold income for the mother country but also as a peer with first-hand experience of this huge colony.

That was why he had cultivated government members of all callings, and had had several interesting meetings with the Governor, Sir Gerard Smith, and the Premier, Sir John Forrest. He believed that federation of all the Australian states – or colonies, as they were known at home – was imminent, despite the accepted opinion in Westminster, and was looking forward to his return. Excited about it, in fact. He would stand up in the House and proclaim this as fact, encouraging his peers not to fight this movement or they would lose Australia as they had done America. The derision that his speech would attract, at this stage, would only add to his stature when he was proved right. Gerald Kengally would make his mark at last, as a man of vision. A man who had been there and talked to the colonials, who understood that their aspirations were no reflection on the Crown.

Egotistical pipe dreams, he grieved, wishing he had the cheek to request another brandy as an excuse to stay a while longer, for Lord Kengally didn't know where to turn.

Sadly he took his leave of the clerk and walked out into the street. He was inclined to take a cab and hurry back to hide in his friend's house from the storm clouds of scandal, but instead he squared his shoulders and strode out to the Perth Gentlemen's Club, where he was made most welcome. He picked up a newspaper and retired to the lounge to fill in time before lunch, and there he was greeted by Henery Whipple, a genial fellow, retiring Speaker of the House, who made him promise to attend his send-off on Saturday night.

'Be pleased to, Henery,' Kengally said, with as much enthusiasm as he could muster. 'Should I get up a party?'

'No need, my dear fellow,' Henery said. 'Just come along. They tell me it's a dinner, then they'll clear the decks for a dance. My chums know old Henery. I'm not one for formality.

We'll just have a jolly good time. You'll be at my table, of course.'

'It's very kind of you.' Kengally considered inviting him to lunch, but intimidated by Tanner's threats, thought better of it. He was already feeling like a pariah.

'By the way,' Henery said, 'I've a friend of yours staying with me at present. Robert Warburton.'

'Is he?' Kengally was a little cheered. Warburton, his old friend. 'I'd like to see him.'

'Well, you shall. Join us for lunch. He should be here any minute.'

Never was Gerald Kengally so pleased to see Robert as now. Desperately he hoped for a chance to talk to Robert alone, to tell him his difficulties. Robert would understand. He was a man who disdained common popularity, preferring to keep his life untainted by acquaintances.

But it was not to be. Robert had a considerable number of shares in Londonderry and spent the time bemoaning his losses, with Henery endeavouring to cheer him up. Kengally felt it would be bad form to spoil Henery's luncheon entirely by adding to the woes, so he turned the conversation to the safe field of botany, their mutual interest.

Certain that he was right in believing that Price and Deagan had bribed if not Addison, then someone else in the Mines Department, Edgar went in search of Clem, first at the United Services Hotel and then at that ridiculous cottage where his wife was staying. It pleased him that Thora was still living apart from her husband; he hoped she'd keep it that way. Their marital arrangements had become rather a joke round town. Clem, it was said, had visiting rights only, a droll comment on his situation. And serve him right, thought Edgar.

He paced angrily up the street, determined not only to confront Clem with his accusations, but to return with the police if necessary. The game was up, and if Clem refused to admit to his treachery then he could suffer the consequences. A night in jail would loosen his tongue. The thought of sending Deagan back to jail was a bonus that quickened Edgar's steps as he pushed open the gate.

Thora was delighted to see him but concerned at his appearance. 'You look tired. Have you been busy? You must have a cup of tea. And some scones. Nanny made some this morning and they're delicious. Do sit down, here by the window. Isn't it a beautiful day?'

She was very gay, in one of her bubbly moods, even calling out to him from the kitchen as she herself made the tea. Before taking his seat he detoured round the small sitting room to peer down the passage at the nanny, who was out the back with the child, but there was no sign of Clem. He could do with a cup of tea anyway, to calm him down; he wanted to be in full possession of his wits when he did find Price. Besides, time alone with Thora was never wasted.

Who knows? he told himself. If they are estranged now, when her husband is charged with conspiracy to defraud, that won't help things. Dear Thora will be glad to have a friend to lean on. While he waited Edgar had pleasant visions of the comfort he would be to her, sheltering her against the scandal of a husband who, if he had any say in it, was headed for jail.

But Thora soon shattered that hope.

When he asked about Clem, telling her that he particularly wanted to see him on a business matter, she smiled that lovely, angelic smile that made his heart miss a beat.

'Oh, Mr Tanner, I'm sorry, Clem won't be back until late this afternoon. He's gone out to Cottersloe. He's such a dear, he's building us the most divine house. I'm absolutely thrilled with it. I simply can't wait to move in. This waiting is quite tragic.'

Unimpressed, he had to suffer her enthusiasm for this plain-looking house. She spread the plan before him, anchoring it with the sugar bowl, explaining every detail, interspersing her monologue with glowing references to her dear husband.

Anger and jealousy grew within him as she went on to describe the furniture she had chosen, even dashing away to produce swatches of material for the curtains and coverings.

When he could finally get a word in, he made an effort to bring her back to earth.

'Yorkey failed, you know. The mine.'

'Did it?' she said vaguely. 'What a pity.'

'Yes. There's some talk that Clem might be mixed up in monkey business there.'

Thora stopped, stared at him for a second, and then laughed. 'Clem wouldn't do anything like that. Now look at this. Do you like this blue or the darker blue for the drapes? I'll have lace curtains, beautiful lace, for our bedroom but I want to carry this blue theme through from the other rooms, blue for the ocean, you see. Although Clem says the lighter blue matches my eyes. Isn't he sweet?'

'He'd know, of course,' Edgar said meanly. 'He's a great one for pleasing the ladies.'

Even self-immersed Thora couldn't miss that remark. 'Yes,' she said hesitating, uncertain of his meaning. 'Yes, he can be very charming.'

'So they say,' he grinned, idly turning over a furniture catalogue that she'd produced. 'The ladies at Kalgoorlie, I mean. They'll miss him.'

She put her hand to her throat, nervously fingering a pearl button. 'I suppose so. What ladies? From what I saw on the train it is no place for ladies.'

'I couldn't agree more, my dear, but then some men don't know the difference. Or don't care, one would say. So far from their loved ones.'

'What's that got to do with it?' She was keenly interested now.

He smiled. 'I shouldn't be telling a lady like you these things. Kalgoorlie is hardly civilization. The things that go on there you wouldn't want to know.'

'But I do. What goes on? You can tell me. I'd adore to know.'

'Well, what they say out there is "out of sight, out of mind". From their wives, of course. Since I separated from Mrs Tanner, I consider myself a single man, but even so I kept well clear of the orgies that go on every night.'

'Orgies! Good heavens. I had no idea!'

'Clem never mentioned them to you?'

Thora tossed her head. 'Of course not, that ugly behaviour would be beneath my husband.'

'If you say so. Could I have another cup of tea?'

Her hand shook as she lifted the teapot, and Edgar smiled to himself. You haven't heard the half of it, lady, he mused, revenge taking shape.

'I often felt sorry for the absent wives,' he said wistfully, 'seeing those men spending all their money on wild women. A real scandal, it is. They say there are more whorehouses in Kalgoorlie than there ever were in Perth.'

'More what?'

He sighed. 'There I go again. I'm shocking you!'

'No, you're not,' she persisted. 'I'm a married woman, not a child.' She blushed, lowering her voice. 'I've heard about those places. What exactly are they? Don't be a tease, Mr Tanner, I insist you tell me. Quick, before Nanny comes in.'

'You ought to ask Clem, really. He owns one.'

She stiffened, sitting straight-backed on the cheap, hard sofa. 'You didn't answer my question. What exactly is a whorehouse?'

He coughed. 'All right. If you insist. A whorehouse is a totally immoral place where men go for the sort of parties I wouldn't dare describe to you. Let's just say the everyday trade is in women's bodies. Men go there by the hundreds, they queue up to pay for sex with those disgusting harlots. There. Now you know.'

Thora clasped her hands tightly in front of her. 'I suppose I always knew they were something like that,' she said nervously, 'but they were too horrible to contemplate.'

'As it should be. You don't need to think about it. Look, Thora, I really ought to go now.'

'Please don't go, Mr Tanner,' she whispered. 'Not yet. You said Clem owns one of those places.'

'I've said too much already. That was a slip.'

'Does he or does he not?'

'You won't tell him I told you?'

'Certainly not.'

'Very well. Clem owns the biggest and . . .' He was about to say 'the best', but changed his tune. '. . . and the worst of them. It's called the Black Cat. It's in the main street of Kalgoorlie.'

Thora had trouble digesting this. She was very quiet for a few minutes, and then she stood. 'I have to apologize to you, Mr Tanner, for encouraging you into this sordid conversation, but as for your accusations against my husband, I don't believe a word of it. You will forgive me, but I must ask you to leave.'

Her swift turnabout surprised and annoyed him. 'By all means,' he said. 'I'm sorry you're taking offence. You did quiz me, after all. You women are all the same. You like spending the money but you never ask where it came from.'

'My husband found gold,' she retorted.

'The hell he did! His feeble attempts at prospecting wouldn't keep you in hats, certainly not an indefinite stay at the Palace. Why don't you grow up, Thora? He's no saint.'

She tried for dignity. 'Just because he owns one of those places, which I doubt, doesn't say he frequents them. My husband is not like that.'

Tanner's laugh was harsh. He knew that Clem loved this woman, and now it was time to destroy his marriage once and for all. This would teach him to double-cross an old pal. For, in his rage at being unfairly implicated in that forgery, he had convinced himself that he and Clem were pals, completely disregarding his designs on Clem's wife.

'That's right,' he sneered. 'Let none of this dirt touch you. You don't need to know that whores are earning the money you spend. And of course your sainted husband wouldn't touch a whore! He was a good customer until he met up with Jocelyn.'

'Who is Jocelyn?'

'Ha! You are interested. You know Jocelyn, my dear. She's a little whore from York. Jocelyn Russell. You went to school with her. She was a waitress in York, well known to the young bucks of the town.'

369

'Jocelyn Russell?' Thora shook her head, not wanting to hear any more. She turned away from him, bewildered, gathering up her plan and catalogues and pretty swatches, grasping them close to her as if they could defend her from his voice.

'She's his favourite whore,' Tanner added. 'She was so good to him, he put her in charge of his brothel. She runs it for him, your old friend Jocelyn, and she keeps her bed warm for him. The boss gets the best, doesn't he?'

Thora stood her ground. 'I never realized what an awful man you are,' she said. 'Get out of my house.'

He shrugged, picked up his hat and walked calmly out of the front door, down the short path, out of the gate and into the street, out of sight.

Until that moment, until she could no longer see him, Thora managed to hang on, but then she ran to the bathroom, frantically turning on the taps, filling the bath, tearing off all of her clothes and stepping in to cleanse herself of this filth. Of Clem.

She was so long in the bath that Nanny had to urge her to come out, finally insisting, wrapping the naked woman in towels. 'You'll get a chill, madam. Why, you're shaking all over! Put on this dressing gown. You'd better get into bed and warm up. There's no warmth in the sun today. I'll make you some cocoa.'

Thora tried to sleep, to erase all of that horror, but she dreamed she was back in York where everyone was sneering at her, pointing at her, and she was running through the town half dressed, ashamed, frantically trying to find clothes to cover her flimsy shift, and her father was there, shouting at her while her mother turned her back in shame, and Jocelyn Russell was standing in the doorway of that hotel, with her arms about Clem, gloating, ignoring her. She ran to them, begging them to take her in, but they couldn't hear her, or see her, and her sisters were throwing stones at her. But they still couldn't hear her screams.

'What is it, madam? What's wrong?' Nanny was shaking her. 'Shush now, you're dreaming. You're frightening Lydia.'

'Who is Lydia?' she demanded.

'Your girl. Your little girl,' Nanny said, shocked.

Thora clutched her hand. 'She's not mine, Nanny,' she whispered urgently. 'They think I don't know. But I do. My baby died. I remember now. I was all mixed up before, but it's clear now. My baby died, so they gave me this one.'

'Oh, no, madam. That's not right.'

'It is, it is. You have to listen to me, Nanny, before they come. Give that little girl back, quickly, before they find out.'

'Oh, glory be, madam. Who should I give her to?'

'Her mother, of course. She was there. A dark-haired girl, thin, frail. She'll want her baby and I've stolen it. Too cruel, Nanny. Too cruel.'

'Yes, I'll do that. I'll find her, madam. Now you just sleep. Mr Price will be here soon, he'll know what to do.'

Thora sat up with a jolt. 'No, he won't. For God's sake, don't tell him. You mustn't tell him anything.'

'I'll make you some hot milk.' Nanny stoked the stove and hovered over the saucepan impatiently, adding a dash of brandy for good measure, then rushed it into her mistress.

That done, she picked up Lydia and ran through to the back entrance to the hotel, in search of Miss Devane, for she dared not mention the problem to anyone else. But Miss Devane was away and not due back for two days. Poor Netta. She thought of calling a doctor but she wasn't sure she had the right to do so. If it was the child, she wouldn't think twice about it, but Mrs Price? She'd probably put on a worse turn than this one.

'Oh, well. All I can do is hope she stays in bed until Mr Price comes.' She put the child on her hip and marched grimly back to the cottage.

In another of her swift mood changes, Thora's fears were replaced by anger.

Why am I hiding in here? she asked herself. I haven't done anything wrong. He has. He's to blame for my nerves and I won't put up with it any longer.

She fossicked about in the cupboards for her most colourful clothes, adding ill-matching scarves and a shawl to her outfit, and tied her hair up garishly with bright ribbons. Then she found the lip rouge that she used sparingly on rare occasions and smeared it on her lips and cheeks, remembering those ladies on the train.

Those women, she recalled. They dress like this. Clem likes women to be showy. She was disappointed that no matter how she tried, her wardrobe lacked the blazing purples and reds that made up that look, but she'd done the best she could. She would show him that she was every bit as attractive as they were.

'What are you staring at?' she demanded of Nanny.

'Nothing, madam. Would you like your lunch now?'

'Yes, please. I'll have scrambled eggs and a glass of wine.'

'A glass of wine?' Nanny's eyes widened.

'You heard me. Are you deaf or something?'

'No, madam.' She fled into the kitchen.

The afternoon was long and chilly as Thora waited for him. A cloud bank hung ominously over the city, and thunder rolled from the hills, giving a promise of rain that never came. Tree branches brushed restlessly against the side windows, and a dog barked fitfully. Nanny took a nap with Lydia in her room, and later, rugged up, wheeled out the pram to take the child for a walk, without bothering to ask permission. And still Thora sat staring at the door, her embroidery untouched beside her.

When he did come in, noisy, laughing, to kiss her on the cheek, she froze, along with all the things she had intended to say to him. If he noticed her appearance, he did not comment. Instead, with a flourish, he presented her with a large box of chocolates tied with a big red bow.

'The house is looking good,' he said. 'The plasterers are doing a fine job. Next week I'll have the furniture sent out and you can come to tell them where to place everything. Don't you want to open your chocolates?'

'Later.'

'Are you feeling all right? You seem very quiet.'

'I have a headache.'

'You should take something for those headaches. They say that milk of magnesia works.'

'Who says?'

'I don't know. Everyone.' He took off his coat. 'You know, I was thinking. It's stupid for me to be at the hotel. I'll move my things in here.'

Thora looked away from him. 'No. I don't want my arrangements upset.'

'Don't be silly, Thora. I won't upset your arrangements, whatever they are.' He strode into the kitchen and she could hear him sawing bread, opening the meat safe, making himself a sandwich, as if he was a good husband, going about normal things, not the owner of one of those evil places, not a man who had a whore for a lover and had the cheek to come to her bed.

She saw him now as he really was, and all those accusations were on the tip of her tongue, but they wouldn't allow themselves to be said. They were too awful to put into words.

When he returned, he did notice. 'You're looking all jollied up. What's the occasion?'

'No occasion. I want you to go. To leave me alone.'

'What?' He gaped, the sandwich suspended in midair.

'Is everyone deaf around here?' she said coldly. 'I would like you to leave.'

'What the hell for? What's wrong now? Just as we were getting along so well. Last night you were so loving, Thora, I thought . . .'

The very mention of last night sickened her. 'You took advantage of me,' she cried. 'Don't you dare mention last night, ever again.' She looked nervously at the door, thinking Nanny might be returning and hear this.

'I'll mention it as often as I like,' he growled. 'We're married. The way you're carrying on you'd think it was a sin.'

A sin? He talks about sin! This is too much. She jumped up and dashed past him to her bedroom, slamming the door, but he pushed it open and followed her.

'Get out!' she screamed. 'Get out! You go off and leave

me and think you can just walk back into my life. Well, you can't.'

'Oh, Jesus! Not that again. I thought we were over that.'

'Don't swear at me. How dare you use the Lord's name?'

He stood in the doorway, thoroughly confused. 'It's about time I had a say in this marriage, Thora. I've been doing the best I can for you, and it's time you gave a little.' He took her arm and sat her firmly on the bed. 'Now you listen to me. I'm not going to put up with this much longer, having to come and go at your whims. If you want to be rid of me, I can make arrangements of my own . . .'

'I suppose with another woman?' she flared, surprised that she was at least able to hit back at him.

'Why not? I'm wasting my time with you. Now, if you want to see me, you'll find me at the United Services Hotel. You're the most spoiled, contrary woman . . .'

'Go away,' she wept. 'You've spoiled everything.'

'This is getting to be a habit,' he muttered as he stormed away from that damned cottage once again. 'Time I put a stop to it. She can come looking for me now.'

He walked down to the river, bought some fish and chips from a kiosk by the pier and sat glumly on a bench, trying to fathom Thora's latest mood. He really was tired of having to pander to her all the time, and for the first time he wondered if this marriage would ever work.

It was probably a mistake right from the first, he mused. She never loved me, and I was so smitten by her I had to have her just the same, believing we would share love in time. Plenty of marriages are arranged, and they work. Or rather, I think they do. They seem to.

Determined to put her out of his mind, he walked for miles along the river front, enjoying the chill wind, wishing he was back at Lancoorie. He'd had enough of the city as well.

Finally, he took a deep breath and turned back. As soon as that house was ready, he'd take Thora out there for a week or so, then they would have to head home. If she didn't want to come back to Lancoorie she could stay there, stay anywhere she pleased, but the game was over. And the marriage too, if that was what she wanted. He didn't care any more. It wasn't a real marriage anyway.

He slipped into the hotel by the side door, in no mood for socializing, and went up to the room he shared with Fred Vosper.

'Where the hell have you been all day?' Vosper shook him awake.

Clem sat up groggily. He had kicked off his boots and flung himself on the bed to rest a while, but must have fallen into a deep sleep. 'What time is it?'

'It's eight o'clock and the night is young. Stir yourself, man, half the town is looking for you.'

'Why? What's wrong?'

Fred sat on the other bed. 'You tell me. Tanner's been on the search for you. He came up and knocked on the door. Didn't you hear him?'

'No.'

'Ah, the sleep of the innocent. That's a good sign. Didn't you read the papers today?'

Clem wanted to go back to sleep. 'Did I have to?'

'Then you didn't know that Londonderry crashed?'

'Did it, by God! That can't be right. She was a beauty!'

'Was. They opened the mine and found the cupboard bare. But word has it that Yorkey's a dud too.'

Clem was wide awake now. 'Who says so? Where'd you get that story from? Yorkey's bearing well or Kengally wouldn't have bought it.'

'Well, there's trouble brewing.' Vosper went on to explain that he'd read about the rumour in the paper after Clem had left, but since he couldn't find him, he'd gone over to have a chat with the editor, and that had led him to make enquiries at the Mines Department.

'Not good news, Clem.'

'Impossible.'

'It turns out the Chief Assayer was in town, and he recalls that his report on Yorkey was unfavourable. He claims it has deeped out, that the quartz he saw isn't bearing enough gold for company investment.'

Needing to clear his head, Clem marched over to the washstand, poured cold water into a china basin and splashed it on to his face.

'What brought this on? I never heard such rubbish. Addison did the assay, he would have written the bloody report. How can he change his mind now?'

'I don't know. What do you think could have happened? Tanner is furious. That's why he wanted to talk to you.'

'So he should be. He organized the sale, he wouldn't want it to collapse at this stage. Neither would Kengally, he's gone public. There'll be hell to pay.'

'That's true,' Vosper said quietly. 'But the Mines Department backing Addison. Do you know him?'

'Yes, he's the very best. That's why I got him. But there must be some mistake, just another wild rumour. Addison wouldn't change his mind. He couldn't.'

'He hasn't. He claims the report that Kengally has is a forgery. And Kengally is now inclined to agree with him. All the fingers point at Tanner. Word has it that Tanner forged the report to keep Kengally on line.'

'Surely not!'

Vosper shrugged. 'Apparently Tanner is trying to wriggle out of it. He's blaming you.'

'Ah, Jesus! Have they all gone mad? Blaming me for what?'

'He claims there was a conspiracy. You and Deagan and Addison cooked the reports so as not to lose the sale.'

Clem laughed. 'Addison! He'll love that.'

'Oh, yes, he does. He's threatening to sue Tanner for slander.'

They talked round and round the mystery for a half-hour, but Clem wasn't too concerned. 'They're all chasing their tails. I'll go to the Mines Department tomorrow and sort it out. There has to be a simple explanation. It's bad luck that Kengally panicked, that won't do his shares much good. But that's his problem. Is there a card game on tonight?'

'Yes, we've got three starters. Are you in?'

'With bells on. Wait till I change and get rid of these whiskers.'

Vosper, a keen fisherman, read *The Angler's Weekly*, his favourite paper, and waited for Clem.

'By the way,' he called. 'I've got two tickets for the big shindig tomorrow night. The send-off for Henery Whipple. You could take Thora. It'll be a good show, a reception and dancing to follow.'

'Forget Thora. She's throwing another one of her tantrums.'

'But she'd enjoy this party with all the nobs.'

'Good. I'll tell her about it afterwards.'

They joined two other men for a game of euchre in a small room at the back of the hotel, agreeing, as usual, to a friendly game with modest stakes.

As they settled at the table, McRae, a heavily bearded union man, shuffled the cards and grinned at Clem.

'Now what have you been up to, Clemmie, me lad?'

'Watching my house grow. You'll have to come to the housewarming, Mac.'

'No. With that mine of yours. The Yorkey.'

'He hasn't been up to anything!' Fred said crossly. 'Deal the cards.'

'It's all right,' Clem said. 'He was only asking. I must be the last to hear about this. As far as I know there's no problem at all, but I can tell you there's no way Addison would be mixed up in any shady deals.'

'What about Tanner, then?'

'He's all right too.'

The other man intervened. 'Is he a mate of yours?'

'Yes.'

Fred saw the two men exchange glances. 'Was,' he warned Clem. 'He's claiming you set him up. Gave him a forged report.'

'How could I? I wasn't even there. I left town before the sale was finalized.'

McRae nodded. 'That lets you out, Clem. But I'd watch Tanner if I were you. He's always been a shyster. He took off from the bank in York after granting himself a fair-sized loan without any collateral.'

'What?' Remembering the 'fair-sized' loan that Tanner had allowed him, Clem was shaken. 'I didn't hear anything about that. I come from York.'

'You wouldn't hear,' McRae said. 'The banks keep that sort of stuff under their hat. Bank managers, you know, pillars of the community, they don't air their dirty washing.'

'The money's on Tanner,' the other man said. 'Looks as if he forged the report on your mine, Clem, to get Kengally to buy. So you'd better stop telling people he's a mate, or you'll be in the bog too.'

Clem reached for his cards. 'Can we leave this? I don't know what's going on. I'll find out tomorrow.'

McRae looked to Vosper. 'Hearts trumps, partner.' As the game commenced, he concentrated on his cards but offered an aside, in passing. 'They say, at the Mines Department, that it was a bloody good forgery. Addison had to use an eyeglass to spot the difference. Sorry about your mine, Clem.'

'Don't give up on it yet. I'll go back there and check it myself.'

As the game progressed Clem tried to forget the confusion over Yorkey, still convinced there was a mistake, but something they'd said was bothering him, worrying him. What was it?

Only when it was his turn to buy the drinks, when he was standing in the bar waiting to be served, did it hit him.

'. . . a bloody good forgery.'

'Oh, Jesus, no!' he groaned. 'You didn't?'

Addison had left for Kalgoorlie, but Mr Rivett at the Mines Department was willing to discuss the matter, since Clem was polite, only interested in finding the truth.

'I'm not making any accusations,' Clem said, his stomach like lead.

'That's a welcome change. I had a most unpleasant day

378

yesterday, Mr Price. Most unpleasant. You say you and your partner were the discoverers of Yorkey mine, and you sold to Lord Kengally?'

'Yes.'

'You sold direct? There were no intermediaries involved? You didn't buy the mine from someone else?'

'No. Mr Tanner arranged the sale with my partner after I left. But I had already agreed to it.'

'And the sale was contingent upon the assayer's report?'

'Of course.' Clem was stepping carefully.

'And Mr Tanner's role was as promoter. He would have been paid commission by you and your partner?'

'Yes. Ten per cent. And he was paid his percentage out of the sale monies.'

'Very well.' Rivett led Clem into a small office and placed two pages on the desk. 'I want you to examine these reports carefully.'

With a sinking heart Clem stared at two reports on Yorkey, signed by the same man. Two differing reports.

'And Mr Addison says this one is correct?' he asked weakly.

'Yes. Sit down, Mr Price. What's your reaction?'

Clem shook his head. 'Yorkey yielded extremely well to start with. I knew it was slipping back, but it's hard to tell when you can see the flecks of gold. We just had to keep going and wait for the final yield by the ton. Now, looking at both of these reports, I wish I'd stayed a bit longer in Kalgoorlie. But I had private business to attend to. Neither of these reports would have given me any joy.'

'How is that?'

'This one: according to Mr Addison, Yorkey has deeped out. That's very disappointing, because I was certain it was a winner. This report would kill the sale, no doubt of that.'

'Do you think Mr Addison made a mistake?'

'Not at all. He's not a prospector, that's not his job. I just happen to believe, rightly or wrongly, time will tell, that the rest of that rich reef isn't far away, or far down. But that's only my opinion. Now, as for the other report, the one Mr Addison claims is a forgery, I'd agree that it is.'

'You would?'

'Without even studying the details of differing letters and so forth that you mention, if I'd seen this, I mightn't have sold Yorkey. Certainly not for the amount paid.' Despite his worries, he grinned. 'This report is better than the original. I mean, it's better than the first strike. At first glance I would have called the sale off, but common sense would have brought me back to earth. I was digging Yorkey myself, Mr Rivett. It couldn't possibly have been yielding as well as this, not in my wildest dreams. This report is ridiculous.'

'But that's the report that encouraged Lord Kengally to buy.'

'Of course it would.'

Mr Rivett scratched his head. 'So you're backing Mr Addison?'

'Yes.'

'Well. That's a relief, coming from the previous owner. But now what, Mr Price? Who carried out that forgery?'

'Beats me,' Clem lied. 'It'll be hard to prove without involving both Tanner and the Mines Department.'

'My people had nothing to do with it!' Rivett exclaimed.

'I believe Tanner says the same thing. And for that matter, so do I. The finger is being pointed at me too. I have to protect my good name the same as you people do. At this point it's your word against Tanner's.'

'He's a dreadful person.'

'And slander is a nasty business, so be careful what you say. We've got to try and retrieve the situation.' Clem was deliberately involving Rivett and his department to keep him on edge, while he tried to think of a way out of this mess.

'I'll go to Kengally today and hand him back what he paid us. That'd be a good start, wouldn't you say?'

'Indeed it would. Very decent of you, Mr Price. Legally, you're not under any obligation to do so, but it would cool the air.'

'Neither of us really have to do anything, Mr Rivett. On

second thoughts, perhaps I should present you with the cheque to give to Kengally. Less Tanner's commission, of course, and I'm sure Mr Tanner will be pleased to follow suit. It would make it more official, coming from you, rather than my handing over a cheque on the quiet.'

'But what about the forgery?'

Clem sat back in the chair and lit his pipe, stalling, searching for the right words. Deagan would know what to say; he had the gift of the gab, the stupid bastard. Clem was struggling.

'Sooner or later someone will get to the bottom of it. I'm damned if I know. It's enough that I have to refund the sale monies. I'll not lose more on a slander charge. I won't even speculate. And you'd be wise to do the same.'

Rivett gave a sigh of relief as Clem wrote the cheque.

'It's been an exhausting morning for me, Mr Price,' he said. 'I had reporters on the doorstep from the minute I arrived, what with that awful Londonderry crash. What about joining me at the Crown and Anchor for a drink before lunch?'

'Be glad to,' Clem said wearily. Lunch with Rivett wasn't his first choice, but a show of unity in that very popular hotel wouldn't do any harm to his reputation. It would certainly scotch rumours that there were any problems between the former owner of Yorkey and officialdom.

He waited while Rivett sent a messenger to Lord Kengally, requesting an appointment that afternoon, and then the two men strolled across the road, both looking forward to a drink to ease the tension.

Clem was right. The Crown was the place to be. The hotel, he presumed, was built along the lines of an English tavern, with the interior featuring warm dark timbers and shining brass fittings, which he found very attractive, but he wondered vaguely if real taverns were as sedate as this. Being the haunt of senior public servants and professional men, the bar they entered lacked the noisy camaraderie of other Perth bars, for which, at this time, he was grateful. Numbly he followed Rivett's progress along a red carpet runner to the fourth wooden booth by the mullioned windows, and a waiter in a striped apron was immediately at their side. Clem gathered from Rivett's rather pompous conversation that this was his 'usual' table. And that was fine with him, anything was fine with him as long as he could get through this day without trouble.

Other customers stopped to chat with Rivett, mainly about the Londonderry débâcle, which was of far greater importance than the Yorkey problem, and Rivett, just as keen as Clem to control any more damaging rumours, made a point of introducing Mr Price. Clem had to admit he was going about his business very smoothly.

They were early, in no hurry to order lunch, and as Rivett held court, Clem dwelled on his whisky, vowing to throttle Mike Deagan next time he got his hands on him.

Why? he kept asking himself, having no doubt that Mike was the guilty party. He had the track record of a forger. Tanner did not. Unless Tanner had unpublicized talents in that direction, which was possible, Clem had to admit, though unlikely. To Clem, at least, Mike was the obvious suspect, but Rivett was convinced that Tanner had done the deed. He and Clem had gone over and over the progress of the report, from hand to hand, and given the facts, Tanner seemed to be the only one who could possibly have made the switch.

But why? Clem worried again. Tanner wasn't that stupid. If, between collecting the report and handing it to Kengally, he'd made the switch, he would know he'd have to be caught. That sort of scam, Clem was well aware, from all the wild tales he'd heard at Kalgoorlie, was only pulled for fast money and a quick exit. Otherwise it was pointless. Tanner had no motive.

Neither did Mike! Clem stood again for another introduction and paid for another round of drinks, which Rivett seemed to take for granted.

Mike didn't need the money from Yorkey. If it had deeped out, then so what? The first strikes at Yorkey had paid them well for their labours. The Black Cat was still the best earner out there, forget prospecting. Reminded of the brothel, Clem was glad to be rid of it. Amused that Jocelyn, obviously with Mike's help, was purchasing his share. That Mike! He hated bringing strangers into his life. For such an outgoing character, Deagan played his cards close to his chest.

Ah, well, Clem mused. Good luck to the both of them. His life was taking a different direction. At first he'd only begun the search for gold to upgrade Lancoorie and please Thora; then, like everyone else, enough wasn't enough. He was a wealthy man. The Black Cat and Yorkey, plus good seasons at Lancoorie with wool prices skyrocketing, had seen to that, and with his knowledge of the goldfields, he'd traded successfully in gold shares, his bank balance improving daily.

Money makes money, he told himself as Rivett left the table, temporarily, to pay homage to his own boss, the Secretary of the Department, who had just arrived with his entourage. No doubt he was telling him he had the ex-owner of Yorkey in tow, and was hosing down any looming unpleasantness.

Clem looked about the room, nodding to faces familiar to him, men who sat on the same boards, and made a mental note to come here more often. Because it wasn't just money now. Clem was ambitious. Vosper had given him a taste of the high life, of the élite of Perth, of Western Australia, the power-brokers, and he enjoyed this company. He had no interest in Vosper's path, in the fight for a seat in Parliament, he preferred the company of the men of the land, the squatters, the graziers, the cattle men, because he felt comfortable with them. Some of the men from the north had properties that were said to be the biggest in the world. He smiled, recalling that men from the great Forrest and Durack families had shaken his hand, and congratulated him for standing strong against the urbanization of this great state.

'Hardly likely, in your territory,' he'd said to one of the younger Duracks, a man his own age.

'That's right,' came the reply. 'But we're up against distance, the necessity for good ports and roads, cattle tick, lack of scientific advice, a whole range of things, so you have to keep in touch with what's going on here, right in this town. Don't bury yourself on your sheep station, but don't let it go either. These days the government is flat out backing anything to do with gold. They'll build that damn railway to Kalgoorlie, and there's a whisper abroad they're going to pipe water from the hills here all the way to Kalgoorlie as well.'

Clem was shocked. 'That would cost a fortune! There's no need. We get a little rain out there. It just runs off. They could dam it. They can bore for water. They just need more condensers . . .'

'These Perth johnnies and their public servants don't care, just so long as they're making a splash. At our expense.' He sighed. 'All I'm saying to you, Clem, is, don't desert your property. That's your life. But you keep a bloody finger hard on the pulse here, where all the decisions are made, or your wool will end up on some wharf, forgotten.

'Problem is,' he added, 'these blokes wanting to get into Parliament, like your mate Vosper, can only think of wages, and the public servants who run the show can only think of one thing at a time, and that, right now, is gold. We don't count.'

Clem knew the advice was important, but he also knew that he would enjoy the challenge of becoming a voice for the pastoralists in Perth. Of joining the famed six families of the massive western state that was his homeland.

These were the things that he wished he could talk to Thora about, but she'd never listen. She went off into her fantasies when he tried to tell her about the men of vision he had met at meetings and luncheons and at his less posh hotel, where most of them preferred to stay. She disdained country men, for some reason, as if they were somehow socially less acceptable than city people, although she didn't seem to know any of those, as far as he could make out. Except for Lord Kengally. To her he was the pinnacle of status.

Rivett was taking his time with his superior, so Clem ordered another drink, not caring. Another whisky. He had his own problems.

It was beginning to dawn on him that Thora was a very foolish woman. She might be the daughter of a doctor, but it hadn't gained her much. While he'd been working to build his reputation here, she'd been behaving like an idiot, pretending she was staying at the Palace when in fact she'd been pushed out to that stupid cottage. It worried him that that had happened at all, but he put it down to another of her whims.

Over the last month or so, he had been invited to various private functions and dinners with his wife, but he had declined, claiming prior engagements, because he was afraid to accept. Afraid that she would refuse, or change her mind at the last minute, which would be worse. She had him constantly afraid. Afraid that she didn't love him, because he loved her so dearly.

Or did he? His patience was running out.

Her enthusiasm for that beach house, his holiday house, was another worry. She was now crazy about it. Couldn't wait to get there. But it was isolated. Just a beach house for the summer. It was no more the centre of Perth social life than was Lancoorie, except that it was only a few hours from town, but Thora hadn't seemed to notice. She was even referring to it as 'home'.

'Mr Price!' Rivett was standing by him. 'Do forgive me, but our Minister has arrived.' He smoothed back his greying hair, tired eyes brittle with excitement. 'I hope you don't mind. He has asked me to join him for luncheon.'

Only then did Clem notice the worn cuffs on Rivett's sleeve, and the shine of his suit, and that depressed him. 'No,' he said kindly. 'I don't mind at all. We only came for drinks. But I want you to know that I'm going out to Kalgoorlie tomorrow. I'll see Mr Addison and we will both issue a statement, after we reassess. It appears that the statement will be to the effect that Yorkey is not viable. You can pay Lord Kengally and that's the best I can do.'

'It is a most honourable position to take, Mr Price, and I must thank you. My Minister, I am sure, will be relieved to hear it.'

Left to his own thoughts again, Clem knew he wasn't out of the woods yet. None of his new business associates would want to know him if it came out that somehow his own partner was the forger. Who would believe he wasn't involved? There were two very serious questions to be answered here. How the hell had Mike managed the switch? And how could Clem resolve the matter without dobbing in his partner, and, by association, himself. He couldn't let Tanner take the blame.

Speak of the devil, he said to himself as Tanner pushed open the heavy doors, stood for a minute, and then strode over to Rivett.

'I'll horsewhip you, you bastard!' he shouted, dragging Rivett from his chair. 'Call me a forger, eh? We'll see about that!'

Rivett's companions, stunned by this sudden violence, pulled back as Tanner, holding Rivett by his lapels, shook the helpless man.

Clem moved quickly down the aisle to force Tanner to release Rivett. 'Cut it out,' he hissed. 'Don't make things worse.'

'I might have known you'd be here!' Tanner shouted. 'Birds of a feather! You're for it too.'

'Outside!' Clem grabbed his arm and shouldered him past startled newcomers until they were in the street, but even then Tanner was so enraged he was ready to fight him.

'You're trying to fit me up as a forger, Price,' he snarled. 'And you won't get away with it.'

'Be your age!' Clem said, pushing him away. 'Cool down or I'll flatten you. I never said you were a forger, and I don't believe you are.'

Tanner stopped, surprised. 'What?'

'I don't think you're that stupid,' Clem said angrily, 'and you can quit calling me a conspirator round the town. I'm not stupid either, if you don't mind.'

Perplexed, Tanner stared at him. 'Then who? What the hell is going on?'

'I haven't got the faintest idea, but I'm going to Kalgoorlie tomorrow and I'll sort this out myself. There's been some mix-up, but the first thing to do is have another look at Yorkey.'

'Sure! Talk to your mates out there and get your story straight!'

'Don't push your luck, Tanner. I'm giving you the benefit of the doubt, while it doesn't seem to me that anyone else is, so shut your mouth. I'm your way out of this mess if you think about it.'

Tanner stepped back grudgingly to digest this, and then, still not convinced, turned to Clem. 'I'm coming with you. I'll be watching your every move.'

Clem could do nothing about that. 'Suit yourself.' He shrugged. 'I'll meet you at the train in the morning.' Tanner could dog his steps but he couldn't listen in on the private conversation Clem intended to have with one Mike Deagan.

Mr and Mrs Deagan were back in York, staying with Jocelyn's family, prior to leaving for Perth. They'd had a short holiday with George and Alice at Lancoorie, all happy in their roles as newly-weds. Jocelyn liked the pair immensely, and was thrilled that they'd made her so welcome. She'd enjoyed Alice's company, and they'd all found great humour in George's insistence that Mike made himself useful during his stay.

'Which he did,' she smiled, proud of her husband, as she told her mother all about their visit to Lancoorie. 'Of course, he groaned and teased George that this was no way to treat a visitor, but it was all in fun.'

Mrs Russell was happy for her daughter, who'd been fortunate enough to marry a man who had struck gold out west, and who was obviously very fond of her. She knew of Mike's background as a convict, but having met him, she had no complaints. After all, her own grandfather had been transported from England, so, she reckoned, people in glass houses shouldn't throw stones. Mike was a lot older than her daughter, but that too was unimportant. He would look after her, and that was all that mattered. She was sad to hear they had chosen to move to Melbourne, but was philosophical about it. They knew their own minds, and besides, they had promised to come back and visit. In all, it was a very satisfactory marriage.

Jocelyn's husband was in town to book seats on the coach

to Northam, en route to Perth, for they were leaving the following morning. First, though, he called in to a pub for a drink and picked up a newspaper, interested to read all this drama about Londonderry. A big shock. Following that story carefully, he came to the last passage about Yorkey.

'Cripes!' he muttered. 'How did they get on to that so fast?' Then he laughed. Tanner would get the blame. No one could figure out how he'd had a hand in it.

But a worry lodged. Except Clem, maybe. Clem wouldn't be too pleased to find out Yorkey had failed, and that there was something fishy about the sale. No, he wouldn't be too pleased at all. This mightn't be the best time to visit his partner.

Instead of booking for Northam, he bought two tickets on the coach service that went south, and that would take them to the port of Albany.

'Why Albany?' Jocelyn asked. 'I thought we were going to Perth.'

'My darlin',' he explained. 'It saves time. The ship from Perth has to go south and round the bottom of the continent to sail east, calling in at Albany. A feller was telling me that all ships run into mountainous swells down from Perth, where the Indian Ocean collides with the Great Southern Ocean, and they have been known to tip right over on their sides.'

'Yes. I've heard that,' Mrs Russell said. 'They say it's a fearsome experience.'

'But I thought we were to call on Clem in Perth.'

'Oh, Clem will keep. He won't mind.'

'Jocelyn,' her mother said, 'Mike is right. You sail from Albany. It'll be much safer. I'd be worried out of my mind if you go the other way.'

So it was agreed. Albany was a lot further than Perth, but compared to the trek from Kalgoorlie it was a pleasure trip, because the south-west corner of Western Australia was known for its scenic attractions, as well as many pleasant little towns where they could break their journey.

Before he left, Mike sent a short note to Clem. He had already written to tell him the grand news that he had sold out of the Black Cat altogether, that he and Jocelyn were wed and that they looked forward to seeing him in Perth before they took to the high seas. But now he decided that an explanation would be timely.

Dear Clem. Sorry we won't be coming to Perth. About Yorkey. That was only a joke. Letter following. Mike.

Rather than draw more attention to himself, Clem didn't return to the Crown. Instead he trudged over to his own hotel, where he found a letter from Mike, written from Lancoorie.

The news startled him. He was amazed that Mike had sold the Black Cat after all. He'd always assumed his partner would have hung on to the place for a long time yet.

To Clem, income from the Cat had been money up the sleeve, kept in a personal bank account so that Alice wouldn't ask too many questions, especially since payments were still being made even after he left. He'd always had Lancoorie to fall back on, but for Mike, the Black Cat was his main source of income. Clem shook his head. Wonders would never cease! And they were married, Mike and Jocelyn. Another surprise.

'Good news for a change,' he muttered, his own worries about Thora and Yorkey still dominating. Mike hadn't mentioned Yorkey at all. And now he wasn't even there, dammit!

Clem was now in a quandary. It would look very strange if he reneged on his promise to go to investigate Yorkey, but it was Mike he'd really had in mind to investigate. Addison would be rechecking the mine output. Maybe Clem should wait for Mike to get here. With Jocelyn.

Jocelyn?

'Oh, Christ!' Her fame as the madame of the Black Cat had spread to Perth with the countless numbers of diggers and businessmen who travelled back and forth from the goldfields. He'd often heard her spoken of in male company while he had pretended that the name of the brothel and its madame meant nothing to him. Now Mike was bringing her to the United Services Hotel. Why had Alice told them where he was staying?

He knew he was being unfair to Alice. They wouldn't have

said a word to her about Jocelyn's previous occupation, nor of the Black Cat, for that matter. But just the same, surely she could see that Jocelyn, who had begun to follow in Glory's footsteps by decking herself out in flashy clothes, would not be well received by Thora?

Clem was fed up with them all. It was time he took charge of his own life. He couldn't be expected to entertain Jocelyn – this wasn't the bush – nor to protect Mike, nor to wet-nurse Tanner. And as for Thora, she could stay in that cottage until the lease ran out, to be practical. Because from that day the money would stop. Not another penny. She would live exactly where he chose, and when, or she was out on her ear. She could go home to her parents in York, for all he cared. They'd all pushed him too far, making a fool of him.

He was hungry now, feeling that he could shed these problems just by being assertive, and followed his nose to the dining room, where he could already smell those sizzling roasts of pork with generous hunks of crackling. His favourite meal.

Vosper, who was already seated, waved him over. 'Where have you been? You missed my campaign meeting.'

'Busy,' he replied shortly. Answerable to no one.

'Then sit down. Take the weight off. I hope you're not too busy for tonight.'

'What's happening tonight?'

'Henery Whipple's send-off. The big shindig.'

'Oh, that!'

'Yes, that. Everyone that's anyone in Perth will be there. Have you changed your mind about taking Thora?'

'No, I have not,' he said firmly. 'I'm not going near her. She can stay home and cool off.'

Vosper smiled. 'With all due respect to Thora, that's a relief. I'd hate to miss out, and I can't get any more tickets. It's a sell-out. But you're coming, aren't you? We'll have a grand time. There's always a surfeit of young ladies at these shows when there's a dance on.'

Clem was about to refuse, but thought better of it. 'Why not?' he said. 'I haven't been to a dance for ages. We'll have to get out the glad rags, I presume?'

'The chambermaid is pressing them for us.' Vosper laughed. 'I guessed you wouldn't want to be left out. And by the way, I've borrowed one of your shirts.'

The waitress came to take Clem's order. 'Sorry, Mr Price,' she said. 'The pork's off. So is the beef. But we've still got roast lamb.'

'That'll do,' Clem said, watching Vosper devour pork. 'It's just not my day.'

All day Thora waited for him to come to the cottage. She had slept soundly, thanks to a foul-tasting draught, a white mixture, that Nanny had obtained from a store, and so she felt better able to deal with him. He would come to her, begging and pleading as usual, but she would have none of it. This time she would tell him what she really thought of him, and make him suffer too. She would tell him she knew about that evil house, and the whores, and he would get the tongue-lashing he deserved before she ordered him from her life for ever. She pictured herself standing tall like the avenging angel, pointing, ordering him to make amends for his sins before darkening her doorstep again. It was a dramatic picture, and it excited her. He had sunk to the lowest of depths and she doubted that even God could forgive him, so it would take a very long time before his wife could be sure he had repented.

In righteous mood, Thora ate all her lunch: soup, cold meat with pickles, and treacle pudding, and Nanny was very pleased with her. She even sipped a delicious white wine, and that cheered her immensely. Gave her confidence.

'We shall be moving shortly, Nanny,' she said. 'I want you to make sure that Miss Devane knows.'

'I'll do that, madam. Is the beach house ready?'

'My home will be ready soon,' Thora corrected.

Nanny was enthusiastic. 'It'll be so exciting to be living in a house with the great ocean right before us. I can take Lydia to play on the beach, she can paddle and we'll build sand castles and all. And with Mr Price there to look after us.'

'What are you talking about? We don't need looking after.

I certainly don't, for one. I am quite capable of running a household without him.'

'Yes, of course, madam. I meant it will be nice for you to be together again, as a family, the house being so big and roomy after the cottage.'

'Yes, we are cramped here. Wait until you see all the beautiful furniture I've bought. It will be the most perfect house. You will have your own room, and a nursery for Lydia, and my room will be exquisite. We don't need Mr Price. He's not coming.'

She saw Nanny's sharp turn of dismay and looked at her with a pitying sigh. 'You're very young, you're just seventeen. You'll learn, men are evil. You be warned by one who knows. Have nothing to do with them, they can ruin you.'

'My mum says that too,' Netta said glumly. 'She's always going on about it. But Mr Price, he's nice.'

'There! See how gullible you are. He's one of the worst.' Thora smiled with satisfaction to see Nanny gape at this pronouncement.

The afternoon wore on and still he didn't appear, and Thora became more and more agitated. She decided to write to Alice and tell her about all these foul things she had discovered, to explain that she could not live with a man so steeped in evil, knowing that Alice would be just as horrified as she was.

The letter began with the formalities, with her hopes that Alice was happy and all was well at Lancoorie, but soon Thora realized that she couldn't ignore the fact that Alice was now married. Poor Alice. Her pen ran on, taking charge. She considered it essential, Alice being her only true friend, to warn her too about associating with men. She commiserated with Alice about having to suffer the indignities of marriage, and offered her the best advice she could. That if she ever needed refuge, Thora's beach home was the place where she would always be welcome.

From there to more and more pages, Thora rambled on. About her divine home, about it being so new and clean and pure, untainted by *them*. By men who brought their filth home from whorehouses, by men who bedded whores, by men who seduced shy young women. Men who associated with loud, gaudy whores, like that Jocelyn. She'd seen them, she told Alice, sluts, floozies, jezebels, on that train. No woman was safe from their disgusting flauntings, from the way they seduced men.

Her pen flew, seducing Thora into a wildly erratic diatribe in which, at times, she confused Clem with Matt Spencer, and yet at others she spoke grandly of mixing with real gentlemen like Lord Kengally. But gradually, inexorably, it came out, hidden deep in the scrawled black ink like a lurking shade, glimpses, glances, flashbacks, horrific images, teetering together on the edge of fact. It was there, feebly outlined, guiltily said, among all this rigmarole, the story of a young girl raped, of the shock and disgust at the violent assault, of the pain and the misery and the shame, the never-ending shame.

Nanny looked in. 'I took Lydia to visit the girls at the hotel. They always love to see her. Chef gave me a lovely potato pie to bring home. Would you like some, madam? It's still hot and I've got a pot of gravy to go with it.'

Mrs Price didn't reply. It was a battle to keep ink on the pen, a nuisance to have to keep jamming it in the inkwell when one was so totally involved in this matter of such importance.

She had forgotten she was writing to Alice; she was just writing, angrily now, guilt assuaged, confession over, floundering her way to the present, to a man who called himself her husband, a disgusting creature who employed whores, who did *that* to whores like Jocelyn Russell.

Exhausted, Thora put down the pen. She riffled through and found the first of her ten pages, addressing Alice, and she felt so sorry for Alice, because her sister-in-law didn't know, was too innocent to know about the vileness in the world.

And yet Alice would have known Jocelyn Russell, growing up in the district, just as she had. That vulgar waitress whose father was just a ditch-digger, and the mother a nobody who'd taken in washing. Alice was entitled to know the sort of women her brother bedded while pretending to be a faithful husband.

She would be shocked, but not to the extent his wife was. She couldn't be.

Dusk had settled like gloom on the afternoon, and Thora left her pages on the dining room table to walk out to the front gate, expecting him any minute. But the street was quiet, ominous. Where was he? How dare he ignore his wife? Did he think that by bringing a cheap box of chocolates he could buy her respect? That would do for the likes of Jocelyn, but not for decent women.

Jocelyn invaded her thoughts, and stayed, an unwelcome guest, sniggering, laughing behind her back, poking faces at her from the mirror in the bedroom, until Thora confronted her.

'You needn't think I'll stay here and put up with this,' she said. 'I'll see him about you. He'll listen to me, don't think he won't. I'll have you put in jail, that's where women like you belong!'

She called to Nanny. 'Could you come in here? I want you to help me dress my hair.'

They brushed her long fair hair until it shone, tonged it into soft waves about her face, then, using the tongs again, Nanny built a cascade of long curls at the back, pinning them into a bunch from the crown.

'Oh, madam, it does look lovely,' Nanny said. 'I'm really getting better at it. Are you going out?'

'Yes. Now I'll have that very full petticoat with all the frills. My blue silk sits out beautifully over that.'

The image of an elegant woman with her hair classically arranged caused blowsy Jocelyn to flee from her mirror, and Thora smiled disdainfully. 'You couldn't possibly hope to compete with me,' she murmured.

'What was that?' Nanny asked.

'Nothing. Fetch me my cloak. No, not that one, that's for day wear. The dark-blue velvet, it's nice and full too. I can't wear a skimpy cloak over this dress.'

Finally, with the cloak tied in place, Thora twirled about the sitting room, the voluminous cloak and skirts swishing in rich folds. 'How do I look?'

394

'Wonderful! What time is Mr Price expected?'

'He is not expected. I'm taking myself out.'

'But it's dark out there. The streets are not safe for ladies at night. Should I try to find you a horse cab?'

'No. They never come down this street. And anyway, I don't need one. I shall walk.'

'Where to?'

'The United Services Hotel, of course. He is staying there.'

Nanny tried to dissuade her, but Thora would have none of it. She sailed out into the street, unconcerned by this poorly lit area and too intent on her own mission to worry about lurking dangers. Once free of Nanny's silly protests, she stepped out swiftly and firmly. She knew the town well now, and she headed straight for his hotel.

The hotel foyer was poky and drab, and it smelled – Thora sniffed – of boiled cabbage and tobacco, quite third class compared to the Palace. She couldn't imagine what he was thinking of to even suggest that she should move in here. On her left, under the staircase, was a set of leather armchairs, guarded by a drooping fern in a brass jardinière and a pinkish plaster statue supporting a lamp.

The wall on her right was jam-packed with photographs and plaques, military and naval memorabilia, and she inspected them to provide herself with purpose while she waited for someone, anyone, to present themselves, for this entrance hall was deserted. Two corridors sped away from the foot of the staircase, and the muffled noise from both ends might have led her in either direction had she not read on frosted glass doors that one hid the bar, and the other the dining room. She pulled back quickly, clutching the soft collar of her cloak.

There were no porters and no reception desk, just what appeared to be an office, totally enclosed except for a frosted window that was firmly shut. She knocked timidly and jumped when a voice rumbled: 'Office is closed.'

'I can see that,' she replied through the glass, and knocked again.

There was no movement for a while, but eventually the small window shot up and a plump-faced youth glared. 'We're booked out.' He was wearing the buttoned-through uniform of lowly hotel staff, and it was obvious to Thora that he was enjoying a snatch of rest in this hideaway, with a newspaper and a bottle of beer, prior to her interruption.

'Did I ask for accommodation?'

He peered out at her, reassessing. 'No, miss, no. I'm sorry.' He was impressed, she was pleased to see, by the lady before him.

His pale eyes gathered light and he smiled quickly, all attention now. 'Were you looking for the dining room? I can take you down there.'

'No. You have a Mr Price staying here. Be kind enough to get him for me.'

'Ah, Mr Price. Clem. Yes, let me see. He's probably in the dining room. No, wait a minute. They've gone out. Quiet night it is here tonight. Nobody much in the dining room now.'

'Gone where?'

'To the big show at the tTown hall.'

Thora felt her knees giving way. It hadn't occurred to her that he wouldn't be in. She clutched the wooden ledge for support and struggled to keep her voice firm. 'Oh, yes, I forgot.'

Clem went to a lot of meetings, he was always talking about his meetings. That was where he would be. At a meeting in a hall.

'They'll be right into the swing of it by now,' the young man said wistfully, no longer anxious to be rid of her.

'Of what?' she asked.

'Of the big party. For some politician. I wouldn't mind going. Our cooks did all the catering, you know. Grub like you never saw. Makes the mouth water thinking about it.'

'Really?' she said, encouraging him. 'A formal dinner, is it?'

'And the rest. An orchestra and dancing. A ball, you could say. You new here?'

'Yes. And you're sure Mr Price went?'

'I saw them leave myself. All dressed up formal like. Matter of fact, I got Mr Price some cigars, now I come to think of it.'

'That's nice. He enjoys a cigar.'

The clerk looked at her sadly, wondering what he could do to help. 'You must have missed him,' he said lamely. 'Is there any message?'

'No. I'll wait for him. In his room.'

He looked about nervously. 'I dunno about that. It's against the rules.'

Thora gave him a tender, winning smile. 'And you are quite right. But don't worry. I'm Mrs Price. Just direct me to his room,' she said, removing her glove to display her wedding ring as she found a coin in her purse for him.

'Oh, well, in that case . . .' he faltered. 'I suppose it's all right. But he might be late.'

'No, he won't,' she lied. 'He's expecting me. I should prefer to rest in his room rather than sit down here in a public place. What number did you say?'

'Room thirty-three. Up the stairs. First floor, to the right. Can I get you anything, Mrs Price?'

'No, thank you. You've been extremely kind. I'm most grateful.'

She could feel his eyes on her as she walked, with the utmost grace, up that tall staircase, and then, when she turned to the right, she heard his window shut as he returned to his evening vigil. She found room thirty-three without difficulty, opened the door and walked in, relieved to find the lamp was still on. Then she slammed the door in a rage, leaning against it, taking deep breaths to control her pounding heart for fear that she would faint, so shocked was she at this latest outrage. This insult! Her face was still hot and flaring from that horrible demeaning conversation. That fellow must have known how ridiculous she looked, searching for her husband while he was out with his floozy.

'I saw them go,' he'd said. Not once, but twice, twisting

the knife. Laughing at her. *Them*. He was with Jocelyn! His whore. She actually mouthed the word.

'Oh, he'll pay for this!' she said, prowling the room.

She had forgotten that he'd said he was sharing a room with Vosper, temporarily. To her, this was simply his room. Everything in here belonged to him, the man with two faces.

And there were two beds in the room.

Was Jocelyn living here with him? Sneaking in here? Or did he flaunt her? Marching down that staircase with his floozy on his arm, showing her off, while his wife, a decent woman, was kept out of sight in the cottage?

She pulled the covers and the sheets from the beds, hysteria rising, furious with him and wildly thrilled that she was at last able to retaliate. 'I'll show him!' she said, upturning the mattresses and dragging them to the floor.

There was a wallet under one mattress, and it wasn't his, so she deduced it belonged to *her*. That went out the window.

Systematically she went round the room, opening drawers and cupboards, hurling the contents about willy-nilly. She found his razor, the blade slim and sharp, and slashed the air with it, excited by the power it gave her. The floor was strewn with clothes, ideal targets for this fine blade, so she picked things up, shirts, jumpers, trousers, singlets, slicing and ripping at them and throwing them down again.

In the corner, past the heavy wardrobe, she spotted two fishing rods, standing on a small case, so she cut at them too, but since she wasn't making much headway, she tossed the razor aside and took great delight in snapping the rods over her knee. Then she went down on one knee to open the case, surprised to find his revolver inside, nestling with a box of bullets in green felt.

'Look at that!' she sneered. 'See how much you take care of things these days!' He had always treasured this wooden gun case that had belonged to Noah, keeping the wood polished and the leather straps well oiled. Now it was worn and battered, and the felt inside looked as if silverfish had taken up residence. It didn't occur to her that Clem would not have had any reason to bring a gun to the city, that it could have belonged to someone else, nxx preparing to make Perth his permanent home.

Not that it would have mattered, because Thora now had the revolver and she loaded it expertly, as she'd been shown so often at Lancoorie as protection against snakes that often slid into the house. Although it was Alice who always dealt with them, Thora recalled. She was terrified of snakes and would grab the baby and run until it was all over.

'But I'm not frightened of guns,' she said proudly, nursing the cool steel and the smooth wooden handle.

'He will be, though, if he walks in that door and finds a gun pointed at him. This is a lesson he'll never forget. This will teach him to lie down with whores. All that talk about meetings, they were lies. Lies to cover what he was really up to.'

Gleefully she pictured the scene, the shock he would get, but she would have to prepare.

She placed the revolver carefully on the dressing table and looked about. The first thing one saw on opening the door was that bed, so she would sit there.

She lugged the mattress back into place and dragged out the thick white bedspread to cover the ugly ticking. She smoothed it down, picked up the revolver and settled herself facing the door. She arranged the folds of her dark velvet cloak so that it presented well against the white, and left it open in front so that the contrasting pale blue of her dress completed the picture.

Satisfied, Thora folded her hands on the gun on her lap and waited. As soon as he walked in, she would aim it straight at him.

Chapter Twelve

After Minchfield, the two-storey stone house, flush to the street, with a small garden at the back, was a disappointment to Lillian, who had expected Henery Whipple to occupy a grand mansion here in St Georges Terrace, but it was neat and cosy and his guests settled in easily. She and Robert each had their own rooms, which irritated him as much, she thought, as if they'd been lodged in the same room. Robert, being a contrary man, always found something to fuss about.

'Henery knows our circumstances,' he whispered. 'And you know I dislike having to sleep alone. It upsets my digestion. You speak to him.'

'Just for now, dear, it would be best not to say anything. Henery will be sure to have other visitors while we're here, and he probably feels he's doing the right thing, not encouraging talk. He simply has two guests, that's all.'

'I am not concerned with talk,' he grumbled. 'One should not be inconvenienced by below-stairs gossip. You be sure to bring me my hot milk and brandy before I retire, and the rubbing lotion. You did remember to pack it?'

'Yes. Now you go on down and I'll unpack for you.'

Robert was jealous and Lillian was delighted. He couldn't help but notice the big bear-hug Henery gave her when they stepped ashore from the river boat, and the over-long kiss he planted on her cheek.

'Why, Lillian,' he'd said, 'you look a picture on this fine sunny day! My word, Robert, you'd better watch out or the lads of Perth will be stealing this beauty from you.'

And Robert! After that welcome he would have stepped right back on the boat, with her in tow, given half a chance,

400

but Henery had his buggy waiting for them, and they were whisked away.

Lillian loved the room Henery had assigned to her, looking down over the wide street, a far cry from Merle's poor boarding house, her last Perth residence, and she was glad to be free of Robert.

'You'd think he was ninety,' she muttered, 'the way he coddles himself. He has to get his sleep, but he snores and takes all the blankets and flails about, keeping me awake. This room to myself is heaven.'

Not that she had any thought of retreating from the situation. Minchfield House was her home, and Caroline's. Her daughter was growing into a beautiful child, cheerfully and chubbily finding her feet, and so sweet she was beloved of all the staff. Lillian still worried about leaving her but she was in good hands, with Cook, who spoiled her, watching over the nursemaid that the mistress had appointed. Lillian was no longer referred to as the housekeeper.

Robert took little interest in the child, and that suited Lillian. She wanted no interference from a bachelor who knew nothing about children, or from anyone else for that matter. Caroline was hers, and she would be brought up the way her mother decreed. Her child would be a young lady; she would never have to rough it. Lillian would sleep with a hundred Roberts if she had to, to ensure Caroline's future. She would go to the best schools, and meet the right people, and if she ever met her sister, who was also living in the lap of luxury out there at Lancoorie, she'd have no reason to feel deprived. Sometimes Lillian felt she was competing with the other child, the one she also called Caroline, racing against time to keep them on an equal footing.

Their days were busy. When Henery wasn't entertaining visitors, they shopped, they went sightseeing, they visited the government offices and even attended a soirée at the magnificent Government House, along with a hundred other guests. Henery took them to the Odeon Theatre for a vaudeville show which Robert hated, but she and Henery just loved. They laughed themselves silly, and sang along with the fancy lady

...green dress who stood centre stage, encouraging ...n with her. She had a lovely voice.

...n't believe a man in your position would enjoy such a ...nmon performance,' Robert complained, as they left the theatre, but Henery laughed.

'That's the best show I've seen in years. Give us a smile, Robert. You're altogether too dismal when there's no need. Look at Lillian, I think she's fair aching from laughing.'

That night, before she retired, Lillian went in to rub Robert's back, stiff, he said, from sitting for hours on those hard theatre seats, and he was in a very bad mood.

'You seem to be getting along well with Henery.'

'I must do, Robert. He's our host.'

'You were laughing like a hyena at that concert!'

She pushed his face into the pillow and slapped the lotion on his back, massaging gently to ease his irritation, since his flabby white back had no real need of her ministerings.

'I think you're getting altogether too fond of Henery,' he complained, and deliberately Lillian took her cue.

'Why wouldn't I? He's your friend and he is such good company. And he's making sure that we have a really good time. You have to admit, there's never a dull moment with Henery about. And he knows so many people. These Perth people are much nicer, much better mannered than the folk in our district. You've said that yourself.'

He struggled up to a sitting position. 'Why are you doing this to me? Haven't I taken care of you? Haven't I looked after you?' he whined.

'Doing what?' she asked innocently.

'Preferring Henery to me. It's so obvious, I'm humiliated. Don't think I don't see,' he cried, almost in tears. 'He's trying to take you away from me. Since his wife died he's been a very lonely man. A woman like you, who could run his house better than the harpies he employs, would be a godsend to him. And you are encouraging him.'

Lillian sat back and sighed. 'Goodness me, Robert. As if I'd leave you. I have to admit that Henery lives an exciting life in the city, compared to our quiet ways, but that shouldn't bother you.'

'Well, it does. Where's this fellow Cornish?'

'Who?' That did surprise her.

'Your husband.'

'Oh, him. I have no idea. I told you before, he deserted me, and good riddance. My mother said it was a mistake to marry him.'

'Obviously your mother had more sense than you.'

'You are right. I won't argue with you on that.'

'I don't like arguments of any sort.'

'I'm sorry. Are we arguing? What is the matter with you, dear? Perhaps you shouldn't have eaten those braised onions, you know they don't agree with you.'

'Posh to the onions!' He climbed out of the bed and put on his dressing gown. 'I was talking about that fellow you are married to. I want you to get rid of him.'

'I am rid of him.'

'Legally you're not. I will take you to a lawyer and we'll make an end to it. For desertion.'

Lillian remained calm, but her heart was beating faster. This was something she'd contemplated for a long time, but she had not known how to go about it, or what it would cost. Women talked, they all knew it was easy for a man to divorce his wife, but hard lines for women who tried it. This time, though, a wealthy man was about to make a run at it, on her behalf.

She shook her head dismally. 'Can that be done?'

'My word it can. We'll see my solicitor on Monday. But not a word of this to Henery. Do you hear me? We'll make some excuse and take time on our own.'

'Oh, Robert, if you could do that, I would be so grateful.'

'And so you ought to be. But it doesn't mean that once you are a single woman again, a divorcée, you should go rushing to Henery with the news.'

'Why ever not? He'd be hurt that we're keeping things from him.'

'Because you'll be marrying me, not Henery. It's none of his business.'

That night, Lillian made love to Robert for a change. She

warmed him and excited him and nurtured and nursed him and excited him all over again with a passion that had him whimpering with pleasure, and then in the early hours she flitted back to her own room. Triumphant. If Robert hadn't been so blinded by his own jealousy, he would have noticed, as Lillian had, that Henery was a naughty lecher. She wasn't the only woman whose breasts and buttocks attracted his straying hands.

The farewell reception was not held at the Esplanade Hotel as previously planned, because of the numbers that had accepted the invitations. Henery was a very popular man. Instead it was held in the town hall, a sit-down supper for two hundred of Perth's finest, and afterwards, when the tables were cleared away, a ball, led by an eight-piece orchestra.

For days before, even Robert was caught up in the excitement, fussing at the tailor's over his new dinner suit and insisting on choosing Lillian's gown. She had no complaints, for, to give Robert his due, he had excellent taste. He utterly rejected the red satin that the exclusive French boutique owner suggested, calling it common, despite her claim that it would look magnificent against madam's dark hair. He called the pale dresses insipid. He hated the gold taffetas as ostentatious, and remarked that the white gown with red beading looked vaudevillian.

The more fractious he became with the 'rubbishy' gowns they displayed, the more Lillian despaired. They were running out of time and this was the very last shop.

'Let's take that blue one,' she said. 'Let me try it on.'

Lillian would have bought any one of them. Never in her life had she seen such magnificent evening gowns, and she was appalled that Robert was treating them, and the elegant boutique owner, so rudely.

He put on his glasses and peered at the voluminous silk gown, that had tiny pearls stitched over the bodice.

'It's beautiful, Robert,' she whispered, 'just beautiful.'

'Let me see what else you've got,' he told the woman, and when she disappeared he silenced Lillian. 'Be good enough to bear with me, please. We may have to take that blue thing if it fits you, but it's just not right. If you are to be my wife, I don't expect you to turn out looking like everyone else. I've seen the blue, with variations of the beading, in every shop window. It's just too common, Lillian.'

The woman returned nursing a superb gown of deep cream satin.

'Now we're getting somewhere. Try it on, Lillian.'

'But you don't like satin.'

'I don't like red satin. This is entirely different. It's actually a champagne colour. Very understated.'

That marvellously elegant dress, with its low-cut neckline, nipped-in waist, smooth bustle and short train gave Lillian a confidence she never dreamed she could attain. As she walked out in it and saw his smile of satisfaction, Lillian felt power, the power of seduction. Her breasts swelled milky white against the luscious satin, forced up by tight corsets to such an extent that they felt almost bold displayed like that, but Robert had no complaints.

'Excellent,' he said. 'We'll take that gown. Are alterations needed?'

'No, sir,' the shop woman said, 'it fits madam perfectly. Being satin, of course, the best satin, it is rather more expensive . . .'

'As I thought,' he told Lillian without bothering to lower his voice, 'they keep the best to last, hoping we'll buy other people's cast-offs.'

In the dressing room, Lillian apologized to the woman. 'I'm sorry. He didn't mean to be rude. It's just his way.'

'You look splendid, madam,' she replied. 'It could have been made for you. And don't apologize for the gentleman. I'm sure he knows best.'

Lillian glanced at her, realizing that this woman also had to pander to Robert, and she sighed.

Henery Whipple raved when he saw the dress. 'It's gorgeous, just gorgeous! Try it on for me, Lillian.'

'There's no need,' Robert said. 'You'll see it on the night.'

'Then wait a minute.' Henery rushed off and came back

with diamond drop earrings. 'Take these, dear heart. They'll set off the dress. They belonged to my mother, who gave them to my wife. Now you shall have them. What do you think, Robert? Perfect, eh?'

But on the night of the reception, when Henery had gone on ahead to be at the receiving line, Robert waited until they were ready to leave.

'You can take those earrings off now, Lillian. They have no colour. I want you to wear these.'

He handed her a small pair of ruby earrings set in gold.

'Much more appropriate,' he said, and Lillian fastened them on, examined them in the mirror and kissed him.

'You always know what's best, my dear.'

The town hall was festooned in foliage and flowers and balloons.

'Like a barn dance,' Robert commented.

Henery and several of his colleagues greeted everyone at the door and ushered them into the overcrowded hall, where they sat stiffly at a table among strangers as the courses of oysters, soup, chicken and vegetables, and wine trifle were served with a generous supply of wines.

Lillian loved it all: the official table with its important personages, the speeches and the presentation to Henery of an illuminated address, followed by a retinue of political gentlemen who insisted on a chance to say a few words. She felt so proud of Henery, up there accepting the accolades, as cool as you like, making jokes, even bursting into one of his ditties, which brought the house down. People clapped and clapped and cheered him and drank the health of dear old Henery, and Lillian thought she would burst with excitement.

Not so Robert, who found the food disgusting, some of the jokes totally out of order with ladies present, and Henery's lack of decorum a shame. Worst of all were the wines.

'Frightful!' he said. 'How dare they thrust this cheap rubbish on us?'

'Well, it is free,' Lillian said.

'What's that got to do with it?'

'I don't know,' she sighed, sitting before the long trestle table in her lovely dress, thinking she might as well have worn a skirt and blouse for all anyone cared.

But then the orchestra began to play. Tables were whisked aside and chairs set along the walls. The well-sprung floor was swept quickly with wide brush brooms and sawdust scattered for the dancing.

Lillian shrank behind Robert as Henery strode purposefully towards her, because it was the guest-of-honour's privilege to open the dancing, and he was holding his hands out to her.

Apart from feeling Robert's resentment, Lillian was overcome with shyness. 'No, Henery, I can't,' she whispered.

'But you must,' he insisted. 'It is my prerogative to choose any lady I wish, and I can't go past our Lillian. You're looking absolutely beautiful, my dear.'

As he led her out on to the floor he smiled. 'Give you a chance to show off that superb gown.'

The whole room burst into spontaneous applause as Henery whisked her into a circular waltz, smiling broadly, enjoying himself.

'You dance well,' he said. 'Where did you learn?'

'Country dances, that's all,' she murmured, grateful that he was an excellent dancer and could lead her expertly under the gaze of all those faces, but at last others began to join in and she was spared any more of this terrifying exhibition.

When Henery returned her to the sidelines, Robert was nowhere to be seen, but they were surrounded by a jolly crowd of people, all anxious to talk to Henery, and as the music began again, a gentleman invited her to partner him in the Lancers.

She looked about her, bewildered, searching for Robert, and unable to think of an excuse, she accepted.

The Lancers were always fun. Once on the floor, Lillian felt more confident, moving happily about the circle in the familiar moves until she came face to face with him!

Of all people! Clem Price! Looking so handsome in his formal attire.

He beamed at her as she circled round him and reached

out to the next partner in the chain, and Lillian blushed, suddenly nervous, thinking she really had no right to be here. He intimidated her.

When she came round again he took her hand. 'Don't I know you?'

'I don't think so,' she gulped, moving on, remembering that she and Ted Cornish were supposed to have gone to Adelaide.

The dance was endless. Lillian kept praying that it would stop and free her, but he was there all the time, smiling at her.

'May I ask your name?'

'Lillian,' she said, trying not to face him. 'Lillian Warburton.'

Apprehension kept her ducking her head, looking every which way but at him, while she tried to decipher her emotions. She wanted to grasp hold of him, take him aside and ask him about her daughter, Caroline's twin. Ask him if she was growing into a pretty little girl with soft dark curls . . . if she was well and happy. But she knew she must not do that. Not here, anyway, not yet. Confusion caused her to miss a call, to move to the right instead of the left, causing amusement, but Clem Price was there to rescue her, to turn her about.

'Might I have the next dance, Miss Warburton?'

'I can't,' she breathed.

'Then the one after. My name's Clem Price. We do have mutual friends.'

'We do?' she asked, startled.

'Friends of Mr Whipple,' he said as he moved on again.

As she was leaving the floor with her partner, he caught up with her. 'The dance after next then,' he said firmly.

Robert was still missing, for which she was grateful. Thoroughly shaken by the encounter, she began to reassess. Why was she feeling so guilty? Why shouldn't she be here? What business was it of Clem Price where she chose to live? None at all. Lillian's natural ability to fight back began to emerge, and she realized that she was battling shame. She was ashamed of that skinny wretch of a girl she'd once been, a pitiful mess, down and out, pregnant and married to a no-hoper, scraping a living on a dirt-poor farm. Robert didn't know her then, he couldn't imagine. But Clem Price did. The girl who had handed over one of her babies to his wife.

And where was Thora Price? She searched the room surreptitiously for fear of catching her eye. Clem Price wasn't the problem after all, he was a nice fellow, but Thora . . .

'My God!' she whispered to herself. 'I'd hate to meet Thora here! That snob. She'd cut me dead if she recognized me. And more so if they eventually told her she had my baby. She'd be on the defensive.'

Lillian measured mother-love in her own terms. Caroline was the most important being in her world, she loved her desperately, and she expected Thora would be the same. Lillian still mourned the loss of her other child, given up under duress, but she had to accept it, for the good of both children. And, as it turned out, she kept reminding herself, she had made the right decision.

She could see Clem Price at the end of the hall, talking to a group of men. Thora hadn't been on the dance floor, nor was she with him now. With a huge sense of relief, Lillian decided that Mr Price must have come to town without his wife or she'd have been here tonight. Reinforcing that belief was his eagerness to dance with other ladies.

Mischief lightened her heart. Wait until I write and tell Mum about the ball, and that I even danced with Clem Price from Lancoorie. She'll be impressed.

But the music started again, and she felt a fool sitting there alone, so she went in search of Robert and found him outside, smoking a cigar. Sulking.

'Heavens, Robert! I've been looking for you everywhere.'

'I can't imagine why. You seem to enjoy making a spectacle of yourself.'

'Why? Dancing with Henery? You can't mean that. I was petrified.'

'Not just Henery. I saw you kicking up your heels in that vulgar reel.'

'Oh, my dear. Not so. You'd left me alone, and when a

gentleman invited me to dance I couldn't think of an excuse not to.'

He shrugged. 'I think it was very poor of Henery to sit us down with the also-rans.'

'But he explained that. He told us he'd have to sit at the official table with his colleagues.'

'Lord Kengally isn't one of his colleagues, he's *my* friend.'

'Never mind, dear. You wouldn't have wanted to sit up there on show. You don't need that.'

She managed to talk him back inside, and even persuade him to partner her in the Pride of Erin, but halfway through the dance he complained that his shoes were pinching, so they left the floor.

'Those musicians are appalling,' he said, settling beside her. 'God knows where they found them. The noise is giving me a headache. I don't believe I can stand this much longer.'

Lillian was stunned. This was the first grand ball she'd ever attended and she was still dazzled by it all. Surely he wouldn't make her leave so soon?

'Can I get you a glass of water?'

'No. Where's Henery? We can't leave without paying our respects.'

Fortunately Henery was lost somewhere in the crowd.

'There's a refreshment bar in the foyer, dear,' she said, resorting to guile. 'A brandy would help your headache. Shall I go and get you one?'

'From a gentlemen's bar? What are you thinking of? I shall go myself. Henery is probably there.'

She watched him walk away. No sign of sore feet. At least she'd postponed their departure. Pleased with herself, Lillian gazed about the room, admiring all the beautiful gowns and at the same time keeping an eye out for Thora Price. If Thora showed up she'd be only too willing to retreat with Robert.

Then she saw Clem Price coming towards her! Defiantly she decided she would dance with him. It would be just too bad if Robert disapproved. She could talk her way out of that. A dance with Clem Price would be intriguing, and a feather in her cap. She'd always had a soft spot for him.

But what would she say if he recognized her?

Don't cross your bridges, she told herself. We'll just see what happens.

'Do you know a Miss Warburton?' he asked Vosper.

'No. Let's breast the bar. We're celebrating tonight! I just got the word from Charlie Rogers that he and his Leftists have agreed to back me, so I've got the numbers.'

'What numbers?'

He punched Clem in the arm. 'Pay attention, friend. It means that by Monday night I'll be the endorsed candidate for the Labor Party in the seat of South Perth.'

Clem was delighted. 'Congratulations. That is good news. What happens then?'

'I'm over the first hurdle, the next will be a shoo-in. With the workers and the miners behind me I'm a certainty. Forrest and his bigwig mates are in for a shock.' He was so thrilled he clapped his hands and shouted to all about them: 'Up the Australian Labor Party!'

A few responded with cheers, but most stared at this odd chap, who was wearing his hair in a long plait, wondering who he was and what on earth he was on about. But Fred didn't mind.

'They don't know who Vosper is yet.' He grinned. 'Not in this company. But they'll know soon enough. Come on, Clem! To the bar!'

'I can't. I've got this dance. Are you sure you don't know Miss Warburton? I'm certain I've seen her somewhere before. She was the lady Henery danced with. The first dance.'

'If you want to be introduced, ask Henery.'

'I've already introduced myself.'

'Then what's the problem?'

Word was out! Other Labor Party supporters descended on Fred to congratulate him, and they headed for the bar.

'Are you coming, Clem?' Fred called over his shoulder.

'After this dance.'

Being a newspaperman, a reporter of happenings of great moment and little import, but nevertheless happenings that affected lives far beyond their fleeting news impact, Fred Vosper wondered later what the outcome might have been had Clem accepted his invitation to celebrate at the bar. Had he not stayed for that dance.

For a long time Thora waited. She was in no hurry. Occasionally she turned her head to primp in the dressing table mirror, oblivious of the disarray about her, but her exhilaration was only a façade. As time passed it began to slip from her like a protective covering, exposing a woman who knew she was fast becoming a bundle of nerves.

But the gun gave her confidence. She cherished it. Talking to it. 'He'll be sorry when he walks in that door to find his wife sitting here. He thinks I'm a fool. He probably thought I'd never find out that he owns a house full of whores. That he didn't make his money honestly from gold but from the wages of sin. The money that I'm expected to spend.'

Suddenly the enormity of that statement struck her.

'Oh, God help me!' she cried, tears brimming. 'Is that what I have come to also? Am I as much to blame as he is? What will people say when they look at him, at us? Will they say "There go the Prices, they own a whorehouse"?'

Now Thora knew why Mr Tanner had been so rude to her. He despised her and her husband, and he had good reason.

Fretting, frightened, she tried to think her way through this. She wished she could walk about, look out of the window, but she couldn't leave this position, it was important to stay right here, for a reason that was becoming obscure.

What if her parents found out about this? Her family? All of those people in York, that hateful town? She'd thought she was free of that humiliation, having moved away as far as she could possibly go – right at the edge of the ocean she would be soon – but now it was starting all over again.

Thora looked back at the mirror in great sorrow, shaking her head. No one cared about her, she was only Thora Carty who'd committed the worst possible sin. Got herself in the family way. That curse was just the beginning of her punishments. She would never recover from it.

'Maybe it would be best if I just put a stop to it now,' she wept. 'I could shoot myself and be done with it. Who'd care? No one.'

She pushed the barrel of the revolver against her heart in a dramatic pose, checking the mirror again, seeing Jocelyn there, laughing at her. At least she thought it was Jocelyn. To be truthful she'd forgotten what Jocelyn Russell looked like, but the face was only too familiar. It was a face from York.

'Oh no you don't!' she snapped. 'You don't think you'll get rid of me this way, do you? I know your type. With me out of the way, you think you can keep him.'

'Keep who?' the mirror replied.

She had trouble saying his name. She rarely said his name. Somewhere, some time, she had loved him, she recalled, with a surge of nostalgia like remembering a dear old song, but when exactly that was, she didn't know. She'd even told him once.

'Clem Price!' she said firmly. 'My husband.'

'Not any more,' the mirror woman sneered. 'He's mine.'

Thora put the gun down and studied the woman. How had Clem come to this? He was a good man. He was. That first day he'd stood up for her, asking if she really wanted to marry him. The day was burned like a brand into her brain. Her parents outside, trying to dispose of her. Her sisters eavesdropping. And Clem there, shy, not really understanding. No one understood because she couldn't tell them. You couldn't tell anyone about that.

'Clem tried,' she said. 'He tried to help me. He is building that house by the ocean as far away from York as possible, to make me happy.'

'You're a poor fool, Thora Carty. You always were.'

Once again Thora wondered how Clem had come to change from that nice country man who was never concerned with small-town gossip, secure at Lancoorie, untainted by wordly affairs, into an associate of whores. And then it came to her. Jocelyn! To Thora, all evil sprang from York.

Jocelyn Russell came from York. She had seduced Thora's husband. Just as Matt Spencer had seduced Thora.

413

'You're to blame for all this,' she said, feeling that she was at last solving this dilemna. This time there was a place to lay the blame. She wouldn't allow Clem to be castigated as she had been. He had been led astray, that was all. She would tell him she understood. He had been seduced by that woman and led on into a den of iniquity, with no one to say him nay. Thora saw herself not as his redeemer, because that was for the Lord, but as his champion, and it was a heady role.

'We won't look back,' she said. 'We'll never look back again. We'll go to our house by the ocean and we won't ever have to worry again.'

'Your house?' the woman in the mirror said. 'You forget. You're the one sitting in this disgusting dingy room. I'm at the ball with him. He doesn't care about you.'

Thora clapped her hand to her mouth. It was true. She'd been sitting here fooling herself. Making excuses. Daydreaming again. When all the time he was out there, in public, with his whore. Enjoying himself.

'I told you, you're stupid, Thora Carty,' the woman said. 'That house by the ocean. It's not yours. It's mine.'

'No,' Thora whimpered. 'Please, no. Don't do this, Jocelyn.'

'Why shouldn't I? You never gave Clem love or care. You pushed away the only person who really cared about you. I know. He told me.'

'The house. You wouldn't go to our house?' she begged.

'Try and stop me.'

The mirror was blank. Thora couldn't even see her own face through the cloud of tears.

Thora Carty sat for a while. Worrying. Thinking back. Who was Jocelyn Russell anyway? A nobody. A cheap slut from York. Everyone knew what sort of a girl she was. And she, Thora Carty, was the eldest daughter of Dr Carty, of the best-respected family in the district. Educated. Better looking than Jocelyn could ever be, and better dressed, always in good taste.

Gradually Thora Carty began to assert herself. The battle was not about all those horrors that had been inflicted on her, it was between women like Jocelyn and women like her. If it hadn't been for the likes of Jocelyn, then Matt Spencer would never have taken it for granted that he could have his way with her too. If it hadn't been for the likes of Jocelyn, there wouldn't be any brothels where men like Clem were led astray.

She took her handkerchief and dabbed her eyes. Looked at the blank mirror with a hard, resolute smile.

'You are wrong, Jocelyn,' she said. 'You're not a patch on me and you never were. I remember you at school, you couldn't spell cat. You think I'm stupid? Well, we'll see about that.'

Thora stood, straightening her dress, brushing flecks from her cloak, and went out into the passage, a firmness in her step now, a sense of purpose. Proudly she swept down the staircase, disappointed that the window was closed again. She really ought to bid the hotel boy good night, let him know she was leaving, but it was not to be, so she turned about and went out to meet the night. Such a beautiful night, clear and bright, with dew in the air, fresh, clean dew, welcome after that male-smelling hotel room and its odour of tobacco and leather.

Clutching her cloak to her with her left hand, Thora walked calmly up the street, and soon she was drawn forward by the sounds of music and gaiety from the town hall. Outside it was well lit, and several men were standing about. As she crossed the road towards them she blinked with surprise that she'd arrived so soon. She was experiencing another one of those blank times. She couldn't recall anything since she left the hotel.

But there'd be no more of that, she told herself, ignoring their stares as she walked proudly up the stone steps towards the lobby. After tonight her nerves would settle once and for all. It was a wonderful feeling of relief.

Thora was proud and confident as she entered the crowded lobby, knowing she looked her best.

The dance had started, a slow waltz, and couples were already taking the floor. A group of rowdy men were making for the bar, and Lillian's heart sank when she saw Clem Price was with them. He'd forgotten. Or maybe she hadn't really accepted. In the confusion of meeting him, she couldn't remember quite what she'd said in the end. Except that her name was Lillian Warburton.

A young gentleman approached her, asking for the dance, but out of the corner of her eye she saw Mr Price turning towards her, and declined politely.

'Is this our dance, Miss Warburton?' he asked her, and she nodded, smiling, almost giggling, because this had become a lark and she was entitled to a bit of fun.

As they circled into the crowd, Lillian had nothing to say, she was enjoying the waltz too much.

'Do you live in Perth?' he asked, finally.

'No.'

'Where are you from?'

'Upriver.'

'Ah.'

Gleefully she savoured the fact that she had no need to question him; she knew all there was to know about Clem Price.

He tried again. 'You're a friend of Mr Whipple?'

'Yes. I'm visiting. Staying at his house.'

'You are? That's nice. I only met him this evening, but my friends tell me he's a fine gentleman.'

'Oh, yes, he is. Charming.'

He moved back to look at her. 'Might I say that's a very beautiful gown, it suits you. Are you sure I haven't met you before somewhere?'

'Maybe you have, Mr Price.'

He laughed as they resumed the dance. 'I wish you'd tell me where.'

'It will come to you,' she said mysteriously. 'It's a wonderful evening,' she added. 'I can't remember when I last enjoyed myself so much. And Henery is having a marvellous time. I'm really thrilled for him.'

'Yes. It's very well attended. I only got a ticket at the last minute. A friend talked me into coming and I'm glad I did now.'

They were at the far end of the hall when the dance ended, so he took her arm to escort her back to her seat near the entrance. 'Perhaps I could call on you,' he said. 'And we could work out where we might have met before.'

Lillian didn't reply. She was staring at the doorway.

Lord Kengally was enjoying a drink at the bar with Henery and Robert Warburton when he saw her come in. Alone.

'Why! It's Thora!' he said, moving towards her.

'Thora!' he called, but she walked straight on past him, her long cloak sweeping the floor, and went into the hall without bothering to remove it.

'Who was that?' Robert asked.

'Mrs Price. Thora Price. A charming woman. I saw her husband here earlier and was surprised she wasn't with him.'

Henery laughed. 'Oh well. Better late than never.'

Lillian clutched his arm. 'Oh my God! It's Thora!'

'Who?' he asked, staring down at her. How did Miss Warburton know his wife's name?

Then he saw her himself. It *was* Thora!

Clem groaned. What was she doing here at this hour? With her head tipped high and her jaw set hard, she was obviously furious with him, and he hoped to God she wasn't going to make a scene. As it was, she was already attracting attention, standing there in her cloak, glaring at him. But courtesy still demanded that he return Miss Warburton to her place, so he drew her forward with him.

The only thing he could do, he decided quickly, was to get Thora outside, where she could yell as much as she liked about being left out of this party, and then take her back to the cottage. It was a damn nuisance having her turn up like this, and typical of her to twist things about, playing the role of the neglected wife. He'd have something to say himself.

Thora was angry. And triumphant. Now she knew she was right. One glance at the familiar face of the woman with Clem was enough. There was no mistake. That woman was from York! She'd recognized Clem's wife immediately. Thora had been watching them come towards her and she'd seen the woman clutch his arm in fear.

'Oh my God! It's Thora!' she'd said to him.

It was Jocelyn all right. Jocelyn the seducer, the whore, dressed to kill in satin and jewels, probably bought for her by Thora's husband, who had the gall to be still hanging on to her for all the world to see.

And Jocelyn had every right to be afraid of Clem's wife. Thora sneered as she lifted the gun from under her cloak and pointed it right at her.

'Now it's my turn, Jocelyn,' she called without so much as a tremor in her voice.

Women were screaming, pointing, and there was a rush as people scrambled away, but others were rushing in from the lobby, so she moved out on to the floor, away from them, waving the gun just for a second to keep them back but returning to keep Jocelyn in her sights.

The whore was hiding behind Clem.

'Not so smart now, are you?' she said, watching her prey cringe, but Clem was shouting at her, reaching out to her.

'Put the gun down, Thora!' he cried, pleading. 'Put it down, please.'

'You stay back,' she ordered grimly.

Then she heard a man's voice calling to someone. A nice voice, educated and very calm. 'Lillian,' he called. 'Slowly. Walk away. Just walk away. Leave them to it.'

Thora had no idea who Lillian was, nor was she interested. There was a great deal of muttering about her, and she heard a woman reply, 'I can't.' They were confusing her.

'Yes, you can,' the voice said. 'It's Robert. I'm coming for you.'

A strange man stepped out from the crowd and, hands outstretched, began to walk towards Clem and Jocelyn, who were now alone on the floor.

'Get away,' Thora said to him, irritated. This was none of his business.

Just as she said that, she saw Jocelyn emerge from behind

418

Clem, white-faced, terrified, moving towards that gentleman, getting away!

Thora aimed the gun, following her, and fired and fired again, but she had not, for that second, seen Clem coming at her.

The noise of the shots was shattering! Terrible! Clem threw his arms in the air, right in front of her. He seemed to be lifted high and then he crashed to the floor, an awful redness spreading on his white shirtfront. Thora couldn't take that in; she was searching about for Jocelyn, but she had disappeared in the crowd. A man struck her from behind, a vicious, cruel blow that brought her to her knees as he grabbed the gun.

Choas followed. Screaming. Shouting. Thora had never heard such an uproar. 'Let me go,' she screamed. 'That's Clem down there. I have to see to him.' But men were holding her, dragging her away.

'You've done enough, lady,' a man said grimly.

The mob about her grew, and Thora was terrified, hardly able to breathe. They were jostling and pushing her. Someone punched her in the back and she stumbled; heavy feet trod on her cloak; it was choking her as she tried to stand, dragging at her throat until the buttons gave way and it was jerked from her, swallowed up in the mêlée. Somewhere in the distance she could hear voices screaming for doctors, for the police. The ground gave way beneath her and Thora felt she was falling into hell with all this malevolence, but she was pulled back and bumped down the steps. A woman spat at her, causing a man in uniform to shout: 'Enough of that!'

Two policemen were there, rescuing her, shouldering those awful people away from her. She was near to fainting but she clung to them, thanking them, as they surged out into the street, and then mounted police came to their aid, shouting, their snorting horses shoving back the mob as she was pushed into a carriage.

Thora fell inside, her dress torn, a shoe lost, her arms stinging from scratches as she cringed, weeping, in a corner. Someone jumped in after her, thrusting her cloak at her.

'It's filthy!' she wept.

'Never mind, my dear. Put it around you.'

Warily she peered at him in the dim light, afraid he too might attack her.

'It's Kengally, my dear,' he said quietly. 'You remember me. Now, just calm down, you'll be all right.'

'Oh, thank God,' she whispered. 'Will you take me home, please? I want to go home.'

'Yes.' He nodded. 'Of course. I'll come with you.'

A persistent clatter of bells heralded the arrival of the ambulance, and Fred Vosper talked to Clem as the doctor did his best to staunch the blood from his wounds with all manner of cloths that were handed to him by frantic guests.

'We're going to shift you now,' he said, even though he wasn't sure Clem could hear him; he was still breathing but barely conscious. 'You're going to be all right.' He glanced about in despair. 'What's taking them so long?'

He looked up and saw a shocked Henery Whipple standing at the front of the circle of horrified guests, keeping them back, and thought what a picture this must make, what headlines Henery's send-off would provide for the press.

'How is he?' he asked the doctor again.

'Bad. Here they come with the stretcher.'

Fred was relieved that the ambulance driver had chosen to urge his horses down the side lane, away from the mob at the entrance, so they could move Clem out quickly through the kitchen. As soon as they had him aboard, Fred climbed in with the doctor. The lane went on through to the back street, so they were soon away, the horses charging through the deserted streets, urged on by the wild cacophony of the ambulance bells.

'What's his name?' the doctor asked.

'Clem Price. He's a sheep farmer from York.'

'Who was the woman?'

'His wife. I wonder what's happened to her.'

The doctor shrugged and spoke to the ambulance attendant. 'Does he have to go so fast? He's bumping my patient all over the place.'

'We're nearly there.'

'Another doctor went on ahead,' Fred told him. 'I didn't think we needed two back there.'

The doctor nodded aproval. 'That's good thinking. We'll have to operate as soon as possible. He's taken a bullet in his chest and another in his thigh.'

'Will he survive?' Fred asked anxiously.

But the doctor wouldn't comment.

Fred followed them into the hospital as far as he was permitted to go, then he turned back to find himself confronting reporters who had been at the dance.

'Nothing to tell you yet,' he said shortly, pushing them aside, but one man laughed.

'Come on, Fred. If you still had your paper you'd be in the front row here. Just let us get the story straight.'

'He's probably going to write it himself,' another said, but he backed off when Fred turned on him.

'Shut your mouth!' he snapped. 'Or I'll shut it for you. Clem Price in there is a mate of mine. His wife shot him, that's all.'

'The hell it is. This is a crime of passion. Who was the other woman? His lover?'

'What other woman?' Fred, who had come running with everyone else when he'd heard the shots, was genuinely surprised. 'There wasn't another woman. He didn't bring a partner.'

But they wouldn't have that. Questions were fired at him from all directions.

'Tell us another, Fred! Who was the woman?'

'I saw it all. The wife didn't fire at him, she fired at his girlfriend.'

'He's a hero! He leapt forward and took the bullets meant for her.'

'Who is Jocelyn?'

'Yeah, he's a hero. Tell us more about him.'

'If he didn't bring a girlfriend, why didn't he bring his wife?'

'She's a looker, the wife. Can you get us some photos of her?'

'What's his girlfriend's name?'

A policeman arrived, and Fred grabbed the opportunity to disappear with him into a quiet room and close the door.

'From what they're saying, there seems to be more to this than I know,' he worried, after he'd given the law all the details he could. 'They're talking about another woman, but that's not how I see it. Clem did have a row with his wife, I know that, she's rather temperamental . . .'

'To say the least,' the sergeant commented, drily.

'But he definitely was not with another woman. I've been rooming with him ever since we came to town. There is no other woman, I can assure you of that, he loved his wife. I won't have him maligned in this way. The man could die, Sergeant, give him a fair go.'

The sergeant wrote his notes laboriously. 'Just the same,' he said, 'witnesses back there say the wife deliberately shot at the other woman. Not at him.'

'All right. She's off her head. Went berserk. Came to the dance, saw him dancing with someone, anyone, and out of jealousy shot at a woman she didn't even know.'

The policeman turned back his notes. 'The woman's name is Lillian Cornish. Do you know her?'

'Never heard of her. Clem didn't know her either. I remember, now, he was enquiring about the woman who opened the dance with Henery Whipple. A very pretty woman.'

'That's her. He was dancing with her.'

'Right. But he didn't know her. He asked me who she was. I don't know her either. So there's your proof. There was no other woman.'

Suddenly he stopped. 'Oh, Christ! Their daughter! What's going to happen to her? She's only a little tot. With Clem here and the mother in jail, what will become of her?'

Robert kept his arm about Lillian as they watched the bearers carry the victim from the dance floor. They had both been too shocked at Lillian's narrow escape to join the mob that had converged on Thora Price, but they too had their questions.

Lillian was still shaking. 'What did you do that for, Robert?

You could have been shot.' Never before, not even in her imaginings, had a man stepped forward as he had to save her, to bring her to safety. Right in front of a loaded gun. No incident in her life bore any comparison, but one thing was clear: Robert Warburton was the bravest man she'd ever known. By that one act, Robert had wiped the slate of all those notions she'd had about him, that he was a hypochondriac, a wimp and a whinger. When the chips were down, Robert, the true gentleman, had shown his colours.

'I couldn't just leave you there,' he said. 'I had to do something.'

Lillian wept. She'd never cried like that, given way, in all her life. He really did care about her, and all this time she'd just been using him, and, too, thinking the same of him. That to him she was only a convenience, a good house-keeper and bedmate whom he'd recently decided he might as well marry.

He'd never said he loved her or even that he cared for her. And, for that matter, she'd never brought real emotion into their relationship, she wouldn't have dared.

He and Henery took her into the cloakroom for privacy.

'Come on, old thing,' Robert said to her. 'Buck up now. It's all over.'

But Lillian blubbered to Henery, 'Did you see what he did? With Thora waving that gun about? He could have been killed.'

'Yes, I know, my dear. There were two heroes here tonight, proof that our gentlemen are not lacking in courage. Robert stepped out into the line of fire, and Mr Price did likewise. Unfortunately he took the bullets. But you said "Thora". That, I believe, is his wife's name. You know them, do you?'

'Yes. From York. A long time ago. But she must have thought I was someone else. She called me Jocelyn. I don't know anyone called Jocelyn. Oh, God! Oh, God! She was going to shoot me, Robert!' Lillian's voice rose to hysteria. 'I feel sick.'

'That's quite enough, Henery,' Robert said. 'You see to your guests. I shall take Lillian back to your place. Would you be good enough to request a doctor to call. She will need a sedative after such a frightful shock.'

'Yes, yes,' Henery agreed. 'The musicians have been asking me what to do. Should they play on? What do you think, Robert?'

'It's a great pity, and I am extremely sorry that these people have ruined such a lovely evening, but I do think it would be for the best to call it a night.'

Lillian listened as Robert delivered his calm advice to Henery Whipple, former Speaker of the House, who was hardly able to cope at all.

'Are you sure?'

'Yes. People are beginning to leave anyway. I think if they played "The Queen" you'd be doing the right thing under the circumstances. Make a formal end to it.'

On the way home in the cab, Lillian still couldn't contain her tears. 'I have to tell you about Thora Price,' she said to him.

'Not now, Lillian. Tomorrow. When you're feeling better.'

Lillian feared that on the morrow she would have to tell him the whole truth. Clem might die. Thora would be jailed. So what would happen to her baby? Caroline's sister. Even if they let Thora out, there was no way Lillian would allow her daughter to stay with a mad woman. She wanted her back and she would get her back somehow, but she'd have to step carefully. Maybe not tell Robert too much, on second thoughts. He may have reacted well to that situation, but Lillian was a practical person, and she knew that once back home to his routine he wouldn't change. He mightn't be too happy about marrying a woman who now wanted to bring a second child into his household.

She sighed. Robert hated notoriety, and thanks to mad Thora, his fiancée was involved in a drama that would have all Perth talking. If anyone found out that Thora's baby was actually hers, God knows what the newspapers would make of that.

Lord Kengally, too, was battling his way through confusion,

trying to protect Thora. He had accompanied her to the watch-house, where she was placed in a cell despite his protests.

'Can't you see the woman is ill? She's almost catatonic, she doesn't know where she is.'

When they'd first arrived, the ugly brick building had been quiet, but that didn't last long. Every policeman in town must have risen from his bed to be in on this drama. Reporters clamoured and busybodies crowded in as well, with no one bothering to challenge their right to be hanging about, craning with curiosity.

At last the chief inspector arrived, still in his dinner suit, but he wasn't inclined to listen to Kengally either.

'What do you expect me to do? I can't let her go. She has to be formally charged, maybe even for murder. We don't know yet. She's not as uncomfortable as her poor husband. A cell won't kill her.'

'That's where you're wrong. She needs a doctor.'

'Then perhaps you can find her one, sir. I realize your plea is humane, and it's very good of you, Lord Kengally. But she might be better served to have a lawyer. I presume you are not a relation?'

'No. But as far as I know, her only relation in town is her husband.'

The inspector nodded. 'Then perhaps she should have thought of that before she shot him. I will interview her myself.'

Yes, of course you will, Kengally thought angrily. And you'll grab the headlines at the same time.

'Could I be present?' he asked. 'I doubt she'll make much sense. If you could only let her rest overnight, she might be clearer in her head about what happened.'

'And give her time to concoct a good story?' the policeman said harshly. 'Not likely.'

He turned his attention to the crowd. 'If you'll all be patient, I shall make a statement shortly.'

'What are you charging her with?' someone shouted.

'Attempted murder.'

'If the husband dies, will she hang?'

'She'll hang,' the chief inspector responded grimly.

Kengally accosted him as he made for the cells. 'This is monstrous! You've pre-empted a jury decision, sir! If she goes before a court at all.'

The inspector untied his bow tie and removed the studs from his stiff collar, loosening it. 'Why don't you go home? This is none of your business.'

But Kengally persisted. 'Are there any ladies here who might attend to Mrs Price?'

'What ladies? This is a police station, for God's sake!'

A young policeman standing nearby sniggered. 'There's one in the cell with her. Old Maggie Ryan got run in again tonight. She's sleeping it off.'

Despairing, Kengally thrust his way outside and strode down to his carriage. He considered calling on the Governor, but at this hour, he would probably only aggravate the man, and by the time he found a lawyer and a doctor, the inspector would have completed his so-called interview.

'It will be short and sweet,' he muttered to himself. 'That self-seeking upstart won't want to keep his audience waiting. I really can't do any more until the morning.'

He hoped that some of Thora's lady friends would bring her aid in the way of fresh clothing and toiletries when they discovered she was in need, not realizing that Thora had no lady friends.

There was nothing more Fred could do at the hospital. The doctors were still operating to remove the bullets, and only one of the reporters was left, dozing, in the waiting room.

He decided he'd better go to the watch-house to see how Thora was faring, and try to discover what this was all about. Surely she hadn't shot Clem just because he went to a party without her? There had to be more to it. And he'd need her advice on what to do about the baby, since it was obvious she wouldn't be released for quite a while.

'Pray that he survives, Thora,' he muttered, 'or your next stop is the Fremantle jail, and that place is hell on earth.'

Faced with the prospect of a long night ahead, he went back to the hotel to change out of his evening clothes, noting sadly that his shirt, Clem's shirt, was stained with Clem's blood.

The devastation in their room shocked him. He stared at the mess in disbelief.

'Who the hell did this?' he asked, appalled, as he stepped over the clothes and effects strewn everywhere. He heard a small snap and looked down to find he'd trodden on one of his favourite fishing rods. No, part of one. Even they were destroyed. He stared at the corner where he'd kept them, and saw his gun case standing open.

Well! He nodded numbly. No need to ask where she got the gun. It's mine!

Angrily he stormed downstairs to rouse the night porter, who was slumbering in the tiny office.

'Did you see a woman go up to my room?'

The youth peered groggily from his window. 'Yes. Mrs Price. She went upstairs to wait for her husband. What happened to you, Mr Vosper? You've got blood on your shirt.'

'Get the boss!'

'I can't do that. He's gone to bed.'

'Get him, I said, and be smart about it.'

'Yes, sir.'

Bloody stupid woman! Fred fumed. No wonder Clem couldn't get any sense out of you. How dare you destroy my belongings!

Vosper was, as usual, very short of cash. He'd been glad to have Clem in the room with him to share expenses, but now he realized, ruefully, that that had been penny-wise. Their clothes had been slashed; he doubted if he had anything wearable left to his name.

He vented his anger on the publican, who was equally shocked. 'Who did this?'

'Mrs Price, I'd say, before she shot her husband. But that doesn't alter the fact that my goods and effects were here in this room, supposedly in safe keeping, and you allowed this to happen. I deem this hotel responsible. Your fellow there let the woman into my room.'

Fred knew he was being unreasonable, but he had to have some recompense as soon as possible to be able to buy some new clothes. He toured the room, noisily assessing his losses, including his fishing rods, with the bewildered man apologizing, agreeing, bemoaning the wreckage, offering him another room free of charge.

One loss Fred did not mention. He'd seen a way to recoup at least something from this débâcle. He said nothing about the gun. He was the only one, so far, who knew where it had come from, and that would give him a head start on other writers.

Appearing mollified by the manager's efforts to appease him, Fred offered a compromise. 'I don't suppose it would go well for the hotel's name for this to get out today. You'd have police and reporters tearing up and down your stairs to get a look at the havoc she caused before she shot her husband.'

The publican gazed about the room, his face reflecting his misery. 'God spare us! I'd appreciate it, Mr Vosper, if you could see your way clear to keeping this quiet. The hotel would turn into a circus.'

'Count on me,' Fred said. 'But I have to get out of these duds. Can you find me something decent to wear?'

'Right away.'

Later, in borrowed clothes, using hotel stationery, Fred sat in his new room and began making notes. This wasn't just a local story, he could sell it to the eastern papers as well, the big newspapers, and with luck, London papers too. And it wouldn't be one or two articles; he would write this story from the beginning and serialize it, drag it out to its finale. A scandal like this would be lapped up by the public and would earn excellent remuneration.

He went first to the watch-house, where an unusual number of police were on duty at this hour, and asked to see Mrs Price.

'No reporters, Fred. Strict orders from the chief,' a sergeant said.

'But I'm not a reporter. I sold my newspaper. I'm a personal friend. How is she?'

'Struck dumb. The chief couldn't get anything out of her. He don't know nothin' about her, not even where she comes from, but he gave the reporters a lot of guff about her being the typical jealous wife who will face the full force of the law. I tried to tell him it wasn't the husband she was trying to shoot, from all accounts, but he wouldn't listen. Not him. He's already got it cut and dried.'

Fred was delighted. The more the chief inspector stuck to his version, the better chance Fred would have of reporting the real story.

'What's your name?' he asked. 'I know you from somewhere, Sergeant.'

'John Bonnington. My mates call me Bonney. I was at your rally. I'm on the committee to establish a police union.'

'Good man. You'll meet opposition, but a police union is essential. Keep up the good work. But now . . . I'm a friend of Thora and Clem Price.'

Bonney grinned. 'There's a start, eh? Her name's Thora. The boss didn't even find that out. My witnesses told me that she called out the name Jocelyn. Do you know who she is?'

'I've been thinking about that, and I've got a fair idea.'

'Was she at the party?'

'No. You let me in to see Thora and I'll give you the background before anyone gets on to it. How about that?'

'Done. But if she's asleep, no go. She seems a nice type of a woman, pretty too. She ought to get some rest.'

He took the keys and went down the back steps, returning to beckon Fred.

She was sitting primly on a stool in the cold stone cell, her cloak grasped about her, and she didn't even look up when Fred entered.

'You should be resting, Thora,' he said softly. 'You should lie down.'

When she didn't reply he lowered himself to the bunk and sat looking at her. 'It's Fred Vosper. You remember me, Thora. I'm here to help you. You shouldn't be in here. I'll try to get you out. Perhaps I can get you a cup of tea?'

He reached over and took her hand. She looked terrible, her hair tumbling down, uncombed, and her face white and drawn, but Fred had visited many a jail and that didn't surprise him.

'Fred,' he persisted. 'We had a lovely time together at the Palace. You looked stunning, the prettiest lady in the room.'

That brought a reaction. Thora nodded. 'Yes. Fred.' She clutched his hand anxiously. 'Where's Clem? Will you get him for me? I don't like this place. It's horrible. I want to go home. You tell Clem I've had the most horrible time. Look at my cloak, it's ruined.'

She stood up. 'Thank you for coming, Fred. I didn't know how to get out of here. Take me home, I have to explain to Clem.'

'Explain what?' he asked cautiously.

'That I don't mind any more. I understand what happened to him. I've been thinking about it, and none of it was his fault.'

'What happened to Clem?'

Thora drew back from him, fear in her eyes. 'That's private. We'll never speak of it again. Can we go now?'

He was overwhelmed with sadness for her, and upset that he had to tell her that he couldn't take her home just yet, but once outside the watch-house he was cross with himself for having allowed sentiment to interfere with his work. After all, she had shot her husband, and she had wrecked his possessions.

'Dammit! She's got you just as confused as she is,' he muttered as he set off, making for the cottage.

The sun was glimmering behind the ranges, outlining them with a glow of gold, and Fred nodded. 'There's a sign, if ever I saw one, of the treasures out beyond those hills.' As a newcomer to the west, he was still in awe of this wonder, still enjoyed the thrill of seeing the sun rise from the cover of mountains instead of lifting from the sea as it did in the eastern states. He'd often ridden over to the seaside to watch the sun set as if into the ocean, painting the surface of that vast expanse with a kaleidoscope of colour; every evening a different hue, from reds to pinks to golds, depending on the mood of the departing day. He never tired of this simple pleasure.

He walked towards the imposing Palace Hotel, unimpressed by this man-made wonder, the pride of Perth. Obviously Thora was, though; she loved the place, even though she'd moved to the annexe cottage. Apparently she'd been staying in the hotel itself for quite some time before Clem arrived. That must have cost him a packet.

The cottage was quiet, no one stirring yet, so he sat in the park across the road rather than wake the nanny and the child too early, and lit his pipe. There was much to consider. He'd never been quite clear on the reason for the problems between Clem and Thora. She might have been angry with him for staying too long on the goldfields, but when he met her she was happy and comfortable in her husband's company. They were a handsome couple, no doubt about that. He wondered if he could find a photograph of them together. Handsome people made better copy than the uglies, created more interest. He would have to get some decent clothes to Thora, and take her photo looking her best as soon as possible.

The thought gave him a small wrench of conscience, but such a photograph, he argued, would not do a disservice. She was a proud woman and would care about these things. And that brought him back to the matter of money.

Thora dressed well, her clothes were expensive, her husband never skimped with her, and given their situation it was damned generous of him.

Then again, Clem was a wealthy man. To the average onlooker he was the owner of that big sheep station, and he'd made the rest of his money on gold and investments, but Fred wasn't the average onlooker. A newspaperman from the goldfields, he knew about the Black Cat, even though it wasn't common knowledge that Clem was part-owner.

He'd ribbed Clem about that. 'I gather one doesn't make mention of a certain house in Kalgoorlie?'

'I'd rather you didn't.'

'Your secret is safe with me, mate. How did you get into that business? A boy from the bush?'

431

'By accident. After my accident, when I got speared that time. Our mine was next to useless, so my partner got the bright idea of buying the Black Cat from Glory, who was ready to sell because she'd run up too many gambling debts.'

'Ah, yes. I knew Glory.'

'So when I arrived back in the land of the living I found I was half-shares in a bloody brothel. I was cranky as hell about it, but when I saw how much that place was taking, every night, I had to rethink.' He looked at Fred sheepishly. 'I was embarrassed, but it was too good to give away. Money up the sleeve, you could say, while I was going about my own business of prospecting.'

'Some sleeve!' Fred laughed.

It was only a couple of weeks ago, Fred now recalled, that Clem had finally taken the plunge and divested himself of his interest in the Black Cat. Sold to Madame Jolie, alias Jocelyn Russell of York.

Jocelyn! Fred blew a cloud of smoke from his pipe into the thin morning air. It would be worth his while, once this section of the story calmed down, to go back to Kalgoorlie and interview her. No one here would have a clue who she was, so far just a name plucked from the air.

He shook his head. Reporters would be ratting about in Clem's background now, and his former interest in the famous Black Cat brothel would surface sooner or later. Half the world would be claiming they knew him, to feel the touch of fame.

Fred whispered a small prayer for Clem, who would be battling for his life now with a bullet in his chest, and added: 'Pity you bothered to sell the Black Cat, mate. It'll all come out now, but small beer compared to being shot by your wife, the lovely Thora.'

He saw the girl open the door of the cottage and stand blinking at the morning. She was stodgy-looking, with fair plaits, only about seventeen, and was dressed like a good nanny in a cheap blouse and black skirt.

'I'm sorry, sir,' she said as he approached. 'There's no one

432

home.' Obviously she wasn't about to inform a stranger that her mistress hadn't come home last night.

'Fred Vosper,' he said. 'You may have heard them speak of me, miss. There's been trouble. May I come in?'

Her name was Netta Barnes, and as he'd expected she was thoroughly shocked, disbelieving. He answered her questions as clearly as he could, at the same time noticing that she was the motherly type and that the baby, still sleeping, was in good hands. The cottage was immaculate.

For a second there he took fright. He should have come here first. What if Thora had gone on the rampage here?

It was Fred who made the tea and found some bread, butter and jam while Netta sat weeping at the kitchen table.

'I was surprised,' she said at length, 'when Mrs Price went out last night on her own. It was dark, and I was worried about her. I didn't know she had a gun!'

Fred let that pass. The ownership of the gun was his secret. He also let her go over and over what he'd told her, as people are wont to do, listening carefully as she added her own part of the story. 'I dressed her hair for her. Tonged it into curls. She looked so beautiful. But I thought Mr Price was coming to call for her like he does. I don't know how she found out about that big party in town. She never mentioned it to me. She was quiet all day. Spent a long time writing a letter, left it on the table out there . . .'

'I see. Where is it now?' Fred asked carefully.

'Oh, there were pages and pages. I stuffed them in the drawer, tidying up like, after she'd gone.'

Fred saw her blush and guessed the reason. 'Did you read the letter?'

'Oh, well.' She hesitated. 'I sort of looked at it. Not being nosy, just something to do. But I didn't read much, it just went on and on, not a newsy letter, boring, so I gave up. It was written to someone called Alice.'

'Do you think I could see it, Netta?'

'I don't know. Would it be right?'

'Put it this way. The police might call, and I'm sure she

won't want them reading her private letter. Things are bad enough. I'll keep it safe. I know Alice.'

'You do?'

'Yes. I'll give it to her. But you'd better let me see it before the police get here.'

Poor Netta was more concerned about the police than the letter. She rushed to get it and gave it to him. 'I don't want the police here. What will I say to them? And what about Mr Price? Will he get better? Who's in charge here with her in jail? Oh, that poor little girl in there. What's to become of her?'

'Don't worry,' he murmured, trying to read Thora's letter. 'I'll take charge for the time being. I won't let anyone bother you or Lydia. Her family will come in from the country, I'm sure. The main thing is for you to stay on. You won't leave, will you, Netta?'

'No, I wouldn't do that. There's Lydia now. I have to see to her.' She began to cry again. 'Poor baby.'

Fred scanned the letter quickly, becoming more and more aware that here was a woman in a serious mental state, and by the looks of things it wasn't a sudden problem. The long, rambling letter was a shriek of anguish, barely intelligible. It would require study, but not just now.

Before the doors of the telegraph office were opened, Vosper was knocking impatiently, and within minutes he'd sent his message to George Gunne, Lancoorie, via York.

Urgent you and Alice come to Perth immediately. Family in need. Fred Vosper. United Services Hotel.

That would get them moving and keep their identities under wraps for the time being, he decided. It would take them a couple of days to reach Perth, which would give them time to see a newspaper somewhere and understand the gravity of his call. And, he hoped, allow them to dodge reporters all along the line. By the time the news reached York, they would have left.

Then he did the rounds. The hospital, to find that Clem had survived the operation but was gravely ill, and not permitted visitors. He waved aside the doctor's apology. 'No, that's as it should be. Keep the police out too. He's not to be bothered. If there's any change in his condition, notify me right away at the United Services Hotel.'

The events of the previous night had taken place too late for the morning papers, although the shooting was mentioned in a Stop Press column on the back page of the *Western Mail*, giving no names. Saving up for the evening editions. He nodded. By five this afternoon every paper in Perth would have sold out.

Next the cottage again, where he found a Miss Devane waiting for him.

Fred was known for his brusqueness, and right now he didn't have time for interfering females. 'Who are you?' he asked.

'She's the hotel housekeeper,' Netta rushed to tell him. 'And she says I have to get out of here, with Lydia. I said I don't go nowhere until you came back, Mr Vosper.'

'Good girl. Now, madam, kindly remove yourself.'

'I'm sorry, sir, I can't do that. I have my orders.'

'So did Napoleon's troops, and look what happened to them. Now buzz off.'

She stood up, and when she did so she was his height. That irritated him too.

'You are aware no doubt of the unfortunate occurrence last night,' she said. 'As a result, the hotel manager requests that Mrs Price vacate these premises.'

'Bad for business, eh?'

'It's not the sort of behaviour the Palace can tolerate. Our clients, you will understand, cannot be associated with such a scandal.'

'But they are not. As you see, Mrs Price has vacated. She is, in fact, in jail.'

That moved her not an inch. 'At the minute, yes. But there is a possibility that she will be released for one reason or another, and she is not welcome in this hotel.'

'You could hardly call this an hotel.'

'My instructions are plain, sir. We only permitted Mrs Price to stay here as a favour. She caused enough trouble in the hotel itself with her antics.'

What was this? Fred shifted ground, remembering the letter in his pocket. 'Miss Devane, I can understand your position, and I'll do my best to accommodate you, but I dislike your reference to Mrs Price's antics. Be good enough to explain yourself.'

She was not only good enough, but eager. He listened to her complaints about this demanding woman who'd put on a disgraceful show of temper in the dining room and had to be escorted out, and who at private functions had abused several ladies with no provocation at all. And whom they'd banished to this cottage out of kindness, while she waited for her husband . . .

'It didn't occur to you,' he asked gently, 'that this lady might be suffering some sort of breakdown?'

'Had that occurred to me,' she said tartly, 'she would have been out of here sooner. This is hotel, not a mental home.'

'I see. Your kindness to her is awe-inspiring. Are the accounts paid up to date?'

'Mrs Price has a lease on the cottage,' Netta said, with a defiant glare at Miss Devane.

'Ah. That's interesting. For how much longer?'

'We're terminating the lease,' Miss Devane said.

'How much longer?' he insisted.

'The money for the last three weeks will be returned,' she said. 'If we can find anyone to hand it to.'

'There's no need,' Fred informed her. 'Her relatives will be arriving shortly and they will be staying right here. And tell your manager from me that if he doesn't back off, then I shall make a point of advising the press that Mrs Price is a good customer of yours.' He knew that any journalist worth his salt would ferret that information out very shortly and there'd be no mention of the cottage. They'd probably have her staying in the best suite. Wealth and beauty were a great combination in any news stories.

'I shall tell him,' she replied. 'But I'm very sorry that you're taking this attitude.'

'It's not an attitude,' he said as she departed, 'it's a fact. You can write the names of Mr and Mrs George Gunne into your lodgers' book.'

'You fixed her,' Netta said gleefully. 'Where did she expect me to go with the baby?'

'It's only the beginning, Netta,' he told her sorrowfully. 'From now on Mrs Price will be the target of every vicious attack and rumour that can be devised, but you must not be concerned. Mr Price's sister and her husband will be here soon. You'll like them. They're very nice people. Now I want you to tell me about Mrs Price. What was she really like?'

Later he returned to the watch-house, this time with a suitcase packed for Thora by the loyal nanny.

From what the girl had told him about Thora's nerves and depressions and odd behaviour, an entirely different picture of Thora was beginning to emerge. Adding that to the letter and Miss Devane's report, he knew he was entering troubled waters. He had information that was both worrying and fascinating, and he hadn't heard the last of it yet. They couldn't try a woman like this, could they?

An idea began to form in his mind, of writing two separate stories. One, the straight-out drama of the shooting and its players; the other, which would take a lot longer and a lot more research, a case study of a woman pushed to the edge of sanity by rape. Because it was evident from the point of Thora's letter to Alice – when she did, finally, get to the point – that the poor girl had been raped. Fred had read some German writings on hysteria that had a bearing on this case, but he would have to read more on the subject.

He'd have to think about all this later, because he certainly could not and would not print Thora's private hell, not under her name anyway. It would send her over the edge completely.

On the other hand, the letter might save her from the gallows if Clem died.

Only as a last resort, he decided. He would seal the letter and put it in the hotel safe, after taking a copy, with names deleted, to think about. To worry over.

Thora did have another friend after all. Lord Kengally was delighted to welcome Fred at the watch-house, immensely relieved that someone had thought to bring her clothes and necessities.

A doctor had examined Thora and found her in shock, which, to Kengally's disgust, was all he could offer. 'Otherwise,' he had pronounced, 'Mrs Price is in excellent health.'

'There is a hatred abroad,' Kengally told Fred. 'You'd think she'd shot the Queen of England. No pity for her anywhere.'

'To be expected.' Fred shrugged. 'Hatred's a cheap drug. Can we get her out of here?'

'I believe so. Not too far, I'm afraid. I brought along a lawyer, who will speak for her in the magistrate's court this afternoon. She will no doubt be charged with attempted murder, and he intends to claim mental incompetence, which is neither here nor there at this stage, but she will not be allowed bail. The chief inspector has the bit in his teeth and he'd burn her at the stake if he could, to please his public. He has never heard of mental incompetence, he claims.' Kengally took Fred by the arm and led him away from interested observers. 'The mirror could assist his education,' he added.

Fred laughed. 'That's our lad. Where can we take Thora from here?'

'To the Barracks. That's the best we can do. At least she won't have to share a cell with drunks and harlots. It's a huge building, she won't have to deal with curiosity-seekers, and women do work there in various capacities.'

The two men from opposite ends of the political world found, to their surprise, common ground in their concern for Clem and Thora. While Thora was spirited out of the watch-house via the stables to avoid the crowd already gathering by the entrance, they walked to the nearby military barracks that had first housed troops guarding transported convicts.

Sergeant Bonnington was waiting for them at the great central archway. 'My wife came along to help Mrs Price,' he said. 'She'll look after her. Help her to tidy up for her court appearance.'

Then he turned to Fred. 'You promised to help me out.'

'I haven't forgotten. Mr and Mrs Price own a sheep station called Lancoorie, out past York. His sister and her husband will be coming to town and staying at the cottage attached to the Palace Hotel, where Mrs Price was holidaying.'

Bonnington took out his notebook. 'Names?'

'Mrs and Mrs George Gunne. But keep it quiet. We don't want them bothered.'

'Gunne? George Gunne? A heavy-built stocky bloke? English? About forty?'

'Yes. Do you know him?'

'Sounds like it. He's well known to the law. An old lag, a convict. Where does he fit into this?'

Fred groaned. Could anything else go wrong? 'Nowhere,' he said. 'He struck me as a decent bloke. Married to Alice Price and leading an exemplary life.'

'You didn't know he was a transportee?'

'Why should I?'

Bonnington shrugged. 'I'll have to check him out. He's come up in the world from Fremantle jail to the Palace.'

Chief Inspector Smythe deemed it imperative that he interview Mrs Cornish himself, since she was staying at the home of the former Speaker of the House. Henery Whipple may have retired, but he remained a very influential gentleman in Perth.

'It's very good of you to come personally,' Henery said, welcoming him into his drawing room. 'My guests are not accustomed to being involved in police matters, and after that horrendous shooting last night, they are dreadfully upset. As am I.'

Smythe was sympathetic. 'I can't tell you how sorry I am about the ruination of your wonderful send-off, Henery. I've seen a lot in my day, but this is the most blatant crime I've come across in years. It is hard to believe that a woman should choose such a happy occasion to vent her spleen on her husband.'

'Her husband?' Henery said. 'She wasn't shooting at Mr

Price, she was shooting at Mrs Cornish. My guest! It's damned disgraceful.'

'You're wrong there, Henery. It was the husband she was after. I just came to assure you that your guest will not be importuned further. I shall take the lady's statement and leave it at that. There'll be no need for her to appear in court; her ordeal last night was harrowing enough.'

'Just a minute.' Henery left the room and returned with his two guests. 'Might I introduce Mr Robert Warburton of Minchfield House. You know it, I'm sure.'

'Of course. A beautiful house. A credit to the family. I'm delighted to meet you, sir.'

'And his fiancée, Mrs Cornish.'

Smythe bowed. She was a good-looking woman, with dark glossy hair and a fine figure, much younger than Warburton, and she appeared very nervous, which was understandable.

'Delighted to meet you too, Mrs Cornish. I am shocked to think what that dreadful woman put you through, but be assured, she will be punished.'

'How is Mr Price?' she asked.

'Dangerously ill. He may not survive. We will most probably have a murder charge on our hands.'

'I'm so sorry,' she said.

'However,' Henery intervened, 'to get back to the other matter. Robert and I talked this over last night and we are of the opinion that Mrs Price was attempting to kill Mrs Cornish.'

Lillian looked up, stunned. She had hoped to be left out of this. Other people had converged on Henery's house when they'd arrived home last night, and they all seemed to be of the opinion that this was a crime of passion. That Thora had marched in with the gun to kill Mr Price.

'But you said . . .' She turned to Robert.

'Yes. We did think Mr Price was her target, what with everyone batting the event about. But after they left, and you went to bed, Henery and I talked it over.'

'And we came to a definite conclusion,' Henery said to Smythe. 'You are quite wrong, Inspector. Any number of witnesses insist she called a woman's name, and when Mrs Cornish tried to run away she turned the gun on her. Had Mr Price not intervened, she might have been the victim.'

Lillian didn't dare say a word. She was thinking fast. Marriage was a long way off, the divorce had to be arranged first. This was not the time to admit she had another child. And yet it would establish more sympathy for her case if she spoke up now, told them that Thora had her child. She could claim that Thora took the baby when Lillian was in no state to make a decision, with them praying over her, insisting it was her Christian duty to hand over the child. She could even say that was a possible reason for Thora's actions. Hatred for the mother of her adopted child.

She twisted her handkerchief in her lap while the men argued, nervously composing a tale that would paint Thora as a cruel, calculating person, not just a woman involved in a marital dispute.

Apparently the inspector was not pleased with Henery's interference.

'Am I to understand,' he asked Lillian, 'that these people, Mr and Mrs Price, are known to you?'

'By no means personal friends,' Robert was quick to state, and Lillian was equally swift in her reaction. That other story would have to keep. For now.

'Known to me,' she said sorrowfully. 'Only inasmuch as one does know people in a country town like York. But we did not socialize. Thora Price was the daughter of the local doctor, but she had quite a reputation.'

'What sort of a reputation?' he asked.

Lil gazed at the pattern in the carpet as if unwilling to reply, but they were waiting.

'One doesn't like to speak of these things, but if you must know, she scandalized the district by becoming pregnant. But not to Clem Price. He stepped in and rescued her.'

'What do you mean, rescued her?' Robert wanted to know.

'Well, she was in trouble. He came forward and married her in a quiet ceremony out of town. I happened to be passing the church on that very day. They kept it all rather hush-hush. So you can see, Mr Price is a very good man. Obviously I owe my life to him now.'

'But why would she want to shoot you?'

'I haven't the faintest idea. She would not have known that I was present, and she wouldn't remember me anyway. She's just plain crazy.'

'There you are,' Robert said. 'You have the story now, Inspector. Mrs Cornish was only dancing with Mr Price because she knew of the gentleman. Otherwise it has nothing to do with her.'

The inspector scratched his ear. 'Maybe not. But this does complicate things.'

'Far from it,' Henery insisted. 'The woman marched into the hall and took a potshot at Mrs Cornish, thinking she was someone else. Someone called Jocelyn. For all we know, it could have had nothing to do with the husband either.'

'That's what I'm afraid of,' the inspector said unhappily.

'You'll sort it out,' Henery said. 'Now, if there's nothing more, Inspector, I am exhausted. I shall have to rest. I never thought my career would end with such a wretched event.'

'But your send-off will be long remembered.'

Robert was not impressed. 'I hardly think Mr Whipple can find any consolation in that. It is something we hope to forget.'

'I quite understand, Mr Warburton. Cruel, it was cruel. I won't keep you any longer.' Smythe took out his notebook. 'I understand you are just visiting our fine city, Mrs Cornish. Could I have your home address, please?'

'Minchfield House.'

He hesitated. 'Oh, I see. Well now, I won't need to bother you now until the trial date is set. I shall let you know as soon as possible.'

'Why?' Robert was appalled. 'What has it to do with Mrs Cornish? We've made it quite plain to you that she was, in fact, just an innocent bystander. She can't be involved in a scandal like this!'

'Had I continued on my original course,' the inspector replied smugly, 'that should have been the case. But since

442

you and Mr Whipple insist that Mrs Price was shooting at a woman, not at her husband, then it will be necessary for Mrs Cornish to give evidence.' He picked up his cap. 'Mr Whipple, I can't tell you how sorry I am that this infernal woman chose your big night for her crime, and everyone else is just as disappointed that it had to end that way. Even my wife is hugely distressed for you. Now, good day, gentlemen. And Mrs Cornish.'

After all the excitement, Minchfield House was a relief. Everything was in order. Caroline was thrilled to see her mother again and to show her the rag dolly that Cook had made for her.

Robert had given Lillian strict instructions on the boat on the way home that the shooting was not to be discussed with anyone; he never wanted to hear it mentioned again. For fear of upsetting him, Lillian obeyed, keeping herself aloof from the endless staff gossip about the woman who shot her husband. She was biding her time.

Surreptitiously she examined the newspapers every day, refolding them with care, but Robert ignored them. He didn't even turn them over, making it plain that he had no interest in what was happening in the outside world. But Lillian hung on every word, and there was plenty about the Prices, taking up page after page. Clem Price was still critical. His sister Alice and her husband were keeping vigil at his bedside. Thora had been formally charged with attempted murder and was imprisoned at the Barracks, awaiting trial.

A photograph of Thora standing at the top of the courthouse steps surrounded by police was reprinted several times. Lil wouldn't have recognized her. She was no longer the tall, slim girl she'd seen swanning about York before she married Clem Price; now she looked absolutely breathtaking, like those mannequin women in the ladies' journals. Strangely, Lillian could not recollect what Thora had looked like at the hall. The gun remained the focal point of that picture. She shuddered every time she recalled those terrifying minutes, and the fear of the gun caused her to cry out in her sleep still, disturbing Robert.

Thora Price would pay for that too, she vowed.

Then she found it. A photograph of her daughter, Caroline's sister, under the caption: *Innocents suffer*.

It was a lovely oval photograph of the child's face, right on the front page, a little angel with a mop of curls and the sweetest smile, the image of Caroline, and Lillian wept.

This time she didn't hesitate. The newspapers not yet read by the master were piling up in the broom cupboard, awaiting his instructions. Lillian had been tempted to cut out a photo of Thora but decided against that, but she wanted that photo of her baby, so she took the whole paper and burned it after cutting out the front page, hoping that, if Robert ever decided to go through them, he wouldn't notice one was missing.

Robert's newspapers, of course, were not the only ones that found their way to Minchfield House, and Lillian waited for someone on the day staff to comment on the likeness between her Caroline and the Price child, who was known as Lydia, but it didn't happen. It just didn't occur to anyone, and Lillian began to breathe more easily again.

Every day there was some reference to the shooting. Witnesses gave their versions, some quite outlandish. One woman even claimed the intruder was sent by an outlaw to rob ladies of their jewels. Opinions were freely given on whether or not she should hang, even if the husband survived, and on the whole it was thumbs down for Thora. Hangings were still a regular occurrence at the Fremantle jail. Nothing was said about the mysterious Jocelyn, or about Mrs Cornish, and she guessed Henery had seen to that, temporarily. She walked down to the jetty and stood looking at the velvety flow of the river.

'What would have happened to my babies,' she asked, 'if that idiot had shot me?'

Mrs Cornish was in a very dangerous mood, not unlike Thora's gathering storm, except that Lillian was far from confused. She was taking one day at a time, with the utmost care.

Above her the moon was high and hard, stars glittered like pinpoints, reminding her that, gradually, she'd come to realize all was not well with Robert. Not that he'd said a word, but he'd drifted back into his lethargy, spending most of his time in his library or in the rose garden, venturing out occasionally to confer with Jordan about the farm management. There was nothing untoward happening, but Lillian could feel those pinpoints in the air when Robert was about, as if he were silently needling her.

She tried to shrug it off. Early summer had set in with a vengeance, tomorrow gave promise of yet another ferociously hot day. That was why she'd strolled down this way, appreciating the slight breeze the river provided in its kindness. She wished she could throw off her clothes, especially the damned corsets she was doomed to wear these days, and dive in, as she'd done in those carefree droving times.

No one swam in the river by Minchfield House, no matter how hot the day. Robert disapproved, as had Lavinia.

He hates the summer, she reminded herself. Maybe that's all it is. He will insist on dressing like the gentleman, no matter the heat, with a jacket and tie and waistcoat over his flannel singlets and silk shirts. Hard to feel sorry for him.

The following day she read a profile of Chief Inspector Smythe, who seemed to enjoy the publicity that the Thora Price case was providing for him, and a comment by someone called F.C.B. Vosper, who was talking about Thora as if she were some sort of Joan of Arc. He claimed she was being railroaded by public hysteria when in fact the lady was suffering from a nervous breakdown and not responsible for her actions.

'Try having a gun pointed at you, chum,' Mrs Cornish snapped. 'You wouldn't be so clever then.'

She read that Clem and Thora were separated. She had been staying at the Palace and he was at the United Services Hotel, both apparently visiting from the country.

'Ha! I bet that's where Jocelyn came in.' She smiled. 'Clem had a lover.'

Another item caught her eye. A goldmine, known as Yorkey, which had belonged to the victim, Clem Price, and his partner, had failed in mysterious circumstances, and Lord Kengally, on behalf of the present owners, had preferred charges against a Mr Edgar Tanner for forgery and fraudulent uttering. However, Mr Tanner had so far eluded the police. Pains were taken to impress on readers that Mr Clem Price had no part in any shady dealings.

'Nor would he,' Lil said loyally. She wished she could visit him in hospital to thank him, but there was no point in even thinking about that. Robert would have a fit. Besides, Clem Price, if he survived, would be in the enemy camp. By now he would regard Lydia as his daughter.

'Hero or not,' Lillian murmured, 'your wife's a loony. You don't get to keep my kid. I never thought I'd see the day when Caroline was better placed than her sister. At least Caroline's mum isn't a criminal. Nice for the kid to have to grow up with that tag.'

Three weeks had passed. Robert made no further mention of arranging her divorce, and neither did Lillian. She was waiting for him to settle down again. Everything, with Robert, took time.

Then, at breakfast one morning, with the windows closed and the shades drawn against the heat, he finished his kidneys and bacon and sat back.

'You have the cook well trained, Lillian. Breakfast these days is a delight. The kidneys were delicious and the gravy as light as it should be for this hour. Now don't leave me, my dear, I need a word with you.'

'Certainly, Robert. More coffee?'

'If you please. And just a smidgen of cream.'

That done, Lillian waited.

'Ah, perfect,' he said, sipping his coffee. 'I have to congratulate you, my dear. I shall miss your menus. I have decided to go away for a while. I enjoy travel, you know.'

'I didn't know.'

'Ah, yes. Widens one's outlook. I am interested in the arts. I shall do a tour of the arts, European, of course.'

'European?'

'But of course. London for a base, but thence to Paris and on to the hub of the art world, Florence.'

'Florence?' she echoed stupidly. 'Where's that?'

'Italy, my dear. Italy.'

'Oh! When?'

'Didn't I say? Tomorrow. I have been in touch with a shipping line and I am assured of a stateroom on the East India Company liner *Mandalay*, sailing shortly from Fremantle. I realize it is short notice, but it won't take long to pack my trunk. Perhaps you could make a note of anything I might need that I can purchase in Perth.'

Lillian was stunned. What about me? she wanted to ask. What about your proposal of marriage? What about that? But she nodded, dumbfounded. 'Yes, of course.'

Was he teasing her? Perhaps he meant to take her with him?

Not very likely by the sound of this, she concluded.

The day was a flurry of packing for the master. His shirts had to be starched – 'Plenty of starch,' Lillian gritted at the washerwomen – his standing trunk to be aired and his dinner suits steamed and pressed, his pyjamas folded neatly into their compartments, socks and shoes separate. Initialled handkerchiefs had their place with ties, cuff links and pearl tie pins in the small stud drawers. Rage building within her, she packed his pigskin suitcase with the necessities required for a short sojourn in Perth prior to boarding that ship, remembering that this was the second time a man had left her.

'When will you be back?' she asked him nervously.

'Who knows, my dear? When I tire of the European scene I shall flee back to Minchfield. You know me, Lillian, I am easily bored.'

'I see. But you want me to stay on here?'

'Of course. No one can manage Minchfield like you. I have arranged for Jordan to pay your wages, so there's nothing to worry about.' He took her hand. 'I'm relying on you, Lillian. Please don't let me down. I will write to you and you must write back, letting me know how things are going here. Promise me you'll do that. It will be exciting for us to

447

be able to keep in touch by mail. At least I'll have interesting things to tell you. I feel I am stagnating here.'

All of the staff were assembled at the jetty to farewell Mr Robert, and as he stood on the boat surrounded by his luggage, which included the two extra suitcases he'd needed at the last minute, they smiled and waved as if they cared.

Lillian did too, as if she was happy for him, as if she hadn't noticed that he'd taken leave of her as formally as he'd done Jordan and the others. As if she was not aware that the staff were laughing at her behind her back. She might have been sleeping with the boss, but now he'd dumped her.

But she kept smiling, she waved happily to him and when the boat pulled away she picked up her skirts and walked up the hill towards the house, where she assembled her staff.

'Just because Mr Robert will be away for a while,' she said cheerfully, 'we mustn't drop our standards. Admittedly since we don't have the master to attend to, there will be a little less work . . .' She saw their grins at that statement, knowing their minds, but she was ready for them.

'But as long as you all pull your weight, I won't put anyone off.'

That shut them up.

Mrs Cornish, the housekeeper, did not relinquish her status. She saw to it that the dining room table was set for her that evening, and she dined in her usual place, having decanted a bottle of his best red wine.

'That will be all,' she said to the waitress when the main course of roast beef was served. 'You can clear up in the morning.'

Then she sat, in solitary splendour, enjoying her meal. The roast and the accompanying vegetables were cooked to perfection. On the sideboard, in a silver frame, was a photograph of Robert, taken, as he often reminded her, in the grounds of Government House in Perth, and she raised her crystal wine glass in a toast to him.

'You bastard!' she said.

'I hate to leave you at a time like this,' George said, but Alice would not hear of him staying.

'The train will be leaving in a minute, George. Please get on board. It's shearing time. You have to be back at Lancoorie before the shearers arrive.' She kissed him. 'Don't forget, Mrs Postle is sending over a cook. Let her do the ordering, she'll know what she needs in the kitchen to keep the shearers fed. And don't you go doing too much.'

He stepped on to the train as it began to move. 'You telegraph me if you need me, Alice. Don't let them put anything over on you.'

'Don't worry. I'll be all right.'

The whistle blew and the steam engine huffed and huffed as it gathered its clanking carriages into motion and pulled away down the track. Alice moved back to escape the gritty smoke but remained on the station until the train was out of sight, unwilling to turn and face the day ahead just yet. She would miss George so much, she wondered if she really could cope without him. All that week he had been a tower of strength in his quiet way, overcoming with stubborn resolve all the difficulties that had been placed before them.

She had been shocked, almost paralysed by Mr Vosper's telegram, unable to think what to do, needing an explanation, but George had insisted they leave right away. He'd left her to pack while he rounded up the farm hands to give them their instructions but when he returned she was still in a daze, wandering about the house doing little more than picking things up and putting them down again, so George had packed for her, hurrying her out to the buggy.

'We'll go direct to Northam,' he told her, 'rather than waste a day waiting for the coach.'

All the way to Northam, she worried. There couldn't have been a death, Vosper would have said so. What had happened? 'Family in need.' That could only be Clem and Thora and the baby. What need?

'Whatever is wrong,' she said to George eventually, 'I'm sure Clem could attend to it. Some people are apt to panic. Do you think Mr Vosper is just panicking over some trivial thing?'

'We'll see.'

And that they did. They stayed overnight at a Northam hotel, were early at the station to wait for the train, and there they saw the newspapers. At least George did. He bought a paper and pocketed it until they were settled on the train. Until she was sitting down, she recalled gratefully. Or she would have fainted on the spot.

She walked out of the station and sat on a bench in the sun, feeling faint again at the remembering.

SHOOTING AT TOWN HALL, the headlines screamed.

'You'd better read this,' George had said.

Alice couldn't believe her eyes! Thora had shot Clem!

'No. This can't be right. She wouldn't shoot Clem. She couldn't have. Thora! I don't believe it.'

But she'd had plenty of time as the train bore them towards Perth to read it over and over again, to weep for Clem, to pray for him, to wonder what had come over Thora, and eventually to try to contain the fierce anger building within her.

'I'll never forgive her,' she said to George. 'It's a terrible thing to say but I hope God punishes her for her wickedness. She'll go to jail for this, won't she?'

'We'll see.'

For his part, George was as shocked as Alice, but somehow not too surprised. He'd guessed all along that Thora was not right in the head, but he judged that even now it wouldn't be the best time to tell Alice that. Not until they'd heard the full story. The paper was full of stories about the ugly event, but no motive was presented, no reason given as to why Thora would do such a thing. And very little about Clem, except that he was gravely ill.

Alice was usually a fair-minded person, but her initial reaction was furious condemnation of Thora, and George listened, glad of this long train journey so that his wife could get her emotions in shape. She so loved her brother, he mused, that in the first rush of rage, given the chance, Alice would have turned a gun on Thora herself. Gradually, though, she eased down and he took her hand.

'All you have to worry about is Clem. The rest will take care of itself. Try to rest, Alice, I'll watch the road.'

She smiled wanly, appreciating his attempt at humour, and put her head on his shoulder. 'You're so good to me, George.'

Fred Vosper met the train and took them straight to the hospital, where they were relieved to find that Clem had survived an operation to remove a bullet from his chest and another from his thigh. He was conscious but, as the doctor explained, too heavily drugged to ease the pain to be aware of what was going on. Alice wept at the sight of him; she clung to his hand, whispering to him, and eventually when they persuaded her to leave she came away, angry again.

Reporters rushed them, harassing them with questions that they were unable to answer, so they pushed through, heads down, saying nothing, until one man threw a question at George.

'Is it true you're a convict, mate?'

'Was.' George shrugged, but Alice flew at the questioner.

'How dare you! How dare you address Mr Gunne in that manner!' She slammed at him with her handbag. 'Get out of my way, you ruffian!'

They were then escorted to the cottage where Thora had been staying, and along the way they heard, to their astonishment, that Clem and Thora had been living in separate establishments.

'Clem never said so,' George explained, 'and we never heard from Thora. She stopped writing when Clem arrived in town. What was wrong?'

He thought Vosper was about to say something, but instead, Clem's friend shook his head. 'I've told you all I know. They seemed to be getting along quite well, looking forward to moving out to the beach house, but they did have a tiff a few days ago. I gathered it wasn't all that serious.'

'Must have been,' George commented. 'Did you know Thora?'

'Met her a couple of times. She was charming.'

'And you don't know why she went off like this?'

'No.'

You're lying, George thought. But we'll leave that for now. Clem will know.

Vosper left them at the cottage and Alice ran on ahead to sweep Lydia up in her arms. 'Oh, my dear little love. It's your Aunt Alice. Don't you remember me?'

She didn't, but they soon became acquainted again, and Alice embraced the nanny, thanking her profusely for looking after the child under such difficult circumstances.

While they talked, George prowled the house, searching for a hint that might explain Thora's behaviour, but it was neat, everything in order, even in the drawers and cupboards, just like Thora's room back home.

'Where did she get the gun?' he asked suddenly. 'Did she have one here?'

'No, sir,' the nanny said. 'The police asked me that. I've got no idea where she got it. But there was never one here. I'd have seen it. What will become of Lydia now?'

'We'll take her back to Lancoorie with us,' Alice said. 'She was happy there, it's her home. Do you think you could stay on as her nanny until we go home, Netta?'

'I'd be glad to, Mrs Gunne.'

Alice refused to visit Thora. 'I can't believe you'd suggest such a thing,' she said to George.

'Then I'd better go.'

'You? Why? We want nothing to do with her.'

'Someone has to go.'

'She boasted about all her fine friends. Let them visit her.'

'I'll just see.'

George knew the Barracks well. He'd been held over here himself on various occasions. As he walked through the great arched gateway, he shuddered, and it took a real effort for him to pass through there voluntarily, the fear of arrest still lodged, permanently, in his soul. Crossing the wide flagged courtyard he stopped, embarrassed, finding that he was shuffling, from habit, from the echoes of leg-irons. He had to take a few deep breaths to regain his composure before he could move on, but he was determined to do what he saw as his duty. Few knew the horror of prison as well as George, and he understood the impact it would have on Thora.

'If she was a bit askew before she came in,' he muttered to himself, 'prison will finish her off. A woman as fragile as Thora can't survive that life. The other women will give her hell, for a start.'

He was burdened with pity for Thora, despite her crime, as he approached the guardhouse, where he requested to see Mrs Price, explaining that he was her brother-in-law.

'No visitors!' the guard replied.

'On whose orders?' George snapped.

'Just orders.'

'The court gave no such ruling! Fair enough to keep out them as have no business here, but I'm family. I'm entitled to see her.'

'You have to put your request in writing then.'

'Don't give me that. Get your super.'

After a prolonged argument with a young lieutenant who obviously found Thora's presence in the barracks an ongoing source of annoyance, a hindrance to his daily routine, George was permitted to enter the premises.

She was alone in her cell, which George saw as a blessing, and it wasn't too bad, he'd seen worse. At least there were clean blankets on the cot, and the barred window was low enough for her to see out, if only to another courtyard.

Thora threw her arms about him. 'Oh, George! Thank God you've come! Where's Alice? Can you take me home? Other people say they will but they don't. They go away and forget about me.'

He managed to quieten her, and knowing he wouldn't have much time, put the question straight to her:

'Thora. What's this all about?'

She began to cry, hysterically, babbling about the cruelty, the food, the humiliations, her clothes, how she'd been deserted by all her friends, until he took her firmly and shook her.

'Stop it, Thora. Stop, for God's sake. I know it's hard, but sit down here now and try to pull yourself together.'

He produced a handkerchief. 'Here. Blow your nose. Calm down, girl. Calm down.'

'You don't understand, George,' she whimpered. 'It's horrible in this filthy place. Where's Alice?'

'They wouldn't let her in. Now listen to me. What's this all about?'

She tossed her head. 'I don't know. I'm sure I don't know.'

'Yes, you do. Now tell me.' He marvelled that she could manage to look so neat, even elegant, under the circumstances, with her hair neatly brushed and pinned into a fall at the back and a white blouse immaculate under her grey suit. Only the redness round her eyes gave any indication of suffering. 'You're looking well, Thora,' he added, to please her. 'But then you were always very beautiful.'

'Do you think so, George? Do you really think so?'

'My word I do.'

'Clem doesn't think so. Or he wouldn't have other women.'

'Is that why you shot him?'

She jerked back, shocked. 'Don't say that. People keep saying that. I didn't shoot Clem.'

'Then who did? Someone shot him.'

She gazed at him, her head on the side. Then she spoke. 'Did I shoot him, George?'

'Yes, Thora.'

'Oh, God! But he didn't die, did he? They say he didn't die. Are they telling the truth?'

'Yes. But he's very ill.'

Thora sighed. 'Can I tell you something, George?'

'Yes. Anything.'

'It's my nerves, George. I've got bad nerves, you see. And I forget things. I do stupid things and I forget, and when I remember they frighten me.'

'Do you remember shooting Clem?'

'I think so, but I was shooting at *her*, not Clem. And now I can't remember why. It will come back to me. I'm in prison, aren't I? Will you tell Clem I'm sorry?'

A guard banged on the heavy door, and George turned to

her urgently. 'How do you feel now, Thora? Apart from being stuck in this place? How are your nerves?'

'Shot to pieces. What do you expect?'

'But you are clear in your head right now?'

She looked up, surprised. 'Yes, I really am. The nerves come and go, you see. It's quite tragic.'

'Yes.' He nodded. 'Now listen to me carefully. Whatever you recall about the shooting, about the gun, or any of it, for God's sake don't tell anyone.'

'Why not? You don't know how frightening it is when you can't remember things.'

'That's all right. It's good for you to remember, and you can tell me, but no one else.' Desperately he took both of her hands and held them tight. 'Get smart, Thora. You're not a stupid woman. You're in jail and you'll bloody stay in jail for a very long time if you spout any of that. You have to say you can't remember a thing. Nothing. And keep on saying that. It's the only way you can save yourself.'

She thought about that for a while, and there were tears brimming when she replied. 'You want them to think I'm mad?'

He nodded. 'Yes. There's no other way.'

'And do you think I'm mad?'

'I think your nerves got the better of you, but you're all right now. You are, aren't you?'

'I hope so.'

'Then prove it, Thora. Shut up. Just keep saying you can't recall, and I'll know you're not mad.'

Her eyes narrowed as understanding came to her. 'I just have to keep saying I don't remember even if I do? That's lying.'

'They won't know. Thora, you have to save yourself. No one else can. Grab hold of this now and hang on, no matter what they say to you, or you'll end up in jail for years. Say this after me: "I don't remember."'

'But I don't want people to think I'm mad,' she whimpered.

'They already do. You shot your husband even if you

did mean to shoot someone else. It's the same thing. Say it!'

'I don't remember,' she whispered. Then, in a stronger voice: 'I really can't remember.'

'Good. Keep it up. Later on we'll try to work out what this is all about, but it's not important now. I have to go, Thora. But I will be back, I promise you.'

At the gate George was interested to hear a portly fellow in a bowler hat engaged in a similar argument with the guard over his right to visit Mrs Price, so he joined them.

'My name is Thomas Forbes, I am her lawyer,' the visitor claimed. 'I insist on seeing Mrs Price.'

'She's already got a visitor,' the guard retorted. 'You'll have to come back. And make your application in writing.'

'I have already made my application in writing!'

George intervened, introducing himself to Forbes. 'I was the visitor,' he explained. 'Nothing to stop you going in now, sir.'

The lawyer drew him aside. 'Family, eh? I am pleased to meet you. How is Mrs Price today? I'm having a difficult time with her. She's very depressed, I can't seem to make any leeway at all. She doesn't seem to understand she is in prison.'

'No,' George said heavily. 'She wasn't able to explain what happened at all. It's very peculiar. I don't understand how she could forget that she shot her husband.'

'Ah, yes, difficult for a lay person. But I have studied these cases. Shock, you see. Especially for a fine lady like Mrs Price. She's a friend of Lord Kengally, you know. Our mutual friend. That's how I came to take the case. His Lordship turned to me immediately.'

'What happens if she can't remember? Can you still defend her?'

'I shall do my best. That may even work for her. Remorse. So struck with remorse at such a violent action, she has blotted it from her mind.'

'Is that right?' George said ingenuously. 'You might find

her calmer now. She was pretty het-up when I first arrived, but having someone from the family walk in the door has cheered her, I think.'

'Excellent! I'm sure that helped. She is in a fearful situation.'

'I wonder if I could call on you tomorrow, Mr Forbes? It is very difficult for my wife and me to understand all this, and the papers are too confusing. We should appreciate your advice.'

'Certainly. Say eleven in the morning? My office is in the Royal Arcade. Forbes and Staybrook. But there's one thing I need to know, Mr Gunne. Who will be paying my accounts? I mean to say, one can hardly send the bill to her husband.' He coughed. 'Delicate situation, what? Does the lady have private funds?'

'I don't think so, but her father will stand by her. He's a man of means. Well known in the Avon Valley. Dr Carty is his name. Based in York.'

'Oh, thank you. Good. Now, if you'll excuse me, I must see to the lady.'

George heaved a sigh of relief as he strode up the street. That was a curly one. Who would pay Thora's bills? Alice was in no mood to cover them. He doubted Carty would be too thrilled either, but he'd had to nominate someone, so let Carty worry about it.

He managed a smile at that bit of fast talking. 'Mike would be proud of me,' he murmured. But where were Mike and Jocelyn? They should be in Perth. Surely they hadn't left already! He had to find someone who could give him an inkling as to why Thora had gone berserk like that. It was all very confusing, from beginning to end, even the town itself. Alice hadn't realized that this was the first time he'd set foot in Perth a free man.

Strange, Thora mused, of all the people I know, who'd have thought that dear old George Gunne should be the one I feel I can talk to? He's such a lump, a born farm hand, but he cares about me. I could see it in his eyes, he means what he says. I'll have to try to do what he suggests. No, insists!

Mr Forbes had been and gone, seeming to be satisfied that she didn't remember the shooting at all, talking about this and that, trying to keep her calm. Promising he'd get her out soon. They all said that.

The soup was awful, and the stew was worse, but she ate every scrap, sopping the soup with stale bread, determined not to lose her figure.

This place, this cell, was horrible, the worst thing she could ever have imagined happening to her, but she was strong now, and she mustn't allow herself to fall back into all that crying. It just wouldn't do any good.

Ever since George had asked her squarely if she had shot Clem, some things had come into focus. This time there were no sudden drifts of memory, as she'd had before. This time it wasn't a vague frightening picture flashing before her eyes, but a clear memory of what she'd done. And even though she'd landed herself in the most awful trouble, there was a sense of relief. Thora decided she wasn't mad at all, thank God. She'd only done what she had to do, at the same time frightening off her own demons. She'd slept in that horrible cot night after night without one nightmare, and that was a blessing in itself. One should count one's blessings, she told herself.

Mr Forbes had talked about remorse, and she did feel the most dreadful remorse. She'd never meant to shoot Clem, although he deserved it. Wait till Alice hears he owns a whorehouse.

She'd only tried to shoot Jocelyn. The whore. The home-wrecker. But Clem must have got in the way. Yes, she had remorse about that.

The last few days were total confusion, but that was understandable, with people dragging her about and policemen pounding questions at her and mobs of ugly faces glaring at her. In here at least she was safe from them. She dreaded being dragged out into the public again.

A policeman was here this morning, a Mr Smythe. An older man, a gentleman. He'd wanted to know where she'd got the gun, and to be honest she still couldn't figure that out, but it would come to her. All she could tell him before her nerves reduced her to tears again was that she'd left the cottage and gone to that hall.

He'd asked her about a Mrs Cornish so many times, Thora had become exasperated. Bad enough that she had been frightened out of her wits for days by all those great big men, without him nagging her as well. 'Why do you keep on?' she'd cried. 'I told you I don't know her. Never heard of her.'

Still he'd pressed her. 'She's engaged to Mr Robert Warburton. Perhaps you know him?'

'Why should I? Who are these people?'

And yet now that she was feeling better, with George and Alice in town at last to take care of her, the name was somehow familiar. It rang a bell, faint, though.

'Oh, Lord,' she said impatiently. 'I can't be bothered trying to place her, I've too many other things to worry about. Poor Clem! I never meant to shoot him. Pray God he's all right.' Suddenly it occurred to her that she should have asked the lawyer to take her to see him, to explain. To tell him she was sorry.

'Surely I would be allowed to see my husband, when he is so ill. They can't deny me that. Next time he comes I will insist. I'm so stupid not to have asked before this. I don't know what they must think of me.'

She sat on the bunk, staring at the whitewashed walls, trying to recall all the events of the past few days, and reassembling the incident that on George's instructions she must say she couldn't recall. It was a very arduous task, but she had to concentrate; his warning had not been lost on her. Thora's emergence into reality had begun, and with it a sure knowledge of the dangers ahead if she did not watch her step.

'You went to see her after all? Even when I asked you not to?' Alice was furious.

'It can't hurt,' George said, stirring his tea.

'And what about my brother at death's door? Did you think of him? Does she care about him?'

459

'Yes. She's sorry.'

'A bit late for that! And Lydia? Did she stop to think about this poor child? Not her. She shoots Clem, knowing she'll be arrested, leaving the child with strangers. What's she got to say about that?'

Nothing, George recalled. She didn't even ask about the child, and he was too busy trying to sort her out to think of Lydia either.

He shrugged. 'She's very upset, Alice. She doesn't remember much about any of it.'

'That's a good excuse!'

Maybe so, George pondered, but it's the best she's got.

'I met Thora's solicitor,' he offered.

'And who's paying him? Not us, that's for sure.'

'I suppose not. Alice, I don't want to go behind your back, so you should know I will visit Thora again, and you know why.'

'You're wasting your sympathy on her!'

'I never had a visitor,' he said quietly, leaving a large section of his life unremarked.

'Oh, do what you want!' she said gruffly, relenting.

Every day he called on Thora, listening to her talk, hearing that her nerves had been bad for years – an understatement, he thought. Hearing that her friend Lord Kengally had visited her to say farewell because he was leaving for England any day. Patiently absorbing the familiar tearful complaints about the prison, the warders and the food, without mentioning that she was receiving star treatment here, compared to a real jail. Possibly, he mused, because of the influence of Kengally. But at no stage did she give any indication as to why she had shot Clem.

His time was running out, soon he'd have to return to Lancoorie, so he began to lean on her.

'If you didn't mean to shoot Clem, you must have been trying to shoot his dance partner. Why? You have to tell me.'

She chewed her handkerchief. 'I can't. It's too dreadful. You'd be shocked.'

460

George grinned. 'I wouldn't think so.'

'Yes, you would. You can ask Clem.'

'He knows, does he?'

She thought about that. 'Maybe he doesn't know I know,' she said mysteriously. 'That's why I want to go to see him. But they won't let me. It's too cruel of them.'

'Don't worry about that now. Why did you call out to Jocelyn?'

Thora drew back. 'You know about her? You know her?'

'Yes. She's Mike Deagan's wife. They were married in Kalgoorlie and they've gone to live in the eastern states.'

Thora leapt to her feet and turned on him. 'You're lying! She's here in Perth. She was dancing with Clem.'

'No, she wasn't. She never came near Perth. I found a note from Mike to Clem, telling him they wouldn't be coming to Perth. They left weeks ago.'

'She married Mike?'

'Does that bother you?'

Thora's gaze was distraught. 'He said it was Clem. He said she was his . . . his . . .'

'Who said?'

'She wasn't here at all?'

'No.'

'Was he lying about all the rest of it too? I thought I saw her. She was in that room with me. I just wanted her to go away. Oh, God. Did I imagine it all?'

She began to weep, and George was worried that he'd caused her even more confusion. He put an arm about her. 'You didn't imagine too much, dear. Just take it quietly. Everything will be all right, you'll see.'

He sat with her a long time, just being company, because she had drifted into her own thoughts as if she'd forgotten he was there. Before he left he tried one more question.

'Who told you that stuff about Jocelyn?'

'I can't remember,' she whispered, and George wondered if she was lying.

★ ★ ★

461

He called on Forbes, who couldn't hold out much hope for Thora.

'I've engaged a barrister, Mr Gunne, but it's a difficult case. So many witnesses to the crime.'

'Can't he turn it around? She didn't mean to shoot Clem, and the woman wasn't harmed. She did discharge a firearm in a public place, but that's not so bad. A minor crime.'

Forbes smiled. 'Ah, you bush lawyers! Mrs Price has been charged with attempted murder. Attempt, you see, therefore intent. That's what we have to worry about.'

'Will she plead guilty then?' George asked miserably.

'The barrister says definitely not. It's an important case. Mr Conway intends to fight the charge.'

'How? With all those witnesses . . .'

'Remains to be seen,' Forbes said vaguely, and George had the impression that he wasn't too hopeful.

'Will she have to go before a jury?'

'Oh, yes, of course. Supreme Court.'

'Poor Thora. Oh well, I'd better go, I have to collect my wife at the hospital.' He picked up his hat. 'By the way, who was the woman that Thora shot at? There's no mention of her in the papers.'

'No. The lady has friends in high places.' He searched his papers. 'Ah! Here we are. A Mrs Lillian Cornish, of Minchfield House, affianced to Mr Robert Warburton. Well-known family, that.'

'Thank you.'

George made his exit quickly. He had not mentioned his conversation with Thora, for fear of saying the wrong thing, and now this! Lillian Cornish? Ted's wife? Could it be the same person? He hoped not.

George called into a pub for a drink, a workmen's pub where he could stand at the bar and think without folk bothering him. Alice's photo had been in the paper, with Lydia, so everywhere they went people besieged them, some kind, some simply meddlesome, and it was hard to get rid of them without being downright rude.

The first pint quenched his thirst and brought with it a sigh of relief; temporary, he knew, on both counts as he ordered another pint.

'Jesus,' he muttered. 'Mrs Cornish! Lil Cornish. I thought I had a handle on Thora's exploits in Perth. What the hell has she really been up to? Mrs Price is gettin' me as confused as she is.'

He turned to stare out at the day. A hot day, worse in town than out in the country. You could fry an egg on the footpath. He let his mind stray to his early days in Perth, working in a chain gang, sweating, straining like a horse, dodging the whip. Built half them bloody roads out there, he said to himself, astonished that he should now be standing watching a passing parade of cabs and buggies and trundling wagons, as if the memory belonged to someone else.

'Savage days,' he muttered. 'Best forgot.'

He saw a man in a black frock coat stride by the window, and only after he'd noticed the fellow's long hair did he realize it was Vosper. He dumped his glass on the counter and ran after him.

'Vosper! Wait!'

'Ah, George! How are things?'

'A bit of a mess.'

'So I hear, but at least Clem's coming good.'

'He is? When was this?'

'I've just come from the hospital,' Vosper said. 'He's awake but dopey. Alice won't have anyone tell him what happened yet, so watch what you say when you go in there.'

'I'll do that. I'm on my way now. I've been to the jail to see Thora . . .'

'You have? That's good of you. I've been meaning to get back to see her but I've been busy.'

'So she said,' George replied drily. 'Everyone promises to come back to see her, but they never do.'

'Hold on,' Vosper said. 'I've been doing my best for Thora, but it's a busy time for me. The elections were announced yesterday. I've only got four weeks to campaign for the seat.'

'Yeah. I forgot. But I need a favour, Fred. I don't know who else to ask.'

He could see that Vosper had other matters on his mind, and it was an effort for him to intrude, being a shy man, but he had to know. 'Please,' he said. 'Just give me a minute. You remember the woman that Thora shot at, Mrs Cornish?'

'Yes. I didn't meet her, though.'

Fred was so offhand in his reply, George was given to wondering whose side he was on in this.

'That doesn't matter,' he said. 'I just want to know who she is. You could find out for me, couldn't you?'

'Why?' Now Fred was interested.

'You're busy. We'll talk about that another time. All I need to know is this: has she got a kid, a baby girl?'

'That's a rum question.'

'True. I could be barking up the wrong tree. But if you can find the answer to that, and anything else about her, it will square it for me.'

Until now George hadn't noticed that Fred was walking with friends, but now he turned to them. 'You go on ahead, mates. I want a quick word with Mr Gunne here.

'What's going on, George? Has there been a shift in the story?'

'No. Thora can't remember a thing. I just need to know who this woman is.'

'Why? Is her lawyer sniffing about?'

'No. Just me. And you. Look, Fred, I'm as unpopular at home as the rats for going near Thora . . .'

'I can understand that. Alice would hang her up by the bootlaces if she could. She never said you were visiting.'

'No.'

George saw the glint of understanding on Fred's express-ive face, and smiled. 'You know, don't you? That I'm an ex-con.'

'Your business!' Fred's gruff reply reminded him of Alice.

'Well, that's history. But Thora and Clem were good to me. I'm not taking no sides. You find out what I want to know, and if it's got anything to do with this bloody mess, I'll tell you.'

Now George was lying. If this Mrs Cornish was Lydia's mother, then she had to be kept in the background. Out of it! By the sounds of things, she was of the same mind. Mrs Cornish, whoever she was, had influential friends and obviously wanted no part of the scandal. If she had no part in it.

Having extracted the promise from Vosper, he went back to finish his pint, but it had lost its flavour.

The doctor met George on the front steps of the hospital. 'Good to see you, Mr Gunne. A harrowing time for the family, is it not? I heard a whisper that you've been visiting Mrs Price. How is she? How is she taking all this? The papers don't tell one much, just rehashing the story to date.'

Irritated, George changed the subject. 'I believe Mr Price is awake now.'

'Who said so?'

'Fred Vosper.'

'Ah, yes. Fred sees what he wants to see. The same with his politics. He's convinced he can come from nowhere and walk into a seat in our Parliament against our established representatives. Friend of the worker! God help us! What next?'

'Do you mean he's wrong about Clem Price?'

'Not exactly. Mr Price has rallied, but he's feverish. He doesn't know where he is, raving on yesterday about being attacked by Aborigines; today it's sharks. I've been trying to quieten him. He thinks he has been in the ocean and was attacked by a shark, keeps calling out to people in some house to come and help him. Mrs Gunne says he does have a beach house. Maybe that's what he's thinking of.'

'Or maybe anything but the truth,' George said. 'He loved Thora very much. Maybe he's just trying to give himself an explanation without having to face what really happened.'

The doctor wasn't listening. His time, too, was precious. He dashed away to welcome an elderly couple: 'Congratulations! You have a grandson . . .'

George passed through the lobby, glancing at a lady in a black coat who was wrestling with an irritable boy in a sailor suit, and on up a flight of stairs to a long corridor cluttered with the skeletons of iron beds and gaping cupboards. Crutches lay askew by the door to a ward, and he had to shove aside a large wicker laundry basket to make his way on to an overpass that led to Clem's ward in the east wing of this maze.

The patient was sleeping, but Alice was still sitting by the bed, looking so pale and wan, George was depressed. He hated to see her upset like this, when everything had being going so well for them, but eventually order would be restored. It was the way of things.

He kissed her and felt Clem's forehead. 'He's still in the fever. Can't they cool him down?'

'The doctor's very kind, he's doing everything he can.'

'What about you? Can I get you a cup of tea or something?'

She shook her head wearily. 'No thanks.'

He pulled up a chair and wedged it in the narrow space by the wall, wondering about prisons. This was Clem's prison for the time being, but Thora had two prisons to worry about, the one with huge brick walls and the other inside her head. She was still a long way from escaping that one.

'I met Fred Vosper,' he told her, for something to say. 'He's all excited about the elections. It'd be funny if he won, wouldn't it? I've never met a Member of Parliament before.'

'Yes,' his wife said listlessly.

George wondered what her reaction would be if he mentioned Lil Cornish. Although no one in the family had said that Lydia was not Thora's child, he and Mike had known all along. Old Sadie, the Aborigine woman, had told them. Sadie never missed much that was going on at Lancoorie.

Eventually he persuaded Alice to go back to the cottage for a rest. 'We can come back after tea,' he promised her.

She had no time for cabs – 'A useless extravagance,' she'd said – so they walked, taking a short detour along the river bank, which they always enjoyed, though that route necessitated passing the imposing front entrance to the Palace Hotel.

'When I look at this place,' Alice said, 'I could scream. She wasn't always at the cottage, you know. She was staying in there, paying an absolute fortune, for weeks and weeks.'

'Yes,' George said.

'If the United Services Hotel was good enough for Clem, why not her? He was too soft on her, that was his trouble. He spoiled her rotten, that was her trouble, thinking she could get away with anything. Has she told you why she shot Clem?'

'She didn't mean to.'

'That's what you keep saying. But why did she want to shoot someone in the first place? She couldn't have found a better husband than Clem. He wouldn't do anything to hurt her.'

'I don't know.'

'Then I can't see the point in visiting her. What do you talk about?'

'Nothing much. Not much to say in prisons.'

Angrily she quickened her pace, and he hurried to keep up with her.

Rest, though, was the last thing on her mind when they arrived back at the cottage to find Dr and Mrs Carty waiting for them.

'Oh, no,' George groaned. Unsure of Alice's reaction, he drifted into the background.

The meeting was tense, lightened only by the presence of Lydia, who brought some joy into the room by clinging to Mrs Carty in an effort to walk, and endeavouring to pronounce 'Grandma', on request.

'My, how she's grown!' Mrs Carty kept saying, while Dr Carty was more interested in the state of Clem's health.

'I'd like to visit him,' Carty said, 'but thought it best to seek your permission first, Alice.'

George was sure that had he not been a doctor, Alice would have rejected Carty out of hand, but she placed Clem before her own priorities. 'I'd appreciate that,' she said. 'Perhaps you could do something for him. We're very worried. He still has the fever.'

'It's the climate,' Carty said. 'People are more prone to fevers in this heat.'

'We're so sorry.' Mrs Carty turned to Alice, tears brimming. 'So terribly sorry. I don't know what could have come over Thora. She was always high-strung.'

While they talked, with Alice grudgingly accepting their apologies, it seemed to George that Dr and Mrs Carty were sorrier for themselves than anyone else, moaning about the shock to them, and the newspapers, and all the fuss this had caused in York.

'We were glad to get away,' Mrs Carty said. 'We're staying with my sister and her husband here in Perth. They could hardly believe it themselves. And do you know, Thora's been in town all this time and she never once called on them? Not once. Not even to take Lydia out to see them. Of course, given what's happened, I think they're rather relieved, although they haven't said so. They're respectable people, preferring to keep their distance from such a scandal.' She mopped tears from her eyes. 'I don't know if I'll ever be able to hold my head up again. Every time I picture my own daughter walking into a ball in Perth with a gun in her hand, I feel quite faint.'

George collected his pipe and wandered outside to sit on the veranda and have a smoke in peace. He hoped the visitors would not stay long. Alice had offered them tea, out of politeness, but not a meal, and he was hungry. There were a dozen nice fat sausages waiting in the meat safe. To pass the time, he let his mind drift into the familiar nothingness of years of incarceration, until he heard raised voices.

'What now?' he sighed, heaving himself out of the canvas squatter's chair.

'You will not!' he heard Alice shout. 'I absolutely refuse. George! You talk to them.'

'About what?'

'About Lydia. They've come to take her back to York.'

'As her grandparents, we have every right!' Mrs Carty said firmly.

'What does Thora think about this?' he asked them.

'Thora!' her father cried. 'She has forfeited any rights to the child.'

'But have you asked her?'

'No, we have not. We haven't been near her. There's no need for Mrs Carty to put herself through such humiliation, visiting a daughter in jail. We have other girls to think of. What do you think this will do to their reputations?'

'But you will go, Dr Carty?'

'Oh my word, I will. As her father and as a doctor. She is mad, she has to be mad to commit a crime like this. I'll have her declared insane and put away. That will put a stop to all this speculation about her guilt; it could go on for years. I'll have her committed as soon as possible.'

George looked to Alice, but she was more concerned for Lydia.

'The child stays with me. She knows me, Lancoorie is her home. You hardly ever came to visit her anyway. How dare you march in here wanting to take her away! You're strangers to her. She still has no idea who you are. She's Clem's child too, remember. He won't permit it. You're just doing this to spite Thora.'

'I haven't noticed you care one whit about Thora,' Mrs Carty said icily. 'Clem will listen to us. You'll see.'

'Don't bank on it,' George said bluntly. He'd had enough talking for one day. He walked to the door and stared out as rain began to fall, swishing like broom strokes across the veranda, cutting off his escape from them.

Chapter Thirteen

Clem knew he was in trouble. A soak of red met his hand as he passed it across his chest. He let his head fall back, exhausted by that feeble effort, but forced himself to think.

Where am I? What happened? What the hell is going on?

He breathed in short gasps, keeping them light, feathery, because his chest flamed at any further intrusion, and he kept very still, closing his eyes again, drifting towards memory.

The spear! That's what it was. They'd speared him, those desert natives, and then they'd pulled the spear out again. He could still feel the sickening wrench. Hear his own howl of agony.

Damn their black hides! Why did they have to do that? I didn't mean them any harm. Bastards! I've got no quarrel with them! Never had. But where are they now? I have to get out of here before they finish me off.

Hands held him down. He was shouting at them, cursing them, trying to escape, but choking pain warned him that the struggle was costly. He was outnumbered anyway. Cunningly, he retreated into the darkness.

In the still of night he surfaced again, warily, listening for them, refusing to move or make a sound as his mind toiled after answers. He was hot, burning up. Sweating. This can't be right. It's night. The desert is cold at night. Freezing. Where are they? Have they gone?

He heard his father's voice. Noah.

'Of course they've gone, you fool. That was a long time ago. Wake up to yourself! I don't know what you were doing out there anyway. Lancoorie not good enough for you, eh?'

Clem pushed him aside. This was not the time to be debating that question. But Noah was right. That had happened a long time ago. Had the wound opened up again?

He could hear the steady swish of rain, welcoming it, but none fell on him, not a drop to cool his burning skin. He turned his head, hoping for some relief, yearning for the chill waters, but they were denied him.

The sea, he decided, that's what I can hear. The swish of the sea. Not rain. I'm adrift on the beach. By my house. But it's dark. That's why they can't see me.

As he lay there, waiting for someone to come for him, to help him, an image flashed through his mind and he recoiled, startled. Shocked. Refusing to accept it.

I know what happened, he told himself, deliberately erasing that memory, replacing it with his own version of recent events. 'I was swimming. I was attacked by a shark. I managed to get myself up to the beach but can go no further. And I'm hurt. Badly hurt. No wonder it has taken so long for me to get my bearings.'

He could not recall the attack, but that was understandable. He'd had to fight for his life. He was still fighting.

'Shark!' he screamed. 'Shark!'

'No,' Alice was saying. 'No. That's not what happened. Can't you remember, Clem?'

It was there again. Something. Just for a second. Terrifying. All wrong. Not possible! He jerked away from it, reviving the pain, but he didn't care.

'Shark!' he said defiantly. His chest had been savaged, and his leg. Couldn't she see that?

Thora was standing up there on the high dunes, her dark-blue cloak flapping about her and her lovely fair hair blowing in the wind. She wasn't looking at him, she was looking to someone else, so he called to her, but his voice came out a scream:

'Thora!' It echoed and echoed.

Alice took his hand and pressed it to her face. Her soft, warm face. Reassuring. Coaxing.

'Have I got sunstroke again?' he asked her.

'No, Clem. You're in hospital. The Perth hospital.'

'What are you doing here?'

'We've come to visit you. Me and George.'

'Where's Thora?'

When they gave no reply, his head reeled and he knew all the rest had only been a postponement.

'I've been shot,' he admitted, finally, and their stricken faces told him that the present had caught up with him.

'Will I die?' he asked, seeking a preferable solution.

'Oh, my goodness, no!' she cried. 'Don't even think that, Clem. You're coming along just fine. The doctors say you're as strong as an ox. They can't get over how fast you've pulled up.'

'Good living,' George joked in the background.

'Is he a good husband?' Clem responded.

'The best,' Alice smiled, 'but he needs taking in hand a bit lately.'

'You'll manage.'

He rested then. Nothing was said. Nothing important anyway. Nothing he could recall.

The next day a doctor inspected his wounds and a nurse bandaged them again, padding his chest and back, which were stinging from bloody stitches.

'Did the bullet go right through me?' he asked her.

'No, sir,' she said in a matter-of-fact way. 'No, sir. It creased your lung. They tried from the front but couldn't reach it, found it lodged near the back. You've got a few broken ribs as well. Your fall did that, they say. You fell heavy.'

'And my leg?'

'Landed in your thigh muscle. That'll badger you for a while too.'

He stared up at the grey hair poked into a mob cap. 'You're no stranger to bullet wounds?'

'No, Mr Price,' she sighed. 'Grew up in the Kimberleys, where the first thing you learn is how to shoot a gun and the next how to dig out bullets. I could show these doctors a thing or two, but they don't want to know from women.'

472

Clem liked her. She finished the bandaging, straightened his bed and plumped the feather pillow.

'Would you do me a favour?' he asked.

'Surely.'

'Talk to me.'

'What about?'

'About who shot me. The subject seems to be taboo. It was my wife, wasn't it?'

'Yes.'

'And?'

'I only know what I read in the papers.'

'That'll do.'

It was enough. She apologized at the telling and brought him a cup of cocoa for solace.

Clem thanked her. The nurse had given him the facts as she knew them, unemotionally, as if wives shot their husbands every day. And maybe they do where she comes from, he mused, trying to make sense of the tale and at the same time despairing of Thora. He turned his face to the wall and spoke to her.

'Why do you hate me so much?'

The days brought more knowledge, more visitors, more confusion and anger. They fuelled an anger that was easier to bear than heartbreak. The police, Alice, Dr and Mrs Carty, the nanny with poor little Lydia, even Henery Whipple himself, who commiserated on the horrible event, announcing that he was recommending Clem for a bravery award, which Clem resented:

'You will not!'

Thora was in jail, where they had convinced him she belonged, not realizing how much that hurt him, even though he was furious with her. He was not well and he knew it. His emotions were tumbling about like rocks down a cliff. Sometimes he hated Thora, but left to himself at night, he dreamed of having his arms about her, protecting her. His lovely Thora. But he couldn't tell them that. What a fool they would think him, yearning after a woman who had almost killed him.

And Noah was there in his dreams. Laughing. 'Dora would never have shot me.'

'How do you know?' Clem fired back. 'You just used her as a bedmate.'

'Ah. How times change. What did you want of Thora? You lusted after her, not to have and to hold in the true sense of the good book. She was a trophy. All part of your ambitions to be what you're not.'

'I can be what I want to be,' Clem shouted.

'Yes. Look where it got you.'

The nurse was by his bed. 'Mr Price, you're dreaming. You'll wake the other patients.'

'I'm sorry,' he said, but he knew he wasn't dreaming, he was just beginning to wake, to face what had to be done.

At last George had a chance to talk to Clem alone, but he'd cut it fine. He wouldn't have left without a few words to him about Thora, but it would have meant insisting that Alice step out for a while, and that would be upsetting for her. She still disapproved of his visits to the Barracks, and it had become a subject that they both avoided. Today, though, she was busy washing and ironing his clothes, packing his bags, because he was leaving for Lancoorie in the morning. Shearing time.

Clem was sitting up now, anxious to quit the hospital, impatient with the doctors, who refused to release him.

'Can't you do something, George?' he said. 'I have to get out of here.'

'Only a few more days. You might as well have the bed rest here as anywhere else. Where will you go when you get out?'

'Back to the hotel for a few days, and then I want to take Alice and the baby out to the beach house, if that's all right with you?'

'Of course. Alice should stay as long as she's needed, and I'll be back later.'

'Did you hear what happened at the hotel. With Thora?'

'No.'

'Good. Vosper's keeping that quiet. I especially didn't want

Alice to know; she's cranky enough with Thora as it is.' He went on to explain Thora's rampage. 'I'll have to recompense Vosper and the hotel, and it's important not to have any more said about it. Thora's in enough trouble.'

'How do you feel about Thora now?'

Clem sighed. 'She's my wife, George. There has to be an explanation for all this. I don't know what got into her. Carty's insisting she's mad and wants her committed, and he's upsetting Alice wanting to take Lydia, but that's not on. If they can't be helpful – her parents, I mean – I wish they'd just go home.'

'What about Thora?' George insisted.

'Ah, yes. Thora. I could be the world's biggest fool but I still love her, George. I have to get her out of this somehow, but there's not much I can do.'

'I'm glad to hear you say that. Thora's worth fighting for.'

'Vosper told me you were visiting her. I'm grateful to you. Tell me about her.'

George explained about his visits now that he could speak freely, but he also had more pressing matters to discuss. 'What were you up to in Kalgoorlie?' he asked. 'Someone's been talking to Thora but I can't find out exactly what was said. Whatever it was, I think it triggered her explosion. She says you know.'

'Know what?' Clem asked.

'You tell me. Jocelyn was a whore, wasn't she?' He looked at Clem's startled expression. 'I didn't come down in the last shower.'

'You didn't tell Alice?'

'Cripes!' George said angrily. 'She was Mike's wife, visiting our home, that was good enough for me. But I'm not stupid and neither is Thora. Someone told Thora a story about you and Jocelyn, and more. I reckon Thora hasn't been well for a long time . . .'

'You never said so. What do you mean, well?'

'A bit mental, if you must know. You think about that. I don't know what went on with you two here in Perth – that's up to you to sort out – but it's my guess that you're holding something back, Clem, and it will all come out in the wash. Why haven't you mentioned that you were dancing with Lil Cornish?'

'I was not! You're the one getting confused now.'

George shook his head. 'No. I had Vosper track her down. She's been working at a place called Minchfield House, a mansion upriver. But you'd know all this . . .'

'How the hell would I know? That woman was a Miss Warburton. She told me her name. Come to think of it, I thought I'd seen her before somewhere . . .'

'She's not Miss Warburton. She was playing games with you. She's engaged to marry Robert Warburton. It's Lil Cornish all right. She was working at that place as his house-keeper. He's a bachelor, so they got together.'

'How did Vosper find all this out?'

'From an employment agent here in town. He places domestic staff. It's definitely Mrs Cornish. She's got the child with her.'

'Where's Ted?'

'No mention of a husband.'

'Oh, Christ!' Clem said. 'I remember now. She recognized Thora! She called out her name.'

'That's her,' George said moodily. 'Turns out Mr Warburton is a mate of Henery Whipple's, and that's how they happened to be at Whipple's send-off.'

A nurse came by to check on Clem and straighten his bed, so George wandered over to the window, glad of the opportunity to think this through. He was relieved that Clem had not known who he was dancing with; the alternative would have complicated the situation, causing him to question Clem's integrity. As it was, there was still Jocelyn. More to that than Clem was saying.

'Jocelyn,' he said to Clem when he returned. 'Thora called her name. You saw a familiar face in Lil Cornish. Maybe Thora did too. Only she made a mistake, she thought she was Jocelyn. Why was she so crook on her, Clem? You better think about that.'

'I am. Thora never went out much. Hardly at all. Whoever

upset her must have called at the cottage. George,' he said urgently, 'ask Netta if Thora had any visitors before all this happened. And one more thing. Would you ask Thora's solicitor to come here? I have to see him. We can't let Thora go to jail, it must be bad enough for her now.'

Jail or the madhouse, George thought miserably as he headed back into town, wishing he'd spoken up earlier about Thora's mental state, wishing they'd stopped her going to town, sent for Clem, done something. He had spoken to Netta about Thora and now had a clearer idea of her downhill slide. But so had Thora's solicitor. What would her defence make of all this?

'I have conferred with Mr Conway about your request,' Forbes told Clem on his second visit, 'but he will not approve. He is aware that you are leaving the hospital but he insists that under no circumstances are you to visit your wife. Mr Conway is gradually gaining Mrs Price's trust, she is beginning to talk to him and he wants no interference.'

'But I wouldn't interfere. She needs me. She needs my support. George Gunne has left town, she has no other visitors.'

'Mr Vosper will be permitted to visit, in company with me or Mr Conway. If you really want to support your wife you'll keep out of this, and let Mr Conway prepare his case in his own way.'

'Do I have to wait until she's condemned?' he asked bitterly.

'Mr Conway is an excellent barrister,' Forbes said.

'The police have been to see me,' Clem said. 'I have told them I will not give evidence against my wife. Doesn't that prove that I'm on her side?'

'Very commendable, but Mr Conway is adamant. It's important that you do not interfere. I shall convey your good wishes to Mrs Price. You know, of course, that she is extremely remorseful over the whole affair.'

Alice walked away from the station. She'd miss George. He'd

been so good through all this trouble, so calm. It would have been hard to handle everything on her own. But it was just as well he was leaving, he was becoming too concerned about Thora.

'Poor Thora be damned,' she said. 'She almost killed Clem and they expect me to feel sorry for her. She twists those men round her little finger! Even Clem.'

She was angry that Clem was still worrying about Thora, as if nothing had happened. Well, he'd have to get over that. A jury would deal with Thora, they wouldn't be taken in by her. The charge was attempted murder, as plain as day, no getting away from the fact.

As soon as Clem was out of hospital they'd move out to the beach house she'd heard so much about, away from the town and all the talk. It would be a blessed relief. The days were beginning to drag, waiting about in that foolish cottage with nothing to do. At least at this new house there'd be chores to take her mind off things. Setting up a new household from scratch wasn't as simple as Clem seemed to think. She'd have to see what he'd already bought and shop for the rest herself. Alice smiled. Knowing Clem, she wouldn't be surprised if he'd bought furniture and forgotten the cutlery.

He was pleased to see her but she wouldn't allow any talk of Thora or the forthcoming trial. 'It was a pity about the Yorkey mine,' she said. 'But at least you made your money before that terrible mix-up. I don't know how he thought he could get away with it.'

'Who?'

'Tanner, of course.'

'It wasn't Tanner,' Clem said wearily. 'Tell him I want to see him.'

'You can't. He's gone. Absconded with trust funds too. Good riddance, I say. You should never have been mixed up with him in the first place. He's not welcome back in York, I can tell you that.'

'I doubt he'd make York a priointy.'

'Someone switched the reports on Yorkey,' she persisted. 'If it wasn't Tanner, then who was it?'

478

'Mike. He sent a note to my hotel. Vosper brought it in. The bloody fool did it for a joke.'

'A poor sort of a joke,' she bristled. 'How did he do it? He didn't have an opportunity.'

'God knows. I can't figure that out, but I guessed who was behind it when they told me it was an excellent forgery. Deagan up to his old tricks again.'

'Oh Lord,' Alice breathed. 'But now, about tomorrow, I've got the cottage packed up. I'll take you home from the hospital and you can stay overnight, and the next day we'll move out to the beach house. Do you think you'll be well enough to travel?'

'I wanted to talk to you about that, Alice . . .'

But she wasn't listening. 'Netta won't be coming with us. She's been hounded by the police, and even Thora's solicitor. Damn cheek of him! She wants to go home to her mother and I don't blame her. A harrowing business for a young girl. That solicitor, Forbes, even quizzed her about Thora having gentlemen callers, piling up scandal upon scandal, I say. The poor girl hardly knew what to say.'

'And did she have any visitors, Alice?' he asked quietly.

'Only one, that awful Tanner, but he was looking for you, Netta said.'

'Tanner?' Clem was grim. 'Oh yes, he'd be looking for me, thinking I'd set him up on that forgery charge. What did he say to Thora?'

'How would Netta know? She's not one to eavesdrop. The poor girl told Mr Forbes, over and over again, that she only heard him come in, asking for you. And later she heard Mrs Price raise her voice. She was angry. Telling him to leave. At least Thora had the sense to get rid of him. Pity she couldn't have a bit more sense . . .'

'I thought we weren't going to discuss Thora.'

'I'm only saying what I think. Anyway, Netta will be leaving tomorrow, but it doesn't matter. I'll be able to take care of Lydia myself now that you're leaving the hospital.'

Clem was worried about what Tanner might have said to Thora, but what was done couldn't be undone. More urgently, the presence of Lil Cornish was real cause for concern. How would Lydia's natural mother be reacting to all this?

'Alice,' he said, 'I've changed my mind. It will be a while before Thora's case comes up. I think it would be better if you took Lydia home to Lancoorie as soon as possible.'

'But I thought you wanted us to come to the beach house. I was quite looking forward to it.'

'Another time. The child has been moved about too much already. Lancoorie's her home, she'll be happier there with you and George.'

Alice was surprised, but not displeased. 'I thought that would have been a better solution all along. But what about you?'

'I'll be all right. I'll move back into the hotel until I've got my sea legs again. I still have to let the doctor keep an eye on me.'

'You see you do. Then you should come home. It's all been a terrible shock for you, Clem. You need a good rest.'

He nodded. 'One day at a time. But I'd feel a lot better with you and Lydia settled back home.'

Away from Lil Cornish, he told himself.

The scandal of the Price woman had slipped from the front pages to inner columns and thence, it seemed, to obscurity, but Lil soon found that a great deal was taking place behind the scenes.

When Inspector Smythe and another policeman stepped off the jetty she knew her hopes of anonymity were lost.

She showed them into the library and apologized: 'I'm afraid Mr Warburton is not here. He has gone overseas.'

'That's quite all right,' Smythe said, settling himself by Robert's desk. 'He called on me before he left, to make a statement, but there wasn't much he could offer, any more than the many other witnesses. I'm hoping you can throw some more light on the incident, Mrs Cornish.'

'I've already told you all I can.'

'Ah yes, but do bear with me. It is still not clear why Mrs

Price shot at you. No matter what she said, what name she used, she did look directly at you and fire. You'd agree on that?'

'I suppose so.'

'How well did you know Clem Price? You seem to have a good opinion of him. Could it be that Mrs Price was jealous of you?'

'Of course not. Are you insinuating that there was something between me and Mr Price?'

'I'm not insinuating anything. I just have to look at the facts, which are that you did know Mr Price prior to the incident, and you were dancing with him.'

'Nonsense! He didn't even remember me. I only ever met him once before.'

'Oh. And where was that?'

Lil hesitated. If she'd had any doubts before as to why Robert had left so suddenly, they were dispelled now. He'd talked to Smythe, so he must have known that she'd have to face another interview and possibly, by the sound of things, be dragged into court. Smythe's attitude had changed too. He no longer had to fear offending Robert and Henery; they'd dropped out of the picture, for the time being anyway.

She worried about how much she should tell the inspector. After all, the whole damn circus had nothing to do with her. So far, she knew, there was only a lull in the publicity; it would start again. She didn't want Robert hearing too much about her yet, about the other child, Lydia, and her real connection with Clem and Thora Price. She'd rather tell him herself when he came home. In her own good time.

'Did you hear me, Mrs Cornish?' Smythe persisted. 'Where did you meet Clem Price?'

'In York.'

'Yes. It's a lovely town. I shall be going out there shortly myself. Where exactly in York? What was the occasion?'

'At Lancoorie, his sheep station,' she said. 'My husband worked there.'

'Ah, did he? What's his name? And in what capacity was

he employed by Mr Price?' He nodded to his companion to take notes.

'Ted Cornish. He worked as a farm hand at Lancoorie. On and off.'

'I understand you are still married?'

'I am divorcing him for desertion.'

'And yet you claim to be Mr Warburton's fiancée?'

'I don't claim,' she said angrily. 'Mr Warburton introduced me as his fiancée. Or rather Mr Whipple did. We are planning to marry as soon as I can get the divorce.'

'When will that be?'

'I don't know. Mr Warburton was going to arrange it with his lawyers. I suppose it will have to wait now until he comes home.'

She watched, suddenly very nervous, as Smythe made a sucking noise through his teeth.

'That might take time,' he said. 'It is my understanding that Mr Warburton will be in no rush to return to Australia. In fact, he has put this house on the market.'

'He has what? I don't know anything about this.'

'No doubt he will inform you all in good time.'

Lil refused to succumb to the tears that began to well. Instead, she swallowed hard. 'Oh well, that's his decision.' It didn't matter now what Smythe found out, but he was being so unpleasant, Lil was in no mood to co-operate.

'Is there anything else?' she asked, trying to dismiss him. Jordan and the rest of the staff would want to know that Robert had done the dirty on them too.

'Yes,' he said. 'I have a letter here from a Mrs Dodds, wife of the vicar at St Luke's Church in the district of York. She sent it to the bishop, who passed it on to me. She writes asking for forgiveness for her part in what she calls a ghastly mistake. She insists that Mrs Price, having committed this terrible crime, is not a fit person to have charge of a child who goes by the name of Lydia Price, and she wants her made a ward of the state.'

He looked up. 'Your name is mentioned, Mrs Cornish. Do you want to tell me about this? What exactly is your relationship with the Price family?'

Lil sat very still. 'Did Mr Warburton know about this letter?'

'Naturally I asked him if he knew any of these people. He was quite shocked. He had no idea you had any more than a passing acquaintance with Mr and Mrs Price.'

Lil smiled bitterly. 'Shocked? Not him. He's just totally selfish. What does he care that he breached his promise to me, though I've done nothing wrong? And what about all the staff here? Not a word to any of them. He just slinks away, not man enough to face any of us.'

Surprisingly, Smythe nodded. 'I rather had that impression.' In a kinder tone he continued the interview. 'I don't know if this has any bearing on the case at all, Mrs Cornish, but I need you to tell me about Thora Price and the child Lydia.'

Numbly, Lil explained what had happened at Lancoorie, and then went on to tell him how she came to be at Minchfield House. He listened without interrupting, for which she was grateful.

'So you see,' she said in the end, 'if Clem Price didn't recognize me, Thora wouldn't have. She thought I was someone else.'

'And you don't know anyone called Jocelyn?'

'No. Thora might have, in York, but I didn't know many people there. I only came there when I was married. I knew Thora by sight, prior to that, because she was who she was. Well known in the town.'

They talked for a while longer, and Lil, relenting, brought the policemen tea and sandwiches because they'd have to wait for the return of the ferry.

'They won't make Lydia a ward of the state, will they?' she asked, eventually.

'Can't see it. You're here, and Mr Price is a respectable guardian. I gather there was no formal adoption?'

'No.' Lil was despairing. 'When Thora blew her top like that I made up my mind I'd demand they return Lydia to me. Since I was engaged to Mr Warburton and, as I thought, well settled, I was in a position to take care of her myself. But now . . . If this house is to be sold, I'll have to look for another position. It'll be hard enough with one child. Everything has fallen apart now.'

'I'm sorry, Mrs Cornish. Maybe the new owners will be helpful.'

'Will I have to go to court?'

'Yes. As a witness for the prosecution. She did fire at you.'

'She must have been really cranky about something.'

'Yes. But we still don't know what it was. I'm inclined to agree with you, that she mistook you for someone else, this mysterious Jocelyn. When we unearth her we'll have the answer.'

'What does Clem Price say?'

'Nothing. He's refusing to throw any light on this at all.'

Lil hid a small smile. Good for him. She wished she could refuse to give evidence. She dreaded having to appear in a courthouse in front of all those people. In front of Thora Price.

'I never liked Warburton,' Jordan said angrily. 'He's a shifty character, never done a stroke of work in his life.'

'Well, whoever comes here, they'll need staff, so I don't know what you're worrying about,' the cook said, but Lil wasn't so sure of her situation. If a family came in – and there never would be a more ideal home for a family – the lady of the house wouldn't need a housekeeper.

'How can he sell the house with all these precious things in it? There's all the silver and the paintings and the beautiful lamps, and what about the furniture?'

They were soon to hear. An agent arrived, armed with written permission from Robert Warburton to take an inventory of the contents of the house.

'My, oh my!' he said to Lil. 'This will take a while. I've never been inside Minchfield House before. It's very grand. Looks like we'll have to get a valuer here as well. I can't put this stuff to auction without a very clear idea of what we're handling.'

'Auction?' Lil echoed, shocked.

'Yes. It's the best way to dispose of the contents. We couldn't let all this go with the house. Quite a bit of the furniture will have to stay to assist the sale, though. Not easy in the present financial climate to sell a house this size, even with the gold boom. Big outlay, you see. And big upkeep.'

'It is an expensive house to run,' Lil agreed, hoping that would deter buyers.

She took him on a tour of the house, as requested, and from upstairs he looked out over the fields.

'Mr Warburton was right,' he told Lil. 'The house is one thing, but trying to sell a lovely home like this with the farm as well is quite another. I envisage the buyer as a professional man, someone who would delight in entertaining. He wouldn't want to be worrying about the farm.'

He opened a door and peered into Robert's bathroom. 'Oh, my! Would you look at this! It's as big as my bedroom. I must bring my wife out to see this place! Yes, as I was saying, we can sell the farm separately. You wouldn't get much more for the house with all the land, but dividing the property would certainly be a much better proposition.'

'That would be a pity,' Lil offered defensively, but he had his own opinion.

'Not at all. These big estates are too cumbersome. Subdividing, it's going on all the time. Well, I'd better get to work. I'll start at the other end of the house, downstairs.'

As soon as she was rid of him, Lil dashed across the fields in search of Jordan.

'They're going to subdivide the property,' she puffed. 'There's an agent up at the house right now. He says the farm will be sold separately!'

'Why?' Jordan was bewildered.

'To make more money for Warburton! Why do you think? And everything in the house, bar the normal furniture, is to be sold by auction. He's up there now taking an inventory.'

'That bastard Warburton! He never did care about Minchfield Farm. He'd look damn silly if Lavinia came back.'

So would I, Lil thought. Out of the frying pan into the fire.

Gloomily she walked with him towards the barn as he worried over their prospects.

'You'll get another job,' she said, 'but I'll be hard pushed. I won't even have a reference.'

'Damn the references. I'll write them,' he said angrily. 'By God! Old man Warburton would turn in his grave.'

For the first time, the next morning Mrs Lillian Cornish found her name in the paper.

The front page was taken up with the results of the elections. A Mr Vosper had ousted a long-time Conservative member, and Henery Whipple's seat had also gone to a Labor man. Lil only read all this because Henery's name was mentioned. She sat at the dining-room table, flipping over the pages, until her own name caught her glance.

It was an article headed: *A Woman of Tragedy*. Only a small piece, and for a change, it was kind to Thora. It described her as a beautiful young woman, daughter of Doctor J. Carty of York, who had grown up in a tranquil country town and married Clement Price of Lancoorie Station.

Lil found the article pointless, just going over Thora's background even down to music lessons, and stating she was the loving mother of her small daughter Lydia.

So what caused her to storm the town hall and attempt to shoot Mrs Lillian Cornish? the paper asked. *What brought a beautiful young woman to this plight?*

No answer was offered, no speculation, but Lil was more interested in the presence of her own name.

A lot of good references will do you now, she said to herself. You're stuck dead in the mud of that scandal. And mud sticks.

By late afternoon, everyone knew. The girls buzzed about her with questions, vastly impressed, and Lil answered them coolly.

'I just happened to be there. In the wrong place at the wrong time,' she said.

'Did you wear that satin dress you've got in your cupboard?' a housemaid asked, giving away that she'd been nosing about

Lil's things, but Lil didn't care now. She wouldn't be the housekeeper much longer.

'You're a celebrity!' Cook said. 'Why didn't you tell us that Mr Robert took you to that ball?'

Even Jordan came up to see her. 'Do you know that woman?'

'Sort of,' she said.

'Why did she try to shoot you?'

'I haven't the faintest idea.'

'Is that why Warburton dumped you?'

'Probably. His good name and all that. But I think he must have been plotting to sell up here all along.'

'Bastard. You know, quite a lot of people in the district weren't too pleased at the way he grabbed this place. I'll have a talk to some of the neighbours to see what they can do. Minchfield wasn't left to him, it was left to Lavinia.'

'Who is in the madhouse.'

'What if they could get her out?'

'Oh, God!' Lil didn't want to hear any more. She took Caroline for a long walk along the river bank. 'We might as well enjoy it while we can, darling,' she said. 'I don't know where we'll go from here.'

But the neighbours were busy, encouraged by Jordan. They called a public meeting to express outrage that the property of Miss Lavinia Warburton had been usurped and was now being sold without her consent.

'Why didn't they speak up before?' Lil asked Jordan.

'Because it was all over before they found out.'

'But Robert owns her power of attorney, or whatever you call it. He's legally entitled to sell, or that agent wouldn't have been here.'

'The power of attorney can be revoked,' Jordan said gleefully, 'if she's in her right mind. The local doctor is taking a delegation to visit her. And his lawyer said you are to refuse the agent entry to the house until this matter is cleared up.'

'How can I do that?'

'He's sending you over a letter that will stave him off for a while.'

Any delay suited Lil. In the meantime she sold the lovely satin dress to a local dressmaker for eight pounds, pleased to see the last of it, convinced it was bad luck.

'I'll never get an opportunity to wear it again,' she told Cook, 'so I might as well have the money.'

Weeks passed. The wages were still being paid, but two of the maids left for more secure employment and were not replaced. The agent didn't return, obviously aware that there could be a problem of ownership of the property, and Lil drifted into a lethargy, finding it difficult to cope with all this waiting.

When Jordan told her that the doctor and his friends had called on Miss Lavinia and were hopeful of her release, Lil thought she might do better to pack up and leave, but he persuaded her to stay on. He went to see Miss Lavinia himself, and came back shocked.

'She's old and thin, bloody wore out,' he said, 'but she's as sane as you and me. Don't ask me how, I never saw such a place in all me born days. Disgusting it was, filthy, all your nightmares about a madhouse rolled into one. Inmates lying in their stink, drooling, dribbling, screeching and pinching and fighting. I was almost afeared of me own life in there, bloody shame it is.'

Lil thought of Thora Price and shuddered. There was talk that she'd end up in the asylum. By the sound of things, jail would be better.

'They're demanding Lavinia's release,' Jordan continued. 'Even taking a petition to the Governor. Your Mr Warburton is as popular as the rats.'

'He's not my Mr Warburton, if you don't mind. But what about Lavinia? I signed the papers that put her away. If she gets out she'll kill me.'

'You signed what he told you to sign. If you hadn't you'd have been out on your ear. I talked to Miss Lavinia. She remembers you.'

'I'll bet she does.'

'She remembers you pulled her out of the fire. Her hand is still scarred from the burns.'

What about the rest? Lil wondered. Maybe she was too drunk to remember what went on before that. With luck.

'I don't know about all this,' she muttered. 'If she comes back, the trouble will start all over again. She was a bully. And cruel. You know that, Jordan, you can't pretend you don't.'

'Can't you hang on for a while, Lil? She's too sick to bully anyone. She cried like a baby when she saw me, but she still wanted to know about Minchfield House, how everything was going.'

Lavinia arrived back at Minchfield House as suddenly as she'd left, escorted this time by a doctor and his wife, who helped the broken woman from the boat.

In her own interests, having heard that there was a possibility that Miss Lavinia would be released, Lil had removed herself, and Caroline, to a section of the original cottage on the other side of the kitchen. It was definitely not main house, not up to the standard of her previous accommodation, but neither was it staff quarters. A compromise. The last thing she wanted to do was to antagonize Miss Lavinia, who couldn't be expected to approve of a former maid living in her house.

Jordan was pleased, helping her to make the cottage habitable again. 'I was hoping you'd move out, Lil, but I didn't like to say so.' They hung fresh curtains, put heavy mats on the stone floors and commandeered furniture from the storerooms, and Lil was delighted with her new abode, even though she knew it could easily be short-lived.

Despite Jordan's warnings, she was not prepared for the change in Miss Lavinia. The woman was haggard. Bowed. She was hatless and she had bald patches on her head. There were sores on her face, and worst of all, she smelled of stale urine.

The doctor saw Lil recoil and whispered to her, 'We did the best we could. We wanted to take her to a friend's place first before bringing her here, but she insisted on coming straight home. A hot bath is in order, Mrs Cornish. Could you run one, please. Right away. And bath salts too, if you have them.'

When the woman was finally put to bed in her own room, it was Lil who took up her tray; she wanted to be visible, to give Miss Lavinia the opportunity to dismiss her and get it over with, but her employer had nothing to say. She smiled wanly at Lil and looked eagerly at the chicken broth, as if waiting for permission.

'You should have it now while it's hot,' Lil said, feeling guilty, feeling very sorry for the woman.

Lil became Lavinia's nurse. She bathed and dressed her, gradually making the change from an invalid diet to heavier food, to build up her strength; assisting her downstairs to sit in the garden with Caroline, and it was from here that Lavinia began to assert herself again, but in an unexpected way.

The woman who'd ignored the baby was delighted with Caroline because the child had taken a liking to her. Caroline toddled about her all the time, bringing her toys and dumping them in her lap, even climbing up to sit on her knee.

When Lil tried to stop her, Lavinia wouldn't have it. 'No, let her be. She's a dear little girl.'

Caroline amused her. She walked with Lavinia, holding her hand, and for some unaccountable reason, she called her May.

'No. This is Miss Lavinia,' Lil said, respectfully.

'You can't expect her to produce a mouthful like that,' Lavinia laughed. 'May will do perfectly well.'

It occurred to Lil that she'd never heard Miss Lavinia laugh before, and certainly the woman wouldn't have found anything to amuse her during her long sojourn in that place. Which was never mentioned.

As Lavinia's health improved, she began to take more interest in the house. 'I'm pleased to see he kept the place up to standard,' she said to Lil one day. 'But I suppose that was your doing.'

'I've done my best,' Lil said. 'Would you like me to bring the housekeeping journals to you now?'

'No,' she replied vaguely. 'Some other time.'

But having inspected the house and the farm, and found everything in order, Lavinia seemed at a loss. She did not resume her previous role, content to leave the housekeeping to Mrs Cornish, and spent hours sitting on the front veranda looking out over the river, with only Caroline for company. At night she sat out there again, a lonely old woman.

'I wonder how long this will last?' Lil asked Jordan. 'I keep waiting for her to break out and start ruling the roost again.'

'Ah. It's that place,' he said. 'It's broken her spirit.'

'Not her. I still see flashes of it. She notices things. The bathrooms need a paint, door knobs missing, the crystal chandelier needs a good wash, told me to see to them. But at least she's not drinking.'

Apparently Lavinia wasn't just sitting ruminating. She invited Lil to sit with her one afternoon and pointed at a river boat that was passing by.

'Not all the people on that boat come upriver for a purpose,' she said. 'They take a joy ride to view the scenery, and I notice they like to stare at this house.'

'Yes. Minchfield House is quite an attraction.'

'It is. Yes, it is. I was thinking of inviting them to tea.'

Lil was amazed. 'You want to have an afternoon tea party?'

'Certainly not! I want to serve them morning or afternoon tea, and have them pay for the pleasure. The drawing room is the biggest room, with access directly from the front of the house. I could put tables in there and serve decent fare. Tea, cakes, that sort of thing. Do you think this cook is up to it?'

She'd better be, Lil thought. That wasn't really a question. She listened, intrigued, as Lavinia outlined her plan, right down to involving the ferrymen.

'They'd be glad of the extra custom that the Minchfield Tea Rooms would bring,' Lavinia said. 'And visitors would be glad of the opportunity to have a better look at the house and grounds. I'm sure they'd be happy to pay.'

'We'd need smaller tables for that room,' Lil said. 'And more chairs. And a waitress.' She knew she should have said two maids to replace the girls who'd left, but she was anxious to please. If Miss Lavinia went ahead with this idea, then her own job would be secure.

'I've thought of that,' Lavinia said. 'We'll make a list of the necessities tomorrow. I think it should be very interesting, as long as' – she glared over her glasses at Lil – 'we serve the very best, as befitting the tone of my house.'

The doctor's visits had ceased, but his wife and a couple of other ladies called occasionally, and eventually they came to hear the news.

'What's this about a tea room opening up here?' they asked Lil.

'You'd have to ask Miss Lavinia,' she replied.

Later, she heard them congratulating her. 'It's a perfectly splendid idea, Lavinia! But surely you wouldn't have just day trippers. You must allow us to come too. It will be such fun!'

Obviously that was the boost Lavinia needed to take the next step. Prior to this she'd made tentative enquiries of the ferrymen and drawn up endless lists, but nothing definite had come of it.

Now the women gave her confidence. They seemed to be at the house daily, even more enthusiastic about this new project than the lady of the house, helping her to plan everything right down to the last detail, and Lavinia emerged from the meetings beaming. Not only had she found something to interest her at last, she had friends, and that went a long way towards what Lil called 'the benigning' of Lavinia.

The drawing room was transformed into an elegant tea room, with small tables set with starched white napery, for Lavinia despised the rustic look. They were discussing an opening date when Lil received notice to present herself at court for the trial of Mrs Thora Price.

Her heart sank. She'd been praying they'd forget her, but it was not to be. The moment she had long dreaded was at hand, and dared not refuse to attend. Not only would she have to ask Lavinia for some days off, she would have to explain why, and that meant admitting she'd been at that dance with Robert. And how that had come to be.

492

Oh well, she decided. I'll stay at Merle's boarding house and look for another job from there.

Finally she plucked up the courage to approach Lavinia, asking, lamely, for time off.

'The court case, is it?' Lavinia asked coldly.

Lil flinched, surprised. 'Yes, ma'am.'

'No need to look so silly at me. I know all about it. People talk. I was even advised to get rid of you, to avoid involvement in the scandal. Do you think I should?'

'I would hope not, ma'am. I like working here.'

'Yes. Results show that. And I shall need your help for this new enterprise.' She walked to the french windows to bat at a fly that was buzzing about, and closed them firmly. 'It seems to me that the Warburtons were on their way to creating their own scandals even before you came into the picture. I'm a living scandal myself now.'

'Oh, madam, that's not right.'

'Really? Do you think people are likely to forget I was committed to the asylum? No, they are not. That's why I can't live here as a recluse and be known as the mad woman of Minchfield. I will be seen, and publicly, and by those means I shall try to restore the good name of the Warburtons.'

'Oh!' Lil was impressed by her reasoning, but too nervous to speak. This interview was not over yet.

'I believe you nearly got your head shot off,' Lavinia said with a sniff. 'A great pity she missed my brother. You do what you have to do. I don't want to hear any more about it. And get back here as soon as possible.'

Chapter Fourteen

His victory celebrations over at last, Fred was caught in a round of meetings with constituents and delegations, even though Parliament was not due to sit again for a few months. He worried too about his all-important maiden speech, writing and rewriting it every few days, cross with himself that as a professional scribbler he couldn't get it right.

'It's a lot easier to write speeches for other people,' he claimed. 'I always used to know what politicians should say.'

But he hadn't forgotten the Price family, and Thora's letter. He went to the cottage to hand it over to Alice Gunne, who should have been the recipient – after all, it was written to her – but the cottage was closed down. Enquiries at the Palace reception desk revealed that Mr and Mrs Gunne had gone home. That eased his conscience. All along, aware that Alice had no sympathy for Thora, he'd known that if he gave it to her, it wouldn't have helped. Alice was firm in her opinion that Thora was mad.

In the end he decided that Clem should read it. Clem should know more about Thora's state of mind than what she was portraying on the surface, so that he could come to a better understanding of her motives. And be gentle with her, he added dismally.

He had tried to see Thora, to apologize for his absence, but was informed that he could only visit her in the company of her lawyer or barrister, and despite his protests, he was turned away. But he also learned that Clem had not visited her either, and that was ominous. Fred had seen Clem at the hotel on several occasions, even though he hadn't had a chance to talk to him. Or to thank him. For Clem had squared the hotel for damage and had left a cheque for his former room-mate, with an apology. The authorities now knew that Thora had stolen Fred's gun from the room, but the rest of it was hush-hush, the proprietor grateful that his hotel was spared the attention of sensation-seekers.

'Time I took a day off anyway,' Fred told himself as he rode out to Cottersloe, armed with a bottle of Hennessy's brandy.

'For medicinal purposes,' he said, handing it to Clem.

The house pleased him. It had tall windows but no curtains as yet, and they seemed to be sitting right among the grass-scattered dunes with a fantastic, untrammelled view of the ocean.

'I'm batching here,' Clem said, 'but you're welcome to take pot luck with me if you'd like a feed.'

'Count me in,' Fred replied. 'How are you? You're looking better. Got some colour up.'

'Damn plaster on my chest still. That's healing, but it gets itchy. The leg's giving me the devil. Busted muscle's taking more time to get back into shape than my ribs.'

'Keep off the leg.'

'Thanks. You're a big help.' Clem opened the brandy. 'I didn't get a chance to congratulate you before, you always seemed to have the flock about you. Well done!'

The house was sparsely furnished with only the bare essentials so far, but the men preferred to sit on the wide front steps, looking out to sea as they talked. Later they cooked steaks on the top of the stove, sizzling them with Worcester sauce and sandwiching them between thick slices of a damper that Clem had cooked that day.

When he could no longer resist, Fred asked why Clem had not been to see Thora. It seemed the best way to gauge his attitude.

'I'm not allowed,' Clem said angrily. 'When you go back, will you talk to Conway? It's outrageous. I can't make any sense of it.'

'Maybe she doesn't want to see you.'

495

'I don't believe that. You can understand, Fred. I need to talk to her, to find out what this was all about.'

Fred considered this. 'Conway's a good man. If he says you can't see her, he must have his reasons. I know that's very hard on Thora, but he is working on her defence. It's a famous case, he'll want to win.'

'But can he?' Clem asked, despairing. 'Tell me the truth.'

Fred couldn't bring himself to say he doubted it. 'Perhaps Conway is looking at why she did it. He might think that if you are allowed to visit Thora you'll distract her from whatever course he has in mind. It's a desperate situation. She's got the best barrister in town; you have to let him run the race his own way.'

All the while, Fred debated with himself whether or not to show Clem the letter, studiously weighing the pros and cons, but then, conscience prevailing over logic, he placed it on the table.

'This was in the cottage. I confiscated it before the police stumbled on it. It was written by Thora before the event.'

Clem unfolded the pages. 'It's to Alice.'

'Yes, but she hasn't read it yet . . .' He sat back as Clem began to read.

'It doesn't make a lot of sense,' Clem said, bewildered, turning back to reread the first page, but Fred made no comment. He walked outside to gaze at a ship far out on the horizon, feeling older than his years as he waited for Clem's reaction.

'She was raped!' Clem said miserably when he returned. 'Why didn't she tell me?'

'How could she? It's all there. Why don't you tell me the circumstances of your marriage, then we might be able to piece all this together. Would you mind doing that?'

'No. I want to talk it out. George Gunne told me he thought there was something wrong with Thora earlier in the piece, and this seems to bear that out.'

'There's a lot more to it than that. Did she know about the Black Cat?'

'It's my guess that Tanner told her. Payback for me, when

496

I wasn't accusing him of anything. It wouldn't sound too pleasant coming from him.' He groaned. 'I wish I could go back a year or so. Poor Thora, I feel sick every time I think of her in jail.'

'You've no hard feelings?'

'Of course not. She didn't know what she was doing.'

They went over the letter, page by page, and Clem was ashen, shocked as the full measure of Thora's breakdown became evident. He was able to fill in the gaps, from the time he met Dr Carty up to the loss of Thora's baby.

'She knew all along,' he said desperately, 'but I suppose having Lydia was some consolation. She just never talked about anything. She was always so composed, as if she didn't have a worry in the world.'

'She doesn't sound too composed if she refused to have sex with her husband.'

'Easy enough to say in hindsight.'

Fred would have liked to accept Clem's invitation to stay overnight, but he could not, he had too many other commitments. Like Clem, accustomed to the quiet of the bush, he did not find this a lonely place by any means. In fact he envied Clem his splendid retreat.

'Would you give Thora's letter to her barrister?' Clem asked him.

'Are you sure that's the right thing to do?'

'No, I'm not. But Conway's on her side. He has to be appraised of all the facts.'

'It might encourage him to go for a plea of guilty but insane. She could end up in the asylum.'

'Wouldn't that be preferable to jail?' Clem asked bitterly. 'At least I could see her. Try to get her out.'

The letter worried him, but Fred did as Clem asked. He delivered it to the barrister and was disappointed when Conway perused it without comment. Instead he seemed more interested in the state of Clem's health and his attitude to Thora. He asked what Fred knew about their relationship, the marriage, the family, a certain whorehouse. And about Jocelyn.

Knowing that Clem wanted him to co-operate with Conway in every possible way, Fred answered the questions as best he could. He wasn't asked, so he did not mention Thora's destructive bout in the hotel room. Both he and Clem were adamant that Thora was in enough trouble; the less a jury heard about that the better.

The next day he went with Conway to visit Thora, who was pleased that Clem was now out of hospital but distressed that he did not visit her.

'The authorities won't permit it,' Fred told her. Conway had warned him that if he blamed her barrister it would ruin the relationship he had built up with Mrs Price. She'd lose trust in him.

'But he sends his love,' Fred added.

'Oh yes,' she said sadly. 'From afar, as usual.'

The courthouse was packed. Stifling. Outside, a bigger crowd craned. When the town hall clock chimed ten, the judge walked in, intimidating the room to silence.

Fred Vosper looked about him, but there was no sign of Clem. He had been threatening to disobey the prosecution's instructions and come into the court, but must have thought better of it at the last minute.

When they brought Thora in, there was a muffled gasp in the room. Fred stared. She looked sad, wan, but so beautiful. Astonishingly beautiful, all in white. Stage-managed by Conway, he thought, because he had bypassed her elegant and expensive clothes to present her in a simple white muslin dress, hatless, her long blonde hair streaming down about her shoulders, not a comb or a bow in sight. She held a tiny lace handkerchief.

The charge was laid, attempted murder, and the wheels of justice began their slow turns. Thora was permitted to be seated in the dock. She looked straight ahead, never once turning her head to the crowd. Another precaution, Fred noted. He wondered how long she could sit this out.

When the prosecuting attorney began his preamble, Fred saw her lips quiver, and looking over to the jury, he didn' think they'd even notice, or care, the charge seemed so cut and dried. And dried it was. By the afternoon it had almost become dreary, the prosecution stating the case and producing witnesses, and the defence seemingly unable to make any headway against this barrage of facts. Fred thought Conway's opening address was weak, referring only to this gentle lady, a good mother, of high standards, talking only of her good name.

The next morning, after the police had their say, Thora seemed more relaxed, the first ordeal over without incident, until Mr Clem Price was called to the stand. She put her hands to her face and those blue eyes looked appealingly at him. What could he do but smile gently at her and move on?

She wept as he answered the questions put to him, stiffly and to the point, volunteering nothing. Incredibly the defence did not wish to question him at this time, so Clem's evidence was over in a very short time, producing nothing new at all.

It was only when Mrs Cornish came to the stand that the court really began to sit up and take notice. It became clear to the jury that Mrs Price did know this woman, that Mrs Price had adopted one of Mrs Cornish's twin daughters shortly after the birth. But Mrs Cornish was not a well-behaved witness. Despite instructions from the judge to stick to the point, she kept insisting that Mrs Price had not been shooting at her. That it was all a mistake.

The defence took a different line. Conway was not interested in Mrs Cornish's previous statements, except for one point.

'Is it a fact that this poor woman, Mrs Price, lost her baby? It was born dead?'

'Yes.'

'That would be a terrible blow to a woman, would it not?'

'Yes. Of course. She wasn't well. She was upset.'

'And is it true that Mrs Price was told your child was hers?'

'I think so.'

'And yet she knew in her own mind that that was not true.'

'Did she?'

'I can assure you she did, but now her family were pressuring her to accept this child as her own. As a mother, would you be confused in those circumstances?'

'Yes.'

'And upset?'

'Yes.'

'So here we have a young woman, confused and upset, who was already carrying the burden of previous difficulties. Is this not so?'

'I don't know what you mean.'

'Ah, but you do. Weren't you aware that Mrs Price was pregnant when she married Clem Price? That in fact her family forced her into this marriage?'

He continued these harsh questions, prising agreement from her that Thora was a victim, and Fred nodded approval, wondering if that line could be sustained, for what it was worth.

Shocked, Thora had stopped weeping, but two red blotches were evident on her face as she gazed at the floor in shame.

From then on, Conway attacked. He had Alice on the stand, presumably to attest to Thora's good name, but Alice was not a good witness. Her antipathy towards Thora showed.

Stupid of him to use her, Fred thought, but Conway soon had her trembling in her seat. 'Did you ever tell Mrs Price that the child, Lydia, was not hers?'

'No.'

'You deliberately sought to confuse this frightened woman, who was brought to your house under duress. Farmed out, so to speak.'

'No, it wasn't like that. We thought it was for the best.'

'And did her husband go off and leave her with you on that isolated farm for more than six months?'

'Yes, but . . .'

'A newly-wed young lady, unused to the solitary life, from a big family, was dumped on you. Was she happy there?'

'Not really, but . . .'

He turned to the jury. 'Gentlemen, we're starting to see the other side of the picture now. You are entitled to ask what brought a young lady to this pass. Indeed, you must ask. Some of you are fathers yourselves. Were this your daughter, this would be the first thing you'd ask.'

Alice was dismissed. She stepped down unsteadily, shattered. When she passed through the main body of the courtroom, Clem was in the lobby to assist her. 'I'm so sorry. I didn't realize how bad it would be.'

Angrily she thrust him away and ran, weeping, into the street.

George Gunne fared better. He was unfazed by the prosecution's efforts to destroy his credibility as a person who could vouch for Thora, calmly agreeing that his criminal record, which was read to the court, was correct.

By this, Fred was squirming in his seat. But did the prosecution realize they were playing into Conway's hands by citing George's history? Soon the barrister was addressing Mr Gunne.

'When Mr Price went to the goldfields for an indefinite stay, were you the only male company he provided for his wife and sister? A convicted felon?'

'Yes.' George was unmoved. Fred had the impression that George had a better idea of what was going on here than he did. Mr Gunne made no attempt to explain that he was now a free man, or even draw attention to the fact that he'd married Alice Price. It seemed to Fred that Conway was building up this victim angle to prove that Thora was insane, but not once had he even suggested it.

But at last it came. Fred experienced relief. The sooner this was over, the better.

'What would you say was Mrs Price's mental state,' he asked George, 'when she was living at the sheep station, without her husband?'

'I'm no expert.'

'No, you're not. Would you say she was fretting?'

'Yes. Hurt. She was vague. She seemed to have a lot of things on her mind.'

'Unhappy?'

501

'Yes.'

Conway turned to the jury. 'And why wouldn't she be? A young girl, lost and lonely, with another woman's child foisted on her.'

To George: 'Did you speak to Mrs Price? Ask her why she was so unhappy?'

'No. It wasn't my place.'

Conway nodded, approving. 'That's true, Mr Gunne. It was not your place. It was her husband's place, but he was elsewhere.'

On that day, Dr Carty got the worst of it. Another reluctant witness, Fred had heard, he was, however, prepared to take the stand and tell the court that Thora came from a good family, had had an excellent upbringing in York, and yes, had done well at school.

'You'd say she was a well-behaved girl?'

'Yes, indeed. All my girls are.'

'Then wasn't it strange that one of these well-behaved girls should misbehave to the extent that she could find herself pregnant?'

'These things happen,' Carty said, mortified.

'Not in the sort of family you describe, it does not. Young ladies of that age and background are well known to seek the gentility of romance.' He smiled to the jurors. 'They can even be quite giddy about it.'

A couple of the jury members nodded their heads.

'You have already told me that of your daughters, Miss Thora was the most dignified. Very reserved, in fact.'

'Yes.'

'Then did it occur to you that Miss Thora might not have entered willingly into sexual relations with this fellow, whose name we are not permitted to mention? That it was a far worse shock for her than for you. That she might have been raped?'

The court was in uproar.

The letter! Conway was using the letter. His evidence from Thora was first hand. Fred glanced over at Thora, who sat, head bowed, thoroughly defeated.

502

For a while legal argument ensued, but Conway had Dr Carty back on the stand, haranguing him unmercifully.

'Did you or your wife even ask Miss Thora about the circumstances of her pregnancy? Or did you just point the finger of blame at her? Have you no faith in your own daughters?'

Carty blustered, denied, agreed, trying to find a way out of this maze. Then Conway struck another blow.

'And is it not true that you, as a doctor, hell-bent on protecting your good name, demanded that your daughter allow you to abort her?'

'No!' Carty shouted.

'And she refused?'

'No!'

'You mean she didn't refuse?'

'Yes, she did.' Carty was thoroughly confused.

'Thank you,' Conway said swiftly, and the courtroom subsided to a horrified silence.

But he still wasn't finished with Carty, and Fred was worried. Clem wasn't coming out of this too well.

Conway turned her dowry into a bribe. He extracted the circumstances of the wedding from Carty, threatening to recall Alice Price if he couldn't unravel the truth. By dint of harsh questioning, he described the heartless wedding wherein the bride was not even permitted to enjoy her day with her family.

'After that secret wedding in a lonely country chapel, did you or any of your family go on to the reception?'

'What reception?'

'Answer the question, Dr Carty. To the reception provided by the groom's sister?'

'No. We had to get back.'

George has filled him in on all this, Fred said to himself, fascinated. It could only have been George. No one else would have thought of it.

'So you not only snubbed Alice Price, who was trying to do the right thing, having prepared a wedding breakfast, but you snubbed your own daughter! Washed your hands. Wedding over. We're rid of her. Have you any idea of the humiliation that wrought on your daughter? She sat through that wedding breakfast in a strange house, surrounded by a motley collection of strangers, her new family, some neighbours that she hadn't met before, and farm hands.'

He seemed close to tears when he addressed the jury. 'This girl might as well have been a virgin. Rape is an awful business. Could she discuss it with her father? Or her mother? Not possible. She wouldn't have known how, nor would any decent girl. And now here she is, flung into even more humiliation. Didn't anyone care about this lovely girl? It seems not. I ask you to look at her, gentlemen of the jury. I, for one, would be proud to call her my daughter. She is the epitome of our fine West Australian girls, not some hussy dredged up from the slums. And what did they do to her? Think about that, gentlemen.'

That night Fred joined a collection of local and interstate journalists at Paddy's bar. He had not posted many of the articles about the case that he'd originally intended to submit. The others were still in his room, lengthy but unfinished, because he'd become too close to his subject. Wanting to help. Afraid he might hinder. Seeing little hope for Thora as things stood.

The journalists argued, taking bets on whether she would be found guilty or insane. Or both.

Some felt very sorry for her. 'She's had a tough life.'

'The hell she has!' another disagreed. 'Living high on the hog. My mum wouldn't mind a day of her life.'

'But, ah, she's beautiful,' an aged journalist said. 'I'm in love with her. Give her to me, Judge.'

'You silly old bugger. She'd shoot you quick as look at you.'

'But what about that rape stuff? Who's the bloke? There's another story.'

'She's not so sweet. She had a boyfriend, Lord Kengally.'

'They say the husband doesn't want to know her.'

'Why would he? He might forget to duck next time.'

A young reporter from Sydney liked her. 'She's gorgeous. I can't stop looking at her,' he told Fred. 'Neither can the blokes on the jury. Some of them are drooling, I tell you. But her barrister can't seem to get to the point. I mean, what is he after? What's the point in menacing all the people who are trying to put in a good word for her? He's ripping into the wrong ones.'

'So what?' another man said. 'She's done for. All this talk is just solicitors and barristers earning their keep. She was there to shoot someone.'

And that's the crux of it, Fred thought as he munched on a pork pie at the bar. Was she? Or was she just reacting to a litany of miseries? Worn down to a fragile mental state? No. She had intent.

Clem was on the stand again, and right from the outset Fred realized that Dr Carty hadn't got the worst of it after all. Clem was being crucified by Conway. No wonder Conway didn't want him talking to Thora, interfering in his case. Clem Price was now the victim, not Thora. She even cried out in his defence, several times, but Conway was relentless.

He took Clem through the circumstances, bad enough, of their meeting and marriage, with no thought given to a honeymoon. And prised from Clem the admission that his wife was not interested in sex.

'This from a so-called hussy? From a fallen woman. Who by all accounts was not a virgin when she married. Did this not strike you as peculiar? Did you not seek advice from her father, who is a doctor? No. You couldn't speak of the problem any more than your wife could speak of the assault perpetrated on her person.'

Inevitably, as Conway ground on about the humiliations heaped on this poor lady, he asked Clem if he was, or had been, the owner of a famous whorehouse in Kalgoorlie known as the Black Cat.

To the jury, he posed the question: 'What would be the reactions of your wives if they discovered that you owned not a famous, but an infamous whorehouse? Think about it, gentlemen. The reaction would be horror. Humiliation.

Fear. Fear for your good name and the good names of your children. And confusion. Utter shocking confusion! On top of everything else, this happened to Mrs Price. Did she hear it from her husband? Oh, no. She had to hear it from someone else.'

Clem, his head in his hands, suffering this diatribe in front of Thora, answered truthfully, directly.

When she shouted at Conway to stop, Clem shrugged, shaking his head for her to leave it be, answering the questions in a monotone.

'So who is Jocelyn?' Conway asked. 'Mrs Price did not aim her humiliations at you, nor at Mrs Cornish. She was mistaken, as Mrs Cornish has attested. She was so further mortified by the nightmares her family and the Price family had heaped on her that she simply struck out. Isn't that so?'

'Yes. I don't doubt that for one minute.'

'So who is Jocelyn?'

The courtroom was agog as Clem admitted that she was, or had been, manager of the Black Cat brothel in Kalgoorlie.

'Not manager. *Madame*,' Conway said, sternly.

'I told you that.'

'And was she known to your wife?'

'In York. Yes.'

'And did you ever have sex with this woman? This whore?'

Clem hesitated.

Say no, Fred urged from his seat in the third row. For God's sake, say no. Who's to know? You can't take this punishment, Clem, it's all wrong.

'Yes,' Clem said quietly. 'Yes, I did.' He looked over at Thora. 'And I ask my wife's forgiveness.'

Alice and George had hurried to Perth when they were advised that a date had been set for Thora's trial, but Alice was very nervous of having to appear in court.

'Why me?' she asked. 'What's it got to do with me?'

'Her lawyers will want to show that she comes from a good family,' George told her. 'You can't refuse to help, Alice. People will think you don't care. She is your sister-in-law.'

'Worse luck.'

She refused to stay at one of the city hotels, preferring to take Lydia to a quiet boarding house that catered for country visitors, and, fortunately, was very happy there.

'We ought to take Lydia to see her mother,' George said.

'I've told you before, I will not set foot in a jail.'

'Then I'll take her. And I want no more argument about it.'

Fearing that he might be turned away with the child, George called on the solicitor, who agreed to accompany them on condition the visit was short.

Thora was overjoyed. 'How well she looks! Come here, my darling, come to Mother. Look, we can see out this window all the Queen's men marching up and down.'

She turned to George. 'At least she doesn't know what sort of a place this is. Do you think she'll remember?'

'I don't think so.'

They stayed for more than an hour, until, tearfully, Thora admitted that the child was becoming bored and restless. 'It's no fun, is it, darling? You go along with George.'

But before they left, she was concerned for Clem. 'Have you seen him? Is he well? They won't let him come here, it's so cruel.'

'Don't worry about him, Thora. He's fine. He didn't leave town, he's been busy fixing up the beach house for you.'

'Will I ever see it, though?' she asked miserably.

'Of course you will,' Forbes said firmly. 'You just have to be brave. Get through this court case. Remember what Mr Conway said: pretend you're at a play, don't look at the audience.'

'It'll be dreadful, won't it?' she said to George.

George grinned. 'Come on now, Thora. I'm an old hand at courts, they're just plain boring. Let it all go over your head.'

But it hadn't been boring. Alice was in a terrible state after her day in court, refusing to see Clem.

'I'll never forgive him,' she wept. 'He let them put me

through that nightmare, making me out to be a horrible person.'

'He had nothing to do with it,' George protested. 'He was just as upset as you were.'

'The hell he was! He's besotted with that woman. He doesn't care about anyone else. Mrs Carty was hysterical outside the court after what they did to her husband. She's finished with Thora for ever.'

'I thought they already were,' George murmured. 'You'd better stay home from now on. I don't think they need you any more.'

'Wild horses wouldn't get me back there!'

But she could read the papers, and it wasn't long before she discovered that her brother had owned an infamous brothel in Kalgoorlie that was run by a Miss Jocelyn Russell. Alias Madame Jolie.

'You knew about this!' she screamed at George when he returned from the court.

'No, I didn't, and keep your voice down or we'll be thrown out of here.'

'She stayed in our house!' she hissed. 'Mike brought that whore to our house!'

'She's not a whore any more, she's his wife.'

'What difference does that make? Lies. It's all been lies. Clem didn't make his money from gold. It was from that brothel. They deserve one another, him and Thora. They're as bad as each other. My God! If I'd known he was running a whorehouse, I'd have taken a gun to him myself.'

'Then you can understand how Thora felt. It must have been a hell of a shock for her to find all that out. On top of everything else. None of us knew she'd been raped.'

Alice clapped her hands over her ears. 'Shut up! I don't want to hear another word, it's all too awful. Can't we go home, George?'

'Won't be long now. It'll be over soon.'

The case dragged on. Finally the prosecution wrapped up their case, the stolen revolver produced again to prove that this woman knew exactly what she was doing. That she coldly and calmly, with no care or regard for the safety of so many innocent folk, walked into the town hall with this loaded gun. That she aimed squarely at an innocent woman, a guest of Mr Henery Whipple himself, and fired, attempting to murder that woman. The jury seemed spellbound with the drama of it as the finger was pointed at Mrs Price over and over again. She sat, head bowed, obviously exhausted.

Conway was quieter. Sadder. He spoke sorrowfully of all the humiliations that had been heaped on a young woman from a sheltered background, a young woman who should have had high expectations, indeed, who had a high opinion of herself, and rightly so, until blow by blow, she was struck down not only by society but by her family and friends. Quietly, almost confidentially, he took the jury on what he called a journey of misery, and George noticed an elderly juror remove his glasses and wipe a tear from his eye.

'You've all heard of nervous breakdowns,' Conway said to them, 'and now you've seen how they come about. They're not sudden, these things, they creep upon you, wearing you down, like water dripping on a rock. They're insidious, you don't even know what's happening to you, the burden gets harder and harder to bear.'

He went on to describe how businessmen had experienced breakdowns from the weight of their problems, men who in the end had given up in despair. Who had shot themselves. 'Yes, I have first-hand knowledge of the result of such torment, as no doubt some of you do.

'They are said to have committed suicide whilst of unsound mind. But Mrs Price fought back. She wouldn't give up, something deep inside her kept her struggling. She was alone in the water, drowning, with no one to help her, knowing she was going under.

'Mrs Price has no memory of that final stroke. And why would she? It was not in her nature to fire a gun at anyone. She was in shock; the last straw was being informed of her husband's contemptible activities.'

He talked to the jury confidentially, as if in a family

discussion about 'our poor young woman' who had been so severely tried, and who was still suffering.

'Of unsound mind when she committed this action?' he asked at last. 'Yes. This is true. My client is not the fiend that the prosecution is attempting to project so flimsily . . .'

George sighed. Insanity. Poor Thora. What would become of her now? They'd never let her out.

'Of unsound mind? Yes,' Conway continued. 'And why wouldn't she be? Driven to distraction, that's what happened. You can't commit her to further suffering, because Mrs Price is not guilty.'

There was a rustle in the court, but the barrister ignored it, keeping the jury with him. 'She was driven to an action she can hardly recall. She is filled with remorse. Her husband was injured, but he knows his wife was sorely injured also. You heard him, gentlemen. He won't point a finger of blame at her. No, he asks her forgiveness. Honour is emerging at last! That was a proud moment! One you must embrace as you enter your deliberations, because I am asking your forgiveness for Mrs Price. Society's honour is at stake here. Find it in your hearts to forgive Mrs Price, who is not a criminal but a victim. You cannot point a finger of blame at a woman who just finally broke down. You must invoke the blessed canon of compassion and return a verdict of not guilty.'

The reunion of Clem and Thora caused even stolid George to feel a lump in his throat. He had accompanied Clem to the Barracks which still housed Mrs Price while they waited for the jury to decide her fate.

Their fate, George thought as Clem took her in his arms. They were both near to collapse from the strain, clinging to each other, afraid to let go. He walked out of the cell to wait with the guard by the open door, standing awkwardly, unable to think of anything to say to the stranger, worrying about the verdict that loomed too heavily over them all.

He glanced back to see them standing by the barred window, temporarily safe in each other's arms, neither of them speaking, and he sighed. Too much had been said.

As they left the courthouse, Lil Cornish had approached Clem nervously. 'I'm very sorry, Mr Price. Really sorry.'

'Thanks,' he muttered, moving on, but she persisted.

'I'd like to have a talk with you when you have time.'

'What about?'

'Lydia.'

'She's all right, Mrs Cornish. Don't worry about her.'

'I know. But we still have to talk.'

'Not now,' he said angrily, brushing her aside.

George could see even more storm clouds on the horizon with the appearance of Lil Cornish. Will there ever be an end to this? he wondered.

'Thora's holding up much better than I expected,' he said to Clem as they emerged into the hard sunlight from the gloom of the cold building.

'I don't know how she has survived that place,' Clem groaned.

'She still hasn't grasped it,' George warned, but Clem seemed not to hear. Forbes had told George that they had used medical evidence to keep Thora off the stand because they'd been afraid of what she might say.

'There's no cunning in her,' the lawyer had said. 'She could easily make things a lot worse.'

'She'd have broken down anyway,' George said. 'They'd have reduced her to tears, she's not up to it.'

'I'm not so sure. Mrs Price still has vague lapses – away with the pixies, you know – and if that took effect for all to see, she'd only be a sad spectacle. But Mr Gunne, in our opinion she is a lot better, surprising as it may sound, than she was in the first days. Mr Conway has a way with him. He talked to her like a father confessor, he understands her, and she responded. She needed that, not for the court case, but for her own stability. It is my considered opinion that if Mrs Price had been able to talk to someone like Maurice Conway in times past, none of this would have happened.'

They went back to the courthouse, but the jury was still out.

511

'Why are they taking so long?' Clem moaned. 'They've been in there all day. Why can't they make up their minds?'

'To what? Best they keep arguing. Come on, I'll buy you a drink to settle your nerves.'

They stood morosely in a quiet bar, staring at pictures of splendid yachts that hung above rows of bottles.

'How's Alice?' Clem asked suddenly.

'Displeased,' George said. 'Yes, you could say displeased.'

'I suppose she is.'

'You took a hiding in there too.'

Clem nodded. 'Yes. But what the hell! That doesn't bother me. As long as Thora can cope with it.'

'Seems she has.'

'We'll see. Can we go back to the courthouse? I can't stand this waiting.'

The following afternoon the jury filed back in to face a packed court again.

George was so nervous he hardly heard any of the preliminaries. Clem was outside. Bilious. Too overcome by nerves even to approach the door. Conway's demeanour hadn't changed; a large imposing man, he regarded the proceedings with dignified patience while beside him, Forbes fussed and twitched. Mrs Cornish had managed to find a seat at the back, and a crush of reporters wrestled for space across the rear of the court, poised to rush away to the telegraph offices. Alice, of course, had refused to attend, and there was no sign of the Cartys, but the young nanny, Netta, was standing, sadly out of place, among the reporters, staring up at Thora.

When the judge asked the jury foreman for their verdict, George turned, inevitably, to Thora. She was wearing a tailored navy-blue suit, elegant now, and her hair was dressed in the fashionable thick roll framing her face, a shaft of light from a window emphasizing the sheen of that beautiful blonde hair. Her face was pale, but she stood, composed, almost as if she was above all this, and George was glad that in her last appearance before the public she'd been permitted to be remembered as a graceful, stylish woman. Her eyes turned to the courtroom, searching, he knew, for Clem. To give her encouragement, George smiled at her, but he doubted she saw him because suddenly the court erupted.

'What? What?' George asked, bewildered, searching around him. He'd missed it!

'Not guilty!' Voices echoed. People were on their feet. There was a stampede for the door. Two women in black cheered and waved their umbrellas. 'Bloody disgusting!' a male voice shouted, but the man sitting next to George muttered: 'Fair enough. She's had a bad trot.' The judge hammered with his gavel. George sat, unable to stir himself, unable to take it in, and people climbed over him, anxious to exit, as if there was a prize for first out.

He saw Conway walk towards Thora, hands outstretched.

Chapter Fifteen

So Thora was acquitted. When the trial ended, Lil felt an overwhelming sadness that surprised her. She never thought she'd see the day when she'd feel sorry for Thora Price, but having endured her short stint before the court, she realized what a dreadful ordeal this was for Thora. Especially when all that dirty washing was being aired and rehashed in the papers. In the end she was glad that the jurors, too, had found it in their hearts to be sympathetic.

But it didn't alter anything.

I want my baby back, she said to herself, and this is the time.

Conscience nudged her that it couldn't be a worse time for Thora, who had already suffered so much, but she thrust it aside. The verdict only meant she'd been spared jail, or the asylum. She was notorious, she'd never live down this scandal, and besides, it was evident that she was a bit mental. No one attempted to say she was cured. If they refused to hand Lydia back to her, Lil was prepared to claim that Thora was not a fit mother, but remembering the interference of the vicar's wife, with her decidedly un-Christian attitude, she had a twinge of regret. How dare that woman suggest Lydia should be made a ward of the state! Lil hoped it wouldn't be necessary to use that weapon.

She'd tried to speak to Clem Price at the courthouse, but the timing had been a mistake. She'd known it was the wrong time the minute she'd spoken, but it had only been a spur-of-the-moment decision. Then, afterwards, she'd lost him. She'd stood in the crowd on the steps of the courthouse, waiting for him to bring Thora out, a free woman, but there was no sign of them. They must have dodged out the back door, fleeing more public scrutiny. They simply disappeared, and Lil had no idea where she could contact them in Perth.

At least she knew she could always find them at Lancoorie, but there was another hurdle to overcome yet. Miss Lavinia.

Lil found that even Lavinia was not immune to curiosity about this sensational case, and she was full of questions when Lil returned.

'Why didn't you tell me that Caroline has a twin sister? I shouldn't have had to read that in the newspapers. Why on earth did you do a thing like that? Giving your baby away.'

Lil flushed. 'I don't know. Poor. Confused. I thought it was God's will at the time.'

'Stuff and nonsense!' she retorted.

Lil hadn't failed to notice – in fact she was pleased to see – that upon her return to Minchfield House, Miss Lavinia had become a strict teetotaller, without the aid of religion. All of that harsh religious fervour had gone by the board.

'God's will,' Lavinia fumed. 'A lot of hypocrisy. God didn't help me when I needed him, nor did any of his seedy pastors, who shut their eyes to suffering. How did all that come about, leaving the child?'

The telling was difficult, embarrassing, but under Lavinia's steely glare, Lil managed to stumble through an explanation.

'I see,' was Lavinia's only comment when she'd finished, because she seemed more interested in the court case.

'That woman, Mrs Price, what's she like?'

'I don't know. I never really knew her.'

'She was fortunate to be cleared,' Lavinia said with a shudder. 'But what gall! To march into the town hall, of all places, wielding a gun. Her husband will think twice about playing up on her again.'

'He was on her side all the time,' Lil said.

'Really! The papers didn't give that impression.'

'No, they were too busy hounding him too.'

'Well, he asked for it. But what are you going to do now? It is appalling that little Caroline is being deprived of the company of her sister, her twin sister. Outrageous! You should never have got yourself into this fix.'

All very well for her to say, Lil thought miserably, feeling the weight of blame. Guilty as charged.

'You can't let this go on,' Lavinia was saying. 'Regardless of who these people are. One does not wish any more grief upon them, but this should never have happened in the first place. You must reunite those children.'

Lil blinked. 'You wouldn't mind if I brought Lydia here?'

'Why should I mind? Minchfield is hardly a cottage. It's not as if we're short of space, and they don't take much feeding. You're their mother. Why are you so reticent about this? What joy it will be for Caroline to have a little playmate. Can you see her face?'

The Lord did work in mysterious ways after all, Lil mused. It was Caroline who had won the day here, not Lil. Had she not been such a loving child, so happy in Lavinia's company, this woman might not be so keen to welcome her sister. But Lavinia loved Caroline, that was plain, and now she was instructing Lil on how to go about this business.

'You have to keep this as amicable as possible. Write them a pleasant letter explaining your present situation. I'll give you a reference. Let them know you can see your way clear to looking after your own children. Point out that the children should not be separated.' She stopped. 'Oh, leave it to me. I'll draft a letter for you.'

Lil didn't bother to mention that she was quite capable of writing her own letters. Since Lavinia had the bit in her teeth it was best to let her run; she had energy to burn. This was another new project for her. While Lil had been away, all the arrangements for the tea rooms had been completed, and the following Sunday was scheduled for opening day. Lavinia didn't believe in wasting time.

The hate mail shocked Alice.

Thora had been found not guilty, but that didn't seem to matter to the writers of the anonymous letters, who still condemned her in the most vile language.

516

'They're so horrible and cowardly,' Alice wailed, 'they make me sick.'

'Then don't read them,' George said. 'Chuck them out.'

'It's fortunate I'm here to sort the mail,' Alice said. 'They're all addressed to Thora. Heaven knows how she'd react.'

Alice had been relieved by the verdict, in that it would give the family some chance of recovering, but she was still angry with Clem, and she had her reservations about Thora. She'd been afraid that Clem would want to bring Thora straight out to Lancoorie, but he said she desperately needed rest and quiet, so he was taking her to the beach house for a while.

Alice hadn't seen Thora. They'd spirited her away to her barrister's house while Clem came with George to talk to his sister.

Their meeting had been cool. Alice was bristling, ready to say that she wasn't prepared to share a house with Thora. That she and George would move out right away, if necessary. But Clem had one more favour to ask of her.

'Would you take Lydia back to Lancoorie for a while, please, Alice? Just for a while. Thora's very much on edge and we need this time alone.'

'I'm sure you do,' she'd said primly. 'I think it's a very good idea. Lydia needs stability too. We'll go in the morning.'

She was still worried. She and George seemed to be in limbo, waiting for that pair to sort themselves out, more like caretakers on the shared property.

To George, there was no hurry – 'We'll just take one day at a time' – but that wasn't good enough for Alice. They needed to get on with their own lives, not wait to be uprooted when it suited Clem.

When the mailman rode up on his bi-weekly round, he announced that there were new rules: property owners would be expected to place mailboxes at their main gates from now on.

'But I'd have to saddle up and ride the two miles to collect the mail, whether there's any there or not,' she said.

'There's always the papers, Alice. It slows me up too much to have to keep opening and closing gates across these properties to get to the homesteads. Not so bad on the wheat farms.'

'I don't know what the world's coming to!'

He handed over a wad of letters. 'More for Thora,' he noted curiously, but Alice ignored him.

Once inside, she deliberately set Thora's mail aside, turning to the local paper to study advertisements of properties for sale. They might as well start looking.

The other letters sat on the bench for a while, and she almost took George's advice and burned them in the store, unopened, but curiosity got the better of her. Two of them were the same old thing – disgust, rage, abuse – but the third lacked the usual slashes and underlinings she'd come to expect, and it was finished in the polite form, with a real signature.

Alice stared.

The signature: Lillian Cornish! How dare she write! Bad enough that she'd insinuated herself into this affair in the first place, dancing with Clem. And he pretending he hadn't known her – Alice was certain there was more to that than met the eye, Clem had become adept at concealing his activities. Not that Alice wanted to know, she'd heard enough. That woman was supposed to have gone east with her husband. Had they gone to the goldfields instead? That was where all this trouble had started. If only Clem hadn't gone out there . . .

She glanced back at the letter. 'What do you want now?' she asked. 'More money, I suppose.'

But as she read on, tears welled. 'Oh, no! Not Lydia! She can't do this.'

Anger replaced the hurt. This was all Thora's fault. Could she do any more damage to the family? The letter was polite, a request from Lillian to have her child returned to her, but the threat was there, plain to see. By making no mention at all of the scandal, Mrs Cornish had left the obvious unsaid. Alice was so sensitive to all the ramifications of Thora's actions that she was sure they'd never have heard from Mrs Cornish if none of this had happened.

Bitterly, she considered burning the letter, ignoring it, but she knew another would come. Damn the woman! Damn both of them! Could she do this? Could she take the dear child away? In her heart Alice knew she could.

She waited for George to come up for his lunch, and thrust the letter at him. 'Read this. Lydia doesn't even know her. How could she be so cruel?'

'Ah, yes,' George said, reading carefully. 'Mrs Cornish.'

'You sound as if you were expecting to hear from her!'

'It was on the cards.'

'Well, what can we do?'

'Send the letter on to Clem. He'll have to deal with it.'

Clem met Mrs Cornish, alias Miss Warburton, at the Town Hall Tea Shoppe and shook his head at her.

'I thought I knew you.'

Lil sighed. He was the nicest man. 'Are you all right now?'

'Still a bit short of breath, but fine, thanks. And you?'

'I got a fright. I'm still not sure why Mrs Price was aiming at me,' she lied, to spare him.

'It's a long story. Nothing to do with you, really. Where's Ted these days?'

'He deserted me as soon as we arrived in Perth.'

'But you seem to have managed.' He ordered tea and scones for them and came straight to the point. 'You want Lydia back?'

'I'm sorry, yes.'

'We love her very much.'

'I don't doubt that, but it was all a mistake, Mr Price. I don't blame anyone but myself and I really am sorry, but I can't go on without her. As I said in my letter, I am well placed now, and my employer, Miss Warburton . . .'

'The real Miss Warburton?'

'Yes. She has a beautiful house, and she agreed that Caroline's twin sister . . .'

'Her name is Caroline? The twin?'

'Yes. We both agree the girls should grow up together.'

'And you know I haven't got a leg to stand on?'

'Yes.'

The waitress served the hot scones with strawberry jam and thick clotted cream, and they talked, just talked, as he dug into them. Lil wasn't hungry. She was amazed that she could talk so easily to Clem Price, because she'd been dreading this meeting ever since he replied to her letter, inviting her to town.

'Don't let him intimidate you,' Lavinia had said. 'Be firm. Just state your case and leave it at that. There can be no argument.'

He wasn't intimidating, but neither was he offering to hand over Lydia.

In the end she had to ask: 'When can I see Lydia?'

'Tell you what,' he said. 'Let me take you out to see Thora. She has to have a say in this too.'

'Thora?' Lil was taken aback. 'I don't know about that. Is it necessary?'

'She won't bite you or shoot you,' he said heavily. 'I am aware you can claim Lydia any time you like, but you won't get her easy unless you and Thora come to an understanding. She has been through a great deal, I won't have her child just disappear. Lydia is out at Lancoorie at present, well cared for and happy, so you have no worries on that score. You have to see Thora, let her know who you are and where you live, make the change slow and real, not just a sudden break. Will you accept that?'

'I suppose so. Yes.'

He stood up. 'Then we have to get going now. We live at an ocean beach. I can take you there in my buggy and bring you back this afternoon.'

She could smell the ocean, the heady saltiness that had always given her such pleasure, but now it filled her with dread. Clem Price had not upset her, but the very thought of confronting the high-and-mighty Thora Price was another matter altogether, and Lil felt totally inadequate. Was this a trap? Had he guessed that Lil Cornish might regress to that wretched girl who'd been cast up on their doorstep with her no-good husband, and wilt in the presence of his wife? If so, he was right. As soon as the buggy turned on to the sandy road, her courage began to fail, and she would have asked him to turn back, but she didn't have the courage to do that either. Instead she sat primly beside him as he steered the horse away from the softer sand on to firm ground, not daring to say a word.

After all, she worried, even if Thora was batty, it took guts to take a gun and stride into a ballroom in front of all those people. Would she condescend to talk to Lil at all? Or would she lash out in righteous rage? Lil's stomach was churning as they broke away from the low scrub into a clearing, and there was a house, a cool white bungalow with a green roof.

He stopped the buggy at a hitching post near newly painted stables, and helped her down. 'Watch your dress, Mrs Cornish. The sea grass is sharp.'

I know that, she thought indignantly. I'm not a complete fool. The resentment was a defence, emanating from a need to boost her spirits, but she only nodded, numbly, clutching at her skirts.

'You're not going in the back way,' he explained, taking her towards a tall flight of timber steps. 'We built the house back to front to concentrate on the view and the sea breeze.'

Lil swallowed and took a deep breath, but there was no sign of Thora. She had her hand on the rail, which was picked out in green over the white-painted steps, when he said:

'You go on up.'

Lil stopped, frozen. She realized that he might want to unhitch and water the horse, it was a hot day. She wanted to wait for him, but he waved her on.

'Aren't you coming?' she asked, desperately.

'No.' It was definite. 'You are the mothers. You work it out. This is what you wanted, isn't it?'

'But . . .'

'I've said my piece. Go on up. Thora is waiting. She's expecting you.'

Lil found herself puffing as she mounted only ten steps, that she would normally take in her stride, and entered a latticed back veranda, stepping, almost tiptoeing, across the polished boards to wipe her shoes busily on the mat before reaching out to knock on the open door, as timidly as one might expect of the wife of Ted Cornish, their part-time farm hand.

Thora, Mrs Price, came out of the shadows of the central passage and stood before Lil, looking down at her. She was taller than Lil recalled, and her long blonde hair was caught loosely at the back with a blue ribbon. She was wearing a simple blue muslin dress, no match for Lil's best travelling suit of beige faille, beautifully tailored, bought for her by Robert in his short-lived foray into marriage plans. But it wouldn't matter what Thora was wearing, Lil thought miserably, she'd win, she looks so damned elegant. Self-consciously, Lil touched her own dark hair under her wide, fashionable hat, laden with curled ribbons and silk flowers, and mumbled something as Thora invited her in, leading her through to a summery room that looked out over the ocean.

'This is very nice,' Lil offered, for something to say.

'Yes. Tea?'

'No thank you.' Lil was too nervous even to consider trying to handle their china.

'Then you must have a cold drink. We have lemon barley.'

'That will do.' Why did I say that? Lil groaned. Why couldn't I just accept gracefully. *That will do.* How awful.

She gazed at Thora when she returned with a jug of lemon barley and two glasses. She didn't look mad. With her flawless skin, high cheekbones and those baby-blue eyes, Mrs Price looked so beautiful, so serene, that Lil felt a stab of jealousy. No wonder Clem Price was so dotty about her that he'd put up with anything she did. Oh, for a man like that, she thought. Again.

'Thank you, Mrs Price.' Lil took her barley water and tried not to gulp at it, even though her throat felt dry and coarse. She looked out over the beach and saw Clem Price walking along the sand.

'There's Mr Price,' she uttered. Stupidly. As if his wife didn't know.

'Yes,' Thora said. 'He's feeling very bad about this. About Lydia. More than he says. He keeps telling me I shouldn't bottle things up, I should talk things over, every little thing, not be brooding, but look at him! He's brooding, worrying, won't admit he's upset. Do you brood, Mrs Cornish?'

'Oh! I think so. Probably. No. I try to make things work my way, but I usually get it wrong. I've learned to go quieter. I mean, everything's all right now.'

'Except for Lydia.'

'Please don't think badly of me, Mrs Price. You must understand why I've come. They're twins. They should be together. I couldn't cope with both babies back then, but now I can.'

'Yes. Clem explained that to me.' She was calm, but a flush of colour appeared on her cheeks. 'I don't think badly of you at all. I hope you'll forgive me. I do remember what happened in that hall now, in bits and pieces anyway, but I don't recall seeing you there, and that's the truth. I'm so sorry.'

Lil was embarrassed. She'd thought that subject would have been taboo, too sensitive even to touch upon.

'That's all right,' she muttered.

Thora looked about her nervously. 'I don't know if it will ever be all right, but thank you. It was a terrible thing to do to you.'

'I'd rather forget the whole thing myself,' Lil said. 'It was a bad time for me too. Everything went wrong.'

'What became of Ted?'

'He deserted me a few weeks after we arrived in Perth, but I don't worry about that now. He's no loss. I'll divorce him as soon as I can. I'm very happy where I'm placed, and the lady I work for, she thinks Lydia should be with us too. You won't object, will you? Minchfield House is really beautiful, I wish you could come and see it.'

Thora surprised her. 'We will. As for Lydia, we can't object. I've come to accept that and I feel better now that I've met you. Clem will talk to you about the arrangements, but before he comes up . . .' She leaned forward. 'I love Lydia, who would not? But I'm glad you've come. She does belong with you, if you can manage . . .'

'I'll manage,' Lil burst out, 'truly I will.'

'Yes, Clem said he'll see to that. He intends to give you some financial support.' She smiled wanly. 'He says Lydia's entitled. But I think she's entitled to her own name.'

'Oh yes?' Lil said flatly, not understanding.

'I don't want her growing up as Lydia Price. They even had her photo in the paper. Daughter of that scandalous mad woman. It will be a long time before I ever live that down, and it's a cruel start for a child.'

Lil fluttered her hands, feeling it would be rude to agree. But hadn't she thought of just that herself?

'Her name will be Lydia Cornish,' Thora said urgently. 'I couldn't insult Clem by saying that in front of him. He'd be so hurt. It's his name we're talking about too.'

'You must love him very much.'

'I never knew how much,' she said sadly, 'until I nearly lost him.'

They both watched as he came trudging over the dunes and up the steps. Thora went out to meet him, and Lil saw the question in his expression.

Thora nodded, smiling, and he kissed her. 'Good girl.'

Over lunch they worked out the arrangements that Thora had mentioned. Clem was very kind, but firm. Lydia was presently at Lancoorie with her aunt and uncle, who, he hoped, would always remain so. They would bring her to Perth as soon as possible, but to just hand the child over to Lil – who was, after all, a stranger – would be too much of a wrench, too upsetting for a little girl, so Clem proposed a period of transition.

At first, Lil was disappointed. She'd seen herself returning triumphantly with Lydia, taking for granted that the child would be delighted, but now she saw their logic. It would be dreadful trying to deal with a fretting child.

'Lil says that this Minchfield House is a very beautiful place, Thora. We should visit. You would enjoy a cruise upriver. And we'll take Lydia with us. There's the beginning.'

He turned to Lil. 'And you must bring Caroline here to visit us, as often as you can. In the meantime, I promise to take Lydia to see you once a week, Lil. The changeover must be gradual. I hope you will accept that you must get to know Lydia. It will be easier on everyone.'

She nodded,

'I know I seem to be dragging this out, Lil, but I want you to trust us. Lydia is your daughter, you love her too. It will be up to you to decide when she is ready to stay with you permanently.'

When they were preparing to leave for the drive back to Perth, he turned to the two women. 'Oh well,' he said cheerfully, 'think of the twins. They'll have doting uncles and aunts now, so I suppose we're not a total loss.'

Thora brought out a photo of Lydia in a silver frame, and gave it to Lil. 'This is for you, and Caroline.'

Coda

Not five years after his election to the state parliament, F.C.B. Vosper died. He was accorded a state funeral and the cathedral was packed to overflowing even before the choir of Welsh miners assembled by the grand new organ.

As if loath to see him go, hundreds of people followed Fred's funeral cortège out to the cemetery, among them, the barrister Maurice Conway. He had come to know Fred Vosper quite well and although he did not always hold with the flamboyant politician's views, he respected his integrity. Vosper had wholeheartedly supported the working man, especially the rights of miners, and had proven a fine advocate. The western goldfields were booming, there seemed to be no end to the glittering treasure hidden in that arid land, and miners' rights had become an important political issue, ignored by governments at their peril. The lessons of the Ballarat uprisings had been learned, thanks to men like Vosper.

With the graveside service in progress, Conway moved back to the sparse shade of a straggling gum tree. He was feeling the heat, and this dry parched cemetery littered with baking white tombstones was hard on his eyes. There was a haze of smoke in the air, and the familiar acrid smell of bushfires wafted down from the hills to add to his discomfort. As the priest droned on, sprinkling holy water over the coffin, Conway looked about the gathering, taking in the faces of friends and acquaintances but there was one man he had trouble placing – a lanky, dark-haired fellow with the tanned face of a country man, standing apart as if in private communion with the departed.

It wasn't until the last sod had been strewn on the coffin,

and the mourners were moving away, that Conway recognized the man. He strode down the sandy path after him.

'Mr Price! How good to see you. How are you?'

Clem turned back. 'Mr Conway! I didn't realize you were here. I'm well, thanks. And you?'

'As best as can be on this sad day. He was too young to die, wasn't he?'

'Yes. Bad luck. I always had a lot of time for Fred. I'm glad I could get here in time for the funeral.'

'Still out at Lancoorie? Your sheep station?'

'No. We never went back there.'

'Ah.' Conway was prepared to leave it at that. After the trial Price and his wife had disappeared. Some said they'd gone overseas, but he'd taken it for granted that they'd eventually found their way back to their home.

Clem fell into step beside him as they trudged down to the gate. 'My sister and her husband have Lancoorie now,' he said, 'and they have a fine son. They called him Noah, after my father, who pioneered the area.'

Maurice smiled. 'Ah, yes. Mr and Mrs Gunne. Have they forgiven me for those days in court? I was hard on them.'

'Forgiven us all, you mean!' Price grinned. 'George is a placid fellow, he took it in his stride, but Alice required some persuading. It was the girls, the twins, who saved the day. Alice was as heartbroken as we were at losing Lydia, but she had to face reality.

'In the end,' he continued, 'she had no choice. Lil, with the girls, Caroline and Lydia, has become close to us. We've stayed good friends, so Alice had to choose. It was either patch up with us or lose touch with Lydia altogether, and she couldn't bear that, so she settled down. Nowadays, the Gunne family come to stay with us quite often so I try to arrange for the twins to be there at the same time. They're beautiful little girls.'

'They are indeed. I see them occasionally.'

'You do?' Clem looked at him in surprise.

'Yes,' the barrister said. 'Henery Whipple is an old friend of mine. I was in London when he married Lillian last year, but

I've seen quite a bit of them since I came home. They seem to be happily settled and, from my observations, Henery is a doting stepfather. He always was a jolly fellow. Last I heard he was teaching the girls to play the piano.' He stopped, uncertainly. 'I say, I hope I haven't put my foot in it. You don't resent him, do you?'

'Of course not. I was very relieved to hear Lil had divorced that first husband. That was always a worry for me. I wouldn't have wanted him around those children. From my point of view, Henery was heaven-sent. They'll be safe with him.'

They passed through the squat stone columns at the entrance to the cemetery and Conway watched the crowd of departing mourners heading back to town. 'They're having a wake for Fred,' he said, 'mostly miners and union men, I believe. I don't think I'd fit in. Would you care to join me for a thirst-quencher at that pub over the road?'

'I'd be glad to.'

Other men, emerging from the cemetery, had the same idea and the bar of the small timber pub was soon crowded, so Clem and Maurice took their drinks and stood by an open window, watching as the hearse, its work done, rattled out of the cemetery and turned down the road.

'You knew Edgar Tanner rather well, didn't you?' Maurice asked Clem.

'Yes. Why?'

'I'm preparing his defence on several charges of fraud and fraudulent uttering. He has been extradited from Adelaide to face these charges.'

'I'm sorry to hear that. Is he guilty?'

'That remains to be seen. But I could do with some background on him. There was that trouble about your Yorkey mine, for instance. What was the truth of that?'

'Tanner was completely innocent in that débâcle,' Clem said. 'The man who did forge the assayer's report left the state.'

'Where is he now?'

'I don't know. He went to Melbourne with his wife. I had a letter from him in which he promised to refund his share of the monies we were paid for Yorkey, but that never happened. I lost touch with them years ago. Eventually I sold Yorkey, didn't get much for it. Then it was sold on again as not much of a goer, but the third owner struck gold. He did well out of it.'

'That must have been disappointing for you.'

'Oh no. I didn't do too badly out of Yorkey in the first place and I was quite cheered to hear it came good again.'

Conway looked at Clem with a sly grin. 'I don't suppose you'd be interested in stepping forward as a character witness for Tanner?'

'After what I've seen you can do to character witnesses? No fear! But apart from that, we both know Tanner treated Thora cruelly, to get revenge on me for perceived hurt. I'll never forgive him. I hope he rots in jail.'

Conroy shrugged. 'Oh well. We'll see.'

Clem set his glass on the weathered windowledge. 'I can't wish you luck this time.' He looked towards the haze of hills and said rather wistfully. 'Sometimes I think Mike has a lot to answer for with that stupid forgery.'

'Mike who?'

'The name doesn't matter. For some reason he had a grudge against Tanner. The forged assayer's report was part joke, part malicious. He knew Tanner would be blamed. But his actions set Tanner after me and resulted in all the trouble.' He sighed. 'All in the past now though. I'd better get going, I've a long ride ahead of me.'

'You're not at the Cottersloe house?'

'No, that's just our beach house. We bought a property down south, near Bunbury. Beautiful country.'

'Glad to hear it. And Mrs Price? How is she?'

'Recovered, thanks to you. And very happy down that end of the world. We still don't see many people, only family really, which now includes Lil and Henery as well as the twins. The property isn't as remote as Lancoorie and it's smaller, more scenic. Thora helped me choose it, so she takes a real interest in it.' He smiled. 'She's the boss, you could say.'

'Did you ever tell her that her father refused to pay her legal fees?'

'No. When I said family, I didn't mean them.'

'It was good of you to foot the bill for Carty.'

'Worth every penny to get my wife back. We'll always be in your debt.'

They shook hands by the cemetery gates which were now firmly closed and Maurice walked over to his sulky. He patted the patient horse then divested himself of his coat and waistcoat, placing them neatly on the leather seat. His duty done on this day, he saw no further need for formality.

Just as he was preparing to climb aboard and make his way home, Maurice turned to watch Clem ride away, wondering if Thora really was cured. He doubted it.

Kitty Rainbow

Wendy Robertson

When the soft-hearted bare-knuckle fighter Ishmael Slaughter rescues an abandoned baby from the swirling River Wear, he knows that if he takes her home his employer will give her short shrift – or worse. So it is to Janine Druce, a draper woman with a dubious reputation but a child of her own, that he takes tiny Kitty Rainbow.

Kitty grows up wild, coping with Janine's bouts of drunkenness and her son's silent strangeness. And she is as fierce in her affections as she is in her hatreds, saving her greatest love for Ishmael, the ageing boxer who provides the only link with her parentage, a scrap of cloth she was wrapped in when he found her. Kitty realises that she cannot live her life wondering who her mother was, and in Ishmael she has father enough. And, when she finds herself pregnant, deprived of the livelihood on which she and the old man depended, she must worry about the future, not the past. But the past has a way of catching the present unawares . . .

'An intense and moving story set against the bitter squalor of the hunger-ridden thirties' *Today*

'A rich fruit cake of well-drawn characters . . .' *Northern Echo*

'Fans of big family stories must read Wendy Robertson' *Peterborough Evening Telegraph*

'A lovely book' *Woman's Realm*

0 7472 5183 5

HEADLINE

A Mersey Duet

Anne Baker

When Elsa Gripper dies in childbirth on Christmas Eve, 1912, her grief-stricken husband is unable to cope with his two newborn daughters, Lucy and Patsy, so the twins are separated.

Elsa's parents, who run a highly successful business, Mersey Antiques, take Lucy home and she grows up spoiled and pampered with no interest in the family firm. Patsy has a more down-to-earth upbringing, living with their father and other grandmother above the Railway Hotel. And through further tragedy she learns to be responsible from an early age. Then Patsy is invited to work at Mersey Antiques, which she hopes will bring her closer to Lucy. But it is to take a series of dramatic events before they are drawn together . . .

'A stirring tale of romance and passion, poverty and ambition . . . everything from seduction to murder, from forbidden love to revenge' *Liverpool Echo*

'Highly observant writing style . . . a compelling book that you just don't want to put down' *Southport Visitor*

0 7472 5320 X

HEADLINE

If you enjoyed this book here is a selection of other bestselling titles from Headline